Finding Love with the Fae King

Vera Foxx

Contents

Chapter 1

Melina

"Melina, we are Werewolves," my best friend spoke to me at the edge of the forest.

"I'm sorry, what?" I shook my head calmly and folded my arms against my chest. Did she really think I had time for this?

"It is true, Melina. The signs are all there. All the questions you had of our community growing up are there! Just put the pieces of the puzzle together."

"Tulip..." I sighed, and her new boyfriend held her close from behind. He continued to nuzzle into her neck, smelling her. What a creep. I couldn't understand why he was here. She just met the guy a week ago at her community dance mixer that I had always refused to go to. They always talked about meeting their mates or soulmates or whatever. I wasn't about to get put into that drama. They had been glued to the hip ever since.

"I am telling the truth. Just watch." Tulip took off her clothes, first her top and her pants. Panicking, I grabbed her arm.

"What in goddess' name are you doing!?" Her new boyfriend, Alec, smirked. "What's so funny?" I snapped.

"The way you used 'goddess', it's referring to the Moon Goddess. Werewolves kind of worship her."

I stared at him blankly. It was just a slang term her whole family used, and I picked up on it. Heck, I practically lived with them for years. I rolled my eyes and turned back to Tulip. She was standing in just her bra and underwear, and I swore I heard Alec growling.

Tulip's body grew hair and break into pieces. She didn't scream once, and within seconds, she had turned into a large brown Wolf. It was larger than your average Wolf, and she stared into my eyes. Her bright blues looked back at me and gave me that signature wink she liked to give.

I stood completely still, my hand still out from trying to grab her arm as she took off her clothes. Alec smiled and puffed out his chest like he was so proud of her. My breathing had stopped, and Tulip slowly walked up to me, nudging my leg, and letting out a whimper. Looking down at her, I wasn't afraid. It really was her.

Holy cow.

Thinking back on the little remarks of them talking about an Alpha, sometimes slipping the word, 'pack,' and people checking the 'territory,' smelling me, smelling each other, her exceptional speed in gym class. It was there staring at me in the face and I was blinded by it all with stupidity.

My best friend is a Werewolf.

***

It had been like any other morning. I had woken up at the cabin that my parents left me at, at only thirteen years old. After thirteen years of marriage, they decided it was over. They never fought, at least in front of me. They both had their own jobs, and it required that they travel a lot.

When I was young, I met my very best friend in a sandbox at the park, Tulip. To match her favorite color of tulips, she always wore a purple dress. I couldn't tell you what sparked my interest to go talk to her, because I was a very shy child. I did though and sharing my shovel with her to make the best sandcastle out of the entire park made her day. She didn't have many friends either and we left that day knowing we would be best friends till the end.

Our mothers noted how well we got along. Several more times we met at the park and my mother finally asked for Tulip's mother to have regular playdates. That soon turned into Tulip's mom babysitting and, even more so, spending the night. However, Tulip's mother didn't mind me.

She took me in like her own and I think she felt sorry for me. My parents weren't always around. My dad was a traveling physician, and my mother was an airline flight attendant. They had multiple nannies that took care of me, but when you have your best friend and her mother loves you like her own daughter, it becomes free childcare.

Several times growing up, I would accidentally call Tulip's mother, Rose, mom, and she would brush it off. She said I could call her anything I wanted, and that was that. Rose seemed happy to call her that, so I continued to do so for the rest of my younger days. She was more of a mother than my incubator, anyway. The few days a week I was actually at my home with my actual parents. They were busy on the computer and making calls. No time for me. I hated it there, and I was officially over it. There were several arguments as I got older, begging them to spend time with me, go to the mall, or even just sit down as a family, but they never did.

I questioned why they even had me if they were going to be so busy until one day I found out. I had just tucked myself into bed and I could hear them talking in the next room. They weren't home enough to realize just how thin the walls really were.

"I just can't do this anymore, Matthew." My mother sighed.

"I know, but we have a few more years with her and then it will be done," he said to my mother, Kathryn. "We used to be so in love. Did a child really break us apart?"

"I just can't believe we were that careless that one time. I never wanted kids and now she is begging for time with us and I just want to focus on my career. You aren't happy. I'm not happy. Maybe having a child *did* tear us apart because of one careless mistake. It ruined everything. We should just have a clean break right now," my mother choked.

I had had enough. I got up from my bed and pushed their bedroom door open. "Is that it? That is how you feel? You never wanted me?"

The look of shock and guilt was on their faces. It was the truth, yet they couldn't speak it in front of me. I stood my ground and folded my arms together.

"That's fine. Now I know the truth." My face was stern. I knew my maturity was more so than my peers at thirteen. I had to be. There were nights I was too embarrassed to go to Tulip's; I didn't want them to know my parents were gone again, so I did things on my own.

"If you all would be happier, get a divorce," I spat. "Just get me a house near Tulip and some money to live from until I turn eighteen and I won't contact either of you again. A clean break, just like you wanted."

In my heart, I hoped they would say they were being selfish, that they really cared about me and would never wish it. That they were going through a rough patch and were saying things they didn't mean. My heart was crushed even more when they agreed.

Tulip's mother got permission from their community that they lived in and put me in a cabin on the edge of their land. Rose was given full guardianship of me without hesitation. She would often tell me how she felt I should have been the daughter of their family. Tulip's father, Elm, a man of few words, told me I was welcomed into their home, but I had refused. They had taken care of me for far too long and the guilt crawled up my spine every night. My now, new mother scolded me for the longest time until she finally allowed me to stay at the edge of the property. She always said it was a safe place to live and I would always be taken care of and protected, but I brushed it off as just some motherly, calming words to ease my mind.

Rose made sure that I had food and a clean house, but I had everything taken care of. She didn't have to take care of me. I became very independent through the years of already being alone, but she still checked. I loved Rose and her family to pieces. They included me in everything.

Or so I thought. There was one secret they kept from me was now staring at me in the face.

I sat down in the grass while Tulip went behind a tree to change.

Alec squatted next to me. "Hey, are you all right?" He put his hand on my back in comfort and I pushed him away.

I think the one thing I was most deprived of was touch. Tulip's parents often hugged me, but it just wasn't the same. I couldn't tell if it was a pity hug or not. If Tulip was given a hug, one quickly followed for me as well. I'm sure their intentions are good. They have always been there, but the doubt is still hovering over me. I could thank my biological parents for that.

"I'm fine." I waved him off. I waited to talk to Tulip. I didn't know Alec from Adam and Eve if those people were even real now that my entire beliefs about the world had just come crashing down.

Tulip tugged her sweatshirt back on over her head as she came from behind the tree. Alec acted like he hadn't seen her in a week and pulled her in for a kiss. I sighed and started coughing to break them up. I don't need to watch them have sex out in the open.

Tulip turned to me and held her arms out for a hug. She was really the only one I thought loved me unconditionally, but now, after dropping the biggest bomb of the century on me, I wasn't so sure. I have told her everything about me, from my heartbreak of my parents to crushes in high school to my questions about her parents really caring for me or just pitying me. I told her everything, yet she kept this secret. Hurt was the only thing I felt right now.

I let her embrace me; I needed some sort of contact. My arms slowly slid up her back, and I laid my head on her shoulder. "I'm sorry I didn't tell you. We are supposed to keep it a secret until necessary."

"So, all of you, your whole family?" Tulip nodded. "This is called a pack then, right?" She nodded again. The pieces of the puzzle fell together. The large house where everyone hung out, people training early in the morning, which I could never watch, people eating large quantities of food without gaining weight. They were all Wolves. Every single one of them. I let out a gigantic sigh. At least I wasn't freaking out. I was taking it quite well honestly.

"Hey." Tulip put both of her hands on my face. "Once I got permission, I told you as quickly as I could. Humans aren't supposed to know. It's for pack safety, understand?"

I nodded my head. Even though the stab in my heart hurt, I couldn't fault her for having to follow some Alpha leader dude. If they functioned anything like actual wolves, I understood that.

"Why are you allowed to tell me now?" I looked up at her. Being only 5'3" was annoying as heck. Everyone was taller than me.

"Well—" Tulip reached for Alec's hand. "I found my mate, my soulmate." Her eyes sparkled as she looked at him, and he grabbed her by her waist and kissed him.

"Soulmate? How do you know?" I questioned.

"His smell, is magnified to me, and he smells of my favorite aromas. Sparks fly across our skin as we touch, and we have this instant connection. Wolves call it mates."

"Oh," I acted sheepishly. "What does that mean, then?"

"It means we will be together forever," she smiled up at him. "Our souls are intertwined with each other, and we are having a mating ceremony, like a wedding, and I'm going to need my best friend to be there with me." Her smile had a glint of mischief in it and stood in shock.

"You just met the guy! You can't do it now!" I squealed.

Alec growled and pulled Tulip closer, and I gave him a glare.

"It is different with Werewolves, Melina." Tulip looked back at Alec. "The Moon Goddess picks our mates. She spends time with each soul and once they are bonded together, it will be forever. I have an everlasting attraction to him, and he does me. He will only have eyes for me and me to him—no cheating, no leaving each other. We are mates forever."

This was all happening so fast. How could they think I would be okay with this? She'd known the guy for only a week and now she wants to spend eternity with him? Knowing that they were Werewolves and this is a common occurrence, I guess I could let it slide. If that is how she truly feels and her parents want the same, why should I stop them? They are whole different species, and I don't even know my best friend anymore.

My eyes teared up. I wish I could believe that mates could be forever. After dealing with my birth parents' marriage that ended up failing because of me, two people that were supposedly in love, in my heart, I didn't believe it. I gave Tulip a fake smile. "Well, when is this mating ceremony and what do you want me to do?"

"The thing is—" Tulip's eyes shone at Alec again with so much love and lust. "—we are going to do it at his home pack in Bergarian."

"Where is that?" I had never heard of such a place. Alec grabbed my hand and pulled us toward the community, I mean, packhouse.

"Let us tell you all about it," he said with a wink.

Chapter 2

Melina

There was silence as we walked through the forest back to the packhouse. Tulip and Alec had their hands intertwined with one another, and I couldn't help but look on. It must be nice to just fall in love like that, but really, will it last? I saw none of her family members or people from her community; I mean pack, get a divorce. They all seemed really in love, but was it love or this bond thing they kept talking about? Did they have a choice? Maybe humans were just different, never really knowing if you supposed over half will leave.

Some Moon Goddess made them fall in love. There was no choice. Sure, it was great in some ways that you don't have to really find out about someone's personality before you settle down. You automatically know it is going to work out, but what about their choice? So, they can't go off and date and decide for themselves to love someone? What if their mate was unappealing to them, they had a third eye, or couldn't please them sexually? Not that I would know what that's like. Rolling my eyes, I continued to walk up the steps and heard the kids shouting at the playground not too far away. To think all those little kids Werewolves, and I never knew.

As we walked into the big foyer, Tulip's parents stood at

the entryway of the massive kitchen. Melina explained to me the roles of the two leaders of this community I grew up in. The supposed 'alpha' of the community was Ramirez. He stood tall with his wife, whom I always thought was just the community mother figure, but was in fact, called a Luna.

Ramirez was a nice guy, kind of gruff, and had a terrible habit of keeping his office messy. I swore when I stumbled upon his office several years ago, I thought I walked into a hazard zone. Food, drinks spilled all over the place and most of all his budget was laid out in the open with bank account numbers written across it.

It was only then I told him my fascination with numbers when he walked in on me, staring at the numbers on the sheet. I was good at math, even better with budgets, since I controlled all the money my parents sent me to live off of. From then on, I took care of the accounting of the entire pack. Little did I know it was for a bunch of Werewolves.

Ramirez' wife was called the 'Luna,' Tulip had briefed me quickly before we walked in. The Luna waved me over and motioned for me to sit down.

"Does she know now?" the Luna asked excitedly.

Tulip nodded her head excitedly and Luna came over and gave me a hug. She had always been a delicate woman, always doting on her husband and making sure people feel welcomed. I was no different; she made me feel like this was my home even though everything I lived here was a lie. I gave a brief smile as she went to stand with her husband, Ramirez.

"I'm sure you have questions," Alpha Ramirez spoke. "We were hoping you would take it well, and it looks like you have. I mean, you haven't run away in terror." He let out a loud laugh.

If he wasn't so well built, I would have thought he was Santa Claus with that laugh. Several other wolves chipped in on the laughter, but I remained pretty stoic, not sure what emotion I should be emitting.

"Um, well. If you haven't eaten me by now, I figured I was

all right," I started. "I am a little hurt that you couldn't trust me with this information for all these years. I mean, I did graduate high school with a lot of your members and here I am, 20 years old, just finding out about it." Folding my arms, I felt a few traitor tears trying to trickle down, but I held them back. *I can't show how upset I am and be some weak human now, can I?*

"I know, Melina, I'm sorry," Rose pitched in. "We just have certain rules and laws we must abide by, and we couldn't tell you. It would put you and us in danger. It was only recently we could tell some humans our secret by the Royal Council. Even then, it still must go through the council here in the Moon Light Pack. All the council members know you and, without hesitation, they agreed you would be a human that knows."

I nodded, accepting it.

"You graduated with some of their grandchildren. We all care about you, dear." Rose petted my hair, and I couldn't help but jump off my seat and give her a hug.

I grew up with these wonderful people, er uh, Wolves. They wouldn't hurt me, and I would have never told them their secret. Some things are out of their hands, I suppose, but who is the Royal Council? Why am I allowed to know now? Sitting up straight and composing myself, I dared to ask my question.

"What is the Royal Council then? Do you have a king and queen Werewolf or something? Do they live in the pack or somewhere else?"

Tulip's eyes lit up and grabbed my hands. "They are a king and queen and their representatives. They just recently passed a law for humans to be allowed to visit Bergarian, and that is where we are having our mating ceremony! You will love it there, the way you love reading fairy tales with elves, fairies, and Sirens. I know you will never want to leave!"

"Hold on there," Tulip's father, Elm, said. "Give the girl some space. This is a lot for her to take in."

My head was spinning. Are there more of these fairytale characters? I shouldn't be surprised. They are Werewolves. What else could there be?

"Are there Vampires, too?" I squealed worriedly. Everyone looked at each other and nodded. "They aren't Twilight-style Vampires, are they? If they sparkle, I don't know if I could handle it."

Tulip burst out laughing and shook her head while the others just chuckled.

"All right now, since you are taking this way better than expected, let's go into the living room and sit down. We have a lot to discuss."

We followed Alpha Ramirez to the large, warm living area with tanned leather couches. They were set up near an enormous fireplace and two stone wolves that flanked the chimney. Honestly, I didn't know why I had never seen it before. I must have been too busy wallowing in pity since my own parents didn't want me. Time to get over that real quick.

Ramirez stood next to the fireplace, one elbow leaning against the mantel as we all sat down. Tulip sat next to me, holding my hand while her mate held the other. I wanted to strangle this boy that thought he had a hold on to my Tulip. I gave him a glare, which he only responded to with a wink. Dumb mate crap.

Ramirez rubbed his hands together and began talking, "Now that we have our guest of honor here—" He tipped his head over to me and I blushed and tried to sink into the sofa. "—My niece is getting married and has decided her mating ceremony will be at the Crimson Shadows Pack in Bergarian. This means we are going to have to travel lightly. Most clothing will be provided except for the actual mating ceremony." Everyone nodded, and I sat there dazed and confused.

"Now, Melina, we need to discuss Bergarian with you."

My eyes widened, ready to hear about this fairy tale place Tulip had just mentioned.

"Bergarian is another realm. It is much like Earth, yet it is meant for the supernaturals that the gods had placed here to protect humans from gods that weren't so, well, friendly. As humans strengthened, they became scared, violent, and hostile, so the gods created a whole new realm just for us. The supernaturals. There are, like Tulip said, Werewolves, Fairies, Sirens, Pixies, Shifters, Dragons—you name it. They are there and have been hiding for a long time. We go through a portal that is about two hours from here, and once we go through, we will be there in the next realm."

I should have been freaking out about this, but I wasn't. I was nodding my head like I was in a trance. I felt like I should go there and check this place out. "How long will we be there?"

"Two weeks," Rose said. "That will give us time to have a brief vacation after the mating ceremony. Elm and I will show you around and we will come back afterward."

I nodded and then paused. "Wait, will you be coming back, Tulip?"

Tulip gripped Alec's hand tightly and shook her head no. My heart was crushed at the thought my best and only friend would be gone from my life.

"You mean, you are moving there?"

Tulip bowed, and a stray tear dripped down my cheek.

"That is why it was so important for you to be there, to know where I was because I didn't want to disappear, and you did not know where I went."

I choked back a sob and put my hands on my face.

Rose came over and gave me a hug and pulled me to her chest. "You will always have us, baby Melina. We will be here." She looked down at me, but my heart was already broken. I have lost my best friend.

"Why are you staying?" My voice cracked.

"Alec is to be the new Delta in a few years. It is a higher position in the pack. He can't leave. Werewolf mates go live where whichever mate has the highest position."

Letting out a shaky breath, I pulled my legs up to my body,

not caring if I got my muddy shoes on their furniture. I lost my best friend to her mate, and she made all the decisions without me. Maybe I was more invested in this friendship than she was.

"I think I need to be alone now. When do we leave?"

Tulip glanced at me with sad eyes as I stood up and wiped a few pieces of invisible dirt from my jeans.

"Tomorrow afternoon. Will you be here?" Tulip stood up and grabbed my hand again.

Looking at it, I didn't feel the same warmth of a friend I had pictured throughout our childhood. I told her everything about me, my fears, my hopes, and dreams. Granted, it wasn't a lot, but it still meant a lot to me. Now she was telling me she was a Werewolf, could never tell me about it, and now she had found her mate, whom she drops everything for and was planning on living in a faraway place I may never visit. As far as I was concerned, my friendship with her was cracked like a fine piece of old China.

Could I be the friend she wanted during her favorable moment? Even though I did not understand the whole mating ceremony, the true traditions of Werewolves, I would be a sucky friend if I denied watching the 'happiest moment of her life' and seeing her off into a new one with her mate.

"Yes, I'll be here," I whispered.

Tulip hugged me, and I hugged her back. When I let go, I gave Alec a death glare and held up two fingers and pointed to my eyes and back to his. He gave out a laugh. Trying to be a good person, I held out my hand to shake his, and he shook it gladly. He gave me a smile and brought me to him to give a hug. I was taken aback at the sudden engulfed hug by a complete stranger that was marrying my best friend after only a week of dating.

"Thank you," he whispered in my ear.

Stepping back, I left out the side door of the living room back to my cabin. It was a good 15-minute walk. It was close to winter, and the leaves had fallen off the trees, so my footsteps caused constant crackling beneath my feet. My hands were stuck in my pockets because I didn't think ahead of time and now the tips were freezing. The jacket hung loosely around my body while I kept my eyes straight ahead. I didn't want to look at all the homes around the territory. I didn't want to watch kids play fighting and wrestling like they always had as I grew up here. Now it all had a different meaning to it.

They were training to be something lethal.

They were Werewolves.

Taking my tenth enormous sigh of the day, my small cabin came into view. It wasn't much. It was a small one-bedroom with a kitchen, living room and one bathroom. My parents had sold our previous house and gave me and Rose the money. Rose always thought of me being mature enough to handle finances, but I let her hold on to the extra, just in case. The cabin had been free, saying no one else was using it. Now I wondered if it was meant for some lonely Wolf that couldn't find their mate.

Holy sad story.

Stomping up the small steps, I heard something rustling in the bushes. Normally, things like that wouldn't bother me. I'd lived here seven years and was never scared of anything now finding out there are other creatures out there. I wasn't so sure anymore. Stepping back down the steps, I looked in the bushes to see bright yellow eyes staring back at me.

My breath hitched only for me to calm a bit and put my hand on my chest. "I know you guys are Werewolves now, whoever you are. Stop being a creep." Walking backwards and fully turning around to get back in the cabin, I unlocked the door and slammed it.

Stripping my jacket off and stoking the fire with the iron, I heard a knock at the door. Probably that dang Wolf. I stomped to the door and opened it abruptly to see none other than the bane of my existence, Esteban.

Chapter 3

Melina

Esteban was hot, I mean on fire. That being said, he was also a player. He could get into any girl's pants at the high school we went to. The popular girls, the athletic ones, drama nerds, and even the awkward social butterflies. The one pair of pants he did not get into, the one skirt he could not lift, was mine.

I was part of the awkward social butterfly's club. I knew how to have fun with a small group of friends, but not great with sizeable crowds. I stuck to Tulip and her crowd, which are now known as the Werewolves.

Now that I know I did better socializing with Wolves as friends also means that I just don't get along with my own kind, humans. Major sigh right here.

"What do you want, Esteban?" I put all my weight on one foot and rolled my eyes as I held the door open.

He gave me that smirk that all the girls go for, the one where it was kind of crooked and part of his teeth show. The kind of smile that made his pearly whites stand out even more with his tanned olive skin. All except me, and that bothered him. It has always bothered him.

"I came to see my favorite girl." He walked past me and

headed to the kitchen and grabbed an apple out of my fruit basket. Throwing it up in the air once or twice, he took a large bite and set it back on the counter. If I didn't know about his past, I could see myself falling for him, but I knew better.

There were many nights in the pack house where we were all in the large living room watching movies. He would try to sit beside me, but I always got right back up and sat in between some girls. He would leave in a huff or come to pick me up, but Tulip would always come to the rescue.

"I don't really have time for your flirty games. I've had enough drama for the day, and I just want to go to sleep."

Esteban tsked his teeth and walked towards me while I sat at my small bistro table in the kitchen. Even though the cabin was small, I gave it my small little touches to make it feel like my birth mother decorated it. I wondered if she would have liked how I turned out without her. Did she even care anymore? Probably not, haven't even heard from her in years. One could still hope, right?

Esteban sat across from me and grabbed my hand that was holding my chin up and caressed my knuckles. If he wasn't such a playboy, I would think he was sweet. "Listen, Melina, I know I appear as a flirt and an ass."

I laughed while he gave me a worried smile.

"I do care about you. Hell, we grew up with each other. I know I've fucked every she-Wolf and half the high school, but I've always had a soft spot for ya."

I blew some air through my nose and rolled my eyes.

"Werewolves have a high sex drive, all right? I was just a little more open about my ways." he winked.

I took my hand back and wiped it on my leg, acting like it was dirty, and he laughed.

"Listen, I know you have had a bad day, so I'm just going to come out and say it." He ruffled his shaggy brown hair and looked up with his chocolate brown eyes. He looked nervous; I could see the beads of sweat on his face. He rubbed his hands together, gathering his thoughts.

"Are you all right, Esteban?" I asked, concerned. I'd never seen the suave Esteban get nervous. He had a way with women to get them in his bed, or in a closet, or even in his car. I shivered at the thought of how gross it was when I found him doing the cheerleading captain in the back of his car. I wasn't sure if he knew I saw him.

"Uh, yeah. Just know that I know you are going to Tulip's mating ceremony, I was wondering if you would be, uh, my date?" Esteban said it so fast, I almost missed it. Esteban was asking me out on a date for the mating ceremony. *Hell has frozen over everyone!* Esteban did not ask girls on dates. He asked if they wanted to go have some fun or gave his favorite line, "Hey, do you wanna get out of here?"

Staring at him for a moment, he looked at me with puppy dog eyes. Ha, how funny that saying is now. He was being serious about this, asking me out on a date. I wasn't the prettiest girl in school; I was the awkward one. Boys didn't give me a second glance, not one date. I didn't even go to the high school prom because I refused to go without a date. I didn't want to be one of those girls that sat in the corner sulking. Now I had Esteban in the palm of my hand, asking me out on a date.

Honestly, it felt good to be wanted. I would not let it get to me, though; he was just trying to take the one thing I have kept all my life and would only give it to someone I trusted and loved.

I sighed heavily and uncrossed my arms from my body. "Fine."

Esteban fist-pumped the air and jumped up and gave me a hug.

"A couple of conditions, though!" I interrupted.

Esteban straightened out his shirt and pushed his locks behind his ear.

"No trying to get in my pants. There will be none of that. No kissing either."

Esteban nodded. "I will never disrespect you." Esteban

smiled. "Anymore, never again, I swear. Only good intentions!" I hummed at the response.

"This is just for the mating ceremony, nothing else." I waved my finger around.

Esteban frowned. "But what if I win your heart?" He gave me that stupid smirk. I rolled my eyes and waved him off.

"Get out, I need to sleep."

"Challenge accepted." He bowed gracefully.

"You can't win, you know."

His back was to me as he opened the door. He turned his head to glance back at me. "Why do you say that?" he asked, acting confused.

"You have a mate out there, just like Tulip. All of you guys do. I'm looking for a long-term relationship, Esteban. I don't play around with my heart."

Esteban gave a small smile, and I swore I heard him say, "I *am* looking for the long term," under his breath.

Shaking my head, I locked the door and started doing my nightly routine. Today was maddening, and I was over it completely. I threw a few things in the washer and dryer so I could have clean clothes for the trip and washed the mugs before setting them out to dry. I watered my small window plants from inside the house and made sure they were locked tight for my departure tomorrow.

The small living room was already clean, the single bathroom was spotless, and my bedroom was warm and inviting. The past seven years of being on my own had made me grow up, maybe too fast. Even before the time my parents left, I had grown up too much for my own good. I was tired of taking care of myself, tired of being independent. There were so many women who begged and fought for independence so they could do what they wanted, but to me, it felt like loneliness, and I had been alone for too long.

I dragged my feet to my bedroom. I had painted it a light purple and Tulip helped me put a faux tulle canopy around my bed that hung from the rafters of the cottage. The comforter was white and lacy; there were times I would spend hours just playing with the extra fabric on the comforter when I felt lonely. Several stuffed animals adorned my bed, including one that Tulip's mother gave me, a medium-sized Wolf to snuggle at night. She got it for me when I was only eight. It was my most prized possession, and now I can just laugh at the irony of it.

Grabbing my stuffed animal, I held it close.

It was my own fault for isolating myself from Tulip's family, but I didn't want to be a burden. I wanted to show I was strong. On the outside, I was strong. I showed no fear and acted like my parents were nothing. Not one tear was shed when they dropped me off at Tulip's home and left me with my bags and a wad of cash. Why would I shed tears when I knew they wouldn't shed any for me? They waved goodbye while I sat on the porch and stared at them and watched them drive off into the distance.

They didn't love me.

And I wanted to be loved.

✳✳✳

The two-hour drive to the portal was long. I couldn't get over how much Tulip and Alec could sit there sniffing and holding each other. It made me want to gag. Tulip went from, "You can't tell me what to do," to, "I'll do anything for you!" I started laughing as they kissed and several wolves in the back started throwing paper, telling them to get a room.

When I walked up to the packhouse with my single suitcase, Tulip engulfed me in an enormous hug. "Thank you so much for coming! This means so much to have my best friend here."

Laughing lightly, I patted her back and looked up the stairs with Alec leaning on the door frame. He watched her like she was his prey. It was almost scary. Letting go, she grabbed my bag and threw it in the back of the SUV.

"Are we all ready to go?" Alpha Ramirez spoke loudly for all to hear. Tulip squealed yes and dragged Alec into the large vehicle. He smiled at me, and I gave him a mock salute and headed to the side of the car to get in.

"Well, I want to see my date for the mating ceremony. Just give me a minute!" I could hear Esteban yelling at some of his friends. His friends were laughing and pushing him around, joking about having a date. "You all laugh now, just you wait. She's stunning!"

I blushed with embarrassment and jumped in the car, hoping he wouldn't find me. Tulip saw my reaction and elbowed me in the gut.

"Pssst," she whispered, "are you, his date?"

My face turned red, and she smiled wildly.

"Holy shit, he was serious."

"Serious about what?"

"He thinks you are his mate."

"What!?" I squealed. Before I could ask any more questions, Esteban poked his head into the car.

"There she is—my date! I wanted to make sure you were still coming and not stand me up." He winked.

"I-I am here! Ready to go," I said nervously.

He blew a kiss with his lips and hopped out of the car and went back to the van he was riding in. Glancing at Alec and Tulip, I asked again. "What do you mean, he thinks I am his mate? You said you instantly knew when you were mates?"

"It's a long story, but Esteban lost his mate when they were still young." I frowned as she spoke. That sounded horrible. "Anyway, not my story to tell, but he thinks you are his second chance mate. They are rare, but they happen. Second chance mates can happen slowly, almost like human love. Slowly you both will feel the sparks when you touch if it's a true second chance. Or he just loves you on his own and when he marks you, then you feel the sparks."

My eyes grew wide. *Mark?*

"What the heck is a mark?" Alec smirked and nuzzled Tulip's neck.

"A bite," she said nonchalantly, and Alec pulled down her shirt. There was a white scar with teeth marks on it. "It lets other wolves and supernaturals know you are taken." Tulip rubbed noses with Alec.

"Gracious," I breathed.

After that conversation, I was silent and watched the other wolves harass the new couple.

Chapter 4

King Osirus

I'd been sitting here for the past hour watching the unmated Fae maidens dance with barely any clothes on. Their thin material was catching the small breeze coming from the large balcony window. It was a tradition that every few months they sent in dancers from across the Fae country to woo me into picking one of them for a queen. The parliament was a pain in my wings. Little did they know I had no desire to pick any of them. Never.

For the past 800 years, I had built up a reputation for myself, only to protect the throne and appease my parents. I've been told I was heartless, conniving, a womanizer, and a trickster with some things I had supposedly done. Some of them are true. I was a trickster with parliament. That is in a Fae's nature, to trick and play games. I was just only enhancing it a bit more than others.

I smiled at the center of the room where the women danced, remembering one of my tricks. We had gathered for a large banquet in honor of the sun. We were the Golden Light Kingdom, so celebrating the Second Sun Season was expected. The food was laid for all to see, many delicacies from around our nation.

Lotus flower candies, chocolate sponge cakes, strawberry souffle, and ginger tea, amongst others, sat around the tables. Everyone had seated and was waiting for me to raise my hand to begin the feast. Before I could begin, a loud scream came from across the garden as several fauns chased a woodland fairy sprite, who was completely naked and in an enlarged form. She was laughing and playing as she jumped and fluttered over the table; the fauns, going through their rutting season, stepped on all the food and cutlery, causing the entire feast to be ruined.

Once the trampled food lay in a giant heap of trash, everyone looked up at me in shock, waiting for me to be angered.

What was funny was, that everyone thought if I lost my temper, I would end them. Being the largest Fae and King could give you that assumption, but it was quite the opposite. I hated these ceremonies as much as the sleazy concubines I had to keep stored away in a harem on the other side of the castle. Pointless.

I waved my hand, stood up, put my hands behind my back and, trailed off with Alaneo, my advisor and best friend, by my side. He was the one I put in charge of making them think of me how they do. That way there was no threat. No one dared to stand up to me and the throne. To be heartless. That was what my father wanted of me, not just to protect the throne, but for our family as well.

The one thing they never pushed for me was finding a queen. Faes are more lenient with mating with non-mates or chosen mates. Faes crave companions and power. Many nobles mated with those that would give them more power or status in the Court, but it never worked. I stopped accepting chosen mates' unions into the Court for that reason. It helped with corruption greatly. The Moon Goddess chose our mates for a reason; why not honor it?

The girls were still dancing a good hour later, and I was growing bored. I haphazardly leaned on my elbow on the throne and threw my leg over the armrest, my signature sitting style, for when I was getting impatient. The music stopped after the chorus and I waved my hand for Alaneo to make the announcement. He knew the drill.

"Thank you all for coming this year. His highness must regretfully inform you he will not be taking a chosen mate this year. If you will, please exit the throne room, we will see everyone at the Winter Ball." There were groans of protest, but I ignored them, putting my arm over my forehead, and staring at the ceiling.

The ceiling was made of marble tile and painted with the most skilled painter over 1200 years ago. The painting was called "Meeting of Mates." Several women were dancing in scantily clad clothing, and male Faes were reaching for their mates. Their eyes locked on one another, and they smiled. The one way a Faes could find one's mate was by staring into their eyes and looking into their soul.

Taking a gigantic sigh, I heard Alaneo clear his throat.

"Yes, Alaneo?" I rolled my eyes.

"Still pouting?" Alaneo sat beside my throne in his appointed chair and leaned on the armrest nearest to me.

"I'm just tired of waiting. 800 rotations of the light sources and I still haven't found her. Maybe my reputation to scare off enemies has also scared her too."

"That is not the case. You said so yourself that Clara claimed the Moon Goddess was giving you one soon." Alaneo was always the voice of reason. Only he could lift my spirits.

Clara or also known as Princess Clarabelle, became my second closest confidant besides Alaneo. She could see right through the facade I put on for my kingdom. To appear strong, but on the inside, I was a weak man waiting for his beloved soulmate to grace his life. She brought a message of hope that my love would be graced to me soon but would be like a little wisp that tries to defy anyone that tries to take control of her.

For the last few hundred years, I had become depressed, and my usual entertainment had bored me. There was a time

I had a few favorite concubines, but I hadn't laid a finger on them for the past 300 years. The Goddess must have been punishing me.

Before I could reply with a response, Daphne walked into the throne room without knocking. Alaneo and I both groaned in annoyance. You sleep with a woman one time, and she thinks she owns the place. Hell, it was well over 350 years ago, but who's counting?

"Yes, Daphne? How can we help you?" Alaneo said in a groaning tone, not acting professionally. I gave him a smirk and light chuckle so she couldn't hear.

Overall, Daphne was decent in her looks. She was naturally slender, with medium-sized breasts that were always on display. Her red lips were a bit overdrawn, and her eyes were an alabaster grey that matched her dull personality. We grew up as friends a long time ago, but as she grew older; she realized what influence her family had over the parliament. She wanted to get into the laws and tax some people more heavily to get a bit more money in her and her family's pockets. I saw right through her greediness, right after I slept with her. She started bossing my servants and trying to dock their pay all within one night of sleeping with her. Daphne was quickly thrown out and put back in her spot as Duchess. I never planned on keeping her around, anyway; it was a one-time deal just like all the others.

"Your Majesty, I come bringing news of the Fae Council regarding the Peace Treaty of the Cerulean Moon Kingdom," she said sweetly.

Upon hearing the news, I sat up. This peace treaty and alliance with the Cerulean Moon Kingdom would benefit both of our nations. Protection for both of us and seeking justice for those who cannot do so alone. That was Princess Clara's ultimate plea and immediately drew me to her. To help those that couldn't help themselves.

"I see," I spoke with no emotion. Standing up from my throne, my robes danced across the marble as I started down the stairs. "When does she want the treaty signed?" I stopped in front of her, glaring.

"There is a mating ceremony tomorrow at the Crimson Shadows Pack. She said she would have time afterward. You are welcome to come to the ceremony and enjoy the festivities," Daphne said, fluttering her eyelashes.

"Tell her I'll be there." I turned and waved her off.

"Would you like an escort, Your Majesty? I am free tomorrow." I stopped in my tracks and turned my head so I could lay one eye on her.

"No." I continued to walk out of the room while I heard a large huff come from her lips as she stomped to the door.

Melina

I groaned as Tulip and Alec continued to suck faces beside me. Tulip always made sure I didn't feel like the third wheel when she dated before, but I sure felt like one now since she found Alec. Many times, I thought about licking the window just to feel like I was doing something instead of hearing, lip-smacking to my right.

"How are you doing back there, Melina?" Alpha Ramirez spoke.

"Just peachy." I rolled my eyes. Ramirez laughed with Elm. Elm was sitting with Ramirez in the passenger seat talking about pack duties I had no clue about. Something about rogues, witch enchantments, and meeting some conniving Faes in the Bergarian world.

We came up to our destination packhouse about 30 minutes ago. They let us through once our caravan had shown proper pack IDs. I had my special permission slip form from our elders and was let through.

There was a pack that guarded the portal to the other world, the Ever Green Pack. They had their own operations here. Small shops, bakeries and s, hotels. If a human stumbled into this area, I don't think they would know the difference. It was just a small town full of Werewolves living their daily lives.

We continued through the town and drove to a dirt road that took us farther into the woods. The path was nearly covered with brush and trees, so no one could really see it unless you were looking for it. A large two-story garage was beside a large double tree archway. Nothing looked particularly special about it. If someone wanted to get married there, it would be nice, though.

Alpha Ramirez had everyone get out of the cars and had us carry one bag each. The cars were taken away and Ramirez was given a ticket for each car they brought. They were parked on the second floor, and we would get them back once we were done with our business in Bergarian. Sports cars, SUVs, Jeeps and a few motorcycles littered the garage. Some people must be insanely rich.

Tulip grabbed my hand and pulled me with her and Alec, and Rose kept a close eye on me. She gave me a smile as we came to the tree archway as we listened to the Ever Green's Alpha.

"There are many of you that have not gone through the portal, so I will let you know the instructions. Once you step foot through the portal, there will be a silver path of stones. Do not step off the path or you will be stuck in darkness forever and not be able to find your way back. Continue to follow the path until you arrive in Bergarian."

Those that hadn't been through the portal looked at each other worriedly, but Rose came up to me and clasped my hand. "Don't worry, Melina. I'll be here with you, all right?"

I nodded at her. Tulip had such a wonderful mother, it almost made me jealous.

Esteban was now walking up, just exiting the large passenger van he rode in. He gave me a wink and stood next to me. "Hey there, doll!" He nudged me with his shoulder.

Rose looked at him warily; she wasn't a big fan of Esteban

or his friends.

"I forgot to ask, what color dress are you wearing?"

"Um, teal. Why do you need to know that?" I asked.

"No reason." He smirked and gave me a shoulder-side hug. I never let my hand go from Rose as he walked away.

"What was that about?" Rose asked worriedly.

"Esteban asked me to be his date for the mating ceremony. Tulip says that Esteban is telling everyone I might be his second chance mate." I rolled my eyes. "How would I even know if I was a mate to someone? I'm human."

Mom hummed in response and looked at her husband and smiled.

"I am not sure about humans, but I know with Werewolves we have an undeniable attraction to each other and when our touch touches another part of our mate's skin tingles erupt all over our bodies. Then there is a pull when the bond traps you in its web and makes you inseparable. It's beautiful." Rose continued to look at Elm as she spoke.

Smiling at the thought, I looked back at Esteban.

He was an attractive guy, and I could see the appeal, but I didn't have that attraction or pull that she was talking about. I wasn't sure about any tingles because I had never touched his skin before. Shaking the thought, our line moved for us to pass through the portal.

People lined up. Tulip and Alec were first, and Tulip eagerly looked behind and saw me, waving her hand childishly at me. I waved my hand back and gave her a small smile. Two at a time, we went through; Rose and I were next to go through and I felt the butterflies in my stomach.

Just yesterday, I found out about Werewolves and the supernatural. Now I'm going into a world full of fantasy creatures from fairy tales. Who knew so much could change in just twenty-four hours?

Chapter 5

Melina

Once we were in the portal, it was eerily quiet. People in front of us kept silent as we walked through the silver path. Looking off the path, there was nothing but darkness, a void. No sound, no wind, utterly silent. One would think that the quiet would calm someone's nerves, and bring peace to your mind, but this was not as expected. My hand tightened around Rose's as we continued to walk through the path.

As if night suddenly turned into day, the light shown above us. Squinting my eyes and looking at the sky, I immediately saw differences from Earth and this world. The sky was blue but with a hint of purple. There were not one but two suns that lit the sky, one larger than the other; perhaps the smallest was a dwarf sun.

Being captivated by the glorious sight, I saw a shadow engulfed us over our heads. Looking up, it came to the view that it was an actual Dragon that had flown over. My head bent back in awe, watching the large, red-scaled lizard flap its gigantic wings around us. The breeze was warm as it continued to fly onward as we looked out over the mountain where we stood.

The portal led us to the side of a mountain, a cliff separating us from the large farmland and communities below. There were no cars to be found, and many people were taken to horse and carriage. "There are no cars here?" I questioned Mom as she led me to the carriage.

"No, we want to keep the land pure, unlike humans that spoil the Earth. This has been maintained to keep it as a Garden of Eden. We do have electricity, though; the windmills and several dams keep us a little civilized." She chuckled as Esteban opened the carriage door for me.

Esteban held out his hand to lead me up to the carriage but was stopped abruptly by Tulip.

"Just shove her in there. She's fine!" She giggled as Alec shook his head and Esteban gave her a glare. "Come on now, Esteban, you have all day tomorrow to bewitch her. Now go on with you and your posse!" Tulip, the ever so romantic girl.

I laughed and waved Esteban goodbye as he set his lips in a pout. Tulip continued to push me to the other side of the carriage, and I sat still.

We were all sharing the carriage, Alec, Tulip, and her parents. The carriage took off with a jolt and I opened up the curtained carriage as we continued down the mountain. There were different castles scattered across the land. One could see the Cerulean Moon Kingdom, as Alec pointed out, home to the future queen, Clara, and her mate, Kane. They were waiting for Clara's training to be completed before they took the throne; thus, she still ran the Crimson Shadows with Kane as their Luna. We would travel there, just beside the Cerulean Moon Kingdom.

Over to the East was the Fae or Golden Light Kingdom. There were different types of Fae as Alec pointed out. There were Pixies, who were tiny and a bit of a handful, no pun intended, since they fit in the size of your hand. When they spoke, they sounded like little bells tinkling in your ear.

Then there were the Fairies, bigger than the Pixies. They stood twelve inches in height and could shrink and grow their size. They could only stay in their grown form for so long until they revert to their smaller selves. Pixies were the keepers of the land; they helped the flowers grow all over Bergarian but were considered to be controlled by the Fae King. Many other types of Pixies lived here such as forest, water, garden, and darkness. Some are sub-cultured pixies that were too rare to mention, as Alec put it.

The Golden Light Kingdom was a vast contrast to the Cerulean Moon Kingdom. Everything was brighter, and it looked like the suns favored the kingdom. The flora was brighter; the water was cleaner, overall, it looked as if it were a heaven on Earth, I mean Bergarian. "You mentioned a Fae King. What is a Fae then?" Alec and the other wolves stiffened at the mention of the word. Instead of Alec, Elm spoke.

"The Faes are tricky creatures, as any type of Fae or Fairy. However, Faes are more like us, part human, with a hint of something else." He shook his head. "They walk and talk like a human, but they still hold on to the fairy inside of them. Faes are much more powerful than all the other, smaller cultures of themselves; they are said to have strengthened over time and not actually created by any god. These are all rumors, of course." He smiled.

Listening intently, I put my hands on my face and my elbows on my knees to encourage him to finish the story.

Everyone laughed at my twinkling eyes as I pouted. "Fine, fine. I forget the child in you, Melina." Satisfied with my efforts, I sat back to listen more.

"Besides what I have told you, there isn't much more to tell. They are private. They don't go around blabbing their history to us Shifters, Vampires or Demons. Even the King himself hasn't left his palace in over 300 years which changed just a few months ago."

"That has got to be brutally boring, and 300 hundred years?"

Alec nodded. "Yeah, supernaturals don't age past thirty and we continue to live unless something kills us. The oldest supernatural I've heard of was 3000 years old."

My mouth dropped. How wonderful to live that long, to see your great, great, great, and maybe a few more great-grandchildren grow up with their husbands and wives. Humans really got the short end of the stick.

"Tulip, I'm going to be old and grey, and you are going to still look beautiful, no fair!"

Tulip chuckled but didn't laugh as happily as I did.

"What's wrong?"

"There will be one day that you won't be here anymore," she said with sadness in her eyes.

I hugged her tightly and kissed her cheek. The thought of them not telling me what they were was out the window. Tulip really care about me and knowing she would be this upset after I was gone was proof of that.

"Don't cry, dear Tulip, or you will start to wilt," I spoke in an American Southern voice.

"Pray to Selene she has a mate. There is a rumor that more humans are becoming mates of our kind," Rose interjected. A wicked smile played on her lips; I wonder if she knew more than she was led to believe.

I squinted my eyes, giving her the 'do you know something?' look. Patting my hand, she then looked back out the window as the conversation never happened.

"Anyway, before I was interrupted—" Elm coughed for attention.

Tulip sat up and nuzzled into Alec's neck in which Elm rolled his eyes.

"The Fae King actually *did* leave the castle during the brief rogue war three months ago and is rumored to be coming by tomorrow for the peace treaty signing after both Alec and Tulip's mating ceremony."

Tulip's eyes grew large, and a sizable, unnatural-looking smile was plastered to her face.

My eardrum just about exploded as Tulip howled inside the carriage. Everyone was covering their ears, and I finally had to stick my head out the window. The horses were yipping and neighing and warriors on horses were looking in confusion. I laughed and giggled as we continued to roll down the cemented path towards the Warrior Pack.

Only a few hours later, we arrived at the pack territory. Again, papers were assessed that looked like passports and with a quick push of a gate, we had entered another territory. We had passed by several areas that had gates, and some that had none. Wolves kept their land in line, but there were other shifters besides wolves. Panthers, lions, and even Dragons littered the area.

"Welcome cousin!" I heard a deep laugh come from the door of the massive mansion. It was made of white brick with large columns and a small girl that stood beside the beast of a man. He was adorned in tattoos and piercings, while the girl next to him was just my size. Petite, as Rose would say. Her stomach was enormous, looking to pop with a baby at any given moment.

"Alpha Kane, look at you now!" Elm encountered the other large alpha.

Alpha Kane easily towered over Elm, and I thought Elm was the tallest I had ever met. The girl beside him patted Alpha Kane on the shoulder and waddled to us.

"Welcome to the Crimson Shadows Pack, Tulip. You look just like the photos your mother sent! You look just as radiant!"

Tulip blushed severely and bowed to the short stature woman and muttered a thank you. "Hello, you must be Tulip's best friend?" She smiled warmly at me. We were easily the same height and I no longer felt short around these Wolves.

"Yes, I am. My name is Melina. It's a pleasure to meet you, Luna Clara, and thank you for allowing me to be here," I tried to say politely.

"Oh, none of that. My name is Clara, and you can call me such."

"T-thank you."

Clara gave me a knowing smile and led us into the house to our rooms.

We were led to our rooms as the day was about to be completed. I wasn't sure what to say. Were they really suns, or did they call them something else here? Shaking my head, I opened the door to my room. It was just the size I liked, small and quaint, with a little charm. It was bigger than my bedroom at home but still had the beautiful finishes I liked so much. It was so girly. I loved all the girly things since I could not indulge in it as I grew up.

Running and bouncing onto the comforter, I let out a little squeal of excitement as I rolled around.

"Enjoying yourself?" I heard from the door. Esteban stood there, leaning on the doorway smirking in my direction.

"Of course, I'm on my very first vacation, why wouldn't I?" I straightened myself from the bed and regally went to my suitcase to unpack. I brought little since that is what they preferred. New clothes were being made, so we matched the surrounding areas. Honestly, excited to see what we would wear. Tulip mentioned everything made of Elven silk, strong, sturdy, soft and waterproof.

"You need to let your little wall down, doll. It isn't a good look on you." Esteban came by me and flicked my hair as he looked out the window. My window looked out to the East where the Golden Light Kingdom should be. My interest in the Faes was growing and was hoping to check out the pack library tomorrow.

"I'm doing just fine, no wall here. Now, I think you need to leave. It isn't appropriate for you to be in my bedroom— people will talk." I walked to the door to show him out, but he didn't move. I kept pointing to the door, and he chuckled as he walked by me with his hands in his pockets.

"You are something else, you know that?" Esteban was now standing in the hall, and every bit of my body wanted to slam the door in his face.

I didn't like the fact he slept with a ton of women and then expected me to forgive and forget and let him be my date. If he had truly cared for me at all during his time in high school, he wouldn't have done it. Then again, maybe there was no bond to be held and now he is just growing fond of me because of a bond that I couldn't even feel. Who wants to fall in love because of a bond, anyway? It should be of my own choosing and nothing more.

"I'll show you a good time tomorrow, doll. Trust me. I'll sweep you off your feet and maybe by the end of the night, you will feel it, too."

"Feel what?" I rolled my eyes.

"My growing love for you." His finger was coming up to touch my face when Tulip burst through her bedroom door in the adjacent hallway.

"Melina!! Come quick! They have Crème Brulé downstairs!!" Tulip grabbed my arm and pulled me down the stairs, leaving Esteban in the dust.

We laughed all the way down until we saw the large dining room. There were hundreds of Wolves in this mansion, all were getting their food in a buffet style fashion. Several women and men were serving the plates, and the smell finally reached my nose.

"Wow, that smells amazing," I whispered to Tulip.

Heads perked up from the dining room table on the far side of the room. Not wanting to look over, Tulip led me to the buffet and piled the food on for me. Laughing, I had to remind her I didn't eat as much as everyone else did.

Sitting down with a large plate of dinner and the famous Crème Brulé, I was about to take my first bite when three males sat down across from us. Tulip nudged me to say something, so I said the first thing that came to mind. "Hi?"

The men chuckled, and one leaned over the table. He was tan like Esteban, his curly, unruly hair was highlighted with golden blond wisps. His eyes were a brown, earthy color. Even sitting down, he towered over me.

"I hear you are new here." He leaned in for a smell. I didn't move and looked at him confusingly. "You smell fantastic."

Tulip choked on her food and quickly wiped her mouth, holding back a laugh.

"Is that supposed to be some Wolfy pick up line? Because it just isn't working for me." I go to my fork and stuck the large piece of meat into my mouth. The boys beside him were smirking.

"Ah ha, no, not a pickup line. It's just that me and the guys here noticed your smell. It is unique."

Tulip's eyes went large, and she looked over at her mother for help. I kept my eyes peeled for this guy in the middle.

"Listen here. If you dare say anything about being my mate or some crazy supernatural crap like that, I'll stick this fork in your Wolf's eye, pull it out, and make you eat it." I stabbed my fork into an opposing blueberry and put it in my mouth, letting the juice dribble on the side.

"Damn," the two other boys said in unison.

The Wolf in the middle smirked. "Hi, I'm Carson."

Chapter 6

Melina

"Warriors, huh?" I spoke.

Carson nodded his head as he took a chunk off his steak and stuck it in his mouth. "We are the top three, meaning we are in the special forces. We can do secret missions for the royals, spying, fighting, tracking, you name it. In fact, we just did one a few months ago. Our team found our Luna in the rogue territory."

"Yeah, we got so much pussy after that," Rex, the guy on Carson's left, said. The guy was decent looking too, cocky just like most Wolves, though. He had sun-bleached hair and a few tattoos on his arms.

"I'm guessing no mates for you guys yet, then?" I questioned.

All of them were silent until Carson spoke up. "Not yet. They are out there. When we find them, we'll chase 'em and mark 'em just like they did in the old days."

I gave a shocked look while Tulip giggled. Alec gave Tulip a wink while I just rolled my eyes. Something tells me Alec ran naked through the woods to pound Tulip into the dirt.

Most of the nice-looking guys I've met were horny Wolves. I don't even know why these Wolves have mates;

they are screwing anything with two legs. Then again, there may be centaurs out there for all I know, then it would be four legs. They were, however, more respectful after I told them their adulthood was at risk of being cut off later if they tried to touch me. Which they found hilarious and now want me to stay near them to protect me from other horny males.

"Being human gives you special privileges since you are weak," Carson told me.

Gee thanks?

"Are there a lot of missions? Do you go spy on some mermaids in the water, taking their tops off?" I jested.

Carson threw his head back and laughed. Other wolves looked over and I couldn't help but shrink a little. *Keep comments to myself, duly noted.* Once Carson had his fun, he went back to eating and never replied.

"Ew," I whispered to Tulip.

Sean, the other Wolf that was up Carson's butt, was on the quiet side. He seemed nice and, most of all, tolerable. There were several times I caught him staring. Maybe the complete human being in a house full of Wolves gave off an unpleasant smell. Before I could ask Sean what he thought about all of this man-whoring around, Esteban walked up, and he looked ticked.

"Melina, doll, how are you?" He gritted his teeth.

Esteban sat his plate next to mine and almost came arm to arm with me. I scooted over, which only made him scoot closer.

Sensing my distress, Carson glanced at Esteban. "Hey, pup, I think she wants some space." Carson gave a deep growl and Esteban only glared in return.

"I'll do what I want, you glorified tracker."

Carson stood up abruptly and puffed out his chest while Esteban followed. I've never seen a brawl from this close with Werewolves, so I took it as my cue to leave. Elbowing Tulip, she took the hint and let me out of the seat.

"She's my date tomorrow. I can talk to her all I want!" Esteban yelled.

Looking back, it was only getting heated. Part of me wanted to stop it. I didn't want anyone getting hurt because of me. I ran back to get in between them and put my hand on both of their chests.

"Listen, let's calm down. Everything is fine. I was just giving Esteban some space. Esteban, Carson is my new friend, all right?

Carson stepped back a but grabbed my hand to pull me away. Esteban's teeth elongated, so I ran to him and put my hand on his chest again. His teeth retracted.

"Esteban, just stop this, Okay?"

Esteban stepped back, but Rex and Sean had already stood up ready to help Carson.

"What's going on here?" we heard a deep voice.

Looking toward the voice, I saw it was Alpha Kane. Neither of the boys were going to say anything, so I spoke up. "I'm sorry, uh, Alpha, sir. Just a misunderstanding. They won't fight anymore, right, guys?"

I looked at both, but their eyes had not left each other.

"Both of you, in my office. Now." The amount of authority and heaviness in his voice was suffocating.

With that, Alpha Kane left the dining room with two wolves tailing him. Every Wolf in the dining room was staring at me. I let out a small sigh and walked to the side door leading to the backyard. Tulip was still with Alec and the way my mood was, she knew I needed time to myself.

It was what I knew anyway, right? To be alone?

Carson

We made the long walk to the Alpha's office. I hated being dragged in here. It had only happened a few times since Alpha Kane had taken over and it was not the most pleasant experience. His Wolf was massive, and he can half shift, something that takes precision and skill and usually only someone of royal blood could accomplish.

Alpha Kane has held it for three days straight when he hunted for his mate from the rogue battle a few months ago.

"Can someone tell me what the fuck was that?" Alpha Kane growled as he sat behind his desk chair.

Esteban, the smug idiot, sat in the chair across from him and folded his arms against his chest. The fucker had the audacity to roll his eyes in front of the Alpha, which was a death sentence.

Alpha jumped over the desk and gripped Esteban's neck so fast he didn't see it coming. He was pinned to the floor, choking for air, and I couldn't help but chuckle to myself. "Want to lose the attitude?" he roared as the room shook.

Thank the Goddess the Luna had the walls reinforced. After his first couple 'meetings' with rowdy Wolves, she had had enough listening to the chastising.

Esteban tried to nod his head, but only a gurgle came from his lips, so he tilted his head to show submission. Alpha gave him one last squeeze and got up and went back to his desk. Esteban coughed and regained his breathing, sitting back in the chair. I was already on the Alpha's good side by not fighting back. Heh, go me.

"Do I need to ask my question again?" Alpha spoke in a whisper, which was almost as scary as him yelling.

"Yes, Alpha," I spoke with as much confidence as I could muster. "There is a human, Melina. Esteban looked like he was getting up in her space and she wasn't comfortable with it, so I spoke to him about backing off. He started giving attitude and eventually Melina had to calm us down."

Esteban scowled at me as I finished my turn speaking.

"Esteban? Sound about, right? Anything to add?" Alpha spoke calmly.

"She's mine. I don't have to listen to a damn thing this tracker says," Esteban spat.

"Is Melina your mate?" Esteban paused.

"Don't lie to me pup, I don't take to it kindly," Alpha growled.

"Technically, second chance mate," Esteban said lowly.

"Chosen or fated?"

Why the hell would he ask that? Does it matter? I thought.

"A bit of both. I have a powerful attraction to her, and I've always wanted her. Her smell calls to me." Esteban looked away. Something wasn't right, but I couldn't detect a lie.

Alpha shifted in his seat as he stared at Esteban. His fingers tapped on the desk and looked out the window, mind-linking someone.

"Does she feel it? The bond?" Alpha tilted his eyebrow.

"I don't know. She won't let me touch her—her skin, anyway. Just touches through the fabric. She's hesitant, considering my past and reputation."

I scoffed. No wonder she wanted to be far away from the prick and all the rest of us. She would not have a horny bastard. *She's got standards, good for her, sorry for the poor guy whoever gets her.* When she sat down at the dinner table, I knew she was a 'no nonsense' kind of girl. She was smart, she knew what Wolves do even when they are destined for a mate.

Alpha pointed his finger at Esteban. "If she shows signs or if she tells you to back off, you back off. I'm trusting Carson and his team to monitor you. One slip up and you're out, you hear?"

Esteban acknowledged reluctantly.

"In my opinion, Esteban, she isn't your mate. I suggest you move on," Alpha said gruffly.

Esteban furrowed his brows in question. "How would you know? You don't know Melina."

"I've got my sources. Now back off. Dismissed." With a no-nonsense tone, we both left the office and went our separate ways.

Melina

Walking through to the backyard, there was a massive lake. Kids were on the other side and the sun was setting. The weather was still warm from the afternoon sun or suns, and I went to put my feet in the water. The small pier led to about a quarter of the way into the lake. I rolled up my skinny jeans and took off my sandals and dipped my feet in the refreshing water. It looked so clean and so clear. You could see straight to the bottom. Small fish swam around in vibrant colors, you would think would only be in the ocean.

I smiled to myself as I sat and observed for a while. The larger sun had set and the smaller one lingered on the horizon. It was getting dark, but the view of this new world intrigued me too much to go inside. Instead of seeing fireflies, I'm guessing the Pixies are lighting the way. They danced around the leaves on the trees and often would come to the lake and skip across. It was so magical to see them laughing and their voices sounding like little bells.

How could a place like this exist and no human could know about it? Humans were the actual monsters, it seemed, ruining Earth, and using all the natural resources until they were completely depleted. The air here was so clean and fresh, making me feel like I could live forever and not age myself.

My bum was getting numb from sitting so long, so I switched positions to my stomach. Legs were in the air, swaying back and forth. My head lay on one of my arms as I took my other hand and had my fingers dance along the water. Small frogs could be heard on the outskirts of the lake. A few splashes from the fish, jumping to get away from a predator. At peace, I felt at peace. For the first time in a long time, I didn't have the aching feeling in the back of my head from my parents.

Never mind, they just came back. Letting a gigantic sigh escape my lips, I tried to think of things besides them. Besides them leaving me alone, never loving me and a brand on my heart, thinking no one else could love me.

Sure, Tulip and her parents cared for me and even said they love me, but it wasn't the deep-rooted love a blood parent could give. Heck, their own love for each other was broken. Humans weren't meant for that. They are the veritable monsters and I got stuck being one of them.

Who could love me anyway? Even if there was such a thing for me to have a mate, I think I would have a hard time. My brain was too messed up with too much emotional baggage. Someone could do better. I'd made it this far with no one. I could go through life without someone loving me.

Could I though? Maybe I was meant not to be loved. The love I wanted, Esteban and any of those stupid Wolves couldn't give me. They just wanted a hand in someone's pants.

A small tear dropped out of my eye and landed in the water. My fingertip dropped into the water to skim it across the skin of the water, humming and faintly singing my favorite tune.

Chapter 7

King Osirus

The ride was long, but I enjoyed the scenery. It had been a few months since I visited the Cerulean Moon Princess and I had missed her. Over the months, we had sent correspondence frequently regarding the new peace treaty between our kingdoms. Princess Clara was the only Wolf, and former human, I would trust. Her aura was pure and calming, which got her into so much trouble since she met her mate. Every male wanted her; luckily, she had one of the strongest males of the whole Bergarian realm as her mate.

Since I rarely left the Golden Light Kingdom, few people knew or noticed me. Instead of wearing my royal robes, I donned just plain tan riding trousers and a loose white tunic. My chest was bare to bring in the sunlight to give me energy for my power if we were ever stopped along the way by bandits. I made sure that we traveled lightly, even forgoing the usual royal carriage. It was nice to be out and be among the norm, not worrying about what the Fae Court or Parliament were saying.

Even though I wasn't wearing my royal attire, many would look at the small riding caravan. We were riding the best-bred horses; expensive and highly trained were written all over these mares and stallions. Our kingdom was known for our horses with a slight sheen to them. It was in the special bristled brushes we used. The finest bristles were made by a special tree that grew on the Eastern Ocean, the Melloway tree.

Montu, my white stallion, reared as we entered the Crimson Shadow Pack territory. It could sense the strong shifter, Alpha Kane, and he didn't like the strong shifter nearby. It wasn't often he was met with an animal more ferocious than he could be. I named him Montu for a reason, it means 'god of war and of the sun.' His bright tan coat was all but a reminder of his great strength.

Patting his neck lightly to calm him, I heard a small gasp from up the path that led into the large mansion. Princess Clara skipped down the stairway with her rounded belly. I gave a smile, something I didn't often do but when it came to her, I couldn't help it. It wasn't anything remotely romantic, just another close friend that I would entrust my life with. I dismounted my horse and gave it to a standing omega waiting.

"Osirus! You came!" Clara continued to waddle and trot to me as I ducked down and gave her a hug. Alpha Kane wasn't too far behind, scowling as he saw me. Werewolves were still leery of me, and for good reason. Until the treaty was signed, they would continue to be that way.

"Alpha Kane," I nodded and pushed my long hair to my back. Reaching out and grabbing his forearm, we both shook vigorously while I gave him a smirk. His Wolf was growling, and it was great to taunt the Wolf.

"It's great you could make it. Clara hasn't stopped talking about it." He rolled his eyes. "Always about other men," he grumbled.

Clara pushed him to the side playfully and gave him a kiss.

"I have you and your men staying in the royal cabin, to the right side of the packhouse."

She pointed to the large cabin, which wasn't really a cabin

at all. It was three stories high and made of some rich, dark wood from the Vermillion Kingdom. The lights covered the outside and several whisps came around looking into the windows.

"It's perfect, Princess. Thank you for accommodating me. My men and I are ever grateful." Clara's eyes glowed as she clapped her hands playfully.

"I've had dinner delivered to you and your men. There was a disturbance in the dining hall today and I think you would much rather take a rest in your quarters."

I gave a smiled. "Trouble in paradise already?"

Kane looked annoyed, meaning it was dealing with his warriors.

"Yeah," Kane continued. "Some visiting Wolf tried to stake a claim on the adopted human daughter of my cousin's family. It's been taken care of." Kane ran his hand through his hair.

"A human?" I questioned. "Has the law finally been passed by the Supernatural Council?"

The Supernatural Council was a panel of a large mix of different species in Bergarian that decided what was best for the realm. They had talked for years to let trustworthy humans visit, and it looked like it had been granted.

"Yes, but a thorough background check must be done. This girl has lived with Werewolves all her life, unbeknownst to her, though. She just found out just yesterday we exist, and she took it quite well," Clara bragged. "She's such a cute thing. I finally have someone the same size as me!"

Kane chuckled at his mate.

"I'll have to meet her. I've never met a human. You were changed by the time I met you."

Clara nodded in agreement. "Oh, you will meet her, all right." She giggled and winked at Kane, who rolled his eyes. "Anyway, enjoy your dinner. I still must help with preparations for tomorrow. Please make yourselves at home!"

Clara and Kane left, and my men had already walked into

the cabin. The horses were tended to by a few omegas that wanted to help. "Be sure to give him extra oats. This was his first long journey." The omegas smiled and bowed several times before leaving.

Resting my hand on my sword and checking out the surroundings, I headed out for a walk. The men were inside taking care of a few things, and the restless beating of my heart made my chest quake. I felt a rush of adrenaline, the flow of my magic inside me. It could very well be the thought of our kingdoms finally being at peace and bringing more light to both of our lands. Our kingdoms would be unstoppable, being the largest companionships of them all.

The Golden Light Kingdom and the Cerulean Moon Kingdom were the largest, followed by Vermillion, which was under a complete renovation of its court and parliament. Queen Diana demanded it and being born half-witch she could accomplish it. There are smaller territories scattered throughout the lands, but none as large as the three.

The last of the light sources had fallen across the horizon, and now the Light Pixies lit the edge of the forests. All was quiet except for the natural sounds of nature. Many Wolves had retired to their homes, and some just going out for the nightly patrol.

There was a small melody of music that led me to the complete opposite side of the pack territory. A lake with lights glowed around in the middle of it. The soft voice was hypnotizing. Gripping my sword with one hand and the sheath in the other, I came closer. The singing became louder, and the sound made my ears tingle. Sirens stayed close to the coastline unless they had inhabited large lakes now. She would be out of her territory and would have to be removed.

Bushes lay near the waterside. Creeping down and looking through the brush, I saw a girl. She was lying on her stomach on the pier. She wasn't a Shifter, a Fae or even a Fairy. I continued to stare at her while I listened to the humming and gently parting her mouth letting a smooth melody escape her.

The music filled my ears, and I felt the sorrow as each note left her lips. Her fingers continued to dance on the water's surface and pieces of her hair fell in. A few drops of tears left her cheeks and dropped into the water. Why was I so captivated by this creature? What was she?

"Your Majesty!" a large voice boomed from across the courtyard.

"Shit," I whispered, and I peered through the bushes again to glimpse the woman. I couldn't see her face, and in my heart, I knew I had to see her.

"Your Majesty!" the voice boomed again and as I looked again; she had run back to the pack house.

"Dammit, what is it, Alaneo?"

Alaneo looked at me, taken aback and raised his arms in question. "What the hell?" His long braid got caught in the wind and a nearby fairy grabbed it and gave it a tug. "Not now, Lydia! I'm working!" He swatted his hands in her direction.

"She followed you all the way to the Cerulean Moon Kingdom territory? She must have it bad." I chuckled lightly.

"You have no idea," he groaned.

"I told you not to mess with a Fairy. They get obsessed until they have had their fill, then they will leave you alone."

"Yeah, yeah. At least she can't grow to Fae size for another 24 hours. I've been telling her no for years, but one time wasn't enough for her."

Slapping him on the back, we headed back to our cabin. "The men were waiting to eat until you arrived."

"They could have eaten without me. I'm here on vacation, away from the political shit. You should have told them."

"They refused. You know your most trusted guards worship you."

"Just because I saved their village and families doesn't mean they need to follow me around all the time," I groaned.

I was just a small Fae when it happened. Vermillion

wasn't always as secluded as they are now. Rogue vampires invaded villages across the Golden Light Kingdom, and luckily, I was visiting my aunt when a small band of them entered. That was the first time I had to use my sword and magic to fight off an enemy. I'd saved the village and earned the title of "The Fearless" because I was only 80 years old. Not near enough time for the full training of a king or knight.

"Everett, Braxton, and Finley, what ails you? Could you not feed yourself and expect your dear King to feed you?" They all laughed, drinking a large pint of Fae wine they had carried with them from home. It wouldn't last the night.

"Nah, dear King. We just wished for ye to enjoy our spoils before the party tomorrow. There are to be many unmated women coming across to the territory, hearing of your arrival." I groaned.

"Pass the flask, Braxton." A loud cheer came from the group.

I could only be myself around Alaneo and Clara; my guards had pledged their life to me, but I could not let them in. There were too many dangers around. I had to keep the entire "Fearless King" facade in place for as long as I could until I found my mate, that is. With that in mind, I will have to let everyone else in as well. I was just scared of the results. If I could fight with her by my side, it would be all the better. I just hope she can trust me enough to understand the dealings we will have to go through together to change a nation and rid it of the Court and Parliament's oppression.

"Are ye ready for the ceremony tomorrow? The wolves do it differently from us, so I'm excited to watch," Everett spoke. His fiery red hair, along with his brothers', was always up in a bun as their beards grew long.

It was uncharacteristic for Fae to wear long beards, but it suited the brothers just fine. They had grown up in the village, away from the courts and away from the stupid mannerisms, one had to have if growing up royalty. Most of his village sported them and the women preferred them.

I took the pad of my finger and traced the flask. "Yes, I've been to one before. Clara and Kane's was quite interesting. You can see the love in their eyes. It makes one quite jealous." I lowered my eyes and took another sip of the strong ale. The men were quiet, not sure what to say.

"We will all find our mates one day. Goddess Selene has promised." Finley slammed his pint down. He was the most dramatic of the group. "I just pray I don't have to share a mate. I don't think I could handle seeing my other brothers' cocks in my woman."

Braxton let out a boisterous laugh while Everett spit some of his ale on Alaneo. Laughter invaded the table, and I let out a small chuckle at the antics.

"It doesn't work that way, idiot," Alaneo spoke. "You aren't identical triplets. You don't share a soul. It'd never work."

"Never say never." Everett laughed. "The Goddess just put humans on the supernatural mating list. Things could change." Everett took a sip. This conversation was going from fun to ridiculous theories. I excused myself and went up to my quarters.

The room was large, and the king-size bed looked inviting. Taking off my belt with my sword and dagger, I laid it on the chair next to me. Riding boots, trousers, and linen shirt, I threw them to the chair as well and sunk into the enormous bed.

Beds always felt lonely, but this night, it felt even more lonely and cold. Very cold.

My thoughts drifted to the little Siren by the lake. Her voice was calming. It reminded me of Clara. Her hair was so dark that it cloaked her face just enough to where I couldn't see her. The thought crossed my mind that if she had only looked up, I could have seen if she was mine. I had never been so captivated by a woman. My heart continued to race at the thought of her.

Putting a hand on my chest to calm my heart, I thought

nothing of what she sang to help me get to sleep.

Chapter 8

Melina

The two suns were close to being high in the sky by the time I woke up the next day. I didn't sleep well at all from the night before. I was too bothered by the feeling I was being watched at the lake. Then there was the constant calling of "Your Majesty!" that was coming from the far end of the courtyard. I didn't want to be caught outside at night and being a 'defenseless human,' it was best if I hightailed it out of there.

There was a loud knock at the door. I had an inkling I knew who it was but was trying my best to ignore it.

"Melina!!!" the voice shrieked, and I put the pillow over my head.

The last thing I wanted to do was get breakfast or lunch in the dining hall. There were too many eyes on me yesterday, and I would rather starve myself than deal with that social awkwardness again. Before I could mutter a "go away" in response, Tulip burst into the room and jumped on the bed.

"Goddess, woman, get off me!" I wasn't the most wonderful person to wake up to.

"Get up. Mom, me and you and even Luna are going to get manis and pedis and do the whole spa thing! They have their own room dedicated to it! Hurry and shower and meet me in five!" Tulip patted my butt and threw the blankets off my bed. I quickly curled up to warm myself and then I heard another light knocking on the door.

Surprise, surprise, Esteban. "I could get used to that view." Esteban licked his lips as he walked into the room.

I sat up and gave him an evil glare as I picked up the fluffy duvet and wrapped myself up. "Now, I'm a burrito, not cute at all."

"Ah, yes, you are still a cute burrito," he purred. "Are you finally up? Everyone was wondering where you were this morning. You aren't sick, are you?" Esteban asked, concerned.

"Uh, no. I didn't sleep well last night, and I didn't want to subject myself to another brawl in the dining room, so I slept instead." I hobbled over to my suitcase to pick out a pair of yoga pants and a tank top.

"Yeah, sorry about that." Esteban rubbed the back of his head. "I kind of lost it there."

"We are just friends, Esteban, nothing more. You can't stake your Wolfie claim on me, all right?" I shook my head as I walked to the ensuite bathroom.

"But what if I wanted to be possessive of you, Melina? I really do like you, whether or not you think so. Why do you think I keep coming for you, pursuing you and wanting to protect you from those damn mutts downstairs?" Esteban gritted his teeth.

I clung to my clothes and looked at him warily.

"What's wrong? Why are you getting angry with me?" Esteban took a step closer, and I took a step back.

"I just want you to know. I do care about you. I do have feelings for you. I haven't experienced these feelings before, so it is all quite new. Just give me a chance, Melina. I promise you won't regret it. Please." The begging Esteban was back; he seemed honest in his tone, but his eyes held something else. I knew the wolves could get possessive in the little time I've been around them, but this was something different.

"All right Esteban, I'll give you a chance. Now, I have to get ready. I'll see you tonight?"

Esteban nodded and gave me a kiss on the side of my unruly bedhead. It felt unnatural to me, almost scary.

Once I was downstairs, the girls already had their pedicures. Omegas quickly led me into the room, giggling and laughing as they picked out the colors that would match my dress. "Teal, you say?" one girl asked as she scrubbed my feet.

"Yes, a light-colored teal."

Luna Clara started shaking her head. "Oh, no, dear, I have a special dress for you!" Her eyes beamed. Both Tulip and her mother looked at her questioningly. "I have this dress that would look beautiful against your skin, and I have been waiting for someone to wear it. Please, do it for me, please!" Clara was pleading with me to wear this dress, and I couldn't help but smile.

"I'd love to, Luna, thank you."

Clara clapped excitedly as she told one omega to have it prepared and sent to my room.

"Are you excited, Tulip?" I asked, changing the subject.

"Very much! I mean, we have already taken care of the mating part, now it is just for show!" I shivered listening to that. Who in the heck wants to get bit in the neck like that?

"How are you and Esteban?" Tulip wiggled her eyes while Clara and Rose stopped speaking, now glancing at me. I pursed my lips together and clenched my hands. Rose came over and put her hands over my clenched fists.

"Did something happen, dear? What's wrong?"

"Just some things he said today. It just put me off a little," I mumbled.

"What sorts of things?" Clara demanded.

Looking at both Tulip and Rose, I told them what happened in my room and what he had told me back home. He thought I was his mate. He wanted to court me and take things slow but doesn't like it when I deny him. The way he would grind his teeth and hold his fists tight frightened me, and it didn't bring me comfort at all. I had no feelings for Esteban, they just weren't there for me. However, it was very real to him.

Clara sat back in her massage chair. Her eyes were glazed, meaning she was speaking to someone.

"I don't want to get him in trouble. I just don't think I am anyone's mate. I've got emotional problems. Being alone is something I am used to. Even if I were Esteban's mate, I think I would just push him away."

Clara's eyes softened and stepped out of the foot tub to sit with me. "Melina, what Esteban is doing to you is wrong. A mate shouldn't feel that way. If he was really your mate, you would like the possessiveness. Obviously, he is not your mate," she growled. "I want you to trust me. Come tonight and I will be sure to have Esteban busy. He won't bother you."

I smiled and let out a sigh that I didn't know I was holding.

An enormous burden was lifted from me, knowing I wouldn't have to deal with Esteban.

***

Tulip was having the final preparations done for her dress and could not be seen until she walked down the aisle with her parents. I had just left my room, completely in awe of my dress. It was a lightly glittered gold dress that fit my body like a glove. It dragged on the back, but the high gold heeled shoes kept it off the floor, mostly. If I was ever asked to dance, it would still be all right. My dark hair was done up in loose curls and small gold pins with small diamonds placed in my hair. I kept telling Clara I couldn't outdo Tulip, but she shushed me anyway.

I strolled to the back of the packhouse. The back courtyard was filled with white chairs and at the end of the walkway, where they would give each other vows, was a massive archway filled with white and yellow flowers. I smiled, looking at the flowers decorating each chair.

Still holding onto the doorway, a hand came to pull it away. Spinning my head, I saw Carson and his friends. All three were wearing lightly colored suits with different colored roses in each of their pockets. "Y'all clean up nicely," I joked.

"We could say the same for you, Melina." All three looked me up and down and I folded my arms across my chest.

"Hmhmm, horn dogs." They all chucked, and Carson held out his arm for me to take.

"Luna has instructed us to escort you tonight, if that is all right with you." The three of them bowed, and I giggled.

"Why I would be delighted," I fluttered my lashes mockingly.

Carson held out his arm. I accepted it and they led me to the front row, reserved for the head Alpha families and close family. I smiled, realizing I was sitting in the sibling section. My three bodyguards sat behind me and told me about the high-ranking warriors and leaders that were being escorted in and put into their seats.

"That's Elder Maxum. He is old and a bit of a perv. His wife likes it, though. One time I caught them in the packhouse doing the deed in the laundry room." Carson smirked while Sean rolled his eyes. Sean still talked little, but he was a comfortable soul to have around.

"What about the Fae King? I've never seen a Fae before."

Carson stuck his nose up and grumbled. "Yeah, King Osirus is a trip, that's for sure. They say he sleeps with anything with two legs and tosses them out of his palace once he's done. He's a trickster and his own court can't stand him."

"Well, you Wolves do the same, and you know you have mates out there." The boys sat back and gave a sigh. "Clara talks so highly of King Osirus, though. All day today, she talked about how wonderful the Fae King was and how much she respected him." Carson rubbed his stubbled chin.

"I don't know why they have such a good relationship, but the word around here is that the Shifters should stay away.

He'll use his Fae powers to bewitch any woman in his bed." My heart sank a little. Clara didn't mention that at all about him during our spa day.

Clara talked about how wonderful he was, passionate about the Fae kingdom, warmhearted, but was deeply misunderstood. Even she had trouble cracking the King of the Faes, letting him know that his mate would grace his presence one day to finally break the unbreakable wall he instilled.

Things got quiet. The only thing you could hear was the playing of the string instruments. Many were mumbling softly. I continued to stare straight ahead, listening to the music until Carson tapped my shoulder. "That, over there, is the Fae King." Looking to my left on the other side of the aisle from me, was the epitome of a Fae King.

His hair was long and white as first fallen snow, with a few braids that were longer than his actual free-flowing hair. His robes were pristine white with small amounts of green leaves embroidered into the expensive material. Gold threading was easily seen throughout his tunic and trousers. His cape matched his royal clothing, pristine white as the underside sparkled with gold. He wasn't a Fae, he looked like an angel. Features were sharp and even just from sitting down so elegantly, he looked tall. If I stood next to him, I'm sure I would see him eye to eye. I was holding my breath as I took in this beautiful creature. Not once in my life had my heart skipped a beat for any man, even in my youth crushing over some boy. There really was a time for everything then.

Carson shook my shoulder, and I blinked a few times and turned to him. "Are you all right? You spaced out there."

I shook my head and realized that Tulip was getting ready to walk down the aisle. Everyone stood up and when I turned my body to face Tulip as she passed between the Fae King and me, my eyes looked directly into his.

His face was perfect. There was no other way to describe him. The sharp jawline, his unwavering stare, and his beautiful golden eyes felt like they reached the depths of my conscience. My heart fluttered as he stood there, unmoving, and unemotional. I swore I saw a faint curl of his lip, but Carson grabbed my hand quickly and had me sit down.

"Melina, what is wrong?" Carson whisper-yelled at me.

Carson and Sean were looking around and staring down at the Fae King. I was too embarrassed to see what was going on, so I stayed in my seat and continued to look forward. My heart pounded in my chest, my hand brushing the heat of my chest away with my fingertips.

What the hell was that?

Clara stood up at the front as Tulip and Alec were saying their vows. A few times, she would glance at me and give me a wink. Everyone is so weird.

I could see why so many women fell for this Fae King, sleep with him one night and be satisfied with that. He was breathtaking. An angel, if not a god. If I could hear his voice, it would make it all the better. My heartfelt tight, thinking that I couldn't pursue any of it. He was just a player, like the rest of them. All men were. They just wanted one thing. My heart was already broken enough to be used and thrown away like that. I wasn't one to give away their love so quickly.

As the ceremony continued, I could feel the warriors behind me on the edge of their seats. Their body language showed they were upset, and the constant whisperings weren't helping me concentrate on the ceremony. I was just a human. The Fae King was just curious about what I was, just like Carson, Rex and Sean were. I'd do my best to stay away from the god beside me because I would not become just another one of his bedmates.

Chapter 9

Osirus

"Do you think your mystery Siren girl is here somewhere?" Alaneo mentioned as I pulled my cape around my neck.

The brothers had slept late, clear until we were supposed to be there in just under an hour. They had drunk all their ale and then went into the packhouse in the middle of the night and stole some Werewine. Werewine was much more potent than ours, so of course they got drunk off their arses.

Alaneo woke with me early, as always, and we trained in the Wolves' warrior training arena since most were tending to the Princess's requests for cleaning and preparing for the mating ceremony. She had really gone overboard, more so than her own mating ceremony; it only made me wonder what Clara has up her sleeve.

Alaneo came back over and slapped me on the shoulder. "Did you hear me at all, your Majesty? Is your head in the clouds?" he chided.

I gave a small smirk and took the cufflinks off the dresser. "I don't know, Alaneo, but I pray to the gods she will be there." Alaneo slumped down in a vacant chair as we heard the brothers screaming at each other to stop using the hot water.

"You know, maybe she *was* a Siren. The way you talked this

morning on the training fields about her singing, she might be one. She just has you captivated under her spell until she will lure you into the waters."

"She is not a Siren," I sighed. "She was fully clothed and ran from the water like someone was running for her life because some nitwit wanted to come find me." I scoffed as I finished checking my appearance in the mirror.

If I was to find this damsel, I was damn well going to look like a king. I'll take whatever crutch I can get because this girl, woman, was different. I could sense it through my magic. It zapped my heart like electricity.

"Let's go, I want to get a good seat," Alaneo said as he walked out the door.

If this girl was who I think she was, this might be the last day I spend alone. I could have my mate in my arms. Letting out a heavy sigh, I followed Alaneo to the packhouse.

The inside of the pack house was pristine. Everything had been dusted, cleaned, and flowers flowed over the foyer. Even though the party was to be outside, Clara had made sure the essence of the mating ceremony trickled into her home. Alaneo had already made his way to the kitchen, sneaking snacks and what not. While I waited for him to return, I headed to the back part of the house where the back deck stood and where most of the Wolves had retreated. I was to be one of the last ones to be escorted since I was of high nobility.

A glimmer caught my eye as I looked to my left. It was a girl standing next to the stairs, looking through the large window. Her eyes were wide with curiosity as her hand laid gently on the clear pane. Her hair was done up in loose, dark curls that framed her face, the tendrils touching her neck and shoulders effortlessly. I was completely enamored by her; she was more beautiful than Aphrodite herself. Her aura was glowing more so than I had ever seen. Golden light whipped around her with small bits of dark smoke that would encompass her heart. She may have looked lively and happy on the outside, but her aura told me something different. She was sad and conflicted, possibly depressed.

Faes were known for reading auras. My ability was much more powerful due to me being a high ranked, but any Fae could see the dark that surrounded her she kept hidden. My heart lurched to comfort her.

Could this be the girl I had seen last night at the lake? Her hair might be the same, but it had covered her face so delicately I couldn't see.

"Your Majesty!" Alaneo finally shoved me playfully.

Looking at Alaneo, annoyed, I watched three Wolves go up to my mystery girl in gold and started speaking with her. "You have dreadfully bad timing," I spoke.

"What now? Oh! Is that the girl over there? Damn, Your Majesty, she's gorgeous! Are you looking for just a good time? It's been so long; I can't be the only man getting some tail!" Alaneo jokingly jabbed, but a switch was let off in my brain.

Grabbing him by the neck and going to the nearest utility closet, I opened and shut the door hastily. His head was slammed against the wall, and I could feel my fangs descending.

"Shit, Osirus!"

I felt my teeth and realized they had indeed descended and covered my mouth. Showing fangs as a Fae had become taboo. We were supposed to be more sophisticated than the Fairies and the Pixies. One doesn't go baring fangs or showing their wings so freely.

"I-I am sorry." I straightened my shirt and cape. "I don't know what came over me." Alaneo looked like an idiot as I wiped my brow. "What is it, Alaneo, speak!?"

Frustrated, I opened the closet door and stormed out. The girl in question was gone, and I put my hand through my hair.

"You liiiike her," he said sing-songingly. "I've never seen you like a girl like that before! Oh, gods, is she your mate? Damn, you are finally going to get some!" Alaneo squealed quietly, like a little girl.

"You know, if another Fae saw you act like this, you would be reported for not representing the Court properly."

"Who the hell cares, Osirus? You are going to change all of that, anyway."

"And I will, but not until I have my mate by my side. I swore to the Moon Goddess to reform the entire kingdom, but not until my own soul has been sated!"

Alaneo quieted down, and an usher came forth to bring me to my seat.

"Good luck, Your Majesty," Alaneo winked, and I followed the usher to my seat.

The gods had blessed me, and I was to be seated right across the aisle from my golden goddess. I was only two arm lengths away from touching her. Her skin was slightly tan, and her hands were the smallest I had ever seen.

She was small. I'm sure if she stood beside me while I sat, she would still barely reach the top of my head. What was she? Surely not a Shifter or a Witch. I glanced at Clara, who was smiling giddily at me. She had something to do with this; she was sneakier than a damn Fae and it was nerve-wracking.

Clara winked at me and nodded her head to the side where this girl was. One Wolf started speaking to her, making her laugh, and that was when I knew I had found my Siren. The different pitches in her laugh were so recognizable, almost like Fairy bells ringing to the tops of my pointed ears. She was the girl by the lake, singing that sad song. I gave a smirk and, looking back at Clara, she did the same and let off a little wink. My princess knew something, and I was going to find out what it was very soon.

The mating ceremony had officially begun, and the girl, Tulip, was coming down the aisle waiting for her parents to give her away. As Tulip passed us while we were standing, waiting for the officiant to tell us to sit, our eyes met.

The light sources didn't seem bright anymore. Her bright

blue eyes bore into mine as if she was reading my own soul. Fireworks erupted over my skin, my magic trying to leak out of my body as I felt her gaze on my very own face. Her pouty lips were parted, shining with the lip paint. I wanted to take her there, kiss her lips, and let her know I would take care of her throughout eternity. Reassure her I would do everything in my power to make her happy and she would never be sad. She was mine, and I didn't care who knew.

Her eyes were soft and warm, so much warmer than any other woman I had seen. Somehow, I knew her eyes were made for me, her body would be easily encompassed in my own as I took care of her and showed her how much that I would love her.

Our stare was broken by the dumb, dumb, and dumber trio that pulled her to her seat. They took her hand and asked her what was wrong, and I could feel the possessiveness take over me. I've never been one to act irrationally, but now that I found my mate after over 800 years, I damn well wasn't letting her go. By no means necessary would I let her go. I gripped my hands in a fist and saw the wolves eyeing me from afar. I glared right back to show I would not back down.

Once the ceremony was over, everyone got up from their seats. My Siren stood up and greeted the newly mated couple and gave the female Tulip a hug.

"Congratulations, sister," she whispered quietly.

Melina

I could still feel the King's eyes from the back of my head. It didn't feel uncomfortable. I was more nervous, but the moment I looked into his eyes, I wanted to get to know him. He held secrets and hearing from two different people about what he could be like, I was utterly confused.

The stage was being quickly taken away, even while I stood there with Tulip and her family. We all laughed at some of Alec's annoying jokes and instantly there was a dance floor covered in a small area of the courtyard. The omegas had set up tables and chairs in record time and the DJ had quickly set up his equipment and started playing music. Many Wolf couples took the floor, while several went to the buffet table and grabbed plates of food.

It was a beautiful affair. Luna Clara did a wonderful job, especially with the colors that Tulip picked: whites and yellows. Being able to come here to the Crimson Shadows Pack was such a blessing, especially since most of her family lived here and not on Earth. I meandered around the different decorations, watched the kids run around tables and dance on the dance floor. They really worked like a unit here, a family. Everyone cared for each other.

If only humans interacted that way.

The heels ached my feet from wandering around, so I sat alone at one table. My warriors were chatting up with a few girls. I didn't want to be a cock-block to them if they were trying to 'get some,' as Carson would say.

Many times, I was offered champagne, but I quickly declined. I wasn't much of a drinker and from the looks of it; it was made with super Werewolf alcohol because some of them were getting drunk, which were mostly the warriors. Alpha Kane was giving them a harsh scolding as Carson, Sean and Rex came up to me.

"Enjoying the party?" Carson taunted me as I sat at a table by myself. I wasn't much for mingling. I was always the people watcher.

"Yes." I smiled. "Just relaxing for the first time in a few days, taking in the scenery, I guess."

"How about you get up and dance with me? I'll be good to ya, I promise."

Looking at Carson's hand, I contemplated going to dance, but Clara put her hands on my shoulders.

"Actually, boys," Clara interrupted. "I have someone I wanted to introduce her to. Your services escorting her will be done for the evening. Just keep an eye out for that one fellow we discussed." Her head tilted to the direction of a stewing Esteban at the bar.

Carson nodded and gave me a small smile as he retracted his hand. I gave a wave and Clara helped me out of the chair.

"Have you enjoyed everything so far?" Luna Clara pried.

"Yes, very much." I twiddled my fingers as we walked. I was being led close to the dance floor and my heart raced. Who was this mystery person she wanted me to meet? I saw a very tall man with his back facing me. He was wearing a white cape with decorative green stitching of leaves. My heart fluttered faster. It was King Osirus.

She wanted me to meet *him!*

"Melina, I want you to meet my wonderful friend, King Osirus."

Osirus turned around with a drinking glass in hand. He looked down at me and gave the sexiest smile I had ever seen. Clara giggled humorously as I stood there, dumbfounded. Osirus was as cool as a cucumber. He was as regal as any king should be. The braids that hung throughout his hair held cusps of gold bands. His nose was straight, and his complexion was flawless, skin almost glowed white and his golden ember eyes bore into me. His jaw was so sharp, and I could swear you could see his cheekbones protrude out of his face. Oh, goddess and I'm gaping like a fish out of water.

"It's a pleasure to finally meet you, dear Melina." King Osirus slightly bowed and gave a smirk.

Do I bow? Curtsy?

"It is w-wonderful to m-meet you too, Your Majesty." I looked at Luna Clara for some guidance and whispered to her, "Do I bow or curtsy?"

Clara laughed out loud, and King Osirus chuckled.

"None of that," King Osirus replied. "In fact, please call me Osirus." Osirus held out his hand and as I was about to take it, until I heard a loud growl behind me and a harsh pull on my waist.

"She's mine. Get away from her, Pixie!"

Chapter 10

Melina

Large gasps were heard through the crowd. Alpha Kane ran up beside Luna Clara and held her from behind tightly. Esteban was panting, his arm securely around my waist and not showing any signs of letting me go.

Looking at Elm and Rose in panic, I felt my eyes on the verge of tears. I had never felt so scared in all my life. Esteban's claws were piercing my gold sequin dress and soon it could pierce my skin. Living among Werewolves, even though unknowingly, gave me a false sense of security as I lived among Tulip's pack, where they looked out for each other. Now that I was seeing the aggressive side of the Werewolves that I just learned about I wasn't so sure anymore, especially with Esteban.

"I said, stay back, you overgrown Pixie," Esteban growled.

King Osirus seemed unfazed. Instead, he looked rather amused. Four large Faes appeared, three of which looked like brothers. Three were sporting Fae military uniforms with head and beard full of red hair.

"I suggest ye watch yer tone, puppy," the tallest Fae said. His voice was gruff with a no-nonsense tone. "Let go of the girl and no one gets hurt." He reached for his sword. Esteban's grip tightened around my waist, and I let out a small whimper. That was going to leave a bruise.

King Osirus glared his eyes at Esteban and before Esteban could say another word, I was being pulled into a large chest with a blanket covering my backside, pulling me impossibly closer to warmth. The gigantic wall in front of me was cozy, and I wanted to instantly melt, but before I could find any comfort, I heard yelling and growling.

Peeking my head out from under the blanket, now realizing it was King Osirus' cloak, I blushed furiously. Being insanely close to this angel gave me the butterflies I had always heard about in my stomach. Plus, he smelled insanely good. It was a sweet spicy and I could roll my eyes to the back of my head at how wonderful it made me feel.

Esteban's eyes went dark, and another Fae had his grip around his neck with a silver dagger pointed at it. He smiled evilly, piercing Esteban's skin. His growl was deep, and you could see he was in pain.

"Impeccable timing as always, Alaneo."

Alaneo looked up through his lashes and gave King Osirus a wink. "Anything for a future queen." Alaneo again cut Esteban's skin, and I whimpered a bit.

Wait, what?!

"Come now, darling, you don't need to see that." King Osirus took his cape and covered my face, which had me burying my face in my chest. It felt so intimate, but the fear that was floating through my veins pushed it aside as I gripped his cloak tighter. Osirus' hand rubbed up and down my back as the cloak shielded me from unwanted eyes.

As if reading my thoughts, Tulip spoke up. "Did you just say, Queen?" Tulip squealed as Alec held her closely, not being fond of the threat before him. Many Wolves looked on, many in shock. Tulip's mother glanced at Luna Clara in acknowledgment and let out a smile.

"Yes, Melina is my mate, future queen of The Golden Light Kingdom," King Osirus said as smooth as silk. Putting both my hands on his chest to back away, he only tightened his grip on me. "You're safe now. No one will ever hurt you." Before he could touch my cheek, Esteban let out another roar.

"She is mine, fucker. She can't be yours!"

My head darted to Esteban, who was now restrained by Carson, Sean, and Rex. All three started tying silver ropes onto his limbs while he struggled.

"Stand down, Esteban!" Alpha Kane growled while Esteban backed down, showing his neck. Many wolves looked on in amusement on how this was going to play out. One Wolf was claiming me while the Fae king was also saying I was his. *Who was my mate, really?*

"How about we do a mating test? I just read about it in one of the history books!" Luna Clara chirped. "That way, there is no question if Esteban ever was her mate. It is really quick and effective and then we can all move on and let the love birds go on their way!" Clara started taking Alpha Kane's black-tie off and came up to me and pulled me out of King Osirus' arms.

"I know this is a lot," Clara whispered to me. "Trust me, everything will work out. I know Osirus is your mate. The Goddess told me not too long ago." Osirus didn't let his face show much expression, I had gathered, but I thought I saw a faint smile across his lips.

"Luna, I'm human. I can't have a mate. I'm not even meant to be here."

Little does she know I had double meaning behind that statement. One, being here in a supernatural world and two... My parents said I was an accident. I really wasn't supposed to be here.

"It will come in time. The Goddess mentioned you were stubborn and would not easily accept it, but you will soon promise." I scrunched up my nose in defiance and she put the tie around my eyes.

"Everyone, listen!" Clara's voice demanded. "Melina will stand here and hold her hand out. We will have several unmated males come up and hold her hand. Whichever one she feels the bond with by just holding her hand will be declared her mate."

"That sounds too easy. How can you go off by touching who your mate is?" I rolled my eyes into the blindfold and crossed my arms. Many people laughed, which only added fuel to my anger.

"Trust me, you will know," Clara sang.

The crowd went silent as one by one male came up and held my hand. After a few seconds, they would take their hand away and another would replace it. The crowd was dreadfully silent, and my anxiety was at an all-time high. I could feel eyes staring at me as these males came up, waiting for something to happen. Rose came up behind me and put her hands on my arms. "Melina, it's all right. Nothing is going to happen, me and Elm are right behind you. You're safe." I nodded slowly, feeling some comfort, but not enough to take away my insecurities.

Another hand came to mine, and I felt a squeeze. It was a possessive squeeze, and it almost burned my hand at how uncomfortable it was. Stepping back, people whispered but were quickly silenced by a growl.

A few moments later, I felt another hand slide into mine. Out of all the hands, I felt, this one felt the most welcoming. Butterflies, no, large birds, soared in my stomach. It took me to a place of comfort I never knew. My chest felt warm, and I could almost feel love in it. Love in a touch, it was something unheard of. My mind told me to pull away, but my body did the opposite. It wanted to lean into it and feed from it. Fill in the holes of my soul of the pieces missing.

"What is it supposed to feel like?" I whispered slowly to Rose. My voice was shaky, scared of the unknown. The hand squeezed me a tad tighter, only confirming the comfort it gave me.

Mom bent down and whispered in my ear, "Like nothing you've felt before. It fills you in places you want to be filled."

There was a long pause, and I sighed heavily. "Him," I whispered so low that I was afraid no one would hear me. There was a growl and large applause that hid away someone's frustration. The blindfold was taken off of me and there, stood before me, was the angel that I could never take my eyes off of.

For the first time, I saw an enormous smile on his face; it was captivating, and I couldn't help but blush at the way he looked at me. My mind was yelling at me to stop, but my heart pulled me into another direction and that was to be near him.

"Take Esteban away until he can be taken back to his pack," Alpha Kane commanded as my friends Carson, Sean, and Rex drug him away. Esteban was thrashing about, throwing out profanities, but I was quickly redirected by Osirus' hand to look away from him.

Alpha Kane addressed the crowd to disperse and to enjoy the party, not just a mating ceremony party any longer, but the celebration of the Fae King finding his mate. Fists clenching my dress, I saw the crowd continue to murmur and disperse while still looking at me, some with jealous eyes and some with cheerful faces of congratulations.

Osirus held out his hand to me and I couldn't help comparing his large one to my small one. "Come, darling. I'm sure you have questions."

With my hand in his, he led me to a more private table and pulled out my chair as I sat down, and a drink was automatically set to my right. His arm was draped over my chair and kept me close to his side. I should feel uncomfortable the way his side is pressed up against mine, but I wasn't.

Tulip waved at me from my peripheral, and I couldn't help but look her way. She was smiling and drawing little hearts in the air while Alec tried to pull her to the dance floor, rolling his eyes.

"Melina, I want you to meet some very important people of mine. They will keep you safe if, for whatever reason, I am not around. Trust only them, all right?" I gulped a wad of spit audibly, wanting to question why only trust these few men and not other people in his kingdom.

"This is Alaneo, my right-hand man, my advisor." Osirus displayed his hand out to show me Alaneo.

"'Tis a pleasure, your Majesty." He bowed and kissed my hand while I blushed.

"Please, just call me Melina." Alaneo looked to Osirus for confirmation, and he nodded his head.

"And these—" He sighed heavily. "—are my personal guards, Everett, Finley and Braxton."

"Aye, it's a pleasure, Yer Majesty. You do not know how long his Majesty has waited for ye. The past years of pouting have been long without him getting some-"

Osirus cut him off with the wave of a hand. "That will be all Everett. Go mingle." With that, his crew left and dispersed into the crowd. I raised a brow at Everett's statement.

Osirus bent down and came close to my ear. I was frozen in place, not sure what he was going to do or say. "I've waited for you so long." His warm breath tickled my ear. It made me hold my thighs together, and I didn't understand why.

Chills invaded my skin as he breathed down my neck. It was an unfamiliar feeling, and I wasn't sure if I liked it or not. Quickly scooting my chair over, he sat straight and cleared his throat.

"I'm sorry." He pulled the collar of his tunic. "I fail to realize you are not versed in the mating bond given to us by the goddess."

I hummed, my snarky attitude long gone out the window. My emotions and hormones were all over the place. Heck, puberty wasn't this bad.

Osirus, ignoring the space that I had placed between us, came close again. "How about we dance, loosen up a bit, hm?" His hand was extended, and I hesitantly took it.

Pulling me up, he guided me to the floor with his hand on my lower back. Taking one hand in mine and the other at my back, he held me close. There was no space and even when I tried to back away, he wouldn't let me.

"I know you are hesitant, Melina. You've been thrown around the past couple of days, but let me tell you, I'm here to take care of you. You are mine; you were made to be mine, and I was made for you." His voice was smooth as silk as he spoke. Those words had me entranced by his beauty and grace. He was different from the Wolves. He wasn't a growling territorial mess as I saw some Wolves were to their mates. Osirus was cool and collected.

I stayed silent, letting myself wonder, which proved to be a bad thing. This cool and collected behavior could be cockiness, knowing that since I was his 'mate', he could get what he wanted from me. Carson said he was a player, and used magic to get women to bed. What if he was using magic on me now? Was he seducing me like he did with Shifters, to get another notch on his bedpost? How could I be certain he wasn't another Esteban? Another horny guy? Everett said about him not getting any for a while, meaning he was getting some from somewhere. The hurt and fury carved out the once empty holes that were filled with him.

"Darling, what's wrong?" He stopped dancing and pulled my chin up to look at him. His eyes glued to mine; confusion set in them. "You are angry. What can I do to fix it?"

"I can't be here right now. I need some space to think." Letting go of him, I tried to walk away, but was quickly grabbed by my forearm by his hand.

"You can't go anywhere without me," he said calmly. "You are my mate, and I am to protect you," his voice held gentleness. Was I going to fall for his charms like every other girl? Absolutely not.

"I did fine before you, and I'll be fine now. I need some space, now let me go." Twisting my head, some pins fell out of my dark hair, and it was now cascading down my back. Osirus didn't let go. In fact, he pulled me back and put both hands around my upper arms, and pulled me close.

"No, you cannot. You are mine as I am yours. I just found you and will not let you go. No one tells me no." All right, so apparently all supernaturals were territorial, not just the Werewolves. I sighed, frustrated.

"Well then, Your Majesty, maybe you should take this as your first lesson in humility by getting your first rejection from a woman." My lip wanted to quiver, but I held it back. I was going to be the strong, independent woman I had always been.

Not needing pity and sympathy or someone to take care of me. The look of amusement fell on his face, and he gently let me go. Before turning around to get away, he grabbed me by my hips and threw me over his shoulder while I squealed.

Wolves started howling and clapping their hands, but my face of mortification was seen by Rose. Softly smiling at me, she gave a wave while Tulip was whistling. "Put me down, you barbarian! You're no king! Where are your manners?" I screamed, hitting his back. No one was going to help me, not even my adopted family.

"Live a little, Melina! He's your mate!" Tulip gyrates her hips and Alex shook his head and put his arms around her waist to make her stop.

"Luna Clara! Please help!!" I pleaded.

Osirus continued to walk off the dance floor while I continued to yell. Instead, the sea of people parted as he walked to the side of the packhouse.

His guards were flanking him while Alaneo had a dirty smirk on his face as he cleaned off the dagger from Esteban.

"Where are you taking me?!" I continued to yell.

"To our room, darling."

Chapter 11

Osirus

Being able to publicly claim Melina, my destiny, was a freeing and joyous occasion. Most of the crowd was happy at the occasion that their new ally will soon have a queen and one that was so closely knit with the Werewolf community. The extra tie to the Werewolves was always a plus.

My thoughts of Melina being much more docile and accepting in the beginning as I led her to the dance floor proved to be completely wrong as I felt her aura shift quickly from confused and concerned to angry and hurt. As soon as I asked my darling what was wrong, she instantly pushed me away. I'm no mind reader, but it seems to be that she took what Everett said to heart. That was the only thing that quirked her in our first few moments of meeting.

"Let me go, you barbarian!"

I had just secured my mate over my shoulder, something that Werewolves liked to do, and earned instant gratification from the crowd. I smirked as she kept squirming above my shoulder. She-wolves looked on in jealousy; if only my mate could comply so willingly, however, I was told from the beginning I was to have a difficult and stubborn mate.

Melina's friends made crude gestures of mating rituals

which only caused her to still and her whole body heat in embarrassment. My entourage only laughed and jeered at each other as we took her back to our sleeping quarters.

"Where are you taking me!?" she screamed into my back.

"To our room, darling," I replied sweetly.

"You will do no such thing!" Her arms pushed off against my shoulders and I gave her a swat to her arse. Hearing her gasp gave me a slight satisfaction as the guards covered their mouths and snickered.

Melina remained quiet as we came up in the royal cabin. We filtered into the main living space, and I turned to my men. "Go get some fruit and cheese and bring it to our room." Without haste, I walked up the stairs while Melina huffed and growled low behind me. We entered the large space, and I gently sat her down on the love seat. Giving her a smile, she crossed her arms, giving her breasts an ample squeeze upwards in frustration while I poured us some honeysuckle nectar.

"Now, darling, surely you know something about mates and destined love since your sister is a Werewolf?"

I handed her the drink, which she just stared at. "How do I know you won't drug me and then have your way with me?"

My heart ached that my mate would think I would drug or use her in that way. I wanted to love and cherish her, not treat her as my concubine or slave. "Melina, where did you get an idea like that?" I mumbled, hoping she would feel the emotion in my voice. Her eyes softened and looked away while biting her bottom lip. By gods, I wish I was the one biting that lip, but it seems that may be far into the future.

"I-I was told some things. Your reputation..."

I nodded silently and placed the nectar on the table in front of her. "I understand." Sitting beside her, studying her.

"Y-you do?" Her arms uncrossed and her body turned to mine.

"I do. I have a reputation, but I can promise you most of the things you have heard are untrue. You may ask anything you wish." I put my hand on hers, stroking her knuckles.

My heart ached not to hold her in my arms, to sit her in my lap and kiss her neck and reassure her it was all a lie. Lies that I allowed so that I could look like an uncaring king until I had my mate beside me. If only she knew the power of a mated Fae couple. I despised every bit of what my nation has become, as well as my parents. They just weren't strong enough, but thanks to the gods, I was born with more power than my own parents combined. With my mate and her ruling beside me, we could change everything.

"Anything?" she asked questioningly.

"Anything for you, darling." I stroked her cheek.

She didn't shy away, which made my soul happy, but she was still skeptical. "The women, they say that you use your magic to get them to your bed…" Her eyes looked down and blushed in embarrassment.

I chuckled, but then she glanced back in annoyance. "Darling, does it look like I need magic to do that?"

"Well, aren't you a cocky thing, huh?" Her arms went right back to being folded under her breasts. I grunted a bit and adjusted my collar. She doesn't know how much that little gesture made her chest look more appetizing.

"I've never used my magic to put anyone to bed. I don't take away people's agency unless they grant it."

"Grant it?"

"Yes, I do have an ability where I can enter someone's mind and use their body as if it was my own. It is a gift that Fae don't normally discuss. I've only told you because you are my mate, and I hope you respect that."

"That's a lot of trust you just put on me," Melina whispered.

Melina

"Why would you tell me that?"

"Because, darling, I will never keep secrets from you, nor will I lie to you. I've looked for you for centuries and I'll be damned if I lose you now." Chills went up my spine as he held my hand. Before I could ask my next question, there was a knock at the door.

Alaneo came in holding a tray of fruits, cheeses, and biscuits; that looked delicious. Since I wasn't able to eat anything during dinner, I quickly grabbed some and put some on a plate. Osirus chuckled and did the same.

"Tell me, Melina. Do you like it here in Bergarian so far? I know you are from Earth and the realms can be quite different." Osirus spread some cheese on his biscuit as he sat back on the sofa while he ate.

"So far, yes, I've really enjoyed it. It is like something out of a book. Never in my life would I think a place like this exists," I said passionately as I ate a strawberry.

"How was it where you used to live, then? Where did you live? I heard you lived amongst Werewolves, and you didn't even know it," he chuckled. Thinking back on it made me cringe. How could I not see? I was so blind.

"I live alone in a cabin on their territory after my parents left. The pack house was not where I was all the time. I kept to myself, took care of myself, and lived off the money my parents left me until Tulip's Alpha realized I was good at numbers. Now I am his accountant." I smiled. I was a spreadsheet goddess and created the perfect point, click, type to watch all the spending.

"Your parents left you? Did they leave that world?" Osirus asked, concerned.

"It just wasn't working out, so I told them to leave and give me money to live off of and I would be fine on my own near Tulip's parents." I waved my hand absentmindedly, like it didn't bother me. Jokes on me, though.

It still bothered me.

"You can't get rid of a child like that! Who do your parents think they are?" Osirus raised his voice.

The calm facade he radiated slowly dissipated and a new side of the king was coming out. Everyone talked about how King Osirus was always calm and collected, having Alaneo speak for him in most cases because he lacked the drive to really give anyone the time of day. Now he was doing something I wasn't expecting. Emotion. Anger.

"They made it perfectly clear they didn't want me." I picked up the glass of nectar. "I said it would be best for them to just go, so I didn't live with a fake family. Not that they were around much, anyway. Tulip became like a sister to me, and her mother and I got close. I even call her mom sometimes. I owe them a lot. They were much more family than my own blood." My voice became lower as I spoke to him. A few straggly tears left my eyes. I felt so vulnerable in front of him; I hadn't cried openly in I didn't know how long.

Osirus picked me up and put me on his lap, something I had seen a lot of supernaturals do with their mates, especially Elm and Rose. Osirus' hand went to the side of my face and held me close to his chest. I didn't fight it. I let him guide my face to his neck as I breathed deeply. There was a constant thrumming in his chest; if I didn't know any better, I thought it was his heart.

"Is that your heart? Beating so fast?" I whispered. It was so fast it was inhuman.

"Yes," he said huskily. "It is compared to a hummingbird. I believe Earth has those as well." Hearing his voice made me shudder, and I pulled away from him and sat back down on my side of the couch. The disappointment was evident in his eyes.

"I'm sorry. I'm just not used to that much contact, I guess. Touching you, it's just so overwhelming." I blushed while fiddling with my dress. "I'm just not used to all the attention." I chuckled, trying to lighten the mood. Not that I didn't want him touching me. It was the fear in the back of my mind he would leave, too.

Just like my parents.

Osirus grabbed my hand again, the constant touch was something he craved and maybe I did too. "Don't lie to me, darling." His golden eyes grew to a dark amber. I gasped as they changed, and they quickly went back to his normal golden color. "I won't lie to you, so don't lie to me. I'll bend you over and spank you myself to let you know it." I blushed bright scarlet. I couldn't look at him any longer. He wouldn't dare, would he? He did smack me earlier, though!

Another knock was heard at the door, and it was opened with a small creek. Luna Clara came in with several Wolves in tow with my bags. "Wait, a minute. Why are you bringing my stuff here?" I said, agitated.

"I told you, this is our room." Osirus got up and took the bags from the men carrying them.

"Don't worry, Melina, I packed your things," Clara said happily while Osirus found a place for them. "So—" She wiggled her eyebrows. "—how is it going so far?"

"This is weird to me," I whispered.

"It was to me too when I first met Kane. There was an undeniable attraction, and I'm sure you feel it too." I looked to see if Osirus was listening, but he was talking to a few of the attendants.

"Yes, but what if he leaves me? I can't get attached." Clara gasped at my question.

"Not with a mate bond. He would never, he has waited for you a long time. He may have a different past, his culture might be different, but he has wanted you for so long." She grabbed my hands, that were folded nicely. "Just tell him you want to take it slow. I promise he will. He's a good friend of mine and means well. He must put up a strong wall there because of the difficulties in his kingdom, but he will show you his true self." She squeezed my hand once more and got up to tell Osirus goodbye.

"Go slow with her, Osirus." Clara pointed her finger at his chest. "I mean it."

"Of course, Princess." He bowed. "Nothing less for her."

Clara waved and walked out the door as Alaneo walked in.

"Your Majesty." He bowed.

A lot of bowing around here. Do I need to be bowing?

"The horses will be ready at dawn. Did you need anything else for the night?"

"That will be all. Thank you, Alaneo." Before Alaneo was fully out the door, I spoke up.

"Oh, you are leaving tomorrow?" I questioned innocently. *Will he come back?* Both started laughing while I sat, confused.

"Darling, you are coming back with us to the Golden Light Kingdom. I can't stay away for too long. I was just here to sign a treaty and return henceforth."

My mouth dropped. "Who said I was going anywhere?! I don't know you. I can't just go ride off to some kingdom. I came here with Tulip, Rose, and Elm. I can't leave them!" I threw my hands in the air. "You can't tell me what to do. You are not the boss, king, mate, or whatever you are to me. I am my own person and can decide for myself and I am not going!" I stomped my foot for beneficial effect.

Alaneo snorted and gave a good pat to Osirus' shoulder while Osirus looked dumbfounded. Didn't anyone tell this guy, 'No?'

"Good luck, Osirus. I'm glad I'm not you."

Alaneo gave a smirk after I stuck my tongue out at him. I don't care if he was dangerous with that dagger he was waving around earlier. I didn't need his comments.

Osirus strolled up to me. If we were the same height, we would be nose to nose, but my nose only came up about mid-chest. "Darling, remember, you are my mate, and you will come back with me. I'm trying to be patient, but this attitude of yours is quite irritating."

"Why? Because I don't bow at everything you say?" I snipped.

Osirus grinned and took a step closer to me. In turn, I took a step back. He towered over me, and the glow of the room was fading as I retreated to the far corner. There was nowhere else to go as my back felt the rough surface of the logged walls. One of his hands came up on one side of my head and then the other. His head dipped down, his nose traced the underside of my jaw. His breath was hot, and I put my hands up to push his chest away, which was futile because he was too strong.

"I meant what I said, darling." His lips tickled my neck, and I felt an odd sensation in the lower part of my belly. This darn zoo in my stomach was going to kill me. "I will bend you over and spank you until you thank me for it if you don't be a good little girl and listen," he huskily whispered in my ear. "I won't tolerate bratty behavior."

Chapter 12

Melina

All night I had laid in the bed, with my back to Osirus. The morning light was coming into the room, only reminding me that today I would tell Tulip and her family goodbye and be taken to a kingdom that I had never heard of until a few days ago. My heart ached knowing I wouldn't be going back with Elm and Rose; they were all I had left and now I really had nothing. Even though this king said that I was his and he was mine, I couldn't help but feel the doubt in my heart.

He wanted to love me and care for me, but with all that good intention, could also bring great pain. My own parents had good intentions of keeping me and turning their relationship into a marriage that would hopefully turn out to be a happily ever after, but we all know how that turned out. Me, getting the one left alone, abandoned, and unwanted by very own parents.

Last night, I had little strength for arguing anymore. Osirus told me to get ready for bed and for once, I listened and did what I was told. The enormous bathroom was easily five times the size of my own bathroom back in my cabin. The tub was large and lavish and held many oils and soaps. Sitting there all night looked like a great idea, but the emotional rollercoaster I was on just wanted me to get into bed.

I put on my baby pink shorts with a matching camisole. If I had known I was going to have another man sleep in the same room as me, I would have brought better nightwear that covered my entire body.

Osirus was already in bed, no shirt, and reading some papers in his hand. One hand reached behind his neck, which showed the stretching of his muscles. He was not built like a Werewolf with big and scary large muscles all over; he was leaner, with muscles encompassing his entire body. His skin was pale and not an inch of a scar or freckle on his torso. I gulped and kept my eyes on the ground as I hopped into bed.

The massive number of pillows that I had on the side of the bed was brought up by me and I built a massive pillow wall between us.

"What do you think you are doing?" Osirus smirked as he put his papers on the nightstand.

"Creating a wall so you don't come to my side in the middle of the night." I put one last pillow that caused me to have to really sit up and look over. "Goodnight," I said sternly and quickly covered myself.

He was making me sleep in the same bed as him, a man I have only known for a few hours. *How scandalous is this?!*

I never went to sleep, and I think he knew it. I could hear and feel him tossing and turning all night. Sometimes mumbling something, probably cursing me because I wouldn't let him near me. If I had my stuffed Wolf, I'm sure I would have slept better. I didn't think I'd ever slept without him until then.

Goddess, I'm such a child sometimes. My eyes finally grew heavy with the morning rays coming into the room. I felt warmth encompass me and I finally drifted off to sleep after six hours of fighting it all.

The next time I woke, the sun was high in the sky, and we had obviously missed our window of leaving, remembering what Alaneo said about the horses being ready at dawn. Blinking a few times and trying to sit up, I realized I was restrained. Glancing behind me, I see Osirus in a deep sleep. I should be angry with him for holding me like this, but I have a feeling he could sleep too since we were closer.

His face was so perfect, not a pore to be seen. Osirus was chiseled from marble itself. His lashes weren't black, but brown with hints of gold. His ears that I had never concentrated on before were, in fact, pointed just like I thought a Fae's might be. The hair that fell between us was stark white and soft to the touch.

Being this close should certainly have bothered me, but it didn't. The sparks continued to flow freely between us, but instead of feeling the intensity of it yesterday and the comparison of today, it felt more natural. It felt like it should have been there all along.

A bond like this shouldn't happen so quickly, right? When humans fall in love, it takes months if not years and even then, that love isn't certain. Taking my hand, I cupped the side of his face, which he only leaned into. I smiled at how just a little touch, even in his unconsciousness, he reacted to.

"Are you all right, darling?" His rough voice said as he opened his eyes. "I was afraid you might be sore with me doing this, but I feel that we both slept better, didn't we?" I nodded my head in agreement, a bit shocked he was awake with me staring him in the face.

"This is what a bond does, makes us more comfortable with each other, to help trust one another. I know you don't trust me and are uncertain. We will take our time. Just don't fight it."

I hummed in agreement, blushing a bit. Osirus gave me a kiss on the forehead and got up from the bed. He was wearing a type of jogger pants, made of light material, that hung dangerously low. Spinning my head, I covered up, realizing what little I was wearing.

"Get dressed, darling. I'll go to another room." Within

minutes, he was gone to leave me to my own devices.

***

The smell of baked goods filled the large cabin as I walked down the stairs. A large table spread of cheeses, fruit, croissants, pancakes, sausage, and several other items on the table I didn't know were displayed expertly on the table. "I wasn't sure what you wanted, so I got a bit of everything," Osirus said behind me, which caused me to jump. Both his hands landed on my shoulders, and he guided me to the table.

Alaneo, Everett, Finley, and Braxton came in and sat as well. Everyone sat in silence while I looked around, confused. "The queen is to let her subjects know when to eat," Alaneo said proudly.

"I'm not a queen." I shook my head.

"But you will be," Osirus interjected. "Might as well get used to it and learn a bit about our traditions, hm?" Osirus placed a napkin on his lap, as well as mine. Everyone was still staring at me, so I said what I thought was best.

"All right, dig in?" The brothers all laughed and loaded their plates full of food. *Does everyone have their metabolism in overdrive?*

"Your Majesty, your request to extend our stay an extra day was confirmed with the council, and they will expect us no later than tomorrow evening," Alaneo said.

"Excellent, thank you, Alaneo. You didn't mention Melina, did you?"

Alaneo shook his head. "No, Your Majesty."

I placed my fork full of eggs back on my plate. "Why do you not want them to know I'm coming?" I asked, confused.

Osirus sighed and leaned back in his chair. "If they know you are coming, either someone from the Court or Parliament would want to either plan some sort of coup before we even arrive, and we want to have the upper hand. They have been trying to marry me off for years to several high-ranking nobles to get their own families involved in the country's running, but I won't allow it." Osirus' voice grew louder. "We will take things slow, darling." He grabbed my hand and placed a kiss on my knuckles. "I know you probably feel you were dealt a bad hand here, but trust me, with you, all things will come to light in our kingdom. I just know it."

"Y-yeah, no pressure or anything," I said with a shaky voice. "I have no qualifications to help you run a country, let alone live here in Bergarian. I'm human and new to everything!"

"And that is why you are perfect to be queen. You don't know our laws and traditions. You could shed new light on how things could be dealt with. New ideas, new thoughts... You were made for this, Melina," Osirus pleaded.

My mind was still telling me to run, but I continued to hold on to the little of the broken heart I had left. For once, I would not do what my mind has always told me to do. Trust and rely on someone other than me. It will be a change, but I will try. I wouldn't go in blindly, however.

Sensing my inner battle, Osirus brushed my cheek with the back of his hand. The coolness of his hand felt soothing against my feverish face. "We will go slow, just enjoy what we have now. Don't worry about the future. I promised you last night I would always be truthful."

I nodded my head slowly, not knowing what to say. "Gods, you are so beautiful, Melina," Osirus whispered to me. Even though there were others at the table, I felt like he and I were the only ones in the room. My heart raced as his thumb traced my lips. "I've been blessed with a soul more beautiful than Aphrodite herself." My cheeks grew embarrassingly red.

A loud banging noise came from the front door, and everyone's heads whipped to the commotion. "The 'ell! I haven't even eaten me breakfast, yat!" Everett shouted as he stomped to the door. The loud banging was silenced only to see Tulip with my stuffed Wolf on the other side.

"No!" I whispered as she came in. Jumping up, I took the

Wolf from her and started pushing her out the door. Everyone kept staring, I shut the door behind me. "What do you think you are doing?!" I whisper-yelled.

"I thought you would want your wolfie to remember us! See, he was so sad!" Tulip held up my stuffed Wolf and made a whining puppy noise.

"Ugh, I didn't want them to see! They will think I'm so childish," I pouted.

"Well, you kind of are. I mean, you threw a temper tantrum in the middle of the dance floor last night," she rolled her eyes as she stuffed the animal into my stomach. "So, where is your mark?"

"My mark?"

"Yes, your mark! Where do they put theirs? Wolves usually do it around the neck area. Oh gosh, did he do it on your inner thigh?! You little kinky slut!" My red flushed as I threw my hand up to her mouth to shut her mouth.

"Are you crazy!! We didn't do anything! We just slept."

"You smell like him, so I guess sleeping in the same bed will give that off. Anyway, I was wondering if you want to do something fun before you leave tomorrow."

Tulip was known for her crazy adventures. There was one time she snuck out of the house to meet me at my cabin in the middle of the night to go tee-pee the packhouse. We giggled through the whole thing until we were caught by the Alpha and got a good scolding. We had to help serve breakfast, lunch, and dinner for an entire week.

"I can't really go." I threw my hands up. "Osirus and his guards are up my butt and around the corner saying I can't go anywhere! They even stand guard by the bathroom. I bet they heard me poop. All my freedom is gone," I whined. Tulip stood silent for a moment, rubbing her chin mischievously.

"All right, we do it at midnight," she whispered.

"What??"

"Sneak out while everyone is sleeping. Meet me at the lake. It will be our last hurrah before you get whisked away, my dear princess." Tulip gave me a wink so I couldn't even object.

"Tulip! Come back!" I yelled, but she had already pranced around the house, leaving me with my Wolf stuffed animal. Letting out a huff, I turned around and bumped into a great-smelling wall.

"What was that all about?" Osirus raised his eyebrow.

"N-nothing, just wanted to tell me goodbye and all." Osirus narrowed his eyes and led me back into the house.

"Whatcha got there?" Braxton asked with a smirk. Looking down at my Wolf, I threw it behind my back. "Nothing! I'm going to freshen up a bit, all right? All right, bye!" Running up the stairs, I heard snickers and laughing but Osirus quickly shut them up.

Chapter 13

Osirus

"Aw, she's such a wee babe!" Finley cooed as he stuffed a large roll into his mouth. "Did ye see the way she hid it from us? The lass is adorable!"

I slammed my hand on the table, causing the dishes to rattle and a few cups to fall over. "You do not speak so casually about your future queen!" I said furiously.

"What has gotten into you, your majesty? Your once emotionless expressions are now written all over you. Has your mate already broken your tough exterior?" Alaneo chided as I huffed and laid the napkin across my lap to finish my meal while straightening my back.

It was true. I never let people see my authentic emotion. Always the stoic face. That way, no one can see what true intentions I have up my sleeve. "Only when it comes to her," I whispered. "Be sure you show her some respect. Don't make her feel inferior, do you understand?" All four of them agreed instantly, and we finished our food in silence.

I found it heartwarming that she had something such as a child's stuffed animal. It shows her innocence in the world. Hell, she didn't have a childhood. Her own tough exterior will be tough to crumble and maybe treating her or spoiling her like a child could break that. Get rid of her worries, get rid of the walls of untrust, and have her fall for me.

Melina came back down the stairs, wearing the tight black jeans and white off-the-shoulder top she had on earlier. Her hair was put up in a high ponytail, exposing her slender neck and collarbones. I've been with her for under 24 hours and I already wanted to mark her with love bites to let everyone know she had an intended. Her body was certainly made for me; it was taking all of my strength not to slip my tongue into her mouth and claim it as mine.

"Would you like to go for a stroll, darling?"

Her shy demeanor had once again resurfaced as she nodded. I'd noticed in times of stress and uncertainty that her sass and battiness were clear. A coping mechanism I was hoping to destroy. I wanted her to be herself and see the smile she had the other day while her friend was introduced to the Warrior pack. Melina's smile was held with pride for her sister and soon my darling's smile would captivate our entire kingdom. She had yet to smile at me, but I would be sure to change that today.

Melina reluctantly walked toward me. I lifted my arm for her to take. She gave an uncertain glance to me and hooked her arm with mine.

Leaving the cabin, I had us stroll down the path to the small merchant area of the territory. I knew they had small shops for clothing, food, and other items. Her eyes grew wide in amazement as we walked through the town.

Melina

The small town looked like I stepped back in time. Nothing was used in excess here. There were gardens behind everyone's homes, the buildings had exotic plants growing out of the roofs to be used as cover, everything was so natural, everything was part of the scenery. Each home and store had its own unique design, yet still blended in with the natural part of the forest.

I noticed women were wearing a variety of different types of clothing. Some women who were shopping were wearing dresses one would see out of the renaissance back in the Earth realm. They weren't extra fancy, exotic, or expensive —just enough to get them through the day. Then there were some women who had more yoga-like pants with a variety of different styled tops. The men were different and wore linen pants and open tunics.

"There are Shifters. They wear what's comfortable and easily removed in case of a need to shift," Osirus commented.

I continued to watch as Osirus guided me through the small market. Fresh fruits, vegetables, breads, grains, and water were on display. No one was rendering any money or taking more than what they needed for food. The only thing costing some sort of coinage was clothing, baskets, and other knick-knacks one could buy. It was a small utopia for the pack members. I smiled, looking at how everyone was happy. No one was going hungry, and no one was trying to steal. They were in their own bliss.

"Is it like this in the Golden Light Kingdom?" I looked up at Osirus.

His lips were pressed into a line as he squeezed my arm tighter. "Not yet. We will get there, darling."

Not saying anything, he led me to a shop that had a sign called *Maxine's Organic Materials.* The opened door caused an invisible bell to ring as we walked in, Osirus going first and scanning the room.

"Welcome!" A tall woman came back from behind the counter. "Oh, Your Majesty." She bowed, realizing who was in the room. Osirus did a silent nod in return.

"I'm afraid we just have ladies' wear, not unless you are shopping for your mate that you have found! She was certainly a beauty. I saw her last night." Her eyes continued to stay down, and I kept hidden behind Osirus, unsure of her true intentions. Too many supernatural beings around here for my liking. My social bar had already been exceeded for the day. My hands stayed fisted in his cape.

Osirus turned around and led me around from his cape. "Yes, it is for my destined." His velvety smooth voice spoke as I continued to look into his eyes. Not only were his looks captivating, but so was his voice. He could read a phone book and put me right to sleep.

"She is certainly more beautiful up close! Come, miss! I have just the collection for you to try." Maxine grabbed my hand, and I looked back for help, but Osirus just waved his hand for me to go. I was led behind an elaborate curtain, and she pulled at my clothes.

"Easy there!" I squealed.

Maxine looked at me, confused.

"I can undress, sorry."

Maxine smiled, grabbing fabrics from the corner from a previous customer. "I keep forgetting you are human. I heard they appreciate their privacy." She grinned. "You will have to get over that more quickly here, child. I heard the Fae kingdom is freer with their bodies." My face paled as she threw some dresses onto the chair next to me. "Come on, chop, chop! We want a show now! I have been blessed to have Luna Clara. You both look about the same size!" The one dress that was left in my hands was staring at me in the face as I grasped it tighter.

"Freer with their bodies?" My breath hitched. "Good gracious."

After a few minutes of trying to get the dress on, and Maxine checking on me multiple times, she huffed while finally tightening the strings on the corset. It was a simple A-line dress in the color of champagne.

Gold threading wove through the fabric, and small white and black flowers stood out on every hemline. It was exotically beautiful and something I would have never picked for myself. Maxine came behind me and pulled my ponytail down, letting my hair cascade down my back.

"He's going to love this on you!" She squeezed my shoulders as she whispered.

The front was low, but not overly so, just more so than what I was used to. The x-shaped cross on the front of the corset and the tie in the back made it look elegant.

Maxine threw the curtain open with a loud grunt, and in front of me was not only Osirus, but his men. Osirus sat on a lounge chair, with a leg hanging over the side, acting like he owned the place. Heck, he probably could. An instant shade of red was felt from my cheeks down to my toes as I saw everyone staring at me. My heart was racing, and I scooted to the side of the curtain to hide, trying to hide.

"Everyone out," Osirus' smooth voice spoke as he stood up and straightened his attire.

"Oy, is he going to take her 'ere?" Finley said, smirking. Alaneo smacked the back of his head roughly as he began to push the other guards out. "Hey! It's a fair question! I know I would!"

Braxton laughed loudly as the door shut behind them. Maxine still stood at the far corner of the store watching Osirus steps toward me. Not one footstep could be heard from him as he sauntered over.

His hand came up to my cheek and instantly felt the sparks fly. Listening to my body, I let him rub his thumb over my chin as I bent closer, our eyes never leaving each other. "You are utterly breathtaking," he whispered. Osirus leaned in and kissed my cheek, close to the side of my mouth. A small gasp left my lips as I held my face where his hand was. "Do you like the dress?"

"Yes, i-it's beautiful." I looked down, twirling it around. I started swaying it back and forth, amazed at how the dress flowed with the floor.

My biological mother never bought me fun dresses like this as a kid. You know how all the girls would run around in tutus and beautiful princess dresses on their birthdays? I envied those girls, instead, I wore secondhand jeans and a Dora the Explorer t-shirt that had seen better days. They had the money but preferred not wasting it on clothes I would grow out of in a year's time.

"Good, we will take the lot." Osirus untied his waistband next to his sword's sheath and tossed a small bag of coins.

"Your Majesty?" Maxine looked wide-eyed as she looked at the coins.

"You heard me. Pack them up and I will send someone to pick them up." Osirus took my hand in his and led me out the door.

"You can't just buy me a bunch of clothes!" pulling back on my hand, Osirus' eyes grew wide. "I don't need them! I was given some to wear during the time I was supposed to be vacationing here."

Osirus chuckled as he grabbed my hand again. "Darling, get used to being spoiled because I intend to do it more."

"I'm not your sugar baby. I can buy things myself. I've got my own money." Osirus continued to drag me out of the small town and onto the path in the forest.

"Now I won't hear any more of that. You're a queen now and will be treated as such. Nothing less for my love. Besides —" He paused and whispered in my ear. "—I'll be ripping them off so often you should have an extensive wardrobe of the finest clothing." I gasped and pushed him off me, which was difficult to do since he was menacingly tall.

"Pervert." I scoffed while he just laughed. An honest laugh he did, the first time I had ever heard him. It was so joyous it reminded me of a Christmas I had always dreamed of. Sitting with your parents and opening presents and hearing Santa Clause movies on the television was a dream of mine. Yeah, that didn't happen to me, but it reminded me of it. I hoped to spoil my children with everything I didn't have. My heart instantly warmed, and I gave him the biggest grin.

"What are you smiling about, Melina?" His smile was enormous, showing off his perfect teeth. There was a twinkle in his eye that I saw the moment we first laid eyes on each other the day before.

"You." I blushed. "When you laugh, it is just a pleasant sound. I can't explain it, it just reminded me of something."

"And what did it remind you of?" My smile faltered a bit. Sensing my battle, he squeezed my hands a few times. "Come, I want to show you something."

We walked for the next twenty minutes through the dense forest but always stayed on the path. Some parts were darker than others and you could see brief flickers of light from Pixies and Whisps. Many would come by and buzz around Osirus' head, some even bowing and making tinkling noises, while he would just smile and nod at them. This continued for the next few minutes until I couldn't take it anymore.

"What are they saying? They are talking to you, right?" Osirus nodded, and another Pixie flew up, this time sitting on his shoulder and looking down at me.

She cupped her hand and tinkled in his ear to tell him a secret and came down in front of me. I held out my hand so she could sit on it. She was small, just under six inches. Her face had the same features as a human but was more pointed and slender. Small leaves and cloth were woven to fit her curvy body. Her eyes were enormous for her face and her ears not only pointed outwards but had feather-like tendrils falling to her back. When she smiled, her teeth were full of sharp, pointed teeth. This observation didn't scare me like I thought it would, but maybe it was because Werewolves had fangs and so far, I hadn't been bitten.

The little Pixie started talking to me like she knew me and told me about her day. I was confused the whole time but nodded my head for her to continue. As she was done, she flew up, kissed my cheek, and flew away.

"What was that all about?" I giggled.

"Leah was letting you know how excited she was that you are to be queen. That she hopes you could help with a few requests for the Pixies. When you nodded your head, you agreed to let the Pixies have a representative at court." My mouth opened wide.

"I'm sorry! I didn't mean to do that. I was trying to be nice!" I panicked.

Osirus snaked his arm around my waist and pulled me in closer.

"Not to worry, a lot of things are changing, and it would be an excellent idea to involve the Pixies. In fact, having a representative of all the Fae cultures in court instead of nobility would be preferred."

Osirus continued to lead me through the path until we saw some light at the end of the forest.

The uneasiness of all this was daunting. How could I, a human, someone that wasn't supposed to be here, end up in this situation? I mean, I should be back home and working on Alpha Ramirez's accounting books and worrying about what I should make myself for dinner. I had lived in a cabin alone for a lot of my life and now I was being thrust into a whole new culture and now I had to rule in it.

"Do not worry, darling. We are taking our time." Osirus always knew my feelings, which I found extremely weird. It was like he had a sixth sense about it.

Another question for another time, I supposed. That list just kept on growing...

Chapter 14

Melina

Coming out of the dense forest and into the sunshine, we entered a bright meadow. Colors here in the Bergarian world were much more vibrant. The grass was so deep of a green you could almost see hints of blue in it. The sky wasn't just blue but also had purples swirled into it while the white clouds continued to float by. Several exotic birds, Fairies and Pixies flew through the sky and even deer roamed the meadow. None were afraid as we came deeper into the tall, lush grasses.

At the top of the hill, Osirus took my hand again and pointed to the east. "There, that is where we are going tomorrow." The sky was so clear you could see for miles, just like on the mountain where my family arrived here. The forest was cut away from an area and a mighty, light-colored castle stood amongst the valleys.

"That is our home, the castle."

Feeling his gaze on the side of my face, I continued to stare at it. It appeared so far away, but even from here you could understand how gigantic and majestic it was. Osirus tugged at my hand again and had me look to the West.

"And this is the Cerulean Moon Kingdom, the Shifter kingdom."

It was just as majestic as the Golden Light Kingdom, but the forest was dense around it, hidden from the light. "They like their cover, so they don't have to shift in the middle of everyone." He laughed. "I don't know why. The Faes aren't really concerned with covering their bodies much." Letting out a large gulp, Osirus squeezed my hand. "Don't worry, they don't walk around naked. Some women just like to wear scanty clothes, is all."

Osirus led me to the South side of the hill and sat down, putting a long piece of grass in his mouth.

"This place is amazing," I said while sitting down. "Were there humans here before? All of this is in fairy tales and story books back on Earth."

Osirus nodded as he took the grass from his mouth.

"Yes, actually. There was a time where humans did roam around with us. Some supernaturals took it upon themselves to torture them, use them as slaves and blood bags—then Luna Clara's parents took the throne, they took it upon themselves to put them all back on Earth. That was about 1100 years ago. I'm sure those that were here benefited from creating some stories about the magical parts of the land. Some stories were greatly obscured."

"Like what?" I began picking some of the purple daisies around us and tying them together.

"For one, Witches eat little children. Ha, that Hansel and Gretel story around here gets a great laugh. Little Red Riding Hood? Wolves don't eat people either."

"That's a relief," I sighed. "I've been thinking about all those stories since I first found out about this place." I chuckled. "What about Vampires, though, do they...?" I paused, waiting. Osirus rubbed his eyes and placed the grass back in his mouth.

"Yes, unfortunately, they do drink the blood of humans. They forced them a long time ago, sometimes going crazy and draining them completely. There are Vampires on Earth now, but they are from a descendent that knew how to control their blood lust well. The vampires here get donations from several supernatural groups, such as Witches and Shifters and even wild animals. Queen Diana of Vermillion has strict laws in place now that we are allowing humans to enter Bergarian again."

"That's good then. I hope they can continue that." I resumed to fiddle with flowers.

Osirus continued to stare out over the view and a few questions popped up in my mind again. The rumors of how he was, what was true, what was not. He said he would always tell me the truth, but when was the right time to bring it up?

"Osirus?" I peeked up at him, catching him staring at me. My cheeks flushed, and I looked back down at my lap of flowers.

"What is it, darling?" His fingers pulled my chin up. I felt extremely guilty asking and being nosey, but if I was to stay here, I had to know.

"You said you didn't trick women into being with you, but what about the willing ones? Did you... date?" I looked down, embarrassed.

"Date?"

"Yes, like taking girls out, I guess woo them? Court them?" Osirus chuckled lightly, then a big hearty laugh left his lips, and I couldn't help but smile.

"It isn't funny. I'm serious!" I gently pushed him, and he gave me a mischievous smirk. After he was done laughing, his face became more serious.

"No, I did not, 'date'," he put into air quotes. Osirus sighed and crossed his legs in front of me. "I'll be honest, there was a time I thought I would never find you." He grabbed my hand and laced his with mine. "I had lived for over 800 years, a long time without a destined one. I had relations with several—" He cleared his throat. "—concubines."

I gasped and took my hand away from his. I instantly regretted it as his face fell. Feeling terrible about it, I grabbed his hand back.

"Sorry, I know our cultures are different. I shouldn't react like that."

Osirus gave a soft smile. "But I shouldn't have, knowing I had my destined one waiting for me."

"I wasn't even born yet; I think you are fine." Even though it hurt me, I couldn't blame him for it. At least he wasn't doing it now.

"I have done anything like that in over 300 years now. I've been searching for you since then. I'm sorry." His eyes were soft, begging for forgiveness.

"You have nothing to be sorry about, Osirus, that's a long time and I think it was honorable of you for waiting that long."

"Gods, I don't deserve you." His finger trailed down my cheek, and I bowed my head, afraid he would see my giddy grin on my face.

"Don't hide from me." He lifted my chin back to his face. "I've waited so long to see your face; I don't want to miss any blush."

I giggled like a little girl and shoved him playfully. "Stop that," I whined.

"What about you, darling?" he quipped. "Did you, 'date'?"

I laughed at the stupid question. "Definitely not. I was too busy taking care of myself to worry about anyone else. I was the awkward teenager that hung out with the popular kids. The pack of Wolves as I know of them now. People stayed away from that group as well as me." I finished up the flowered crown I was making in my lap. "I had a few guys I liked, but nothing came of it. I didn't care that much about pursuing it. Besides, I'd figured they would leave me like my parents did."

Once I finished my flower crown, I let go of Osirus' hand. I stared back up at him. His face was somber with a slight tick of his jaw, so to lighten the mood, I took my flower crown and got on my knees, careful not to fall over my dress. Osirus looked confused until I placed the flower crown on his head.

"There, now you are king of the magical meadow!" I laughed, sitting back down, and falling back. I felt my hair strewn across the grass as I continued to laugh. Big 'ole kingly man now has a crown of flowers.

He looked so cute with a flower crown. Now he looked like a girly Fae you would see in some crude painting from a pervy artist. He was just so, not pretty, but handsome. Everything about him was alluring, drawing me in. As much as I want to fight it, the longer I was with him, the more comfortable I became.

Osirus finally smiled as he saw me laughing; he laid down beside me, propping his elbow on the grass and tilting his head towards mine. "King of the magical meadow, huh?" I giggled again and bit my lips from laughing too much. It felt so good to laugh.

His eyes wandered from my eyes to my lips and his thumb came up to my chin to pull my bottom lip from my teeth. "Don't do that, darling," he whispered. I tilted my head to the side, cocking my eyebrow.

"Do what?" I whispered back.

"Gods," he sighed heavily. "Darling, can I kiss you?"

Osirus' eyes were so intense, I felt like he could read everything that was going in my mind. When I didn't answer, he leaned in closer. I was still lying on the ground, mulling over his words until I finally let out a faint, "Yes," as his lips brushed mine.

Not to sound cliché but when his lips touched mine, time stopped. His lips were much softer than I thought they would be. His normal pursed thin lips when he was hiding his emotions came out of the woodworks. There was so much passion as his lips moved against the slickness of my lip gloss.

My body responded almost immediately, kissing him back. He tasted like my favorite cotton candy, and I couldn't get enough. I continued to kiss him, like I was always meant to do it, and his hand came down, cupping my cheek. The pad of his thumb stroked my jaw and I let out a sigh. My hands quickly went up around his neck and he pulled me up and had me straddle him.

My dress hiked up my thighs, but not enough to expose anything. Straddling his lap, his arms came around my waist, pulling me closer to him. Osirus' tongue gently licked my lips, praying I watched enough romance movies, I opened my mouth only to be greeted with his tongue massaging mine. He groaned as his grip went tighter around my lower waist. My hips did something I never thought possible and started rocking into him.

Goddess, it felt good. Once I realized what I was doing, I quickly stopped and continued to kiss his tasty lips.

I let out a gigantic sigh, and he then squeezed my rear end, causing me to stop kissing him and gasp.

"I'm sorry, darling, I got a bit carried away," he whispered into my mouth as he caressed my face.

"Sorry, I was surprised." I giggled.

He smirked as he pulled a few strands of my hair away from my face.

Osirus

Holy fucking goddess. My love let me kiss those pouty lips. They were so succulent, so ripe, just for me, and the best part about it was that no other man, Fae, or Shifter had touched what was mine. She had saved herself for someone she cared about and being blessed by the gods, she gave that gift to me. My poor heart was beating faster than it had ever done before, faster than any adrenaline rush from any battle or war.

Melina made me feel. She made me have emotions that I had hidden away for several human lifetimes. She'd broken down my walls, and she didn't even realize it. Here she was, sitting on my lap, facing me with those beautiful eyes. Those eyes beckon me to take her, to spoil her, and give her all the love and attention that she had been denied most of her life.

I will spoil her, even though she swore she didn't need it. She was too thoughtful, too independent. I wanted her to depend on me for every damn thing in her life.

I couldn't stand it anymore. Her in that dress made her curves so appetizing. Most Faes are slender, stick thin, and lacking in certain departments that I always seemed to love about shifter females. No shifter could ever compare to her, though, my darling. Her lush body, I will claim soon. It will be mine to devour, to treasure, pleasure, and place my angry cock into.

Things heated quickly in our kiss. When she began grinding her hips onto my cock, I tried to keep it light, not wanting to scare her. I wanted to make love to her there, out in the open. I didn't care if any Dragon flew by and saw what we were doing. Hell, let them watch. Then they would all know how the Fae King took his bride.

When she stopped, however, I was so disappointed. I knew she stopped because she started thinking, not knowing what she was doing. Not knowing the foreign feeling between her legs. She was damn innocent, and I loved it. When I squeezed her arse, I knew I went too far.

When she said she was just surprised, it gave me hope maybe we could go a step further next time. Her cheeks were flushed and her hair a bit disheveled and that in itself turned me on all the more.

"Darling, we should head back. Dinner will be soon, and I promised your family one last meal together before we leave tomorrow." Melina nodded and gave me a smile. Before she could stand up, I picked her up and gently set her feet on the ground.

My white horse, Montu, trotted towards us, and I held my hand out for him as he nuzzled into it. "Where did he come from?!" Melina squealed excitedly.

"Being a Fae, I am closely connected to nature. He knew

I would want to come back soon, so he sought me out. Now that he knows you are mine, he will start to understand your aura, too." Her eyes grew wide as she petted the side of his neck, and he gave her a nibble on her shoulder.

"I've never ridden a horse before. Do you think he will let me ride him?" Montu instantly nudged her, letting her know it was all right. Fae horses are extremely intelligent creatures, all done through our rigorous breeding programs. "You are such a handsome boy! You are!" Melina encouraged him and he let out a neigh.

I mounted Montu bareback and held my hand out for Melina. She was as light as a feather as I pulled her to the front and held onto her waist as Montu trotted back into the forest, back to the packhouse. The entire ride, her arse was bumping against my cock, and I groaned trying to adjust myself, which proved challenging. I wasn't sure how much longer I was going to be able to take it, I knew we needed to go slow, but gods, it was so damn hard.

Chapter 15

Osirus

Once we arrived back at the Royal Cabin, I helped Melina dismount off Montu, and I led her back to our room. Her dresses were already packaged nicely, ready for us to head back to our home tomorrow. We both cleaned up before heading to dinner in the packhouse with her adoptive parents, along with Clara and her mate.

"I'm just so happy for her," Rose cooed at her adoptive daughter. "I always wondered what would happen when she aged and realize we weren't aging with her. It would have broken my heart to let her know then." Rose kissed Melina on the cheek, and she just hugged her back. I wanted to ask more about Melina's biological parents, but I resisted. I'd love to hunt them down and destroy every bit of happiness in them for making my soulmate suffer most of her life.

I noticed Melina craved attention but hid it very well. She didn't want to be one of "those" attention-seeking girls Even though she builds a powerful fortress around her heart, she craves contact and that makes her sweet and lovely. She's eager to love but resists. Her aura lightened when she was near me and the blackness surrounding her heart was slowly fading, but I knew we had a long way to go. Years of neglect and love had only beaten her down as she strived to show everyone, she was strong and capable. She is capable and strong, but now that she has me, she can be the weak girl she never got to be.

"I can visit whenever I want, right?" Tulip quipped.

Alec gave a scowl. He was one of the warriors and received little time off. "Only if I accompany you, Tulip," Alec tried to soothe his mate. She glared at him right back.

"But you never get time off!" she whined. "Besides, I'm sure His Majesty has plenty of guards."

Alec grabbed Tulip and put her in his lap and gripped her waist tightly. "Don't argue with me. You can't leave me."

Tulip pouted and nodded. Clara started laughing and petting Kane's arm.

"Oh, that is like us, isn't it, babe?" Kane nuzzled into Clara's hair as she sat in his lap. The stronger the warrior, the more possessive they were with their mates, and Kane was no exception.

Melina continued to eat silently, being quiet as a dormouse sneaking cheese in the kitchen. "Darling, wouldn't you like for Tulip to come visit sometime? Even Rose and Elm?"

She nodded enthusiastically and swallowed her food. "Of course, I would!"

"It's settled then. Our bonding ceremony will be a month from tomorrow, and I hope to see you all there." Everyone talked excitedly about the announcement. Few Shifters come to the Golden Light Kingdom; many Faes in the government could be quite harsh in judgment, so other supernaturals stayed away.

As people talked at the table about our upcoming ceremony, Melina pulled on my sleeve a bit aggressively. "Excuse me!" she whispered harshly. "What do you think you are doing? You didn't discuss this with me! A bonding ceremony? I didn't even know what that is with Fae!"

"It's just a statement, saying we are destined soulmates.

You can dress up and wear a beautiful dress at a fancy party. It is like Tulip and Alec's mating ceremony," I said off-handedly. "It will be extravagant and beautiful, everything you have ever wanted at a party." I picked up her hand to kiss it until she pulled away.

"Um, no. First, you didn't ask me, and now you are putting a timer on me. You said we were going slow. This isn't slow!" Her family was staring at us, so I took Melina's hand and led her outside; as I looked back, Elm gave me a scowl. I sighed and pushed open the door, only to see Melina crossing her arms and stomping her foot.

"I can't believe you! You can't announce something like that without talking to me!" she continued to speak in hushed tones.

"Darling, a month is a long time. Traditionally, I should have taken you the first night. I thought things were going so well." I held out my arms to comfort her, but she walked away. My heart ached to see her so angry.

"I'm human, Osirus. Humans sometimes take years before they get 'married' or have some sort of ceremony. We just met!"

The anger radiating off her was clear, but my own pride was getting the best of me. No one just tells me no; no woman has ever told me no to any advancements I have made.

"A month is slow around here, Melina. I'm sure some Shifters are already talking about us not being marked yet. I suggest you calm your bratty attitude," I growled.

"I'm human, and I was understanding about your concubines. Now you need to be more understanding of my traditions."

A stab to my heart. My heart stopped a few moments, only to feel the pain of that statement. She was right. Humans took time, and she had been thrown into this colossal mess of a world she knew nothing about.

"Darling—" I softened my voice. "I do not want to do anything you do not wish."

Her eyes looked up at me, begging me to listen to her, and my heart wanted to comply. This time I couldn't listen.

"Finding your destined one is a beautiful bond, a gift, and many take that gift and make sure that no one else will take it away. If I lose you and someone tries to mark or make you theirs, I will die of heartache. Literally. I must protect you. Many would kill at the opportunity to see you and I hurt."

Melina's eyes softened, and she slowly dropped into her arms. "I love you, Melina. I know you don't understand the bond yet and you don't have to tell me you love me back. We must do this for the both of us. Let's plan it and see where it goes, hmm? If you are that opposed, then we can talk about it."

Her eyes were down, the disappointment and sadness were written all over her aura. I walked up to her and held her close; she didn't wrap her arms around me. I knew she was angry, but this was the best way to protect her. I'd always be able to find her if she was ever taken from me. Petting her hair softly, I gave it a quick kiss. "How about we go back to dinner? You won't be able to see them in the morning, so we need to say our goodbyes tonight." She kept her head lowered. I knew she was upset I'd have to explain more later.

The rest of dinner was somber. Even Clara looked sad for Melina. Clara was born human. The gods refused to give her a Wolf since she was blessed with other gifts by the goddess Charis. Clara was only gifted a Wolf after her mate, Kane, marked her. She understood what she was going through. However, Clara embraced the bond more so than Melina. Clara didn't have trust or abandonment issues. Elm continued to glare at me as Rose petted Melina's hand. Often, she would whisper in her ear, and she would smile a bit.

All the while, Kane sat silently as he finished his steak. The brooding alpha always had a scowl on his face unless he was addressing his mate. We all stood up and said our goodbyes while a few tears were shed. Her family reassured her everything was going to be fine and to not fight the bond. I was sure she was going to fight even more now.

"Melina," Kane spoke up, which shocked everyone. He glared at everyone to leave, but I stayed close to the door to watch. Clara grabbed my hand and gave it a gentle pat.

"Being a strong supernatural is hard," Kane mumbled. "I had a hard time with Clara in the beginning. I had to go slow. I was fortunate that Clara didn't resist the bond. When you are troubled, I want you to think of Clara or your friend Tulip. They may have not had troubles like you did growing up, but they are both now happier than they ever were. Their souls are completed now, you will eventually feel whole. I'm not saying give in, but to give him a chance. He's holding back a lot for you. He's also king, which comes with tremendous possessiveness for you, but he only wants to protect and love you. He isn't lying, he will not play with your heart." Kane gave a tight-lipped smile as he patted her shoulder. "And he is Okay, for Fae," he mumbled.

I swelled in pride thinking that Alpha Kane would say that about me. We never got along, he was doing this act of kindness more for his mate than me, but the words of encouragement made me thankful. Melina smiled and gave Kane a hug, surprising him. He patted her head, and she walked over to me and held my hand. Smiling, I mouthed a 'thank you' to Kane, and we went back to our room.

Melina

Osirus led me back to our room and, while he was talking about our plans for tomorrow, I shut the bathroom door. We had such a wonderful afternoon, and he had to go and ruin it by making decisions without talking to me. Sure, I know we were going slower than what his kind is used to, but hell; I gave him my first kiss on the first date. That was something, right?

While I've been stewing, I've been sitting in the bath.

The steam continued to come off the tub, never losing its warmth. Must be some Fairy magic. I leaned back on the headrest of the tub; every once in a while, Osirus would knock to check on me. Another reminder of how he is way up my butt and wanting to know where I am, always.

Raising my hands, I know I've become pruny, but I don't really care.

If he had just said, "Hey, we really need to show that we are a couple. Can we do this in a month?" I would have been cautious at first, but I would have agreed. I'm not going to put out because of some bond, though; no one tells me when I'm ready to further a relationship, even if it is the Moon Goddess. Continuing to wash my hair, which now smelled like that honeysuckle drink, I stepped out of the tub, and I heard shuffling on the other side of the door.

Seriously? Has he been listening to me breathe? I let out a huff and heard footsteps walk away. That's a bit better. You know, I could be ready in a month, be ready to commit because I know this bond is holding us together. However, he didn't ask. I squinted my eyes at the mirror, talking silently to myself. "You got this, you don't give in. Even if he is extremely hot. You hold your ground." I nodded my head to myself and pointed my finger to my reflection for extra effect.

I turned around and smirked at myself. If I was to be queen and always have someone at my side, whether it be Osirus or a bodyguard, I should have one last hoorah, right? I was going to ask him to visit Tulip tonight to be nice and considerate, but that is out the window. He didn't ask me if I wanted a bonding ceremony, so I will not ask him for me to go out alone. Insert evil laugh here. I giggled.

Once my hair was dry and my joggers were on, courtesy of Tulip after I told her my embarrassing moment of wearing a skimpy thing to bed the night before, I threw on a sweatshirt for good measure. I walk out of the bathroom, steam blowing behind me as I saunter to the bed. Osirus was sitting with his back against the headboard, watching my every move.

"Have a good bath, darling?" His voice was soft, like velvet, and almost made me want to go weak in the knees. Almost.

"Yes, thank you. I'm tired now. I'd like to sleep." Rolling over so my back was to his face.

He slithered closer to me until I could feel his breath down my neck. Now that I knew what his breath did to me when we kissed, it made me shutter. Osirus wrapped his arms around me and whispered *good night* and it was all I could do not to turn around and snuggle in closer to him, but I was a strong, independent woman. I could take care of myself.

Osirus breathing evened out. His rapid heartbeats were now not as fast. The small twitches in his fingers let me know he was out cold. Glancing at the clock, I saw it was close to midnight. Tulip would be at the front door any minute.

Gently picking up Osirus' arm, I slid out, only to replace his arm with my pillow. It smelled like me from the night before, so I hoped he didn't have any strange Wolfy smells, so he won't know the difference. Mentally high fiving myself, I slid out the door, not even bothering with shoes.

Tulip was waiting impatiently at the bottom of the stairs. "What took you so long? I thought you weren't coming!" she whisper-yelled playfully.

"After that show of dominance at the dinner table, you really thought I would back down after that? Let's go cause trouble." Tulip snickered and led me to the back of the courtyard, just beyond the row of trees.

Remembering my first night here, I knew where we were going. The lake was lit up magically with the evening Pixies dancing across it. Some flew up to me and gave me a little bow and a kiss on the cheek. "Word has gotten around. They must know you are the new queen," Tulip mused. "Come on." She pulled at my arm as we stood on the pier.

"All right, strip!" Tulip threw her shirt over her body and her pants were discarded quickly as she jumped into the lake.

That was going to be cold.

"Tulip! I am not skinny dipping! I am not as comfortable with my nudity as you are!"

Tulip resurfaced and laughed. "Then keep your panties and bra on, you twit, and get in!"

I guessed it was kind of like a bathing suit. Everything was covered, and this was my last night to have some fun. Taking my sweatshirt and joggers off quickly, I jumped into the lake so I couldn't back down.

The. Water. Was. Freezing.

I resurfaced, and immediately my teeth chattered. Why was the lake so cold?! It was supposed to be summer outside here! Tulip swam up behind me and dunked me in the water. I stayed underwater and quickly pulled her leg and brought her down with me. As we both resurfaced, we started laughing a bit too loudly and heard some footsteps not too far away.

"Well, well, well, what do we have here?" we heard a playful voice say.

Quickly, I swam to the edge of the pier to cover myself, but Tulip sat under the water in all her glory. She smacked her lips in annoyance and gave a glare. "Carson and the goons, check it out, Melina." I peeked over the pier and gave a small wave.

"Shit, Melina, you can't be out here. I just thought it was Tulip. The King is gonna be pissed. Well, you too, Tulip, because your mate is looking for you right now." He let out a laugh.

Tulip scoffed. "Let him come. I'm up for some angry sex." My face paled. Oh, my gosh, what is Osirus going to do to me?

That was something I didn't think about. I'm half-naked, swimming in a lake in the middle of the night, future queen, and all. Whoopsie. The sudden guilt had me pale as I heard growling from the bushes; I couldn't hear any footsteps, but the rapid breathing and the white hair reflecting across the top of his head—could only tell me one thing.

Osirus, and he was mad.

Chapter 16

Osirus

Melina wouldn't even look at me as she came to bed. I saw the frustration in her eyes, but she refused to cry. She was closed off, not wanting to show any weakness towards me, but I knew better. She was hurting and felt betrayed that I wouldn't discuss the bonding ceremony with her. With any other woman that understood our world, they would be thrilled; however, Melina wasn't from here. She wasn't any other girl and in my stupid mind, I thought she would love it.

She's fighting it, every step of the way, and I didn't know how to break down her walls. All supernaturals were beasts compared to humans. There were some aspects of our bodies we had trouble controlling and each minute with her, not having her as mine, completely pulled at my soul. Melina may not feel the pull as strongly as I do, but I know she will feel it once we are one.

My thoughts continued to ravage my mind as I held onto her, the only way I knew to keep her protected. I hoped my touch would calm her and we could talk more in the morning as we traveled back to our home. I couldn't wait to show her the palace, her new home. I had already sent word to prepare the royal bedchambers to my most trusted maids and to keep silent about it. If word got out that my mate was to arrive before I was ready to announce it, there would be repercussions for their actions.

My thoughts of Melina finally letting go and trusting me gave me a warm feeling as I drifted off to sleep, hearing her even breathing.

Feeling a chilly breeze enter the room, I sat up, confused. The bedroom door was open, and Melina wasn't in the bed. In fact, it felt cold.

"Melina? Darling?" I sat up and threw the covers off me as I jumped to check the bathing facilities.

"Melina?"

The water closet light was off, but I still threw the shower doors open and checked the tub. Nothing. Running down the stairs in just my linen sleep trousers and bare chest, I looked in the kitchen. I panicked, hoping she didn't wander into one of the guards or even Alaneo's room.

"EVERYONE UP!" I yelled, and within seconds, everyone was standing in the living room.

My breathing had picked up, my chest heaving, and my own teeth pierced my lips.

"Your Majesty, you need to calm down." Alaneo came up to me from behind, but I grabbed him by the collar quickly and stuck him to the wall. "We have to stop doing this." Alaneo rolled his eyes.

"Where is my destined!?" I roared in his face.

Everyone stilled, not knowing what to say. Not only did my fangs descend, but I felt the rest of my teeth transforming into their wild state. I hadn't done this since I was 100 years old at the Battle of Erund fighting stay Ogres over land territory.

"W-what do ya mean?" Finley said, putting on his shirt. "She was with you. We haven't seen 'er." My wings haven't left my body in a while now, but I could feel them twitch inside me, wanting to fly out of the house and search the area.

Alaneo, seeing my struggle, patted my hand, and I let him

down. "We'll find her, come on—" Alaneo started spouting out orders and I immediately left the house. Running toward the woods, thinking whoever took her must still be traveling. She couldn't have gone far.

Several Pixies flew far away from me, seeing my state. My back was still twitching, but I kept them at bay. My teeth were sharper than I remember, and I know my eyes have gone black against my white skin. Hearing a twinkle above me I stopped my pursuit to look up. It was a Pixie named Nia. Nia quietly sat on my shoulder as I waited for her to speak. Tink, tink, tinkle, tink was all that anyone else could hear, but since I was bred to rule, I could understand all the Fae creatures.

"She's by the lake. She went with her friend," Nia said. *"They were laughing and skipping by not too long ago."* I nodded for a quick thank you and sprinted in the lake's direction. You could hear squeals of screams and laughter until they halted.

Male voices infiltrated my ears as I continued to run forward and brush the bushes to the side. "Well, well, well, what do we have here?" I heard the voice of the familiar Carson. That Wolf liked Melina; I could feel his disgusting aura of wanting a mile away.

"Melina, what are you doing here? The King will be pissed you are here..." The mumbling continued as my anger clouded my hearing. Pushing the last bush aside, I see my Melina, at the end of the pier, soaking wet, with her eyes as large as tea saucers. Fear was in her eyes as I looked at her.

She was afraid of me.

Carson stood back as he heard a roar come pouncing from the bushes on the other side of the lake. Alec's Wolf stood tall and circled back around where we were all standing. Tulip cowered in fear as Alec transformed in mere seconds. "Tulip! What the hell are you doing!" Tulip swam to the pier and grabbed her clothes and put them on while she was still in the lake. Her body had been completely naked, and Alec's anger was getting the best of him.

"All of you leave. This is a mate matter!"

Carson, Sean, and Rex turned and looked at Melina. She was still hidden under the pier and waved goodbye to them. Carson eyes hardened as he looked at me. "Don't fucking scare her, I don't care if you are king of some fucking Fairies." I grew my stature taller and bared my teeth at him and hissed. I easily towered over the average sized Wolf. He may have muscle and a Wolf, but I was a king. I had more powers than he could even fathom.

My nails grew into golden claws as I gripped his neck. "Mind your business, pup." I picked him up as he struggled. His friends stood back and slowly walked backwards until they were at a safe distance.

"I know what is best for my mate. Get that through your head." For a Wolf, he was quite scared of my appearance. Fae have been shunned into not releasing their anger of their true forms long before he was alive, so this was a first for him and his friends to see. Even Alec and Tulip stood stunned as they continued to back away.

Dropping the piece of bulky meat, I glanced over at Melina, who was shaking in fear. Controlling my breathing, I tried to calm my anger, but it was no use. Everyone had their backs turned to us and were walking away. Feeling afraid to speak, I motioned her to come to me, but she was hesitant. I turned around, giving her privacy. Hearing her pull herself out of the water, I continued to concentrate on my primitive side to make it still. The soft pitter patter of her feet came close, but I stayed turned around, afraid she would run seeing my face.

I knew my teeth were still razor-sharp, my eyes have been dilated and my ears even stretched farther than their normal size. It was primitive; it was animalistic, that was what we really were on the inside. No matter how much my race and I tried to hide it, it would always be there. I was just relieved my wings did not emerge; this was going to be a lot for her.

Melina's hand slid into mine, and she looked up at me. Her eyes were glazed with tears, fighting for them not to fall. I wanted to urge her to let them fall, let all her sorrow out, but I couldn't. My voice was hoarse, raspy, like gravel rumbling in my throat. My darling had heard enough when I yelled at Carson.

"I'm sorry," she whispered. "I was angry. I don't have control anymore and I wanted to have fun one last time."

She doesn't think she will have fun anymore? Gods, what the hell is going on in that head of hers?

I got on my knee and motioned her to sit, and she listened for once. Picking her legs up under one arm and supporting her back with the other, we headed back to the cabin.

It was late, and dawn would approach in a few hours. I laid her on the bed, her hair still wet as I covered her body with a blanket. I stood up to go downstairs until I could fully calm down, but she called for me.

"Osirus?" Turning around, the worried look on her face made me giddy and made me happy in a sick, twisted way. Maybe she cared about me. "Please stay." Her voice was barely a whisper. Letting out a sigh, I came around the bed and laid down; she automatically glued herself to my side and buried her face into my chest.

"I'm sorry," was the last thing I heard as we both fell into a deep sleep.

Melina

Instead of riding on Montu, Osirus had us ride in a carriage that Alpha Kane and Luna Clara let us borrow. All the dresses that Osirus bought, as well as everyone's luggage, were stored inside with us. The seats were well-cushioned, and you could hardly feel the bumps along the road as we traveled.

Osirus had said nothing about last night, just that I should shower before we left so I wouldn't be uncomfortable during the day. Osirus was mostly reading parchment paper and reading notes as I sat by the window and looked at the scenery.

We passed through most of the dense forest where most of the shifters stayed. Now we were at the plains area where there were still some shifters, such as lions and panthers. The occasional forest would come up and bears and tigers would come trotting by. There were several children that would run up and pat on the carriage, in which Osirus would groan at the loud noises. He was being such a grump.

One child ran up to the carriage and gave me a bouquet of beautiful flowers and I couldn't help but smile and blow him a kiss, which caused the other children to complain. Pulling in the flowers, I smelled them; they smelled of citrus fruits like oranges and lemons. No flower could compare to this back on Earth. They were orange and yellow with hints of purple inside each petal. They stood out brightly against the olive-green dress that Osirus had me wear.

"What do you think, darling?" he asked suddenly.

"Hmm?" I continued to look at the exotic bouquet.

"The flowers? Are they to your liking?" Osirus gave me the first smile of the day and it was nearly noon.

"Yes, they are beautiful. I've never seen flowers like these before. Are there many flowers around the castle?" I inquired.

"Darling, there are many gardens around the palace. You can pick as many as you want and make bouquets for our chambers." I smiled at the thought. There weren't a lot of flowers around the cabin I used to live in; it was mostly trees and not enough sunlight to reach the ground.

"Osirus? About last night..." I started, but my voice quickly faded at the mention of last night.

"How about we forget about it?" Osirus cut in quickly. His hand came up and brushed a strand of my dark hair. "We both did and said things yesterday we regret, and it is best we put it behind us. We will be more open with communication from now on. Hmm?" I sighed and grabbed his hand.

When I saw Osirus' fangs last night, the deep guttural growl and the way his ears had elongated like that, like an animal, it made me fearful. I know he cannot word-vomit everything out in just two days of knowing each other, but it was certainly a sight to see.

"I wanted to ask you—"

Osirus cut me off quickly. "I know about my appearance." His eyes darted to the view outside.

The waterfall we were passing was beautiful and I could have sworn I saw a mermaid, but I dismissed it. Talking to Osirus was more important.

"There are things about Fae that aren't spoken. One of those things was what happened last night. I lost control..." Osirus paused as he looked at me. He looked so lost and broken, I didn't know how to comfort him, so I did the one thing I thought would help and that was to sit in his lap. Werewolves liked it. Why not him? I giggled when his eyes shot up with surprise.

"Go on, let me hear the story," I mused.

He let out a deep chuckle and continued. "Faes are said to be descended from Pixies. Pixies can be mean little creatures when angry. I believe there is a story about some tooth fairy that takes teeth away from children back on Earth?"

I hummed in agreement.

"Well, there were some angry Pixies over some land disputes once upon a time and the Pixies attacked their enemies while they were sleeping, they used their magic to pull out all of their teeth." I gasped and Osirus gave an enormous smile. "It was all true. It is in their history."

"Makes my teeth hurt." I laughed.

"Anyway, they have been dubbed feral and unsocialized creatures by many Fae, but you have now come to know they are a quiet, pleasant creature. However, that stigma still stays. The gods created all the supernatural, so they just took the Pixies as a blueprint and experimented. Next, they had the Fairies and then the Faes. That was when they stopped after they created the Fae. Many generations ago, many believe the Faes were the ultimate creation of our kind, so that must mean we are the superior. We now have to keep ourselves in check and not succumb to some Pixie tendencies that run in our blood. Which I succumbed to last night."

"But it's normal," I chirped, not afraid of who he was last night, more shocked. "That is part of your nature. It is the same with all supernatural. Werewolves do it when they are upset, especially about their mate. All Shifters do it. I even heard that vampires throw hissy fits too and become more demon-like! I'm unsure about witches and such, but that is just who you are! You shouldn't have to suppress yourself and not be the supernatural you are!" I was getting worked up and Osirus rubbed his hands on my arms.

"It's all right. I'm fine now," he brushed me off.

"Well, I'm not fine!" I pouted. "I enjoyed seeing you all mad. It let me know you cared. Even though it is kind of weird for me to see that." I blushed. "You are supposed to do that. No one has ever gotten so protective of me, and I liked it when you got mad at Carson. You stood up for me, claimed me, protected me. I wouldn't want anything less. What do other Faes do?"

Osirus pondered for a moment. "Outlying territories, they are more open to who they are. They show forms of aggressiveness and possessiveness. They protect their mates ferociously as long as no one from the capital is nearby."

"Well, why? You should change it," I demanded.

"Really, my queen? If all this talk about change and accepting who we really are, is that important to you, does that mean you will accept who you are, the Queen of the Faes?" Osirus smirked.

Chapter 17

Melina

"W-what? What do you mean?" I questioned Osirus as his hands slithered against my hips, pulling me into his lap.

"I said," he answered in a husky voice, "shouldn't you accept who you are meant to be, and who you are meant to be with?"

Osirus' breath was in my ear. It was warm and smelled just like cotton candy, I had a taste of it just the day before. His nose traced around my ear as he gently nibbled at it, causing a slight whimper to escape my lips. Why does this feel so good?

Osirus turned my body, I was now straddling him, my dress was hiked up to my upper thighs, and I blushed in embarrassment as I tried to pull it down. "You shouldn't be embarrassed, darling. One day I'll get to see that pale skin of yours." His lips continued to grace my jaw, leaving small kisses in their wake. His voice was sultry, inviting, and incredibly sexy.

Osirus could top any actor if he was trying to play me. My breathing hitched when he pressed his lips to the crook of my shoulder where it meets my neck. "Mmm, found it," he mumbled.

I clenched my thighs as his tongue licked such an erotic part of my body.

Feeling my heartbeat between my thighs, I desperately wanted friction. It was a feeling I had never experienced, and I was unsure what to do with it. I wanted one thing, though; I really wanted his lips on mine.

Osirus continued to tease me. I was becoming a panting mess. He sucked on my neck and chuckled every time I would squirm in his lap.

"Ohh, goddess," I whimpered.

"You know," he continued to kiss up and down my neck, "If a Fae releases its true self, you get not only possessiveness and our true form, but you also get something else entirely."

I hummed in agreement, hardly paying attention. His lips felt so good. I wanted more.

"You also get a Fae's urge to please their mate, to make them feel pleasure over and over and then one day—" He kissed my cheek. "—they decide to make their own little Pixie."

My cheeks flushed as I put both hands on Osirus' shoulders. Osirus' eyes went dark, just as they were the night before, but these weren't of anger, they were of lust. Eyelids were hooded, and I felt nothing but the heat from his body against my chest. My chest was heaving, my breasts almost spilling over my dress.

"Osirus—" Before I could say another word, his lips crashed into mine. I moaned as he held me close. One hand was around my lower back and the other was fisted in the back of my hair.

He didn't want me to pull away; the joke was on him because I didn't want to either. His tongue swiftly entered my mouth, and I mewled at the feeling. This was intense, not sweet like yesterday. There was passion and desire in it. And I craved it.

I didn't even think my body took over. The thoughts of doubt and untrustworthiness toward the Fae King were gone. At that moment, I wanted him to dominate my mouth and my neck. Osirus had given me no reason to not trust him. His words were always soothing. Even if we had a disagreement, he could quickly resolve the problem. *Why am I thinking right now?*

He groaned as I rubbed against him. Quickly realizing his growing problem and my pulsing lower region, he gripped my waist, pulling me down harder on his member. I gasped as he kneaded my rear.

I pushed myself further into his grasp, and he groaned as he nipped at my bottom lip, pulling it slightly. Quickly letting go, I kissed down his neck, he leaned his head to the side as I sucked on the same spot he had done on me. He continued to rub my core against his throbbing member.

"Osirus," I whispered while panting, continuing to bury my face in his neck.

His groan only fueled something in me, and I didn't know what. "Do you feel my need for you?" he growled lowly into my ear. "Do you feel my desire to take you right here in the carriage?" Osirus' hands slipped under my dress, palming my ass tightly. "I want nothing more than to have you, Melina."

"I-I d-don't know this feeling," I said as I gripped the front of his tunic.

A purr left Osirus' chest as I spoke. The heat of his breath fanned my neck as he pulled me back to see my face. His lips were parted, and pleasure was carefully written on his perfectly sculpted face. The tingles from his touch reached every part of my body, especially to one specific part.

My body was about to explode, and the foreign feeling had me worried and confused. The desperation on my face must have been clear because I was climbing an invisible mountain and I didn't know my destination.

"Shhh," he cooed. "Just let it happen. Let your body fall."

With that velvet voice, it became my undoing. I let out a frantic moan, not sure how I was falling, but warmth wrapped around me cushioned the feeling. Osirus let out a large growl in his throat which he grabbed my ass hard as he seemed to be falling from the same mountain I was on.

Both of us, a panting mess. I kept my head in the crook of his shoulder. One hand remained on my rear and the other was rubbing comforting circles on my back.

"Wow," I breathed as I sat up.

Osirus looked at me with worried eyes, assessing the aftermath. "Are you all right?" His hand came up to the side of my face and brought me forward, giving me a gentle kiss on my forehead.

"Yes," I whispered. A twinge of embarrassment came to mind since it felt like I just completely drenched myself.

"Don't be worried. Everything is normal. What you feel both emotionally and physically is normal." Osirus' words were tender as he brought me closer to him to give me a comforting embrace. "I couldn't control my desire for you, darling. I hope you aren't upset."

"No, I'm not." In fact, I loved it. The awkwardness was painted on my face, but I tried not to let it show. Osirus chuckled and pecked my lips lightly.

"How about we get cleaned up, hm?" he whispered while I sat up.

My cheeks turned a few shades of darker red and he just laughed.

"Darling, it's normal. I had my release, too. We both need to clean up, all right?"

I nodded, feeling utterly shy. *Not going to ask questions about that.*

Osirus took his bag and pulled himself out a new set of clothes. All while I searched through my own and put on a lilac dress of the same design features of the last. Osirus, being the gentleman that he was, kept his back turned and eyes closed while I dressed. However, when it came time for him to change, without warning, he started stripping.

"Whoa there!" I squealed, surprised.

Osirus smirked. "What is it, darling? I'm just giving you

a preview of what else you could see later." My face blushed scarlet, and I turned my head in a huff while giggling excessively.

The sun was setting, and I had fallen asleep multiple times on Osirus, who gladly took it upon himself to hold me through the entire rest of the ride. His warmth, along with the swaying of the carriage, only kept me in my deep sleep.

The carriage slowed and a few large bumps in the road jostled me awake. "We're here, darling." Osirus took in a large breath and held me close. "We're home."

The carriage door was suddenly opened. Alaneo smiled back at us with warmth. "Come, Your Majesties, let's get you to your chambers."

Osirus left the carriage first, only to turn around and grab my hand and gently put my feet to the ground. The palace was grand, huge white marble and granite adorned the outside. Looking upwards, it reached to the sky as if it was part of the clouds. The suns were setting to the West, casting an ethereal glow on the colorful stained-glass windows of fairies and Fae.

"Here." Alaneo produced a cape and put it around me.

The cape was enormous and white, with a hood on the back, gold swirls of flowers and thorns along the outside of the edges were there.

Osirus put the hood up. It was huge enough for me to see out of and to cover my face from prying eyes. "For tonight, I want to get you inside before we announce your arrival. I want to be sure my most trusted guards and soldiers are on our floor to protect you."

I nodded and interlaced my hands with his, giving him a large smile. His smile was also substantial. It made my heart flutter finally trying to let my walls down and that we may truly will be together.

Maybe this would not be so bad, our two souls becoming one someday. He was the first male that I have ever had this much desire and care for, after all.

My hood kept me hidden, but it didn't obstruct the views I was desperately trying to see. We had arrived at the servant's entrance at the back of the palace; many Fae were working in the kitchen as we entered, and several stopped to watch their king walk through, but Alaneo cleared his throat and they all continued with their work.

Swiftly, I was led to a hallway with large windows with the sunset streaming in. The long hallway had pristine golden carpet, not an ounce of dirt laid anywhere on the intricate detail of the golden threads. There was so much gold, but I guess it was the Golden Light Kingdom. The clanking of some of the metal behind me, being that of Everett, Finley, and Braxton, continued to follow us as we reached an enormous staircase.

Statues of Fae, Fairies, and Sprites in crystal decorated the large space. Many had limited clothing on their bodies, just enough to cover their private areas. On Earth, there were statues like this, so I couldn't judge too harshly.

As we passed by a window, I saw a massive garden filled with beautiful flowers, and I couldn't help but stop. Pinks, maroons, reds, yellows, and orange-colored flowers littered the garden, all in a specific order to give it an orderly and decorative look. The path in the garden wasn't hard cement but beautiful blue stones with large clear orbs along the edges of the path. Each orb had a faint light glowing inside. I'm sure it looked magnificent in just the glow of darkness.

Osirus

My little darling was staring out at the garden. It had been specifically manicured today for her arrival. Once I saw her gazing at the bouquet of wildflowers from a panther cub, I couldn't help but have her pleased. Alaneo was quick to tell a local Sprite to send word to the head servant of the East Wing to decorate with flowers. I'm sure many are talking and making her happy was superficial, but I didn't care. I wanted it to feel like home.

Once we arrived in our royal bed chambers, she would be even more surprised at the flowers that will be presented there. Squeezing her hand lightly, I led her away from the window and down the East Wing corridors. These corridors were specifically for us and our future family once we had children. No one was to come down these halls except specific servants, maids, and guards. The royal family was to always be protected; growing up here with my parents along with several brothers proved to be enjoyable.

Now that my family had moved to the far north of the kingdom, away at the Winter Quarters part of the territory, it was just me, albeit lonely but rewarding in some ways. I could wallow in self-pity for having no mate.

The hallways had been cleaned, and vases of flowers and decorations of small, delicate trees lined our way to our room. Taking a deep breath, I prayed to the gods it was ready. This was to be our home, where we would complete our bond when she was ready to have me. Our first child would be born here and many, many mornings and nights of lovemaking would be done in this one room.

My chest tightened at the joy that she should hopefully have here. Opening the door, Melina gasped at the glory that it stood.

The large living area had a chandelier, covered in rubies, diamonds, sapphires and other precious gems known to Bergarian. The carpets were plush, white as snow and the sitting area looked to be out of the gods' celestial kingdom on Olympus.

Melina's mouth was agape, hoping she was enjoying the view. I put my hand on her lower back and escorted her into the room.

"What do you think?" I bent down and whispered in her ear.

She continued to walk forward, touching the plush

couches, and looking out at the overly large, windowed balcony doors. The east ocean sparkled as the last bit of the light sources faded on the other side of the palace. "It's b-beautiful. I've seen nothing like this." Her voice was raspy from not speaking, but the tone of it was light. She was happy, in turn making me nothing but elated.

"I'm glad you think so." I grabbed her waist and pulled her close. "Let me show you our bedroom." Melina giggled and gave me a 'no nonsense now' look. Alaneo and the guards still stood in the living area, awaiting their next orders.

Cracking the door first, I could see dozens upon dozens of flowers in vases and pots scattered in the room. With one final push, hoping to see flower petals across the bed and floor, I saw none other than the bane of my existence.

Daphne.

Chapter 18

Melina

"Daphne," Osirus voice rang out harshly.

I peeked around Osirus. Most of his body was covering my view of the room and after hearing some name with such a harsh tone, I knew I had to see.

Little did I know, curiosity killed the cat.

"Who is Daphne?" I turned back to Alaneo, who had his eyes widened at the sight.

He said nothing but looked onward, like seeing a ghost. This Daphne was wearing close to nothing. The tulle she wore that covered her breasts still showed her nipples proudly, and the netting down below on her private area barely left anything to the imagination. She was everything I thought a female Fae should be.

Graceful, beautiful, such an exquisite creature. I immediately frowned when she stood up and walked to Osirus. The sway of her hips, her confidence, and just her presence had the room still.

Osirus looked at her, eyes furrowed, and his lips spread into a thin line and into a frown. At least he wasn't too happy to see her. "Daphne." Osirus' tone was full of warning as she walked closer. Her face was innocent as she held her shoulders up and then down.

"What is it, your Majesty?" Her voice was sickly sweet. "I saw several of your servants getting the royal bed chambers ready. I thought you had decided and chose me to be your chosen mate." Her feet stopped just a few feet away from Osirus, her hand about to touch him until I cleared my throat.

Osirus' hand found mine and gave it a squeeze. "Who is this?" Her voice was now seemingly normal instead of her candy-coated voice from earlier. "Did you bring a concubine for your harem?" Daphne ticked. Right there, fires have been shot. Who did this woman think she was?

Before I could speak, Alaneo put his hand on my shoulder, making sure I didn't take off the hood of my cloak. "Gracious Daphne, I must ask you to leave. You are breaking many laws by being in this room alone." Alaneo's voice was serious as Braxton came over and grabbed Daphne's upper arm.

"What do you mean?" Again, with the candy voice. "The king and I were the last ones to be intimate with each other. One would only think that these chambers were made for me." Daphne blinked her eyes a few times as she stared at Osirus. His face never changed. He continued to stare at her with such malice.

He had yet to say a word to her.

"You must remember," Daphne purred. "Our romp on the beach just a short time ago." Her manicured finger got close to Osirus' shoulder until the spark in me blew a casket.

"Well, obviously he doesn't remember if you have to remind him," I spat. Daphne's head turned so fast, the wind direction could have changed.

"What did you say, you little whore!?" Her hand flew back, ready to strike me but Finley quickly intervened.

"Aye, that's enough there," he taunted.

Daphne's anger didn't falter as she tried to struggle, looking to Osirus for help.

"First-tier prison," Osirus spoke with command, and our two friends took Daphne out kicking and screaming.

Daphne was literally dragged from the room, and the plush carpet still had her feet impressions after they drug her through. Osirus stepped forward, letting go of my hand as he leaned against the foot of the bed. Alaneo snickered and came forward to take my cloak.

"That was brilliant," Alaneo whispered as he held out his hand.

Giving it a quick smack, I lifted the corner of my mouth in acknowledgement as he closed the doors behind us. Osirus continued to stare off into the distance of the ocean. The suns had finally set, and the stars and moon came over the horizon of the ocean.

"Melina, darling, I'm sorry."

My head whipped back to him, and I walked to the foot of the bed, sitting on it while he continued to lean.

"It has been over 300 years since I have had relations and unfortunately, it was with that woman. We were childhood friends, but over a drunken stupor we ended up doing things I deeply regret. While I was sleeping, she took it upon herself to try and change things in the castle regarding my staff, and I then knew her true intentions. To become my chosen mate."

I gasped a bit. Supernatural beings, from what I gathered, were dead set on having their true mate. Sure, they would have relationships before they met their intended, but both parties understood that once their true mate showed up, they would discontinue the relationship. At least, that was what I understood.

"You see, Melina, the Golden Light Kingdom isn't all rainbows and light." Osirus went to a nearby cabinet and pulled out a dark liquid and poured himself a glass. "The past several thousand years, Fae wanted to marry for power instead of love and happiness. They wanted a piece of the pie, a piece of the power one could have under a King. They brushed away a gift from the Goddess Selene just so they could have riches."

Osirus took a long sip while he poured water in another

glass. The clinking of the ice cubes tickled my ears as he looked at me, handing me the glass. "In the past 250 years, I have been able to block any marriages or bonds of convenience to come into the Court. That in itself has proven a pain, but I've kept it up." He sighed and led me to a small seating arrangement near the windows.

"It is the first step in changing how this kingdom is to be run. Get rid of the money and power-hungry nobles and replace them with a new court. Representatives from each Fae order around the kingdom. The sprites, the fairies, the Fae, whisps, Nymphs and even Sirens. No more nobility, no more high taxes to keep up their lavish lifestyle. Live more like the shifters do.

"Take what is needed for food, help one another by building homes, taking care of orphans when needed. The basics of life taken care of by the kingdom and with the taxes of goods they earn will be filtered back into the kingdom to create better lifestyles. Help pay for the army and their basic needs as well. People will earn what they want to have, not have it handed to them."

I sat in awe as I listened. I hardly realized I was basically on his lap listening to him. The conviction and passion in his voice soothed my soul at how he wanted to help his own people.

"There are too many times I've seen dirty children running the capital. They look starved and hungry, yet the Court turns a blind eye. They want their diamonds, precious things, and fancy houses," he spat. "This castle was originally built by the people of this nation, gifted to the first king with the finest materials. In turn, that king gave the basic needs for everyone that needed it. If they did not have jobs, he supplied them. If there were no homes, he helped build them." Osirus cleared his throat.

"At the time, the Court was there to help oversee it all. But it has turned wicked and in turn, parliament can't do a damn thing about it. The court are the votes of parliament to make sure a king does not have too much power, but now the Court holds the power. And it is making the people suffer, especially when they have their own small armies."

I frowned at hearing his speech. A king is a king, the last commander and speaker of a nation and now the Court holds all of it? It doesn't sound like he can do much at all. He was just a glorified person and the face of the Golden Light Kingdom. My heart clenched at the thought of hungry children with no food.

Osirus sensed my distress and held me tightly. "Do not worry, with you by my side, we will accomplish much." He kissed my forehead. "I have special places where children and the poor have access to clean food, water, and shelter. It is just not an open service to keep the Court at bay while we plan another way." I sighed a bit as I rested against his shoulder.

"What about Daphne?" I whispered.

Osirus sighed deeply and leaned back into the cushion. "She is a high-ranking court member. Well, at least her parents are. Mated for convenience and now want their daughter to be my chosen mate. I've refused, the Parliament cannot force me. However, her being in this bedchamber was the perfect opportunity so I could lock her up for a while and get her out of my hair," he chuckled and I couldn't help but laugh.

"Then why did you freeze when she was walking towards you? You said little of anything. I thought you were going to go to her."

Osirus looked at me in surprise. "Darling, never." He kissed my lips. "I don't show emotion to anyone except you. My mind was wandering about the best way to handle the situation and Alaneo is usually my speaker. Apparently, he was speechless himself the way she was dressed. It was quite brazen, even for a Fae."

I nodded, accepting his explanation. If Esteban came to me half dressed, I don't think I would know what to say either.

I just hope I was beautiful enough. She looked like an angel, like him. All the Faes were equally beautiful but here I was, a human looking oddly plain against all of them.

Osirus and I sat in each other's arms until we heard a knock at the door. Quietly, a cart was rolled in with food, and Osirus seamlessly waved them off as he approached. The main living area also had a dining room, along with a refrigerator and small kitchenette for light cooking if needed.

Osirus had me sit down at the table and served me himself. A king was serving a poor, lowly peasant. I grinned as he sat down, waiting for me to take the first bite. When I finally put the chicken into my mouth, I let out a breathy moan. The chicken fell apart in my mouth and the garlic butter sauce gave it just enough flavor. Osirus would flick his eyes over from time to time to catch my appearance at how I loved the food.

When Osirus would look at me, it gave me butterflies. He made me feel like I was the center of his world. Everything I did, he noted. He would always eye me as I patted my napkin to my lips or when I would wiggle in excitement for the next course of the meal.

After the rest of dinner, we talked about our childhoods. His, being much longer than mine, was full of adventure. There were battles he won, women and children he had saved, such as Finley, Braxton, and Everett. They were young Fae, just barely able to grow their beards when Osirus saved his family from rabid vampires going across their territory. Now they say they are indebted to them saving their mother.

I felt my own stories were nowhere near as exciting, yet he listened on with interest. I was just a bookworm in high school, reading every fairy tale of adventure I could find. I even told him of my child-like bedroom I had back at my cabin. Frilly lace, a bed canopy, and tons of stuffed animals still adorned the bed back home. The thought made me a bit homesick, thinking I would never see any of my things.

Osirus assured me he already had servants gathering my

things, even my clothes, so I could always have them. Pictures, my childhood toys that held some memories, blankets, and clothes, would all be here in the next few days. My heart skipped a beat as Osirus told me. He was very thoughtful and attentive to my wishes. Maybe one day I could gift them to my children, *our* children if things worked out.

After dinner, we headed to the bedroom. Even though there had been only two nights of sleeping in the same bed, I had come to like it and was ready for a restful sleep. Before getting ready for bed, I looked at the massive four-poster bed. It was almost like a gigantic canopy bed with tulle colors of whites and creams that came from the ceiling and tied at the poster part of the bed. The bed itself was larger than a king, possibly doubled in size. I tiled my head in question. What do you call the size of this bed? It wasn't a king-size, Ultra King Plus?

Osirus stopped gathering his things and came behind me as I continued to look onto the bed. "What is it, darling?" His hands wrapped around my waist.

"Why do we need such a gigantic bed?" He chuckled and kissed my neck.

"Because my sweet, I plan on using every inch of that bed to pleasure you in positions you never dreamed of." My eyes widened and I let out an audible gulp.

Osirus sauntered to the bathroom, until I called out, "You sure you aren't just compensating for something?" I held in a laugh as he slowly turned around. His eyes had turned black, and I saw his neck vein protrude a bit. If I didn't know better, I would have thought I hit a nerve.

Osirus took long strides to me and grabbed the back of my ass and picked me up as I automatically wrapped my legs around his waist. He flung me on the bed, and I landed with a squeak. His leg spread over mine and he put the weight of his body on my lower half. His member was painfully hard as he rubbed it across my core. I let out a brief sigh as he took my wrists and pinned them over my head. I didn't fight or struggle, concentrating too much on the heat in my lower half.

"Does this feel like I'm compensating for something?" he breathed as his hips rolled into mine.

I let an involuntary moan escape my mouth as his lips kissed my neck. He resumed his assault as his hips remained to hit a sweet spot. One hand continued to roam the side of my body. Up and down from the right side of my rib cage to my lower back and finally my ass, giving it a hard squeeze. As I gasped at the roughness, he took this as time to stick his tongue into my mouth.

My tongue quickly followed and rubbed against his, tasting his sweet mouth. He pushed his hand onto my ass again, making his member inexplicably hard against my core. I wanted more. I didn't want to feel just the hardness; I wanted to feel the heat.

My dress was slowly rising as he continued dancing with his hips against me. My hands fisted his hair as I pulled a bit too roughly. He groaned and lifted his hand to put on the back of my leg. The warm hand slid up the back of my thigh as he lifted it up and put it around his waist. His member was now rubbing painfully hard against my entire core.

"Osirus," I breathed as he continued. His hands pulled down on my bodice and he freed my breast which made him stop his assault on my lower region. He pulled the other side of the bodice down, exposing my chest to him. Osirus eyes were dark while he looked into my eyes.

"May I continue?" he rasped. The Fae stopped to ask my permission? A face that was full of desire had me trembling. I could see his ears had already elongated, his fangs were in his smile and his eyes were black as obsidian. I didn't fear him.

My mind is telling me to stop, but my heart tells me something completely different. Trust the bond? For now, I will meet just halfway and think with a clearer mind later. Something that felt this good couldn't be wrong. Feeling this pull towards him couldn't be wrong.

"Just no sex," I whispered. Osirus' smile grew, showing

his four fangs in his mouth. I never knew that seeing fangs would make my body ache for him to gently nip at me.

The mischief in his eyes told me I was going to be in for a ride.

Chapter 19

Osirus

Melina's eyes widened as she nodded her head 'yes.' I couldn't take it too far with her, but I wasn't planning on it. Her mouth tasted so sweet against my own. She was the drug I had been searching for all my life and I could now get a sweet taste.

My cock was painfully hard as I continued to rub against her, her dress and my own clothes were getting in the way, so I instantly took off my tunic that only exposed the upper part of my chest. She untied her bodice as I slipped my trousers off and with one swift motion, she was bare in just her under-garments, as was I.

Her breasts were supple and plump as a juma fruit in summer in the highlands, and I bet they tasted just the same. Pulling down her lace bra, I sucked at one nipple while grasping the other. Her hands went into my hair and gave it a tug. I groaned at feeling the slight pain from my scalp as I gently nipped and sucked her tits.

Melina's body was squirming underneath me. I would normally scold her, but since she was feeling so many new sensations, I let her continue. Her waist was narrow while her hips were larger than a Fae female, but that seemed to turn my body on more. She could carry more than one Fae-ling child with those hips and that made my chest swell further.

My claw ripped her undergarment down the middle and her breasts pooled outward. I grabbed her neck with my hand, giving her a bit of pressure on her throat, and she gasped. It seemed my little darling liked it a little rough. I kissed her harshly, and she nipped hard at my lips in warning, but it only made me hungrier.

"Osirus," she moaned as her hands slipped to my biceps.

"Do you trust me?" I whispered as I continued to pepper kisses along her jaw.

She thought a moment before I finally spoke.

"I would never hurt you," I breathed.

Nodding her head in agreement, I continued to kiss her neck and back up to her mouth as I slid my hand near her underwear.

Cupping the apex of her thighs let me know she was enjoying me as much as I was enjoying her. Her pussy was wet, dripping, and even soaking the sheets of the bed. A growl left my throat, which caused Melina to gasp slightly.

"You are so wet," I rasped.

Her face grew hot and tinted with the color of rose petals. "That is what I want. I want you drenched for me. The day I finally take you, I want you just like this." I bit her neck slightly, that caused a shudder to go through the left side of her body.

My hand searched for her pleasure nub, and it was found quickly. Her skin was completely bare, not a single sprig of hair was left on her body, which made me involuntarily rub my erection on her thigh. "The things you do to me," I growled. Melina paid no attention as my finger rubbed her numb up and down as she held onto me for dear life. Little did she know she was moving her hips along with the rhythm of my finger.

Before she reached her peak, I stopped, which caused a

whine to escape her lips. "Osirus, what—" Before the next word fell from her lips, I thrust my finger inside of her. Gasping at the intrusion, I began to vigorously suck her breasts while gyrating my hips next to her hip. It was involuntary and damn, it felt good to have my dick so close to her skin. Letting out a low moan, Melina gripped my hair tightly again at the scalp. My finger continued to thrust into her. I swear I don't think I could get another finger in her. She was so tight.

But I was going to try.

Her hips moved along with my finger, wanting it to go deeper, so I added a second.

"Ahhh!" came from her sexy pout of a mouth as I started thrusting faster. Her breasts heaved up and down and I started leaving love bites and marks all over her chest. "Osirus, please!" she whispered as I started rubbing on her special spot.

"Come for me, darling. Show me how much you like me pleasuring you."

With a sharp yell, Melina came undone and the grip on my head was tight, painful. It was a good pain. It showed how long her orgasm lasted as I continued to thrust my fingers in and out. Cum dripped down her legs and down my hand. Her body was specifically made just for me. The smell and the taste almost made my wings rip open from my back.

Melina looked up at me with exhaustion and watched as I licked each finger individually. Her haze was short-lived when we heard a knock at the door.

"Damnit," I whispered. I wrapped Melina in a warm blanket and hid her under the covers. The embarrassment was rolling off her as I walked to the door.

Cracking it, I saw Finley at the door. "What is it?" I growled at him.

He stood back but quickly regained his posture. "It's a few court members. They want to meet with you tomorrow. Apparently, word has gotten out about Melina." A scowl quickly formed on my face. I wanted more time, but of course, things don't work out the way you want them to.

"Fine, they can meet in the Court chambers at noon," I spoke harshly and shut the door.

Melina sat up in the bed, wrapped up in layers of blankets. Her hair was a mess, and her cheeks were tinted pink. If I didn't know any better, it looked like she had been through a romp in the hay. "Are you all right, darling?"

"Yes," she whispered playfully. The playful side of my intended was showing, the brattiness wasn't clear as it had been.

After we both took showers, individually, to my disappointment, we gathered into bed. Melina made no hesitation to curl up beside me and lay her head on my chest. My heart was screaming in happiness at having her by my side. I knew she still had reservations about me and this whole new world, but I was hoping to continue to show her our new way of life as we battled for a new era in our kingdom.

Once mated we both would be unstoppable. She may even well turn into a Fae. This would be the first time a Fae has joined with a human, so questions will arise soon. I just pray to the gods her body didn't change too drastically. Her fine hourglass shape had me in a trance, the extra hold I had on her would be amazing during our bond. My mouth watered just thinking about tasting her skin in my mouth as I bit her marking spot.

I palm my growing erection, just thinking about placing it inside her. The tightness of her body, the way she would milk me for my seed as I planted every bit of love I have for her in it. I groan lightly and hear Melina stir. She was just the right size for me, the right bit of everything.

Closing my eyes, for the first time in a long time, I felt more complete than I ever have. The thought of finally making her fully mine and feeling even more of this love was indescribable.

Melina

Once I fell asleep the night before, I don't think I hardly moved. The bed and Osirus were so comfortable I had a dreamless sleep. There were many times when I would dream and would always be running, running to my parents asking them to stay that it was a mistake. That we could be a family and I would try harder to make them happy.

In those dreams, I always woke up tired. I had run all night in my head and my body seemed to think I honestly did in the real world.

Feeling the surrounding sheets, they felt cold. Osirus was not in the bed, but the imprint of his head was still left on the pillow. I face-planted into his pillow; it smelled just like him. He smelled so sweet to me, a smell I couldn't possibly describe except for cotton candy, just like his lips. I blushed at what we did last night.

I had done nothing like what we had done yesterday. Not once, but twice! In the carriage and now in bed. If things keep progressing, we were going to be having sex by tonight! I needed to get my head together, think this through. There will be NO sex tonight, that was for sure. Now, I was too hot and bothered to think. Then again, I was told not to over-think things when it came to a mating bond.

When I am with him, though! My heart is a flutter and I feel like a hormonal mess. I want nothing but let him have his way with me. I just couldn't think straight with him nearby.

Taking a quick stretch, I let out a loud yawn, not being lady-like in the slightest, and hopped out of bed. My over-sized joggers and large black t-shirt that came down to my knees were wrinkled and in a mess. Scratching my head, I went over to the closet to grab a skirt and a shirt that I had brought from home.

The tank top was a light color yellow, and the cardigan was white with small diamond decorations spread throughout. I paired it with a white pleated skirt that came midway on my thighs and some sandals. I brushed my hair and pinned up my bangs so they wouldn't get in the way.

Now my mission was to find Osirus. I skipped to the door, only to hear a knock when I tried to open it. Unlocking the bedroom door and slowly cracking it, I was then pegged in the face with the corner of the door as two flying Fairies came in. They were giggling and laughing while I rubbed my face, trying to get rid of the pain.

"Oh, dear! I am so sorry!" the pink haired one said as she looked at my face.

"Yes, yes, so sorry. People don't normally like to kiss the doors in the mornin'," the green-haired one replied.

I groaned and shut the door again. "It's all right, I just didn't know what to expect," I continued to rub my face.

"You must be Melina! Er, I mean, Your Majesty!" They both bowed in mid-air.

I waved them off. "Just call me Melina, I'm not a queen yet," I laughed.

"Well, obviously, I don't see a mark yet. How the Hades are you holding back from that hunk of a Fae? I mean hello! Swoon!" The pink hair fairy fluttered her hand and fake fell before flying back up to speak. "And I'm sure he is a great lover, he is so tall and has such enormous feet and you know what they say about..." the pink-haired fairy was cut off.

"But you are His Majesty's mate, we must call you that," the green-haired fairy said, giving the pink-haired fairy a look of reprimand.

I continued to blush but nodded shyly. Talking so brazenly about sex like that had me hot and flustered.

"May I ask for your names, then?"

Both fairies blushed and giggled.

"We are so sorry! My name is Primrose," the pink one bowed and kissed my hand.

The green hair fairy flew up and kissed me on the cheek. "And I am Peoni, at your service," she giggled. "We are your Fairy attendants, we are here to get you dressed for the day, keep your schedule and such," Peoni spoke while staring at my attire. "It looks like you already did our job so far."

I laughed. "Yes, I'm used to getting dressed myself." I stood up and started heading to the door.

"Wait! Where are you going?" Primrose flew to the door and shut it.

I gave her a questioning eye and tried the door again. "I'm going to find Osirus. He left me this morning and didn't tell me where he was going. I'd like to see him."

Primrose shut the door again, and I crossed my arms at the situation. "Excuse me?" I said, annoyed.

"We are sorry, Your Majesty. His Majesty said you are to stay in the room until he fetches you." My brows furrowed in anger, and I let out a huff.

"Well, you can go tell 'His Majesty' that he can get his butt back here right now, then!" I growled out. Osirus was already locking me up, and I wasn't even his mate yet. This was what I was afraid of.

"W-well, we can't really do that. He is in a meeting with the Court. It was very last minute, and he had to go. It should be over soon." Peoni shook as she sat on the doorknob. Feeling sorry for the Fairies just carrying out orders, I sat down on the plush couch. "Fine, I'm sorry I yelled. However, he has one hour to get back here or I'm leaving." I held up one finger as both the fairies nodded in agreement.

"I'll make sure, Your Majesty!" Peoni flew out the door while Primrose came to sit on the couch.

"So, you are really human?"

I gazed down at Primrose. "Last time I checked," I snorted.

"Many girls will be jealous that you are queen. I bet you are ecstatic! You get a handsome Fae, all the beautiful dresses, and to play games and go to parties!" Primrose continued with her rant of how great it would be to be queen. Parties, games, social events? None of it seemed like me at all.

"That's not what I want, Primrose." I sighed.

Primrose looked at me in confusion. "What do you want, Your Majesty?"

"Freedom," I sighed. "Not to be held in a golden cage and locked away. I want to be out of these walls and help those that need it. I don't want to play with politics. People should just live their lives and be happy. From what I've heard, there are many that aren't happy."

Primrose smiled and flew over and sat on my leg. To get my attention, she spread her wings a few times to fan me and had me look into her beautiful cat-like eyes. "That is exactly what His Majesty wants for our kingdom."

I raised a brow.

"Except the part where you are kept in a golden cage." Primrose laughed. "He would never do that. He would probably chain you to the bed instead."

Chapter 20

Melina

"I'm sorry, what?!" I squealed, causing Primrose to fall back on the couch. Her laughing was going borderline crazy as she finally dusted herself off and stood back up.

"Like I said, he would probably chain you to the bed instead. Fae males are kinky as shit." Primrose flew to the enormous bed and pulled out the drawer. "See this?" There were handcuffs, silk ropes, blindfolds, feathers, and even a small riding crop.

"The hell is this?!" I jumped back. "What is that all used for?!"

Primrose looked at me blankly as she flew up to me to stare at me in the face. "You seriously don't know?"

I shook my head in confusion.

"Wait, you've had at least sex before, right?"

I shook my head no, and Primrose's eyes lit up like a Christmas tree.

"Oh, my gods! A virgin! You have so much to learn! Come sit, sit!" She waved to the bed as I sat down. Fear dripped from my body as she explained.

"Listen here. You have done some things, correct?"

Looking angry and crossing my arms, I huffed. "I know

what the birds and the bees are. I know what sex is and I don't need an explanation! I need you to tell me what those devices are in the drawer!" This was getting out of hand.

That wasn't part of sex, now, was it? There is a penis and a vagina, and it goes in some places. You can do things with your mouths and fingers but the whole, handcuffs, blindfolds, and that crop were not in my explanation of sex in school.

"I would rather talk to Osirus about this. This is private," I gritted.

Primrose giggled and held her hand over her mouth. "Oh, honey, I'm just trying to help. Fae can be a bit adventurous when it comes to..." She looked around before whispering, "Intimacy."

"Do you use these things?" I asked in disbelief.

"Some and other things." She laughed and gave me a wink. "My boyfriend and I are a bit more adventurous. You know, public places." She threw her head back dramatically and showed me her shoulder.

"Goddess, Primrose, what if you get caught?!" How could anyone want to do that sort of thing in public?

"It's exciting, the thought that someone could walk up and see you doing the horizontal limbo, the sticky tango, the love rub..."

I started covering my ears and hummed.

"Anyway." Primrose giggled. "It's exciting!"

"That's nice and all, not my style." I got up from the bed and headed back over to the couch. I thought everything was going to be smooth sailing from here, but more and more questions seem to be running through my mind. Is he into beating his lovers? Pain? Those things look painful to me. What if I didn't want to have anything to do with that sort of thing?

Osirus was dominant in bed, but how far would he go? What if we mated and then he brought all this up? My head hurt—my heart began to hurt. I have barely done anything, heck I've never even seen a dick in real life and here we are talking about tying me to the bed and letting him have his way with me! What if that was the master plan? He will tie me to the bed and force me to stay!

Nope, not going to happen. I could feel my heart closing off right now. The things we did last night seemed like a distant memory. It was a nice memory, but if we are to move forward with anything, a lot of my questions needed answers.

One, being locked up in this room, and two, what he expected from me sexually because we went from 0 to 100 real quick.

Osirus

"You are late, your highness," Alaneo reminded me for the second time as I fixed the sleeves on my jacket. My cape felt unusually heavy today and my heart. I had to leave my mate alone in the bed so I could attend a court meeting regarding her.

This was not what I wanted, to be stuck in a meeting for who knows how long regarding the future of the kingdom. I wanted her to feel comfortable before presenting her to the people, but that has been completely ruined.

"I know, Alaneo. The meeting doesn't truly start until its king is present anyway, correct?" I gave him a side smirk while he patted my back.

Entering through the double doors that the guards held open, I walked up to my table in the back center of the room. All the noble families were already in attendance, ready to spout whatever nonsense they wanted to do with the kingdom. I stood at my desk, assessing to see if everyone was present, and I sat down, signaling everyone to follow.

Cosmo Cottonfleck stood from his seat and walked to the center of the stadium-style room, built enough for fifty members. He sauntered to the podium and had several papers he organized before facing me with a stern face.

"Your Majesty," he spoke arrogantly. "There is a rumor in the kingdom that you have found your mate." Cosmo paused as I rested my hand on my cheek, looking at him unamused. Cosmo waited for me to speak, but I just waved my finger at Alaneo to speak for me. It was better that way. People think I'm passive or too pissed off to speak. I let them think what they want.

"His Highness is aware of the rumor. What of it?" I think Alaneo needed a raise, or maybe a better home, inside the castle. He put up with so much shit for me.

Cosmo cleared his throat, irritation was clear in his voice. "Is it true?" he demanded.

I sat up from my seat, getting quite uncomfortable about where this was going.

"What does it matter to you?" I growled at him.

Many members of the Court were shocked that I spoke out loud to a group of people. Many began whispering to each other, concerned over my outburst. Alaneo was my speaker, if there was something to be said, he spoke for me.

"Y-your Majesty, we need to know if you have found your mate. It is your duty to claim her and let the people know of your intended." He gave a sly smirk.

The whole point of him wanting to expose her was to make up flaws, so my subjects would say she was unfit to be queen. The damn nobles and their pride. Their minds had been twisted into thinking the Moon Goddess couldn't properly match. This could cause a coup in the Court, Faes trying to overthrow me and try to take a new king. Cosmo had eyed the throne for a long time.

This would not happen. Little did they know the Werewolves and a few Shifter communities were on our side. I just needed to keep Melina safe until she allowed me to mark her as mine and complete the bond.

"Who are you to say that your king doesn't fulfill his duties?" I rose from my seat. The aura he was spilling was fear, but his face remained stoic. I knew he wanted my crown. He wanted it when my father had it, but this time I will make sure he will rot in the grave.

I pulled the magic within my body and let it seep through my fingertips. The anger and fury I felt were indescribable. My fangs descended and there were gasps within the room. My fangs made them terrified but more so as my ears elongated. Since meeting Melina, she told me she wasn't afraid of my true form, that every Fae should embrace it, even more so when protecting a mate or our kingdom.

Cosmo stood back in shock. "Your M-majesty! What is the meaning of this!" he screamed while only a few others yelled in agreement. I stood on the desk and jumped down in front of him. My claws grew as I approached him and grabbed his neck.

"I will bring forth my mate when I am ready and none earlier," I growled. "Do not tempt me in using my instincts and killing you now." I pulled Cosmo closer and whispered in his ear, "I know what you are doing, and trust me, I will stop you." I dropped him to the floor and walked out of the room.

I could hear Cosmo's mistress run to him to help him up, but he just took his arm away from her.

"That went well," Alaneo joked as he jogged to my side. "And what do you think that accomplished?"

I stopped in my tracks and faced Alaneo. "I have no control when it comes to my mate's safety. Exposing her now would only endanger and overwhelm her. I can't lose her." I started walking again but felt a small tap hit my chest.

"Your Majesty!" It was Peoni, one Fairy that I had looked over Melina in case she woke up.

"Is Melina all right?" I asked, concerned.

"Oh, yes, yes! She said, however, if you do not come back into the room in an hour she would leave and go back to her cabin with the Wolves, though."

I groaned while she laughed.

"Hi, Alaneo," Peoni said flirtatiously while adjusting her

breasts.

Alaneo only bowed at her and winked before she giggled and flew away.

"Your mate is feisty, huh?" Alaneo said, amused.

"I wouldn't want it any different. She challenges me in things other women wouldn't." Alaneo laughed as I headed back to our room.

***

Without knocking, I walked into the room to see a very flustered Melina with Primrose sitting on the bed. Melina's eyes didn't look at me with love. No, she had nothing but confusion and hurt in her eyes.

"Darling, what is wrong? I'm sorry it took so long to come back." I rushed to her side and put my arm around her. She continued to be stiff. My hand cupped her cheek and for the first time, I felt a tear come from her eyes. She had been strong for so long and now I finally see her break.

"Darling, talk to me," I whispered.

The next thing I know, she pulled up a set of handcuffs beside her lap and dropped them in my lap. *Oh shit.*

"Leave," I told Primrose and Peoni, who had followed me in. Both cowered at my tone and flew out a nearby window.

"What are these, Osirus?" Her voice cracked.

My heart wanted to pick her up and bury her face in my neck, to comfort her and show her that everything was all right. Things were not all right for her, and she felt betrayed. I kept silent, trying to gather my words.

"Are you going to force me to stay here, to mark me? Are you going to tie me to the bed while you have sex with me?" Her voice grew higher with each word.

"Darling, please let me explain," I begged.

Looking into my eyes, she stood up and walked across the room, and sat in a decorative chair.

"Explain from there. When you are close to me, I don't

want to forgive you too easily."

Damn, she was smart. She was trying to go around our bond to make sure she was making the right decisions. She will be the perfect queen if she will have me.

"Like I have said before, I would never force you to mate with me. I would never take your freedom like that. I want you to love me with your own heart. These things—" I waved to the handcuffs, the ties, and several other items in the drawer. "—are ways to make intimacy more pleasurable, and enjoyable. We don't even have to make love to use them. It is just a way to put a twist on pleasure and make it more exciting."

Her head tilted in confusion. My heart skipped a beat, excited that she wanted to know more.

"This—" I held up a blindfold. "—will take away your sight, so your other senses are heightened. You will feel my touch a little bit stronger, the excitement of where my hands will be next."

Melina's breath hitched and looked at the other items in the drawer.

"These—" The handcuffs clinked as I held them up. "—make it so you can't touch me, but I can touch you. You may want to run your hands through my hair, my body, but the anticipation of you wanting to touch me will mean so much more when you can. This crop is to be used for touching you, tickling you, and maybe a light smack or two."

Melina released a breath and rubbed her thighs together.

"We don't even have to use these things!" I threw the things back in the drawer and slammed it shut. "I just want you, and you only. I don't need them to make me want you. It is just a way to play, that's all," I pleaded.

"So, you aren't forcing me to stay or try to hurt me or take anything away from me?" She sniffed as my heart clenched.

"Darling, I would never," I pleaded.

It was a dangerous move putting those there, but I had little time to move things around before she arrived. Fuck,

I was dumb. She was so innocent when it came to intimacy and here I am holding things in my drawer, making her think I would hurt her.

"I swear to you, baby, I would never. Please, can I hold you? It's killing me seeing you like this."

Melina nodded, and I rushed to her side, kissing her forehead.

"I'm sorry, Darling. I should have moved all of that out of here." I continued to pepper her face with kisses, and she finally started laughing.

"You Fae people are crazy." She laughed. "Maybe after a while, once I'm comfortable with other things, if we progress, we could try it."

"Are you sure, darling?" I answered seductively, nipping at her ear. Hell, we were going to progress, I could promise that.

"Yes," she whispered as she leaned into me.

Chapter 21

Melina

"Are you sure, darling?" he whispered in my ear while pulling it with his teeth. The shivers running down my spine reached my toes. My body instantly leaned into Osirus'. I was so mad at him earlier. How can my body betray me and forgive him so easily?

"The bond is making you forgive me more easily," he whispered. His hands rubbed up and down my arms as he swayed, dancing to our own song.

"How do you do that?" I nuzzled into his chest.

"I can feel your aura. I can see how you feel. Every living thing projects colors. Not all Faes can read into auras, but I can." Osirus kissed down my neck and instinctively I leaned my head to the side to grant him more space. "I can tell when you are sad." He nipped my neck. "When you are happy." His nose nuzzled into the crook of my neck. "I can feel the apprehension you have for me in your heart." Osirus sucked on the sweet spot he found a day ago, and I let out a breathy moan. "I can also read how your body wants mine."

My eyes grew large, and my face flushed. Osirus chuckled against me.

"It's all right, I love it. I love that you have a desire for me like I do you." His hands that were tracing my arms lowered to my waist and lifted my shirt, so his thumbs were crazing my hips. Looking up at him, his eyes were black against his white skin. Leaning down, he captured my lips again and lifted me up, so my legs wrapped around his waist.

"Do you see how your body responds to mine?"

I hummed while his tongue dove into my mouth. Leaning me up against the wall, his kiss deepened, and his hands started to wander. Small grunts and purrs left his mouth and chest as I pulled on his hair. I wanted more than his mouth. I wanted to kiss his neck like he did mine.

Ripping away and with a reluctant growl, I kissed down his jaw, letting him know I wasn't done. His member rubbing my core and the small little rubs and grinding got me instantly wet. My breath hitched as I sucked his neck.

"Darling, shit."

I left little love bites down his neck just as he did to my chest. I looked at my work and started giggling.

"Something funny, darling?" he playfully growled.

"No." I giggled more. This was fun.

Osirus reached under my skirt, playing with my lacy white panties, and moved them to the side. His hand was absent for a moment until I felt a large smack that hit just below my butt cheek. I squeaked and gripped onto his jacket.

"Are you sure there is nothing funny?" His eyebrows raised in mischief as I continued to shake my head.

Another smack was left on my other cheek, and I grew red. His lips crashed back into mine as he kept me pinned to the wall. "You like getting spanked, don't you?"

Osirus kissed under my jaw and then sucked vigorously on my neck. A loud moan left my mouth and another smack to my butt caused my core to clench. My grip became increasingly tighter as he pulled me from the wall.

"You are so wet for me, I can feel the heat between your thighs," he said seductively as he sat on the bed and had my belly on his lap.

"Osirus! What are you—?" SMACK. I groaned. Why did this feel so good? This was so wrong.

I wiggled, trying to get up, but Osirus held me pinned to his lap. "Stop right now, or I'll make it, so it doesn't feel good," he growled.

I stilled, not out of fear but excitement.

"You want this?" He rubbed my butt as he pulled on my underwear with one of his fingers. They gently pooled at my ankles and dropped to the floor as I held onto Osirus' pant leg. My breathing was heavy, not sure what he was going to do next. Osirus lifted my skirt, my butt now on display for him to look at.

"Excited, are we?" he taunted.

I wanted to be a smart mouth but refrained. My butt was in the air and at his disposal. This was so incredibly hot to me, and I couldn't understand why. He palmed my butt again and massaged it. "I'm going to give you five spanks, and I want you to count."

My breath hitched. Five? I whimpered against his pants.

"Do you want me to stop?" His voice held concern.

I looked up at him. He would stop if I asked, that much I gathered. But I was confused. Why did I like this so much? Just a few minutes ago I was crying about handcuffs and crops. Now I was willingly letting him smack my butt like a child. It just felt so good when he did it!

Feeling my inner struggle, Osirus lifted me back up and had me sit on his lap.

"Melina, talk to me." His hand removed a piece of fallen hair from my face.

"I-I don't know," I whispered.

"You are uncertain," he stated.

I nodded, barely looking at him in the eyes.

"It is all right to be excited and even turned on by it, especially when it is with someone you trust or care about."

My heart leaped. I had cared for him in such a short amount of time. We still had a lot of cultural differences to talk about, but I felt safe with him. Safer than back on Earth by the cabin.

"I just never knew about these things," I said shyly. "I do like it."

Osirus' face held an enormous grin. "If we do something you don't like, I want you to say 'red,' can you do that?"

I nodded my head yes, and he swiftly put me back on his lap like the conversation had never happened. I squeezed my legs together in anticipation while I held onto his legs.

"Count, Melina."

SMACK.

"One." I winced.

SMACK.

"Two." I locked my thighs tightly together.

SMACK.

"Three." I moaned loudly, which made Osirus' hand falter while he groaned himself.

SMACK.

"Four!" I screamed.

SMACK.

"FIVE!" I laid limp on his legs until he spread my legs. A finger trailed into my core.

"Gods, you are soaked." Osirus groaned as his member poked my stomach. His fingers quickly parted my lower lips and stuck one finger in. I squeaked as his finger thrust in and out of my body. My core was clenching around his finger as he was roughly pounding me harder.

"Fuck, darling, you are so damn tight. I can't wait to bury myself in you."

Moaning into his thigh and gently biting him, he growled in approval as he continued his assault.

"You'd like that, wouldn't you? Have my cock fuck you senseless?"

You could hear the dampness of my core as he inserted another finger. Two fingers were almost too tight. I winced as he stretched me. My breasts itched, wanting to be touched.

His dirty words were stirring something deep inside me. I liked how he talked so dirty.

"Osirus," I gasped. "I need you to touch me." With one swift movement, he had me on my back, his fingers never leaving my cavern as he continued to push into me more. My white tank top was ripped from top to bottom as he fought to grab my breast. His tongue assaulted my nipple and pulled it with his teeth.

"Osirus! I—!"

"Cum, for fuck's sake, cum all over my fingers, darling. Let me feel you squirt your essence on me," he growled in my ear. *Those words!*

Between his husky, commanding voice and the fingers that had entered my body, I screamed his name. My breathing was hard as I came down from my high, my fingers entangled in his long locks of hair. He looked well spent himself as he panted into my neck. We both lay there as I rubbed his head and continued to kiss my breasts.

"Gods, you are perfect, Melina." He nuzzled more into my chest.

I started giggling and held onto him tighter. "That—" I paused. "—was something else. Who knew I had been missing out on so much?"

"And there is more, little one, much more." Osirus came up and pecked me on the lips and rolled me onto his chest, cradling me.

"We should get ready for dinner, darling. They will be expecting us."

I propped my head up to stare into his eyes. They were so beautiful. Tiny shimmery golden flecks sparkled inside with hints of black speckles.

"I'm allowed to leave the room?" I half joked while he gave me a stern look.

"Of course, I'll show you around where it is safe for you to be. Everett, Finley, and Braxton are always to be with you if I am not around if I must attend to things. Staying on the east side of the palace would be for the best. I'm still trying to keep you somewhat hidden from prying eyes."

I nodded and gave a brief salute.

"When you are ready, darling." Osirus cleared his throat nervously. "When you are ready to accept me to be your mate for eternity, please let me know." His eyes were pleading. He wanted an answer, but I still had so many questions.

"I promise to give you an answer soon. It's just so much. I just want a little more time to get to know you."

"Like a date?" he chided.

My eyes lit up. "Yes! Like a date! I've never dated before. It would be nice to go on one before I get hitched." I laughed out loud.

"Hitched?"

"Yeah! Like marriage, bonding, that sort of thing." I waved my hands around between us.

Osirus' eyes widened in realization. "So that is what you want, a little bit of this dating thing that humans do?"

I nodded my head enthusiastically. "Yup, and you can be my boyfriend!"

Osirus scoffed, but gave me a smirk. "All right then, we will 'date.' How long does dating last before one gets 'hitched?'"

I snorted at the way he used my terms.

"When I fall in love with you," I smiled shyly.

Osirus smiled widely, mischief swirling on his face. "Challenge accepted, darling."

Osirus had me wear one dress that was made for me by the royal seamstress. They had gotten my measurements from Maxine back at the Crimson Shadows Pack, and they had already made me dozens of dresses. I told Osirus I didn't need that many, but of course he didn't listen.

I explained to him, however, I do like to wear pants every now and again so I could get them messy. After riding Montu a few days ago, I had fallen in love with the idea of going horseback riding. All Osirus kept telling me was "soon" I could go riding again.

Osirus had his arm held out as we walked down the corridor to the dining room. Osirus wanted to have our dinner in our room originally, but I haven't even seen half the castle and was curious who all lived here and other rooms that were mostly empty.

Servants, tons of servants, lived here. Most of the Court that Osirus spoke of lived in their own homes surrounding the palace in the capital but often came to the palace to use the library, genealogy room, and a room specifically for the elders of his kingdom.

"They are currently working on our mating ceremony," he muttered.

My eyebrows furrowed in confusion.

"Just in case you say yes," he gave a small smile. "You are human, and I am unaware of what could happen once we are mated. There has never been a Fae and human bonding written within the last 1500 years. They are scouring the history books to see what we may have to prepare for."

"Prepare for?"

"Consider this—with Werewolves, which have more common pairings with humans recently, humans can be 'changed' into Werewolves themselves."

I let out a long "oh," in realization.

"Right," he sighed. "With Faes, I'm not sure what will happen to you. You could remain human, or you could turn into one of us. If you turn into a Fae, you could be asleep for days and will need special care until you wake up." The thought of turning into a Fae didn't deter me. It was rather exciting. I would be looked on as one of them, not an outsider and maybe more fit to rule a kingdom. Those thoughts had gone through my mind in the carriage just the day before. A human in a Fae world?

"That would be amazing if I turned into a Fae!" I said eagerly.

Osirus gave a grin while he snaked his hand around my

waist.

"If only you guys could fly, that would make it outstanding!" I squealed.

Osirus stopped in his tracks and stared off into the distance.

"What's wrong?" I tilted my head.

Osirus looked down at me and tucked a bit of his own hair behind his ear. "We have wings, darling," he gave a solemn frown.

My eyes lit up. "Really!? Why don't you fly!? I would fly everywhere! I don't think I would ever walk!"

Osirus chuckled and held my arm again in his. "Darling, remember when I said that the Fae repress certain emotions and transformations?"

I nodded enthusiastically until the realization dawned on me.

"They hold back their wings. They don't fly."

Disappointment within my heart left me feeling empty. "That's so sad." Osirus hummed in agreement.

"We will make it right." He patted my hand. "Soon, everything will change. With change, things take time and the least amount of lives lost would be for the better."

I acknowledged as we continued to walk down the hallway.

"Your wings though...?" I asked. I had seen his muscular back before, but there were no wings. *How does he hide them?*

"Ha," he laughed. "Faes can hide their wings, unlike the Pixies and Fairies. They can come out when I will them to or under aggression or heightened sexual arousal."

I blushed thinking of them flying out during something 'exciting.'

"Calm yourself, little one, or I'll take you into my office over my desk." Osirus' look became dark, and I straightened my posture quickly.

As we reached the dining room, the vastness of the room was overwhelming. One could let out a loud yell and hear it repeated over and over. The table was long and made of marble. There was no way they could move this giant table around the room. It was long, and only an eighth of the table was set.

Alaneo and the red-headed guards sat waiting for us patiently. "'Bout time ya showed up. We were goin' to send a search party for ya!" Everett shouted.

Osirus chuckled, and everyone stilled.

Tilting my head to the side, I asked, "What's wrong?"

"The man never smiles, looks like his queen is already doing wonders," Alaneo said hopefully.

We all sat down and were immediately served with the finest of foods. I did not know what many were. The first course was a salad and there weren't as many greens as you would think. Small flowers covered the entire plate, and nectar was the dressing that tied it all together. The entire plate was sweet, almost like a dessert.

The main course was a type of meat that tasted like chicken but had the texture of tofu. Osirus was talking to Alaneo about some political policies that I wasn't aware of, so I continued to stare at it until Braxton spoke up. "It's a Peryton." I looked at him in confusion. "It is a cross between a stag and a bird. That is why its meat is light, so it can fly."

"It reminds me of tofu," I continued to poke the meat.

"Toe Foot?" Braxton asked while I laughed at the failed attempt.

"No, *tofu*! It is made of plants, a substitution for meat."

Braxton shook his head while I continued to feast on the desserts that were then set on the table.

"Darling?" Osirus grabbed my hand as I looked at him at the head of the table. "Tomorrow, I have several meetings and I don't want to burden you with them as of right now. You are welcome to explore the areas I showed you or even have the guards take you into the marketplace and see the city."

My eyes lit up. "I'd love that!" I clapped my hands excitedly.

He would not leave me in his room all day. I can finally see what the Fae kingdom was all about. Osirus was trying. I could almost feel the reluctance in his voice. He mentioned several times I could be in danger if people found out I was his mate, and he was going to great lengths for people not to find out just yet. The Cerulean Moon Kingdom nobles were becoming aware because they were preparing for the uprising he had mentioned.

It was just sad his own kingdom must be the last to know until I really knew that I loved him and was willing to be a Queen. The pain of guilt settled at the bottom of my heart. "None of that," Osirus whispered and kissed my knuckles. "I'm glad you are taking this seriously. I'm looking forward to more of a chase." He winked.

I blushed as he squeezed my hand again.

"And tomorrow night, I'm taking you out on a date." He smiled brightly.

Chapter 22

Melina

Osirus had already showered and had his crisp royal garb on. It was olive green with hints of white and beige with gold threading. He was wearing a gold crown that looked like an intricate weave of vines, branches, and thorns. In the center near his forehead held a single yellow diamond that sparkled when the light hit it just right.

"Are you sure you will be all right?" He fixed his collar and tugged on his sleeves. The cape or cloak, I'm not sure what to call it, made him look more dashing. Osirus looked like one of those regal kings or princes, ready to go off into battle and claim what he wanted. My poor body was shuddering at the thought of him claiming me.

"Yes, I'm sure!" I chirped as I stood up from the sitting area.

He picked out my dress again today, something he liked to do, and I enjoyed. It showed me he cared what he put me in and dressed me. My parents never once thought to look at the clothes I wore at school to make me look good. Several years of yearbook picture at school proved that time and time again. I really looked like a two-year-old dressed me for years.

"And I'll listen to all the rules you gave me." I rolled my

eyes.

"Good girl," he purred as he walked closer. "You know the punishment if you don't."

Giving him a small smile, I chided him, "But is it really a punishment?"

"It definitely can be if you don't behave," Osirus growled in warning.

"I will be good, I promise. Don't leave the guards, stay quiet, don't draw attention, wear the cloak, hide my face," I started spouting off all his rules until he silenced me with a finger.

"That's all I ask until you have fully decided." Osirus pecked my lips and walked to the door, his white cape trailing behind him. One last look at me and he was gone.

Peoni flew up behind me and sat on my shoulder. "Damn, he is one fine specimen. If I wasn't banging Alaneo, I'd try to get up on that." She waved her finger around and stuck it in her mouth.

"Excuse me, but he is my mate!" I pushed her off my shoulder.

"A Fairy can look. And, hon, you need to make up your mind, or some other Fae is going to come in and grab that fine piece of ass."

I rolled my eyes and grabbed my olive-green cloak that matched Osirus' color of the day. "You remind me of my friend Tulip, a piece of work."

Peoni tinkled a laugh and woke up Primrose who was sleeping on the bed. "He sure worked you yesterday. All that hand to butt slapping was turning me on and I wasn't even in the room!" I gasped as my face turned tomato red.

"You heard that!?" I yelled.

Peoni and Primrose begun laughing.

"Fuck, come for me baby!" Primrose mocked a deeper voice while Peoni squealed, "Oh, I'm coming!" as she fakes fainting.

My entire body turned red as I ran to the bathroom and

locked the door. The laughs and the catcalls coming from the other side of the door were deafening. I couldn't believe they heard all that. How could they hear all that?!

"Melina, dear! The guards are here! Come on, so we can get to the marketplace before it gets too crowded," Peoni sang.

"No! I can't face you any longer! I have never been so embarrassed!"

Primrose came closer to the door and whispered into the keyhole, "Fine, I'll go tell the red-bearded brothers of your frolic in the punishment department!"

I quickly opened the door, face still red and a few tears hiding behind my eyes. "How. Did. You. Hear?" I spat my words out.

"We just want to be the first to know when you are bonded. Gossip runs wild around here and, being the first to spread, it is high status to us," Primrose giggled. "Don't worry, we won't do it again. His Majesty felt our aura and scolded us." I let out a frustrated sigh and grabbed the bag of coins that Osirus gave me and met Everett, Finley, and Braxton in the living room.

"Aight, lass, you ready?" Finley spoke as he took my bag. All three of them were dressed in regular clothes, no royal uniforms, or emblems of any kind. "His Majesty wants to keep a low profile. I will stand beside you while my brothers keep a lookout on other sides." I skipped towards them understanding and we headed out the door.

After dodging a few royals behind the palace, they led me to a door that opened straight into the marketplace. It was already busy for it being so early, and food vendors around every corner. There were many foods I recognized but many that I did not. Finley tried to tell me what animals they were, but I stood there frozen, not understanding what animal, fruit, or vegetable he was talking about.

Once we passed the food section of the market, we came upon trinkets, clothing, jewelry, and even animals up for sale as pets. Finley kept trying to get me to look at the jewelry, but

I continued to walk, not interested. I've never owned a piece of jewelry my entire life and I wasn't really wanting to start now.

Many foxes in an assortment of colors caught my eye and I instantly fell in love with a white one with light blue tips on its ears and feet.

"That there is a frost fairy fox."

The fox gazed up at me sadly through the bars of the cage. The poor thing appeared so lonely. I pet his head in sympathy as it nuzzled into my hand. This wasn't the normal fox you would see on Earth. This one had several tails behind it and was about the size of a raccoon.

"They get larger," Finley spoke as he gave it a nut to eat. "When they are captured, they purposely put them in a small space and the fox shrinks down to a comfortable size inside the cage.

"That's awful," I whined. I wondered if Osirus would let me get a pet. I'd never had one before, not unless you counted Tulip as my Wolf pet. Snickering to myself I petted the poor things head.

Yelling on the other side of the market grabbed my attention. A small boy and a food vender holding onto his arm. The boy was crying for him to let go, but the food vender ripped the large loaf of bread out of his hand and continued to scold him.

"I've told you how many times to stop stealing from me! I'm having you arrested!" the Fae sneered.

"Please, sir, I'm sorry. My sister and I are just hungry!"

The man growled. "I don't care, half the kingdom is starved, I will get paid!" He pushed him to the ground, a guards walked up with their hands on their swords. "This boy tried to steal from me!"

The young child was about five years old, dirty face, hands, and clothes. He was alone and had no one to stand up to him. Finley was talking to the pet vendor, so I grabbed my coin bag quickly and ran up and stood in front of the boy.

"I'm sorry. I forgot to give him some money. Will you please accept this for the misunderstanding?" The sign said one pence, so I grabbed the smallest coins that had 'pence' written across them. "Here, double the price for the trouble." I kept my head down and the bread maker swiped the money out of my hand.

"I guess this will do." He scoffed. "Don't let me catch you around here again." The man walked off as some of the guards looked at me warily.

"Who are you?" one of them spoke cautiously. "Are you new here?"

"Um, yes! I am just traveling. I'm visiting my friend in the Cerulean Moon Kingdom and thought I would sight see." It wasn't a lie, so I hope he bought it. "I asked the boy to get me some bread because I am not familiar with your city and forgot to give him money."

The boy grabbed a hold of my cloak and didn't let go.

"Let us see your face," one of them bellowed. "We don't allow many strangers here."

My heart was beating in my chest until Finley showed up. "Ah, Fargus!" The guard turned around. Finley waved his hand for me to go, and the little boy grabbed my hand and nodded his head to the alley.

Following the boy, several kids in the alleyway staring attentively at the bread. They quickly divided the bread and ate. The little Fae children were so small and dirty, and I was sure they were homeless. I could hear Finley still speaking with the guard and Everett and Braxton showed up.

"Melina, ya sure do know how to get in trouble quickly. What were ya thinkin'?" Everett scolded.

"I couldn't let him get in trouble. It isn't his fault he was hungry! Why are the children like this? Are there more of them?" Everett cleared his throat, looking at them sadly.

"Ya, there are more. There is an orphanage just outside the capital that houses them. I'm not sure why they are here." The little boy grabbed my hand and pulled me down to talk to him.

"There is no more food and the women who take care of us don't have any money. They work during the day so they can come home and feed us, but we were just so hungry." The little boy's eyes welled up with tears.

I grabbed him and held him to my chest, holding on to my pain these children are having. I pulled him from me and moved his hair away from his face. "What's your name?"

"Cricket," he sniffed

"Well, Cricket." I stood up and dusted off my dress. "We are going to get some food to take back to the orphanage."

The kids looked up excitedly.

Braxton walked toward me with a suspicious look. "Your Majesty," he whispered, "you are to keep a low profile." I glared back at him.

"And we shall," I smirked. "We will split up the money three ways and meet at the edge of the city. Finley can come with me while you and Everett gather the rest. The children will take us to the orphanage once finished." Braxton scratched the back of his head, questioning my decision.

"It's an order, Braxton." He looked down into my eyes and gave a right lipped smile. "Aight, let's get to it then." Finley, and once briefed, Finley agreed to my demands. We gathered as much food as we possibly could with the coins Osirus gave me, which was a substantial amount, and headed to the orphanage.

Once we left the main part of the city, the homes were more dispersed. Some homes were shacks, while others were well maintained. Each home was equipped with a garden and a few hen-like creatures and maybe a cow. The orphanage was the furthest house from the initial break away from the fancier homes in the city.

It was a modest building that said *Her Love of Light*. It reminded me of a smaller packhouse and older, way older. Bricks were misplaced, and steps were broken, but the roof, walls and doors were intact to keep out the weather and animals. Walking in, a large living space with rugs, couches and books laid in the room.

Children ran up to us wondering what we were doing in the home. Many children called out the name *Nana* and Cricket quickly told us she took care of the household. During the day, she and three other women work to earn money so the children can eat but can only bring back so much a day. They run errands and send messages to nearby towns of The Golden Light Kingdom, which doesn't pay much. The women needed a flexible schedule to come back during the day if needed.

The guards, being big burly men, did not know what to do with the food or with all the extra little eyes watching them, so I motioned for them to put the food on the counter. Taking off my cloak and hanging it on the hook, many children gasped while the guards groaned.

Right, wasn't supposed to take that off.

"What are you!?" Cricket came up to me and held my hand again. The children, equally absorbed with excitement began pulling and poking my skin while I laughed or gasped as they pinched me.

"I'm human." A noticeable gasp left their lips again.

"I thought they were Fairy Tales, like the ones that get eaten by witches!" A wide toothless grin smiled from across the room. The Fae children snickered as I snorted back a laugh.

"No, we are real. Where I come from, we all think you are not real!" They all stood in shock as they took the new information.

"No way!" Cricket yelped.

I nodded my head. "Yes, way!"

After introductions were concluded and they could touch my ears and check my back for any wings, I got to work stocking the kitchen and making them a warm pot of chili with the meat that Finley had picked out.

"Your Majesty, all these children know who you are now,"

Everett hissed at me.

I waved my hand and continued to chop the onion. "If you keep saying, 'Your Majesty,' then they are really going to know. They just think I'm passing through. Don't worry about it." I continued to chop while the infamous brothers bickered in the corner.

Peoni and Primrose, who had been absent since we stepped foot into the marketplace, fluttered in the door and sat on the kitchen counter while I cooked. "How did you find me?" I asked, unamused.

"It's a secret." Peoni giggled.

I didn't trust Peoni and Primrose one bit. These Fairies always had something up their sleeve or up their dresses.

"Peoni was visiting a, ahem, friend," Primrose said cheekily.

"Yes, and Primrose was also visiting a, ahem, friend." I rolled my eyes as I threw the rest of the food into the pot.

The smell was wafting into the air. Children began sitting at the table waiting for me to pour them a large portion of chili when the door came open.

Four exhausted Fae women walked through the door and hung their cloaks, but immediately perked up as they smelled the chili on the stove cooking. Cricket came bursting through the kitchen and held onto the more worn-looking Fae woman.

"Nana! I met a friend today! She made us all food!"

Nana whipped her head into the kitchen and stared at my giant posse behind me.

"I-I," she spoke as the shocked look on her face dwindled. "T-thank you."

I smiled at her warmly and handed her a bowl of chili. "Here, come sit." I gathered her at a table and gave her the first bowl. She didn't look old by any means because aging wasn't a thing here, but she oozed experience. The worry she held in her eyes, the pain, the suffering was all there. Older children grabbed rolls and bowls for the younger ones and fed themselves. Nana kept glancing at my ears and my short stature but didn't utter a word.

The three girls continued to hold on to their cloaks and looked at my bodyguards with wide eyes. Once the infamous redheads looked up, their own eyes opened wide. Confusion was set on my face until they all said one four-letter word...

Chapter 23

Melina

"FUCK!" they all screamed and ran towards each other. Hugs and cheek kisses were all around as Nana and I scrambled to cover the little one's ears. Many of the older kids sat wide-eyed while the younger children happily slopped their chili on some bread rolls.

"Oy! I haven't seen you in forever!" Finley blasted as he gave one girl a swift kiss on the cheek. All the girls all laughed as they put their fingers through their beards.

One girl, a tall woman with long golden hair, gave Everett a pat on the chest. "Mother will be so sorry she didn't get to see her favorite nephews." Oh, so they are cousins.

"Melina, we want you to meet our cousins, Elana, Eve and Wind." The three girls all curtsied beautifully and were equally stunning in their looks, sporting various shades of blonde.

"A human!" Elana gasped. "I've never seen one before! Welcome!" The other two girls gave a slight wave and whispered to each other, pointing at my stature and point-less ears.

Elana turned to her red-haired cousins and clasped her hands. "This is such a surprise! When we moved to the capital just a year ago, we were wondering when we would find you three. Our paths never crossed, so we figured you had moved on to another place."

Braxton laughed. "Nah, we are creatures of habit. Our loyalties are with the King and the King alone."

Eve scoffed and crossed her arms. "I don't know why. These poor children are starving, and he does nothing about it." My eyes furrowed in confusion. Didn't Osirus say he sent money to those just outside of the capital to help them?

"That's not true," I spoke up. The three sisters turned to me in confusion as to why I would defend their King. "He sends aid. There must be a mistake for this. If he knew there were children starving, then he would have surely sent more!" Wind turned her back to me and hung up her cloak.

"Listen here, little human. You know nothing of the Faes. The King is heartless and lets small children starve while the nobles are eating high-ranking meats and vegetables and discarding the scraps for their pets. Not even these children are said to be deserving of such a treat."

Anger boiled inside me, in my heart, I knew Osirus would never allow such a thing to happen. He just said he helps aid them the best he can! Before I could speak again, there was a harsh knock at the door. Nana stood up, clasping her hands, and walked to the door carefully.

Once opened, we all stood and stared into the eyes of none other than Daphne. I felt my jaw tick seeing my mate's former bed warmer. Braxton stood by me and put his hand on my shoulder, noticing my distress.

"Well, well, well, looks like a party in here this afternoon, hmm, Nana?" Nana stood back and gripped the child behind her that was still clinging to her dress.

Daphne was beautiful, just like every other Fae but she had lean muscles and a strong posture that oozed strength. I wondered if the Fae trained as much as the Werewolves.

"What seems to be the occasion?" She walked in and started smelling the pot. "Hm, not a Fae dish." Daphne turned to me and narrowed her eyes. "You," she growled. "What is a concubine doing here? Are you too good to warm the King's bed now?"

The women in the home looked at me confused, and my face blushed red. "I don't see how that is any of your concern." I stood from the table in defiance. This woman wasn't going to tear me down. She's just a jealous hoe that wants Osirus, my Osirus.

And I just claimed him, goddess help me.

Daphne sauntered over and my stance didn't waver. The room went quiet as some of the little children continued to eat their food. "You have more of a backbone now, huh?" She tsked her teeth. "What are you, human?" She continued to walk around the table, inspecting the food laying on the table. "We don't get many of your kind around here and my job is to make sure—" She picked up a crust of bread from the table and tossed it back down, landing with a small thud. "—that the Fae kingdom stays a pure race, and your polluted blood is ruining it. You must be a good lay."

My fists balled up in anger, but Finley was shaking his head behind her. "You are planning on leaving, correct? Just a tumbleweed in the wind? Just a notch on the King's bed post?" *This bitch.*

"Oh, you mean just like you?" I said sweetly.

I saw irritation in her eyes as she slammed her hand down on the table. "You will not speak to me that way! I am of noble blood, and I can have you ended with the snap of my fingers!" she bellowed. I gave a little smirk and patted my napkin on my lips before I walked around the table to meet her gaze. "Is someone jealous?" I whispered. "The mighty noble that can't get the King to put his cock in the same hole again? You must be too loose." I snickered. "Now a little human comes along and has the King wrapped around her finger. I thought being of noble blood, you would be better at hiding your jealousy."

The women in the room all clasped their hands to their

mouths in unison while the *Red Fury* as I'd dubbed the guards, stood in surprise. There was no doubt I was going to get spanked over this, but I would not allow that ugly Fae to get the best of me.

Daphne stomped to the door and swung it open. "Nana, just so you know, the donated land taxes were higher this month, and donations by the Fae Kingdom's subjects weren't enough to help. You still owe coinage to the Court of Fae." Daphne slammed the door and shook the overhanging decoration above the door.

Nana looked defeated; her shoulders slumped downward while the sisters looked at me in heartache. "How? We are barely getting by now." Wind sniffed. "Then we will all go hungry."

"It's all her fault!" Eve pointed at me. "If she hadn't riled her up, then we could still scrape by. Now we are officially screwed!" The pang in my heart as she pointed to me made me take a step back. Cricket looked up at me with his wide eyes, and I stomped my foot in determination. I'm not giving up yet.

"No, you will make ends meet. There will be enough money for food and help fix up the place. I'll be sure of it." I grabbed my cloak and Peoni and Primrose quickly helped me tie it.

"I think you have done enough," Nana said solemnly. "Just leave us to our own devices. The King won't help, he never has. You are only a concubine. Someone not even worth mentioning." Finley gave her a hard look and stepped forward to say something, but Braxton stopped him with a wave of his hand.

"Nana," I mumbled. "I know you don't believe me, but I am going to help. The King has told me personally he was helping all of you. I'm not sure why you aren't seeing the funds. I'm sorry if I angered her further, but she needed to be knocked off whatever high horse she was on. These children will be clothed and fed with full bellies tomorrow night." I tightened the knot on my cloak and pulled up the hood.

The children that met me in the alley came up and gave me a quick hug. "You will be back, promise?" Cricket held me tightly on my dress.

I sat down on the floor and rubbed his cheek full of butter from his bread. "I promise, Cricket. Everything will be just fine."

The walk back was quiet. I continued to stew about what Daphne had said to me, as well as Nana. Now every Fae woman I have met so far in the blasted kingdom thought I was a harlot. I was far from that. I have done nothing of the sort in my life until I met Osirus.

However, if someone called me that in front of him, would he say anything? He said he was protecting me until I chose this life with him, but right now, I felt like a dirty little secret. Finley stepped up to me and put his hand on my shoulder in comfort.

"Are ya all right, lass?"

I nodded, fearing if I spoke, my voice would crack.

"Listen, don't pay attention to them. They don't know who you are, and Daphne is a bitch. She wants the crown more than anything and putting down others is what she does." Finley spat out a wad of tobacco. "Everybody hates her, the Court only tolerates her, anyway."

"I know, but I feel like a dirty secret being hidden away. I should just accept all this so Osirus can claim me, but I can't help but feel scared. I didn't grow up with this. I'm used to being alone and over the years, I kept myself out of relationships so I wouldn't feel hurt again. My own parents were supposed to love me and care for me and didn't. What makes me think a bond can keep that together with Osirus?"

"Your Majesty, listen to me." Finley stopped and tilted my chin up. "Bonding is something you don't understand because you didn't grow up with it. Bonds are for eternity. He would never betray or forsake you. Every mated pair I have ever known are still together and I've been around a long time." Finley smiled and nodded his head slightly.

Maybe I was overthinking and should let my heart be open. The past few days, I have felt closer to him than even my best friend and her parents. He'd made me feel wanted and cared for. Every morning he buttered my croissant and, for the life of me, I didn't know how he knew how I liked it. Buttered lightly with a hint of strawberry jam.

His little snores at night were so endearing. Osirus might have been the King, but he looked like a little prince when he slept. My heart would soar when he would say my name while he was dreaming. This had only been a few days, feeling so strongly about someone shouldn't come this easy.

The only thing I could do was open my heart to him. Accept him. Take a chance to love him wholly. Not just because I've been called a whore or harlot, but because it's time to move on and be happy. Time to love and be loved in return and not fear rejection.

Osirus had shown me nothing but kindness and love throughout it all. He never said one thing that hurt my heart, even if it had been a few days of knowing him.

Tugging my cloak closer to myself, we entered the servant's quarters at the back of the palace. "Finley? Where would Osirus be now?" Finley's eyes twinkled in amusement, possibly thinking about our recent conversation.

"The throne room, should I lead you there?" Giving him an enormous smile, he led me down several large hallways and up a few flights of stairs. "This is the backside of the throne room. I figured you didn't want to walk in with a room full of people."

"Thank you," I whispered, and opened the back door of the room.

I could see Osirus' leg swinging on the side of the chair, something he liked to do when he was bored to show how unamused he was. His long hair was dripping off the other side. I couldn't help but feel giddy to tell him I wanted more, that I wanted to be his mate. He would be excited, and I couldn't wait until the end of the day to tell him. Sneaking up behind him, I stood behind his chair getting ready to scare him when I heard that sickeningly sweet voice.

"Your Majesty? You are looking well today." It was that damn woman. Could she not just let it go? He rejected her in front of the guards and Alaneo. Why not be a little humble and admit defeat?

"What is it you want?" Osirus' bored tone had a hint of irritation. "I thought you were still in confinement."

Daphne gave a fake laugh. "They thought it was a mistake." She waved her hand. "They let me go fairly quickly."

"Or your father threw a tantrum," Osirus mumbled, and I stifled back a giggle.

"I came here to find out about the girl you brought to your chambers. What is she to you?"

"I suggest you watch your inquisitiveness, Daphne. It will get you into misfortune," Osirus spat, sitting upright in his chair.

"I only ask because she is human. You know I'm in charge of new species coming into the kingdom and keeping records. I need to know how long she is staying. Are you just using her as a concubine for the long or short term? These questions must be answered for the sake of the Court and taking charge of the census." Daphne's voice was docile, begging for answers. My heart knew what I wanted Osirus to say. The question was, what was he going to say?

Hearing the small mumbles in the throne room, people were scattered about with parchment paper. Asking questions, writing down notes and some were laughing at jokes their partner had said. Osirus blew out a breath and looked out the window.

"Come on now, Osirus, we have been friends for years..."

Osirus banged his fist on the arm of the chair and leaned down on his throne to whisper-yell at her. "Yes, she is my concubine, a woman to warm my bed, and let me say this. She gives me more pleasure than you ever did. I'll keep her as long as I want so I can keep you out of my damn hair!"

My breath hitched as I covered my mouth. He didn't really mean that, he really didn't. Finley said mates were for eternity that we would love each other and would never break each other's hearts with rejection or pain.

But why did I feel my heartbreaking when he spoke about me like that? He was trying to protect me, that was what he was doing, but why did hearing it escape his lips hurt? I peeked around the throne to see Daphne smirk at me.

"Ah, I see. Just a tumbleweed in the wind." She jotted it down on a small pad of paper. "I will put that on the census that she won't be here for long."

Standing up quickly, I burst out of the back servant's door of the throne room. Finley started calling my name, but I didn't stop. "Melina, wait!" he called. I continued to run down the hallway, keeping the hood over my face. "He didn't mean it! You know this!"

Windows flew past me my dainty slipper shoes slapped the hard-marbled floor as I turned sharply down a servant's corridor. Finley's voice continued to fade as my breaths became brash. I would not stop running until I felt more pain in my limbs than my heart.

He didn't mean it, he was protecting me, I chanted over and over in my mind.

Then why did it hurt?

Chapter 24

Osirus

I didn't want to leave her. Every day she grew more and more beautiful in my eyes, her confidence in herself was growing and her trust in me was not far behind. She was opening her heart bit by bit and I was going to make sure she saw how much I loved her and wanted to take care of her tonight.

With my day filled with nonsense meetings, social gatherings, and plans to overthrow the Court with several trusted Parliament members. On top of it all, I needed to woo my mate. Clara wasn't kidding when she told me that I would have my work cut out for me. Melina was a stubborn little human, but precious and worth it all.

Today, I gave her a cape that matched my attire. She might not have realized it, but it was a Fae tradition to dress alike when courting to symbolize our proposed mating intentions if one mate was reluctant. Outside of the Fae kingdom, many might think a delayed mating would be a recipe for disaster, but it showed the strength and the seriousness of a bond.

I was reluctant letting Melina go out into the market-place. However, with my personal guards plus two boisterous Fairies, I was sure she would be fine. No one would know who she was and be none the wiser. I also had a willing Pixie that took a liking to Melina the night she ran from me, Leah. She agreed to be my little spy to watch Melina as she traveled through the marketplace and report back to me quickly if there was a need to.

"Your Majesty!" I rolled my eyes internally. "I'm glad you're back. I'm sure your trip to the Cerulean Moon Kingdom was fruitful?" Cosmo strolled up to the throne. He has been harassing me for decades for me to marry his daughter and I have never swayed in my decision.

"Yes, Cosmo, it was. The Faes and the Shifters are now at peace for at least 500 or so years," I said facetiously. I popped a grape in my mouth, only to keep my mouth shut about his whore of a daughter.

"Good, good, now that is settled. Why don't we talk about you finding a queen? It has been too many years of you being alone and my own daughter is holding out for you. The perfect match you both would be!" He smiled brightly. "In fact, the Court even approves it! It's a match made in paradise!" I continued to munch on my grapes absentmindedly.

"Thank you for the concern, but I'll hold out for my mate. If you will excuse me, but there are other people in line wanting to speak with me." My hand waved behind him.

Alaneo snorted back a laugh as Cosmo gave a leery eye.

"You can't be single forever, you know." I raised my eyebrow at the hellion.

"There is a law by your 820th birthday if the king has not found a mate that he would marry one of the court member's daughters." He smiled radiantly. The dark Fairy thought he had the upper hand on me, didn't he?

"Thank you, Cosmo, that will be all." I waved my hand again for the guards to step in if needed, but he bowed graciously with a smirk on his lips.

"The man doesn't give up, does he?" Alaneo spoke.

"That he doesn't. Luckily for me, my birthday isn't for another two years, and I don't think my mate will wait that long." I popped another grape into my mouth and savored the taste.

Oher court members brought me their problems, issues, proposals, and some subjects of the kingdom arrived for help of their own. I paid more courtesy to them than to the court and tried to help direct them the best I could.

There was a lull in between the next appointment when Leah tinkled silently in my ear. "*Your Majesty,*" her sweet bells rang.

I slightly grunted for her to continue while she was on my shoulder, not to bring attention to us.

"*Melina has found the orphanage. It looks like the funds you have been sending have not been going to the children. She promised Nana, the head of the home, that they would be sure to take care of them only to be insulted. They called her a meaningless concubine, and she didn't reject the name-calling.*"

My hands tightened around my chair. Alaneo put his hand on my shoulder in warning.

"Anything else, Leah?" I whispered.

"*Daphne was there. She might be the one intercepting the monies and taxing them on top of it. She was very degrading of her Majesty.*" A snarl left my lips. "*They are heading back to the palace now, Your Majesty.*"

I nodded my head, and she flew out the nearby window.

That damn woman. Daphne was going to be hard to get rid of. I couldn't hold her in the dungeons once we took over. She would either be banned from the city or death itself would rain on her. No one would talk to the future queen in that manner.

I've only got to keep her secret a little while longer. If word got out now, it would be over. Assassins would storm the castle to try and kill her. If we were mated, no one would dare touch her because to touch her would be to kill me and the next in line of the throne would ascend and there really would be a war outbreak.

Thousands would die in the process, and my plan had the least amount of fatalities. Protect the queen, protect the kingdom. My brothers were not as sympathetic as I was, even though I acted tough in the Court. They trained with the warriors in Clara's pack, they could be brutal when they wanted to be, they were not fit to run a kingdom.

Speaking of the demoness herself, Daphne sauntered up to the throne. She did an obnoxious curtsey and started babbling nonsense about Melina. She must have gotten under her skin if she came right away after seeing her at the orphanage. Half listening, half daydreaming of feeling Melina's skin on my fingertips, she asked a question that irks me.

"Is she your concubine?" was the general question.

She had danced around with her words and now she wanted me to come out and say what Melina meant to me. I had to protect my destined but saying these words alone made my own heartache because she was far from it.

"Yes, she is my concubine, a woman to warm my bed, and let me say this she gives me more pleasure than you ever did. I keep her so I can keep you out of my damn hair!" The words stung my heart, the pounding in my chest as I spoke it. It was all lies. I had to protect her. Just a little longer.

"I see, just a tumbleweed in the wind," she said cunningly.

Walking away, anger flared in my eyes. How dare that woman! She will be the first to go.

"Your Majesty, we have a problem." Finley walked up behind the throne.

"What is it? Where is Melina?" I stood up, causing the entire room to go silent. Finley leaned in and whispered in my ear.

"She came to see you, to tell you something important, but she heard your conversation with Daphne."

A deep growl reverberated in my chest and echoed into the room. I felt my fangs growing, but I shook my head and felt my nostrils flare. "Where is she?" I whispered.

"I'm sorry, she ran. I don't know where she went! Please have mercy!" Finley got on one knee and lowered his head. The crowd saw my distress as I looked around the room. I stared at Alaneo for support, and he quickly stepped up. "This will conclude our meetings for the day. His Majesty has other matters to attend to. Please leave any important documents by the door with the servants. Thank you."

Alaneo was still talking as I heard his voice fade away. My steps were heavy as I untied my cape and it fell to the floor. "Where would she go? Where did she go today?" Finley continued to run beside me as I unbuckled my cuff links to roll them up my sleeve.

"We went to the market and the orphanage. She was too upset after what happened at the orphanage to do anything else. Braxton and Everett are out scouting those areas." We continued walking to the east side of the palace while Peoni and Primrose flew up beside us.

"Your Majesty." Primrose bowed while still hovering in the air.

"Where is she?" My voice was deep and not a hint of playfulness residing in it.

Primrose shuddered and bowed again. "I'm sorry, I have looked in your chambers as well as the dining room and library, and she is not there."

Changing my direction, we headed to the stables. She couldn't have gotten far in the amount of time this all transpired. To know where she would go, in a land she was unfamiliar with and unsure of, would be the challenge.

Walking up to my shining white horse, I spoke to him hurriedly, "Montu, I need you to concentrate." Montu perked up his ears. The one-time Melina rode with me should be enough for Montu to pick up on her smell. "Find my destined, Montu. A bushel of apples and oats will be in your stall waiting if we find her by sundown."

Montu grunted in approval as I mounted my steed bareback. I adjusted my sword and dagger. No time to saddle, we were going to find her.

Melina

I ran until I couldn't run anymore. The trees diffused, and the houses became far between. I ran until I finally hit the East coast. The past two mornings, I had watched the suns rise above the water, giving a beautiful purple, blue and pink glow. Many times, I could see dolphins and fish jumping through the waves, but right now the waves were gone. It was peaceful. Somewhere I could rest my weary mind.

The whirlwind I had been put through and the emotions that I have felt made the ocean even more inviting. There were dark rocks that adorned some areas that looked dry and flat, like its own pier into the ocean. I stepped on a few stones, slipping a few times since my slipper-like shoes were not meant for the terrain. I hopped over pools that stood still in the crevasses until I reached the end of the natural pier. Bits of sand still dusted over the rocks.

Taking off my cloak, I laid it down on the rock and my body with it. The run felt good. The pain was stronger in my legs than in my heart. He's trying to protect me. I knew he was; I knew he wouldn't lie. The pain from my parents was what was keeping me from going to him. They rejected me and hearing him say words so strongly like that only reminded me of them.

"*I didn't want her, we didn't want her,*" my mother's voice rang in my head.

"*She's just a tumbleweed in the wind.*" I understood why he said I was a concubine, but hearing it come out of his mouth only made my memories rear their ugly head.

I sighed heavily. Minutes ticked by and the ocean rose. I could lay my head on my arm and put my hand into the water. It was cool and fresh to touch. Closing my eyes, a small tear escapes me. It runs down my cheek, onto my chin, and drops in the water below me. Then I do the one thing I've always done when I'm upset and that was to sing. It started when my own parents wouldn't sing to me when I was a young child. Not even Twinkle, Twinkle Little Star.

The tears were free-flowing as I sang a few notes of melody. I couldn't even sing anymore. I let out small sobs into my arm. I was letting it go. I was letting go of all the pain my parents had caused me because they are just dragging me down after all these years. I was going to be happy. I wanted to be happy with Osirus. Why didn't I go to therapy when Tulip's parents suggested it?

I dabbed my eyes with my cloak and sat back on my legs. Taking a large breath, looking up at the sky, and breathing out slowly, I felt a cold hand on my wrist. Whipping my head at the person who was submerged in the water from the nose down, I let out a petrified scream.

It was a man, his dark hair wet from swimming. His skin had a blue-green tint to it and his eyes were yellow. He slowly rose out of the water without letting go of my wrist as I tried to pull it back. My heart was beating erratically, and my breathing had picked up. I had never been more scared in all my life. This creature before me was something I had never seen.

Once I finished screaming and stopped struggling from the tight grip, he held onto me and rose, so the water was just below his hip bones.

"Took you long enough to stop screaming, gods," he said sarcastically as he whipped his hair back to take care of the excess water. He had a bright white smile, showing a few fangs. "I'm Lucca."

I continued to look at him in confusion as he held onto my wrist. "C-can you let go?"

"What if I don't want to? Besides, you might run away." Lucca gave a grin. "Come on now, I just wanted to hear you sing some more. I thought you were another Siren, but low and behold, it was a land dweller."

"Huh? What?"

"You aren't a very smart one, are you?" Lucca gave a flick of his tail and launched himself out of the water to sit next to me without letting go.

I gasped at the sight. His tale was a gorgeous blue and green that led right up to his six-pack that turned into skin. He had gills underneath his ears yet lungs to let him breathe air.

"Are you done staring, precious?" He wiggled his eyebrows at me.

"I'm sorry. I've seen nothing like you."

"That's what all the ladies say. Now, I never got a name from you. What is it?" Lucca leaned in and pulled on my arm so I could get closer. I pulled back but heard a loud *shing*, and a pointed metal object pointed right at Lucca's jaw.

"Damn, forgot you Fae are stealthy little shits." Lucca chuckled as he glanced up at Osirus.

"Let go of my destined Siren," Osirus spoke deeply.

Sitting on the rock, looking up at Osirus, he appeared imperial. The way the wind blew in his hair, his sword tickling the neck of the Siren, his commanding voice, it gave me chills how magnificent he seemed.

Wait, he called me his destined, his mate, in front of someone else?

"Do I need to say it again, Lucca?"

Chapter 25

Melina

"Do I need to say it again, Lucca?" Osirus' voice was filled with anger, and it was really damn hot. Lucca continued to glance up at Osirus with a devilish grin and his fangs on display. Lucca let go and kept his hands in the air all while Osirus grabbed me and pulled me to his side. His body was warm as he held me close while his sword was still on Lucca.

"I let her go, don't do anything brash," Lucca stated.

Osirus sheathed his sword and picked me up and carried me off the rock mount. His breathing was heavy, his nostrils were flaring, and his ears had extended but were trickling back to the normal form I usually see.

"I'll see you later, Your Majesty!" Lucca chanted.

Osirus turned around once more to glare at Lucca, but he was already gone back into the sea.

Osirus carried me until we reached a grassed area where Montu was grazing. He stared up and shook his head while he stomped at the ground and flicked his ears. Osirus gently put me down feet first into the grass and held me tight by my waist.

"Melina, that was brash and uncalled for, you leaving the palace. You could have been taken or even killed! If I hadn't gotten there in time…" He threw his hands up in the air and raked his clean hair back. "You would have never surfaced again." His voice cracked, and an overpowering cloud of guilt covered me. My crying session had not been over for long and I felt the tears coming back, this time I let them fall.

Covering my face to hide, Osirus kneeled to the ground, so he was close to the same height as me now. He pulled my hands away and gazed into my glassy eyes.

"Darling, I am so sorry." His fingers rested at the base of my neck while his thumb tickled my jaw. "I was trying to protect you and I said some things that even hurt me as well. You are not a concubine and never will be. You are my queen, my angel, and my light. I would never treat you in such a way. I wish you could feel the sorrow in my heart for hurting you." Osirus' thumbs continued to wipe away the tears that fell into the palm of his hand.

My emotions had taken the forefront of my mind over the last seven years after seeing my parents drive off. The wall had been broken, and I was going to let him in. Osirus was sincere, more so than any man or Fae I had ever encountered.

"I'm sorry," I whispered into his hand, cupping my face. "I don't know what came over me." As a child, I was a realist. I took life for what it was and if something was good, it was good, if it was bad, it was bad, but the grey area I was in with Osirus was different. I had to figure out my emotions myself and not rely on the bond. However, I couldn't deny the pull I had to him.

I flung my arms around his neck, and he wrapped his around my body. He rubbed the back of my head and cooed gently into my ear. "I'm here, and I'm never leaving. We will always have each other. If you run, I will find you and bring your arse back home. Do you understand?"

I placed my head on his shoulder, sniffing into his neck. Osirus pulled me from his neck and put his index finger on my nose. "And I will spank your arse until it's bloody pink!"

I giggled and let in one big sniff, so I didn't have snot falling out of my runny nose.

Osirus rubbed my arms up and down and stood up, leading me to Montu. I watched Osirus get up on his back and Montu turned his head and nipped at my shoulder and sputtered. "I know, I'm sorry, I won't run again."

Montu rose his head up and down, stopping the ground in recognition. Once mounted, Osirus had me sit in front of him while he held the reins, and we trotted back to the city. My cloak was long forgotten as we started entering civilization, and I had nothing to cover my face.

"Don't worry about it, darling. I will not have people think you are some lowly concubine. You are my queen and will be treated like one. Wolves from Clara's pack are on their way to protect you since I cannot tell which of my soldiers are truly for the rebellion. No matter what, I'll protect you." He squeezed my waist as we came up to the Capital gates. He didn't even take the back entrance like we did my first night here.

Osirus' posture was rigid. He sat up straight and tall as he held onto the reins with one hand and another around my body. My one hand came up to his, and I interlaced our fingers. He smiled down at me and kissed my forehead tenderly as we walked through the town.

There were whispers, gasps, and cheers that came through the windows and doors of homes. A few of the small children from the orphanage ran up beside Montu and gave him a few carrots. Cricket was beaming with pride, calling out for me, even though he didn't know my name.

"I told you she was an angel! Now she's gonna be queen!" Nana and the three sisters stood in shock as they carried the smaller children with them.

They all bowed, and Osirus untied his coin bag and tossed it to them. "You should have been receiving donations. I will get to the bottom of it." He snapped. The women thanked profusely as we continued, never stopping in one place.

A crowd of people formed behind us, walking us to the

palace gates, and when opened, they all cheered as I looked back. Osirus turned his horse as the gates closed and had me look up into his eyes. His face held nothing but love for me. His face was soft as he leaned down and kissed me in front of the crowd of people. I blushed as he smiled down at me and covered my face. He sat up straight and looked up into the crowd just behind the iron gates.

"People of the Golden Light Kingdom, I give you, your future queen!" Osirus roared.

Montu began dancing his own dance while jumping and screaming came from the Faes, Fairies, and Pixies. Pixies flew through the gate, throwing flowers at me and Osirus. I couldn't help but giggle and held a few flowers in my hand, putting one in Osirus' chest pocket. Osirus' face lit up and the biggest grin spread across his flawless face. I'd never seen him smile in public, but here he was, in front of most of his own kingdom, letting down his very own wall of stoic emotions.

He leaned down for one more hot, passionate kiss as I ran my fingers through his hair. I peeked up at him while he kissed me, only to see a large crowd on the balcony above the front doors of the palace. There was no celebration, cheers, or joyous praise. Daggers were in their eyes, especially from one woman, Daphne.

***

"You fuckin' idiot!" Alaneo drawled, pacing the living room floor.

We were in the royal living chambers. The red-headed fury stood by the door while Alaneo was trying to reprimand Osirus. Keyword was trying. Osirus sat in the overly decorative chair of golden tassels and swirls of green and gold while I sat in his lap. One hand wrapped around my waist and another petting my cheek. He made me feel like a little trophy that he had just won.

Smiling like a little prince on Christmas morning, he pecked kisses on my cheek. If he was happy now, wait until I tell him I was 100% sure I wanted to be his mate.

"Do you even think?" Alaneo continued, slapping his palm against his forehead. "All this time of planning, preparing, and keeping your destined safe, you have done the worst thing possible! You painted a target on her back! Do you realize what you have even done, Osirus!?"

There weren't many times Alaneo called Osirus by his first name. Mostly he called him that in jest, but now Osirus snapped his head to Alaneo and gently put me in the chair.

"I suggest you use the correct title when you try to rebuke me. You do know who you are talking to, correct?" Osirus' fists were balled up, his posture rigid. Finley came by to stand beside me with his arms behind his back.

"Yes," Alaneo let out with a sigh. "And I am speaking to you as your friend. You have planned so long to save these people from political persecution and when our Queen has come into the picture, they start to fall apart," Alaneo said softly. Even with Alaneo's soft word, Osirus continued to be riled up, rolling up his sleeves, prepared to get into an altercation.

"All I am saying, we have to protect both the kingdom and Melina," he pleaded. "Leah and her fellow Pixies say the Wolves are on their way and once the Court realizes, it will create suspicion. The Dragon Shifters to help aid us won't be here for another week. We need to send the Wolves away. Maybe Melina, too." Alaneo had sweat on his brow and his hands shaking. "They will come for her—in the night, the day, while she is bathing, while she is sleeping. It isn't a matter of 'if,' it is a matter of when!"

Osirus' claws grew and his fangs descended. His body was shaking in pure rage and grabbed Alaneo by the throat, throwing him up against the wall, feet dangling and all.

I rose from my seat, but Finley held me down with one of his hands. "Let them get through this," he whispered gruffly.

I sat back down, twiddling my fingers.

Did he mean what he said? Will they come for me? My silly little tantrum messed everything up for the entire kingdom?

"Melina will remain by my side. Only more eyes will watch her every move until this rebellion is over. She is mine and no one will take her from me," Osirus continued to growl as his chest heaved. "She will always remain by my side. This could be a distraction that we need. Their eyes will be on her rather than the armies surrounding the castle. Now, if you are finished, leave." Osirus dropped him to the floor and walked menacingly away from him, picking me up from the chair gently, as if he had never had a tantrum.

Looking back, Alaneo was rubbing his neck, waving his hands for the red-headed fury to leave him alone. "I just had to test him, make sure his head was on straight." He winked at me as Osirus slammed our bedroom door closed.

"Primrose!" Osirus shouted and within an instant, she was in front of him. "Find the Wolves, tell them under direction of King Osirus to cease their travels for six days. Tell them code word, 'Axis."

Primrose bowed, and with a small gust of wind, she was gone.

Osirus' eyes appeared tired as he fell to the couch beside me. I walked over to the drink bar and poured him one of the Fae alcohols I'd seen him drink. Strolling to him, I kneeled before him and handed him a drink while his arm was over his eyes. Sensing my presence, he moved his arm and gave me a stern look of determination.

"I will protect you Melina, from that damn Wolf Esteban, the Siren, Daphne and all the Fae kingdom. I will protect you," he spoke with promise and fortitude.

I couldn't help but kiss his inviting lips. They held so much of who he was. His passion, desire, and strength poured from them into mine. In a swift motion, he sat up and pulled me to his lap, straddling him while brushing my back. The kiss deepened and my breasts rubbed up against his chest. I felt my nipples pebbling within my dress. The itch they were causing me was almost painful. I wanted him to touch them, relieve them of their annoyance.

Talk about hot and bothered.

I moaned into his mouth as I tugged his hair.

"I'd walk through the lake of fire for you," he whispered as he trailed kisses down my neck and to my chest. "I'd travel to the end of the realms to get you the rarest of diamonds." Osirus' hand trailed up my dress and close to my core. I gasped at the way it tickled my inner thigh. Small bumps of pleasure erupted over my skin. "I'd fight the most ferocious of beasts... to gain your love."

Osirus continued to kiss my chest, but my arms slackened around his body. He stopped kissing me and put his hand up to my cheek.

"I mean every word," he whispered.

Smiling at him, a lone tear fell down my cheek. How did I get so lucky to be paired with this Fae? An emotionally broken and lonely soul was granted the gift of a handsome man with a passion for me. Me, of all people.

"You don't have to do any of those things," I whispered to him as I cupped his face with both my hands. I stared into his golden eyes. His jeweled eyes twinkled in anticipation of what I was going to say that was on the tip of my tongue.

Call me crazy, but even though we met just over a week ago, I was already crazy for this Fae. He had shown more love to me than anyone. Bond or not, I was in love with him.

"Why is that my darling? Why can I not prove my love for you?" His voice was a whine. He was adorable, a king of a nation begging at my feet for what I am about to tell him.

"Because I already love you."

Chapter 26

Osirus

Dear gods.

She said she loved me. I had been blessed by everything holy in the Celestial Kingdom. This woman before me just claimed that she loved me. The purring in my chest grew painfully strong as I gripped her tighter. Her hips would have bruises for sure, but she just smirked at me. She fucking loved it.

"You love me?" I growled in her ear. I didn't know whether to be sweet and gentle with her or throw her over my shoulder and fuck her senseless.

In all of Hades' Underworld, what was wrong with me? This possessiveness, the protection, the drive to plummet my dick inside her slick cavern was rocking my emotions. Everything before her never mattered. Was never this strong. She would be my undoing.

"Say it again." I nipped at her ear as she jumped slightly.

Her smile tickled my cheek as I continued to kiss down her neck. "I love you, Osirus."

That did it. That woke up the Fae animal inside of me. I pushed her down hard on my erection. Her dress was already up to her thighs and her core was directly over my member.

Thank you for wearing a dress.

Melina let out a mewl of pleasure as I continued to force her down to ride my cock. Damn, she felt good. I needed more. She leaned her head back as I took a claw and ripped right down her dress, which made her scream. "Osirus, stop ripping my clothes," she whined.

I slapped her thigh in warning. "I'll get you more."

My lips were instantly on her pink, perky tits. My tongue ran over her nipple while I thumbed the other. Her hands were on my torso, trying to unbutton my tunic. Keyword *trying.* She was a fumbling mess. Melina's own body rocked into me, grinding on my painfully hard erection. Again, she whined, and I slapped her thigh harder, and she moaned. "You like it when I spank you, don't you?"

The hooded eyes told me no lie. I took her to the bed and grabbed the cuffs from the drawer. Showing her what I had, she nodded eagerly as I cuffed her and tied a rope around the cuffs to keep her hands above her. The rest of her dress was ripped off completely and only a black lace bra and panties graced her flawless body.

Shit.

The handprints where I slapped her thigh made my dick harder than it already was. Seeing the red prints of my hands on her thigh. The strain in my pants was too much, so I stripped down to nothing, this being Melina's first time seeing my dick. Her playful, seductive look quickly turned into worry as it sprung free. Glancing back at me and below my waist, she began to wiggle.

"Shhh, shhh, darling, look at me." I sat up next to her, my dick resting on her thigh. The warmth radiating off her leg causing to leak on her thigh.

Placing kisses on her cheek, she immediately relaxed.

"We are not making love right now; I would never tie you up and do that." I placed my hand on her inner thigh and her body leaned into my hand. She trusted me and I was trembling. Who knew that a week of staying close and helping the bond would put us where we were now?

I slipped my finger into her core and a small whine left her lips. She pulled on the cuffs, wanting to touch me, and I chuckled at her struggle.

"I don't know if I like this," she whispered as I continued my assault. It was more for my advantage, not hers right now.

"Oh, but I do, darling."

Continuing finger fucking her, I kneeled between her legs, spreading them wide open so I could watch her glistening pussy drip with her juices. "Darling, you are soaked."

Melina watched me lick my lips in anticipation as I took one long lick from bottom to top, lingering on her clit. My hands held her hips down as she tried to ride my face, and I sucked on her bud. Gasps and curses swept across her lips and with each curse that left her mouth, I slapped her thigh. My dick was so hard it was hard for me to concentrate.

"You like it when I eat your sweet pussy, don't you?" She groaned, and I slapped her thigh again.

Melina hissed, "Yes," with a breathy moan.

I slapped her thigh again. "Yes, what?" I growled into her cunt.

"Yes—" she paused as she tried to think.

Fuck, call me Daddy. I was chanting in my head.

"Yes, Daddy." Sweet Kronos, Rhea, and Zeus. I plunged two fingers into her core while sucking her berry.

"Osirus," she moaned.

The cuffs were clanging on the headboard, and, without warning, she fell off her high. Her hips thrust into my face again and again until she was spent. Working my way up her body, I released the cuffs, and her arms immediately went around my neck, and she kissed me passionately. While kissing and bathing in her alluring scent, I felt her small hand around my shaft.

I stiffened at the touch, and I really didn't want it to stop. Groaning, I jerked my hips through her hand, hoping she would get the idea, and she did. She held my dick and pumped, her grip tightening and then loosening, she was playing with me.

My lips let go of hers, and I rolled onto my back. She immediately got on her knees, kissing my neck, leaving love bites all the way down my torso. This would be great to explain to Alaneo tomorrow during training.

She reached my hip bones, and I grabbed her wrist. "You don't—" But I was completely cut off before Melina licked the tip of my cock. I threw my head back from how sensitive it was, I could have come right then, but what kind of Fae would I be? Holding back the best I could, I saw Melina smirking as she put her mouth completely around my cock, inching her way to touch my pelvis with her nose.

Good luck with that, darling.

To my damn surprise, she does. In what life did I deserve this?! The woman had no gag reflex and was taking me as one of those human vacuums. She sputtered a few times, and I grabbed her hair. She didn't have to do this but then she put her hand on mine that was on the back of her head.

Dear gods, she wanted me to lead this. *Fuck, fuck, fuck.*

I pushed her down, and she bobbed back up, only to repeat the process over and over. As she was fondling my balls and sucking me dry, my ability to last was gone and I was going to explode everywhere. Hell, had she done this before?

"Darling, get up," I strained, but she was unmoving, well, not moving off my cock, anyway. There was a slight hum, and I released everything I had. Melina continued to bob up and down until I was spent.

Her sultry eyes stared up at me, and I saw her neck strained back and I watched her swallow my seed. We were both hot and sweaty as I hauled her up to my chest. Her nose nuzzled into my neck as I pulled the sheets over our bodies. Letting out a sigh, she kissed my neck and my heart almost exploded.

"Darling—" I petted her hair. "—you didn't have to do

that," I whispered like it was some big secret between the both of us.

"I wanted to. I'm just worried about other things." The blush went from her face down to her chest, and I squeezed her tighter. My cock was already hard. She feared my ten-inch beast. Chuckling in her hair and cupping her cheek, I sucked on her bottom lip.

"We won't do anything until you are ready, darling. No rush. I promise you this." I used my fingers to tickle up her arm. "I will make slow love to you and make you so wet that it won't hurt the first time."

Her doe eyes glanced up at me and raised an eyebrow.

"Much," I added quickly. I cleared my throat. "So, how uh..." I trailed off, and she started giggling.

"How do you know all that...what you just did?" She kissed my neck again. "Well, let's say my adoptive family were very sexual. I may have been scared to do things at first with you because you are my first everything, but I was told how to get down to business. Tulip wouldn't let me be that innocent."

"I should send her a gift then," I mumbled into her hair.

Melina snuggled up against me again, and I could feel her eyelashes tickle my neck. She was falling asleep, and I had an entire date planned out. I would continue to 'date' her like she wanted until she was comfortable mating. Just knowing she wanted me, and she loved me would have me sated.

My thoughts still strayed to what will happen to her once the claiming officially happens. Faes, like Werewolves, bite or make a mark to ward off other males or females. There was no record of a human and a Fae pairing, and that concerned me the most. The goddess wouldn't have paired us if it was dangerous, but Melina could be out for days if the process were to be the same. I could feel my face contort in anger at the thought of anything happening to her.

Some scholars that I had spoken to were still researching, but all efforts were fruitless. We would have to continue to take it a day at a time. Right now, claiming her would be stupid. The rebellion was in six days, and I couldn't afford one day off from training myself and preparing the rest of the Shifter armies that are arriving.

However, keeping Melina safe will be number one. I had felt the heat of their stares from the upper west side of the palace. Every single one of them were pissed. They wanted the Court to have the upper hand, and they thought they were in the lead. In two years, I had to take a queen and now my destined was here and will take the place of Daphne.

I grunted silently, and Melina remained still. Petting her hair and tickling her arm, I could feel the warm breaths bathe my chest. No one will have her, no one will have my queen over my dead bloody body.

Lucca was another to worry about. Lucca was one of the Siren princes and had a nasty streak of stealing women from beaches and putting them in his harem. Once they were sucked into that whirlpool of madness, there was no escaping unless he let them out. He told people he saved them, but he was a crazy fish that even his own parents stayed away from him. Luckily, he was the youngest of the princes and would have no way to access the throne. Having twelve brothers would do that.

***

Melina slept right through our date and on into dinner. I didn't sleep a wink, just staring at her like the obsessed Fae I'd become. Who knew I would end up like the sap I was? Once she stirred, I could hear her stomach growling, and I couldn't help but laugh. Her eyes darted straight up to mine and whispered a small, "sorry," before peeling herself from my body.

"Where do you think you are going?" I pulled her back to bed and pinned her down.

She giggled and tried to push me off. "I have to go to the ladies' room! Let go!" She laughed as she playfully shoved me.

Taking the torn dress off the floor, she tried to hide her body as she tip-toed to the water closet. I've seen all her body and yet she still tried to hide from me. I smirked as she closed the door while she gave me a warning glance.

A banging on the door woke me from my stupor. I grabbed my Elven silk robe and walked to the door. Everett stood with a hand on his blade with a formidable expression on his face. "Cosmo from Court is here to see you, Your Majesty."

I gritted my teeth as I opened the door wide and headed to the living room quarters. He sat on the couch, rustling through some parchment. I cleared my throat and his eyes whipped to mine. Standing up, he took a bow.

"Your Majesty, most congratulations are in order for you and your destined." His voice strained. Returning to his stoic features, he handed me the stacks of parchments. "Here you will find your destined's new schedule. Since she is human, she will need to undergo rigorous training. The Court demands it and I'm sure the Parliament would agree."

I ripped the papers from his hand and studied them. She would be gone from sunup to sundown and even then, she would be forced to sleep in different quarters than I.

"The hell is this?" I growled.

Cosmo stood back and fixed his cloak. "She is human, Your Majesty. She has no previous training; she doesn't know the land or the cultures inside it. It is highly recommended, even demanded. She needs to understand what her duties will be. I'm sure you understand."

"My own mate is not to sleep in the same room as me? Care to elaborate?" I snarled at him.

Sweat was beading on his brow. "It is, so she isn't mated, Your Majesty. We don't know what will happen once a bond is cemented in place with her being human. It is just for precaution. She will be under constant guard. No worries about that." Cosmo waved his hand and turned his back to me as he walked to the door.

I chuckled, and my chuckle grew to a dark, sinister laugh. Cosmo turned around, gripping his small dagger. That's not all that was small. My laugh stopped and Everett and Alaneo were by my side in an instant, wondering about my next moves. Once calculated steps and planning were thrown out the door. My love was now sitting on death row. They were already planning her untimely death by their own hands.

Walking stealthily up to Cosmo, my hand grabbed around his thick neck. For a Fae, he was fat, a typical nobleman. "You can't keep me away from her, you pompous troll." My fangs had already grown three times the size while his eyes grew as large as moons.

"Think, Your Majesty," Alaneo whispered in my ear. My grip only tightened. If I think any more of this Fae keeping me away from what was mine, I will break his neck right here.

Chapter 27

Osirus

"Osirus?" the sweet angelic voice came from our bedroom door. Her head was poking out, her long dark hair cascading next to the door frame. "Is everything okay? I heard some yelling." Her voice calmed me as I closed my eyes, my hands still gripping on Cosmo's throat.

"Everything is fine, darling." I let go, causing Alaneo to release a large breath he was holding.

"Thank you, Hera," he prayed.

Cosmo coughed and rubbed his neck while glancing back at Melina. Rage filled me, knowing he was sizing her up and a small smirk played on his lips. He didn't know I could read his aura, his ill intentions, his hatred.

"I'm sorry, didn't know we had company." She ducked back into the room.

"Come, darling, I want you to meet someone." She blushed and looked back into our room.

"I'm not decent," she whispered.

My body couldn't stand it anymore, and I needed her touch before I lashed out and broke Cosmo's neck.

"Please," I said pleadingly, holding my hand to her.

Hesitantly, she stepped out, and she was wearing a white,

short silk robe. Her long legs were creamy and small bruises were on her outer thighs from me, grabbing hold of her just a few hours ago. I grinned, looking at my handy work. Alaneo and Everett dropped their mouths in shock, her hair covering the front of her body as she played with it nervously.

She appeared like a damn angel. Her bare feet padded across the floor and took my hand, and I held her close to me. Her short stature didn't go unnoticed by Cosmo as he cleared his throat. He knew it would be easy to take her down. No supernatural power, no protection spell, she couldn't even defend herself in this world.

"This is why she needs to be trained, Your Majesty. A queen should always be presentable."

I rolled my eyes at his statement. I was in my own damn robe, and we were in our own fucking chambers.

All the while, he's staring at her, giving her a hard look, and when I thought she would cower away, she stepped forward. "We are in our living quarters. Why the heck would I need to be in a dress? You were the one that came here unannounced."

Cosmo's face contorted from shock to anger while I beamed with pride. "Listen, here," he stated, "You are not queen yet, so I suggest—"

I cut him off. "I suggest you leave," I growled. "Go to the Court and the Parliament to get your order, but she stays with me, and I will take care of what she needs to know." Little does he know that by the time the Parliament assembled to conduct a ruling that it would be too late.

"Fine. Good evening, Your Majesty." Cosmo stomped out the door while Alaneo shut it gently.

"Who was that goon? I got the creeps from him. Why don't you, like, kick his butt or something? You are King, right?" Alaneo and Everett snorted a laugh while I pulled her into my lap and sat down.

"I can't just yet. At the end of the week, I certainly will." I traced my fingers on her thigh as she leaned into me. "There are a lot of moving parts to a kingdom. There are even things I cannot overthrow without the help of others.

"Is that when you plan to take everything over? Take care of the Court?"

I nodded solemnly. "We must. There are too many variables and the quicker it's done, the more I can concentrate on you."

She hummed as she nestled into my chest. "I just want to make sure the orphanage is all right. I'd like to visit them again this week. They have been through a lot, and I'd like to help give those women a break."

"I'll see what I can do."

Melina

The next morning, Osirus woke me at the crack of dawn. The suns were barely over the ocean as he got dressed. I groaned into the pillow, not wanting to move my body. Osirus decided to make me orgasm five times last night before we fell asleep. The Fae had some stamina. His tongue, his fingers, his hands touching every part of my body made me shiver. The thought of one day finally giving my whole body to him gave me tingles in... some places.

There was a point last night where I asked him to take me. I wanted to be his, fully. I wanted him to kiss up and down my body and thrust the beast inside me, but we had to wait. No one knew what would happen to me. We were going in blind once he bit me. My gut told me everything would be fine, but Osirus didn't want to risk it, especially since he thought I would be out for a few days either changing or accepting the bond in my human form so I could live for centuries as he can.

Throwing the covers back, I stepped into our closet and pulled out silk and leather riding pants and tunic. There was a tan leather bodice that goes on the outside of the tunic, giving me a very warrior princess look. The boots were tall and hit my knee, and there were riding gloves tucked into my belt. I loved the outfit almost as much as the beautiful dresses that Osirus liked to pick out for me.

A sharp sting on my butt had me rubbing it fiercely and when I turned around while rubbing the pain away. Osirus was in his work-workout. Loose tunic with an open chest, his lean muscles were on display. Hair was pulled back and showed off his muscular neck. He had a bit of blond stubble to match his platinum blond hair. He was more rugged than his normal clean cut, kingly look, and I loved it. This suited him so much more than what he appeared to be.

Once the Court was demolished and rebuilt with representatives, I hoped he would keep it this way. I licked my lips unknowingly, and he gave me that knowing smile.

"Enjoying the view, darling? Because I am really enjoying mine." His hand slithered around my waist and gave my butt a tug. "Your arse is so damn plump. I can't help but want to spank it until it's red."

I giggled and planted a chaste kiss on his lips. "Maybe later. We need you focused!"

The training fields looked a lot like the ones in Tulip's pack. There were stadium stands, large and tires, but no screens to strip out of clothes to shift. Some ladies liked a bit of privacy back home. Osirus brought me with him, he said I was never to leave his sight, which I'm sure will be difficult for him since he still had meetings to attend. I guess my afternoon naps were over with.

"Melina! Over 'ere!" Braxton waved me over. He was swinging a battle ax and throwing it at some targets while Osirus set up Montu for some riding practice with Alaneo. Braxton took a large ax and swung it towards the target and hit dead center.

"Nice shot!" I clapped.

Braxton did a mock bow while I ran to the enormous, wooded target. It comprised three large tree trunks stacked together with painted bulls-eyes in the middle. Something I would expect of The Red Fury. The axes were thrown so harshly that I had to use my full weight to pull them out. I could only carry one ax at a time back to him. They had to weigh at least 80 pounds apiece. Braxton laughed and took the one from me while he pulled the other three out.

"Are you here to train or just watch your destined and his rippling muscles?"

That didn't even deserve a response.

I pursed my lips and wiggled my mouth back and forth. "Both," said confidently. "Can you train me?"

"Sure," he said brightly as he threw the ax down. "What are your strengths?"

"Osirus says I'm pretty stubborn." I laugh.

"We all know that." He rolled his eyes.

"All right, I'm an excellent swimmer. I'm wicked fast." Back at my old pack, there were many times we would all race across the lake. I'd beat everyone, every time. Now that I think about it, they were Werewolves, and I kicked their tails with their stupid doggy paddle. Maybe Werewolves sucked at swimming.

"Well, the fight will be on land, so water training is out." Braxton got a smaller ax that looked like a toothpick compared to his ax. "Let's start with this." For the next fifteen minutes Braxton talked about the aerodynamics of the ax, the position, how you throw it, and a mini-history lesson on who created them in this realm. I was bored out of my mind. I finally grabbed it out of his hand and got into my stance.

"The hell is she doing!?" I heard Osirus dismount his horse. His light armor he donned looked like it was paper-thin. Braxton mentioned it was light as a feather and made by the gnomes. They worked with the metals of the Earth—I mean, Bergarian. They had perfected the ideal suit of armor for the king himself and his royal armies, and the wonderful armor comes at a price. It was expensive, but Osirus did nothing for the best for his armies.

"She said she wanted to train!" Braxton shouted to him as Osirus continued to walk up with long strides. His walk was powerful, the rippling of his muscles beneath the armor, his large gait and his flowing hair that escaped the band that held it back.

My mate was a fine piece of meat, and it was all I could do to keep my tongue in my mouth. How in the goddess I ever denied him, I'll never know.

"Like hell, she is," he growled. "You will be nowhere near the fight, Melina. Not on my watch."

"I don't need a dang babysitter! All my life, I took care of myself. I don't want to be some damsel in distress!" I huffed, crossing my arms.

"I said no! I will not move on this. Darling, you must see reason. You are human."

I bit my cheek. I was nothing but a porcelain doll on a shelf or a bird in his golden cage. One could reason that I was weak, I was human, but he could at least see that I wanted to be useful in some way.

I strutted up to him and whispered to him, "If you don't at least let me train, I won't let you spank me anymore." I crossed my arms and smiled.

"Darling," he bent over to whisper in my ear, "I think it is you that likes it, so you are really just punishing yourself."

"Tell that to your dick that was twitching while *your* hand trembled at *my* flesh," I whispered seductively back.

Osirus' breathing went heavy, his eyes growing darker by the second as he groaned.

I turned to walk away, grabbing the ax that Braxton set out for me. I knew I would not hit the mark, but dang. I wanted to hit something to let out the frustration. One swift throw and my ax flew and landed straight in the middle of the target. My insides were bursting with excitement at how I nailed the bullseye, but I kept my cool. I couldn't let them show my surprise.

Keeping my face stoic, I turned to Osirus and Braxton that

looked dazed, and tilted my head in amusement. Bring it on now, bitches. Of course, Osirus could see right through me and see my aura of excitement. He let out a hearty laugh as I finally cracked my smile.

Walking back over, I felt a tickle in my hand and held it up to look and found a gigantic black spider sitting on it. I. Lost. It.

Screaming as if my butt was on fire, I flung my hand around only for the spider to squeeze tighter. It was huge; it was holding my hand! Osirus frantically came up to me and held me tight, screaming at me what was wrong.

"SPIDER! OH, GODS! IT IS ON ME! GET IT OFF!"

Osirus snatched both my hands and grabbed it with his bare hand. Braxton, Finley, and Everett were looking on in worry as they had dropped the workout stations they were manning. Osirus opened his hand to find a tiny spider, no larger than a pea.

"Would you see at that? It shrunk! Do they do that here?" I asked, worried, still shaking from the encounter.

The Red Fury's boisterous laughter echoed across the training field. Osirus took the spider down in the grass. My lip wobbled as people were laughing at me. Maybe I couldn't take care of myself and I'm just a joke.

"Darling, come here." He held out his arms, and I buried my face in his chest to hide my face. He petted my head, chuckling along with everyone else. "It was just a spider. A small one, but just know I'll always be here to protect you."

I rubbed my face into his chest, and he kissed the top of my head. "I just don't want to be this frail, useless human," I mumbled.

"You are in a different world, Melina. You weren't bred to be the strongest physically, but mentally you are. On the first day out of the palace, you helped an orphanage. You can spot trouble a mile away. We balance each other out. You will help the kingdom grow in ways I would have never thought of. The Goddess of Pairing chose you for me. Just because you can't fight doesn't make you weak."

I sniffed, and I hugged him tighter.

Osirus always knew the right things to say. I could help in other ways, but the thought of him being alone during the fight troubled me. Where was I to go during all of this?

"You are handy with an ax. I say she keeps training," Alaneo says proudly. "Have some self-defense training. That way, if it is needed, she has it." Osirus nodded and agreed.

"HEY, MELINA!" Braxton yelled across the field.

We all turned, waiting for him to speak.

"How big was that spider again?!" Braxton started laughing, and I narrowed my eyes. He was elbowing his brothers while they were laughing to themselves.

"About as big as your dick!" I snapped.

Howls of laughter seeped through the field. Braxton put his hand over his heart. "Harsh," he mouthed.

Chapter 28

Cosmo

"Daphne!" I screamed in our large home. The home was massive and with just the two of us living here, it might be excessive, but I'll be damned if I had anything less. The cooks, the maids, the servants, and even the willing women were all worth it. All worth giving up my destined mate to have the power within the Golden Light Kingdom, one of the strongest kingdoms of all Bergarian.

"What is it, Father?" Daphne walked out in one of her new expensive gowns.

Lately, I had been showering her in jewels, dresses, and expensive lingerie for her to seduce the King. All now to be insignificant since he has his destined. Daphne should have worked harder, been stronger, smarter, and more seductive. She bedded him once and had the gall to order his servants around and rubbed the King the wrong way.

"Have you seen him today?" I growled.

The little wench should have. I'd ordered her, trained her, and supplied her with all the ammunition. It was just her using it that was the damn problem.

"Yes, Father. He said that little human was his concubine and nothing more." She flipped her fingers out to look at her nails as she fell to the couch. Not a worried bone in her body, that would change.

"Then you know she was in his bed chambers this evening, alone, with her all in a scantily clad silk robe, saying that she was his destined?" I all but growled. Her eyes fluttered up, a deep scowl on her face presented.

"What do you mean?!" she yelled. "He said she was a concubine, a meaningless one. One to even just to get me off his back and stop nagging him. He isn't keeping her!"

"Oh, he is keeping her, and he has claimed her as his. There is no mark, but who knows when that will happen? Did you not hear about the celebration in the marketplace? He claimed her for all to see. Your trip to the throne has been halted!" I threw my hands up in the air.

"For years, Daphne, you have been trained for this, to grab the throne, to put our family name in the history books, for us to gain power, prestige, and a talented army to overthrow the none-the-wiser Cerulean Moon Kingdom that are now sitting ducks at our feet. All for what? To sleep in his bed one night?" Daphne bit her lip back and narrowed her eyes.

"All to be nothing but a whore," I spat. This should have been a done deal years ago and now all of it will go down the drain. "Raised beside the King to be a friend, how many damn years did I spend on you? You are as worthless as your mother was in bed!" I threw the closest thing that was next to me, the family picture frame of Daphne's birth.

Daphne's mother was nothing but a pawn to get to The Court. I had bribed her father with gold, jewels, and information on the whereabouts of his own true mate, and he gave her to me willingly. Once he had his true mate, he was gone. Marriage to Daphne's mother gave me the title I had always dreamed of, being part of the Fae Court. Since it had been established, it had grown from a tiny seed to a beautiful garden of just the Fae people. No Pixies, Fairies, Whisps. The true and elite Fae will only be able to run the country. We are the perfected species.

Daphne screamed at the frame, falling to the ground, and breaking into a thousand pieces. She loved her mother, she still did, but her mother went crazy after Daphne was all of seven years old. Elaine craved for her mate, she was such a docile Fae and did what she was told until the day she could no longer handle my firm hand.

She cracked, refused to eat or drink, and now she was at the Institute of the Mateless. A waste of tax money. *Just let them kill themselves and be over with it.* It would be the first place to go once Daphne's place on the throne was solidified.

"You listen here, Daphne. If you want your mother to remain alive, you fix this. You get that weakling human out of The Golden Light Kingdom at all costs. The quicker the better. There is something brewing, and I can feel it deep within my gut."

Daphne smirked and crossed her arms. "You sure it isn't all the alcoholic nectar you are drinking? It could just be gas." I turned to slap her, but she pulled up her finger to wave it in my face. "Nuh uh, you can't mar this pretty skin if you want Osirus to have it."

I growled at her. She was right. I couldn't lay a finger on her; she was supposed to be my perfect daughter. Running my hand through my dark hair, I slapped the table.

"What are your plans, Daphne?"

Looking back up at me, she shows a devilish smirk. "Well, I have a Plan B since I figured there was something going on with this human the first time I met her. There is a Wolf that has had his eyes on her for quite some time. He came to the palace only a few days after she arrived, demanding to see her. He's chained up in the basement." Daphne rubbed her hands together and smirked.

Rubbing my thumb along my lip, I nod my head. "Show me."

Melina

After Osirus' training sessions in the morning, he had several meetings to attend to. Once it was announced that I was his destined mate, I had to look the part. Peoni and Primrose were in their grown size now, helping me get dressed in one dress Osirus laid out for me.

A gorgeous purple with small pearls decorating the hemming. It was simple and elegant, something in my wildest dreams I never thought I would wear one day. Primrose curled my hair and let it fall loosely behind my back. A small chain with a pink, teardrop shape diamond laid on my neck. It was beautiful, but not as beautiful as Osirus.

Swoon!

A large breath was blown out behind me, and I immediately knew it was Osirus. "Darling, you look gorgeous." He kissed my cheek. His attire was quite like what he usually wears to his meetings. A sharp-looking suit that made him look so much as the King he was. However, it was a deeper purple, matching my dress.

Aww, how cheesy, we match.

I giggled at him, and he gave me a questioning look, but I waved him off. Osirus led me down the corner, my arm in the crook of his, and led me to the throne room. Since he ran out the day before, he had to finish speaking with those he was unable to. The guilt turned in my stomach, but he immediately squeezed my hand, shook his head.

Now that I wasn't hiding behind the throne, I could see the full throne room in all its glory. The massive room was both tall and wide, able to hold thousands of people. There was not one, but five chandeliers in place. No chairs set up in the room, but there were benches that were near the tall windows that reached the sky lights. Groups of people gathered in different corners of the room with a paper in their hands, taking notes and questioning each other.

"These people are from outlying towns and territories of The Golden Light Kingdom. They come for either help, requests, or just giving me their reports for the past month." I nodded slowly, and he led me to the throne. I was expecting a chair beside him so that I could sit, but that wasn't the case. He picked me up and had me sit on his knee like a child.

"I don't think I like this," I side-eyed him.

"Behave, you are mine, and I'll let everyone know it."

"I'm not a child," I whisper yelled.

"No, but you can be punished like one." He nipped at my ear as I giggled. This giggling had to stop.

Cosmo stood in front of the stairs, leading up to the throne, and cleared his throat. I didn't like this guy one bit. He was rude, and pushy and the overall cocky attitude was a turnoff. "Your Majesty, if it be your will, I ask we conduct today's meeting promptly."

Osirus waved his hand, and Alaneo stepped forward. Alaneo was becoming a sneaky stalker for Osirus. I hoped he hadn't heard anything from our bedroom. "Attention, we will now begin today's proceedings. We will resume with the Dayfeather Tribe." Fairies flew up to the bottom steps of the throne. They were so far away that I could hardly see their faces, but the three had specific colors that stood out. The male wore blue and black, while the other two females wore pinks and oranges.

"Your Majesty," the male in blue bowed. "We bring our Fairy count census for the year. We also request aide for your protection." Osirus waved his hand for him to continue while another servant took their census. "We have been troubled with Macklebees." Osirus rubbed his brow and was about to speak before Cosmo broke the silence.

"Macklebees are none of our concern or are worth fighting off. They are insects, not a large animal or supernatural, that can cause actual damage," Cosmo spoke condescendingly.

"What are Macklebees?" I whispered to Alaneo.

"There are bees about the size of fairies, nasty little buggers that pack a punch when they sting. They can kill Fairies instantly." My fists tightened. Cosmo just wants the Fairies to suffer like that?

"Please," the pink Fairy spoke. "They have ruined our crops and several of us have been seriously injured. We can't fight them off in our larger form for a long period and they are reproducing at an alarming rate around our village. Their own natural predator, the bear, doesn't live around us. We don't know how the Macklebees got there in the first place! They are a rainforest-type species."

"That isn't our problem, the King-"

"Will help," I spoke boldly. Osirus smirked and held his hand on my thigh. "The King is supposed to help all his subjects. Why would he not help the village of Dayfeather?" The room became quiet, too quiet. All were looking up at me, but I kept my face pinned on Cosmo.

"They are all but Fairies, Melina," Cosmo said passively.

"You speak to her by her title, Speaker!" Osirus yelled. Faes in the room backed up in fear. "She is right. We help all the kingdom. Alaneo, grab the General of Subject Affairs and relay to him the information and get a team out there." Alaneo did a slight bow and smirked at me. I was still angry and the Court Speaker. He was to speak for the people and obviously he wasn't.

"Easy, darling. I know you are angry, but we must be slow." I leaned back in his arms, and he pulled me close, kissing me slowly and sweetly. He parts our lips and looks into my eyes. "You will be an amazing queen."

"I hope so," I whispered.

The next several hours had passed, and I kept my mouth completely quiet. Cosmo would often butt in to give his own opinion, which Osirus ignored blatantly, which only fueled his fire. I know The Court was corrupted and, even with Cosmo blatantly rebutting everything other than the Fae people, it was apparent things must change. I'm just glad that Osirus cared for his entire nation and species instead of just the Faes.

My eyes were growing heavy, but my bladder was full, so I had to nudge Osirus during a five-minute break between meetings. "I need the lady's room," I whispered quietly, and he only chuckled. I had been so comfortable just sitting on his lap, but I also really needed to stretch my legs.

"I'll come with you," he muttered, and we both stood.

"Your Majesty, a word?" Cosmo gave an enormous smile and held out his hand.

Osirus looked down at him and gave him a firm, "No."

"Your Majesty, it will only take a moment. You can have your guards escort her so we can talk in private. It is rather urgent. It involves the Gnome Chief." Osirus looked to Alaneo and the Red Fury and nodded. I was going to have an entire entourage to the bathroom.

"She never leaves your side," he warned, and he pecked my lips lightly. "Be back soon, my queen." I laughed and gave him one more kiss. If the bond was strong now, I craved what would be next.

Two guards in front, a guard, and an adviser behind me, they lead me to a private bathroom in a secluded hallway. "Be quick, Your Majesty," Finley warned after returning from scouting the bathroom. I gave a mock salute while they laughed at me and entered.

Washing and drying my hands and one quick check in the mirror for any yucky crumbs mascara can leave behind. I walked out to an empty hallway. Not good. This told me bad news was about to happen. I had two options: stay put or run and find the throne room as quickly as I can. Why wasn't my red fury out here?

Preferring not to be a sitting duck, I ran. I continued to run until I hit the throne room doors and swung them open to find no one there. The room was still well lit, but absence of people had my gut churn. There were no sounds, not even birds on the outside and my slippered feet were making all the noise. My heartbeat was thrumming in my head in panic.

The door behind me creaked open, and it was taking

every ounce of power to turn and see who it was. I had not been afraid when I first found out about Werewolves and the supernatural. It all fit into place. My only fear was my emotions and getting hurt again, which I never should have been afraid of in the first place. This time, I have something to be afraid of. I'm the target of the entire Fae Court, Daphne, Cosmo, and who knows who else.

So here it is, I'm going to fight, whatever that might entail, physically, mentally or with my wits because by gods, I was going to get the happily ever after I freaking deserved.

Chapter 29

Melina

"Carson?" His face was no longer carefree, and his brown curly wisps of hair had darkened from the last time I saw him. Small black veins were adorned on his shirtless chest. Carson was the last person I thought I would see here at this moment.

"Melina," the voice was strained as he continued to walk toward me. "I need you to come with me." There was something wrong, all of this seemed wrong, and my legs wanted to move but I couldn't. I was paralyzed in fear.

"W-what are you doing here? Where are Rex and Sean?" I had never seen Carson without the other two, they were the trio that always stuck together to get the women they wanted, yet all yearned for the day they found their mates.

"They are waiting for us. We need to get you to safety. There have been some disturbances in the Golden Light Kingdom and Luna has sent us here to retrieve you and bring you back to the Crimson Shadows Pack, where you will be safe." Carson told me he and his friends were the top trackers in his pack, that was for certain. He tracked me all the way back to the Golden Light Kingdom and knew exactly where I was. He was on suicide missions before to save Luna Clara. Was this really a rescue mission or something more?

"We don't have time, Melina! We need to go. The enchantment will only last so long." Carson took a few steps forward again, but I stepped back. The look was hardened as he continued to hold out his hand. "I told Luna I would keep you safe. I kept you safe in my pack when you visited. You must trust me."

Osirus' face flashed in my head. No, Osirus was to keep me safe. Osirus would have told me if I needed to leave. He wouldn't keep these things from me. What was that code word he used when he told Primrose to halt the Wolves from coming to protect me? Axis. He would need to know that word to execute a plan.

"What's the code word?" I stood firm; my stance unwavering.

His eyes went from confusion to anger. He didn't know. I was in danger from someone I thought was my friend.

Carson lunged at me to grab my arm, but I darted away. I knew I couldn't outrun him, but whatever enchantment powers were on the room was had to fade. I just needed to stay away until then. Carson snarled as I went behind a large table sitting in the room that was used for signing documents. Time, I needed time.

"Why are you doing this? What have I done to you? I thought I was your friend!?" Keep him talking, buy some time. Carson leaped and jumped on the table, his feet were bare and dirty, claws were transforming on his feet and his hands. A large growl ripped through the room as he snarled with drool coming from his mouth. Bits of foam dripped to the sides. Was he rabid?

Carson jumped, and I dove under the table. The claws made his footing slip, and I ran out of the ballroom, closing the door and hastily pushing a large chair under the doors. He could come through that easily, so I ran. Down the hallway and through the lighted windows, I found the bathroom I had emerged from. Instantly drawn to the door, I pushed it open, only to be sucked inside and spilled out of the other. Instead of the bathroom floor, I was back in the hallway with the Red Fury and Alaneo staring at me wide eyed.

"Gods, Melina, are you all right?" Finley picked me up off the floor, sweat was dripping down my face from running, the heavy breaths were tight in the corset I wore. Finley looked me over carefully. He had become a brother I never had how he looked after me. If I wasn't so distraught and confused, I'd throw my arms around him and let him know how much it means to me.

Alaneo approached and saw my confusion. "What the hell happened, Your Majesty?"

"I-I don't know. I was here, but I wasn't! Everyone was gone when I came out of the washroom. Then Carson, showed up, told me I had to come with him, and I knew something was wrong. I told him no, and he chased me! Gods, he chased me until I threw myself back into the washroom and fell out here!"

Everett, the bulkier of the three, picked me up, one arm under my legs and the other behind my back. Being thankful, because I'm not sure if I could walk, he carried me back to throne room with three other angry Faes. Everett's nostrils flared and held me tightly. He was being so protective of me but all I wanted was Osirus.

Osirus' back was to us as he continued to talk to the Chief Gnome. Sensing my presence and knowing I had entered the room, he turned around to smile, but quickly faded when he saw me in Everett's arms. "What's he meaning of this?" Osirus yelled and I wiggled out of Everett's arms.

Running to him, I grabbed on to his neck and pulled myself closer. "Someone tried to take me," I whispered. Osirus' grip became strong as he gripped me.

"Who?" he growled.

"Carson, from the Crimson Shadows Pack." Alaneo walked up to Osirus and put a hand on his shoulder to whisper in his ear.

"Not here Osirus. Let me get a witch to check the enchantment and find the source."

"Good, I'll contact Clara." Alaneo walked away, and Osirus grunted, causing Alaneo to turn.

"Tomorrow," Osirus spoke harshly. Alaneo nodded his head reluctantly once and walked out the door while the Red Fury stiffened.

"This concludes our meetings for the day," Osirus spoke. "We will resume tomorrow at 8am." Murmurs were heard around the room as Osirus pulled me to his side to leave the room.

Back in Osirus' private office, he had me sit on his lap while Alaneo finished his research. Finley was pacing with his sword at his side, fiddling with the handle. Everett continued to sit in his chair and stare at the floor while Braxton looked out the window.

Osirus made me tell him the whole story. No detail could be left out, and he made me repeat the story again and again to make sure. Apparently, women just can't remember things properly or men just have a hard time remembering themselves. It was confirmed that it was an enchantment but from who, where it was cast and if Carson was bewitched, was still up for debate.

The look Carson had in his eyes was barren, empty. I knew it wasn't the same Wolf I met just weeks ago. He was so fun, full of life and happy to be where he was. He obeyed Alpha Kane and was loyal to the Luna.

"Your highness." Braxton opened the window to find Leah, the Pixie flew in and fell on the desk. Osirus held me close while Finley fetched some water and Leah hopped up quickly to guzzle it down before a sequence of bells filled the room. It was frantic and wailing. Osirus' gaze was harsh as she continued to talk while he nodded, understanding every word. The Red Fury sat and watched the interaction, but their faces gave nothing away.

"Thank you, Leah. Please rest." Without another ring, she

left the office for our living room.

"The Wolves and Dragons are on their way; they will arrive just before dawn. This will all be over with in the end of the week." I squeezed Osirus' hand, and he pecked me on the cheek. "As for Carson, he asked for leave three days after we left the Crimson Shadows Pack and was supposed to report back yesterday. Alpha Kane has a search team in place. Even his own posse hasn't seen him." Osirus frowned.

"Why would he come here? I don't understand," I asked.

"You are so blind, Melina. You are a beautiful woman. I'm sure he wanted to have you come back with him," Everett spoke while Osirus gripped me tighter.

"Mine," he growled. The hair on my arms stood up and Osirus palmed my thigh, his nose in my neck.

"No, that isn't it. He talked about finding his mate and how he looks forward to the day! Something is wrong, he must be possessed or something," I said, panicked. The door slammed open and Alaneo walked through the door and did a quick bow to Osirus.

"An entire coven is working against us, Your Majesty. The Blood Coven near Vermillion. The people are following their leader, Sorceress Prinna. She pulled her powers from the coven to create the Enchantment of Projection." The room stiffened, but Osirus relaxed back in his chair.

"Thank you, Alaneo. Where did you get this information from?"

"Pluto, the Seer. He said it was information that should be known," said Alaneo. Osirus pursed his lips.

"What's a seer?" I asked quietly. Alaneo gave a small smile.

"A seer can predict the future but is only allowed to tell certain things. They cannot alter the future but can help those whose future should be the destiny. We don't know who will win this fight, but we know he can tell certain parts of the future. With him giving us this tid-bit, we maybe on the winning side."

"How do you know he isn't lying, though?" My trust

issues come to the forefront.

Alaneo tightened his stance and nodded his head. "We don't."

"Darling, I want you to come meet someone." Osirus' fingers were intertwined in mine, but his face became the stoic king I first saw at the Crimson Shadows pack. He was back into his role, the leader of a nation, one to protect from any outsiders.

Osirus stood up from the chair and had me follow him, leaving his men behind.

The walk felt long as we walked through several corridors and finally outside where the suns were shining. If only the suns knew how dark inside the palace had become. The danger was here, all the danger that Osirus said would come to haunt us was here and now it was not to just get me, but Osirus too. To bind him down and to be ruled over by his very own government that had corrupted themselves.

Rounding the palace, a large rock face cavern. The opening was massive and settled right in the middle of the large stone face. "Horus!" Osirus shouted from the entrance. Large banging against the ground made small rocks tumble from the top of the entrance to the bottom. The pebbles shook violently where they sat until a large animal approached the entrance.

I gasped at the sight. It was a large golden Dragon, its scales almost like mirrors of the suns themselves. His talons were white, long, and sharp, with bits of dried blood between his toes. The jaws of the creature were large as well as the teeth. Some may have been as tall as me. The Dragon itself was taller than two elephants toppled on each other and who knows how long the creature was?

The wings that were neatly folded to his body looked strong, full of muscle and power. The wingspan would be enormous to hold the sheer power of this Dragon's body. Osirus tugged at my arm, pulling me from my trance, and led me forward. I trusted Osirus, but this beast gave a whole new meaning of the word trust. Horus could stomp on my body without a second thought, and I would feel but like a pebble under its foot.

"Darling, this is Horus. He's our Dragon." Our Dragon? My words had left my brain as I wrapped my head around this creature. Fairies, Werewolves, Fae, Shifters, all that registered but an actual Dragon in front of me took the cake.

"N-nice to meet you?" I stuttered. Horus just bowed his head and blew through his nostrils in acknowledgement. Gripping Osirus' hand tighter, he chuckled at me.

"Don't be afraid. He is the most trustworthy Dragon in all the realm." Osirus went to pat him on his neck and Horus purred in contentment while closing his eyes. "Dear friend, this is Melina, my destined, my mate." Horus's eyes lit up and flickered with flecks of gold. He took two mighty steps to where I was standing and rubbed my cheek with his nostrils. I started laughing at how it felt, it wasn't hard like I thought it would be with the sharp scales, but smooth and cool to touch.

Horus was a magnificent creature. No one could even use words to describe how beautiful he was. His eyes were like a cat's, his dark pupils opening and closing as he adjusted his vision to see every detail that was on me.

"Not a shifter Dragon, right?" Horus huffed and growled in his neck.

"No, no," Osirus laughed. "He is a proper Dragon, much stronger than any Shifter Dragon. He is one of the last of his kind that live on the mainland. Most have flown off and stay away from us two-legged folk." I chuckled as Horus came up to me to continue to inspect, rub, and smell me. He was like a giant puppy, enjoying his scratches under his jaw and even rolling on his side for belly rubs.

"Darling." Osirus' smile faltered as he became serious. "With what happened today, I'm going to have to change some plans." Both his hands picked me up from the ground, taking me away from loving on Horus. Osirus' eyes held pain, which only made me panic.

Osirus sighed. "I'm going to have to send you away."

Chapter 30

Melina

"What?" I whispered. "You are getting rid of me?"

"No, darling, listen. I'm sending you somewhere safe, where no one will harm you. The battle is happening tomorrow. It cannot wait any longer. Your life is in danger and the threats are becoming real. I must strike now before all this planning is for naught." Osirus shook his head.

"The only thing I got out of that was that you are making me leave, away from you. You promised you would never leave me and now you are sending me away!" I yelled. My heart ripped in the places he had so meticulously stitched up. The fear of abandonment, my parents driving away in their brand-new BMWs, all came flooding back. I had been alone for so long, so many nights huddled in the corner of a room watching movies, reading books, and looking out the window. Tulip's family was nice and took me under their wing, but it was different. I couldn't help but see it as pity. Their family was whole before I even arrived, and I was just the little extra child forced in with a bunch of Wolves.

"You can't do this," I begged. The strong, independent woman who didn't need anybody now needed someone, him. This man had broken down the fortress around my heart and now all he was doing was solidifying another wall, an impenetrable one. I never wanted to let anyone in for fear of them leaving. The thought of Tulip living in the Crimson Shadows Pack and not coming back with her own mom and dad had me breaking. Now, the man that is supposed to be my mate was making me leave.

Sure, he was trying to save me. He was trying to protect me, but the thoughts of my own parents leaving had ripped open the stitching of my heart. I was bleeding out, and I didn't know if I could recover from this. I was still the broken girl whose parents left her at thirteen, but this time I didn't know if I had the strength to keep going.

"Once this is all over, I will come retrieve you, Melina. This isn't forever, just until we've won." Osirus' face became softer, his hand touching my cheek, wiping away the stray tears falling. "Horus is powerful. He is taking you to the Isle of Dragons. No one can go there unless invited or brought specifically by a Dragon. There is a small cottage there that will have everything you need."

I backed away from him, my hands no longer feeling the tingles that he usually leaves on my body. Now I was feeling nothing but anger, hurt, resentment. He was leaving me and, as selfish as I was being. I didn't care. I had taught myself to be strong, not to rely on others, and he taught me to trust him, to know he would always be there. Now he wasn't. I was confused and conflicted about my feelings. I thought he would send me to some underground bunker where I could stay at least near him and not on some island who knows how far away.

"I see your anger, your fear, darling. This is not forever. I will come back to you. I want you safe. Please understand that." Osirus was pleading with me, pulling me to his chest and rubbing my hair. What kind of queen would I be anyway, being spoiled and not wanting to let him go? He had an entire kingdom waiting for him and I was wallowing in self-hatred and pity. I didn't even have some witty comment to come back with. I really was pathetic.

"I'll do as you say," I sniffed and backed away. Alaneo walked from behind some bushes and held out two large bags and wrapped them around Horus.

"Don't be like that, darling. I love you, and I'll be damned if anything will happen to you." Osirus' fists clenched as he held onto his sword. He came in to give me one last hug, but I stepped back. I was being selfish, sure, but he was deciding things without me. We were a team, and he just shipped me off without talking to me about it.

He should go rule his kingdom and take care of his people. I was getting in the way, anyway. Just like how I impeded my own parents' dreams.

"Darling..." His face was saddened. Even with the stoic kingly face, he had on, I knew he could read my heart. It was broken and all he could do was watch as Alaneo helped me climb onto Horus.

"Could Tulip come with me? Or even Finley?" I asked, without looking at him.

Osirus' gaze fell to Horus as he scratched his chin. "I'm sorry, Melina, but they are fighting, fighting for us." I nodded my head and held back a sob. No one. Utterly no one.

This was it. I was going to be utterly alone for who knows how long. He might physically fight off the country's demons, but in my heart, I was fighting them as well. The loneliness. I was going to be lonesome for a while. All those moments we have already shared, sleeping in each other's arms was going to be fruitless. It was going to be like he was never there. Who knows if I will ever sleep that well while I'm gone from him?

How stupid of me to get so attached.

More sleepless nights, and not because I was going to be alone, but because I was going to miss him. The bond was the most messed up thing anyone could ever have. Even though I was thoroughly angry with him, I still wanted to be by his side.

With a nod, I let him know I was ready to go. My legs gripped tightly against Horus' neck and shoulders. I should be terrified of flying off with a beast that could rip me to shreds, but instead, I was more afraid of losing Osirus.

"I love you," Osirus spoke loudly.

With one last glance, I looked him square in the eye. "I love you too." The worst part was, I did love him. Even though the hovering thoughts of everyone leaving me behind weighed on my shoulders. I couldn't look at him anymore and Alaneo slapped Horus's haunch, and he started running. Horus unfolded his wings as he ran and quickly ascended into the sky as his claws bounced up into the air. I didn't feel the adrenaline rush, the butterflies in my stomach at the thought of flying on some fairy tale Dragon. Daring not to look back, I held onto Horus's neck and cried a thousand tears as he carried me away from the one person who I had let my walls crumble for.

Osirus

Horus had taken flight in the clear sky. The light sources were falling into the horizon as they flew towards it. This was the hardest decision that I had to make, to make her leave to guarantee her safety, but it was for good reason.

Her heart broke into a million pieces. My darling thought I was leaving her for good, but it was far from it. She had no power to protect herself, and I had to have my full head in this battle. This was for us, for her. Being around her had given me enough strength to power through this, and once this is over, I'll make it up to her. I just prayed she would eventually understand.

With the witch coven coming to aid Cosmo and Court members, I knew time was short. He felt threatened that Melina was here, so his very own plans were forced to come quickly. "Your Majesty?" Alaneo spoke softly. Alaneo had mentioned it before, having Melina fly off with Horus and into The Isle of Dragons. I was the only Fae that was allowed there since I saved Horus when he was still a hatchling.

"What is it, Alaneo?" I spoke, sullen.

"The first wave of shifters has disembarked; they are awaiting your orders at the Northside of the territory. Leah has also returned and said the Dragon Shifters should be here by dawn." I continued to stare off into the distance and walked to the stables. Montu was going to have a ride ahead of him. The Northern part of our territory was rocky terrain the last stretch of our journey, but it had to be done. We would get no sleep tonight as we waited for the final rounds of warriors to come through.

As much as I wanted to hold off another day, I feared we may have already lost our timing. Cosmo may have wanted his daughter to marry me to gain more power for himself and control his daughter, but now we are on another level. Cosmo talked to the Chief Gnomes, and once he had left to order some other defenseless creatures from our kingdom around, Osmond was able to give me a warning.

Osmond was a good chief. he was for the rebellion against the government and said he would send the finest of metals and shields for the battle. He could not supply us with soldiers since they are a smaller territory but wished us the best of luck. Food, water, and supplies would be sent if asked. Cosmo had threatened him and his people for their silence during any uprisings the Golden Light Kingdom may have, and instantly, he knew something was going to transpire. It is good to hold alliances with even the minor territories around the kingdom.

"Montu, my friend. Let's ride." With a quick huff, we set out at a galloping speed, along with Alaneo and the Red Fury, as Melina likes to call them. They were all very similar in looks, but their personalities were gravely different. Without them, I don't think I would have had the drive to change the kingdom, however, first seeing how happy and peaceful their tribe was before the squalor with rogue vampires made me realize the Fae people could be happy and not have a terrible caste system like humans used in the middle ages.

To work for what you earn, to help those in need, to give to those that needed it the most, was going to be our stand. The Werewolves adopted this quickly in their early years and somehow the Faes never seemed to acquire it. Now was the time, with me being the strongest Fae King in both physical and magical attributes. We will succeed in a reformation.

The push I needed was Melina. My stony heart broke when I first laid eyes on her. From the instant she spoke about having representatives of all territories and subspecies as the Court instead of just the Faes, I felt pride within my heart. She may not have queenly training or a higher education like most queens were subject to, but she had heart. She thought her physical capabilities held her back and made her weak, but she was far from it. In fact, she was strong. She just needed to see that within herself.

She felt alone all those years and finally breaking through to her gave me hope she would trust me, even when I sent her away. The look in her eyes as she broke into a million pieces crushed my soul. We are not bonded together yet, I felt her pain and the rejection. She understood she could not be here, but just now, coming to love someone and having a bond so strong would break her.

Not understanding what was happening to her, her emotions were running rampant. She loved me. I knew she did. Part of her aura understood that and understood why she couldn't be here. However, her past haunted her again and I will have to save her once again from her fears.

I growled loudly as Montu continued to pound the dirt with his hooves. His angry breaths continued to follow the hidden trail up the path. I never got to take her on a proper date like humans do. There were so many things I wanted to show her, and now the land may be tainted with blood as we fight for the reform.

If I have anything to do with it, it will be a bloodless battle. I didn't want lives lost or blood spilt, but it was inevitable when demanding for power. I prayed to the gods that our numbers could exceed those that want the Fae Court to stay in power. I already felt that the Fae people, the commoners, will be with us in this revolt.

My heart heavy, my sword swinging by my side, we finally arrived at the make-shift camp. Wolves, Lions, Tigers, and Bears were scouting the area, looking to set up their own place to stay. Alpha Kane and Luna Clara come walking forward in their warrior gear, with Clara no longer pregnant.

"Princess, you should be with your pup. Congratulations, however," I smirked at Kane as he rolled his eyes. The Wolf will never like me, not really.

"I gave birth the day after you left and healed quite nicely. Evelyn will be fine with Kane's mother. I'm here for a good time." She laughed while looking at her mate lovingly. I still didn't understand what Clara saw in the Wolf, but they do complement each other well in controlling his beast.

"No word on Carson," Kane butted in. "He's as good as dead for trying to kidnap the future Queen of Fae." He growled.

"Babe, he might be under a spell. It doesn't sound right that he would do that to Melina," Clara cooed at her mate. "I say capture and question. Then if he really is guilty, you can do what want. What do you say?" She fluttered her eyelashes as he grabbed her by the waist and planted a passionate kiss on her lips. "Anything for you."

"All right, thanks for the show there, Princess." Clara blushed and giggled while Kane held her closer. I was ready to have Melina back in my arms and kiss her with the fire that burns within me. Her smell, her touch, and the light inside her...

"Let's talk strategies," Alaneo piped up, stirring me from my daydreams.

Chapter 31

Melina

We hadn't flown for long until we reached the ocean of the Eastern Sea. The water was how I remembered it the day I met Lucca; crystal clear. The dark outlines of large fish and the rocks on the ocean floor were easily seen, even from up in the sky. All and all, it was a beautiful sight. It only made me want to swim that much more in the cool water. Heeding Osirus' warning, I knew to stay away unless I wanted to get sucked down into the beautiful abyss by vengeful Sirens.

Looking towards the horizon, there was an island. Large trees and thickly covered mountains of vegetation hung sat high in the sky. I'm guessing it was the Isle of the Dragons. The waves were rough here in the middle of the sea, if one tried to come to the island, their boat would capsize in an instant. Large white caps crashed down on one another as the sea's tumult roared. Leaning over to get a better look, Horus gave a warning growl, and I sat back up straight in my seating position.

My tears had long since dried once we reached the island. Maybe time away from Osirus would be good for me, show that I am still that independent person and can take care of myself. I did it for how many years, anyway. I still loved and cared for him but was still brutally hurt by how easy it was for him to send me away. His face was masked, something he didn't do with me, but today he did. Possibly he was staying stronger for the both of us because he knew I would cry to still be in his arms.

He proved strong, and I left, not without showing him how hurt I was. I regretted not giving him at least one last goodbye kiss. I worried about him fighting in a war, even though his confident demeanor told me without question we would come out on top.

I let out an angry sigh. I'm so selfish. Got a little bit of attention and now I craved him like a child to candy.

Horus descended onto the beach. The sand was thicker than most, reminding me of oatmeal as my feet sunk further into it. It was warm and welcoming, and I relished every moment until Horus started nudging my back while huffing. He wanted me away from the beach.

I took off the bags that Alaneo had packed for me. There was food, clothing, and other necessities if I needed it, but that won't keep a roof over my head.

"All right, Horus, where is this cabin that I need to go to?" Horus huffed and pushed me into the sparsely spaced-out grand trees. It was enough space for him to wander with me as we came to an old path. The path was overgrown with moss, trees, and bushes, but just enough for me to get through without getting scratched.

Horus was walking slowly behind me and, since I wasn't walking as fast as he wanted, Horus sighed in frustration. "Fine, fine, I can run if you are bored," I said, agitated. I picked up my speed until his nose went through my legs and held me close to his face. I screamed, being lifted so high, but he only chortled at my silliness.

"If you could talk, this would be a heck of a lot easier. If you have all these magical powers, why can't you at least do that?" I crossed my arms and gripped my legs around his snout.

The cabin was small and quaint on the outside. It gave me warm feelings of my cabin back with Tulip's family, but there were subtle differences. This one had shells decorating the outside, and fishing poles hanging on the side of the cabin. The roof was mostly flat, covered in small, crushed shells and cement. If a storm came by, I doubted any of the cabin would move.

Horus let me down and laid on the ground and curled up like a cat. The sun fell directly on the extensive area cleared out for the cabin and Horus took that advantage to soak up the sun. His eyes closed and was asleep before I could walk in.

The cabin was studio like, the complete cabin was one room besides the bathroom. The kitchen sat in the far-left corner while the bed was on the right. A small two-seater table and one couch in the middle of the room. It was quite dusty and hadn't been used in years, so I got to work to clean it with the rags that held my bags together.

By the time I finished, it was sunset. Overall, it was a place I could see myself living in if I had never found Osirus. Who really knows how long I'll be here, so I might get a preview of that? Pulling some bread and cheese from one bag, I ate my dinner in silence.

Just two months ago, if someone told me I was to be on a Dragon Island with people trying to kill me, I think I would have slapped them silly. Now, here I am, eating cheese on a Dragon Island and sleeping in a studio hut in the forest. I started giggling. This was all just crazy! On top of it all, I fell in love with the King of Fae!

If my parents kept me, acted like they cared. I may not even be here. I could travel the world with mom or off to medical school, where my dad had studied. The light in my head went off instantly, all because my parents leaving, I could meet my soul mate. The lonely nights, the years of not being cared for, being loved by them was just a twinkle in time compared to the eternity I could have with Osirus.

Hearing Horus continue to sleep with his loud thundered

breathing made me sleepy, too. Stripping into some night clothes, I crawled into the bed. It was fluffy, soft, and warm. Even though it was comfortable and one of the better beds I've ever slept on, there was something missing. I knew exactly what the missing piece was, but he was far away from me, fighting a battle that his people deserved. *Just a few days of this.* I continued my mantra.

I smiled, thinking about how Osirus would look at Montu. The silver and gold armor dawned on his horse with his sword high in the air, waving around giving orders. Fighting with his men instead of behind his army's lines. Sighing dreamily, I rolled to my back, staring at the walls. I was lucky; he put up with my bratty attitude. I just wished I could say sorry, sorry I didn't kiss him goodbye.

Regret and guilt consumed me as I fell asleep late into the night.

***

The next morning, I was up with the sun. All the crying, self-loathing and guilt racked my mind last night, and I was going to be productive and do something fun. If I can't help Osirus, I could help myself by exploring an island few two-legged people can say they have explored.

Opening the door of the cabin, Horus's head perked up at attention and tilted his head to the side, examining me. He was a magnificent creature. Every time he moved, you could see his scales ripple and hints of light beaming from them. The golden sheen on his scales made him look perfectly clean and royal. Fit for Osirus, I suppose.

"Come on, let's go explore," I beckoned him. Rolling his eyes, he stood up while I continued to walk through the forest. Several animals that I had seen back in the Fae Kingdom: rabbits, birds, the crazy fairy moss that bursts into bits of light when you step on it. Those were the most fun. Every time I came by a patch of the purple stuff, I would stomp on it only to hear Horus chuckle behind me.

We continued walking on the same path for about an hour. There were plenty of stops along the way, looking at sleeping Dragons underneath the tall trees. Dragons napped a lot. They reminded me of cats and how they loved to sleep but also had that fiery spirt about them when they wanted it. Small groups of Dragons played with each other, nipping at each other's tails, and rolling in the moss. When I tried to approach, Horus would immediately put out his claw in front of me and keep me away.

The trees disappeared, and the light shone brighter. I could hear splashing and the rushing of water in the distance. Once we went toward the sound, we arrived at a beautiful spring. The small waterfall barreled down several levels of rock and stone that glistened as the crystal-clear water fell into it.

Immediately thinking of Tulip and our last encounter together, I sighed heavily. I missed her, and I hoped she was all right. Feeling the cool water on my feet, I had a rush of excitement. Swimming sounded so good right now. I smirked. There are no other people here so I should be fine, only Horus and he's a Dragon. Who was he gonna tell? I'm not near an ocean, so no danger here.

Famous last words.

Ignoring the thought, I stripped down to my bra and underwear. Running towards a rock and finally jumping in, I let out a small scream of laughter. Horus purred deeply in his throat as he sat by the water's edge. Both claws were one on top of the other, giving him more of the catlike appearance.

I laughed and swam back under the water, swimming towards the bottom. The rocks were different colors that looked polished. One would look at them and think they were polished jewels for a royal treasury. Picking some up and bringing them to the top, I looked at them in the sun. The one I picked up was a royal blue color, a sapphire. My eyes were memorized by the color until I heard a voice behind me.

"Beautiful, isn't it?" I screamed and threw the rock back in the water behind me and started swimming to the shore, only to be grabbed by my foot.

"Hey, now, not so fast." I was splashing like a mad woman while Horus hissed a laugh. My fear became wonder as I stopped struggling. If Horus wasn't rushing to the rescue, maybe I was all right. Turning to my attacker, I saw none other than Lucca.

"Ya see? That's better." The shock on my face was apparent as he threw back his head and laughed. "You are a strange one. I can't figure you out." Lucca grabbed my hand and pulled me to a nearby rock so I could sit on it. Being fully aware of my situation of just wearing a bra and panties, I grabbed my legs and hold them to my chest.

"Now, what is a pretty girl like you doing all the way out here?" He smirked as he leaned on the rock with his elbow.

"That's none of your business," I snapped.

"Someone grew a spine, eh?" Lucca swam backwards and laid on his back. "Must be something serious to get special permission from the Dragons to be out 'ere."

"Then why are you out here?" I asked.

"I'm not considered a 'two feet,' hence the fin." He waved at it nonchalantly.

"Oh," I sighed. "Well, what are you doing here?"

"That is a good question." He put his hands behind his head. "Every time you enter the water, I'm called to you. Not like a mating call, just a call. I sense your presence, and I'm not sure why." He hummed.

"If that is supposed to be some crazy pickup line, it won't work," I huffed.

"Princess, you are beautiful, but I'm not ready to start a war with the Fae against the water dwellers. Besides, you aren't my type."

"Well, good." I huffed. "How are you here, anyway? This is a freshwater source, and you are supposed to be in the ocean!" Lucca flicked a few stray leaves that were in the water away from him.

"All water leads to the sea, princess. I could swim up a stream or take some underwater caverns from the ocean, which is what I just did."

Lucca swam around on his back while Horus watched intently. A gleam in his eyes danced over to us as he looked between the two of us. An enormous grin showed all his beautiful sharp teeth.

"What's with him?" Lucca asked, and I shrugged my shoulders.

"Anyway," he rolled his eyes, "tell me about yourself, Melina. I need to figure out this situation between us or it will drive me mad."

"I don't think I should talk to you," I crossed my arms. "Osirus said you were dangerous."

"Yeah, what else did the little King say about me? That I abduct women and make them stay in my harem?" I blinked a few times and nodded my head yes.

"HA! Damn fool. Doesn't learn from his own experience?" Lucca throws a rock that pegs off a tree. "You have heard his rumors, right? He had sex with so many women, uses them, then throws them out like yesterday's garbage?"

"Yes, but he didn't, really!" I came to Osirus' defense.

"Same rumor 'ere, Princess. The only girls I take are the ones that ask to be taken to get away from abusing men or looking to start anew. They all have found their mates down here and never return to the surface. I guess the goddess has a funny way of presenting them to me while I look for my own damn mate." Lucca took another rock and threw it harshly against another tree.

"I never thought of it like that. I guess I was quick to judge. I'm sorry. This entire world is new to me. Don't know who to trust and who to stay away from..." My voice trailed away while Lucca raised his hand.

"It's fine. He thinks that way because he saw me take one of the Fae girls that was running to the water. She was trying to get away from some rutting Wolf that wanted to claim her as his chosen mate. I had told her the day before I would take her. She was just screaming for me to take her quickly." Lucca's face was forlorn. His mind was taking him to another place. I had a powerful urge to comfort him, a man I didn't know. His blue-green scales were darker than what they were the first time I met him.

"I'm so sorry, Lucca. I had no idea. What you did for those women, that is very heroic of you to take them in like that." Lucca scoffed.

"Doesn't really matter. I just don't want them to end up like my father did." Lucca bit his lip harshly but gave a sinister smile. "My mother wasn't my father's real mate all for political gains pushed by her. Once she found her true mate, though, she left him, she left us."

My heart broke for Lucca. He may have a family full of brothers and a father but knowing loss of a family member was something I knew all too well too.

"Your father still cares for you, doesn't he?" He nodded his head. "Very much."

"That's good," I whispered.

"And you?" Lucca pried. "Surely they were upset when their daughter got taken by a Fae," he snickered.

"Nah, they didn't care," I mumbled.

Chapter 32

Melina

Lucca and I continued to talk through the afternoon. He was really interested in learning more about Earth, so I told him how different it was from the land here. 'Boring,' is all he said as he continued to pelt rocks to nearby trees. The only good thing about Earth was the music and video games, he said. Even the boys here had their horrible hobbies. Bergarian received a lot of imports from Earth. They just picked and choose between what vices they want.

"You should come visit," Lucca said as I put my dress back on. "It would be significantly easier to show you than tell you about it. Atlantis has far too many wonders to describe with words." My mouth fell open as he spoke of Atlantis. "You mean Atlantis is real?" I gasped.

"Of course, it is, why, do people of Earth talk about it?"

"Yes, but they think it is a lost city that sunk into the ocean."

"No, it was never sunk. It has always been in water. A few sailors were brought there when they accidentally found a portal when they were tossed into the sea during a storm. They were healed and put back in their rightful place. We didn't want humans around the Bergarian world. I guess they couldn't keep their big mouths shut." I nodded my head in understanding. Crazy to think that all the fairy tales of Earth were just in a portal next door.

"I can't visit. Osirus could come for me at any time," I said matter-of-factly. Lucca scoffed and walked out of the water. His fin had disappeared, and a small cloth hung at his hips covering his nakedness. The scales on his body were sucked back into his body and his gills flatted next to his neck to hide.

"You don't seem like a woman that waits on a man." I perked my head up.

"I-I don't."

"Then you should come with me tomorrow. I'll take you to my friend Calista. She's part witch. Maybe she can help us figure out why I can feel your presence near water." Looking over at Horus for disagreement but he just nodded a quick yes. I was putting my faith in a Dragon. Then again Osirus trusted him.

"Fine," I deadpanned. "What do I need to bring?"

"Wear some light clothing. I'll be sure you have everything you need when we arrive. It's a bit of a swim," he smirked. Before I could object, Lucca jumped back in the water and with a flick of his tail goodbye, I gave out a loud groan. "What am I in for, Horus?" Horus huffed and stood up, ready to head back to the cabin.

Once back, I made myself an enormous meal since I had skipped breakfast and lunch. The few ingredients in the bag were able to make a sandwich. I'm sure it was all enchanted to keep it from going bad because the tomatoes and cheese looked fresh. I'll never get over how this world is so different from Earth. It seemed so long ago that I was there and knowing it wasn't home anymore made it all surreal.

After a long bath and bathing myself in vanilla body lotion, I put on a large tunic over my body. I knew it had to be Osirus' because it smelled just like him. My heart ached remembering he was off fighting, and I was stuck here without him. It was unfair. I couldn't imagine being mated to him and having to be away. Tulip said the bond wouldn't let you be without the other for too long or you got physically sick.

Bundling myself up in hordes of blankets, I made my little nest and tried to sleep, but the thoughts of tomorrow's adventure had plagued me. How was I going to hold my breath to get down to Atlantis and what would this Calista girl tell me? I have felt nothing towards Lucca other than something friendly and a bit of trust. Which I shouldn't. I should heed Osirus' warning, but Lucca's arguments were just. He could have been painted in a different light, just like Osirus was.

I growled out in frustration while Horus looked in my window with his eye. "I'm fine. I'm mentally frustrated!" I shouted. His body came closer, his head laid by my window. For a magical Dragon, I haven't seen many magical things come from him, but his ability to feel emotions was uncanny.

My eyes began to flutter faster and faster. I felt like I was falling asleep without even trying and darkness evaded my senses, only to have a bright light shine above me.

The sun was so bright, I couldn't see the figure's face that was right in front of mine. The ground below me was still soft, like the sheets I fell asleep on, but I knew I was outside. Using my hand to obstruct the bright light, I saw none other than my mate. His long hair was blowing in the wind, his tunic was off his body, and he had a smile to greet me. This was going to be an amazing dream.

Reaching for his neck and holding him close as I let a small sob fall from my lips. "I wish this wasn't a dream," I cried. "I'd tell you how sorry I am for acting like such a brat. I'm so sorry Osirus, so sorry!" As his arms pulled me to his chest, I continued to breathe. He was holding me like you would a baby and kept my head in the crook of his neck. "So sorry," I whispered as I held onto his arm that was stroking my cheek.

"I was never mad at you, darling." Osirus' voice was deep as I felt it through his chest. His linen pants tickled my bare thighs as they blew through the light wind. We were on the bed but in an open meadow just like the one in the Crimson Shadows Pack

territory.

"*I wish you were here.*" *I kissed his neck.*

"*But I am here, darling. I've come to you in your dreams.*" *I looked up at him, confused. "Doesn't this feel more real than an ordinary dream?" I nodded. It was different. Everything was de-tailed and wasn't tunnel vision like most of my dreams. I could concentrate on more than one thing, and Osirus would still be in my arms.*

"*I told you I was a powerful Fae. I don't think you really be-lieve me.*" *My eyes watered.*

"*You are here, right now, with me?*" *I asked hopefully. He laughed at my excitement.*

"*Yes, it is one of my gifts. I can control the weak minded or those that let me invade their minds, but also those who are sleeping. I've only done it to my family. Since you are my mate, I can do it with you too.*"

"*Ahhh, like sleep mind-linking, but in color!*"

Osirus threw his head back and laughed. "Exactly!"

I grabbed hold of him again and kissed his cheek. "I'm so sorry. I think I was trapped in a bad place when I had to leave."

"*I know you were. I don't blame you. It was difficult to watch you go, but it had to be done. The battle is almost over and then you can come home.*" *I sighed in relief. "Then I can make you mine," he spoke seductively.*

Looking into his golden eyes, they grew darker. Lust was pour-ing off his body, and my body tensed as his hands came down tightly on my waist. I let out a whimper and his nose traced my cheek. Waiting for the perfect moment, he struck his lips down on mine and kissed me passionately. His tongue licked my bottom lip, and I opened my mouth gladly. He explored my mouth as we both moaned. Osirus' hands pulled up the tunic I was wearing and felt my bare breasts.

"*Gods, did you do this for me?*" *Gripping ahold of my breast, he massaged and pinched my nipple that made my core wet with need. Tingles rushed through my body as I held my thighs together tightly. A small growl left Osirus' lips as he pulled the* tunic over my head, revealing not only my breasts, but my bare pussy.

"You do not know how much I want to fuck you right now." Pushing me to the bed, he sucked on my breasts while another hand inched down to my core. Grabbing his hair, I pulled the harder he sucked and nibbled. "Osirus," I moaned.

A slap to my thigh made me squeak. "What is my name while we are in bed, darling?" My body vibrated as he parted my folds to sneak a finger to play with my bud.

"Daddy," I whispered. His body shuttered and dove his finger into my core. A short scream left my lips as he pounded his finger into my body.

"When I have you, I'm going to stretch your hole so you can take my cock in your wet pussy. I'm going to make you scream my name, so the entire palace knows you are mine." My nipples puckered as he talked, my body reacting to his dirty talk gave me a wave of pleasure. I was close to my breaking point when he removed his fingers.

"Nooo!" I whined, but another smack came to my thigh.

"I will give, and you will take what I give you. You are being punished for being a brat yesterday." I groaned as he flipped me over, so I was lying on my stomach. Osirus pulled my hands above my head and made me grip the iron headboard. Osirus kneaded my ass until I heard a large smack echo in my ears. "Five, my darling. I am going to give you five." I was panting. This was turning me on so much it was driving me crazy. I could feel the juices dripping down my thigh.

After each smack, I replied with a thank you, and I whimpered. "Please Daddy, I want to come." Osirus smirked as he saw me looking over my shoulder. He pulled my hips up and made me kneel on all fours. He looked at his handy work. My butt was on fire, and I'm sure his handprints painted my white skin. One day I hoped he would pound me from behind. The thought only made my pussy pulse. Goddess, I'm a mess.

Osirus' head came between my thighs as he laid on his back, his mouth immediately finding my core and sucking enthusias-

tically on my clit. I tried to ride his face, but his hands came up quickly, steadying my hips so I wouldn't move. "I want you to scream my name when you come, baby." His mouth continued its assault as my legs shook. This was so intense, and this was only a dream!

My body came unraveled, and my arms gave way. Osirus quickly ducked away and pulled me to his side. His mouth came to my ear and sucked long and hard, only making me hungry for more. "I'm going to ravage your sweet pussy with my cock, darling. I'll fuck you so hard and take you over and over." Osirus' mouth made it to my neck, and he sucked painfully hard. A groan mixed with pain and pleasure filled me as I hunted for his dick with my wandering hands.

Gripping him with my hand as he sucked on my neck, I rubbed it up and down, rubbing the pre-cum around with my thumb. Bringing my thumb up to my mouth, Osirus watched as I licked his liquid off.

"Take me in your mouth," he commanded. His pants were off in an instant, not wanting me to have to work around them as I kissed down his delectable torso.

"All mine," I moaned, and he gripped the sheets in agreement.

Licking from the base of his cock to the tip, he sighed as his hand came to my head. With one swift motion, he pushed my head down into him. Gagging, I sucked him, milking him, trying to fill my mouth with his seed. Osirus' body was shaking. He didn't have to guide me. I felt what he needed, and I wanted to give it to him. My thighs were rubbing together as his groans grew louder. "Damn, baby, that's it. Fucking shit," he hissed as he slapped his own high. I sucked until there was none left and swallowed.

Crawling back up to his side, I laid on top of his chest while he petted my hair. "Gods, Melina, what do you do to me?" I giggled and kissed his toned chest.

"Anything you want," I said seductively.

Osirus smiled at me and petted my hair. "It's almost dawn. I'll need to get back." I gave him a squeeze, not wanting to let go.

"Hey now, I'll come visit again tonight." I beamed up at him as he pecked at my lips. "It's almost over Melina. Give me two days to get things settled."

"All right, please be safe," I nuzzled into his neck.

"Always, my love, stay out of trouble."

Blinking my eyes one more time, I was left in my room, alone again.

Chapter 33

Osirus

Waking up with a massive erection, one that I knew a cold shower would have a hard time to relieve. I had just visited Melina in a dream. I was shocked I could do so since she is a strong-minded woman, but while she sleeps and being my mate, I could penetrate her walls. As she slept, I gently eased my mind into hers. Most of her mind's layers were of untrustworthiness, fear, and pain. Untrusting because of the fear and pain of being alone once again.

That was the last thing on my mind as I made her fly off into the sunset with the Dragon Horus that had pledged his allegiance to me. He would have been great during battle but protecting the one thing most precious to me was more important.

I willed us into the dream-like meadow, the one that was near the Crimson Shadows house. You could easily distinguish the Cerulean Moon and Golden Light Kingdoms there. However, I seem to find colors that do not exist while I gazed into her sleeping form. She was the magic of this dream.

This place brought her comfort and happiness and our very first kiss. Melina was still laying on the queen-sized bed that I had left there in the Isle of Dragons on my last adventure with Horus. Many years ago, I had built the small cabin, promising myself I would bring my mate back with me. Unfortunately, she had to go alone to enjoy the small, pleasant life.

While in the dream, Melina's eyes were often clasped shut, her hands fisting at the sheets as she tried to sleep peacefully. The hallucination I had created in her mind felt real to me as I moved the hair from her face. Touch was hard to create while in a dream, but the strong pull I felt to her even now, it was easy to feel.

When she woke up in the dream, she was magnificent. It wasn't just the hallucination that I had willed for both of us. Her own body was beautiful without magic. Her eyes looked into mine and they were as blue as the Eastern Sea. I was drowning as I fell into her soul.

We couldn't help but touch each other as we rolled around in the bed, feeling, sucking, nipping. Gods, she was perfect. The night ended all too quickly, but both her and my mind were at ease where we stood together. Peace, longing, trust, patience.

This battle was about to be over, and she would be in my arms again. We would mate and rule over a new kingdom that she will help rebuild.

I let out a large growl at the thought she may be out a few days after our initial mating. It had been a mere 36 hours without her, and it had been dreadful. My mood soured, and my vengeance on those who have hurt subjects of our kingdom went without mercy.

"Osirus," Alaneo spoke as he entered my private tent. I sat up, staring at his army regalia. Being my right hand and advisor, he was one of the high-ranking officials that could call major plays during battle. "We have caught an intruder that was heading straight to your tent. I suggest you come for questioning." Alaneo's eyes were fierce at the thought of someone coming to harm me. I stood up, throwing my braided hair behind me, and shoved on my trousers.

"Give me a briefing," I ordered as I put on my armor.

"It's Daphne. She had no weapons but was determined to talk to you, saying it will swing the way of the war. It's urgent, and she gave us surrender." I scoffed. That woman won't take no for an answer. Daphne is bartering with her life and her father's. He's the main reason for this battle and here she was doing his bidding, again.

I flung the tent flap open and headed to the general's tent. Shifters sparred while Fairies in full form were putting on their armor. They could only last a few hours at a time in full form, so they have been working in shifts through the night.

"Your Majesty," General Storm bowed. "We have caught the intruder, Daphne, Cosmo's daughter, head of the Fae Court." Daphne was tied to a chair, unmoving. Her eyes were watering, yet not letting a tear fall.

"She came willing You Majesty, in fact, she had no weapons and held a white cloth waving over her head as she entered the camp." A sign of surrender. I grunted in acknowledgement.

"What do you want, Daphne?" I crossed my arms over my chest, my armor making a clanging as each bicep met my breast plate.

"I've come to bargain," she breathed. Raising my brow in question, her face was unmoving. "I know we haven't gotten along the past few hundred years, Osirus."

Alaneo growled out, "You do not disrespect your King!" Soldiers come forward and stiffened as I put my hand up to halt them.

"I'm sorry, Your Majesty." She lowered her head. "I mean no disrespect." Daphne had been a tough woman the past few hundred years, trying to be a seductress and get back into my bed. In fact, she had been relentless, but now I saw the meek and mild Daphne I grew up with. The one that looked to please others and the hard exterior broken. Her aura was oozing regret as she sat in the chair with her head lowered.

"You may speak freely, Daphne. However, I suggest you

choose your words wisely and not let a lie leave your lips." My words were harsh. She had still caused much pain to my mate just a few days ago and her own father was the one I was currently fighting against. He had hidden himself away like the coward, as well as some of his high-ranking officers. Having my own armies fighting blindly in their stead.

The Fae army believed they were fighting for Cosmo because I became unfit to be king. The lie helped along by magical charms of lies and deceit through the witch coven. They will be certain to pay later.

"My mother," she sniffed. "I've been this way because of my mother." Her eyes looked up at me. I didn't break my hardened looked as I nodded for her to continue. "Father wants the power; he wants control over the armies and to create the perfect race of Fae and when I was born, he thought I could win you over and be queen. All the while, he could use me to go behind your back and mold the kingdom the way he wanted it. I didn't want to do it, but he has my mother locked away at the Mateless Institution. If I ever wanted to see her again, I had to become queen. He's threated to even shut it down and let her die alone." Daphne sobbed. "She can barely care for herself. She's never met her mate, that's all she ever wanted!"

I knew of Cosmo and his marriage to Elaine, after his marriage I had forbade for chosen mates be brought into the Court. It was a tough law to pass, but luckily my parents were still available to sway some court members because of their long-standing history.

"I did those things for her. I had to listen to him. I've been playing his side letting him think I was working for her him, I swear!" Tears ran down her face and Alaneo looked to me for a decision. Her emotions were genuine, but I still couldn't trust her.

"What are you wanting in return, and what do you want to give me?"

"I want my mother safe. I want her protected so I can take

care of her and find her true mate," she breathed harshly.

"What will you give me, Daphne? Because right now I only want one thing." I took a few steps forward, standing in front of her.

"I'll give you my father's hiding place, and his nobles. However, I do have information about someone that says they are your friend but works for my father." Few gasps in the room. Someone among us was a traitor.

"You better not be lying, Daphne," I growled. She continued to shake her head, "No, on my mother's life I swear to you!"

"Name the traitor!" General Storm spoke as he banged his fists against the stone table.

"Peoni, Melina's Fairy Attendant," Daphne spoke quickly.

"You fucking liar!!" Alaneo roared. "She would never do such a thing! Where is your proof!!" Alaneo began pacing in the tent, angered that his current fling would do such a thing. I often wondered if it was a fling or something more. They weren't mates, but they had grown close the past year. Many Fae had their steady relationships until they found their mate. Faes didn't fare well being alone. Thank the gods I had Melina.

"Bring her in for questioning," I ordered one soldier. A swift nod from him and a few minutes later, Peoni came prancing in, wearing her armor. "Alaneo!" she whispered while she seductively waved at him. Alaneo's body went rigid and looked at her in longing. One of the soldiers told her to sit next to Daphne and Peoni froze.

Daphne gave an apologetic look while Peoni sat down. Her heart was racing, and her wings shuttered. "What's going on?" Peoni tried to play it off. "What do you need me for?" Primrose ran up to the tent, wondering where her friend could be, but stopped when she saw all the high-ranking soldiers and one angered Alaneo.

"Tell me Peoni," I gritted my teeth and felt the leather on my chest creak as I tightened my muscles in restraint, "When did you start working for Cosmo?" A gasp left her lips as she looked from me and to Alaneo.

"I-I w-would never betray you, Your Majesty!"

"Lies!" I roared. The betrayal was radiating off her like the light sources of our kingdom. Alaneo could sense my reading, and his head immediately fell. A hand went up to his dagger as he pulled it from his side and pointed it at her throat. For the first time, I saw his fangs and his claws emerge from his body. His eyes grew to a bright red as he narrowed them at her.

His own power was going to be shown if he wasn't careful.

"Do you know the penalty of treason, Peoni?" he growled. "Death, that is what you have earned!" I pulled Alaneo's hand with the dagger away from Peoni as she sobbed. "Why?" Alaneo's voice cracked. "Did you just use me to get what you wanted?" Peoni nodded her head as her tears fell again.

"Did you ever care for me? We aren't mates, but I cared for you," Alaneo whispered and put his dagger back in his belt. The room was silent, watching the altercation unfold; it was a damn drama all before our eyes.

"I cared for you, but then I found my mate a weeks ago. Cosmo had him in the cells and said he would kill him if I didn't do what he asked. I do care about this kingdom, but he has my mate!"

"You could have come to me, Peoni!" Alaneo yelled. "I would have helped you! You know I would have!"

A large cry left Peoni's lips. "I just, I just, I was so scared." Daphne let a tear roll down her cheek, the hardened soul of the last few hundred years letting her authentic emotions escape.

"I'm sorry, I didn't know," Daphne said. "I would have brought it up later if I had known he was threatening your mate." Now I had two sobbing women in my midst. Great. Can I just kill someone already?

"What did you do, Peoni?" I asked, trying to bring back

the awkward tension.

"I sprinkled the bathroom door with the alternant dimension portal so Carson could take Melina." I growled out in anger as my fangs descended. Peoni may have done this to save her mate but put mine in danger.

My hands went around Peoni's neck as I choked her with one hand. My inner Fae was screaming to kill her, to end her, for trying to take my mate away from me. I had waited much longer than she had to find her mate, and now I wanted her to pay.

"Your Majesty, please," I heard Alaneo as he touched my shoulder. I whipped my head around to let him know to back off. He bowed out, and I continued to strangle the traitor. "You will be locked in the dungeons until I know what to do with you," I spat.

Peoni dropped to the ground, and they took her to the make-shift prison we made in the northern part of our camp. Primrose had her hands over her mouth in surprise. Tears were in her eyes, her wings had drooped downward, showing her utter grief.

"Daphne, tell me where the hidden nobles are, so we can end this!" I snarled. "I'm done playing games. I want my mate and I want her fucking now, so tell me where they are, and I can't promise you they will be alive when I get my claws into them!"

Even though Daphne gave me the information I wanted, I couldn't trust her. She was put in a cell away from the other prisoners, just like Peoni. My anger rose within me, thinking my closest Fairy giving up all the information on my Melina. Not only did Peoni help put the enchantment on the water closet, but she also gave Melina's where abouts to Cosmo as she traveled through the city. They knew what we had done in the bedroom, watching to make sure I didn't mark her. Fucking sick.

Once everything was over, I would find Carson and Peoni's mate and figure out what to do with them at another time. Too much shit to deal with in such a short amount of time.

My heart hurt, knowing that we could have lost everything a lot sooner if I had not kept her by my side or had my own trusted guards watch her. Along with being betrayed by a close Fairy and the pain it caused, I could feel how dejected Alaneo was. A mate bond was stronger than any force, but Alaneo had fallen for Peoni. Their rendezvous were hot and passionate, and it was the first time in many years he had settled for just one Fairy. I prayed to the gods he finds his mate soon. I don't think he will ever be the same until he did.

The Fae Court cowards, as the soldiers had called them, found the miserable scum hiding in a dugout near the palace. It had running water, food, and electricity to help them hide for decades. They had planned to be safe while thousands of Faes did their bidding.

The Court was now dissolved and running on just my power alone. As much as any king would like to have that supremacy, I felt it was extremely unnecessary. The Court will be the representatives of the different races of Faes, and my say will be the ultimate law. How could a king rule and not listen to the hearts of his people?

I sat down on my bed in the palace. It was dark, with nothing to light the room. Even the moon was resting this night as I took off my armor. Without Melina here, it feels completely empty. The Shifters will stay for three days as we prepared the celebration feast, one that Melina should enjoy. I'll have the finest dress made and we will finally be together again. Afterward, she will become my mate.

Now that the day was done, and the prisoners were locked away, I could visit my mate one last time before I fetched her in the morning. For once in my life, my reality was becoming better than a dream, but for tonight I will now take the second best.

Chapter 34

Melina

"Damn, took you long enough to get here," Lucca complained as I trudged up to the spring. Horus was behind me, snickering and blowing bits of smoke through his nostrils.

I did not feel like I slept a wink the night before, which I guess I didn't. Or did I really? This magic stuff was weird. Osirus had visited me in my dreams and not once was I resting while he was there. The thoughts of him kissing me, touching me, holding me gave me the only energy I had left to walk the hour walk to the spring. Please let the war be over soon, I prayed wholeheartedly.

"Dear gods, what is on your neck?" My hand slapped at my neck quickly. I didn't have any concealer to hide the large mark that Osirus had put on my skin. That irresistible pleasure of him sucking, licking, and kissing could get my core wet in a matter of seconds, but the aftermath left me with a large hickey the size of a silver dollar. How in goddess' name it could show up on my body when he only kissed me in a dream was unexplainable. "Um, nothing," I said, embarrassed.

"Ah, did your king come visit you last night? Staking his claim? Gods, why hasn't he even marked and mated with you yet? Not that I really care for the guy anyway, but it's so damn old-school."

I rubbed the mark gently and stepped up to the spring and gave him a glare. "He's my mate, and I didn't mind it one bit. Now, are we going to get going or what?"

"Geez, all right, Princess." Lucca held up his hands in defense. "Don't go all barracuda on me. There are a couple of things we need to talk about first." Lucca dug in his bag that he had brought with him and held out a necklace to me as he stood on the sand.

"This is an enchanted necklace from Calista that will let you breathe underwater. We are borrowing this, so don't lose it." He glared at me.

"Watch it, fishy boy."

"I'm a damn man!" Lucca shot back.

"Well, half of one anyway. You are still part fish." Lucca growled playfully while I shoved him.

Looking back at Horus, he was shrinking, and my eyes shot open. "Horus!" He continued to shrink until he was the size of Osirus' gigantic horse. "He's going to let you ride on his back through the water. You say you are fast, but you don't have fins. We need to get there quickly so I can bring you back tonight or your little Fairy is going to get pissy."

"He's Fae," I snapped.

"Whatever. Now put the necklace on." He shoved it into my hand. It was a black iridescent shell on the fishing net string. Putting it on, I felt my chest grow heavy and I let out a groan.

"Quick, in the water. We won't be able to talk to each other, so just hang on to Horus." Horus scooped me up by nuzzling his head under my legs. The unbearable pressure on my chest hurt, and we dove into the spring. Lucca was already in his Siren form, looking at me worriedly. *"I wish you could hear me."* I heard in my mind.

I nodded my head at him, hoping he understood. Can I communicate back? The pressure on my lungs continued as

I reached for my neck. I was going to need to resurface. *"I can hear you!"* His face was full of shock as I projected my thoughts toward him. Lucca swam towards me and ripped the necklace from my neck, not thinking anything of it.

"Try to breathe!" I shook my head 'no' at him while unhooking my legs from Horus, but Horus held me down with his claws.

"I'm going to die!" I internally screamed as I held my breath. Lucca grabbed me by the shoulders and looked at me in eyes. His eyes reminded me of a cat's as he focused on me.

"Trust me, Princess. Take a breath. I'm right here." Feeling the overwhelming sense of calm from him, I let go of my neck and took in a breath. I didn't feel my lungs fill with water. In fact, it was like I was breathing normally. My heart evened out and Horus came nose to nose with me. His nose nudged my cheek in reassurance. He knew I would be fine; I wonder what else he really knows.

"This is insane. You must have Siren blood in you. There is no other way for this to be possible," Lucca stressed.

"My mother and father were human! 100% human!" Lucca shook his head in disagreement and waved his hand to follow.

"How can we talk like this?" I snapped.

"All Sirens can talk to each other while under the water. It's the way we communicate. Why you can still puzzles me." Lucca's eyes didn't meet mine as he continued down into the caverns and into the open ocean while I continued to ride Horus.

With the water being so clear, I could see out on the vast ocean floor. An abundance of fish swam by, and I swore I saw some looking at us as we passed. The trench that Lucca had mentioned where Atlantis was hidden was just up ahead. Instead of descending into a dark gorge, we were met with light. An enormous dome covered the entire city. Many Sirens would enter and leave around the same few openings at the base of the dome. Lucca had us swim to the backside of the dome where there were fewer Sirens.

Horus continued to weave his long neck behind him to check on me, but I only nodded and petted behind his horns. Once we came to the base of the dome, I got off Horus' back and swam close to Lucca to see what he would do. Waving his hand over a certain area that had two large dolphin-like pillars and he could step through while holding me close to him. We were instantly pulled in, along with Horus, and we became dry.

"A witch enchanted it, so we didn't have to be wet all the time," Lucca announced as we finally walked through the portal-like structure. Horus' tail was constantly touching me as we walked through the back streets of the city. You could hear Sirens laughing at talking as we took several side streets over, not taking me to the main roads.

"Where are we going?" I whispered as I took in the view. The city was lighted beautifully, decorated with shells, blue coral, and white stones. Lights lit up the street in magnificent orbs that floated in a light pole contraption. Several children ran in between their parents as they giggled and squealed. It looked like any other marketplace or city, except it was all under crystal blue waters.

"To Calista's. She has a small shop right around the corner." Lucca grabbed my hand and pulled me close to him while Horus stayed close as well. I'm getting smothered not just by my two bodyguards but by the stares. Several Sirens saw Horus and tried to follow as we ducked into the shop. Opening the door, shells chimed together, alerting of customers. The store was darker than it was outside, the smell of incense almost too intense.

Jars and globes were covered on the shelves with various objects from seaweed, dried fish, and horse hooves. I silently let out a long, "ewww," and Lucca glared at me playfully.

"Calista! Come out, I haven't got all day!"

Lucca smacked his hand on the counter and waited for Calista to emerge from the back. I took a few steps forward to her bookshelf. History of Atlantis, science, magic, spells, and various other generic books aligned the wall and even an old paperback book that said, "The Little Mermaid." I started giggling until I felt a hand on my shoulder and was turned around abruptly.

The woman had hair in dreads down to her hips, shells and pieces of coral suck out in the most peculiar places. Her face was littered with freckles even on her dark skin. Her eyes were a striking purple, and her scales were there to match. "I'm Calista," she muttered and turned me around in a circle. I complied and did what she wanted me to do.

Up and down, her eyes probed my body until she finally had me stop turning. Her palm went to my forehead while her eyes looked at her toes. Calista snorted and took her hand away as she laughed. "What is it? What did you see?" Lucca urged her to speak, but she continued to laugh. I stood there not moving, afraid she might fall over from laughter.

"Nothing!" she cried as she waved her hand to fan her face. "She was just so serious and did everything I wanted her to do. I thought it was funny." She snorted one more time and went behind the counter.

"This isn't a game Calista; I need to know!" Lucca urged again, losing his temper.

"Why is it so important? Why do you want to know anything about this human girl?" She laughed again as she re-arranged her collection of clamshells.

"Because I am drawn to her. I know when she is in water, she sings and hell she can breathe in water! There is something different, but I can't sense her being one of us!" He pleaded. "I need to know what she is to me."

In the short time I've known Lucca, he never looked like the person to beg. He is a prince and could have easily commanded her to tell him. Lucca was sensing something else, but he wasn't telling me. He continued to run his hand through his hair, and I noticed had small streaks of blue under the Atlantean light.

"Maybe she is your mate, or you have a little crush on the

dear?" Lucca shook his head violently no.

"She is not. I have no attraction to her in that way, no offense," he added. I shrugged my shoulders. The feeling was neutral.

"And what of you? What do you think of Prince Lucca?" Calista directed to me as she continued to mix various spices and fish into the bowl.

"He's kinda cocky, a little arrogant and has 'find the damsel in distress' complex, but other than that he's a nice guy. I trust him," I said with a smirk.

"I am not arrogant!"

"Tell that to my mate." I rolled my eyes.

"You are something else. No one would ever talk to me that way," he laughed.

"I'm just not everyone else," I deadpanned.

Calista finished mixing her potion and would look back and forth between us, mumbling words under her breath. Finally, she called us over and plucked two hairs from our heads, spat on them, and dumped them into the mixture.

"Please don't tell me we have to eat that," I asked worriedly.

"We? We are trying to figure out what YOU are, so I don't have to eat anything!"

"No one is eating anything," Calista growled. With a few more flicks of her wrist, the concoction was completed. Calista grabbed my arm without permission and smeared it on my arm. For a few moments, nothing happened until I felt a tingle, then a burn.

"Ouch! Why is it hurting?! Take it off!" I looked around for a washrag until Calista took it off. A small smile left her lips, and she put her hand on her hip.

"Well, human, I guess you aren't human after all." I looked at Horus and he nodded his head in confirmation.

"You're half Siren and not just any type of Siren blood, but a powerful one." My jaw dropped and Lucca's brows only knotted to confusion.

"I figured that, but what is she to me?" Lucca growled out. Dang, he's like a shark. Chomp, chomp.

"Speak to your father. He will have the answers you seek. He's the only one with enough power and insight to tell you that." Calista smiled and went to the back of the store.

Meanwhile, I was having an identity crisis. I had not moved from the same spot since she spoke those words. I was not fully human. My birth parents were human! I had never seen any signs of them being anything but human! They didn't care for me or each other very much, but they were all, in the sense of the word, human.

Breathing underwater, being able to swim well and Lucca being able to tell I'm in the water were all signs that I could very well be part Siren. My heart squeezed. Either my parents kept the truth from me or my mother...

My mother was not true to my father while they were together if they were even together at all. "Breathe there, Princess." Lucca grabbed me as I began to fall and held me up to sit me in a chair. "Are you all right? This is a lot to process, I'm sure." I nodded my head lightly, still not focusing my eyes on him.

Within three weeks, my life had changed. I knew my future; it was to be with Osirus. My past I had closed the doors not just 24 hours ago and wanted to live the rest of my life in happiness. Now the back door had been burst open again and I must dig into a past that is painful. Freaking whiplash.

"Are you going to breathe? Because it doesn't look like you are," Lucca joked as he pushed my shoulder. Shaking my head, I stood up to find Horus looking at us through the window. The gleam in his eye and the slight nod as he glanced at me gave me the reassurance I needed.

"I need to know," I whispered.

"What?"

"I need to talk to your father. If Calista says I need to talk to him to find out who I am, I need to see him." Lucca rubbed the back of his head, frustrated.

"That will be hard to do, Princess. He hasn't been the same since my mother left to be with her true mate." I nodded in disappointment.

Calista comes back out carrying a purple-colored lei you would find on the Hawaiian Islands on Earth. "Give him this. He will come to see her then." Calista blew Lucca a kiss and went back to her storage closet.

"She is a strange woman but has never steered me wrong, are you ready for this?" Straightening my shoulders back and a new determination running down to my bones, I knew I was ready. I was going to find out my true history and maybe why my parents didn't want me.

"Let's go, fishy."

Chapter 35

Melina

Lucca led us to the main square of Atlantis. People watched Horus and me with leery eyes, but he continued to hold his head up high since he was a proud creature. If only they knew how large and powerful he was, they would cower in fear. Horus continued to stay by my side, always touching me. If not with my hand on his side, his tail was protectively wrapped around my waist.

When we were away from Atlantis, Lucca could manipulate his looks to make him look more human. Here, everyone kept their colorful scales and hair while they walked about, more in their true form minus the tail. I stuck out like a sore thumb, looking every bit of human. Many girls donned beautiful, short skirts that wrapped around their waists with shells beading around their waists. Hair came in an assortment of colors you would find in a thriving coral reef. My hair was dark, and I didn't have the colorful clothing or scales they had.

Many male Sirens looked over, licking their lips, flexing their muscles, and advancing towards our little entourage, but Horus only let out a low growl in warning. Lucca didn't sway in his steps as we continued down the main road up to the palace gates. His eyes were stern, looking like the prince he really was.

Once we arrived, soldiers holding spears came to speak with him while Horus and I stood back. Their eyes glanced back and forth between Horus and me, also eyeing the beautiful flower lei. The guards finally nodded and opened the gate and with one look, we were guided into the palace.

The Little Mermaid movie had nothing on this place. It was grand, stunning, and competed with Osirus' palace. Pearls and marble decorated the floor and pillars and the orb lights lit up the entire dwelling. Women with shell anklets and short, beautiful dresses came prancing in, giggling, and talking. I've not seen one woman in the entire kingdom wear any clothing longer than mid-thigh or cover their shoulders.

"Those are my brother's mates," he nodded in their direction.

"They are beautiful," I whispered.

"They are. They are the perfect complement to my brothers. I'm glad my father only allows us to be with our mates instead of arranged marriages like they used to so long ago." Lucca's eyes fell distant as he continued to lead us down the grand hallway. "Ever since my mother left, he made it to law to follow that of the Cerulean Moon Kingdom and only accept your true mate. I'm surprised The Golden Light Kingdom doesn't follow suit."

"They do now!" I smiled brightly, thinking of Osirus bringing forth a new era in his nation. "There is a war in the kingdom right now. That is why he had me fly with Horus to The Land of Dragons to keep me safe until it was over." Lucca let out a breath in relief.

"Good, I was getting worried about that, Princess."

"Why is that?"

"I thought he was going to keep you on the side and marry someone else to gain more favor with his corrupt Court." I gasped in disbelief.

"No, he would never! He waited for me this long. Why

would he mate with someone else now!?"

"Royal marriages aren't that simple, Princess." Lucca shook his head.

We came upon two large double doors that reminded me of Osirus' to the throne room. My heart fluttered in nervousness as he knocked on the door. Horus's tail wrapped possessively around me but nuzzled my cheek for confidence.

"He's grumpy, but he won't hurt you," Lucca trailed off until we heard a loud roar from the other side.

"I said, I don't want to be disturbed!!" The voice was angered, hurt, and almost pitiful. My heart broke hearing him speak. Lucca looked down at me as he saw the distressed look on my face.

"Father, it's me, Lucca." There was a long pause, and we heard him say, 'enter.'

We all walked into the massive throne room. The king was sitting at the very end, and even at a distance, he was large. He was bare-chested with muscles comparable to Alpha Kane. Wearing a long skirt as opposed to the short ones to the knees that the men wore. His hair was platinum blond, with a neatly short, trimmed beard.

"Who is this, son?" the gruff voice growled as I stood closer to Horus. Horus stood beside me as he sat on his haunches.

"This is my friend," Lucca was quickly cut off.

"Is this some whore!? Do you understand what I told you about mates, son!?" Lucca's father stood up to a towering height. My small body couldn't comprehend what was happening, and it began to shake.

"No father, we come seeking help," Lucca remained passive.

"I'm in no mood, Lucca. I suggest you go elsewhere with this human." He turned and walked back to his seat.

"Sing something," Lucca nudged me.

"What?" I hissed.

"Do it, now!"

"I've never sung in front of anyone before!" I whisper-yelled.

"Do it now or you will lose the chance," he pushed.

My breath hitched; this was going to be tough. The only time I sang was when I felt a strong emotion, which was usually sadness. Now I must sing something, and I wasn't sad. I was conflicted about who I really was.

"Think of Osirus, your mate." Lucca grabbed me by the shoulders." Sing from the heart. That is where your power will be." I sighed dejectedly. This was mortifying.

Thinking of Osirus, I held onto my chest and closed my eyes, playing with the idea no one was around. This was for me, and Osirus was my future. Just getting a glimpse of what I am will give me the final closure I need to move on. I must do this for the closure.

I hummed a random melody with my voice, slowly opening my mouth and letting the notes surround us. It was full of sorrow as I began, almost telling the story of my life. It gradually became lighter, as I remembered first meeting Osirus.

I continued to sing, and I felt the air in the room shift around me. I couldn't feel Lucca and Horus not beside me any longer. It was the song and me, as I continued to think of Osirus. I missed him terribly. Maybe this was a bad idea to come here to find out who I was. It will only lead to more heartache and loneliness. What if I found out I really belonged to someone else? Would they want nothing to do with me, too?

I was ready to move forward to be with my mate and in a world full of things I never would have dreamed of. If Lucca's father couldn't give me the answers I wanted, I would drop all this, all the wondering of 'what if's and 'what could have been?' I'll take my life as is and be with my mate.

My voice echoed through the throne room, the notes rising and falling thinking of the love I had for my mate. He was my constant, he would always be there for me even if I didn't know who my true parents were.

Praying that was enough to get the Atlantean King's attention, I opened my eyes to see him standing in front of me. His eyes were no longer matted together, the barely there lines from his scowl earlier had faded. His eyes had softened, and his posture was relaxed.

The large blue eyes investigated me, and he held out his hand. "What is your name?" His voice was barely a whisper. The scary muscle man from before became a teddy bear in a matter of seconds.

"Melina," I whispered back and put my hand in his. The hand was warm as he gripped it. A small tear left his eyes. Lucca wandered beside his father and held out the purple Hawaiian lay and as his father took it, he looked back at me. He chuckled a few times before his voice became a burst of boisterous laughter.

The hand never left mine in the state of my confusion. "Kathryn was a spitfire; I'll give you that."

"Y-you knew my mother?"

"Yes, intimately anyway. She helped me," he cleared his throat, "forget things." His voice went back to being solemn. "How is she?" I slumped my shoulders.

"I don't know. I haven't seen her in years." His amusement of the situation went from confused to anger. "What do you mean you haven't seen her?"

"We parted ways seven years ago. Mother and father didn't want me. They wanted to divorce and go their separate ways. So, I grew up with my friend with her Wolf pack."

"That man was not your father," he ruffed. "And your Kathryn ended up being a real piece of work." His hand tightened against me and pulled me to his bare chest. Being petrified that this man could crush me, Lucca was looking on in astonishment. The King's hand brushed my hair and gave a light peck to the top of my head.

"I am your father, Melina. Your true father. I swear to the gods I knew nothing about you." He poured his soul onto me, and my heart leaped inside my chest.

"What?" I whispered, slowly backing away.

"I am your father, Melina. By gods, if I knew about you, I would have brought you down here and raised you with your half-brothers." My mouth dropped as I glanced at Lucca and then at Horus, both with entertained faces.

"You're my dad?" His glassy eyes held so much hope that I would accept this information. Could I accept it? Hell, I didn't have a family before my birth mother left me and this guy wanted to take me in. He wanted me. He wanted a daughter, and he was technically my dad by blood. My gut was telling me to trust it, and it didn't steer me wrong with Osirus.

"Yeah, I'm your father. I feel it in my bones. Your song only confirms it. Each Siren has a certain pitch so parents can find their children. You are my daughter, Melina." The determination in his voice made me choke back a sob. I wasn't far from him, but I leaped into his arms and buried my face in his chest. I have a father. A family.

"I've always wanted a daughter," he cooed in my ear. "And now I've got you." He squeezed me tight as we both fell to the floor. Lucca crossed his arms and started laughing.

"Come on, you know you want in," Lucca's father or my dad spoke to him happily. Lucca grinned at his father as he helped us both up.

"I'm sorry, but I don't know your name yet?" I spoke up.

"Ha, right? I'm Girard, King of Atlantis, and you, my dear Melina, are now the beloved first princess of Atlantis." I blushed mightily as I put my hands to my face. This seriously can't be real.

"Father, hate to break it to you, but she's going to be a queen soon. I don't think the princess title suits her," Lucca brought up jokingly.

"What?" he snapped as he looked towards me. He must not have noticed before, but he noticed then. The large hickey on my neck was beaming proudly as he moved my hair to inspect. "What is this?!"

"Uhhh, it's, um, a hickey?" I said innocently. Lucca

snickered, and I threw out a glare at him.

"From your mate?" Dad raised an eyebrow, still hovering close to me. I nodded excitedly. "Who is he? The only known King that hasn't found a queen,..." He trailed off before snapping his head back to me. "Osirus? The Fae King?" he roared. There goes happy dad. I nodded yes again, and he slumped his shoulders.

"I only just got you back and you will already be going back to the surface." This wasn't the response I was thinking I was going to get, but at least he won't keep me away from Osirus. I would have been heartbroken if my father decided I couldn't be with him and with our bond this strong, I don't think I could handle the heartache. I couldn't lose both when I just got everyone back into my life.

Dad sat us both down and talked about why I never noticed my powers before, and it was just because I never noticed them; why would I when I spent most of my time on land? I also never tried to breathe underwater, and I never sang to anyone to lure them to me, which was another history lesson for another time. I wanted to know if I get scales too, but Dad said that I was still only half Siren, possibly more than three quarters because of his strong bloodline. When he switched to a full human form, he mentioned he had darkened hair like I do, which I'm guessing is another trait I got from him.

The conversation flowed flawlessly as we talked about my history, how I was alone for so long, finding out about the supernatural, and finally arriving in Bergarian. My father had his arm around me the entire time we spoke and beamed with pride at how I took my first breath of water just hours ago.

"That's my daughter! You did that better than most guppies! It's the royal blood in you!" I laughed while Lucca shook his head.

"Guess she's the favorite child now, huh?"

"Most definitely. She's my little girl! And I need to meet

Osirus. I dealt with his parents before but never met the Fairy."

"He's a Fae!" I whined.

"No matter," he growled. "Nothing is too good for my baby girl." I gasped.

"Yay!! I'm a daddy's girl!" I laughed and clapped ridiculously. The thought of me calling Osirus daddy too disturbed me. I'll just call my father Dad. Goddesses have mercy.

"Father, we need to get her back. King Osirus will expect her at the cottage after the war."

"Nonsense, my princess will not stay there. She will stay here, and we will all personally take her back to Osirus tomorrow, along with an army. We aren't that far from the Fae Kingdom. We can leave at dawn. I can then size him up and see if he is good enough for Melina, Moon Goddess or not. He will be good to her."

I rolled my eyes, but I secretly loved it.

Chapter 36

Osirus

It's nearing midnight, and she still hasn't fallen asleep. I growled out in frustration as I paced the room. The moon was high tonight, a mere crescent, but the light Pixies kept the entire kingdom lit with their excitement. They would receive seats in the Court and were deemed equals throughout the kingdom.

Small fires were finally put out and now only bits of ash remained as the smoke entails the outskirts of the kingdom's territory. The shifters had all taken shelter in the many dormitories we hold within the palace walls. They are all considered heroes and will forever be remembered as I plan to build a monument with all their names who helped in the good fight.

Not as many lives were lost as we fought. I commanded them to wound many so they could without terminal injury. It wasn't their fault they were fighting with the wrong leadership commanding them. They didn't know, and they were still my subjects. We are to rebuild a kingdom, not have the people mourning loss. This would be a time of celebration and the Shifters who came to help understood my plea to just fight them off and defend, not destroy.

Clenching my fist, I lay on the sofa to try again. Laying on the bed would be more comfortable, but it hurts my soul not having her there. Her smell still lingered on the pillow, and it only made me miss her more.

I must reach her. If I don't, I will spread my wings for the first time in centuries and fly to her. I need to know she is all right. Keeping a promise I made to her, for her to see my wings emerge from my back for the first time in so long would be broken, but it would be just as I go to search for her.

Taking a large breath, I willed myself to concentrate, to feel her aura with me, and that was when I felt it. She was slowly falling into a deeper sleep. Melina was safe. She was comfortable. I could feel her physical body as it sunk deeper into the folds of the sheets around her body. Calmness encompassed me as I began to will us into our own dreamland, one that I would have right here in our own room.

The bed has now dipped with her body laying inside our white linens. I caressed her arm with one of my fingers as I willed her to wake up in our dream. A small smile was gracing her lips. I prayed she was thinking of me. My darling's eyes fluttered open as her long lashes graced her cheeks. The large pearly smile gazed at me with excitement.

"Osirus!" she squealed as she held onto my neck. "You are all right! Is the war over? Can I come home to you?" Her excitement thrilled me she wanted to be back with me. After our last dream together, I was worried she would still be upset.

"Yes, darling, it's over. We've won," I whispered in the shell of her ear.

"Is everyone all right?" her voice said, laced with concern.

"Of course, what kind of king would I be if I let my own subjects die for what we were all fighting for in the first place?" I smirked at her as I took in her attire.

Melina had a blush pink silk camisole on with rather revealing shorts. I don't remember ever buying anything like this. "Darling, what are you wearing?" My voice was laced with apprehension, with a hint of anger.

"Oh, this?" She blushed. "It's a long story, but I found my real father today!" My mouth hung wide. I've missed much, apparently.

"What do you mean? Aren't you on the Dragon's land?" I became irritable.

"Um, no. I'm in Atlantis?" she innocently spoke as my blood boiled.

"Did Lucca find you? How the hell did this happen, Melina?!" My breathing grew heavy and my grip on her tightened. My eyes filled with fear. She placed her hand on my cheek.

"Calm down and I will tell you, my love." The words she cast on me were a spell. I immediately calmed down as I placed my forehead on hers.

"I've been so worried about you, darling. Finding out you are in Atlantis, the one kingdom I needed you to stay away from, and you go there. It's almost impossible for land-dwellers to get there."

"Horus told me it was all right. He brought me here and protected me," she spoke sweetly.

"Horus thought this was a good idea?" I asked, surprised. Maybe I thought too highly of the damn beast.

"He wanted me to go, now listen..."

I listened. Every bit of the story she told was with excitement, large hand movements. The emotions she poured out as she figured out that her supposed father on Earth was just a random man, so her mother had someone to lean on during the pregnancy. The crazed woman pegged her pregnancy on another man.

The darkness of depression in Melina's aura had dwindled down to just a quarter in size. She no longer carried an enormous burden on her soul like she used to. My smile only widened as she got to the part where her father explained how he knew she was his. Happy tears flowed down her face as I rubbed her cheeks with the pads of my thumbs while she straddled my lap, looking into my soul. My little Melina found what she was looking for, the birth family that really wanted her. Not only that but thirteen older brothers.

Holy shit. I rubbed a bit of my forehead as she told me.

"...and we are coming back tomorrow! Dad said he will bring us in his largest chariot, and we will meet you on the beach at sunrise!" She continued to choke back tears. I couldn't take it anymore, her gorgeous smile, her happy demeanor. I just couldn't handle it.

I smashed my lips to her to silence her cries. Even though she was happy, I couldn't stand to see her cry. "My love, I've missed you," I spoke between kisses. She moaned into my mouth as her arms were hurriedly thrown around my neck. "I'm so happy for you, my darling." One hand was held behind her neck to keep her from leaving my lips, while the other held her back to keep her close. I needed to touch her, to be with her. The dream state does nothing but lets me see. We may feel each other in our dreams and feel some pleasure, but our physical bodies' needs are left unstated once we wake.

"I missed you too Osirus, it makes my chest hurt." Her hand fell to cup my face. "No really, my chest physically hurts. I'm so addicted to you," she giggled.

"It's the bond. We need to be together soon. Just a few hours and you will be back with me, and I will claim this body before I claim your soul," I spoke temptingly to her. Melina's lips parted and her nipples hardened under her silk camisole. "Fuck," I whispered, staring at her breasts. Both of our hands were playing with our faces, not wanting to let go.

I was truly happy for her; her tormented mind could be more at ease now that she has a family, but it will help us as we continued our own future together. Taking one of my hands from her face, I rubbed her nipple on the outside of her silk shirt. She moaned and leaned into me.

"Osirus, I need you." Her mouth went straight to my ear as she nibbled, pulling it softly It was so sensual, not just the sexual drive but how we touched and caressed each other, no doubt I was harder than a Dragon's scales, but this was a loving touch, from the both of us.

My hands trailed her arms while small sparks flew across the tips of my fingers and through her skin. Her hand touched my chest and trailed around each chest muscle and my toned stomach. It was erotic, sensual like we were worshiping each other's bodies.

"I want to continue this, darling, but you and I both have had a long day." Nodding her head reluctantly, I covered us with our bedsheets. I brushed the hair from her face as we entangled our legs with one another.

"I'm apologizing beforehand, but I think Dad wants to size you up," she muttered as she closed her eyes while nuzzling into my neck. I chuckled lightly.

"I wouldn't expect anything less from a true father to a beautiful princess of a daughter."

***

It was minutes before sunrise, and I had already warned the servants as well as the Shifters that have been staying with us that this was a momentous occasion, since the Atlanteans rarely surfaced. They were a peaceful people that kept to themselves. They were certainly smaller in numbers than that of the Fae or Shifter kingdoms, but still very powerful.

Visiting royal quarters were prepared for Girard and his sons, and any servant quarters he may need. I wasn't sure how long they planned on staying, but from what I have heard about Sirens, they cannot stay out of the water for very long periods of time. Melina had been granted a splendid gift to be able to be both on land and water.

The sea was churning as the sun came across the horizon. Alpha Kane, Luna Clara, Tulip, and her mate had come with me as well as Alaneo and the 'Red Fury.' They had all missed their friend and were glad she was safe. However, I most of all was glad she would be here returning to me.

In the distance, we saw a large dome-like apparatus emerge from the water, a few more came along with it. I could see Melina waving wildly as Horus swam up from under the water and took flight. His loud roar had Faes on the beach, covering their ears, as he finally landed in his full form.

"You got my mate into a new mess of trouble, didn't you, old friend?" Horus nodded and did a bow as I rubbed his forehead. "I thank you for that." Horus let out a wink and stepped away and took flight again, back to his cave. True Dragons didn't like to spend much time around people. They were a solitary breed, unlike the Shifter Dragons of the northern territories.

Once the dome structures came close to the shore, the dome popped like a giant bubble and Melina came jumping out with her feet landing along the waves. She was wearing an iridescent, short wrap-around skirt that barely covered down to her mid-thigh. Her top was made of clamshells and pearls, just enough to keep her privates covered. Small sea stars decorated her hair. Her dark hair was curled perfectly. Her laugh became contagious as we both ran to each other's arms.

Picking her up and twirling her in the surf, she gave me a kiss on the cheek. "I've missed you, my love," she spoke loudly, no doubt to let her family know that I was hers.

Girard was a large man, almost intimidating, but since I was a King, I knew I could stand up to him.

"Greetings, King Osirus," he bowed as I did to him. Melina stood beside me, looking, wondering what would be said. "I've heard rumors of you, but my son Lucca and daughter Melina have explained it was a farce just like Lucca's endeavors to save distressed women."

"Yes, your excellency. I've waited over 800 years for my mate, and I would wait 800 more." I took Melina's hand and kissed it as she looked dreamily up at me.

"That's what I want to hear," he nodded as he held onto his trident. No doubt it was handed down by Poseidon himself. "Just finding out about my daughter and having to give her to her mate is quite," he paused, "difficult. I hope you understand my reluctance to send her to you." I nodded, agreeing.

"And that is why I want to invite you and your family to stay for the celebration of a reformed Golden Light Kingdom," I spoke proudly while holding Melina close to me. Her smile let me know how proud she was. "We will up the party to tonight. I know you cannot be out of the water too long."

"We would appreciate that. We can stay for one sunrise and sunset and our bodies cannot stand too much of the light sources. Leaving tomorrow at dawn would keep my people safe." Melina let go of me to give her father a quick embrace.

"Thank you for not being mean," she whispered to him, but we all heard and laughed. The men behind her father glared at me. They were all well-built men with blue and green hair. Their scales were missing, so they must be in more of a human-like form. Melina skipped to Lucca and pulled him forward, "Let me introduce you properly, this is Lucca, my half-brother."

Melina beamed at him while he wrapped his arms around her. "You will be just as my full-blooded sister, Melina." All her brothers nodded in agreement as she pulled them out all one by one. "This is Thalamere, Aqualis, Echoete, Jonas, Jarl, Tore, Gudmund, Eirik, Kaare, Atle, Ivar and Hugo!"

There is no way I will remember that.

"Welcome, if you have mates, please bring them tonight and if you don't have mates, well, I'm sure there are some willing Fae and Fairies ready to have a good time." Several laughed and smirked with each other while others went to go grab their mates.

"Darling let's get you cleaned up and in more appropriate attire," I growled playfully. "I don't like unmated males seeing this much skin on you." She giggled and gave me a quick peck on the cheek.

"Eh, Osirus," Girard spoke up and walked towards me. "I don't want to see any hickeys on my daughter while I'm here, do you understand?" His fangs grew until they were protruding out of his mouth. I wanted to laugh and show him some real fangs, but I relented.

"Of course not, sir," I smiled. Melina's face looked on in horror at her father, who ruffled her hair.

Her entire family took up the North Wing of the castle meant for visiting royalty. Alpha Kane and Luna Clara gave their well wishes and headed back to their own territory but leaving most of their warriors for them to celebrate. Clara didn't enjoy leaving her newborn Evelyn for too long, not that I blame her.

Tulip came rushing up to Melina after her father departed and squeezed her tightly and moved her neck back and forth. Melina continued to push her away and blush, but Tulip was not having anything to do with it.

"You haven't mated yet?" she hissed. "You need to give up the v-card already! Damn girl, you are also a lost princess. Who would have thought? That makes mating so much easier, doesn't it? You have supernatural blood in you, you won't be out for days!"

Tulip was right, she wouldn't be out for too many days. A smirk played on my face with the new information. She was half Siren but with royal blood that could protect her from any injury while the bonding occurs.

"Shhhh, we thought I would be out for a while and with the war, he didn't want me helpless while I slept. Now that we know and everyone leaves, I'll be more open to it."

Damn, she going to make me wait.

"Do it tonight after the party!" Tulip whined. Melina shook her head.

"I can't do it while my dad is here. That is just weird." She made a face. "Plus, he has to take me out on a date first."

"You are so damn stubborn." Tulip rolled her eyes as she walked back to her mate.

"You are right. I do owe you a date." I grabbed her hand and placed a chaste kiss.

"You do, and do it right," she playfully jabbed me in the waist. "I want to know more of you now that you know me."

She was right. I've met her family, and I had yet to really tell her about my own. A game of twenty questions and then some fun might be in order. I'll plan the perfect date for her, but tonight we are going to a party and when a Fae parties, it is unlike any other.

Chapter 37

Melina

After dinner having a small dinner in our rooms, Osirus had Primrose come in and help me get ready for the big celebration. It wasn't one of those stuffy parties where you must wear an elegant gown and have your hair to be done just so. This was going to be an out-of-control party where the PDA would be undeniable, and the booze would be flowing. Hips grinding against pelvises and a lot of drunken one-night stands.

I was excited because I never associated myself with any sort of parties. Tulip and the rest of her pack would have their mate gatherings so they could find their mates, but I never went. Just not my scene because I didn't have a date to go with, but now I did. He was the host, and that meant I got all the perks.

While getting dressed, Primrose had the displeasure of telling me what happened to Peoni and being shocked was an understatement. I thought she was my friend and a true rebel for Osirus' new plans for the kingdom. Didn't she want equal rights? Once it was found out her mate was involved, that put a whole new spin on things. My body slumped in the chair. Hearing that her mate was held captive. Osirus hadn't disclosed who her mate really was, just that he was behind bars and has kept them separate until he knows what to do with them. I believe a just and fair trial against her peers would be most appropriate instead of him making all the decisions. This was her mate she was trying to protect. I would have done the same.

Even in Primrose's sad state, she kept a radiant face for me, brushing and curling my hair while she told me how excited she was for me finding my family. My brothers, two or three at a time, visited me and Osirus in our living quarters. Poor Osirus didn't get any time alone with me today and he was certainly restraining himself several times when we would get intimate.

My theory was that my brothers were standing outside of the door, trying to listen to what was going on. On just the first day of knowing them, they became so protective. When Dad called them all into the throne room, they were utterly confused. Only four of them had found their mates and the rest were currently mateless. Some were worried that their father was going to make the same mistake as he did with their mother, take me on as a chosen mate or force one of them to marry me.

Thalamere, the eldest, was about to rip father a new one until a quick clarification of, "she's your half-sister," explanation came into play. Thalamere's temper was quickly resolved. I worried about how they would take it. Lucca was ecstatic that I was a sibling; he said he felt a connection with me, and he was glad this was what that calling was. The rest of the brothers were equally animated, and I was engulfed in the biggest dog pile on the floor.

Once they saw the hickey on my neck, they got a little pissy.

"Who the hell did this to your neck?" Jonas yelled. My brothers had a bit of a temper, it seemed.

"My mate did it!" I squealed, calling it to his defense. He was my mate, and I certainly wanted him, so I didn't see the big deal.

Jarl came around to pick me up out of the dogpile and pulled him to his chest for an enormous hug. "You mean we just get a sister and now we have to give her up?" Several of my brothers shook their heads in disbelief.

"She will visit us, and we will visit her. I am having Calista make something for us so we can spend more time on land. However, Melina can come here whenever she wants. She certainly received good genes in having both land and water abilities." Father spoke.

Even though Osirus left a love bite and no mate mark yet, it upset my whole family. They wanted to know why I waited to be marked, so I had to explain. I thought I was only human and the war itself put a damper on things. I'm not sure they believed it because they were being extra annoying visiting their dear sister every fifteen minutes. Jarl mentioned he didn't want me to be just a side-mate.

Primrose styled my hair down. she curled it in little ringlets and gave it a quick brush, giving it full body. Tiny pearls were scattered around the crown of my head and a deep eye shadow was given to my eyes. In honor of my family, she stuck with blue and green with heavy eyeliner and dark lashes. I looked like an entirely different person, but I loved it. The person in the mirror looked confident and happy.

Osirus picked the dress for tonight. He wasn't thrilled I was only wearing a shell-covered bra when I arrived on the shore this morning. That was the dressing of my people, however, so he tried not to say much. I didn't care for it, anyway. There are many Fae women who wear less, but being a king himself, he was more possessive of his darling. I giggled internally as I put on the dress.

Again, Osirus picked a beautiful dress. It was a strapless, form-fitting royal blue. The entire dress looked like it was fabric wrapped around me with small wrinkles in the material. To top everything off, my father had sent several pieces of jewelry from Atlantis. A pearl tiara, along with a deep blue sapphire covered in diamonds to adorn my neck.

The girl that had no family just a mere month ago has now gained thirteen brothers, a father, a mate, and two kingdoms. My tears welled in my eyes until I felt a warm presence behind me. "Osirus," I whispered as I turned around to greet him. The overwhelming tingles his touch gives me will never become old.

"Darling, you look ravishing." His hands were placed in his, which trickled down to grab my butt and had me shriek in surprise. Before I was about to kiss him, this incredibly handsome Fae, I heard a throat clearing in the open bedroom doorway. My father stood with his arms crossed over his bare chest, eyeing us both.

"She hasn't been marked yet and you have yet to proclaim her formally. I suggest you remove your hands from my daughter." My face turned tomato red as Osirus' hands dropped from my butt.

"Pardon me, Your Majesty, but the reasonings are just. If it will make you feel better, I can announce her tonight during the celebration." Father nodded at him as he approached and took my hand.

"That should suffice, for now." He glared at him. "I'm escorting her since you haven't formally proclaimed. Don't make her look like your flavor of the week," he scolded. I haven't seen Osirus this angry since he saw me skinny dipping. Osirus' face grew red with anger and his ears grew, as well as his claws. I gave him a pleading look and immediately his eyes softened to me.

"As you wish, King Girard." Osirus came and pulled my other hand and kissed it all while looking into my eyes. "I will see you soon, darling," he winked and retreated from the room. Turning to Father, I slapped him on the arm.

"You are being so mean. He has done nothing but protect and love me!" Father chuckled and patted my hand. "Of course, he has, just making him work a little harder. Besides, I'm making up for all the years I missed scaring off boys."

"Don't worry about that. Osirus was my first kiss, let alone a person I truly care about." I rolled my eyes.

"That's my daughter." He leaned down and gave me a kiss on the cheek.

***

The party was in full swing. There really were half-naked Fae women on the dance floor. Many wore tulle skirts and tiny little bells around their ankles, making them look like gypsies from Earth. Many males were dancing with them as the music started pounding the ballroom floor. I still couldn't understand how music from Earth could be played here along with a mix of the Bergarian culture.

Lights were done by the Pixies flying around the room, which I think some might be drunk. I saw one crash into the window but whiffed it off and kept flying in the other direction. The buffet full of food and drinks and was constantly flooded with Shifters as they ate until their hearts were content. Tulip could eat an insane amount of food and still looked like the muscular goddess she was.

The suns had set for the day. My father was taking me around the room with my hand in the crook of his arm. He would comment on how he wished he could stay longer and be with me but understood the importance of a mate bond. He still to this day had not met his mate at 1458 years old. Constantly, he blamed himself for the misfortune, believing that marrying his first wife that gave him his wonderful sons cursed him forever to be alone.

"You will find her one day, dad. I know you will. You deserve it." I gave him a gentle squeeze.

Looking down at me with a bit of sadness in his eyes, "I certainly hope so, and that she will accept the wonderful children I have." I poked his side with my index finger.

"Well, we are pretty amazing. I don't think she can deny us." I smiled up at him and he kissed my cheek again while

he laughed. Before we walked further into the crowd of celebrating supernaturals, the lights were suddenly cut off along
with the music. Everyone murmured, and Lucca came up to
father and me.

"Stay close Melina," Lucca commanded as he and father
shielded my body. The room was then lit up by hundreds
if not thousands of wisps parading the room. Many whisps
lifted the women's dresses and giggled while also pulling
some of the men's hair. Some danced across the indoor fountain that was placed in the middle of the ballroom before the
party, lighting up the entire fountain.

While standing in awe, I felt my hand being lifted by
those familiar tingles across my skin. Osirus.

"Come with me," he whispered, and I gladly joined him
while a leery father and brothers looked on cautiously. Leading me to the fountain where everyone was now staring
because of the blue lights that gave it a luminous glow. He
pulled my waist close to him. His hand cupped my cheek as
he gave me a quick kiss before turning his head to the crowd.

"To the entire Golden Light Kingdom, Cerulean Moon
Kingdom, as well as Atlanteans, I welcome you to our celebration of a dawn of a new time in this land. We celebrate the
reformation of a new Court and Parliament. Not only that,
but the official declaration of your new queen." My heart fluttered as all eyes were on both of us.

"Melina is the princess of the Atlantean King, Girard the
Second and sister to her thirteen older brothers. She is my
true mate, my destined, and your queen. Please welcome her
as we will do so formally during our Royal Binding Ceremony
in two weeks' time," Osirus announced proudly as he held me
close. Bending forward and his lips touching my ear, he whispered, "We may have our formal binding ceremony in front
of our people, but I will mark and mate you before then," he
spoke huskily into my ear. I could feel my core tighten at the
anticipation as I gripped onto his tunic tightly with my fingers. Feeling another presence behind me, I looked up only to

that of my father. His eyes were looking to Osirus' as to challenge him, but Osirus only held out his hand in truce.

My father's eyes softened as I continued to hold Osirus close to me and a small smirk played on his lips. He nodded his head and I gripped Osirus' hand tightly as the room erupted in cheers. Tulip came up behind me and pulled me to her and squeezed me securely. "Now, let's go get you drunk, princess!" Osirus laughed as Tulip pulled me away from the two most important men of my life as I headed to the refreshments table.

"Tulip, I've never drank before," I muttered as the music picked up.

"Exactly, so we are going to get you wasty faced!" Tulip held up a few small glasses of purple liquid and put them to my lips. "Drink this, it tastes like grape jolly ranchers." I sniffed it a few times and downed two of the small glasses. I coughed a few times, and the surrounding men started laughing.

"Easy there, your highness or you won't last an hour," Finley stepped up and bowed.

"Finley!" I screamed and gave him a hug. "I'm so glad you are all right! I was worried about you and your brothers!"

"Do you doubt our fighting, dearest one?" I laughed as Tulip shoved another glass of lime green juice in my hand. Without thinking, I downed it quickly, only to cough violently after.

"Yuck, what was that Tulip?" Finley and Tulip continued to have me try drinks until I had to go to the bathroom. The room was moving under my feet, and I frequently had to stop and check my surroundings. Once I felt steady, I continued to walk to the bathroom, giggling at myself and muttering that I needed to stop.

Osirus kept stealing glances at me as I did him. He was talking to my father, no doubt planning the ceremony at the end of the month, and my brothers continued to watch my every move. Once they saw where I was going, their eyes left me, and I stepped into the bathroom. Lucky for me, my hair and makeup were still in one piece, and I didn't look like a total tramp.

After a double check in the mirror before I left, I felt heavy breathing on my neck. It was warm, but it gave me everything but a warm feeling. Turning around quickly, I saw nothing but an empty bathroom. I could still feel the eyes on me. It raked over my entire body, from my face, my breasts, and even down my legs. A cold draft passed through the room until I decided I needed to leave. No one was here, it was just the alcohol.

Leaving the restroom, the feeling of being watched had left me, but my mind was still unsettled. Walking back out, much more sober than what I was before I entered the bathroom, I saw Osirus with a glass in his hand all alone. My mood quickly picked up for the better and sauntered over to him, swaying my hips. Osirus licked his lips, grinning mischievously after he took one last sip of his beverage and started towards me as well.

"Well, hello handsome," I said with a lower, more sultry voice. Osirus smirked and gave me a wink. "I don't think we've met before. My name is Melina. I'm a princess, you know," I said playfully.

"I have not met such a stunning woman before, let alone a princess. May I ask what has blessed me with your appearance?"

"You looked so lonely," I whined lightly as I trailed my index finger down his chest. "Such a sexy Fae as yourself shouldn't be alone for the evening. You looked so..." I paused, "vulnerable standing here by yourself." Osirus let out a chuckle. He knew I had too much.

"Then will you do me the honor of dancing with me and healing my lonely heart?" I smirked and sassily put my hand in his as he led me to the dance floor.

Chapter 38

Melina

Osirus led me to the dance floor, and the alcohol had given me liquid courage to follow him as the beats of the music picked up around us. The only person who has seen me dance was Tulip, who said I had serious moves but coming from your best friend, that meant little to me. I just prayed to the goddess that I had rhythm as I walked through the crowd of future subjects.

As the song played, Osirus turned me around and made sure his member was right on my butt as he felt the sides of my body. Hands were roaming all over me while I put my hands on his, touching every inch of him. His passionate touches had me panting as we continued to grind against each other. I wanted him before this party started, and I wanted him even more now.

The sexual tension between the both of us was unmistakable. All day, we had been teased and taunted with each other and by my brothers and father interrupting all our passionate kisses, it made us delirious for some alone time. It was like fate trying to impede what we both truly wanted, and that was our skin on each other.

Osirus knew I didn't want to mate with my father in the

same palace as me. Even though I've known him for a day, I just couldn't stomach it since he saw me as his little princess. However, right now, this little princess was getting hot and bothered. I wanted Osirus to talk dirty to me like the previous night, and it made me ache to want to listen to those filthy words from his mouth.

Turning around, I threw my arms around his neck as his hands went straight for my butt, which he has a huge fascination with. I didn't see all the hype, but I liked the way he massages and kneads it while pushing my pelvis into his growing erection and kept inching close and closer to my kitty spot.

Sweat had formed, and Osirus' tunic had become wet. The fevered bodies on the floor didn't help the situation. Couples were groping each other, and more than just a bit of pleasure going as far as orgasming on the floor.

Osirus dipped his mouth to my neck, and I moaned as he let soft licks and kisses trail up to my ear. Gripping his barely dry tunic, I felt a tap on my shoulder. Tulip stood there with Alec by her side, holding up a glass. "Thought you might need a refreshment?" she winked, and I took it, downing the burn in one gulp. Osirus nodded at Alec in thanks while Tulip whispered to Osirus, "You will thank me later." Osirus raised a brow. Still, with his enormous member riding along my pelvis, he quickly ignored it and kissed me with his lustful hunger.

The dancing went on, and our hands roamed each other's bodies until Osirus suggested we take a break. I whined a bit, but that only got me a slight tap on my rear-end. "Behave, or I'll have to show you who's your real daddy," he whispered lowly. I giggled and nodded my head at how silly it sounded. Both of us were drenched in sweat, but the party was in full swing. It must be close to midnight, because I saw my father nodding and waving at a few people as he approached us.

"I'm going to head off to bed, my princess." Father looked at me longingly. He gave a quick glance to Osirus and smiled.

"You don't have to see me out tomorrow, and I'll be back in two weeks for your coronation and binding ceremony. Calista should have something to help us stay out of water for longer periods by then."

"Thank you, dad!" I gave him a large hug and he returned the sentiment. He kissed my head and held me out by my shoulders.

"I'm so happy to have found you, Melina. I wish I could have you a little longer. However, I understand how important it is to find your mate. Come visit anytime you wish, and I mean that." The last part of his sentence was stern, which only made me laugh as I gave him one final hug. Again, he nodded to Osirus as to say to take care of me.

Osirus led me to a sitting area where Alaneo was quietly drinking in the corner, and his eyes never left the table that sat in the middle of the sitting area. His eyes were clouded over as he rubbed his chin several times before laying his head back on the sofa. "Don't bother him, darling. This is how he copes." I hummed in response as the Red Fury took their seats around us as well. Alaneo's mouth slowly parted as soft snores came from his side of the couch.

"No ladies that suit your fancy tonight?" Osirus pried as Everett rolled his eyes.

"Ya, they all want some fish to lie with them, saying it is a rare occasion." I held back a laugh as Finley and Braxton nodded mournfully.

My body felt feverish at my feet and was working slowly up my body. Once it reached my core, I felt it tingle, and I was instantly turned on by whatever this feeling was. The beat of the music was felt within my core, and my nipples instantly hardened. My breath became sporadic, and my head became light and dizzy. I looked at Osirus to see if he felt the same, but he was still talking to Everett about their women trouble.

A song came on that caught my ears and I had the urge to dance, to let my body be free and flow with the music. My head rolled back, trying to catch my bearings, to make myself feel lowered to the ground, but nothing was helping. My eyes became half-closed as I continued to fight with the urge to stand up, but it was a lost cause. What harm would it be to just dance right here instead of on the dance floor?

Osirus

Everett continued to joke how he was spending time alone with his good-ole friend his hand, while Finley and Braxton tried to lighten the mood that the night was in fact still young. Melina was sitting at my side, swaying. The alcohol that Tulip gave her must have hit her harder than Melina intended.

Suddenly, Melina was standing up and swaying to the music. She looked downright hypnotic. I was grateful she was staying right here and not on the dance floor. I think I would have spanked her right there, leaving me here with these nimrods.

The sways became more engaging and seductive, her hips moving to the beat, her arms lifting above her head as she continued to roll her head side to side. My friends looked at her, but I was too entranced by her body and the freeness she was showing. Enjoying the pleasure of how her body moved, I lifted my hand to turn her to me. Her eyes opened, and she saw me, and she gave a playful smirk.

Melina swayed before me in sensual movements as she placed each knee on either side of my waist. My body was so turned on, my mind had been covered in a haze of lust at how she touched my open tunic. Her eyes wandered my body as she licked her lips and sucked her fingers that held my sweat. She was a damn vixen when she would let go, and maybe she should drink occasionally.

"Fuck, Melina you are going to kill me." She giggled as she peeled back my tunic, so my shoulders showed. It pooled to my elbows, my torso was available all to see. Some women looked my way, but all I could concentrate on was this seductress before me.

Her core met my painfully hard erection as I held her hips, guiding her toward how I wanted her to move. "Feel my cock, baby. Do you see how bad you turn me on?" I growled at her.

I was fully aware of my friends watching, but damn, my dick didn't care right now. I needed her as much as she needed me. We had been away from each other far too long, and I didn't have the heart to make her stop and take her to our room.

"Do you like me dancing for you?" she whispered as she captured my lips. Her eyes were full of lust as she eyed my torso, which made me thankful for early morning workouts. My mate loved my body, and this was the first time she was really appreciating it with me knowing.

Her breasts were heaving in my face, the damn material covering what I really wanted. Her glorious tits couldn't stay contained for long. I didn't want to allow them to be free so others could gawk at them, but gods, I wanted them in my mouth. I wanted to feel her nipple roll between my lips as I sucked them till they hurt.

My hands groped her from the outside of the material, hiding those glorious breasts. She let out a moan as she grabbed my neck to kiss me. One hand on her arse and one hand on her breast. I could die a fortunate man.

Another song came on, and she smiled wildly at me. "I love this song," she husked. Her voice was a damn turn on how low it got as she spoke into my mouth. Her head leaned back, and she put both of her hands into her hair and for the first time since that first night in the Cerulean Moon Kingdom, I heard her sing.

It was the same damn voice I heard my first night at the Crimson Shadows Pack. Her voice really was hypnotic, just like her body. The voice was so damn alluring it drew me in to hold her and keep her close. As she continued her assault, giving me the best lap dance in existence, she was suddenly not there. I opened my eyes to enjoy my mate's touch until I saw a Wolf with her in his arms.

"The hell do you think you are doing?" I stood up, going to reach for my mate. Before I could grab her back, the entire sitting area was surrounded by unmated Wolves and Faes. The only ones not affected were the mated and her brothers. Lucca came running in, baring his fangs, while her brothers started shoving them off.

Finley, Everett, and Braxton joined the fight while I jumped over the couches and lunged at the Wolf, whose hands were on to Melina. The sitting area was being torn apart. Unmated and mated men were at each other's throats, some brother against brother as the Wolf who captured her backed to the door during the riot.

Melina's eyes were in terror as he gripped her arm tightly. Blood was dripping down her arm as she tried to pull him off. "Let me go, please!" she cried, and my heart broke listening to her pleading. I was going to kill him, that I was sure of it.

I stood in front of the deranged Wolf, whose eyes were clouded over. Before I jumped to rip his throat out, Lucca grabbed me. "Did she sing?" he panted as he looked at her. I nodded yes, and he quickly took the attention to Melina. "Command him, Melina, don't beg or plead, tell him what to do!" Melina tried to pull his hand away from him but whimpered.

"You must show domination, Melina! Don't show fear, or it won't work!" Melina's eyes darted back and forth between the Wolf and Lucca.

"Darling, you can do this. Don't be afraid. You are strong," I coached her as she continued to pull in silence. The extra encouragement she needed helped as she stood up straight and stopped pulling.

"I demand for you to stop this, right now!" Melina yelled into his ear. A small whimper left his lips as he let go, and she ran to me, burying her face in my chest. I pulled her away from the scene, only for Lucca to stop me from speaking to

Melina again.

"Tell them they are released, Melina," Lucca continued to coach her as she watched in horror of the Wolves and Faes fighting. "Command them all!" Giving her a pat on the back, she stood up straight again. "You are released!" she yelled with authority, and the mutiny that was in the sitting room stopped. Wolves woke up from their hazed slumber, looking confused and dumbfounded.

"Why are we in here?" one of them spoke. Several shrugged their shoulders and went back whence they came. Not questioning any longer why the entire room was destroyed over my mate.

"What happened?" Melina whispered as she was swaying in my arms. Her eyes were closing, so I picked her up with one arm under her knees and one behind her back. Melina's eyes rolled to the back of her head, and her head slumped over my bare chest.

"She compelled them. Sirens used to do it all the time a long time ago to kill off humans who ventured too close to the portal. She must not have had control of her mind. Usually, you have to will it in your mind for it to happen." Then Lucca smiled as he pushed my shoulder. "Unless she wanted to seduce you," he winked.

"My darling was drinking," I said while I stroked the hair from her face. "This isn't something she would normally do. She's never even sang to me before this night. I've only caught her singing while she is all alone. Melina is normally too self-conscious to do what she did."

"Drinking and singing compulsion is difficult to do. It's like trying to ride your horse in a straight line while intoxicated. Melina drank or took something else that made her become sexually active," Lucca spoke harshly as he ground his teeth together. At first, I didn't trust Lucca, but he had become a brilliant brother to Melina. He's as pissed as I am because this would have been a disaster if she wasn't fully awake enough to stop it.

"She's only drunk with me. What about you?" Lucca questioned.

"Nothing, just the one drink from…." My eyes darted to Tulip across the room. I saw a face full of guilt as she cried into her mate's arms.

Chapter 39

Osirus

Lucca let out a low growl as he realized the culprit. "Easy brother, we will deal with this accordingly," I assured him while I nodded to Braxton and Everett to fetch the pair. Alaneo was waking up from his drunken stupor and was looking much better.

"What did I miss?" He rubbed down his face with one hand.

"A lot. Meet me in my chambers," I ordered.

I carried Melina along with Finley, who was standing watch for any other unmated males that could follow, who did not hear her command. My tiny mate went from human to half Siren and had many Wolves and Faes at her beckoning call. They were trying to take her at first but now that we know she can command them and release them from the call, this could be used as a protective tactic later if the need arose.

My anger began to swell, thinking how careless her friend was. Gripping my mate tighter, she let out a whimper as she buried her head into my chest again. A smile graced my lips as we entered our living chambers and I sat down with her on my lap. Pulling a light blanket over her to make sure her skin wasn't on show too much, Alec and Tulip were corralled into the room.

Alaneo sat beside me and put Melina's feet on his lap. If I wasn't so close to Alaneo as my brother, I would have ripped a new hole for him to breathe from, but he truly cared for Melina like a sister. Melina was sweating and shivering at the same time as I continued to pull her damp hair back from her face.

Lucca stormed into the room and slammed the door and got close to Tulip's face. "Do you want to tell me what you gave her?" he roared as she cowered into her mate's chest.

"Watch your tone, Fae!" Alec growled out and shielded his mate.

"You just about caused a full-out war on the Cerulean Moon Kingdom if anything had happened to her! You know she is a princess of one of the most lethal armies of Bergarian!?"

Tulip sobbed again, and Alec stood stoic, trying to comfort his mate. "It was an accident, she didn't mean any malice by it!" Alec replied.

"That's enough, Lucca," I commanded. "Tulip is Melina's best friend. I'm sure there was a reason behind this behavior of hers." I raised my brow at her while she nodded profusely.

"She said she was so nervous earlier about completing the mating and she didn't want to do it with her father under the same roof because it made her anxious. I was trying to get her to loosen up! I didn't know it would cause this much of a problem!"

"For a Wolf, you sure are an idiot!" Lucca hissed. "You knew she was half Siren. She can seduce the entire room with her voice, did you not think?" Tulip couldn't look anyone in the eye while she took her chastising. Alec mouthed a quick, 'sorry,' to me, but I continued to glare at them both. Alec has no balls to deal with his mate. Might as well chop them off and place them on the mantel.

"She never sings!" Tulip cried. "I thought it would be

Okay!"

Alaneo sat his head back on the couch and mouthed a big, "oh," as he put the pieces of the puzzle together.

"I'm never drinking again. I missed too much," Alaneo scoffed while Braxton slapped him on the back of the head.

"This is serious, you ass." Melina stirred in my arms and tried clutching the sleeves to my tunic.

"What did you give her?" Not bothering to glance at the two idiots.

"A seduction potion," she whispered. "There was a potion vendor in the marketplace earlier today."

"From a witch?" I spoke harshly while she nodded. "Fuck," I whispered, looking at Alaneo. Love and seduction potions were prohibited in the Golden Light Kingdom. It was stated as plain as day once entering our lands for any merchants coming to sell at the local marketplace. The only coven that would dare go against that order would be the Blood Coven, the same one that was helping Cosmo and the Court trying to overthrow me. We had yet to deal with that issue of lack of evidence.

"Fuck is right," Alaneo spoke louder. The Red Fury's hands went to their swords and gripped them tightly. We weren't done with this war yet. We may have Cosmo and the traitors in the dungeon, but there were more people out there wanting the throne or to see me suffer.

Cupping Melina's cheek, I left a chaste kiss on her forehead. The sweat was slowly drying, and her eyes fluttered as she went into a deep sleep. "Alec, Tulip, you are not to leave tomorrow with your pack. You are to stay here until further instruction. I will ask Melina what she would like to do and with some insight from her and then I will plan your punishment. You are both to go to your room and two guards will stay in place to make sure you don't leave. You are lucky you are like a sister to Melina, otherwise you would be in the prison for harm upon the future queen," I spoke sternly.

Two guards who were posted outside the chamber door

came in and led them back to their room while Lucca stood with his arms crossed. "Their fate should be death. She could have been raped, imprisoned, or even killed by one of those damn men. Her singing was only heightened because of the seduction potion. She reached clear to mid-dance floor, which was unbelievable." Lucca plopped down on the couch with his elbows on his knee and his hands on his head. "Who knew having a sister would cause so much stress?" he chuckled.

"Wait," his head perked up. "Why weren't you four affected?"

Alaneo looked up and raised his hands in surrender. "I was passed out! I didn't hear a damn thing."

The red-headed brothers looked at each other and then looked away. Braxton mumbled something while Finley had turned bright scarlet. "Men, did you find your mate?" I asked hopefully. They had been without a mate as long as I had; they certainly deserved it and I had seen the mournful looks in their eyes when they saw Melina giving me loving looks.

"No, uh, um, well, we weren't paying attention to her singing." Everett rubbed the back of his neck while looking away from us.

"No, we weren't," Braxton shyly confirmed. Finley stepped away from the group and grabbed a glass of scotch from the table. If anyone was going to talk, it would be Finley. He was always honest and forthcoming, but I have a feeling I will not like what they are going to say.

"We were attending to... other things..." He cleared his throat while looking at me in the mirror.

"What things?" Alaneo sat cluelessly.

"Let's just say, her majesty had some moves that were pleasing to our eyes..." Finley choked as he pulled at his uniform collar.

"What?" I still didn't understand.

"Oi! don't make us say it," Everett groaned as he sat in the chair beside me. Alaneo's eyes grew wide, flabbergasted, and let out a large laugh, startling Melina in my arms while she continued to sleep.

"You didn't..." Alaneo continued to laugh while slapping his knee.

"What are you talking about?" I growled, getting impatient, my fangs descending.

"Chill, chill," Everett spoke. "We kinda got off while you both were uh..." I cut him off.

"WHAT? You did that out in the open? While watching my mate?!" I stood up with Melina in my arms and Melina's eyes opened wide. Her eyes were dilated as she squeaked in surprise. Realizing my mistake, I sat back down and rubbed her cheek.

"I'm sorry, darling," I cooed. "Go back to sleep." Her eyes immediately closed as I glared at the brothers and sighed heavily. "Listen, we all did things we regret today. I say we forget it and never mention it again, especially to Melina." Everyone nodded in agreement.

Lucca stood up and punched a hole right in the wall. "Forgive and forget? What kind of King are you!? They have disrespected the princess of Atlantis. You have put her in a terrible situation allowing her to give you a damn lap dance in front of a crowd. You are supposed to protect her! Not treat her as a sex doll!"

Calmly, I stood up and had Alaneo take Melina from me to put her to bed. Once she had left the room, I walked to Lucca silently as everyone watched in the room. "I am the King of the Golden Light Kingdom, ruler of this land. I don't trust people easily and the Faes in this room are my brothers in spirit. They have risked their lives for me and their nation, and they have given me nothing but honesty. If I had found out from another source that this was done without my knowledge, then I would have their heads. We are bound to each other as we are to his country. I will decide who gets punished." My voice was low and unwavering as Lucca's breaths also slowed.

"Ruling a nation is not about killing or torturing people. It is about understanding and trust. They have not broken my trust. They did not lay a hand on her like the others tried to do. It was my fault that I couldn't get her to stop, but fuck, she is my mate, and I haven't been allowed to mate with her yet and I was under her spell. Of course, my primal instincts are going to not want her to stop. She was protected by my finest men as you saw them fight off the unmated males. If I punish them now, it would be cruel and unjust, and I would lose my best brothers. If anyone should be punished, it is Tulip and her mate."

Lucca nodded his head. "Then good. Make sure she is punished. Nothing less than 20 lashes if not I'm sure our father will see he does something about it." Lucca stood up straight and walked to the double doors and marched out.

"Damn, who does Melina belong to?" Alaneo said with a laugh. Running my hands through my now messy hair, I sat back down and let out a frustrated sigh. This was supposed to be a celebration, and it had turned into a complete disaster. Now I have two more people under watch, including a full prison of ex-court members, a traitor, and her mate that I had yet to meet.

Tulip was like a sister to her. I couldn't just punish her, but Girard will come to find out and really put a noose around my neck if I do nothing.

We all said our goodnights, and I headed into the bedroom. Melina was still in her dress, laying on our love seat. Alaneo must have known I would want to bathe her before bed. Dirty bedsheets were a pet peeve of mine.

I stripped myself bare and gently took all the pieces of pearls and starfish out of her hair, along with the jewelry her father had gifted to her and put them in a newly gained jewelry box I was going to show her today. If we weren't interrupted so frequently, she would have been able to appreciate it.

Her naked body made me have wonderful thoughts of our

dance just an hour ago, but she was sick from the seduction potion as well as mixing it with alcohol. That could have been deadly if she really was fully human. Shaking my head, I pulled her to me, and she automatically clung to my neck. The bathwater was done running and was filled with rose and gardenia petals that the maids had left. I'll have to thank them later. We both emerged into the warm water as she let out a sigh. Her eyes fluttered open and gave me a small smile.

"You are so handsome," she played with my face with her index finger. "So pretty too... such a pretty face," she giggled again. I chuckled as I took the cloth and poured the washing oils on her body. The smell of vanilla and lavender filled the room as her eyes tried to defy gravity.

"We will have pretty babies," she mumbled, and my heart grew ten times the size. Having children with her wasn't on my current to-do list, but one day we would have beautiful children. Once she was bathed and washed, I picked her up to dry her off and laid her on the fresh, clean sheets. My body was already tired and trying to wrestle a barely conscience Melina was not something I wanted to do. Naked in the sheets is what it was going to be. Climbing into bed with her, she immediately rolled over and pressed her naked body to mine.

Normally I would be rock hard but seeing her sleep so peacefully on my chest as she intertwined our legs was too precious to screw up with an erection.

There were so many things we would have to discuss tomorrow. Her friend, the prisoners, Peoni, and I wanted to throw it all away and just spend time with my darling. We hadn't had the most peaceful courtship, but tomorrow night I will give her the date she deserves.

Chapter 40

Melina

There was a pounding in my head, like a hammer to a nail. It continued pounding until my semi-conscious state was reeling in anger to wake up and take care of the pain. Lifting my hand to my forehead, I could feel the constant racking of my brain. "Ouch," I whined, feeling the tears reaching the corners of my eyes. Why was I feeling so terrible?

Groaning, I rolled over and landed on a hard chest. Squinting my eyes so the sunlight didn't rip my brain in half, I saw Osirus' perfectly sculpted chest. I couldn't believe how perfect his body was. Not a single scar. Werewolves were known for their fighting and quick healing abilities. Sometimes they healed so quickly it would leave tiny white scars on their bodies. That didn't happen with the Faes. Even though they didn't have as quick of healing as the Werewolves, their bodies would always heal themselves, so their flesh was perfect.

It was so perfect it made me to want to take my tongue and run it through the creases of his abs. The pounding in my head reminded me nothing like that could happen now and possibly for a week if it didn't let up soon. Is it possible to bruise your brain? I'm pretty sure it is after the splitting headache I have right now.

"Darling?" His voice was raspy. That beautiful silk voice wasn't present as he scooted up to the headboard. "Darling, are you all right?" Giving him a small smile, I nodded my head as I held my forehead. "Yeah, just a little headache." I tried to open my eyes, but my eyes refused and now I had the ugliest face, as one eye was completely shut and the other half open.

"Oh, darling." He chuckled. "I'll have someone get you some bring some potions to help." Throughout the morning, Osirus tended to me like a mother would a child. He checked my forehead and took a cold washcloth to my face to ease the pain. Being pampered wasn't something I was used to, but it was something I really enjoyed.

The pain was so fierce at times, I hardly noticed I was completely naked. Osirus didn't dare look at my body and there wasn't a hint of lust; he just took care of me. Fed me, stroked my head, and even tickled my back while I slept with his nimble fingers. Could this man get any more perfect?

Somewhere between lunch and dinner, I felt my strength come back to me. The small naps we took together helped enough to let me out of bed, but Osirus was by my side the entire time. "I had planned our date for this evening, but you are still weak. How about tomorrow?"

My heart had plummeted into my stomach. "No, I want to go today," I whined like a baby.

Osirus chucked and stroked my hair. "Darling, it's all right. I would rather have you 100%" Placing a gentle kiss on my forehead, he retreated to the closet, where he pulled out a dress for me to wear.

"Unfortunately, there are some things we need to discuss. Will you get dressed for me and we will go talk in the living area?" Taking the dress he picked, it was as gorgeous as all the others. A baby pink sundress with small dots all over that gave such a U.S. 1950's vibe.

While dressing, I tried to remember the events of last

night. How did I even get here? The pounding in my head was gone and the memories along with it. The last thing I remember was dancing with Osirus, his hands all over my body as we kissed, touched, and our bodies rubbing all over each other. Thinking about it was getting me hot, but that was all I could remember. Did we go to bed straight afterward?

Opening the bedroom door that led to the sitting area, I see a very distraught Tulip and Alec on the love seat. Both looked at me with worry until Osirus held out his hand to take me to sit with him. Alaneo sat carelessly in a nearby chair while Lucca had his arms crossed, giving them the evil eye.

"What's going on?" I asked, concerned. Lucca unfolded his arms as came to me and gave me a kiss on the cheek.

"Why don't you ask your 'best friend'?" he spat out those last words.

"Tulip? Is everything all right?" Tulip looked at Alec, who only nodded for her to go on.

"Do you remember what happened last night? After I gave you your last drink?" A flash went through my mind of her handing me a green substance that did not taste like the rest of the alcohol I consumed. Tilting my head, trying to remember more, more flashes came to light. Me straddling Osirus with his lust-filled gaze, me grinding into his member, my breasts almost falling out of my dress.

My face grew white as I realized I had done this in public, in front of his friends, his subjects, my brothers. Mouth agape and my hands flying to my mouth in shock, a lone tear fell down my face. Being mortified was only the tip of the iceberg. Nothing else had gone wrong, had it? Why did I do those things?

"Oh goddess," I cried. "What did I do?" I looked at Osirus with a somber look on his face.

"Darling, it wasn't your fault." The pad of his thumb brushed across my cheek, catching a tear.

"I gave you a lap dance in front of the entire kingdom!

How is that not my fault? I drank too much! They will think of me as some whore!" I cried and Lucca came up from behind me, turning me so he could ease my crying.

My hand never left Osirus' as Lucca whispered. "It isn't your fault, and the entire kingdom will know the truth."

Gazing up at Lucca, I looked at both in confusion. "Truth? What truth?" Osirus pulled me back into his arms and patted my head as my head laid in his chest.

"Darling, Tulip gave you a seduction potion. It was to inhibit your senses. They are not to be sold in our kingdom, but somehow, she retrieved some and spiked your drink." My head darted to Tulip, praying it was just a joke, a mistake. Someone else had done it and she didn't realize it.

"It's true," she whispered, barely audible. "I just wanted you to let loose. You were so nervous, and I was trying to help," she cried. Tulip tried to rush to me, but Lucca stood in front of me and growled.

"Get back, Wolf," he growled as his teeth descended into sharp points.

"How could you Tulip? That was wrong." I sucked in a breath. "You know I like to do things at my own pace. Why would you force this? This is my love story, not yours."

Even though Tulip was my best friend, she had always been the pushy one in the relationship we had. She would argue she was just the leader, which she was. I followed her around like a helpless puppy when my parents left because I had no one else, heck she even wanted it. She took me under her wing gladly, even had me be with her pack which I greatly appreciated. There were times, though, she would push too hard for something.

Like the time at a birthday party when all the Wolves were playing spin the bottle. I didn't want to play, didn't want to give away my first kiss to some random person. I remember running to her mother crying because she made me sit there and when the bottle landed on me, I wouldn't play the game. "Come on Melina, it's just a kiss," she taunted in front of her friends. I couldn't handle it, so I ran. When my parents left, I knew I couldn't live with Tulip because I still wanted my independence, but the small thought in my mind was also fear that Tulip would push too far again.

Even with her mother's pleading for me to stay in their house, I think she knew. She knew I loved her daughter like a sister, but Tulip just had too strong of a personality, and I couldn't say no until I was pushed to the edge.

Last night, that was too far.

"You could have died, Melina," Lucca broke the silence. "If you were fully human, the potion would have been too much. Hell, it was still too much, and you are only half Siren. It knocked you out cold and left you in pain. The only reason you are standing now is that father sent some Siren healing potions."

Lucca looked terrible, Father had left this morning, but he was still here. "Lucca, why are you still here?" The light blue tint to his skin was now a dull grey, eyes were red-rimmed and dark circles under his eyes.

"I wanted to make sure you were safe," he breathed. He came and gave me a kiss on my cheek again. "I must go though. I wanted to stay to see you wake up. I'll be back for the binding and coronation ceremony. Don't fuck up, Osirus," he glared and left the room with the door slamming shut behind him.

Alaneo stood up and straightened his tunic. "Now, we can't have her go unpunished, so what is our next move?" Alaneo threw his hands behind his back and started pacing the room. No longer the funny friend but the advisor to the King.

I sat on the couch in silence as they went over options on how to handle the situation. Tulip continued to sit on the couch with her hands clasping Alec's. It was brought up that she could be a traitor working for the other side of another rebellion brewing since she found the potion in the marketplace. Tulip screamed and cried that it wasn't so, but

Alaneo had refused to let it go. "My lover told me that, and do you know where she is? The prison!" he shouted. My heart clenched hearing him speak those words.

Osirus kept me on his lap and held me tightly, never wanting to let go; and I didn't want him to either.

She remained quiet as Osirus racked his brain for what to do. I really didn't want to see her get punished, but my father knew and had already threatened Osirus with a note that was delivered right after he arrived home. He wanted the girl punished. That made his little girl lose part of her mind for an hour.

I didn't think I would regain the other memories that were told me about the night. I had used my voice to sing to Osirus and called upon so many unmated wolves. Embarrassment flooded through me as I tried to conceal my tears. I never knew my voice influenced people. Had it always been there?

If it had, I could remember singing around my cabin when I would plant flowers, but I always made sure no one was there. I hated the thought of someone hearing me sing because I didn't know if I was good enough to sing out loud. There could have been so much more damage if I had sung around people, and I wouldn't have even understood it.

My head leaned back on the couch as I pondered my thoughts of Tulip. What could I do? It had to be announced that she had poisoned my drink to save my reputation as a queen. Osirus had been drunk himself and my singing, it only made it worse. Letting out a heavy sigh, Alaneo spoke of the master plan.

"We make an announcement, tomorrow," he grabbed a glass of ambrosia from the desk filled with our dinner. "That the future queen was slipped a seduction potion and was under its spell. The culprit has been captured and will receive twenty lashings and one month in the prison with no contact with their mate."

Living without Osirus for just a few days was torture, and

I wasn't marked. I couldn't imagine how that would feel once you were mated. "Isn't that a little harsh?" I spoke up.

"It isn't, for poisoning the queen, it should be death," Osirus' voice was firm and determined he wouldn't be moved. "You are lucky you are her best friend, Tulip. Otherwise, your actions would have cost your life and your mate's." Alec held onto Tulip and hugged her tightly.

"I will not announce your name to shame you unless they beg for a name," Alaneo spoke solemnly. "If the people ask, I must give it. This was the worst time to do this since we are starting over on our government. We must give the people what they want so they can trust in the system again." Tulip nodded and held onto Alec.

"Guards," Osirus spoke loudly, so they would enter our room. "Take Tulip to the level one prison cells." Looking up in question, Osirus answered. "It is one of the nicer cells. It has a bed, desk, and a small window." Giving him a small smile, I saw Tulip stand up and choke back a sob.

"I'm sorry," she choked again, looking back at me. I nodded my head at her. I don't know if I had the courage to forgive her. Tulip had been there in many times of need, but she knew I didn't want to give myself up wholly to Osirus while my father was there, yet she drugged me, hoping I would 'seal the deal.'

Alec stood in the same place Tulip left her. His fists were balled up in anger and he let out a low growl. "You wouldn't do anything, Melina? You just sat there?!" I didn't look at Alec. I didn't even know him. Just that he was my best friend's mate. I knew her better than he did. I've known her since I was three.

"Osirus, can you at least take away the twenty lashings?" The thought of her being whipped turned my stomach in knots. She may have slipped me a bit of a drug in my drink, but she didn't mean for it to be out of control; it was a series of unfortunate events.

"Your father will have my head. He specifically requested

it," Osirus pleaded into my eyes.

"I'll take care of Dad. Just keep her a month away from her mate. I'll figure out a replacement punishment." I gave him a small smile while he sighed heavily. Alaneo shook his head in disagreement.

"You know I can't say no to you, darling." I buried my face in his chest at his understanding.

Once everyone left, Osirus led me to our room. I had slept all day, but the thought of us being alone together soothed me. I needed him, and not just to cuddle. No, I needed so much more. Osirus shut the door behind him and when he turned to look up at me, my arms immediately went around his neck as I pulled myself up to his lips. Osirus' arms wrapped around me impulsively and pulled me to his toned chest.

It wasn't a kiss of love, it was lust. He took care of me all day. He peppered me with love and affection, now I needed something more. Something we haven't had in too long since my departure to the Dragon's Island.

"I want you," I said, breaking the kiss while both of us were panting. My mouth hovered over him as I continued to nip his bottom lip.

"Darling, I don't want you." My kissing stopped, and I looked up into his golden eyes, darkening into a deep whisky brown. "I fucking need you."

Chapter 41

Osirus

"I fucking need you," the words spilled out of my mouth as her panting advanced. She clutched my tunic that was coming off so I could feel her body on mine. "I need you, darling," I begged.

We started pulling off each other's clothes. It wasn't rushed, it wasn't forced. It was pure seduction. I pulled each and every string off her corset. She unbuttoned every button of my tunic. Both of us slid out of our dressings, respectively. Our eyes never left each other's as we continued to pull the clothes off our bodies.

I hadn't touched her physically in days. The dreams could only do so much. They feel great at the time but waking up; I felt alone and empty. Her nipples puckered as they hit the night air of the opened balcony window. Tulle drapes twisted and twirled along the floor as we kissed sultrily while I led her to the bed.

Laying her down gently, I kissed her neck while she looked in the opposite direction, giving me ample access to her pale neck. Her chest was rising, tickling my chest, begging for me to suck her delectable nipples. My dick grew harder as I wrapped one hand around her waist, pulling her flush with my body.

"Osirus," she whimpered as my teeth pulled on her ear. Her hands were in my hair, scratching at the scalp as my nose traced her jawline. "Make love to me." It wasn't a question; it was a wistful order. Stopping my assault on her neck, I lifted my head above hers and dove into her eyes.

"Are you sure, my love?" Melina had been through an emotional turmoil today. Her best friend had caused so much of a commotion I didn't want her to do this out of stress. I wanted her to want me because she needed me, too. "Maybe we should wait." Melina chuckled while she put a piece of hair behind my ear.

"I want to be one with you. I want to feel your love for me physically. Please, make love to me," she begged quietly. Her hand cupped my face and traced the lines of my lips with her finger. The smallest gestures she does makes me love her even more. My eyes closed, savoring her touch. It was sensuous, loving like she was adoring me, which I prayed to the fates she was.

"I need you, Osirus. Make me whole." My lips graced her in small kisses until I spread her lips with my tongue. My member rubbed the outside of her core and her soft mewls got my dick impossibly hard.

"Are you sure?" The growl in my chest was a warning. I was about to unleash my inner beast and take her body. I would take her body, but as for her soul, it will be another time.

Having already put two fingers into her body before, I knew she was extremely tight. This would hurt her and having me mark her at the same time would be just cruel. "I will take your body today, my love. Tomorrow, I take your soul." Her breath shuttered as she held both her hands out and cupped my face.

"Take this body," she whispered into my mouth, and I crashed into her lips.

My hands roamed her breasts while I kissed her, but

quickly, I sucked on one of her perfectly pink tits. I sucked so hard I swear I could have tasted the essence from within her breast. Small pink marks littered her chest. Chills ran across her skin while she rubbed her thighs together. Any other time I would spank her for trying to pleasure herself, but we were making love tonight.

I spread her legs apart as I kissed each hip tenderly. Her weeping core was calling my name, and I wanted to bury my face in her delicate flower. Licking from bottom to top, I had parted her lips with my tongue. Her hips wiggled on the bed but I held her down so she wouldn't get away, she would never get away from me. Hands automatically found my hair as she gripped tightly, moving her hips against my face.

Her core bobbed happily as I lapped up clit and sunk my tongue into her cavern. Melina's legs were trembling as she fell to pieces into my mouth. Shots of her sweet honey filled my lips as I found her gripping her breasts before me, and it was certainly a sight.

"Osirus," she whispered out once she had descended from her mountain. "More." Hades, I will give her more. Climbing on top of her, I lined my cock at her entrance. She wasn't scared at the size any longer but licked her lips in awe. A slight chuckle brushed past her lips for the excitement that was yet to come.

"Don't worry, my love. I'll make it pleasurable." Nodding for me to continue, I slowly sank my furious cock inside her pussy, being careful not to push too far. Melina moaned as I continued until I hit her innocence. "I'm sorry, my love." She looked up in curiosity and I slammed my lips on hers as I thrust forth, causing her to squeal into my mouth while scratching down my back. Hades, it felt good to feel the pleasure in my loins and the pain in my back.

Silent tears danced down her face as I felt the burn in my back. I knew her nails were not that strong, but the burning only intensified. "Please move," she whispered, and I did it delightedly. Slowly at first and then a steady rhythm showed.

Each thrust she met with her own as she gripped my biceps. Her moans fueled my fire for her as she closed her eyes.

"Don't close your eyes," I rasped as I continued to slide into her. "Let me see your soul."

Melina was painfully tight. It felt like a damn vice as her liquids coated me. My back felt like it was on fire now and I could no longer hold back my large scream into Melina's neck. Tearing was felt through my skin as I heard Melina gasp as we both released onto each other. Ropes of my seed coated her walls and into her womb. Her small thrusts became light as she fell with me.

Our breath was in sync, our bodies were one and I would never see myself with another woman for as long as I lived. Her tear-stained eyes looked up at me in awe. "Osirus, your wings," she whispered as she looked behind me.

My wings, after centuries of hiding because of my ancestors, had finally emerged. They were larger than I remembered, a white opulent that could only remind one of that of a bee's. The swirls, the sparkle and the dark tips of the wings only showed my power and right to rule The Golden Light Kingdom.

Melina looked at them in awe as she gently touched the base of my back. Her touch on my wings sent me close to another orgasm as I let out a large groan.

"I'm sorry," she whispered. "They are just so beautiful, and I'm guessing sensitive." I nodded as I glanced at Melina's naked form.

"You are so beautiful, Melina. You are the definition of imperial beauty." My darling blushed as she reached up and pecked me on the lips. My wings fluttered with glee and Melina laughed.

"Do they have a mind of their own?" she asked.

"It has been so long, but yes, they do. You can see my emotions easier. They flutter when they are happy, down when they are sad. Shake when I'm angry or afraid." I traced her lips with my finger, and she opened her mouth to suck it in.

I groaned as she sucked hard against it. "Melina, what are you doing?" I growled.

"I'm ready to claim your body now," she said seductively. Melina rolled me over with her hips, my dick still inside her body as she sat up straight. My wings instinctively were folding back into my body so I could lie on my back.

"Yes, I'm going to claim you." Her hips rolled onto my dick, and I let out a strangled growl. My hands went straight to her hips to help her move. Melina's breasts thrust up and down as she rode me. One hand on her clit and one on her breast. You would think she had done this before, but the blood on the sheets told me otherwise.

Her breasts began skipping up and down, and I sat up straight while she continued her assault on my cock. "That's it, ride the shit out of it, baby." Grabbing her breasts again and forcing a nipple in my mouth, I rolled her nipple between my teeth. Pulling and sucking while my hands palmed her arse, surely leaving bruises.

"Arrrg," she groaned. My mate loved it when I talked dirty.

She lifted again upwards from my cock, and I pulled her off like she weighed nothing and put her on her hands and knees. "Only I get to dominate your body, baby." I slapped her arse and her skin jumped while my handprint showed up pink. "Only I get to fuck this pussy." I slid into her cavern, hitting her cervix. A yip of excitement came from her mouth as I began my assault on her.

What I wouldn't give to sink my cock in her forbidden area. In time, I will dominate every part of her body.

"I will fucking do as I please with this body. This body is mine," another slap across her thigh.

Melina moaned until I heard a whisper. "I need to cum." I smirked. She was so responsive to me. My cock was twitching inside her, pleased with her asking.

"You cum when I tell you," I growled, feeling close to my release. "I control your pleasure!" I willed myself to hold it just a little longer, prolonging the desire we would spill together. The longer we could hold it, the better it would be. My eyes closed as my hands gripped her hips, slamming into her again.

"What's my name?" I growled. My fangs lengthened, and my wings ripped from my back for the second time. It was taking every bit of strength not to mark her right here, right now. Pulling my face back from her shoulder, I could think of one word that could help me. Dear gods say it.

"Daddy!" She let out a strangled cry, and it was enough to tip me over the edge and to hold my fangs back.

"COME," I roared as I spilled more of my seed into her. It flowed outside of her body from our previous session. Her body collapsed onto the bed and my erection slowly slipped out of her, which caused her to whine.

Peppering kisses on her shoulder, I whispered encouraging words to her. I prayed it wasn't too much. "You did so well," I cooed in her ear. "My beautiful baby did so well." I licked her ear that caused small goosebumps to go down the left side of her body. Letting out a small whimper, I pulled away from her body.

"Daddy, wait." Her voice was weak, and her one hand reached for me. I smiled at the nickname that made me so hard coming from her lips.

"I'll be back, darling. I'm going to clean you up." I returned with a warm cloth, cleaning up our essence that was left behind, her eyes slowly closing as I cleaned her. A small whimper left her lips again as I left the bedroom.

Grabbing water from the bathroom, I made her sit up and take a sip of water before crawling under the covers with her. Turning around, she nuzzled into my neck. "I love you," she sighed contently as she shivered against my body.

"That wasn't too much, was it?" I worried over her as her lashes kissed her cheeks.

"It was perfect," she hummed while she kissed my chest. My hand grazed her cheek as I watched her fall into a deep sleep.

Letting out a small breath while I held her small body, my excitement at having her body kept me awake. She was my caffeine and I'm sure I could have gone three or four more times before finally being sated. This was her first time, and she would be sore, delectably sore. I hope secretly she would have a limp to her walk. The thought made my member grow hard again as it rubbed up against her mound. She unconsciously stirred and rubbed against it again.

Shit.

There was no doubt she was my mate. The goddess had it planned all along; she would be an insatiable queen and mother to our children. Kissing her forehead as she slept, I settled down into the pillow. Tomorrow I would give her the date she has wanted before I claimed her soul. I'll bite her hard enough to where I touch her spirit, leaving a piece of me and taking a piece from her so we will be intertwined through all eternity.

My Melina, my love, my mate.

Chapter 42

Alaneo

Melina had been a blessing to Osirus. She trusted him whole-heartedly, and I was happy for them both. However, Melina knew how to work her mate to her advantage because the punishment of her friend Tulip was too lenient. This could be a good or bad thing, I chuckled out loud. This will only leave openings for further intimidation or future assassinations to the throne if Tulip isn't given a better punishment. I hoped Melina has something special in store for her.

In my own chambers, I must sit and wait. Osirus needed to claim Melina, and I knew he was reluctant to do so with her being half-human. The situation has fared far better than expected for her to be half Siren, but we still did not know the repercussions once she was marked. Fae just don't claim humans. It hasn't been done. We will have to leave it in the goddess' hands that she will be all right. I don't think I could stand seeing Osirus hurt if something happened to her. He had gone through so much that he has yet to tell Melina. He let his charm cover the scars of who he really was.

Osirus was in a dark place for at least 200 years in his life. Sure, he had some concubines and messed around and that's what Melina was worried about, but the savageness he had when he was younger was almost vicious. His own family had to stay away and continue to stay in the far northern part of the kingdom for fear of his anger once he took the crown. 'Cool, calm, collected' was the mantra he used to say after his warpath. His own father was in shock as he took down hundreds if not thousands of rogue vampires on his own to save Everett, Finley, and Braxton's tribe from his first battle.

It was marked in the history books as a glorious win and everyone regarded Osirus as a hero, but those who were there to see his savageness would know how it truly was.

Torture and savagery, that was what it was. He fought with more evil in his heart than any Fae I had ever seen. Plucking their eyes out before them and letting them wander the battlefield. There were no swift deaths, just torture, as they called out for their brothers to save them. Osirus wanted his enemies to know his wrath when The Golden Light Kingdom was messed with.

Rogue vampires were vicious, sure. They wanted blood and a lot of it, but his father, Nyx, was worried about his son's savageness. There were rumors of passing the crown to one of his younger brothers. Thank the gods it didn't happen, though. His brothers were more warrior-like than Osirus. A Fae king was supposed to be delicate, soothing, and commanding according to his father, but Nyx's sons did not get that memo. His wife, Nissa, and he had bred a new breed of Fae royalty, which scared them into hiding.

Several hundred years after the battle of the Vampire Rogues, Nyx thought his son should take over after years of classes and meditation to control his anger, only for it to blow up in his face. Osirus was livid and let his father know he was to protect his nation along with an army rather than sit and watch his people burn at his command.

I'd never been one of excitement with King Nyx. He was truly an elegant king that relied on his generals for the bloody warpath they could create. Osirus was never of the sort, only showing what his father wanted until the crown was passed. I was glad about it. Growing up with Osirus, he helped strengthen my own power to protect the people of The Golden Light Kingdom; maybe that was why he chose me to be his right hand.

King Nyx was a passive king that let the Court take over, while his son rectified it. I'm not sure if Osirus would ever forgive his father for the passiveness of his nation yet ruled Osirus like an iron fist.

Taking a sip of nectar, I heard a knock wrapping at the door. It was Finley, I would know that knock anywhere. "Enter." I stood up from my desk as I walked towards the door.

"Finley, it's late. Everything all right?" Finley did a slight bow, even though he knew he didn't have to. He was our brother, but he still felt indebted to Osirus, so he would always bow to his leaders.

"Peoni is talking. She wants to give us information, but she has taken a Faithful Tonic from whoever she was working for and needs the antidote." I rubbed the stubble on my chin.

"In the morning, let her fester on it awhile." I turned to retreat to my bed chambers, but Finley stopped me.

"You can't hold her betrayal to you over her head. You would have done the same if you found your mate." I growled out in frustration.

"No!" I yelled. "I would not have! I would have told Osirus immediately, mate or not. She damn well knows we were like family to the cause, and she chose the wrong path. This is more than just some petty lie she told me she had found her mate. Let her suffer the night and we will send for the alchemist in the morning." I sighed as turned my back to him. He was disappointed in me, and I couldn't bear to look at his face.

I fell too hard for Peoni even though she wasn't mine to begin with, but that was beside the point. We all had an agreement, the brothers, Peoni, Primrose and Osirus, and me. We all agreed to overthrow the Court, and she betrayed us.

"It's been a long two days, Finley. Just let it be for the night. I'm sure Osirus would appreciate some time alone with his mate." Finley left without a word as I continued to my room to sleep.

***

Morning came too quickly; the light sources had barely breached the Eastern Sea as I rose from the bed. My heart sunk realizing I must deal with Peoni today. I wasn't angry with her, just about the situation. She strung me along for weeks while plotting away with the enemy. How could she have lied to me? I thought our relationship was more than that. More than just passionate nights and secret meetings.

I dressed swiftly. The attention of Peoni could not be put off any longer. Osirus needed to know who else could try to get the throne or overthrow the almost mated couple.

The palace hallways were golden as the pink and gold light lit through the windows. There was a reason they called this The Golden Light Kingdom. The light sources were unprecedented. Not bothering to knock on their chamber doors, I marched in right into their living room. It was still early, and I knew they were to be asleep.

Knocking lightly, just enough so if they were still mating, they wouldn't be disturbed. With no answer, I cracked the door sightly. Osirus was curled up next to Melina. She was covered and had her arm over Osirus,' who clutched her waist delicately.

One day, one day, I will have that.

"Osirus," I whispered, gently tapping his shoulder. His eyes flew open and as quick as a snake's bite as he gripped my wrist as his claws buried into my skin. "It's just me!" I whisper yelled. Osirus was not known for being this aggressive and drawing blood to me. Osirus has gripped my neck and thrown me to the wall a few times, but it was mostly in jest. Never enough to hurt me. His eyes went back to his golden color as he let go and looked down at his sleeping mate.

"Get out," he growled as he turned to tighten his hold. Melina whimpered and snuggled deeper into the pillow. Osirus' aggressiveness was back this morning after so long, something was amiss.

"Did you mate her?" I question harshly. If he had mated with her without leaving his bonding mark, this would make him territorial and more aggressive. All the hard work he had laid down so many years ago would be put to the side until he officially bonded her.

There was a rumble in his chest. His ears grew, and his fangs were out of his mouth. Hell, his wings unfolded before my eyes. I hadn't seen him since his last battle some centuries ago. "I'll go, I'll go." I waved my hands in defense and walked out the door.

Osirus

Rage went through my body as I felt Alaneo's hand touched my shoulder. This bed chamber was our haven, Melina's smell was floating throughout the room and Alaneo was in here smelling her, trying to see what was mine. I let out a low growl as I squeezed Melina's body tighter to mine.

She purred and stretched as she turned her body towards me. "What's wrong, handsome?" she giggled as she kissed my neck. Kissing her temple, I felt her body rub against me again, as she put her arm around my body, feeling my wings.

"Darling, don't start something you can't finish." She giggled again, and I pecked at her lips.

"We need to get up. Alaneo needs us in the office area. I think it's urgent." Melina groaned, and I swatted her arse playfully while she shrieked.

"Don't be whiny." I nipped her bottom lip while she

hopped out of bed.

We both dressed, and I held her by my side closely. I had mated her body last night, but my mark had yet to be placed. My body knew she was ours, but our souls were yet to be intertwined and that made me nervous. She could leave if she wanted, and it could kill us both since I wouldn't be able to find her. The bond would always help me find her if she were ever to depart from me.

Going into my office, Everett, Finley, and Braxton stood at the doorway while Alaneo sat in the chair across the desk. I pulled Melina with me and sat her on my lap. She instantly cuddled into me but wiggled her body to get comfortable.

"Sore?" I whispered, nipping at her neck. A small blush went across her cheeks while she bit her bottom lip.

Melina

I wanted to stick ice cubes up my cooter. That's how sore I was, but I would not say it out loud around the boys. Gods in the heavens, when I went to the bathroom this morning, I thought I was going to die from the sting, but it was a good sting. It reminded me of all the pleasure I had last night. He was a regular Casanova. I was hoping for a long bath with him this morning to soothe my muscles, but Osirus wouldn't let me out of his sight. "You can't leave my side!" he told me darkly. All right then.

Osirus had always been possessive, not Werewolf posses-sive, but enough to show everyone I was his. Now he was acting like I was going to disappear. A hand always graced my back or waist, not one inch was separated between our bodies.

Osirus gave Alaneo a slight growl and pulled me closer if that was possible. Goddess have mercy on my lady bits.

"What is going on, Alaneo, that you had to disturb us this morning?" Osirus was pissed, his voice was deep, and his brows were furrowed. Osirus was the calm and collected one and here he was, showing all his emotion on his sleeve. Did I do something wrong? Did something happen?

"Yes, I'm sorry, Your Majesty." Alaneo cleared his throat.

"Peoni has some information to give us, but she was, indeed, given a Faithful Tonic and will need the antidote to free her from her secrets. We need your permission to retrieve an alchemist." Osirus started writing on some parchment while Alaneo lit a candle. Taking the wax stick, he dripped a few drops on the paper and Osirus placed his seal.

"Don't bother us again for the rest of the day," Osirus barked. They all looked at Osirus as he stood up and carried me with one arm behind my back and one under my legs.

"Osirus, you are being all being grumpy. You don't act like that to your friends." Osirus grunted and took me around the desk.

"They are looking at what is mine. I'll take you where I damn well please to get their fucking eyes off you." My heart fluttered and my thighs inched together. Was it me? Or was that extremely hot?

Then Everett took a few steps forward to speak to me, but Osirus whipped his head around and let down his fangs.

"Osirus!" I yelled and gripped his tunic tighter. The grip holding me was so tight, it was starting to hurt.

"He needs to mark you, Melina. The sooner the better." Everett used his deep voice. "You think Wolves are possessive? Wait until you get a Fae that didn't complete the bond." Everyone nodded while Osirus growled again.

"I know what is best for my mate, so stay out of it!" he snapped while he stormed out of the room.

Talk about PMS.

"You need to calm down," I demanded softly. Osirus didn't take us back to our chambers but led us outside. His cape was still dragging behind him as he went down the massive steps at the front of the palace. Guards were stationed in every entryway, and a few followed as Osirus came close to the gates.

"Leave us," he commanded, and the guards stood back, looking at one another. "Did I stutter? Leave us!" Osirus yelled again.

One guard dared to step closer. "Your Majesty, we are checking on the princess. You don't look well." Osirus was about to put me down to take care of the problem until I spoke up.

"Please go, I'm fine," I waved one hand in front of our bodies. "He needs to mark me," I whisper yelled, and both stood back. Taking a bow, they walked backward to watch what Osirus would do.

Osirus' cape fell to the ground as he untied it, and I gripped my arms around his neck. His wings exploded from his body and with one leap, he had us flying into the air. Where we were going, I wasn't sure, but I knew one thing: he needed to mark me today.

Chapter 43

Melina

I didn't know genuine fear until today. As Osirus leaped into the air, I held my breath, fearing that if I let go, I would fall to the ground. It was an irrational thought, but what other control did I have? Osirus was acting like a whole other being; my sweet and gentle mate had become a possessive man with wings of fury.

"Osirus!" I squealed as he continued to rise into the sky. From what I gathered; we were heading northwest, away from the sea into a land I had never been to before. Osirus looked down at me and smiled gently. All his fury had washed away and kissed me gently on the forehead.

"I'm taking you on our date. It's overdue," he rasped, trying to keep his calm. He must have read my aura that I was completely petrified not just being in the air but with his change of behavior. I kept silent, watching over the land below me. The scenery and topography change so quickly in Bergarian. You could be standing seaside and when you go twenty miles inland, you could be in the valley of the mountains.

No matter what part of the land we were in, Bergarian was stunning. From the flows trees to the mystical lakes all the way down to the dark forests to the South. The land was magical and, in some ways, deadly. I didn't know the extent of the danger of Bergarian, but I'm sure it was more deadly than that of Earth. If the supernatural beings were strong, who knows what wild animals one had to look out for here?

Osirus gripped me tighter as he descended halfway up the foothills of the mountains. Luscious trees canopied the forest floor, so no one from towering heights could peek. One tree stood out among the rest, with a small cabin in its branches. From the outside, it looked worn down and nothing to be worth exploring, but Osirus landed on its porch that stuck out on a large limb.

The planks of wood were unbalanced where the tree had taken over and moss started growing on the sides of the small treehouse. "You aren't going to chop me up into little pieces now that I am alone, are you?" I joked lightly as I nudged his arm. Osirus slid his arm around my waist and planted a kiss on my lips.

Silent treatment, nice.

Osirus opened the rickety door, only to be met with a burst of light coming from the room. The room was in sharp comparison to the house outside. It was pristine. The walls were painted white, there was a skylight above us so one could easily look at the stars. A large mattress with many fresh blankets and fabrics with colors I've never seen before all laid to perfection. Pinks, purples, blues, and greens. It was done so one would think you stumbled into a gypsy's hideaway.

A small chandelier hung at two corners of the room and candles lit throughout. "Osirus," I whispered in surprise while touching the small pieces of furniture. How could this all fit in here? The whole treehouse looked like a shack on the outside.

"It's a cloaking spell. I had a friend cast it so no one would ever find this place." Osirus stepped in and led me to the gigantic bed on the floor. He pulled me to his lap and peppered kisses on my neck. "It's a place I used to hide as a child, before my father," Osirus looked away and stared out the large windows that overlooked the valley. "Before he became blind to Cosmo's devious ways."

I used my fingers to tickle his chin as he looked back into my eyes. "There is a lot about me you don't know, Melina, and I wanted to explain that to you today. I want you to get to know me as I have gotten to know you."

Daphne

I continued to sit on the most uncomfortable bed of my existence. I should be used to it; I've been here several times when I got on Osirus' nerves. Damn king doesn't know what he's missing. Letting out a huff, I stood up to pace the floor. It had been five days since he's locked me down here.

Five days, even after I gave up my father, who knows where he could be. Actually, I know. He's down past the dungeons and in the torture rooms. He'd been there before, but never on the receiving end, always the one giving.

Peoni was sobbing across the hall. Peoni had become a good chess piece in all this, finally hammering in the nail that I needed to get my way. My father trained me for this mess. He just expected that I would do it for him, the pot-bellied fool.

I love my mother. I do, but power was more important. Once I get the power I wanted from Osirus after the bonding, I would go back to her. She might not like what I've done but I'll keep her safe. Even if it means sacrificing innocent lives for it.

"Peoni, I'm sorry," I pleaded to her. "I just had to save my mother. You know how cruel my father is!" I let a few tears drip down my cheeks, milking this for all it's worth. Maybe I could use Peoni again. Right now, I'm not sure how, but it is always good to have a backup.

"It's all right. He's the one that imprisoned me, not you. You are just trying to protect your own blood," she whimpered again and rolled over in the bed. Internally laughing, I went and sat back down, only to hear the large dungeon door slam. You couldn't hear much movement, but you could certainly tell it was a powerful presence, one that I have come to know since Osirus makes him deal with me.

"Alaneo!" I cried. "Please, let me go see my mother. I must check if she is all right!"

Alaneo gave me a side glance and ticked his jaw in my direction. "His Majesty is out for the day. I'll have more information for you tomorrow." He walked past me as the bottom of his cloak touched the dirtied stairs as he reached Peoni's cell.

The key made a loud clack as the door was unlocked, which in returned let out a long whine as the door opened. "Let's go, Peoni." Alaneo turned and didn't wait for her to follow. The three red-headed freaks nodded to her sorrowfully as she walked out behind Alaneo.

"What are you going to do to her?!" I cried. "She's innocent! She was just trying to protect her mate!" I gripped the bars and leaned my face as close as I could to get a better look. Where exactly were they taking her? She betrayed them. Surely, she wasn't getting out this soon.

"She's got information, just as you did with us, Daphne," Finley spoke while he eyed me warily.

"Oh, that's good then!" I chirped, "What kind of information?" Finley let out a sigh and continued walking.

"That's what we are going to find out," he responded, annoyed. Peoni couldn't speak too much. She took a Faithful Tonic to Cosmo; any secrets she had with him would never come to the surface, so at least part of the plan where Melina would be killed would still be in place. Luckily for me, I was nowhere near my father during the exchange.

"Good luck, Peoni!" I cheered for her as her head was still low.

"She doesn't need luck. She'll have the antidote," Braxton jeered as he nudged Finley with his elbow. "Yer a damn idiot, did ya know that?" Finley silenced him as I watched them walk out the dungeon door.

My heart spiked. So, they knew she took a Faithful Tonic. Shit.

"You're worried," I heard a low voice at the back of a nearby cell. I didn't even know anyone else was still down here. "Question is, what are you worried about?" Footsteps came closer to the cell that was three doors down adjacent to me.

"Who are you?" I asked.

"Melina's ex-best friend." Her voice was heavy as she paused. "So, what is it? Afraid of what they will find out or afraid for Peoni? Because if anyone knows about fake sympathy, it's me, and honey, you aren't that great of an actress you think you are." I could almost imagine the fake eye-rolling from the smelly mutt.

I gritted my teeth, wanting to spit in her face. I could trick my aura to radiate innocence, but she didn't think I could act. How dare she talk to me that way, the stupid dog. "Why do you care?" I hissed back.

"Because if you are worried about some plan being exposed or have plans to ruin the star-crossed lovers, I want in, and I can help." The woman tried to grip the bars, but it instantly burned her hands, causing her to hiss.

"Why should I trust you? You were a close friend," I questioned.

"Because I'm tired of being ignored. Growing up with her was a pain in my ass. 'Melina this and that, she's so strong. She lost her parents. Look how great she turned out.'" The annoyance in her voice grew louder, almost a yell.

"My own parents thought of her more of a daughter than me! Then I invite her to my mating ceremony so I could be the center of attention for once and she comes to be mated to the freaking Fae King! How unfair is that!?" she whined as she punched her cell wall. All right, a motive to hate her. I could work with this. She's got the muscle I needed.

"All right, say if I trust you. What are you willing to do and what do you want?"

"Anything, take her away from her mate and make her disappear. We can throw her back on Earth or give her to the rogue vampires. I don't care." The voice was filled with malice and disgust. I crossed my arms across my chest as I fiddled with my lips with my fingertips. I'm running out of options and fast. Peoni's mate will only stay underneath the spell for so long; he was probably coming out of it as we speak. I'm going to lose the muscle that we needed to trap Osirus in a bonding marriage to me.

This she-Wolf might be some help, after all. "What's your name?"

"Tulip," she mumbled.

"Hmm, then I think I will have something for you to do then."

Alaneo

"Peoni, are you sure you want to do this?" The after-effects of the Faithful Tonic antidote were going to be brutal. She wouldn't be able to shift into a full size for at least a week or two, which will cause difficulty in her mate claiming her.

I had Braxton go out this morning after Osirus had left to find her mate. He was in a make-shift cell at Cosmo and Daphne's home. Silver chains had scarred his wrists and there were gashes along his torso. Black veins were across his body like a tangled web as his body continued to breathe harshly. His heartbeat was erratic, and his eyes were black with red pupils. All of this pointed to one thing: black magic and the overuse on his body. If he wasn't a warrior and just an omega, he would have died days ago. He was in rough shape and reversing the spell would be difficult, but there were signs he was coming out of it. This Carson, the name I had come to know, was no longer present, just the empty shell.

"Mate, mate," he moaned as we kept him in a portable ironed cage, we had in one of the private guest rooms. He had spent enough time in a dungeon, and it was obvious he wasn't of sound mind when he tried to take Melina. Peoni had stayed in her large form for too long once she reached the guest room, ready to tell us everything we needed to know, but she did it for him.

I could see the desperate look in her eyes as she rounded the corner. A sickening sob from her lips came from her as she rushed toward him. Braxton grabbed her arm, a bit too harshly for my liking, holding her back. "He's still under the spell, Peoni. You need to wait. The alchemist is in the other room working on it." She nodded her head solemnly as we sat her down in the chair.

"Are ye ready?" Everett stood, holding the sickening green concoction.

"Yes, of course," she nodded and downed it all in one go. That was something I loved about her; she was ballsy. Once the last drop touched her lips, she dropped the glass that shattered to pieces. Her hand immediately went to her throat as her body spasmed. Her wings shortened immediately as well as the rest of her body, resulting in her original height of just 12 inches. She sputtered a bit and sat up. Most of her magic was gone and would cause her inability to grow or fly.

"I'm all right." She sat up in the cushioned chair. Carson stared at her with hurt in his eyes. "I'm all right," she waved at him as the faint hint of a smile played on his face.

"Are you ready for this? I'm only saying it once." I need to help him," she cried. "I've been without him too long already." Everett nodded as he stepped away, and I stood forward, ready to listen to the explanation.

"Carson came to the palace gates a few days after Melina arrived. There was a bag in his hand and a note. I'm not sure what it was for or where it went. We immediately knew we were mates, and we embraced each other, and he wanted to take and mark me right then. I was trying to take him into the palace to complete the bond until Daphne saw me and stopped us and beckoned me to follow her back to er house. That it was urgent in matters of the King. I was still undercover to watch him, so I went willingly, along with Carson because he wouldn't leave my side." she blushed.

"Carson didn't know the threat that we were walking into, but there was no way to warn him. I swear, baby!" She looked to Carson, who only stared at her with love. "There was a witch there. I didn't catch her name, but she cast a spell and he was immediately transported to the basement, and I was grabbed, forced to take the tonic. All he had to do was say, 'in this to you, I entrust,' and then I couldn't repeat anything he told me to do. However, the idiot didn't tell me I couldn't say 'I had a Faithful Tonic given to me,' that was the only reason why you know."

Finley snickered in the corner, "Dumb fuck." His brothers laughed in agreement as Peoni continued.

"With the help of the witch, he could watch all my moves through a mirror, so I couldn't tell you all anything. If I didn't comply, they would hurt Carson. They had plans to kill her with Carson and blame it on him and the Cerulean Moon Kingdom." Peoni laid down on the seat. Her eyes were heavy. "I'm so sorry, Alaneo. I didn't want to hurt anyone, especially you." Tears sprouted from her eyes.

"It's all right, Peoni. I understand." I went to pet her tiny head until I heard the bars of the cell shaking violently while the hinges broke.

"MINE!"

Chapter 44

Alaneo

Growls erupted the room while Peoni laid now unconscious on the cushioned seat once she heard her mate's growls. I backed away slowly, holding my hands up in surrender as Carson continued to rattle the cage.

"What the hell is going on here?" the alchemist, Cullen, spoke as he continued to stir the concoction in one bowl. "I can't concentrate on shit when you guys are in here teasing the crippled one." Carson growled at Cullen, who just stuck out his tongue. "Yeah, watch it pal, or my own Werewolf will come haunt your ass. He's a beta, a bit stronger than you are, too. While you are weak like this," he swirled his finger around Carson in the air, "you ain't worth shit."

Carson sat back down in the cage to sulk. He knew he was weak and still technically under the mind-control power, so even if he wanted to attack, his strength wouldn't come to him unless Cosmo was the one controlling him. "Yeah, that's what I thought." Cullen bounced his hip as he laid his hand on it. "He's a damn fine warrior, too. You are lucky I came to help. He hasn't marked me completely, and he was NOT happy I was coming here."

Cullen had just found his mate just two days ago as a

warlock doctor through the Golden Light Kingdom. Cullen found his mate when the Werewolves came back from the battle with the nobles, seeking tonics to help their wounds heal faster for the party. When we called upon him, he was preparing, to move into his mate's pack. "What's going on?" A large burly Wolf walked in. He had platinum blond hair and bright red eyes, his skin was almost white, enough for one to think he was a white Wolf, which only strengthens him to even out his inability to blend in with his surroundings.

"Nothing, dear. This Wolf started acting all naughty, but I brought up your status and he straightened out." Cullen went over and kissed his mate sweetly. "This is Jaison, Jaison, these people," Cullen waved his hand around again with sass, "hired me to fix the Fairy and the Wolf." Cullen put the bowl down and looked over Carson before he administered the tonic.

"You are coming out of the dark magic on your own, but just to be sure, this tonic will flush your system quick, but you will be down for a few days. No shifting, no mating obviously until Peoni can shift back to a full form to complete the bond. Do you understand?" Cullen spoke in a no-nonsense tone. Carson nodded and was handed the tonic to drink. "Once you bond with Peoni, she will stay in a full form because you both feed off each other's souls, in case you were wondering." Cullen winked as he walked away.

The face said it all. It was vile tasting as he made gagging noises. "Give it an hour and he will start vomiting all that dark tar up. Then he should be good to go and let out of the cage." Cullen flicked his long blond locks over his shoulders and grabbed Jaison's hand.

"Let's do this, honey," and walked out of the room. The brothers shivered, thinking about what was about to happen. The newly paired couple had asked for the honeymoon suite as payment so they could brag to their friends as they mated in the Golden Light Kingdom Palace.

"I'm truly happy for them to find each other," Everett

spoke. "But Cullen looks like he is into more kinky shit than we are."

Braxton snickered. "Yeah, think they will let us watch?"

Finley smacked Braxton upside the head. "We already got in trouble for something like that, remember?" Braxton pouted in the corner while the other two shook their heads.

After an hour, we led Carson into the water closet to throw up any of the remaining magic in him. Once he was finished, he rushed out of the room to tend to his mate. The cell was properly taken out of the room and the new couple could help heal each other while they recovered. Staying close with your mate could help accelerate healing, but with the wringer that these two just went through, they will still have some time.

I wanted to tell Carson to take care of Peoni, to make sure she was always happy. This would be the first woman I would ever miss laying in my bed. We would talk for hours about the most irrelevant things. Osirus had no idea until recently of the affair we had. She would dress in different clothes and go as far as to wear a wig and chase me down when we would leave to visit different villages. The thrill of getting caught was a turn-on for her, and let's face it, it was for me too.

Carson carefully picked her up and cradled her to his chest and made sure her wings wouldn't get bent at an odd angle. Immediately, Peoni sighed in contentment and grasped his shirt. Clearing my throat, I said, "We will leave you both to it then. Remember what Cullen said about her, she's going to be weak." Carson growled, sensing my worry for his mate. He has every right to hate me. I was her lover for the past three years and we had formed a wonderful friendship. I can kiss that goodbye.

Nodding them off, I shut the door to the last relationship I will ever have until I find my mate. It hurt too much to accidentally fall in love with someone that wasn't meant to be yours.

Melina

Osirus just spent the last hour telling all his 'sins' to me, some that I should know and other things that I really didn't want to know. Like how many women he had been with. It was making him feel better, so I kept my lips sealed as spilled all his dark secrets. It was almost too much and several times I wanted to speak up and tell him to stop. Weirdest date ever.

Now Osirus has his face buried in my lap in front of me. I'm petting his hair like a small child. Who knew he would be on such an emotional roller coaster after just having one night with me? It was precious but very concerning, which I could only blame for the partial mating we had last night. "Osirus, I'm fine. I don't know why you wanted to tell me all this, but I love you and I'm not going anywhere."

Osirus looked up, eventually sitting up, and pecked me on the lips. "You are too good to me, darling."

Cupping his face once more, I gave him a kiss on the cheek. "Does it bother you that bad you don't have a great relationship with your father? He just thought he was doing what was best. When a son decides on his own path rather than his father's, I'm sure it was difficult for him to understand. Parents make mistakes too."

"You're right. Once they see the kingdom in a better place, I hope they will understand better." Osirus stood up to look out the window while I sat on the bed. It was mid-afternoon and Osirus had just calmed down.

"He will be proud of you. Just wait," I said optimistically as I stood up and wrapped my arms around his waist. Osirus was so tall. He towered over me, and I loved feeling helpless in his arms. Call me cliché, but I loved the feeling of being taken care of. "How long are we staying here?"

"As long as you like, darling." Osirus was being so sweet, but something had awoken in me last night. I wanted more of him, and I kept getting dirty thoughts in my head. We were here to complete the mating bond. We had to before we go back because it would be a disaster if we didn't. We both wanted it so why don't I stir the pot a bit and get this show on the road? I started giggling to myself, and Osirus looked at me questioningly.

"So, now that you have told me all your war stories, what do you want to do now?" I paused for a moment before I laid down the last word to get him going. "Daddy?" Osirus closed his eyes and lulled his head back.

"Don't start something you don't want to finish, baby," he rasped as his grip on my arms became tight. I giggled again, trying to spur something out of him, but he was ahead of me. "Because right now, I don't want to be gentle." A chill of excitement went down to my core. Sensing my eagerness, he backed away from me, which gave me a frown.

Osirus took off his tunic and threw it in the corner and sat down in an old chair with his legs spread. His trousers were loose and let his member strain against the fabric. Refraining from licking my lips in eagerness, I waited to see what he wanted me to do.

"Take off your clothes," he almost growled. His eyes quickly changed to the whisky amber as his breaths became long and deep. There wasn't time to think. I gently pulled the dress off my body, leaving me only in my undergarments.

"All of it." His voice was low and commanding. It showed more threat than if he yelled at me. Osirus' eyes became hooded as he palmed his pants, looking for friction. His chest muscles were rippling beneath his skin, which caused an involuntary whimper to leave my mouth. The Siren in me must be waking up because never in my life had I been this wet.

"You like it when I command you, don't you, baby?" There was a strain in my voice as I tried not to groan at his presence. "You like it when speak harsh." I nodded my head, which earned a growl.

"Speak when you are spoken to, darling."

"Yes," I whispered.

"Yes, what?" he raised his voice.

"Yes, Daddy," I said a little louder than my black thong dropped to the floor.

"Good girl, now lay on the bed, on your back."

My questioning look make him smirk evilly as he nodded his head for me to continue. "Go or I'll smack your ass so hard you won't enjoy it." I squeaked and laid down on the mattress in haste. The excitement of what he was going to have me do next was making me tingle with eagerness.

"Spread your legs," he whispered lowly. My hands were at my side, and I parted my legs. "I want you to touch yourself, touch that pretty pink pussy." Mortification filled me as I took a moment to think. Osirus got up and flipped me over and spanked my butt, causing a beautiful sting. "Don't think, just do," he whispered hypnotically in my ear.

Flipping back over, he got up and stood at the foot of the bed. I've pleasured myself before in the bathtub while he was speaking with Alaneo, I was not a stranger to that but doing it in font of someone else was erotic and a bit embarrassing. What if he didn't like what I did? Taking my right hand, I slowly traced down my belly, which, in turn, Osirus let out a gigantic sigh as he watched me part my lower lips. I was already wet. He had to have known that because as soon as I rubbed my clit I could hear the wet moisture from the movement.

"Fuck, that's so sexy," he growled as he started taking off his trousers. He palmed his erection and pumped it up and down as I continued to rub my bundle of nerves. Feeling a jolt of pleasure, I arched my back, closing my eyes. "Stick your finger in your pussy, baby," Osirus rasped. He laid down on the bed with his head between my thighs, watching up close what I'm doing.

"Another one." Another finger slid into my hole and my other hand was itching to do something. My breasts were out in the open and him not touching me was driving me crazy. Taking my left hand, I grabbed my breast. It was just enough to over-fill my hand as I gripped it tightly. A moan left my lips, and I felt Osirus grip the sheets beside my hips. "Ugh, fuck, go faster."

Taking my two fingers, I tried to force them in harder and deeper, I felt the pleasure at the pit of my stomach as I arched my breasts upwards. "I can't take it," he growled and ripped my fingers out of my body and thrust in with his own. His fingers were longer and thicker than mine, so the sudden intrusion set me off. He pumped hard, making my body move up on the bed. Stars filled my vision as I pinched my nipple as he assaulted me.

The cum coming from my body had already drenched the sheets as Osirus lapped up the juices from my body. I wasn't done yet, and I knew Osirus wasn't either. I felt like going on for hours. This new person inside me wanted more, and I prayed Osirus would thrust his cock into me soon.

"You taste like honeysuckle." He tugged on my lower lips with his teeth as yelped with the sensitivity. Osirus' cock was raging hard and by the looks of it, pre-cum was dripping down, ready for it to be in its rightful place. Osirus stood up, licking his lips, and turned around, showing off his muscular back and toned behind.

Sitting down in the chair, he spread his legs. "Come here." His eyes stayed trained on me as I got up from the bed. My legs felt like gelatin, but the suspense was fueling me to continue what he was going to do next. "Kneel," he spoke in his deep voice, as I kneeled in front of him. I was eye to eye with his one-eyed monster. I looked up at Osirus waiting for instruction. I was incredibly turned on and wanted nothing more than to please him like he pleases me.

"Suck my cock," he spat. Grabbing the bottom section of his dick, I licked underneath his balls which earned a hiss as he grabbed my hair and sunk my mouth around him. "GODS MELINA!" he yelled as I licked up and down his shaft. His dick was oozing cum like it couldn't be contained. He was holding himself, trying not to explode, but he was failing.

345

Grabbing his balls and bobbing my head, I felt his dick twitch, and I readied myself to drink his seed. Osirus yelled out as he spurts his load right down my throat, not even able to swallow.

Before he was even finished, he pulled me up and kissed me. I could taste myself on his lips as he could taste his own. "Ride me," he growled as pulled me onto his lap and centered my cavern right on top of his large member. Osirus was already hard and ready as he pushed me down harshly as my pussy swallowed him whole clenching him tightly.

Using the chair to my advantage, I put my feet on the floor and moved up and down his shaft. His hands were firmly placed on my hips and helped me go faster. His breath was heaving as sweat was dripping from both of us. "Fuck me harder, baby," he moaned. "Grind your cunt into me." My breasts were right in his face as he grabbed on with his teeth, pulling and sucking as I felt the ridge at the top of his cock hit my g-spot.

"Ahhh, Osirus!" Goosebumps erupted over my body, getting closer, but Osirus pulled me off. I whined loudly at the sudden loss, and he slapped my ass harshly. Turning me around he had my ass facing him and slammed me again on his cock. "MORE!" He pushed and pulled my hips to continue riding him. We weren't just going up and down, we were rocking in a full circle and my body was growing tired.

"I want to stick my cock in your ass, Melina. One day I'm going to. I'm going to conquer your body one day at a time." He slapped my ass again, causing me to shutter.

"I'm going to fucking mark you, Melina. You are mine, no one else. Your pussy, your body, I am to do what I please, do you understand? I will fuck you when I want and how I want."

"Yes, Daddy." I leaned my body back so he could bite into my shoulder.

"Cum with me now, baby, cum all over your daddy's cock." Osirus grabbed both of my breasts and pulled me back and bit hard into my shoulder. I felt the blood trickle down as the best orgasm filled my body. My breath slowed as I felt my body become light as a feather. I leaned back onto Osirus' opposite shoulder so I wouldn't fall forward. His teeth were still sunk into my skin as my eyelids closed, blocking out the light from the outside.

Chapter 45

Osirus

My fangs quivered as they elongated, looking at her pale flesh. I thrust into her hard as she took my cock. Her pussy was clamping on my dick, squeezing the life from it as she oozed from her wetness all over my lap. The slapping of our skins could be heard throughout the forest. Thank the gods we were high in the tree.

Lifting her up several times and grabbing her breasts, she leaned back into me. She knew what was coming and it wasn't just my dick. My fangs tickled the crook of her neck and I plunged them into her soft, buttery skin. My fangs went in deep, clear into the muscle. Her body spasmed as her orgasm held out longer as the venom from my fangs was injected into her.

The venom, like every supernatural, is released when marking their mate, causing them to be better matched physically. If a fairy was mated to a Wolf, the fairy could automatically stay larger for longer periods of time to keep the bond strong. Sirens could stay out of the water and be able to live on land if mated with a vampire, and so on. Melina could already always stay with me, so I did not expect her to change much because of her human and Siren genes.

I didn't want to let go, my fangs urged me to stay in for longer and what I've learned about my kind is that if there is a feeling to do something, you follow it. My dick was still pulsing in her body, letting load after load squirt into her. My body had become weaker, and my darling had already fallen asleep.

My fangs retracted on their own as we both slumped into the chair. I held onto her tightly and gently slipped my cock from her body. Still, the damn thing would not give up because it had a mind of its own. I was instantly hard again, watching my mate's breasts heave up and down as she took deep breaths. A small whimper slipped from her pouty lips as I carefully laid her on the gigantic bed full of blankets and pillows.

I marked her first. Now she will have to do the same to me. My venom should run through her body, giving her soul the ability to latch onto mine by the time she wakes up. She may not want to mate again for a few days. I had been rough with her for two nights in a row. She had to be sore. I grinned widely with that thought.

Pulling up the blankets, I wrapped our bodies together and laid my head on her breasts. She was soft in the right places and my dick immediately wanted more. Goddess, please wake up tomorrow, I pleaded with her.

***

Melina didn't move at all in the night, despite me waking up every hour to check on her. She had started to sweat, and her skin had become pale in comparison to what her skin naturally looked. Her cheekbones were more prominent and had an iridescent glow, with slight hints of blue and green sparkle reflected in her cheeks. Her lips were still the pouty pale pink I adored, and the roots of her hair were turning white.

I never knew there would be this much change in her body and features, she was half Siren and already could walk on land just fine. Now she looked more Fae with hints of her Siren family's colors coming through on parts of her skin. The human part of her must be leaving her.

If her whole body was to change, then she wouldn't wake up today; she would sleep until the transformation was complete. Keeping her close to my body, I stroked her arm to let her know I was there. The bond was powerful and even though she was sleeping, her soul knew that I was there watching over her.

I kept myself busy as the days progressed; we had been here for three days and not a movement from Melina. I had already sent word from a passing forest sprite to let Alaneo know we were alive and well and he could figure out the Daphne problem on his own. I didn't have time to sit and think about her release, all I could think about was my destined.

Melina's hair was now white, a stark contrast to her original deep ebony hair. There were hints of light blue highlights that were heavier at the tips of her long hair. My darling was still small compared to me. Her petite features made her look just like a fairy and not a Fae.

A light groan came from the bed as I stood up from the far side of the room. Her arm rose above her head and shielded her eyes. "Osirus?" she croaked. Melina's voice cracked as she said my name and I rushed to her with some water.

"Darling, are you all right?" I picked her up to sit her in my lap. If it were ever possible, she felt lighter to me as she nuzzled into my neck.

"I'm so tired. Is it morning already?" Another yawn left her lips, and it made me want to smash mine into the plump softness.

"Darling, you've been asleep for three days." Her eyes opened suddenly as she glanced out the window.

"It has? No way! What happened? Was I sick?" she asked hurriedly, while I started laughing.

"No, darling, I've marked you. Remember when I said

things may change about your body? Your body put you to sleep so my venom could help with you changing." Melina tried to get up from my arms to find a mirror, but I held her back. "Darling," I whispered.

"Lemmie goo! I wanna see! What happened to me?" Looking down at her legs, she noticed automatically that her legs were blemish-free and milky white. A small gasp came from her lips.

"Come here." I pulled her up to standing and put my hands over her eyes and walked to the full-length mirror. My Melina was stunning before and even with this transformation her body still could give me a raging erection. I was still in awe of her beauty. A beautiful Fae queen, she would make. Her slightly pointed ears started turning red, which made me chuckle out loud.

"Don't make fun. Let me see!"

Melina

He was playing a game, and it was driving me insane. My whole body was different. I could feel it. I felt lighter. My skin by itself looked so smooth and white I could take a cookie and dip it on my skin like frosting. Getting impatient, I jumped up and down and Osirus laughed at me some more.

"Okay, now." He tickled my ear with his lips.

My heart stopped as I took in my appearance. My hair was no longer the dark curls that stopped mid-back. My hair was as white as my father's, with streaks of blue just like my brother Lucca's, and fell to my waist. My cheeks had a sparkle to them with hints of green and blue. Maybe where scales should have been? My eyes never changed, but my facial features were more supernatural than the human face I once wore. My cheeks were higher, and my jaw was sharper. It was definitely a Fae look.

"How are you doing? Do you like it?" he breathed, waiting

for my answer. In all honesty, I was shocked. This was something I never imagined myself to look like. I had never been the most beautiful person in school, but I certainly thought I was all right. Looking at me now, looking more like Osirus and his people, our people, I felt beautiful.

"Osirus," I whispered slowly. His hand came to my shoulder and waist as he moved some of my hair to the other side of my neck. Gently kissing my mark, he laid his head on my shoulder. "You are stunning, Melina. You always have been but knowing that our souls are that much closer to being one makes you more ravishing." A slight pink came to my cheeks.

"Let's see if you have wings." He stood back from me while I stood in the middle of the room. He had me in a short mini skirt that many Fae women wore and a sleeveless top that had an open back. "I want you to stand there and concentrate. I want you to imagine your wings coming from your body. You will feel a slight tingle and then it will go on its own." I took a deep breath, concentrating on Osirus' words.

Could I really have wings too? I can already swim and breathe in the water, but to fly too, surely I couldn't be that lucky. I felt Osirus walk towards me, sensing my reluctance to try. "When a fish is destined for the bird, the goddess will only help the fish grow its wings." A chaste kiss was left on my lips as I smiled at him. He always knows how to say the right things!

Concentrating, I willed myself to think of wings sprouting from my back. There was warmth flowing through my body as the tingle in my back intensified. I swore an animal was scratching through my back as I heard a large whoosh come from behind me. Letting out a scream, I felt the wind blow from behind me. Osirus came and stood in front of me, catching me from falling.

"Darling, look." Staring back into the mirror, I saw two large wings. They weren't iridescent like Osirus', these were colorful. Blues and greens were swirled together that reminded me of a butterfly. Both were symmetrical to each other with the explosion of color.

"You are the perfect combination of both Fae and Siren, love." I willed them to flutter, and they did exactly as they were told. Just like curling my fingers up in a ball when I wanted, my wings listened too. Completely under my control.

"This is amazing," I muttered to myself as I continued to flap and look at myself in the mirror.

"Come on, darling, let's go for a test drive." Fluttering once, then twice and registering what Osirus said, I stopped, frozen in fright.

"Eeeehhhh what?" I spoke in a high-pitched voice. "I'm not ready for that!" When Osirus had flown me here, I was petrified. There wasn't a mighty Dragon beneath me where I had the powerful muscles to catch me from falling. Osirus smiled, and he reached for my hand and pulled me to him; his wings were already out of his body, twitching like a hummingbird. "Come," he commanded, but as we got close to the door, I took my hand from him. I had to think of something fast, a good excuse. I could not jump out of this tree and fall flat on my face. What if I embarrass myself and can only fly in a circle like a rabid dog?

"Darling?" Osirus' voice became worried, but with the split second of a plan I had concocted in my head, I knew this would save the day.

"But what if I want to do something else? Daddy?" I whispered lowly. Osirus took a few steps towards me.

"Do you now?" His nose traced my jaw as his hot breath cascaded down my neck. "Are you sure?" His mouth connected to my neck as he sucked, causing my legs to become weak. His body pressed up against me as I wrapped my arms around his neck. "I think you just want to get out of your lessons." His teeth nipped at my ear as I let a moan slip.

Feeling bold, I lowered my hand to feel the bulge in his pants. "But isn't Daddy supposed to take care of his baby?" Osirus groaned as his hand slipped under my shirt to feel my breast, squeezing it harshly. I let out a squeak and his mouth consumed me. His tongue explored mine as I reached in his pants to hold on to his dick tightly. Groaning, he bit down on my lip hard, causing it to bleed. My little yip caused him to pause and look into my eyes.

"You are being naughty and not listening to your Daddy." Osirus pressed his cock to the outside of my clothes. Too many clothes were between us as and my panting subsided.

"Daddy, my princess parts are tingling," I whined, half giggling as he slapped my pussy. Immediately, I could feel the slick run between my legs. "Please, Daddy!" I whined again now more needy as I gripped his tunic. Before he could slam me to the bed, we heard a woman scream in a sing-song voice.

"OSIRUS!! Are you up there!?" She paused while I looked at Osirus harshly. It better have not been one of his past lovers. I don't care if I forgave him. I didn't need to see any of the sluts. Jealousy was already consuming me as I felt my teeth start to itch.

"There are rumors in the trees you have been here! Get down here before I come up and break down the door!"

Chapter 46

Melina

My teeth were itching. It was the strangest feeling but also the overwhelming of wanting to kill whatever woman was down there. I could feel my wings get agitated as a large scowl landed on my face.

"Who is that?" I growled at Osirus, who stood to look at me in shock. His hand went out to grab me, but I slapped it away. The fury running through my veins was taken over because before he answered, I ran out the door. Not even thinking, I jumped off the broken porch façade of a treehouse and fluttered to the ground.

As I landed, I put one hand out to steady myself. If only Tulip could see me now. I looked like freaking Iron Man about to blow up the terrorists.

The woman before me was beautiful, with long blonde hair with bright green eyes. She had the similar features of the Faes, but one could tell easily she was an elf. The Elven people had a slightly tanner skin than the Fae and their ears were not as pointed. Her dressing was also different as she wore tight clothes that resembled leaves that wrapped around her body like a second skin.

The woman's breath hitched and looked at me in horror.

"I am so sorry. I thought Osirus was up there. I didn't mean to disturb you!" Her voice stuttered as she backed away from me.

"Oh, he is up there all right." My wings jolted me forward as I grabbed her by the neck and pinned her to the tree. I felt Osirus' presence as he grabbed my shoulder. My body instantly relaxed as he kissed my mark.

"Darling, let her go and let me explain." His voice was as smooth as the first time I heard him speak those weeks ago. It calmed me as my teeth tingled once more and were no longer sharp. My grip lessened, but not enough to let go.

"Who are you?" I growled at her. The fear in her eyes was clear. She dared not look at Osirus, only at me, the one whose life I was now holding.

"I'm Lura. Osirus' cousin!" she tried to speak, but it came out small and meek. My face of anger quickly went to embarrassment as I let her go. Lura started coughing, grabbing her throat, and I tried to help her up.

"I'm so sorry, I don't know what came over me! I've never hurt anyone. I'm so sorry!" My words came out rushed, while Osirus and Lura started laughing at my apology.

"It's all right!" She waved her hand around. "I should have been more careful. I heard he had yet to complete the bond with you and from the looks of it you haven't marked him yet, so of course, you would be overprotective. It's normal!" I held my breath. I was so insanely jealous I was about to kill someone. My eyes went glassy only for Osirus to shush me and pull me to his chest.

"Darling, it is all right. It is normal." He kissed my forehead, but the feeling of disappointment in myself was still there. Something else controlled my body, and I didn't like it. "You are both Siren and Fae, you will have trouble battling both, but you will get the hang of it with your emotions. I just need you to mark me before we head back to the palace, so you don't kill anyone." He laughed again. I cringed as he spoke about killing someone.

"Anyway," Lura said as she tried to break the tension. "We are starting a large feast and wanted to know if you both would like to join? It's actually in honor of the new kingdom." My stomach immediately growled at the thought of food. It had been almost four days since I had eaten anything.

"Think that answers your question. Lead the way, Lura." Osirus put his hand on the small of my back and we followed her through the forest. The trees were dense and not much sunlight reached the floor. Several animals scurried away as they heard us coming down the path.

"Father will be pleased to see you. He's so proud of you, Osirus. Being able to not only stand up to the Fae Court but also to your own family. That took some real guts," Lura spoke.

"I only did what was best for the country. It's my job after all." Osirus smiled at me and kissed the temple of my head.

We traveled for twenty minutes and made small talk; Lura was his cousin on his mother's side. His Uncle Zaos was the eldest of his mother's siblings that was mated to an elven woman named Annabelle and moved to the Elven tribe when they met some 600 years ago. Osirus often would escape his father's etiquette lessons and find himself amongst the Elves and played with Lura as she grew. She was the sister that Osirus never had and had a great deal of a soft spot for her.

Lura was very sore with Osirus, not mentioning to her we would stay in their old treehouse. Osirus had to explain it was time for him and me to have some alone time and she immediately understood.

"Everyone will be so excited to see you! The entire group!" Lura spoke wildly, and Osirus scratched his neck nervously.

"They are all mated, right?" he chuckled nervously. I let out a growl and Luna started laughing hysterically.

"Oh, yes, all of them from our group of friends. No need to worry. You were the last one to find your mate and let me say that the goddess did well!" I blushed to hide my face.

"That she did," Osirus agreed as he grabbed my waist and

pulled me in for a passionate kiss. Do we really need to go to dinner?

We arrived at the Elven tribe. Several tribes were scattered around The Golden Light Kingdom, but this was the largest one called The Silver Light Tribe. The Elves had many huts on the ground but also many homes in the trees. A series of rope bridge, ladders and swings were all over the branches, and several simple elevators made of bamboo, assumably to transport large amounts of food or goods to their homes.

There was a roaring fire in the middle of the area along with several smaller ones cooking various foods. The large fire had a massive animal called a Sokeophant that resembled a hairy mammoth. The meat would be cooked and stored in various underground food storage that kept food frozen and cold for the winter months. Elves were very much into nature, like all the supernaturals, and used every part of an animal. Bones, hair, eyes, you name it, Lura said they would use it.

As we walked forward, a long table that could seat at least fifty people on each side stood before us. Small children were running around with sticks and balls as they were whacking it side to side in some sort of game. Girls were playing with marbles while their mothers continued to stir the stew and other Elven men came out of huts holding large plates of biscuits and bread.

My stomach growled again, and Osirus clenched me. "Father!" Lura yelled, waving violently. "Your hunt was fruitful! How did you get such a massive beast down yourself!?" Lura ran up and gave Zaos a hug.

"No, your mate Matteo helped me. Once the beast was brought down, the elders helped bring the beast in pieces." Zaos gave his daughter a peck on the cheek and motioned for us to come over. Zaos gave one look to Osirus and let out the biggest greeting. "OSIRUS! My favorite nephew! What brings you here?"

"Trying to get away from people, but we keep getting

found out," Osirus muttered under his breath. I giggled and nudged his arm and he only sighed while his arm still wrapped around me possessively. "Just trying to have a small vacation before the coronation and binding ceremony. Looks like the trees talk too much for us to hide."

Zaos snickered and gave him a large pat on the back. "Well, congratulations to you both, anyway. By gods, your wings are stunning. I've seen nothing like it!" I blushed and leaned closer to Osirus and murmured a thank you.

Zaos went to touch them, but Osirus immediately slapped his hand. "You may be my uncle, but you cannot touch what is mine," he hissed. Zaos backed up with both his hands up. "Finally, showing some emotion there, glad your father's classes didn't mess you up too badly," he grinned. "How's your father? Have you spoken to him recently?"

Osirus stood back and looked down at me with sorrowful eyes. "No, I know they accepted the invitation to the celebration. Maybe they will come early so we can patch things up."

"You know," Zaos grabbed a pocketknife from his belt and played with it, "He will be proud of you; you both have very different personalities on how to handle things and the way you handled it was best for this kingdom. He will see that when he gets here. And he will love your mate, I can already tell."

"Thank you, Uncle, that means a lot to me." Osirus gave a large smile.

"Of course, we were all rooting for you! That three-day battle, that one will go down in history as the shortest battle to win a kingdom to date!" He slapped Osirus' back again and looked at me. "And certainly, you will too. There have been rumors about you being a half Siren and half-human, now it looks like the Fae blood completed your body and now you are merge of the two. It certainly suits you; you are such an exotic specimen."

"Um, thank you," I smiled sweetly. I wasn't some animal to be gawked at. "Come," he waved. "Come sit. We don't use chairs, just the cushion of the soil. Food will be presented, and entertainment will be provided because of your presence! Malki! Go get the dancers!"

Osirus explained the dynamics to me briefly about how the Elves ran their tribe. Zaos was voted the tribal leader some years ago once he became mated with his mate, Annabelle. The Fae blood made him strong since he had a high-ranking blood like his father before him. Annabelle was the previous Elven leader's daughter. It was a match made by the gods and they had been governing side by side.

The group was coming together quickly. Men and women flooded the tables with colorful foods of bread, meat, vegetables, desserts, and drinks of all kinds. Many I had never seen, much like at the palace when I first arrived. Each tribe had their own unique tastes, and I was about to engorge myself with all of it.

As I was gawking at the food, the heated stares burned my skin. Looking around, I saw males, females, and children staring at both of us. Mostly with curiosity, they were whispering, and I knew they were talking about us. I grabbed Osirus' arm and to silently ask what it was about. Osirus pulled me close and kissed my lips as I tried to hide from the stares. I never enjoyed being the center of attention. I don't know how this world couldn't figure that out, but here we are.

"Your wings, darling. No one in this world has wings as you do." I fluttered them a few times and the little children gathered around my legs, asking if they could touch them. Osirus let out a soft growl, letting them know it wasn't all right. "Wings are sensitive and are only meant to be touched by mates. I'll let it slide since you didn't know." The children nodded their heads before scattering while laughing at how Osirus growled like a Wolf.

Zaos guided us to the head seat at the table, which felt odd; this wasn't our tribe. I wanted to sit in the middle so I can blend in a little. I tried to have my wings folded back into my body, but Osirus urged me not to. "It's showing we are no longer hiding behind our natural state. We are making a statement among the Elves we are changing the kingdom. Even the Pixies and a few Fairies are spreading the word about us being out in the open. Hopefully, when we return, many will follow suit." Osirus brushed my white hair off my shoulder and kissed his mark, that gave me a pleasurable chill. "They are beautiful. You should be proud. Your father will be most pleased you kept your family's colors."

Nuzzling up close to Osirus, we were both gifted large plates of food. There were no utensils, and you had to use your hands to eat, but I was too hungry to care. I saw many licking their fingers and burping out loud. I tried not to laugh, but a few escaped my lips. Annabelle looked over and gave a light chuckle. "I forget you were raised human and don't know our ways. Burping is a sign of thankfulness and how well the food tastes."

I laughed out loud again. "I love it! I just wasn't prepared!" Osirus started laughing at me as we started speaking about the random traditions of the tribe.

Osirus held up a piece of meat up to my lips to feed me. Our eyes lingered on each other as I opened my mouth to take the food. I purposefully sucked his fingers into my mouth, licking the juices from his fingers. Osirus' lips parted slightly as a small groan left his lips. "Darling, if you don't stop, we might need to leave." I smirked at him as I licked my lips.

"I don't think I would mind," I whispered. I held up a piece of a sponge-like cake up to his mouth and his eyes never left me as he opened his mouth and sucked my fingers too I bit my lip and tightened my thighs together as his tongue danced over the pad of my fingers. My chest heaved and Osirus immediately looked at my breasts. I wanted to take him behind a tree somewhere, but unfortunately there were too many people, and they would know what we were doing.

Not long after dessert, the suns had set, and the night was a glow through the enormous bonfire in the middle. Elven women and men came out dancing in vine and leaf clothing as they danced rhythmically to the music of beating drums and wooden flutes. My smile grew wide as the men started doing flips over the fire, some even spitting out a substance that made fire come from their lips. They were all shirtless and were light on their feet as they continued their jumping. The women held large flower necklaces and started placing them on several men in the tribe.

"The women are choosing their dance partners for the next few songs," Annabelle spoke proudly of her people. The pride she radiated as the little ones ran around to their parents, as well as each other, was heartwarming. If only humans on Earth could have close-knit communities like these.

Continuing to look on, I felt Osirus' arm that was wrapped around me tighten, and his gaze shifted to his right. A beautiful Elven woman with long red hair, pinned to the side of her head with intricate braids and flowers, placed a large, flowered necklace over my mate's head.

Chapter 47

Osirus

Melina's body flexed in anger as she saw the flowered ornament hang from my neck. My initial reaction was shocked to utter disbelief. This woman would dare try to claim me for a dance. When flowers are hung by an unmated female to a male's neck, it means they not only want to dance but also to take pleasure after the dance. Of course, Annabelle didn't tell Melina that, but I think she knew from the tension in the air.

Melina stood up and walked around me to the red-headed elf that easily was a head taller than her. Her eyes flashed black as I saw not only the fangs I saw earlier with Lura, but as well as the razor-sharp teeth that a Siren would have. My bite must have awakened her Siren as well.

"What in Hades' name do you think you are doing?" Her throat made a growling noise similar to a sea lion. Melina continued to flick her fingers as she walked closer to the young elf.

"I'm giving a flower ornament to the King. What else does it look like?" she said cockily to Melina. Melina's eyes clouded over as her wings fluttered, making herself eye level.

"Is. That. So," Melina whispered, and with a small breeze caused by her wings, she pushed the Elven woman to a nearby tree, holding her up with her clawed hands. The grip was tight, and blood trickled from her neck. If I thought Melina was angry with Lura, this was something else.

"He's mine, you pile of moldy leaves. I bare his mark!" Melina spat as she took her other hand to slice her arm. Many elves gathered to watch the commotion of their future queen torturing one of their own. Many protested, but Zaos held his arm up for the arguments to stop. "She has every right. Alissa started this mess, and the future queen will finish it." His voice was bold, daring anyone to question. "She gifted the King a flowered ornament." Gasps were heard throughout the crowd, while Melina continued to hold Alissa with one hand.

"Y-you h-aven't m-m-marked h-im," she stuttered through the vice around her neck. "F-ree g-ame." Melina's eyes narrowed and gripped tighter. A snarl ripped through her mouth as she let her go.

Pissed off, Melina was a damn turn-on. I couldn't help it. The way her breath was ragged, the anger in her eyes, the possessiveness she procured in just a matter of seconds got my dick harder than I ever thought was possible. I almost prayed she would fuck me right here on the table and mark me for everyone to see, but I knew she wasn't into that kinky of shit. Plus, the elves were a bit more reserved anyway, the Fae on the other hand...

"If people would stop interrupting us, maybe I could get that done," she bared. Lura blushed in embarrassment and hid behind her mate, who was snickering at her earlier disruption. Melina turned around and ripped the flower necklace from my neck, and stomped back over to Alissa, who was still rubbing her neck. Ripping it in half and taking several flowers, she opened her mouth and stuffed them in. Alissa was choking on the petals while she stood up. "Pray to the gods I don't remember you after my binding ceremony," Melina bent down to look her in the eye, "because I will come back and finish the job if you so much as look at my mate."

Melina quickly grabbed my hand and immediately flew while pulling me. I followed suit, not wanting to make her angry anymore or cum all over my pants.

I'm guessing she was no longer afraid of flying. Her anger overpowered her self-confidence as she led us to a large spring. A small waterfall, no higher than three feet, was at the far end. Several willow trees concealed the area, so we had plenty of privacy from prying eyes. Landing at the water's edge, she immediately stripped, and my eyes went from her breasts to her arse as she threw off her clothes and immediately dove in as her wings automatically retracted.

By the time she surfaced, she was in the middle of the spring. The angry scowl she sported was long gone, and peace had taken over her body. She stood up; the water came just underneath her breasts while her white and blue hair cascaded down her back. The epitome of beauty was staring at me as the water glistened down her body. Giving a small smile, she threw out her hand, and her finger curled up to let me know she wanted me to join.

Stripping off my linens, I entered the water quickly, not sure if anyone was really around, and swam to her. The small blue and green sparkles that littered her body had become larger and looked like small scales. Her legs wrapped around my torso as we headed deeper into the water. My Siren said nothing as she pressed her body against my chest. Her nipples were hard as diamonds as they would brush up against me.

Shivers ran up against our bodies as our breaths sped up. Slamming my lips on hers, we kissed passionately near the waterfall. Small droplets of water dusted our skin as she gripped onto my arms.

"I need you, Osirus," she panted as I grabbed a nipple between my lips. Rolling her nipple in my mouth, she tugged at my hair and moaned feverishly as her hips gyrated over my cock. She didn't just need me, I needed her as well. I aligned myself to her core, and before I could thrust into her, she slammed herself on me and let out a scream.

"Daddy, more. Fuck me hard." Her head lulled back as I pushed her up against the rough, wet rock behind her. I thrust into her harder than I ever have. Her anger and possessiveness over me had turned on something more in my soul. I couldn't tell if it was because I had marked her or she was so fucking hot all on her own. Her groans turned to growls as I sucked her mark, nipping it along the way.

"Do you like it, baby?" I whispered in her ear as I pulled at her earlobe. "Do you like it rough?" She moaned again and went straight for my neck. Fuck, she was going to mark me. My cock twitched harshly inside her, and her pussy gripped onto me. One kiss on the crook of my neck and her teeth pierced the skin. Her Siren, her Fae, had taken over, and she let her instincts were telling her to bite the hell out of me.

My seed roped her womb as she gently rocked into me as she milked not only my cock but my neck. She was sucking, biting, and riding it out. I gripped her breasts to prolong her pleasure because all I cared about was her.

I was becoming weaker by the second as my baby let go of my neck. Licking me lightly, she pulled me from my still raging hard cock and let me lean on her. Her body engulfed mine in a hug as she swam us both across the lake with ease. I couldn't remember much as she pulled me to shore; both of our bodies were naked under the moon, which was now high in the sky.

I didn't have the strength to get dressed as my eyes closed on their own, Melina seemed to be pleased with herself as she snuggled up closer to me as we lay on the thick moss beneath us. A large blanket engulfed us, and the water Nymphs giggled at us as we both as I fell asleep.

***

The night felt only like a blink as I woke through the light sources flowing through the willow's leaves. Looking at my side for Melina, I became panicked. She wasn't there. Standing up with the same suit I wore the day I was born, I looked for her, calling her name. Pixies came around and started snickering as I pulled the blanket back over my hips.

Damn Pixies.

"Where is she?" I ordered, and they stopped laughing.

"She is swimming, Your Majesty. Her Majesty has been down there aa while so she should be right back." The water Nymphs that sat by a nearby rock jumped into the water, and within minutes, Melina stood up by the water's edge.

"Good morning, sleepyhead," she smiled as she stepped out of the water. Her body glistened as the rising sun hovered over her skin. The few scales she had instantly retracted as a Nymph came by and gave her a blanket to cover herself. "Did you sleep all right? I'm sorry I couldn't sleep longer. I'm still angry about that stupid Alissa."

Melina came over and straddled my lap as I inhaled her scent. The towel was covering her breasts, but I couldn't help but pull it down so I could feel them on me. "Osirus! Someone may see!"

"You're right," I sighed. "But I'm here, and no one will, or I will rip them to pieces." She giggled and kissed my mark.

"How are you feeling?" I rubbed the mark she gave me last night. The memories replayed like a broken record over and over. My length hardened as my hands gripped her hip and breast tighter.

"That good, huh?" She rubbed her core over my dick as I moaned.

"Yes, that good." I pecked at her lips.

"Good, now no other unmated chick will come near you. You are mine now," she grinned mischievously. "Now come, I want to test something." Melina pulled my hand and led us to the water. "Turn around, you sneaky Pixies!"

The Pixies started laughing and replied with, "We won't look, Your Majesty!"

"You will too, you perverted little dolls. I heard you talking last night about how amazing our sexcapade was. Now shoo!" They let a series of groans out and flew off into the forest.

Wait.

"Can you hear them, darling? You can hear their language?" Before, all she said she could hear from the Pixies were small bells tinkling in the air. Now she can understand them?

"Yeah, I heard them talking as you were talking all dirty to me last night. They said it was such a turn on, but I was too caught up in the moment I didn't say anything," she blushed. "I'm sorry, I just wanted you to impale me right then because people keep interrupting!" I let out a large laugh as we entered the water together. Damn, my mark must have completely taken over her human side.

"I want you to breathe underwater," she spat.

"What?" I laughed lightly as I pulled her close.

"I'm serious. I want you to try. It will feel you are drowning at first, but after the first large breath, you will be fine. I thought Lucca was trying to drown me, but you don't. If I can fly, I don't see why not you can't breathe underwater."

"Darling, I'm not sure if this is a good idea," I hesitated. Shit, now look who is scared. Sensing my hesitation, she sucked on my earlobe.

"I'll give you a surprise if you at least try." Licking her lips, she glanced down at my erection in the water. A large groan came from me as I nodded my head and she led me into deeper water.

"Let all the air out from your lungs and dunk your head under. I will hold you. If anything happens, I know CPR!" She beamed.

"That is not comforting, darling." Faes don't spend a lot of time in the water. This was insane. I shouldn't even be swimming right now. Melina's lower lip went into a pout, and I jumped at the chance to suck on it while she laughed hysterically.

"Don't change the subject. Come on!" She pulled me underwater before I rejected the idea again. Opening my eyes, I could already tell the water was different from my vision. I could actually see, and not the blurry mess I saw as a child when we went swimming in our local watering holes.

Melina came in front of me, smiling. *"Breathe."* I could hear her voice in my head. My shocked expression made her laugh as she nodded her head. *"Just breathe."* I took one breath in and was surprised I wasn't choking. *"You did better than I did. I tried to fight it. It took Lucca and Horus a good few minutes of fighting to keep me down in the water."*

I was not too fond of that. She was forced to breathe instead of trying it on her own. *"My love, it's all right,"* she patted my cheek. *"Talk to me."*

"Like this?" I spoke in my mind to her, and she laughed again, wrapping her legs around me. We spent the rest of the morning under the springs. There were beautiful fish, a few old boats that sat at the bottom, and even a cavern that she thought led to the ocean. We were far inland, but if she could sense it, I wouldn't question her Siren abilities.

"We should head back." I nudged her as she was petting a few baby otters that had followed us. Heading to the surface, I could immediately breathe the air with no problem as we swam to the shore.

As we got dressed, Primrose came and landed on a nearby branch. "Your Majesties, I'm sorry to intrude." Primrose was out of breath as she came to sit down.

"It's all right! We are both marked now, so I think the tension is lifted," I joked while Melina grabbed me and kissed me again.

"I'm sorry, this can't wait." Melina and I turned to her, now worried. "It's your friend Melina. Tulip has escaped!"

Chapter 48

Daphne

I was curled up on the terrible-smelling cot below me. It smelled of mold and death as I tried to hold my breath from the stench. A plan was forming in my head as Tulip was sleeping a few cells away, but first, I had to get out of here, and acting as sweet as I could be the only way they would let me go.

"Daphne," he nodded as he opened the door. Suddenly, there was a click on the door, and my head immediately jerked up to see none other than Alaneo. The loud squeal it made would be ingrained in my mind throughout my life. I would make sure Alaneo would suffer once I was queen.

"After much deliberation, we decided to set you free. Just know this, Daphne," Alaneo stood above me as I sat with my perfect posture, "we will be watching you closely." I nodded enthusiastically.

"Of course, for the safety of Osirus and the kingdom!"

"And the future Queen, Melina, correct?" His eyebrow raised to test me. I smiled at him again as I bit my cheek.

"Absolutely! Once mated, they will make an excellent pair." Alaneo nodded and opened the door.

"They are already mated. It's a done deal." Alaneo walked

me down the corridor, and I glanced back at Tulip, who nodded a few times and slipped back into the darkness of her cell.

They were already mated. Shit, that put a damper on my plans. I wanted to growl, throw, or hit something, but I wasn't out of the woods yet. There are ways around a bond, but it won't be easy to find someone. The last witch was found and was completely mutilated by a changed she-Wolf, a most unexpected demise for her.

There were others...

"Tell the happy couple congratulations, then!" Alaneo walked in silence as he led me to a side door of the palace. One I used to use every time I wanted to get in quietly. I may have slept with the guards a few times to get in, but nothing I couldn't handle. They were quick to be done, anyway.

"One more thing, Daphne." I turned around to look up at Alaneo, who was standing on the steps with his arms crossed and a scowl on his face. "You may have been pardoned of death for collaborating with the enemy because of your mother, but that doesn't dismiss you entirely. You are forthwith stripped of your title, and you are no longer Duchess, but a mere commoner. Don't worry, most of your friends are too, so don't worry about being alone."

My mouth dropped. This I wasn't expecting. I thought I could at least maintain my title until all of this was through. "You have one week to get your things out of your home, and then it will be deemed His and Her Majesties' property." I couldn't say a word, not without sounding like a spoiled brat and blowing my cover.

"Of course. I thank you again for sparing my life." I bowed my head and walked hastily before he could take anything else away from me. I needed to get to work and fast. There wasn't a way in Hades I was going to give up my home, where I was born and lived for the past hundreds of years. Not in his life.

Marching up the steps, I threw the door open to have the maids packing their bags. "What the hell do you think you are doing?" I seethed.

"Madam, we have received word that you are no longer a duchess, and we have been granted new jobs at the palace," the eldest spoke as she picked up her bag. "We wish you the best, Madam." Several maids, the butler, and the cook all took off through the door. I couldn't even make them come back; they were going to the palace and would tattle on me.

Letting out a large growl, I felt my teeth start to itch, and my claws come forth. Breathing deeply, I tried to think of soothing thoughts. I would not revert to my animalistic ways. We were the superior race. A few breaths caught in my throat as I felt the itch fade from my existence. Now it was time to get to work.

Grabbing my father's mirror from his bedside table, I repeated the enchantment that I had heard thousands of times. The mirror reflection fogged, and in it, I saw none other than my partner in crime, Sorceress Prinna of the Blood Coven.

"It's been a while," her sickly sweet voice spoke. For a witch or sorceress, you would think they would be ugly as they draw some of their powers from the dark. Not Prinna. She was the epitome of beauty and didn't even have to use her magic to make her that way.

"I heard The Court has failed in battle. Why do you summon me, Daphne? I can only do so much with my small coven, and your father got caught in three days. That wasn't enough time to weaken Osirus' army of Shifters."

Prinna and her coven were summoning dark powers of demons of Tartarus that were thirsty for innocent blood since that fuels their own dark power, but it took time. Osirus struck early, and we were left defenseless. If my father wasn't caught, we could have survived, even won.

"Yes, there were complications," I huffed in irritation. Meaning I didn't want my father to have control over me once I was mated to Osirus. "But this isn't over yet if you still want some power over the Cerulean Moon Kingdom." Prinna wanted the power of the Northern area of the Cerulean Moon

Kingdom, specifically the Dragons. Dragon shifter blood was scarce, their skin was tough just like their scales, and they hardly ever flew South near Vermillion. To send her own up the mountain to capture one would not only be suicide on them but as well as her coven since Queen Eden and King Elijah are brutally protective of their own. She would need an army, specifically The Golden Light Kingdom, to storm their territory, and that is what I promised them. An army that was swift and stealthy.

"Fine, what do you need?" she spoke exasperatedly. The Dragon's blood would make her and her coven stronger, so I knew she would take the chance.

"First, I need you to free someone from prison and find someone to break a mating bond." Prinna scoffed.

"I don't have anyone to do that," she growled out. "It would take time."

"How much time?" I pressed.

"I don't know, time. I'd need to find a powerful demon with no blood attached to them from Hades or a god. Both will be hard to find and be willing to work with us."

"Figure it out, and I'll do the rest. I'll get Osirus' mate to you, and you hold her until it breaks. First, rescue the prisoner." I held out three nail clippings that Tulip gave me and dropped them into the mirror. They appeared in Prinna's hand as she took a sniff.

"A Wolf? What will a Wolf do for you?" Her eyebrow raised in question as she crushed the nail in a bowl with various spices.

"Melina trusts her, the Wolf's name is Tulip, and she will deliver her to you," I snickered at the full-proof plan. This was going to run smoothly, and with little manpower, I could feel it.

Melina

"Tulip escaped?" Osirus grew angry. "How did this happen?" Primrose cowered before regaining her footing on the branch.

"We don't know, Your Majesty we think magic might be involved." Osirus grabbed my hand as soon as I put on my skirt, pulling me away from the tree branches.

"We fly back. Just know we will have to walk through the main gates of the kingdom, Primrose. Let Alaneo know of our arrival."

"Yes, Your Majesty!" Primrose sped off quickly as Osirus unfolded his wings as I did mine. With one leap, we both took a flight to head back to the kingdom. Flying over the Elven territory, we saw Zaos and Annabelle, as well as Lura waving frantically. I let go of Osirus' hand and cupped my hands to my mouth and yelled.

"I marked him! He's mine!!!" They all started laughing while waving us off. Osirus only smiled and shook his head as we continued our journey.

It was a lot faster with me flying on my own and not as scary as I thought it would be. The air in my face and the ability to control if I wanted to rise in the sky or lower myself was my own type of comfort.

We were on the outskirts of town when I saw Cricket at the orphanage waving frantically, calling his fellow roommates that were hiding in the trees. Pointing to Cricket, Osirus understood as we flew down to where they were playing.

"You came back! I told Nana you would!" Cricket gave me an enormous hug, and the other children started laughing as they came up to both of us.

"Why are your wings out?" a little girl asked innocently. "We have to keep them away."

"Not anymore," Osirus stated. "This is a new kingdom, and you are to learn to fly and use them. Just as our creators had meant for us to do." The children smiled as they started ripping holes in the back of their tunics. Nana stood in shock as she threw a tunic she was repairing in her rocking chair, mumbling it was useless.

Within minutes, all the children were displaying their wings triumphantly. Many tried to take off from the ground but only hovered. "That's it, Cricket, keep practicing that. You will have to work your way up. You won't be able to fly long distances for another few years. Your full wingspan will come when you are twelve." Osirus ruffled up Cricket's hair while he grabbed my hand.

"We need to get going, darling, or we will not be there until sunset." Before we took off again, the little girl grabbed my hand.

"But why are your wings so colorful while ours are not?" Letting go of Osirus' hand, I brushed her beautiful pink curls from her head.

"I'm half Siren when Osirus and I got together. My other half was human and took on more of a Fae look. The colors are of my family, and I guess it made me the perfect mix between Siren and Fae." The little girl nodded, happy with my answer so Osirus and I could take off again.

Many stood in awe as we flew over the marketplace, several Fae cheering as we flew over the palace gates. Men took off their tunics, and the women made room for the wings to expand. I had never seen so many people so excited about the new proclamation that Osirus had wanted to spread the first day after the battle.

"No more hiding who we are. If you wish to fly, you fly. If you wish to walk among others, then do so. You are never to be afraid of who or what you are, no matter your rank. Representatives will be called to a new Court to help with aiding the different territories. A voting system will be in place so your own territories can select their representative. More information will be sent out as we put it to paper."

More cheers from the crowd and a hot passionate kiss later, we entered the palace, almost forgetting the one reason we were back so early—Tulip's escape.

375

Chapter 49

Under the Moon

The people of The Golden Light Kingdom that had surrounded the gates were in awe. Their very own King and soon to be Queen had flown in on their very own wings. Smiles were gathered around while the older Fae ripped holes in the back of their tunics and dresses. Beautiful wings emerged from the bodies as you could hear the slight tear in the skin.

For many, it has been over hundreds of years since they had let down their wings. Faes that were taught at an early age not to have them emerge were standing in admiration. Their eyes were all aglow, looking at their still young-looking parents and grandparents stand proud. The older Fae encouraged the younger as they let them emerge for the first time.

The first time was always the hardest, but the excitement grew in their bellies at the thought of taking flight. The air was the second home to a Fae; it brought excitement and pride in their bodies to travel long distances without animal or carriage.

One could ask how it all started before and how they were ordered to keep their wings at bay. They were taxed and fined once the original Court decided it was beneath them to fly. The gods didn't fly around the air as they did; they didn't play with each other in the sky, nor did they have fangs and claws. The Faes were said to have evolved from Pixies to Fairies and then to their own bodies. Not flying would have increased the process of evolution.

This was not so.

Small children laughed as they watched their parents take flight for the first time. It was rocky at first, but they could get as high as the marketplace.

Little girls and boys ran around the market, claiming they were the king and queen. "I have beautiful wings!" one girl cried as she tried to flap her wings. Her concentration on her wings looked more like constipation on her face as the others laughed in jest.

Word spread like wildfire. Soon the outlying territories were joyous. They didn't come to the capital that often and had already been practicing with their wings, but now they could fly wherever they wanted.

For once, in a long while, The Golden Light Kingdom was filled with light. The birds seemed to sing louder, and the flower petals were a brighter hue. Things were turning out for the better, especially for their King.

Osirus' face had always been stoic, but upon seeing his happiness, they all knew too well it was because of her. The light that snuffed out the grumpy king and brought forth his playful Fae demeanor back. He was hard as stone, but she polished him up nicely, as if he was the puppy he always was. The future queen may not know it, but she was loved by all, and they knew her story well. The servants from the palace talked about her polite and calm aura, how she looked at the King with all the love and affection, even though she wasn't happy to give it in the beginning.

Melina made King Osirus happy, and the love in their eyes only let the people realize one thing. Soon an heir would be graced to the good kingdom soon and on such a day they would all hold feasts in the cities and territories.

However, even though they were happy for the royal affair and the soon-to-be coronation and binding ceremony, there was still something dark lurking in the shadows.

Melina

I'm a terrible liar.

Seriously, terrible. I remember Tulip's mother, Rose, would come over in the evenings to check on me. "Have you had dinner yet?" I kept my mouth shut, so my voice didn't waver. I nodded, "of course, I had dinner," when I really hadn't. Rose would scowl at me and tsk her mouth and do the dreaded, "mmhmm," most unapproving mothers did.

"Come eat," she would demand, and made me sit down at the table with her. She brought over food from their dinner anyway and watched me eat every bite. It was mostly meat and carbs, not a lot of vegetables, and come to think about it, I should have known so much sooner what they were. I slapped myself mentally at the thought.

Then there was a time Tulip wanted to go to a party with her. She nagged all during school and well into the afternoon. I groaned and complained about it until I finally went. Rose didn't know about it because it was a human party, and she didn't keep up with those certain things. Tulip told Rose she would just spend the night at the cabin and lied straight through her perfectly white teeth she did.

The next morning there was banging on the cabin door, and Tulip and I got up groggily. We didn't get home until three in the morning to much of my protest of not staying out that late. Rose walked in and took in our appearance.

"Have a fun sleepover, you two?" Technically she did sleepover, so we both nodded yes.

"Of course, mother," Tulip's voice was sickly sweet. On the inside, my heart was pounding out of my chest. We were caught. I just knew it.

"So, you didn't go anywhere last night. You stayed right here in the cabin?" Rose's eyebrow raised with her hands on her hips. Tulip nodded again and smiled. Rose looked at me and took a few steps forward, and my eyes widened. How could she look at me and could see the lie written all over my face?

"What about you, Melina? Did you stay in the cabin all night?" My heart pounded several times harshly against the ribcage, and Rose sat back up with a smile. "You both are grounded. Melina, sleep in our guest room until your punishment is over."

How she could figure it out every time there was a lie, I couldn't figure it out. Then, when the Werewolf secret came out, it was quite clear. They can hear heartbeats. They can hear the lies because they were all walking lie detectors. It was so embarrassing. Each lie I ever told, may it be white or not, they knew.

Osirus and I had just arrived back in his royal study. Everett, Braxton, and Finley welcomed us back with wide smiles, even though there was a 'criminal' on the loose. My stomach churned as it dropped lower into my stomach. Faes couldn't hear that well, not as well as Werewolves. They can't detect a lie or deception, can they?

Sure, Osirus read auras and look for deception, but I don't think he reads mine that often. He can quickly glance at my face and can tell what I'm feeling. Panic rose in me. What if he sees?

"Darling? Are you all right?" He glanced back at me as he sat at his desk.

Fiddling with my fingers, I nodded. "Yes, just a bit hungry. We didn't eat breakfast," I mentioned quickly.

Osirus ordered servants to bring in a wide array of food, and to be honest, it smelled amazing. Maybe my mood can change a bit while I stuff my face with some lotus sponge cake.

"Give me the briefing," Osirus spoke to Alaneo, who was by his side.

"It happened about twelve hours after we released Daphne. I don't think the two are linked. However, Daphne seemed thankful to be released. Even when I mentioned her status demotion, she took it well." I internally scoffed. I can't believe they would throw her off like she couldn't do anything. If it weren't for my time in high school watching evil, queen bees of the school, I wouldn't have known either. Her artificially sweetened demeanor was repulsive. Any woman could smell her stench of lies.

I snorted, and everyone in the room looked at me. Popping a grape in my mouth like I had nearly choked, they went back to speaking. Too close. This was too much. I couldn't handle it. If Osirus finds out, he is going to spank my ass so red a demon himself would like he was blushing.

"Darling, are you sure you are all right?" All right? I've been keeping a secret from you for days, and it is burning a hole in my heart! Now I don't know how to tell you!

"Yup!" I popped the p and threw another grape in my mouth. As long as no Werewolves show up and asked me about Tulip directly, I should be fine.

Alec then burst into the room.

CHEESE AND RICE.

I exhaustedly laid back in a nearby chair with my plate of grapes. "Where is my mate?!" Alec growled. "She is supposed to be in the dungeons. Only the guards told me she escaped! My mate would never do such a thing!"

"Think again," I muttered lightly to myself. Alec whipped his head around to stare at me. His eyes blazing in a fury.

Fudge nuggets. Stupid hearing.

"Do you know where Tulip is at, Melina?" He walked closer to me, but Osirus and the brothers immediately stand up to guard me. I feel it. My heart was bursting out of my chest, and before I can even lie, he growled at me.

"You dare growl at the Queen of the Golden Light Kingdom?" Osirus roared as he got into a fighting stance. "She is my mate! We have been gone for the past five days. What makes you think she would know anything?"

I swallowed the big lump in my throat and discarded my plate beside me. Standing up as straight and regal as I could, I folded my hands together. "I..I do." Everyone whipped their head at me as I felt the heated gaze cook me like KFC's extra crispy chicken.

"I'm sorry I said nothing before." My voice was becoming meeker by the minute. "But I didn't trust Daphne, and you were going to let her go." Osirus sighed as he sat back down in his chair, rubbing his temples with his fingers.

"What did you do, darling?" He wasn't angry, more disappointed, and that hurt worse than anything. I kept a secret from him, and I knew it stabbed him in the gut. I didn't have a choice, though. At the time the plan came to mind. She was already in the dungeon, and we had mated, but he hadn't bitten me. He was acting too possessive. I wouldn't have been able to reason with him!

"I swear, I didn't mean to hurt you, Osirus. You were acting so possessive, and you weren't thinking straight. I knew you were planning on releasing Daphne soon, so I did the one thing I thought was best. For Tulip's punishment, I told her to find out if Daphne had any other ulterior motives or plans and to follow her and act like she was angry with me putting her in prison. I wanted to know her plan if there was one at all." The room grew silent as everyone took in the information.

"So, you sent my mate on a dangerous mission without consulting me or anyone else?" Alec heaved with his shoulders, defeated.

"I did, for the kingdom. Tulip and are like sisters and she replied to me she would do anything to help me. She may get on my nerves and push my buttons and boundaries, but that is what sisters do. They also take care of each other, and I did that not letting them whip her twenty times with silver shards."

"Silver?" Alec questioned while Osirus nodded. "Twenty lashes to a Werewolf are silver, to a vampire dogwood, and to a Fae is iron." Alec sighed and sat down in the chair next to mine. I put my hand on his shoulder.

"Tulip is cunning, smart, witty, and an excellent actress. She will be safe. Once she knows the plans, we can halfway execute them and capture Daphne along with anyone else helping her. I think we all know this isn't over yet." Alec nodded in agreement, and his face was now in his hands.

"I haven't had her that long, and I don't want to lose her. I hate not being in control," he sniffed and stood up. "I'm a damn warrior. I should be proud of her!" I rubbed his back.

"She's stronger than you think Alec, you are just getting to know her. It's only been a little over a month?"

The doors were slammed open again, and an angry pair of wolves walked in. At this rate, we are going to have to replace the doors or the guards, one of the two, more than likely both, because they really suck. I'm going to have to talk to Osirus about that.

Sean and Rex walked in, both with worried and frustrated faces. "Where is Carson?" Rex spoke as Sean trailed behind. "We have orders to bring him back for duty. Alpha Kane is getting angry. His star tracker isn't back yet. They are trying to track down some coven that is trying to infiltrate the Dragon shifter territories in the mountains. We need him if you aren't going to punish him."

Primrose, in full size, walked into the room with a cart full of tea. Her dress was higher up her thighs since she was slightly bent over pouring azalea tea for everyone. The large growl in the room startled her as she went to put two sugars in Osirus' drink, the cubes toppled over to the floor. Not thinking anything of it, she bent over only for all of us to gasp as Rex growled again while palming his manhood.

Cheeses.

"Mine," he said playfully. Primrose popped back up from

the cart and looked around, surprised everyone was staring at her. Rex took a few steps closer while Primrose stepped back.

"Mate," she whispered as she darted her eyes at the open window and back to Carson. He tilted his head with eyes full of mischief, just waiting for her to make her move.

Chapter 50

Melina

Primrose gave a smirk. I had never seen this playful side of her. Usually, I saw it in Peoni when they would talk about the 'birds and the bees.' This was something new. Primrose pranced over to the window, only for Rex to jump over the desk in one leap, blocking the window. Primrose stopped as her wings fluttered excitedly as she turned around and dashed for the door.

"Oh, hell yeah!" Rex roared as he ran after her, giggling from the palace hallways. Series of crashes and squeals as we heard Rex rip out of his clothes to shift into his Wolf.

Alaneo sighed audibly. "Your Mother is going to throw a fit if that was the vase from the Pixies." Osirus didn't smile as he looked back at me while I stared down at my feet.

"All right then," Sean spoke up, breaking the tension. "Where can I find Carson?"

"He's in the Northern Wing, just past the library," Alaneo replied while I jumped up from my seat.

"I'll take you! Come on!" I ushered him to walk out the door while Osirus watched me with fire in his eyes as Alaneo and Alec crowded the desk to ask more questions about what to do next.

"Phew, that was a lot of tension in there. What happened?"

I groaned and slapped both my hands to my face. "I happened, I did a bit of a 'whoops,' and now my butt is gonna be sore for days!" We walked past a few servants as they giggled. They knew what was up. I'm sure they could hear his hand echo across the palace when it hit my rear. "I lied to him, well kept the truth from him by omission."

Sean's mouth hung open. "You lied to a Fae? You fibbed to a Fae?" I nodded my head guiltily as we took a quick turn to the northern part of the castle.

"Wow, Faes are known for tricking and playing pranks on people. They aren't used to being tricked back. It's a one-way street there, and you just did it to the king himself." I rolled my eyes.

"Are you trying to make me feel better? Because it really isn't working." I started biting my nails as we came closer to the door. I held up my finger and knocked a few times. If they weren't mated yet, it was best that I was the first to open the door. We didn't need yet another unmated male near an unmated female.

"Your two close friends are almost mated now, so I guess you are next?" I laughed. Sean nodded while he bit his lip. "She will be amazing, I'm sure!" Sean continued to bite his lip and shuffle back and forth.

"What's wrong?"

"Well," he scratched his scruffy chin. This was the most I had talked to Sean, so it was a pleasant change. Sean blended well into the background with Carson and Rex, always just nodding and agreeing with what they said about 'chicks' and pack duties. "I hope it isn't a girl," he muttered. I smiled widely.

"Oh!" I nudged his side. "Playing for the other team, are we?" He smirked.

"Yeah, I just lied about having sex with girls. Sure, I was quiet and flirted with them, but just had no interest. None of my friends are gay, so it was hard to talk about it with any-one. I just played along and kept things to myself."

"I'm so happy for you! You are staying for the coronation, right? Several territories are coming in. I think it will be a mating frenzy." He threw his head back and laughed.

"Yes, I'll stay. Especially for that."

"Sean?" I stopped right before the guest bedroom door. Sean's eyes softened, looking down at me. "Can I ask why Carson came here at the palace with a package and a note? No one knows where any of these things went and I'm curious." Sean scratched his chin thoughtfully.

"I can't say for sure. I know the bag he carried had food, specifically cinnamon rolls," he chuckled. "And I know he was upset how you were carried off by the Fae King. I'm sure the note was just to tell you to be strong and he would help you if you needed it. Carson wouldn't do anything to break any bond. Just being a good friend to you is all he wanted."

Just then, the door swung open, revealing Carson. He looked weak as he glanced back at the bed, looking at Peoni, who was sleeping in her small form. Primrose briefed me on their own situation while we took our long flight back to the palace.

"Come in, Sean," Carson gave a weak smile. "Up for guard duty?" Sean stepped in and patted Carson's shoulder.

"Go get some sleep. I'll watch over the both of you." Carson tilted his head to me, and they shut the door. I couldn't help but feel so much closer to Sean, even with just a brief exchange. Even now that I have so many half-brothers, he seemed like he would be a good fit too. A friendship must be blooming. Like my heart just went out to him like a mini-bond-like attachment. I tapped my finger on my chin; I'll have to make sure there were a lot of unmated males attending too.

Before I turned around, a hand was put over my mouth, and I was engulfed in a warm body as I was dragged from the hallway. Panic rose as I tried to rip the hands off my mouth until I felt that familiar spark. The door next to us was flung open and closed quickly with a slam. The room was dark; no other bodies were in the room as my breath evened out while I was pushed to the wall. I couldn't see anything in front of my face until the snap of a finger let the room come to a light glow.

It was still dark enough to hide details from our faces, but light enough for me to know it was Osirus. "Darling, you've become a sneaky little Fae, haven't you?" His hands grabbed both of mine then threw them above my head, leaving me defenseless against the excessive force he was using. I was no longer scared. No, I was excited, and he could feel my aura leaking my desire.

"Since when do we keep secrets from each other, darling?" His nose trailed down the back of my ear, to my neck and my mark. He nipped it lightly at first, but bit harder as I moaned. "Aren't you going to answer my question?"

"Y-you were unreasonable at the time. I decided for the both of us," I rushed out as Osirus snapped his head up to look into my eyes.

"And that, darling, is where you should have talked to my second. Someone should know the plan, not just you." Osirus' mouth crashed into me as he pulled my lip with his fangs, nipping my lower lip as a drop of metallic blood on my lips. Osirus groaned as he pushed his pelvis into me. "As much as I should be angry, I'm not," he panted as he swiveled his hips into my core. His knee came up to spread my legs so his raging cock could have a better chance of rubbing. "In fact, I'm quite turned on, as you can tell," he smirked as one of his hands came down to trace my pear-shaped figure.

Osirus squeezed my breast with his hand, only for me to whimper at his touch. "Gods, you always feel incredible," he rasped as he ripped the top of my dress. My breast pooled into his hand as I gasped at his dominating nature. My pussy was already wet. I could feel it drip down my leg. I was so ready for him.

"How to punish you," he muttered to himself. "You can't do this again." Osirus' lips went to my nipple as he tugged at it harshly while I yipped in excitement.

"Daddy," I whispered, which only earned a guttural growl from him.

"Fuck," he whispered again as he pulled his trousers so hard, they pooled to the floor.

"I'm going to fuck you on this wall." he ripped the other side of my dress. "That desk." he pulled the remaining bits of fabric from my hips as they dropped to the floor. "And then I'm going to take your virgin ass on the couch." My eyes widened and my thighs tightened together.

"You like that, don't you? That I will dominate every hole in your body. Your ass is mine, baby, and I can't wait until it wraps around my cock." My nipples puckered. I had never thought about doing it in the 'forbidden area' before, but the thought gives excitement, especially when it was Osirus.

Like the rest of my clothes, Osirus slipped the panties from my body and lined up his raging erection, taking one leg and having me put it over his hip. Thank the gods, I was flexible. With one motion, he jammed his cock inside me. I thought I would have gotten used to him, but it always feels like the first time. He's hard, large, and my pussy was tight. There was no more room to accommodate him; he took every space in my body.

"Don't cum until I tell you." He thrust into me. This was carnal. He dominated my pussy like no tomorrow. Like I was his water, and there was no guarantee that he would have a taste of the crisp cool waters. Again and again, he thrust into me. "DADDY! Please!" I screamed.

"Cum!" and I creamed all over his cock; his thrusts became erratic as the sweat dripped from his chest.

I pulled his tunic off with a few claws I let out to take in his chest. I leaned over and arched my back backward so he could get deeper into my core, which he seemed to like. He was grunting like an animal until I was pulled up and my legs automatically wrapped around his waist.

The desk was scattered with papers, important documents, lamps, and writing utensils that were easily swiped away with one arm as our bodies were still connected. Loud crashes to the floor didn't even bother him as he laid me down. Osirus pushed both my legs back, so my knees were touching the sides of my torso. "I love to see you so open like this." Osirus pulled his dick from me as I whined and kept my legs wide open. His head went straight to my pussy. "I can see everything, your wet cunt down to the ass I'm about to fuck."

I could feel my juices pool down my crack. My face was aflame at how he could see every detail about me, even if the room was dim. He licked my clit several times, and I came undone all over again while he chuckled into my core. "I love how you respond to my touch, baby."

"Daddy, I can't," I rasped harshly. I was so sensitive. If he just blew on my clit, I would break all over again. My breasts were tender marks all over them as I looked down at that devilish smirk.

"You can, baby. You can." He rammed his dick into me again as I screamed in pleasure. "Cum again," he commanded, and I did just that. His voice commanded me, and I easily obeyed, not able to control my body. Osirus said this body was his, and it was. I'd give him anything he wanted.

The warmth of his cum flowed through me again as I arched my back on the hard table. My knees were still firmly planted on the side of my torso. Osirus grunted as he filled me, but he still wasn't satisfied. Releasing me from his hold, he picked me up and threw me over his shoulder. Was it wrong of me to feel so turned on yet again? I groaned as I gripped his ass. I hadn't touched him, and I would take every bit I could.

His muscular butt had me entranced. How can a butt look so damn nice? Gripping his butt as he walked, he flexed, and I felt my mouth just water. How is this even punishment?

Osirus had me kneel in front of the couch with my butt

out and he slapped it once, hard. Ahh, there it is. There was the punishment. My core quivered as I felt more of his essence drip from me. Another slap at me, a moaning mess. Why does it hurt and feel so good at the same time?

"I'm going to fuck your ass, baby." My head popped up from the couch; sensing my worry, he cocooned over my body, his head resting on my shoulder. "Slow baby, we are going slow. I will not hurt you, and you just must relax." I nodded my head, not sure what to say as his warmth left my back. He dipped his cock in our juices as he tickled my hole. I held my breath, waiting for him to push forward, but it never came.

"Baby, relax," he cooed as he kissed up my back. The sparks took my mind off the prodding he was doing, and I felt the tightness of his cock slide in. It burned for a good few seconds until it stretched just for him. Osirus rested as he continued to pepper kisses at the top of my back. "So good, baby, such a good girl," he cooed again as he gently pulled out to glide back in.

The fullness felt different. It was tight, but I also felt it down the front of my core. I moaned as he went a little faster as he rubbed my clit with his thumb. "Damn, I won't last long," he whispered to himself as his body spasmed and dropped another load of his seed into my body. He had taken every part of me, and my body felt on fire.

I had fallen in love with the Fae King, who has shown me pleasure in the strangest of places, opening my small mind of love making into something of a wonderland. My body spasmed again as a small orgasm ripped through me as he pulled his cock from the forbidden area. Osirus pulled me to the fur rug as we laid there, both panting and an utter mess. A thin blanket from the couch was pulled by his long arms and covered us.

"Sleep, darling, no one will bother us." I hummed in contentment as I turned and buried my face in his chest. This was my favorite place. Right here, right now, with the Fae.

"Melina?" Osirus spoke as I had almost fallen asleep. "Everyone has an addiction. I never really believed that until I met you. You are my addiction, and I can never live without you." I smiled and leaned in, pecking his lips until we started doing more than just pecking.

Our lips danced with each other until our tongues wanted more. He filled not only my mouth, but my heart with love. Breaking away, panting, "Just when I didn't think I could love you anymore, you go on and say and do the most wonderful things," I whispered into his mouth.

Chapter 51

Melina

I had learned my lesson. No more keeping things from Osirus, and if he is in one of his "possessive moods," go to Alaneo. Good to know.

After waking up from that thundering session and taking a walk of shame with a blanket covering my naked body down the hall, we all had to sit down and form a plan; just because I had Tulip out there listening to the crazy lady's plans didn't mean she was safe, and we weren't out of the woods yet.

Alaneo had been working at Osirus' desk all afternoon while we were away. Several important events had transpired in just two hours. Alaneo even scolded Osirus for being so neglectful of his duties, even though it was the first time in his life that he had ever done so. "Don't make it a habit," Alaneo playfully laughed as he rose from his seat.

"The Dragon shifters of the North are seeing some strange sightings, bursts of light, and even people covered in cloaks, only to vanish into thin air. These sightings are getting closer to the small tribes in the mountains full of the women and children up there."

The Dragon Shifters were an old and dying breed. They

were having trouble finding full blooded Dragon mates, mainly women. A full-blooded female Dragon was extinct except for a few that were already mated and even then, they were only giving birth to males. When the Dragons found a female mate from another race, once they gave birth, they wouldn't inherit the Dragon blood and become whatever their mother was previously. Seers, Healers, and Shamans didn't know what to do. They were at a loss and Dragons continued to pray to the gods that something would change quickly, or they would slowly die off one by one through battle if that was ever to occur.

These Dragons Shifters have power besides their strength. Instead of breathing fire, they could breathe ice or use nature around them to fend off enemies. Now they were being threatened by Witches and Warlocks from what Alaneo had gathered. Dragon blood could enhance Witches own power, but the only way to get a Dragon to give their blood is by willingly or by death. With the fate of the women and children, they were now put at risk since they were weaker and causing some furious, domineering Dragons. With our peace treaty with The Cerulean Moon Kingdom, we will have to go to war with the magical entities threatening them.

We would win a battle, no doubt about it, but the lost lives were something no one wants on the winning side. However, things might be inevitable.

"How is Tulip supposed to contact you?" Finley spoke up. I scratched the back of my head, not really wanting to answer.

"It never really came up," I shrugged my shoulders and Alaneo threw his hands in the air. "Honestly, it was a quick message sent to her by Primrose the morning after Osirus and me... did some things to make him super possessive." I blushed remembering that night. I was going to always blush thinking about the dirty things we do. It was just going to happen.

"How did you even tell Primrose I didn't even see her? I

was right there with you the entire time." Osirus rubbed my shoulders.

Rolling my eyes, "She fell asleep in the linen closet, and once we started to, 'ahem,' she knew she couldn't leave and disturb us, so she slept there, while I was doing some lady business she came out, and I told her what to do."

"This is getting ridiculous. Not a moment of peace around here." Osirus sat down and pulled me to his lap. "What will we do now? We have no way to contact Tulip, or we will cause a scene and give her away."

"Tulip will find away." I looked at Alec. "She's smart, trust me." There was a rapping at the window as a Pixie was trying to get our attention. With him was a note clutched in his hand that was several times his size. The window was opened as he panted harshly, and Braxton brought him to the table in his large hands.

"*Please don't make me do that again!*" he pleaded. "*That Wolf is nuts. She wrote her life story on this thing. I'm not made to be a messenger. The Fairies are!*" The Pixie pushed the note away while he climbed to the glass of water on the table and started drinking straight from the glass. He was an odd Pixie, he had black accents on his body. The Pixies I had seen were bright and colorful. This one had wings that were pitch black, along with this clothing.

His hair was also dark, along with one side of his head shaved and long on the other, giving him a classic 'emo' look I remembered from Earth. I gave a little snort and covered my mouth instantly. Of course, Tulip would have picked this Pixie, and it's so her humor.

"A dark Pixie, I haven't seen one in years," Osirus whispered. "They live in Vermillion, where it is darker and helps handle the plants that don't need as much sunlight."

"*That's right and now I'm a bloody messenger!*" The Pixie wiped his mouth off with his arm and stood in front of us. "*Are you princess, queen-of-whatever kingdom, Melina?*" The Pixie's hands kept waving about wildly, and Osirus narrowed his eyes.

"She is Queen Melina of the Golden Light Kingdom, show some respect."

"*Sorry, sorry.*" he pushed the letter to me, and I picked it up. All that was on the envelope was the letter, 'M.' "*I'm Flix. Nice to meet you.*"

I nodded my head while Osirus spoke for both of us. "Thank you, Flix."

Opening it up, I exclaimed, "It's from Tulip!" Alec jumped from his chair to come to read the letter. I stood up straight so everyone could hear.

M,

I'm sorry I haven't written sooner. It's hard to getaway. I am currently on the outskirts of Vermillion in the Blood Coven with the head sorceress, Prinna, along with Daphne. Your hunch was right, and she purposefully got rid of Cosmo to take the power for herself.

This coven specifically uses dark magic and have found a Soul Unbinding Book. Daphne plans to unbind you from Osirus and will use me to retrieve you the day before the ceremony. Getting here is a problem. We will have to make a plan to get Osirus' soldiers inside. It is cloaked in several cloaking spells, and only certain people are allowed in through the magic. I'll send word the more I know.

M

PS. Please tell A, I love him, and I will be home soon, and I will see you in my dreams.

Alec was beside himself; his eyes were glassy as he held onto the table. "I can't lose her, Melina." His eyes were pleading, begging me to bring her home, but we were so close. If we could find out exactly where this coven was, we could be rid of it, and our problems, along with the Dragon shifters, would be solved without bloodshed.

My shaky breath went unheard as Osirus took a nearby vase and threw it to the floor. Books fell off the bookshelf, and little trinkets smashed to pieces. Osirus' breathing was ragged as his back was to us, heaving up and down, and his wings protruded from his back. This time they weren't outlined in small black lines at the tip of his wings, rather the entire wing and the small intricate designs had turned to black swirls.

I didn't know if I should go comfort him or step back. I had seen nothing like it. Alaneo and the boys stepped back from him and looked at me to do the same. My heart only wanted to comfort him, and since it hadn't steered me wrong yet, I stepped forward, one tiny step at a time. He was still throwing, growling, and hitting the walls with his bare fists. Sweat dripped down his body as his tunic became untied in the front as his chest showed.

Gently touching his forearm, he turned his head to me. His eyes were black while the outer rim of his eyes was red. A creature I had never seen before looked back at me. This wasn't my Osirus. It was someone else.

"Honey," I cooed at him. His breathing hitched and slowed down. The tension in his body slowly dwindled as I felt his anger and frustration through the bond we shared. Turning to Alaneo and the rest of the men in the room, "I think we are done for today. Let's reconvene tomorrow morning. Flix, a servant, will show you to your quarters until we can write a return note." Flix didn't say a word, and his trembling wings were enough to tell me what he was thinking.

Everyone was leaving the room and Osirus' eyes were still pinned on the side of my head. Another one of my hands easily snaked around his arm as I pulled him to sit down in his oversized desk chair.

Grabbing a cloth from the drink cart, I dipped it in some cold water and wrung out the excess. Osirus' eyes were still pinned on me, like I was going to disappear at any moment. Walking back, he kept his eyes glued to mine as a small smile came on my face. This was my job, to keep the King of the Faes calm. Sitting in his lap, I gently put the ice-cold towel on his forehead. He was burning up; his fingertips grazed my hips through the jeans I wore today. Lifting a bit of my shirt so his hands were directly on my skin, I sighed at how he felt. I'm supposed to comfort him, and here he was, helping me.

"Honey, tell me what happened?" I cooed at him while I cooled his neck and chest. Letting out a shaky breath, he gripped my hips a little tighter, and his forehead went to mine.

"No one can take you from me, Melina. I can't let that happen." Osirus' eyes closed as he spoke to me. I felt every word roll out of his mouth and into my ears. He was scared he would lose me, heck, I was scared I would lose him, but we were one step ahead of Daphne.

"We know what is going on. We have a spy in place. We are ahead of the game." I touched his face with my palm, and he immediately kissed it. "We will get rid of her, and if you want to draw her out, I may have an idea." Osirus gave a small smirk.

"You really are becoming a cunning little Fae, aren't you?" I pecked his lips and kissed him again, only letting it linger.

"I only learn from the best." I kissed his neck as he relaxed instantly. "Now, about the Dragons, Carson is down for at least two weeks, so he can't help Alpha Kane." Osirus rubbed his eyes and pulled me into his chest.

"I'll send my best trackers, now they can fly, they will reach the Dragon's territory faster than Carson and his friends, anyway. I may need to go meet with the chief there." I nodded in understanding.

"When would we leave?" I asked quietly.

"I will leave as soon as possible. You will stay here." I threw my arms around my body as I pushed away.

"Listen here, King Osirus, I will come with you. You are basically asking someone to kidnap me while you are away. Do you ever read romance novels?" I arched my brow while I scowled at him. Taking an enormous sigh, he bit down on his bottom lip.

"Do you know how sexy you look when you are angry?" His hands removed my arms as he palmed my breasts.

"Changing the subject won't help. I'm coming at that is final." Osirus nodded at once as he kissed the upper part of my chest.

"I don't think I can handle one other thing right now. Daphne, the Dragons, the witches, the coronation, and the binding ceremony that has to still be planned. I feel like this entire month has been rushed." Osirus' sad puppy face made me giggle.

"Honestly, this is the most exciting thing that has ever happened. I don't really mind it. Let's pray to the gods nothing else is thrown on our plate right now." Osirus chuckled and pulled me close, letting me smell his strong forest scent.

One servant walked in the open door and bowed. "Your majesties, I come to inform you that King Osirus' parents have just arrived by carriage."

Fudge.

Chapter 52

Osirus

What kind of fuckery is this? Are there some evil demons out there that are hell-bent on trying to make my life hard? Not one moment of peace since my love has come to me; everything that could have gone wrong had been slammed in a month, and not one moment I can relish in her beauty. I just wanted to love and cherish her, and so far, I've been to battle, sent her away only to have her come back with the Atlantean army, be drugged and now we face another threat of her being taken away from me.

Just one moment of peace, that's all I wanted.

"Where are they?" My voice was stern. The kingdom thought their King would be in a more playful mood. They were outside the gates celebrating right now, but this was not the case. I'm livid, not even a note letting me know of their arrival. Was father out for a death wish? The invitation I sent to him was instructions to come two days before, not seven days. Now I will have to hear all his "suggestions" on how I should run the nation.

Well, guess what? I changed it all, and the people are happy about it.

"Right here, your highness." The look of fear was slapped

across the servants' faces as my father and mother opened the other door that kept them hidden. Here I was, barechested, as Melina had a cloth cooling off my heated body with her in a rather compromising position. Melina's eyes grew wide, and I felt the heat from her face flow down between her legs, and it wasn't for lust. Pure embarrassment.

Melina whipped her head around and put her head on my shoulder. A small sniff came from her. My darling wasn't one for a crowd, especially being caught in such a position in front of my parents.

"Next time, have them wait in the receiving room. Hmm?" My voice snapped at the servants.

"Is this what you do in your free time, son? Mess with some harlot?" Melina's body flinched, and I felt a damp tear on my shoulder. That's it.

"Father, I suggest you watch your tone. This is the future Queen and my true mate. Do you not have the decency to leave after seeing us like this?" My mother, the follower of the relationship, was almost dancing on her toes, keeping her mouth shut while my father bore his amber eyes into me. My mother's squeak caught my father's attention, and she released her hands from her mouth.

"Can I seeeee herrrrr!? Oh, my baby got his mate!" Mother was the one I confided in the most growing up. If there was a scrape on my knee or I feared the rolling thunder, mother was there while my father was too preoccupied with his duties. He may seem like a stern King, but that was only to his own family. In the Court, he was a pushover, always wanting what was best for them and not the kingdom.

Melina sniffed as she tried to dry her eyes. My darling had certainly opened her feelings the past few weeks together, but even so, this was a bit much for her. "Is this too much? Would you like to meet them later?" I whispered while I kissed the shell of her ear.

"Your mother sounds excited, but your father called me a harlot. What am I to do with that?" She sniffed again and took the once cold rag and dabbed her nose. Damn, her nose was adorable when it was all red and stuffy.

"Spend some time with my mother. She is better than him." I glared at my father while he crossed his arms. Melina nodded her head and fixed her hair quickly before getting off my lap.

"Good evening, Your Majesty," Melina bowed gracefully. "My name is Melina, and I am Osirus'-" before another word was said, my mother embraced her in her arms and lovingly petting her head.

"I'm Nissa, or just mother to you, little one. You are so small! Oh, my, and you have been marked! It's true!" My mother engulfed her in another hug and led her out of the study. My mother was fully aware of what was about to go down with my father and me.

"You marked her already? Do you have no regard for the etiquette lessons you spent day in and day out studying? What the hell is wrong with you? You are to mark her on the day of the coronation and binding ceremony!" I growled at him as my wings flung right back out of my back. There was no more hiding, no more being shied away from what we were.

My father stood back in surprise. He hadn't seen my wings for a long time. "What are you doing?" he yelled again, and I immediately stepped forward. My wings were black, almost charred, the anger of my aura was rolling off me like roaring thunder as he continued to walk backwards and fell onto the couch behind him.

Little did anyone know the bonding that Melina and I completed unlocked a new power in me. I could not only use my light power, but I could touch my ancient ancestor's dark power. Something no Fae had ever done. It has said I was to be the strongest Fae yet, the seers confirmed it the day of my birth and was written for all to see. The Fae people didn't know how powerful, and today it was unleashed by the utter rage of the chance my mate would be taken from me.

"You listen here. You are no longer king of this kingdom. You are weak, feeble-minded, and were easily persuaded into darkness. The people have suffered because of you, you let the Court rule over you when it should be the other way around. Kings pledge to do what is best for the people, not tax them into starvation and giving up their wings." My breath heaved as I tried to rein in my anger. I didn't know how far I could go with this darker power, and I didn't want to test it now.

"We are Fae, and we are to be proud of it. As of yesterday, the kingdom has seen what I have done and has approved it themselves. Now, if you want to stay, I suggest you apologize to your Queen, the princess of Atlantis. Her father Girard is not an understanding man when it comes to his only daughter." My father's eyes widened. He knew he was in some deep shit now, offending a lost princess and a princess of Atlantis no doubt would certainly be the end of him, and hell, I'd have front row seats to that.

"I'm sorry, son." He pulled at his tunic as he tried to sit up. The information was suffocating him and having a shot of brandy might be good for him. I went to the bar and poured him a glass while he wiped his brow with his handkerchief. What caught me off guard the most was those three words I had longed to hear him say, 'I'm sorry, son.'

"I know I'm a terrible father." He put his glass down on the desk and walked to the large window overlooking the marketplace. "I did what I was told in the Court and thought it was for the best. At the time, I didn't know they were conniving little shits because we all grew up together. I thought they were looking out for me." Again, my father picked up the glass and swirled the ice inside. "Part of me still hurts, but I know they did wrong. I didn't want to admit to it. Old habits die hard, but I came back early for your forgiveness. I was more upset that the woman in your lap might not be your mate," he scoffed.

Even though the supernatural didn't age, he looked older.

He wasn't as fit as he used to be, and the worry lines littered his face. A permanent frown had taken over and my mother's cheerful attitude couldn't even help him. "A King shouldn't have to apologize, but a father should. The way I have treated you has been wrong, and I know I have a long way to go to make up for it. I have so much to do to make it up to you, and me fleeing the palace and letting you fend for yourself was also wrong. I didn't want to admit my mistakes. Hell, I still don't. A father is supposed to be someone to look up to, and over the years, it has slowly sunk in how wrong I was to you, Osirus."

The anger that I had felt just ten minutes ago faded. His aura had become significantly lighter as he spoke. He wasn't the father I once knew; he was trying to turn over a new leaf. The question was, could I really forgive him? Just that speech alone couldn't erase everything he had done. He made my life miserable for so long, listening to the wrong people, forcing policies down my throat I didn't agree with.

"We have a long way to go," I walked toward him and put my hand on his shoulder, "we also have a long life ahead of us. May it be blessed by the gods. Now, do you want to meet my mate?" Men don't need to dwell on these things. Women do but not men. I wouldn't mind if we sparred a bit, and we could beat the shit out of each other and call it good, but with everything else on my plate, I don't think Melina would be very appreciative of the primitive things men could do. I couldn't forgive him, not yet. I wanted him to prove himself to me, and with all the shit we have coming up, he could do just that this week.

Father chuckled as he took a large swig of his whisky. "I thought she was one of your old concubines. I will grovel." His face was back to being harsh. He certainly had a much longer road than he thought. Changing one's attitude doesn't happen overnight. He was still ticked that I marked her before the ceremony, but Melina was mine, and I would not let her get away from me. How he waited with my mother. I will never know that kind of strength.

After the long walk to the tearoom, Father explained where my five brothers were. Most of them were off hunting for their mates. I grew up mostly as an only child until I was 300 years old and they started over again. She popped out my brothers one after the other until she was satisfied and now no longer had that maternal drive. All she would talk about before my father took her and my brothers away was how she was ready for grandchildren. That was so many years ago, and now that chance might come sooner than later.

I could feel tingles down in my heart at the thought of Melina being swollen with our child. Having more time with her alone would be preferable, but hell, I was going to use anything to prevent my seed from coating her walls. She could very well be pregnant right now, for all I knew. If her sudden burst of tears of embarrassment was any inclination, I may be on to something.

A silent smirk flew on my face, and I knew my father could feel my excitement. He could also read auras with those he was related to. His hand went to the back of my neck to squeeze his affection at me. "She is certainly beautiful. I'm glad you found her after all these years." I wished Father's gift was stronger so he could read his very own friends that went against him all those years ago in Court.

Even though my father looked like he turned over a new leaf, I was always going to be wary of him. Like I said, years and years of bickering and trying to drill me into submission of the Court was going to lay heavy on my mind and heart. If only he had trusted his son, but as a father, he thought he knew best. I hope not to make the same mistake with my children.

As we walked, I had to explain how most of the Fae Court were in the dungeons, along with his supposed best friend Cosmo. Once I had taken over, Cosmo, father's right hand and speaker of the Court, had dropped my father like a fly and tried to win my favor. Never worked. I could smell him a mile away and his overwhelming stench of horse dung.

Father sighed in agreement and was even understanding of their punishment. The evidence was overwhelming, the papers I had collected, budgets, embezzlement, treachery, treason it was all there, and he would succumb to his own devices and be locked away or put to death depending on the will of the people.

We wandered down the hall as we both felt the pull of our mates and found ourselves in the tearoom. It was a brightly lit room with shelves upon shelves of different teas and sweeteners such as honey, agave nectar, and juley juices from the palace orchards. Melina was sitting up straight as mother showed her the proper ways to pour tea. Melina was really enjoying herself, smiling at my mother brightly.

"And this is Honey Ambrosia Tea. The leaves are dried for at least two years before you can crush them and place them into the small baggies," my mother smiled as she let Melina smell them.

"At least she likes to learn some etiquette," my father said under his breath while he pushed me playfully. I gave an enormous smile as I saw my Melina listen to my mother. The 800 some years of waiting for my mate was worth it. If we could get past this next week, we would be set for a long time.

Chapter 53

Melina

Nissa was such a wonderful person. She made me feel right at home as she took me away from the soon-to-be fighting. When they appeared not only thirty minutes later in the tearoom, but I also knew there had to of been a breakthrough. My thought was right when Nissa looked at both men and gave a large smile and I think I saw a blush come to her face when Nyx gave her a wide grin. Even after all those years, he loved her, even if he strayed a bit.

Nyx profusely apologized, saying he did not know who I was. He wanted Osirus to find his true mate and the rumors of him being a man-whore had spread throughout the kingdom, so he thought the worst. Luckily for Osirus, me being his mate made Nyx relax and be joyful about our pairing. However, now HE felt utterly embarrassed. We were both embarrassed today, so I told him we were even.

Osirus' father was briefed on our current 'situations,' A.K.A. 'the big hot sticky mess.' We spent a good time talking about Cosmo's daughter Daphne. Nyx never liked the daughter of his best friend he grew up with. She was spoiled and was the product of a chosen mate marriage and he was firmly against that, even though in the Fae Court it was allowed.

There were rumors that Cosmo's chosen mate was in a mateless facility for those who don't want to live on without mates, which sparked my interest a few days ago. I had an idea to lure Daphne out of hiding. Daphne had a love for her mother Osirus had mentioned, so why not use that to our advantage even though her mother was innocent? Maybe we could find her true mate once Cosmo was put to death or forced to be in prison. Nissa explained chosen marks could fade or be overturned by Selene's proper matching, which gave me a tremendous sigh of relief.

Nissa was put in charge of finding Elaine, Daphne's mother, and help prepare a room for her. Elaine had been depressed and debilitated with that depression, being married to Cosmo. The evil man only cared about marrying her for her status. Physicians would be brought in to help her hoping to find her mate, and I prayed the goddess looks down on her with mercy.

Along with helping Elaine, Nissa would oversee the coronation preparations. I was asked several times about colors, themes, and so forth, but I didn't really care. All I wanted was to have the attention diverted away from me, which only made her laugh. "All the attention will be on you, sweetheart," Nissa cooed at me while Osirus kissed my head.

"You are already the talk of the entire realm, colorful wings, the lost princesses no one even knew about. You reek of popularity," one servant spoke as said as he poured me a glass of tea.

"You truly are a doll, Melina, coming from the upbringing you had and especially with those Wolves. My son doesn't deserve your kindness and refreshing look at life. Not to mention, quite the beauty." Nyx winked at Osirus, who just rolled his eyes.

"I've already made up for it, father, trust me." Osirus winked, and I turned bright pink with my new porcelain skin tone.

While Alaneo and Nyx oversaw the Kingdom and gathering extra soldiers for the coronation and protecting the palace, they were also left to their own devices to find the hidden Blood Coven. This would have to be done discretely. Sending Pixies into the area around Vermillion. If only we had an alliance with the darker kingdom, but they are currently undergoing their own transitions of power.

The next day, Osirus, Everett, Finley, Braxton, and I were to fly up to the Dragon shifter tribe and let them know about Tulip's recent discovery of witches trying to steal the Dragon's blood. If those witches got their hands on a child, I'm sure the Dragons would burn everything down. They were powerful creatures but also discrete. They often fly in the sky and patrol the shifter kingdom well, but their home was their sanctuary. No one goes in or out unless they have an invitation, and right now, we do not.

Time was of the essence as we took flight together. It was a sight to see. Osirus was by my side while Everett and Finley were in front and Braxton flanking us. The higher in elevation, the thinner air became, and I found it hard to breathe. Fortunately, we didn't have to fly much longer because flying in Dragon territory was an immediate threat. "If you think Wolves are possessive of their territory, you wait and see a Dragon," Everett yelled as the wind howled.

The clouds darkened as we saw rain approaching, making us land earlier than planned. Osirus said it might be okay for me to fly in the rain with my wings, but it would spell trouble for an ordinary Fae. Airing out wings takes weeks and a lot of medicinal creams that were scarce. "We will land there!" Osirus shouted as the wind howled again. Osirus pointed to a cave nearby, and we fluttered over. With a gentle thump, I landed less gracefully than the others. Everett laughed as I stumbled a bit as the pack pushed me forward, wanting to keep going.

"Ah, inertia is a bitch." Everett laughed while I chuckled, taking the pack off.

"We will have to wait here until the storm clears before

heading deeper into the forest," Osirus spoke as we entered the cave.

"Are you sure, Osirus? It is only drizzling. We should keep going," I pushed. Something didn't feel right being in this cave. It was dark but mostly dry. Meaning it could be a perfect place for someone or something to live in.

"We need a rest, we have flown two hours straight," Finley said, not worried in the slightest. Since I was just a newly planted Bergarian, I figured it should be all right if two mighty warriors said it was. I sat down on a small mat and leaned against the cave wall and shut my eyes.

Osirus was speaking to Finley, who had a map of the Dragon tribes and which one they should visit since we didn't have time to see them all. It was decided to visit the largest, the one with the ultimate alpha Dragon, Adam. His wife was a Fae which gave us the upper hand if the Dragons didn't appreciate our intrusion. Faes tend to favor other Faes.

Letting out a gigantic sigh, I felt the wall behind me move. My eyes flew open as I felt behind me. It wasn't a cold cave wall like it should have been. In fact, it felt warm. I rubbed it again, and a slight rumble came out. Sitting up I looked behind me now that Braxton had a fire lit and staring back at me where two gigantic black eyes with a flicker of light from the fire.

Screaming like my pants were on fire, I ran up to Osirus and pulled his tunic while he stared at me in shock. The beady eyes kept staring as I couldn't come up with the words to spill out of my mouth. "THE W-WALL H-Has EYES!"

The men all pulled out their swords, ready to attack with the wall came to life. It wasn't a Dragon. It was scarier than that. Instead of Horus and his beautiful white and gold scales, these were pitch black, covered in scars. The wings were bat-like for webbing but had thin feathers from the top of its head down to its tail. Eyes were as large as dinner plates, and the hind legs were large with foot-long talons.

It never growled but grunted while its white fangs came

over its bottom jaw. Nothing in the storybooks I have read could help me figure out this creature. I had stopped screaming and now looked at it in awe. It was huge, and its head raised to the top of the cave. Osirus stood still, waiting for an attack, but there was none.

Large bouts of smoke came from its nostrils as it circled him, and black glitter sprung forth to engulf the creature as it covered its shrinking body. A few seconds went by and when the smoke cleared, it was a gargantuan man. Scars littered his chest, along with several tribal and Dragon tattoos. His dark hair was long, down to mid-back. A large scar went down his face, going straight through the eye. If he didn't have the scar, he would have been a beautiful man. Even with the scar, the aura of power he leaked was stifling. Four Fae could never bring this beast down in the full form.

"Who are you?" Osirus put his sword away, and everyone followed. The man just folded his arms while the cloth covering his private parts swayed as the wind blew in the cave. To break the awkward silence, I stepped forward. Maybe listening to a woman might help?

"Um, hello?" Yeah, the confidence was out the window now. Great job Melina. "I'm Melina, and this is King Osirus. We have news to take to Alpha Adam, maybe you have heard? Dangers are coming this way, and it affects the tribes."

The brooding man stood there, taking in our words. He looked everyone up and down as his arms stayed crossed over his raging muscles. "You shouldn't have told him anything. He isn't a Dragon," Everett said, and that was when we heard a loud growl from the monster.

"He looks Dragon enough to me," I said honestly. The man's eyes softened for only a second before he turned cold. "Sorry to bother you. We can leave." I motioned for everyone to pack up, and Osirus agreed but dragged me with him by the hand.

"Melina, what were you thinking, talking to that thing?" Osirus whispered.

"He's a person, Osirus. He lives up here with the other Dragons, so he has some relation to them. Why not ask for help?" Osirus' jaw ticked.

"Don't speak to these Dragons, darling. They aren't like the elves and the Wolves, you know. They are more animalistic, if that were even possible." He threw his hair over his shoulder to get it out of the way while I glared at him, and he motioned for everyone to leave.

I let out a huff and turned right around back up to mister scary guy and gave a little bow. "We are just trying to save the women and children from the witches coming over the border and warn your people." Mister scary man didn't move or showed any easement of his stance. Pausing, I came up with a brilliant idea. Singing light heartedly as I could, I sang to the tune of 'Wheels on the Bus', "Please lead us to Alpha Adam's Tribe, Adam's tribe. Will you please lead us to Alpha Adam's tribe? We would be forever grateful."

This was not my proudest moment. I'm sure Lucca would roll on the floor right now.

I heard Osirus growl at me while I turned around and gave him an enormous tongue to stare at. Big Fae meanie. Mister big scary man nodded his head, uncrossed his arms, and led us out of the cave while we followed. Grabbing my bag and glaring at Osirus, I followed closely. I don't know if it was my Siren powers or the fact I just looked like an idiot. I will never know.

"Oy, you are in for it, eh?" Everett laughed as I heard a slap on Osirus' back. "She tamed a wild beast all on 'er own! Must be da Siren blood." I looked back at Osirus, who looked like someone slapped him with a stupid stick.

Mister scary man led us through the forest and in no time, we reached a small village. The area was primitive but also secure and safe. Instead of homes in trees like the elves, the Dragons had huts on the ground made of mud as hard as concrete. Several of them had smokestacks coming out, with one hut looking to be the largest of them all.

As we entered slowly, mister scary man held out his arm for us to halt until a beautiful Fae woman walked out. She must have been Alpha Adam's mate. Her hair was long and blonde and had a sheen of red highlights in her hair. She smiled warmly once she saw our guide and whisper yelled, "Creed!"

That's nice. Now we have a name. Creed just gave a curt nod as she engulfed him in a hug. "As great as it is to see you Creed, you better go. Adam is in a foul mood." Creed did a small bow and kissed her hand as he turned to us and walked past.

"Thank you!" I called to him, but he didn't even turn around. He continued walking down the path he led us down.

"King Osirus, to what do we owe the pleasure?" She curtsied lowly. Osirus came forward, his kingly stoic face was slapped on, and I couldn't help but internally groan. He's pissed at me. I could feel those waves of anger a mile away.

"We have come to warn you of-" A roar broke through the camp. Another large man, well, who am I kidding? Everyone was large. He was at least 6'8", with mousy brown hair, sweat protruding from his body, and only wearing the same type of cloth Creed was wearing. We've got hot Tarzans up in these mountains.

"You are in our territory with no invitation." His index finger pointed directly to Osirus, who stood still with a hand on his sword.

Chapter 54

Melina

Osirus and the Red-Headed Fury all drew their swords in a fighting stance. I stood back, still standing near the Alpha's mate. "You need to leave. You did not follow proper protocol. Who is to say you are here with the right intentions or some damn magical creature impersonating King Osirus?" the man spat.

"It's me, Osirus. If we followed protocol, it would be too late. Now, do you want to hear why we are here?" Osirus looked smug, as if he had won, but the sparkle in the man's eye said he wasn't done. Osirus instantly unbuckled his cape as it drifted to the ground while I stood wide-eyed. I had never seen him in action, so now I got to see a show.

Instead of advancing, Osirus and the man continued to hurl insults at one another, and it was becoming rather dull. "So do you throw sparkles when you fly around the flowers?" the giant taunted.

Everett screamed, "The fuck?!" before he started inching forward. Osirus swung out his hand so Everett couldn't advance.

"Let me ask a question, did you crawl out of your mother's womb, or did you hatch from an egg and eat your brother?"

Burly man gritted his teeth in anger as scales popped out over his body and smoke swirled. I should be scared beyond belief, but I had a feeling it was just a man's argument trying to see whose dick was more extensive.

"Yours?" I pointed to the half-shifted Dragon in front of me. She nodded as she continued watching with a hand on her hip.

"Mine's the one with the tiny pointy stick waving it around at your mate. He's King Osirus."

She made a long, "ohhhhhh," and looked relieved.

"Hmm, would you like something to eat?" The woman beside me spoke, raising her eyebrow in question. The now large red Dragon in front of me let me know she was indeed the mate of this crazy alpha. The reds in her hair and the red in his scales were proof enough.

"Sure! I'm starving!" She held out her arm, and I took it gladly; Finley looked concerned as I waved at him, letting him know I would be in the hut across the central court-yard. All the men gathered and very few females stopped the bickering as we strolled over to the large hut that had smoke dancing from the stack.

"I'm Amora, and that was Adam. Sorry, you seemed to have met him in a foul mood." She waved her hand.

"It's all right. Osirus can be hot-headed. They mean well. I'm Melina." The outside of the hut was like the others. A strong cement-like mud coated the walls, but once you entered, it was a different entirely.

The inside looked magnificent, one that you could see in the palace itself. Dark marbled floors with deep red walls and brightly lit chandeliers lit the entire room. Long, low tables were scattered across the room that reminded me of the din-ing room of a packhouse. Several women led us to a smaller table, still the same height as the others, which was low. Beautiful cushions with intricate beading and blankets scat-ted below the table. Sitting on the cushion, they brought me several kinds of drinks as Amora whispered a few things to the maiden beside her.

"Welcome to the Toboki tribe. What brings you here so suddenly? We aren't used to visitors," she laughed lightly as she poured wine into my cup.

"Yes, well, we are here on important matters. We know we are supposed to go through the Cerulean Moon Kingdom to reach you, but there wasn't enough time." Amora urged me to continue as a plate of steak was placed before me.

"There are witches and sorcerers from the Blood Coven that are after Dragon's blood. They may have been trying to infiltrate the mountains." Amora's fork dropped to the table, causing the entire room of servants to stare at her in shock.

"Come again?" she whispered. "You mean the strange sightings we have been seeing have not been Fairies or Pixies?"

"Why would they be Fairies or Pixies? Osirus said they were forbidden to come to the mountain except for spring to get a jump start on your crops." Amora gripped her fork again, and her wings shuddered.

"We thought it was them, the way they moved and would vanish. I swore I saw one myself. Are you sure they are witches?" I nodded again.

"I have a spy in the Blood Coven, and she sent word they are specifically targeting the Dragons in the mountains. They need the blood to make their spells stronger, and on top of that, they are working with a Fae trying to overthrow the Golden Light Kingdom. It's a big fat mess." I rolled my eyes and crossed my arms.

Not one day of peace.

"This is some news, then. That's why my Adam has been so angry. I told him there had to be a reason Osirus would send Fairies here; there was no way he would go back on his policies."

"I'm sorry for the misunderstanding and the past few weeks with the battle your tribe helped us win and then having to deal with me as a new mate didn't help matters." I took a large bite of the steak in front of me and instantly moaned. "Holy cow, this is amazing. I haven't been served anything like this since living in the palace. Light Fae fish food and little cucumber sandwiches is all I eat at the palace." Amora laughed.

"Yes, it is heavy for me, but once I was bonded, my taste changed. You must be half something else?" Her eyebrows raised.

"I'm part Siren. Before I was half-human, and I loved burgers and steaks." I popped another piece in my mouth and let my tastebuds savor the flavor before swallowing. "Please tell me this is a cow and not some funky animal?" Amora laughed and slapped her hand on the table.

"Oh yes, we have a herding facility that the whole Shifter Dragon colony takes turns taking care of. We have quite a few cows from the Earth realm, and we are the only colony in the Shifter kingdom that has them." I sighed as I took another bite.

"Maybe we can come up with some sort of agreement. I'm sure I'm the only one that would want to eat it at the palace besides some visiting Werewolves."

Amora looked at me with interest. "You are certainly different. I've never heard of a half Siren half-Fae. How do your wings look?"

I gave a blush as I patted my mouth with the napkin. "Oh, it's nothing." Amora continued to press until I finally let my wings out, and the entire room went silent again. Many came forward to look closely at the colors that shimmered on the wings.

"Like a butterfly," one murmured while others commented they look like a hummingbird's wing. I started giggling, realizing what I was drinking was some strong alcohol but was sweet like candy.

Amora and I sat and talked while the boys continued to yell and scream at each other outside. They had gone at it for more than an hour as we talked about how we met our mates, concluding we were both head over heels for our mates. There were a few sentences saying we should go check on them but laughed some more and let them keep fighting. Laughing more at the silly things that alpha says or do when it comes to their mates, to assert their dominance, I had almost forgotten about the one man that really reeked of male testosterone, Creed.

"Hey, Amora, who is Creed?" Amora stopped laughing and had a small smile at the mention of his name.

"He was my childhood friend, but he holds a sweet place in my heart. I am only telling you some of his story since you are the queen and have the right to know." Amora brushed her hair to the side and started to braid it as she continued. "He is Adam's half-brother. His mother was raped at an early age, and no one really knows who the father was. When Adam's mother found her true mate and Adam's father, he still accepted her because he loved her the way she was, with or without a child that wasn't his." I swooned internally with a man that would still accept a woman even though misfortune fell on her. There were too many times I had heard men not pursuing women due to having a child that wasn't their own.

"Adam's mother loved Creed, and when Adam came along, she loved them both equally, as did their father. Adam was still jealous of Creed, thinking he was just a monstrous creature once Creed first shifted. Creed was different and not fully Dragon, but I still cared for him the same because he loved as his mother loved. Without discrimination and with passion." Amora turned as she gave our plates to the servants next to us.

"Adam made Creed look like he was a monster after their parents died during a brawl with a neighboring tribe. Once Adam became alpha, it took little convincing to turn the entire tribe's back on Creed. He was always different, quiet, and brutally strong. Many feared him and feared he would want to take over the tribe even though he was not the first-born son of Adam's father. Everyone turned on him and called him a monster and a beast the way he would fight to defend our tribe. Creed was a true warrior.

"Creed left the tribe because Adam ultimately exiled him, but he is expected to fight their battles. Creed secretly protected the women and children on the outskirts of our territory." Part of me wanted to question why Adam was so cruel to his brother, but I kept silent. How could Amora love a man who could be so cruel to his own half-brother? The bond and love can make one so blind. I'm not that way, am I?

Creed sounded like an outstanding person, even though he was treated harshly. Creed's story pulled at my heartstrings. I hoped he could find a mate.

"You know the worst part?" Amora spoke quietly. "They say he can't have a mate because he was conceived without a bond and through force." I gasped loudly. My heart just crumbled to pieces.

"Surely not, there has to be-"

Amora shook her head. "It's what the elders say,..." She trailed off while I grabbed her hands. She had a close relationship with Creed, which made me wonder if they were once together. A little tear was wiped away as she sniffed.

"He was like a brother to me," she whispered. "Sorry, one of my gifts is light mind-reading, and you are really loud." I giggled, the alcohol finally hitting my system.

"Um, can Creed be persuaded with a Siren song?" I asked curiously. Please say it worked, so I didn't embarrass myself. Amora laughed and shook her head no.

"Sirens have no power on a Dragon. A Dragon's magical abilities are too strong." I groaned and put my head on the table.

Amora gasped while laughing, "What did you do?!" A squeal was heard from her as tears leaked from her eyes. The alcohol must have hit her too because we were both laughing loudly.

"I sang to the tune of 'Wheels on the Bus,' I thought about

what a bus looked like and hummed the song in my head. Amora spit out a bit of wine from her mouth, "And I commanded him to take us here!" I fell onto the cushion dramatically. Amora crawled to me on the other side of the table, and we both held onto each other in laughter.

A few throats were clearing as we both looked up from the floor of our mates, Adam, and Osirus, with amused smirks on their faces. "Are you both done measuring your dicks now?" Amora laughed while I snorted out a giggle again.

"Oh, I can tell you how big Osirus is. It is this..." I held up both my hands to show Amora, but Osirus picked me up and threw me over his shoulder.

"That's enough wine for you, darling," and smacked my butt harshly.

"Again, Daddy!" I squealed, and Amora laughed harder while trying to catch her breath.

"Adam! They have the same kinks we do! I enjoy calling him Master!" Adam turned a bright red and pulled up Amora and whispered in her ear as she blushed profusely. Adam must be shy.

"We will take you to your sleeping quarters and talk more in the morning before you leave," Adam spoke with authority. I groaned as we walked out, not liking the swaying I was currently experiencing upside down. Understanding my predicament, Osirus set me down and kissed me on the side of my head.

"Thank you, my love!" I pulled him in for a quick peck while he gave me a smirk.

We were led outside to the main courtyard and sent to a small hut in the woods, away from most of the other Dragons for privacy. Amora kept explaining to Adam how we were still in our "honeymoon stage" and "no one needs to hear that."

Again, the hut looked small on the outside, but the inside was magnificent. It was just a large bedroom with a small kitchen nook in the corner, enough to make coffee or tea, and had a few things in a miniature fridge such as custard cakes and drinks. The bed was a large king with a deep red comforter with black sheets. The entire place was carpeted and had a warm feeling as opposed to the cold lurking in the tribe tonight.

"We will leave you to it then." Adam gave a solid handshake to Osirus, who nodded in agreement. Once the large door was shut to the hut, Osirus turned around and bit his bottom lip while smiling, which I found extremely sexy.

"Now, darling, we need to talk."

Chapter 55

Osirus

I could hear Melina chatting to the Alpha female of the tribe. Few giggles and talking of a stick left the tent and I prayed to the goddess she was talking about the damn sword. Finley nudged me as the rest of the tribe watched the two women link arms together and enter the main hunt. Alpha Adam stood staring at his wife's arse while I watched Melina's as well.

Having two Alphas, me being a King of Fae and him being the Tribe leader of the Dragon shifters, puts our primal instincts to the forefront. Adam has worked with me before, but unfortunately, his territorial Dragon is throwing a fit with his territory infiltrated by unknown sources. I saw his eyes turn black with fury, thinking I caused the danger lurking.

"You are playing with fire, girly one," his Dragon smirked as he weaved side to side. Adam's Dragon was red and black, the colors of his tribe. His family crest that hung on a flag entering their territory was that of a fire breather, his ancestral family heritage. The scales of a Dragon were almost impenetrable along with their skin. It took a particular poison, an acid, to breakthrough using a sharp sword or bow. Difficult to make, but very potent.

Dragons themselves could speak in their Dragon form, one of the few shifter families to do so. Most other shifters use a mind-link, but it was common for them to speak with this old race. "Are you done throwing insults? Our mates found it petty and left for some other fun. Would you like your code word or not?"

Adam's Dragon was a hot head sometimes, like all Dragons. Once his parents passed away with a rival tribe over a mating issue, he took the position seriously. The tribe had prospered.

"Fine," he huffed as the smoke swirled out of his nostrils. "Out with it." This could have saved so much trouble earlier, but again, Dragons are hot-headed and primal, just like a neanderthal of the humans.

"Axis," I exclaimed, and instantly Adam reverted to his human form. The smoke plumed forth as the dark smoke covered the Dragon's body until Adam was left standing in his cloth. Adam growled again as he approached. His hand came out to grab my neck, but I instantly dodged and used my aura abilities to confuse him with my exact location. I kicked him in the back as Adam fell forward to the ground. He shook his head as he jumped back up while I stood and waited. Dragons were big and bulky, while Fae were thin and agile, a perfect complement to an exciting fight.

The men cheered as Adam became frustrated with me evading his hits, while Everett screamed for me to get it over with. Adam may be strong and a leader Dragon, but he wasn't the Head Elder Dragon, nor was he the King of Shifters that held the most power.

In one swift movement, I grabbed his forearm as I drew strength from the dark force of my new unlocked power and blinded him for a moment. The black smoke covered his eyes as he tried to wave his hand against it as I pinned him to the ground. It was quick and easy, especially for his cocky attitude. Dragon or not, I was Fae, and my power was more substantial than he thought.

"Do you yield?" I smirked as his face was still planted in the dirt. His cloth had ridden up, nearly exposing his arse as I leaned in closer to his ear. "It would be a shame if I had to get your mate out here to see you like this. So helpless." When a male Dragon loses in front of his mate, a female could reject him even if they were bonded. Dragon mate females want their mates strong, but I knew Amora wouldn't do such a thing. She was a full Fae, but Adam didn't understand that Fae would never dismiss a mate, so why not take that to my advantage?

"Fine, yield," he growled as I let go, and he stood up. He dusted off his torso and gave a broad grin, as did I. We both grabbed each other's forearms and went in for a brotherly hug. Cheers went around as we patted each other on the back. "Great sparing," he chuckled.

"Sorry, Your Majesty, with the way our territory is being infiltrated, I had to be sure. There is something amiss, and we can't figure it out. Wolves have been trying to sniff it out, but even King Emilio's team can't track them."

"It's all right. I completely understood. I was prepared to defend my entourage." Finley rolled his eyes as a few beads of sweat dripped from his brow. Finley had a special attachment to Melina, and I knew he feared her safety like a brother would.

I grabbed my cape and tied it back as I laid my hand on my sword casually. Many of the bystanders scattered while his leading warriors stood by to listen to the information I had presented. Adam's face grew red as I explained about the Blood Coven. Fists were clenched, jaw tight, his Dragon nearly at the surface.

"We know something is happening soon, and I had to get here as quickly as possible. We hope to have this resolved at the end of the week, but I needed you on alert to keep your women and children safe. If you feel bringing them to the palace would help, we would be happy to accommodate them."

Adam's stance didn't relax as his men murmured behind him about what they should do. The women were precious, there weren't many mates to produce more Dragons, and when there was a pregnancy, they were born male and not even a Dragon, but of that species of their mother.

"Let me talk to my mate and my men tonight in private and come to a decision." A loud cackling came from the main hut, and a loud crash of a glass bottle hit the floor. Adam groaned and leaned his head back.

"She can be a bit of a lush when new women come into the tribe. I'm sure your mate is plastered." Adam started walking to the hut, and I had a grin on my face. Who doesn't love a drunk Melina? She was a horny drunk, and it was as hot hell.

Braxton started giggling like a fool and nudged Everett, who continued to shake his head. "They won't let you watch, bro." I groaned while Finley started laughing. The day they find their mates will be a gift from the goddess; they have to get a life and stop following me around.

***

Once the door to the hut was shut, Melina stood twiddling her fingers. I wasn't though. I was turned on by her assertiveness but wanted to crank it down a notch, and I knew exactly how to do that. Now, after she directly disobeyed me by talking to the strange creature, I found out was named Creed, heading to the hut without permission and about to expose my dick's size to the entire hut, I should be mad.

"Darling?" I curved my index finger for her to come to me, which she happily did. She damn near skipped to me as her breasts touched my chest. I groaned, and she sashayed her hips, grinding her core into my cock. "Fuck," I breathed. I thought I was the one that was to show dominance. Melina was too hot for her own good. The shoulder of her top fell gently, and she gave me a smirk as she gently pulled it down.

Her exposed neck with my mark made my dick twitch as I wrapped my arms around her waist as I kissed her neck.

A moan left her lips as I sucked on her, and Melina's hands grabbed my cock from the outside of my trousers. "Mmm, Osirus," she palmed it, feeling it spring to life. Her fingers fiddled with the tie around her top as her breasts spilled into the cold air, pebbling along with contact.

I slapped her thighs, and she immediately jumped and wrapped around my waist. Kissing her all the way to the bed, I explored her mouth, that tasted of mulberry wine with a hint of vanilla bean. Another moan from her had me stripping her down to nothing in a matter of seconds as her wet pussy gleamed on the lush, red duvet. The aroma she put out was my drug, and I could smell her scent for days as I nudged my nose around her core.

Melina's hips bucked for me to do more, but I wanted to tease and try something new. Usually, I liked my baby's eyes opened, but while her eyes were closed and feeling the heat of my tongue, I decided to be sneaky. Pulling a device out of my pocket, I put on a small fingertip vibrator as I continued to lick her folds. With one hand on her tits and my tongue slipping into her hole, I placed the vibrator right on her clit. It was silent, so the jump and squeal from her had me panting. She immediately went over the edge, screaming my name as I continued to rub figure eight circles with the vibrator.

"OH GODS!" She screamed again as her orgasm piled up again.

I bit my bottom lip and pulled away, wanting to watch her face contort into mind-blowing pleasure. Melina tried to slow her breathing, but another wave quickly hit her; before she screamed, I slammed my mouth to hers so she could taste her come in her mouth. I flung the vibrator to the side of the bed, getting my next toy, a vibrator ring, to go over my dick. I positioned myself at her entrance.

"W-what was that? Oh, gods, what?" Before she said another word, I pushed into her, and her pussy vibrated around my cock as it tickled her clit. "Oooh!" My baby creamed all over me, and I groaned at the wet slick running down her thigh. I could cum right now, feeling the thick arousal around me.

Pushing into her at a fast rhythm, she opened her legs wider, moved them to the tops of my shoulder. I now could put my hands under her arse and really pound her. Going deeper, hitting her cervix, she screamed for me over and over.

"You like that, baby? Do you like my cock tearing up your insides? Do you want it harder?" The ragged breaths and her eyes staring up into mine as she gripped the headboard, so I didn't slam her head into it, was enough of an answer. I used my wings to push the air behind me as I rammed her harder.

"Yes! Yes!" Melina yelped as I burst my seed into her womb. Her pussy clamped on me just as I spilled into her, milking me, sucking me dry. I collapsed on her. The ring was still buzzing, and Melina continued to have mini aftershocks rack her body. Kissing up and down her neck and nuzzling into my mark, she sighed contently as she tickled my back with her fingers.

"I love you, Osirus. I'm so happy I have you." Her eyes watered.

"Are you all right?" I asked, concerned. I knew I went far, and I didn't want to hurt her.

"I'm just so happy. I never thought I would feel a love like this, and now I have you. I don't have to be alone again." I glanced at her aura. Even after we had mated, there was a tint of blackness still there, the worry, the depression of her past. Now it was gone. There was no dark mass hovering over her heart, and it was a bright light full of joy.

Gently sliding out of her and taking the ring off, I pulled her to me as I peppered her with kisses, petting her face as she traced my chest with her fingertips. Touching was so intimate to both of us. We couldn't get enough. We were kissing, cuddling, and speaking of our future. Sure, the sex was amazing but, this is what I loved the most.

"You should sleep darling, we have to fly back tomorrow." Melina's yawn looked like a small puppy as she nuzzled closer to me. Our naked bodies intertwined again as both of our breathing slowed to take on another step of being safe.

Chapter 56

Nissa

Everything happened so fast! My joy had radiated through the Winter Fae Quarter Place as I got the invitation to the coronation ceremony just a few weeks ago. It took everything within me not to show up the next day at the main palace. My first son had finally found his mate!

Osirus had waited too long for someone to love. He saw what Nyx, and I had, even though his father could be a complete ass. Yes, an ass. With a capital, A. Nyx was different around me; he was tender, gentle, and sexier than any Fae I had ever seen. However, he had his shortcomings, and I wasn't talking about his manhood.

Nyx trusted his friends too much. He had a heart of gold and growing up with his friends meant everything to him since his own father died while he was very young in the Shifter Wars. His mother did the best she good, bless her soul, but once her mate had died, it was up to the Court to raise him, in other words, most of his friend's parents. They preened him into the king they wanted, the docile and respectful king to the court members, which was the ultimate demise of his reign.

As the saying goes, if you throw a toad into a pot of boiling water, it will automatically jump out, so it doesn't die. Take that same toad, put it in a pot of cold water, and slowly heat the water, and it will eventually die of the heat. That was what exactly happened to my dear mate, and he was slowly being boiled alive. The Court overthrew him, gave him less and less power, and he was too blind to see it in those who had raised him.

By the time I came into the picture, he couldn't be swayed. I did the best I could, but to no avail. He respected them as his own adoptive parents, and I knew even our bond couldn't change that. Once our first child was born, Osirus, he tried to instill those same features into him.

Secretly, I showed Osirus the true colors of the Court and how their power had grown too much. The lies, deceptions, and betrayal that went on were too much. Osirus did his own digging when he was older and was outraged that people of his own country would commit treason. Osirus did what he had to do to get the crown from his father, and Osirus may have overdone it.

The last fight that caused us to flee the palace after his coronation was enormous, and with a swift goodbye, I left my eldest. Nyx and I were bonded; we would both become weak and sick if separated.

Osirus continued to write me and send me more and more information that I could never get in my queenly status. The evidence was astounding, starving innocent children, high taxes, and ripping mate bonds to shreds to get higher status in courts. As the years dragged on and as Nyx was further away from the whisperings in his ear, he opened his eyes and see.

For years, he had become depressed for a nation he did not provide for and protect. Our bond had also strengthened more over the years, and with much pushing on my part, he had somewhat forgiven himself. He blamed himself for the torture he made his son go through, realizing just how strong Osirus was.

Osirus was strong, and through much pushing on my part when he was a child, he became a ruthless warrior. His anger grew with his father, but it was for the best. It fueled his drive on the battlefield and the fire within him to change our nation. The many years that Osirus suffered not having a mate were treacherous on his soul. The haunted look I saw in him as we drove away the last day we saw him haunted my dreams.

He was lonely and longing. The rumors being spread about him didn't help either, but that was for the best, he said. It was, so no one got close to him and tried to hold anything against him and knew his true colors.

As Osirus wrote to me, he mentioned how he couldn't do the final push until he found her. The drive was leaving him as he became more depressed, not having a true mate. The pressure from the Court also didn't help as they wanted him to mate with Daphne, the daughter of the speaker, Cosmo. I continue to still roll my eyes at that piece of information. They knew Nyx instilled that into Osirus to find his true mate.

Melina came at the perfect time for Osirus. Who knew she would have a fire within her as well? She's spunky, funny, and able to handle Osirus' temper very well. Melina wasn't one to walk on like a doormat. She didn't fall for the bond initially, and that really showed her strength. A noble head on her shoulders would prove to be a great asset, helping Osirus rule.

I smiled as I stirred my last bit of sugar cube into my coffee. Today, I would hold up my end of the plan and retrieve Elaine from the Mateless Home in the woods of the South.

"My Queen?" Nyx came to me as he kissed my forehead as he sat across the bistro table. "Are you sure going alone is the best thing?" I chuckled at his thoughtfulness as I laid my cup down.

"Of course, dear. Besides, I won't be alone. Sean, Melina's Werewolf friend, is accompanying me. The poor thing lost all his close friends to mates, so he is dreadfully bored." As I stood up and pecked my mate on the lips, I tapped the napkin on my lips. "I won't be long. I should be back by evening if Elaine will come on her own and not by force."

Elaine was part of Melina's plan to get Daphne to surrender and gently stop the Blood Coven. If Daphne agreed to drop the mess and tend to her mother properly and protect her with the promise of the Royal Family, it will save the kingdom from many hassles and unnecessary loss.

"I wish I could accompany you, but sending warriors in blindly has Osirus and I uncertain about their safety. Even though I haven't fought in quite some time, I think I still stand a punch or two." Nyx smiled as he raised his arm to flex. I instinctively grabbed hold and was awed as he flexed for me.

"You are more than capable, my love. In fact, you might have to wish me a proper goodbye while using these." I winked as I pressed my breasts to his chest. A playful growl escaped his lips as Alaneo walked through the door.

"Gods no! Not you two as well! Everyone is getting some but me!" Alaneo sighed as he sat in a nearby chair, sulking.

Nyx went over and slapped him on the shoulder. "All in due time, son. I'm sure it is right around the corner. The goddess won't let you suffer for long. Besides, Sean is still looking, too. Maybe at the coronation?"

Alaneo rolled his eyes and stood back up, adjusting his uniform. "Are you ready, your majesty?" Nyx gave me one long kiss before departing as I walked to the large open window.

The sky was clear, just a few clouds hovering above the palace's highest towers. I had always loved living here. The light sources were bright, and the moon was often just as bright on a complete cycle. I unbuttoned the back of my dress with my nimble fingers and let my wings unfold. They glistened as the sun's rays shone on the lightly patterned swirls.

Sean was waiting at the bottom of the tower next to the

carriage in Wolf form. We weren't aware how bad off Elaine was and if she could fly, so the carriage was our mode of transportation today. Fluttering down and landing with the most grace I could muster since it had been so many years, Sean opened the carriage door for me.

"I'll travel in Wolf form along with the coachmen. We should arrive within the next hour, Your Majesty." Sean bowed as his bare chest flexed to show the power his Wolf held. He was one of the best trackers in the Crimson Shadows Pack, and I knew I would be in excellent hands if things went awry.

***

The carriage ride went faster than I expected. Thoughts ran through my head of what I was going to say. Would Elaine come on her own accord? What will she say when she finds out her daughter was trying to overthrow an entire kingdom and that her chosen mate had been locked away in the dungeons? Would she be happy? Would Elaine be coherent at all? Over the years, they say one will lose themselves slowly, letting the madness of not finding their true mate kill them slowly since she had no say in the bonding at all.

Pain ripped through me, thinking how she was forced. I remember the day vividly as she cried, begging Nyx not to do this. She knew the pain her mother had when she had mated with her father, because he was too impatient. Once he finally found his true mate, he left her birth mother, and she died shortly after, not being strong enough with no bond. Elaine had not had the easiest life; once this was all said and done, I would take her myself all over Bergarian to search for her mate if he was still even alive.

As we pulled closer, the building was more like a cottage. Moss overgrew on the roof, and vines dangled from the rooftops. It was a single-story building with beautiful roses and butterfly bushes decorating the sides of the cottage. The picket fence was in pristine condition and would be a perfect retirement home for a human.

Stepping out of the carriage, I saw several solemn Fae were rocking in chairs, not even looking up to see their unknown visitor. Sean had changed and walked beside me as he took in the sight. Several caretakers came by to make sure they were drinking and eating as they saw us approach.

"Your Majesty!" One of them bowed while the rest in question followed. "This is King Nyx's wife, former king of The Golden Light Kingdom!" Several others went to bow, but I waved them to stop. I was no longer queen, only a servant now to my son and his mate.

"Please stand up, and I don't need any of that. I'm actually here to find someone." Several of the residents looked up, some with confusion and others with sadness. They knew that my husband allowed chosen mates for Fae to climb the social ladder, so I would not blame them if they hated me. I should have done more.

After explaining who I was looking for, the two caretakers speaking with me nodded and led me into the cottage. There was a woman with beautiful, dark purple hair rocking in front of the fire. She had a quilt lying on her lap. Her face was gaunt, she hadn't been eating, and dark circles hung around her eyes. For someone that shouldn't age, she had undoubtedly looked to be much older. The heavy sigh left her lips as she closed them, rocking her chair a few more times.

"Elaine?" I spoke gently as I put my hand on top of hers. Elaine didn't advert her eyes as she opened them and stared into the fire.

"What do you want?" Her voice was void and hollow, with no emotion to her words.

"I need your help. It is about your daughter." Elaine didn't turn her head as a rogue tear streamed down her face. Her face contorted as she looked at me. My heart sunk as her eyes met mine. She had given up on life, and she was almost an empty vessel.

"I will tell you what I told her: leave me. I have lost my chance to find my mate, raped, tortured, and bruised. Let me live what is left of my pathetic life." Elaine's eyes returned to the fire, but I pressed on.

"She is trying to protect you. She wants you safe, but she is doing it in all the wrong ways. She wants to take over the kingdom! Daphne is planning to rip the bond between King Osirus and Melina. Help us," I pleaded with her. Elaine continued to sit in her chair but paused her rocking.

"Is King Osirus Daphne's mate?" I sat beside her in shock, not knowing what to say.

"No, she is trying to take Osirus as a chosen to protect you and to gain power. Osirus' true mate is Melina." An enormous sigh left Elaine's lips as she gripped the quilt. Using as much strength as she could, her voice grew louder.

"I'll come with you. She can't do what her father did." I helped her stand up, thankful she will come along with us.

Men and women eyed us in curiosity, and my heart sunk to the floor. All of them needed help. They just wanted their mates. These people were rejected just before the bond became strong. Their mates took on another instead of waiting, or their mate died after a child was born. They needed a second chance, and if the goddess granted it worthy, she would deliver. She had to, and I had faith in her she would offer these poor souls a second chance.

"You are all coming with me," I spoke loudly, enough for the caretakers to hear. "There is a coronation and binding ceremony at the end of the week, and the entire kingdom and many unmated men and women will be there. I pray the goddess has a second chance for all of you." My voice grew weak as my sentence trailed. Many gave a slight smile, and a few still hung their heads in defeat. They had given up, but I wasn't going to.

I was going to help right the wrongs, and Nyx was going to help me do it. His new attitude and guilt demand it. "Sean, grab a messenger fairy and send for more carriages." Sean beamed and gave a bow as he ran outside to have a message delivered.

The palace would be filled with commotion, but it was the right thing to do, and I know Melina would have wanted it as well.

Chapter 57

Alaneo

Dealing with Osirus' father was not on my list of "most exciting activities." I told him it would be acceptable to go alone and take a few of our warriors, but Nyx insisted. He tried to be chivalric and say he owed the country that much.

A quiet flight through the countryside was what I was hoping for. All the warriors now donned older uniforms taken to storage before we had to hide our wings. Even though there were at least fifty of us in total, you still could not hear the flapping of our wings, like you would hear the bees that look for honey.

These were our stealthiest men. They had their arrows, swords, and several had spears for their choice of weapons and the darker camouflaged clothing to be stealthy enough to hit Vermillion was on point. We made it a clear effort to stay away from Vermillion. It was the darker side of Bergarian and could cause a Fae and fairies' mood to be depressed. We craved the light while they craved the dark. Even though the light sources still shone there, there were just not as bright with the thickly spaced trees and overhanging flora and fauna.

Nyx was struggling to keep up. He had not trained

enough over the years, but I will monitor him. Osirus would appreciate that now that his father had was acting like a parent.

Only 300 years too late.

As we approached the edge of Vermillion, I realized we would have some difficulty maneuvering about with our mass numbers. Breaking up the large group into several smaller ones and having themselves cloaked with a scent neutralizer, we headed in different directions.

Since having our wings expelled from our bodies only a few days ago, many Fae took it upon understanding they can also use the blessed power each Fae has. It could be like Osirus,' who can take control of people's bodies and read auras, or something simpler, like being able to frost the foliage. Warriors asked permission, and it was immediately granted. Their power was to render themselves invisible to the opposing race. We could see them, but other races could not, a beneficial gift in their line of work. They would be promoted as soon as this mess was cleared.

My gift was not as impressive as most, even though I was firm in battle. I had a war tactic ability; I could place my opponents' steps before taking them and go for their weak spots. That was what helped me grab Esteban and have Osirus rip Melina from his grasp.

Nyx stayed with me along with two other warriors as we tread through the forest. Our steps were light, and hardly any sound escaped our feet until we heard rustling through the bushes. We all crouched down, hoping to find the source of the noise. If the goddess were on our side today, the hidden Blood Coven that had been cloaked in the glamor spells would be found.

A small yip and a splash were heard as Nyx, and I looked over the foliage. "What was that?" he whispered, but I quickly shushed him as I saw a vampire girl along the banks. She was climbing up, coughing, and trying to stand up while two Ogres were looming overhead.

"Eh, look here? A weak one, isn't it?" the large Ogre started. Ogres were hideous-looking creatures. They may not be as tall as a Fae, but their body mass was large, green, and they carried a series of warts and small gatherings of bumps on their bodies. The more imperfections you had, the more a female Ogre wanted you. Ogres didn't follow the mating process from Selene, and I even wondered if she continued to try to mate them.

"Please, just leave me alone," the vampire whimpered. Scrapes and bruises adorned her body, a black eye, and bands around her wrists with chains. Her red eyes looked up, pleading with them as the second ogre pushed her back into the sand.

"She's weakened. She has dogwood bands on her wrists," the large one laughed in triumph.

"Excellent, I'll take her first. You wait until I'm done." The largest pulled her by the ankle, causing her dress to ride up. "Ugh, not a single wart. An ugly thing you are. Good thing we ain't keepin' ya." The girl screamed as she clawed at the dirt for him to let her go.

The tightness in my chest wouldn't allow this to carry on. Fighting two ogres with just the men we had was going to be difficult. They were strong, powerful, and could lift a full-grown tree out of the ground. The girl screamed again as the ogre gripped her ankle, easily snapping it in half.

Without hesitation, we all stormed the small beach around the lake. "Unhand her!" I pulled my sword from its sheath as the others followed. I looked to Nyx, who only pushed forward as we took off our capes. "That wasn't a question," I demanded again as I lunged forward. The warriors went to the smaller one as their swords tried hit the beast.

My interest was the largest, the biggest challenge. Nyx stood at my side in a fighting stance. I wasn't sure how strong he would be, so I was counting on myself. The young girl looked me dead in the eye as she tried to pull away from the chaos. Eyes widening, she covered her mouth as I went into a fighting stance.

Mate.

Before lunging forward, I had a shit-eating grin on my face as I looked back at my attacker. His grunts and growls were pounding the ground as I used my light footedness to scamper around him. The ogre's irritation grew as he saw I wasn't even trying. Nyx had a few good hits until he was slammed into a nearby tree. "Stay down, Your Majesty," I yelled back at him while taking another glance at my mate.

"Your name, maiden?" I asked curiously. Her eyes darted from me to the ogre as I continued to jump behind him and hit the brute with the butt of my sword. Swearing, he rubbed his head as I took my sheath and slipped it between his legs, causing him to fall to the ground. I was going to milk this chivalry shit. What better way to woo my mate than to beat up her attacker and whisk her off to my chambers and bed her the same day? All right, maybe not the same day, but it will be damn near close.

"Juliet," she barely spoke as I took another jab at the ogre, who was being insufferable. I had never heard so many swear words come out of one of my enemies as I did this one.

"And may I ask why you have bands on your wrists?" I winked at her as I grabbed a vine from a nearby tree, wrapping it around the ogre's feet.

"I was captured and experimented on. These kept me weak," I growled from hearing my mate might have been tortured, causing a surge of violence to wrack through me as I tripped the beast over and tied his feet and his legs. Ogres were like crocodiles, and they had considerable strength punching outward but hardly any strength as they pulled inward. The wrappings kept him tight as I kicked him in the head for one last measure.

I strode over to my mate, ready to hold out my hand, until Nyx started clapping and looking over my prey. "Well done, Alaneo!" Rolling my eyes, I squat down to help my mate. Juliet was drenched from head to toe, making her hair as dark as a Dragon's cave. The bright red eyes bore into my soul. Ruby's red lips were that of a doll, plump and beautiful. Her skin shivered, and her ankle had taken on a black and blue hue. Just from sitting, I could see how curvy she was. Thick thighs and a good-sized bosom taunted me as she blushed. Goddess, she was meant for me. I knew I would never have a Fae mate because of my actual feelings about stick-thin figures, but this was beyond surprising. I would never have thought this goddess would drop into my lap.

"Let's get these off of you, shall we?" Juliet nodded her head bashfully as I grabbed her hands in mine. We both gasped at the tingles as I ripped the wooden bands and chains along with it. Rubbing her wrists, the red and blistered skin healed along with her ankle.

"Thank you," her voice was sultry and low. It gave my wings a good shudder as she smiled back at me.

"Your name is Alaneo?" I nodded as I pulled her up from the ground. I held her by her waist and pulled her close.

"Repeat it," I whispered into her ear. A shiver ran down her arm as I put my hand on her arm to warm her while she healed.

"Alaneo?"

Pulling her closer, her body came flush with mine, and she gently laid her head on my chest. Her bosom kept her waist apart from me as my dick instantly hardened. Goddess.

"You saved my life, Alaneo. I don't know what would have happened if..." I put my finger to her lips as she quieted down.

"But it didn't, and I'm here now. I'll always be here for you." Her smile widened, and she quickly hugged me again. "I am glad you are safe, but I need to know who put these bands on you so I can go kill them swiftly." Warriors rolled the ogre into the lake, and he was instantly submerged in the water, which would eventually drown him. Piercing the skin of an ogre took special tools and sometimes blessed weaponry, so drowning was our best bet. The smaller was long gone in the water as well.

"Witches, the Blood Coven," Juliet sputtered. "I escaped with the help of a girl named Tulip. There were several of us, and we got separated." Panic surged through me, hearing Tulip's help. Did she get caught?

"Do they know Tulip helped?" Juliet shook her head no.

We made a small camp by the lake. The information that Juliet was about to speak of perked everyone's interest. This would be the first time we had spoken to anyone on the other side of the Blood Coven besides Tulip, and since we left this morning, we had heard nothing.

"They are evil, evil, I tell you." Juliet sniffed. "They have captured several races and have taken their blood. They are trying to strengthen their powers. Each witch has their specific ability, just like Fae do, or so I'm told. Some can summon fire, Bergarian soil, and weather, but only in small increments. They want to combine the strongest witches and take over the supernatural council so they can be the ultimate deliberators on the humans on Earth."

Juliet shivered as I put my cloak around her. "They captured my family, and they knew our family, once aged to be 200, could see the future. They originally wanted the Queen of the Cerulean Moon Kingdom, but she is unobtainable with Kane being her daughter's mate. She's too protected, so we were next. I haven't hacked into my power yet, my blood wasn't ripe, and my family was all older than me and couldn't be controlled, so they,.." Juliet's breath hitched, and she buried her face in her hands. As she sobbed, I looked at the others with a look of disdain, and we were going to have a difficult time. Even if Daphne decided against going after Osirus and the throne, the Blood Coven would still try to take over.

I pulled Juliet from her seat on the log and put her in my lap. This may be too soon, but I knew the bond would comfort her. Juliet immediately stopped crying and held onto me. "My little Rose, how long have you been there?"

Juliet sniffed again. "Eight years. I'm thirty now, and they were trying to invoke my power to wake up sooner. I wanted to die. I thought about it so often. The poking, the prodding, they did. Barely enough blood, just enough to keep me alive." She hiccupped again, and the warriors, along with Nyx, stood up to give us privacy.

"Are you hungry now, my Rose?" Juliet paused but shook her head 'no' as I pulled her from my neck. All I cared about was her and her safety, and now, looking at her, I could see the strenuous life she had led before me. Even with the beautiful curves she had, she was meant for more meat around those delicious thighs. Her ashen body would glow as soon as she ate; in fact, she would heal so much faster.

"Please don't lie, not now," I whispered to her, concerned. She sniffed. I knew vampires could eat solid food, but from the looks of her, she needed blood. Thank the gods for the cultural classes we had to take in primary. Otherwise, I would be lost here. "I want you to drink from me," I pressed.

"No! I can't!" Juliet spoke, startled. "It has been too long since I've eaten, and I don't know if I can stop." I laughed at her as she tried to stand up. Holding her close, I pushed back some of her raven hair.

"My little Rose, you can't hurt me. I regenerate too quickly. Besides, I'm your mate. You are supposed to drink from me, always." The hesitant look in her eyes got her thinking before she whispered, an 'Okay.'

Juliet pulled up my arm near my wrist before I pulled back. "What are you doing?"

"Drinking?" she blushed as she looked back down.

Pulling her head back up to me, I asked, "Why there? Why not my neck?" She gripped my tunic in frustration, and I chuckled at her.

"I have never drunk from there before." Vampires drinking from one's neck was very intimate, and I knew that, but I wanted to tease her. I wanted her to do it most of all. It wouldn't be a marking bite, but a feeding bite, which were two completely different things. I prayed she would mark me soon so I could mark her.

"Can you?" I pressed. "I've looked for you so long, my Rose. It would please me if you would." Juliet smiled as she bit her bottom lip.

"Only if you are comfortable." A mischievous smirk graced her lips as she leaned in. Meeting her halfway, I gave her a light kiss. For vampires being known as cold creatures, she felt the complete opposite. It was warm, and her lips tasted of bright cherries, the same color as her lips. I felt myself purr as she broke away and kissed down my cheek to my neck. She began lightly sucking on my shoulder as I moved my head and felt her sharp fangs tickle me.

In one swift bite, her teeth sunk into my skin, the warmth of her lips soothed the calm flow of blood escaping my body. I gripped her tighter, and she did the same. Our bodies melted together as the slight growl of a purr escaped her throat. She was soothing me, rocking me into a comforting state as she continued.

Chapter 58

Melina

After three rounds of morning fornication, yes, three, we finally arose from the dark duvet of our bed by mid-morning. I could feel the warmth of the air infiltrate the hut as we heard people milling about outside. Osirus was continuing to pepper kisses on my bare back as I hummed in fulfillment.

"Could we just stay here?" I mumbled into the pillow. "No one bothers us here." I felt Osirus' smirk on my back as he reached the nape of my neck.

"I wish we could, darling, but we have much to do in very little time." Osirus stripped the duvet from over my body, leaving me bare and the cold air of the blankets rushing by hit my skin, and I tried to curl up in the fetal position. Osirus pulled me from the bed, over his shoulder, and pulled me into the shower. The warm shower eased my sore muscles. Osirus had definitely given me some yoga poses to work on for the next time he wanted a romp in the park, but for now, the warm water would have to ease my ailments.

After stepping outside and greeting Amora and Adam, we had to discuss a plan in regarding the witches and sorcerers. It was believed that Creed would have to step in and help, despite Adam's reluctance. The Alpha leader of the tribe didn't trust Creed or just didn't like him. Creed had been nothing but hospitable to us, and Amora took a liking to him. The information that Amora graced me with only churned my stomach to think this was all a jealousy thing because he was not the firstborn of his mother and Creed could have had rightful leadership of the tribe. Their mother was the alpha Dragon and the last female born Dragon, so her mate became her equal and both partook of the Alpha roles.

Once we convened and spoke over a few hours of a plan, the Werewolves would come to help aid the Dragons, even with the reluctance of some of the tribe members. Dragons were prideful and wanted to take care of their own but losing a mate or even a child was far more significant when they were gone protecting their territory. The King and Queen of the Cerulean Moon Kingdom were to come personally to help aid them while taking on the Blood Coven on our own.

The treaty that Osirus had signed when I had first arrived at the Crimson Shadows Pack proved to be beneficial to both kingdoms. One protects, while one fights surely making their kingdoms almost incomparable in numbers and strong in defense and offense.

After a heartfelt goodbye to Amora and a stiff nod to Adam, we departed, and the Red-Headed Fury accompanied us all the same. Their jokes and jeers about how some women looked terrified of them gave them the best belly laughs. Many of them hadn't seen Fae let alone powerful warriors of their kind. They were both fascinated and terrified of their red beards and muscular bare chests.

As we began our flight back, I had an aching in my heart as I flew closer to the palace. My mind kept wandering to my father and how he was doing. He was reluctant to leave me with Osirus. He had not entirely accepted him being my mate, nor was he excited to let goof me after just finding me. The nudging in my chest only grew stronger as we landed at the front gates of the palace. Our bags were taken swiftly by some attendants as I looked around at some unfamiliar carriages.

"Whose are those?" I asked Finley as he took off his bag. Osirus had talked to one servant and left me to my devices.

"Those are spare carriages from the storage unit. I'm not sure why they are out?" Finley questioned as we approached. "Goddess," Finley breathed as he opened the door. Looking inside, we saw several gaunt-looking Fae; their eyes were lifeless, and their bodies looked weak. Nissa landed beside me, which startled me, but her hand came to my shoulder to comfort me.

"I'm sorry for sneaking up on you," Nissa smiled sadly. "I hope you and Osirus don't mind, but I brought those at the unmated house here to the palace. With the glorious celebration coming up and many unmated supernaturals to be here, I'm hoping they will find their mate. At least, maybe have a good time and find the light they need to carry on."

My heart clenched at the thought of the seven carriages that held the unmated. Would Osirus have been the same if I never showed up? Several attendants came by and opened doors, helping them all out one by one. Servants grabbed their bags and led them to the palace. Even though my heart ached, there was one person I wanted to see, Elaine, Daphne's mother, and hopefully the redemption I had hoped Daphne will take.

Nissa led me to the first carriage that carried only Elaine. She had a quilt draped over her shoulders to keep her warm. The long, deep purple hair covered her face as she exited—the bright light blinding her, causing her to keep her hand over her eyes. "Elaine, it is an honor to meet you," I spoke as I held out my hand to hold hers. Elaine gave a small smile and took her other hand to pat mine.

"I'm so sorry about my daughter. She knows how important her mates are. I have failed yet again as a Fae to teach her these things." If her eyes could go any darker into despair, they would have. The once light, flawless skin was now grey and lifeless. Shaking the shock at her appearance, I shook my head.

"Daphne has told many how she wants to protect you, I am hoping this is the truth and if she hears your words, I pray to the goddess she will ask for forgiveness and drop this whole thing." Elaine nodded her head in understanding.

"Don't be so sure, Your Majesty," she gave a sad smile. "Cosmo is a cunning man. His words tasted like honey to her. She looked up to him yet despised him at the same time. It is not only me she wants to protect, but her thirst for power is there. His bad blood runs through her veins." Nissa and I stood in shock as Elaine lowered herself from the carriage as we walked in.

There may be no hope for Daphne at all. Her mother had given up on her, and she hadn't seen her for years. Who was this Cosmo, and how could it be so cruel? The few times I had met him, he was cunning, tricky, like the rumors of how Faes were. Brainwashing Daphne may have been his tactic, and there was no hope for her.

I supposed not everyone could be blessed with forgiveness.

I took extra care of Elaine, and I wanted to personally see her to her chambers. Her story had become heartbreaking to me, forced into a loveless bonding, begging for him not to bond her. Her own mother had the same fate, yet Elaine was more substantial than her mother, hoping she would find her mate. However, from the looks of her ragged body, her time was almost gone. If she didn't find her mate soon, she would give up and no longer have the strength to breathe.

Nissa and I tucked her into the bed and left her so she could rest. The trip had tired her out too quickly. Before leaving the room, Elaine beckoned me to her bed and used all the strength she had to hug me. Shocked at the initial contact, I quickly hugged her back.

"Thank you," she sobbed as I rubbed her back. "For trying to give Daphne a chance." Before I could respond, her head lulled into my shoulder, and I saw she had fallen asleep. I laid her down gently as you would a baby. I put an extra blanket over her fragile body and stepped out of the room. As much grief and pain, I felt in my heart, I could also feel a pull, and it was pulling me to another room.

Osirus was in his study, discussing with Alaneo and Nyx the plans for the next several days while Nissa was tending to the unmated Faes. Following the pull, I was led down a quiet hallway I had never gone down. Several servants bowed until the head maid greeted me. "Your Majesty, your father, and brothers have arrived. We have put them in the Southeast Wing on the bottom floor so they can have easier access to the ocean." A smile graced my face as I rushed out a 'thank you' and ran toward the pull.

It was my family! The pull that Lucca used to talk about when I entered the water that he felt. I felt it here on land. Running quickly, my wings fell open all on their own as I pushed in the door to the guest chamber.

My father turned from looking out over the waters of the sea with his hands behind his back. He looked everything like an older king should look—regal, robust, immaculate in his shell-adorned attire. Dad looked everything like a land King would look like. Royal blue suit, cuffed with pearls and his dark scruffy beard for his human appearance, made him look handsome.

"My princess!" he spoke in his smoldering tone while he held out his arms. I ran to him, and he engulfed me while caressing my cheek. "My beautiful Melina, you have changed." He stared in awe as he played with my hair.

"It seems you have more of me in you than I realized. You took on my hair and our family colors after you have mated." Father gritted his teeth at the last part, now knowing his daughter was now deflowered. I blushed, and he pursed his lips as he shook it off.

"All grown up, and these wings?" He looked over my shoulder. "These don't look Fae at all, they look…."

"Like a butterfly, I know. I guess colorful wings instead of scales?" I wanted approval, and his glistening eyes only confirmed he loved it.

"They are gorgeous, princess." Father engulfed me in another hug as he took a sniff into my hair. His body stiffened as his caressing of my back stopped. Pulling away, he held me at arm's length. I was giving him a questioning look. He gave a small smile.

"Who have you been with today?" Not understanding what he was asking, I named off several people until I realized.

Elaine.

"Why are you asking me who I have been with?" My father stiffened again and rubbed his beard.

"There is a different smell to you, and it intrigues me." My eyes opened wide, and I covered my mouth.

"Come with me," I whisper yelled as I grabbed his hand. Father started laughing as I tried to pull his body to the door.

I prayed to the goddess that my intuition would be correct, that this entire problem would be solved. Killing two birds with one stone. My heart leaped as I tried to pull him faster. "What is the rush princess? Where are you taking me?" My father was oblivious. How in goddess name could he not know? Well, he probably gave up, too. The only reason he hadn't succumbed to depression was his sons and me. He had something to live for.

Unlike Elaine. She had given up on her daughter.

We stood outside the door to Elaine's room. Father looked at me questioningly as I cracked the door. The door made a small moan as we entered the darkroom. Holding onto my father's hand, I continued to lead him to the other side of the enormous bed. Elaine had opted to sleep close to the nightstand so she could reach for water if needed. Her chest rose slowly up and down as we got closer.

Her face was pained. She was dreaming of her past with Cosmo or the loneliness in her heart. My father had a look of pain on his face. "Who is she?" he barely spoke.

"Elaine, she has a terrible past, but in short, she is giving up on finding her mate."

My father clutched his chest as he knelt beside the bed. His fingers pushed back the dark, purple hair as he took in her scent.

I backed away from him so he could study her. I wanted to scream for her to wake up, but this was too precious of a moment. His crown stood still on his head as he brushed her lips with his fingers. Elaine moved her head closer to his hand, and my father's fist clutched to his side.

The easy breathing Elaine was exposing was now sporadic. She was waking up. With hardly any movement, she opened her eyes and glanced at my father. Both stared at each other until Elaine gasped.

Chapter 59

Girard

She was here, my mate. The one I had looked for over a thousand years was here, lying before me. Her face was ashen, unhealthy, and her deep purple hair was lifeless. The lips that I desperately wanted to capture were chapped and broken. A glass of water laid full beside the bed as well as fresh fruits and vegetables. Not one thing was touched, as she was trying to keep warm underneath the quilts and blankets. Melina had smelled of her, and I knew she was taking care of her. Someone she didn't know and was unfamiliar with, not knowing this woman was mine.

My heart swelled with the love of my daughter and her kindness.

I felt shuffling behind me, and my daughter gave a small smile as she rounded the bed and slipped out the door. My heart wanted to go to my daughter, embrace her for not only letting me be granted the title as a father, but as well as the matchmaker for my soul. My eyes instantly darted back to the woman before me. Her eyes were wide, and her lips were now parted. I could feel her heart racing beneath the layers of blankets.

She instantly tried to sit up, but I sat on the bed beside

her and nuzzled her back with my hands on her shoulders. "You need rest," my heart raced as I could still feel the shocks of pleasure through my fingertips. Her brows furrowed as I smiled at her; what had my love gone through to cause such a condition?

I realized she showed the signs of a mate withdrawal. Her heart had given up finding me. My chest constricted at the thought she was giving up on me. Even though I thought I had loved before my previously chosen wife who had given me 13 beautiful sons. But sitting on this bed, swimming in this woman's eyes, I never knew what love really was. No wonder my chosen mate left. This bond was something to behold.

"What is your name?" I needed to hear it, to taste it on my tongue before I went and captured her lips.

"E-Elaine," she whispered, still in shock.

"Elaine," I spoke, and I felt the shiver down her body, which only made me smirk like a pubescent teenager. "I am Girard, your mate." Tears rolled down her cheeks, emotion pouring from them as she sat straight up out of bed and held onto me for dear life. I couldn't help but smile. She wanted me after all this time.

If I had known where she was, even an inkling, I would have found her and brought her to my palace. Then again, I never would have found her. I was confined to the sea. Now that Calista has granted us all amulets to be above water for five days at a time, it still would have been difficult to find her. "Mate," she sobbed.

Petting her hair, I immediately felt her grip tighten on me as I nuzzled into her neck. Glancing at her shoulder, I see a fading mating scar that caused me to growl. I had no right to be jealous or upset, and I had a whole family before her. Does she have children too? Sighing, I buried myself deeper into her hair, and she visibly relaxed.

"I'm sorry, I...I don't look-" I pulled her from our embrace and thumbed her tears away.

"Gorgeous, you look absolutely radiant." Kissing her forehead, I pulled her from the bed and cradled her in my arms. The only way for her to get better was to have me, her mate, and the bond. It will bind us together, making her healthy again, and we will enjoy the rest of eternity together.

I didn't regret my time with my chosen mate, and she gave me children I could never have otherwise. I love them all, and I thought I would be in the same place Elaine was if I didn't have them. But here she was, just in time for me to take her away from this land and take her to mine. She will be my queen, and I will dress her in the finest of clothing, and jewelry and worship the very ground she walks on.

As much as I want to mate, mark, and fully bond with her, we will have to wait. Elaine was too weak and fragile. I'd break her. Gods know how long it had been since I had taken a female. Melina's human mother was the last and final straw for me.

"Elaine, I'd love to get to know you," I spoke to her lips. Even after sleeping, her breath smelled of oatmeal cookies out of the oven. A growl ripped through me, and she smiled at my lips. Elaine's eyes closed, and I couldn't help but smash my greedy lips to hers.

Gods, she tasted amazing, more than exceptional. I was having an orgasm in my damn mouth. Elaine's neck leaned back as I pushed my tongue to her lips, and she opened without question. Her hands dove into my hair and trusted my body against hers. Goddess, she was heavily endowed, the things I could do with those tits. My lips, on their own accord, trailed her cheek and down her neck as they peppered kisses where I would sink my fangs into her, her guttural growl grew hard as I sucked it.

I couldn't permanently mark her, but I would damn well leave a temporary one. Her hand gripped my hair as I finished kissing her shoulder. "I need to stop, my love. We should talk and get you healthy." The lust in her eyes told me different that she would accept me for all that I am, but I wanted to be upfront. She may not like the idea I have thirteen sons and a daughter. I couldn't mess this up.

Her blush filled her face as she tried to lean away from me, but I held her tight. "Mine," I whispered in her ear as she giggled.

"LUCCA, WAIT!" I heard an ear-piercing scream. "They might be doing IT!!!" Lucca bursts through the door along with Melina, who is breathing heavily and propping herself up on the door.

"Is it true?!" Lucca grinned and let his fangs grow. He jumped into the bed that Elaine and I were sitting on and crossed his legs. Lucca had always been one that didn't understand the need of personal space.

"Luuuuke!" Melina whined childishly. "Let them have their moment!" She began to pull Lucca from the bed, but he dragged her up and stuffed her face in the pillow next to Elaine. Melina let out grumbling noises as he kept her pinned.

"I'm guessing it's true since the way you are sitting?" Lucca smirked, and Elaine blushed and put her face in my chest.

"Lucca," I gave him a scornful look, and he held up his hands.

"I just wanted to say hey to my new mother." Elaine popped her head up and looked at both of us. I gave a small, hesitant smile to her as I felt embarrassment climb up my neck.

"That was what I wanted to talk about." I loosened my collar while Melina sat up with her messy hair. Lucca pulled her to his side as she laughed at him. They should have been damn twins the way they interact with each other.

"I had a chosen before you, and we did have children." Elaine nodded, not bothered in the slightest. "Not just one or two," I trailed my voice. "But twelve." Her eyes grew wide until Melina cut in.

"You forgot me!" Melina stuck out her lip and crossed her

arms.

"I mean, I have twelve boys and one daughter. We just found out a few weeks ago." I took Melina's hand and rubbed her knuckles with my thumb. Elaine gave a small smile in understanding.

"That doesn't bother me. They are your children. I have one of my own, but things get complicated from there." Melina tried not to show any emotion and played with her fingers.

"My daughter is the reason for all the commotion." Elaine sucked in a breath. "She wants to get rid of Melina and have Osirus have her as queen."

A growl ripped through my throat as I heard this. Trying to clear it from my throat, she looked at me with no judging eyes. "I know this makes things complicated, and I hope she will relent. I think it is best if I spoke with her father and see if he can change her mind."

Melina scoffed and folded her arms.

"What makes you think he will listen to you, Elaine? He tortured you, forced you to do unspeakable things. What makes you think he will speak to you now?" My fists gripped in anger. I didn't know Elaine's complete story, but from the sounds of it, I needed to rip this guy's dick off.

"We have ways to make him talk." Osirus walked through the open door. He glanced at Elaine in my lap and gave me a bow. "Congratulation's Your Majesty on finding your mate." Elaine glanced, turned to look at me, and then looked at my head, adorned with the crown of my ancestors.

"I-I didn't realize," she sputtered.

"And that is why I adore you because you saw me instead of a crown. Now you will be my queen and rule all over Atlantis."

Melina

Well, this is hella awkward. My stepsister was trying to get my mate. How the hell did that end up happening? What are the odds?!

Elaine seemed like a pleasant woman. I could already see the color returning to her face as my father held her in her arms. She was happy. Seeing the white of her teeth told me this would work out for the best. They were mates, supposed to be bonded together. The whole Daphne thing was just a hump in the road. If a bond told me anything, you get past whatever hurdles you may cross.

Lucca looked longingly at our father, as well as me. I know he wanted a mate. Some of his brothers had waited longer, but Lucca wanted it the most. I've thought of all the times he went to the surface to watch for those that needed help and aided them to Atlantis. From what he spoke of, he all found them their mates. Was he trying to help those women that needed help, or was he secretly yearning for his mate? It could be a combination of both. Lucca had a tender heart, and I prayed he found someone soon.

Once Osirus entered the room, the tension was lifted. The alchemist that had helped Peoni and Carson had left several vials of Truthing Serum. These were scarce and very expensive to make since the flowers used in the serum come from near the Dragon Shifter territories. The flowers were gifts to friendly sorcerers or to any that have mated to a shifter.

Elaine was still too weak to walk long distances, so my father happily grabbed her in his arms and carried her along with a quilt holding close to her body. Her head lulled right into the crook of his neck as he held her close while we walked down the hallway to the dungeons.

"Stay close to me, Melina, and do not let go." Originally, Osirus wanted to bring Cosmo to the throne room but didn't want any chance of escape. With no word from Tulip or any threats to the palace, we couldn't take that chance. I shrugged my shoulders and held onto his hand as we descended the dark stairwell that led us underground.

Osirus' grip tightened around me and eventually went

around my shoulders as we passed through several levels of cells and cages. The race of the prisoners was vast. Several Pixies, fairies, and Fae had cells that accommodated the power they held. The Pixies were stored in tiny containers one would find completely barbaric. They sat in glass jars with holes poked in them that were strapped to the wall. I wondered if you could use them as a night light?

"What could a Pixie possibly do?" I muttered to myself. Osirus' frown deepened as we walked by.

"Never underestimate a race, darling. They were spies at the time of the shifter war. They will remain here for another 100 years to finish out their sentence. By that time, their mates have been granted a second chance at a mate or have died. That is their proper punishment." My heart ached, but knowing they went against their kingdom during a time of war was disheartening.

I kept the thoughts at bay as we passed by shifter cells lined with Wolfsbane and silver. Wolves were growling and salivating as we walked by. One grabbed the edge of my dress, and Osirus pulled me away and hissed at the beast. "Double the dose," Osirus barked as a fine mist sprayed through the bars. It coughed and wheezed until the Wolf turned human. He was ragged and dirty, with no soul left in his eyes.

We descended deeper, and it felt we had walked miles until we reached the end of the corridor. A strong scent of metallic seeped through my nose as I held it closed with my hand. Elaine gasped as she looked through the bars where we had arrived.

Cosmo sat in his filth. His stubble of a beard had now grown, and his hair was messily hanging over his eyes. Instead of looking at the floor, his head was leaned back against the stone walls as he took in a large breath of air.

"Elaine…."

Chapter 60

Melina

Elaine gripped onto my father's neck collar as Cosmo tried to stand up but slipped in his own puddle of urine. His eyes were hazed, and an evil smirk tainted his face as he grew closer to the bars. My father gripped Elaine and whispered encouraging words in her ear while Osirus held me back. I never knew just how evil a Fae could look until this moment.

The dark shadows clung to his features, the slight shine of his fangs that had now descended. Feral was the only word to describe him now. No longer the strong Speaker of the Court Fae, he had fallen from his pedestal he had put himself on, and he had given up.

Cosmo gripped the bars and showed his fangs, something he would have never done before coming down here. He was untamed, a monster, and the dirt on his face only enhanced the slimy person he indeed was.

"Elaine…" he hissed. "Never thought I would see you again after sending you away. Did you finally get someone to love your sorry ass?" Elaine stood frozen while my father growled lowly.

"Watch to whom you speak, for she is the future Queen of Atlantis." My father's deep voice made Elaine squirm while

I held back a laugh. She was turned on even though she was scared to death. I knew that feeling all too well.

Cosmo glared at Elaine while he banged the bars with his hands. "Impossible! She has no mate! She was as worthless the day I chose her. The only good thing that came out of her was nothing but a good, forced virgin fuck. Everything else was useless!" My father handed off Elaine to Lucca as he reached through the bars and grabbed his neck. Wings flew out of Cosmo as he tried to struggle and get away. Sputters of spit landed on my father, but never once flinched. His wings banged the bars violently, like a bird in a cage trying to get away from an apex predator.

"What was that? I didn't catch what you said. I swore you said you forced her." The grip grew impossibly tight as Cosmo's face turned a bright red. Veins protruded from his forehead as the blood was trapped in his face.

"Your Majesty, will all due respect, we need him to speak until we get the information we seek." Osirus took his hand to calm my father, but his grip only tightened. Elaine forced herself out of Lucca's arms and ran to my Father as her arms went around his waist, hugging him tightly.

"I'm all right now," she whispered into his back. "We are here together, that is all that matters. Let's save Melina and Osirus from a terrible fate." The grip loosened around Cosmo, but my father's large hand remained.

"The serum, Osirus." Osirus immediately handed over the vile and puckered Cosmo's lips open, and he swallowed. With a hard push, he was forced to the ground and landed in his filth. Father turned and gripped Elaine as he kissed her cheeks and had her bury her face in his chest. "I'll kill him," he whispered to her. "I'll make him suffer a thousand deaths for forcing you." Elaine gave a soft smile while she held onto him. "He will never see the light of day, and I will rip his wings from his back and hang them on my trophy wall."

"That's gross," Lucca whispered while I slapped his chest.

Cosmo sputtered and groaned as he rose to his feet. On

the way down to the dungeons, Osirus said it would take just minutes to work, but the minutes passed by like hours for us. The serum would eventually tell us all we needed to know how to get Daphne to stop the madness. My thoughts wavered at the idea he might want to strike a deal with us, his life for his own daughter, but the way the evil had overcome his soul, I doubted anyone would win at this point.

Osirus stepped up to the bars. "Cosmo, you can no longer hold your secrets, and we plan to extract everything we need to know. For your first secret to spill, we need to know if you are still in contact with Daphne." Osirus' command gave me shivers as I drew closer to him. My hand was holding his as he squeezed it tightly, letting him know I was never letting go.

"That brat? She ratted me out as soon as she could. Who knew my blood would betray me? I gave that bitch everything. The clothes on her back to the political gain. She is just like her mother, a conniving, worthless slave. I'm glad I left her to starve after she gave birth."

Our confusion was heightened after his words spilled from his mouth. "What?" Elaine spoke. "I was never a slave or servant?" It was true. Elaine was born in a noble household and was bartered so Cosmo could take Elaine's status while her own father ran off with his true mate. She has never been a slave or commoner.

"Ha, after all these years, you couldn't figure it out. Does Daphne look anything like you?" Elaine grabbed her heart with one hand and rubbed her stomach with another. Disgust clouded her face as she stared at him.

"I carried her in my womb for four months. I birthed her and cared for her until she could take care of herself. Of course, Daphne is mine! She has lost her way, but I will do my best to set her on the right path. I love her and will do what is best for her. I just need you to talk some sense into her since you brainwashed her!" She cried.

Laughing manically, Cosmo sat in the chair on the far side of the room. His ankle crossed over his leg as he scratched the scraggly beard. "Daphne isn't yours," he whispered. Elaine's eyes watered as she gripped her chest. Father picked her up again as Elaine felt faint. What could Cosmo possibly have done? The filthy man was more screwed up than I thought, and the chances of Daphne coming to her senses were now low.

"Daphne is the product of my true mate," he scoffed as he rose from his chair. He was now pacing the bars as he looked at her dead in the eye. Instead of being the prey, Cosmo tried to be the predator. He wanted nothing but to feel in charge, to break Elaine's soul even more. With my father here, that wouldn't happen. Elaine was in excellent hands now, with a large family to love her.

"I found Opal near the sea, picking shells to sell at the market. Her hair was a chestnut brown, and the rose-colored lips had my dick instantly hard at the sight of her." Cosmo started rubbing himself, and I looked away in disgust. "I had already made my plans to bond with you that night, and I dared not give that position of power." The room grew silent. The only thing that could be heard was the constant dripping of water, hitting puddles in a nearby cell.

"Took her to the nearest, cheapest inn I could. I told her I would give her the world, and she believed it. The poor thing hung on every word, so she took me and my cock." My heart clenched—the poor woman.

"I never marked her, just fucked her. That was the best I ever had. Sorry, sweetheart." His look glanced over to Elaine. "She fought me a bit once I said I would not mark her, but she gave up. She straight-up rejected me, ballsy if you ask me, but she was supposed to be my mate, so of course she was strong. Luckily for me, you both fell pregnant simultaneously, and with my watchful eye, switching them out was but a gift from the gods when you birthed the children on the same day.

Opal was a strong Fae, and our child would be, too. I watched her birth Daphne with only two pushes, and immediately Daphne cried and fought for life on the forest floor. I immediately ran to her and scooped her up into my arms. I knew she was the key, so my family name would rise and have her sit beside Osirus as his bride."

I growled out at myself, startling everyone as I held Osirus close to me. This prick had another thing coming. The urge to take my claws and rip him to pieces was so damn strong, but Osirus kept me in his arms repeatedly, telling me he wasn't leaving me.

"Opal was weak, losing blood, so I took Daphne as my mate passed out. She didn't even know what gender she had just given birth to, so I brought back Elaine's child, a son that Elaine had birthed. Opal knew it wasn't her baby, but she clutched to it like a lifeline. Motherly instincts can be so," Cosmo shook his head as he pensively stared at the wall, "primitive."

"Dear gods, what a sick fuck!" Lucca yelled as he banged the stone wall. It crumbled beneath him as Elaine started crying hysterically. My father's rage was fierce. He wanted to go into the cell and kill him off then. Father's hair became white, his scales ran up his neck, and his claws extended. With great restraint, he held onto Elaine as he neared the cell.

"Where is your mate and Elaine's child?" The rumble was felt through the floor and up to my chest. Osirus didn't let me go for fear I would vanish.

Cosmo started laughing hysterically. "Really? Do you want to know? The bitch hid. She hid from me, she tried to get away, I know she is here in the kingdom, I can feel it, but she put a cloaking spell on her and the child once she figured out who I was and figured out what my intentions were. If Daphne had ever died or didn't listen to me as a child, I would have taken Elaine's child back and worked on him. Opal was damn smart." Cosmo threw the chair across the cell.

"A cloaking spell! A damn good one, too. The child's cloak will not let him grow up, can you believe that?! I looked for years for a witch that specialized in it only to find out she had died after casting it!" Cosmo waved his hand dismissively as he sat back down in the chair. He groaned and laid his head in his hands.

"It's wearing off," Osirus spoke.

Lucca and I looked at each other. Cloaking spell? To not grow up? "Osirus? Can that be done?"

Osirus' jaw ticked. "Yes, it can. It is a powerful spell. If the spell is to be taken off the boy now, he would have to grow on his own. He wouldn't revert to his true age."

This world became much stranger to me than it already was. I knew nothing about the witches, only the elves and the shifters. Witches scared me and learning all that they could do with just a simple spell. Now that we were going up against an entire coven, would we be able to withstand it all? Two kingdoms fighting just one coven seems easy if it was a physical fight, but this will not be a physical fight. It was magical and scary.

Doubts crossed my mind. We were in trouble. Osirus pulled me to his chest as tears brimmed my eyes. Tulip was in more danger than I realized, and we needed to get her back. It was all my fault that I sent her into the lion's den. No word had been brought back, and it had been days. Alec trusted me to bring her home safe. So many supernaturals are on the line, lives will be lost. "Shh," Osirus cooed. "It will be all right, I promise. We will win." Petting my hair, I nodded into his chest.

Osirus had not once told me wrong, and he has always told me nothing but truths. The whirlwind I now called my life was beginning to be too much. There were days I wanted nothing more than to hide in the walls of my cabin, away from it all. The one night in the Dragon territory was heaven. We slept, we loved each other, worshiped each other, but we were leaders. We had to save everyone, or at least forge a plan.

Why do people want power? It was a messy thing. Was it so wrong for people just to live their lives and love each other? They were all so blessed to have the goddess give them mates and find their soul's match. Humans would kill for such a thing. Why make it complicated with power and greed?

Elaine again stepped down from my father's arms and came to the cage. "What is my son's name? Where are they?" Elaine's voice was more substantial than I ever knew possible. She radiated the anger, the contempt, the suffering in her voice. Cosmo's eyes widened at the mighty strength that stood behind her words.

"I don't know what Opal goes by, but the boy's name is Cricket." Cosmo groaned as his body now hit the floor, going unconscious.

Chapter 61

Alaneo

"You are going to be fine. Be sure to drink blood three times a day from a fresh source, preferably through your mate," the on-call physician spoke as he packed up his bag.

The warriors we had taken to the borders of Vermillion had no luck finding the Blood Coven's home. Juliet was already exhausted by the time she was done feeding, and dusk settled. We didn't need to fight the dark as it wasn't acceptable for us to wander around in the dark since our powers would weaken.

I held Juliet in my arms while Nyx continued to bark orders at the warriors. It was like he was back at his station as King, but most warriors welcomed it, enjoying the new personality that he had shone through. "Tomorrow, we look again. Rest up. We will start at first light." The warriors flew off back to their homes to their own mates and families while I held onto Juliet. She wasn't accustomed to flying, and her grip around my neck grew tight, but I savored the moment.

I had found my mate. When everyone else had found their forever, I had found mine. Juliet's smile widened as her fangs shone with the setting sun while I held her close.

That was but a few hours ago, and now the doctor began

his departure. I had stayed in the room the entire time, even though he was a mated Fae himself. I'm understanding how Osirus can be so obsessive of Melina in times like these. It was a sensitive time to establish not only a spiritual bond but a physical one, meaning being damn obsessive over her.

Gods, her holding onto me gave me a massive erection from the flight back to the palace. I needed a third hand just to help me tuck it away. Nyx constantly looked over, snickering at the situation that was causing my distress.

"Can I speak with you, Doctor?" The physician nodded as we both headed out the door. "Is she-"

"Yes, she can mate. Just know she will probably feed on you as your bond, which can make you weak for a few hours. Not that I think you would mind, though." He winked as he walked away.

All right then.

I knocked on the door, a common courtesy, and Juliet sat up from the bed. I had given her one of my oversized shirts, and damn, it was the sexiest thing she could wear. Forget the lacy bras and underwear; just wear my shirt with nothing underneath.

Juliet blushed as she shoved her hands under her straightened legs. How can I be nervous? I've seduced too many women to be anxious about this. But this was her. My everything and my damn mate. This was it. No more partying or looking for someone to satisfy my needs, and I couldn't be happier.

"Um," I scratched the back of my head. "This is my room, and I can sleep somewhere else if you don't feel-"

"Alaneo?" Her sweet voice sang to me. "Please come lay with me." My heart thudded in my chest, and my palms became sweaty. How brazen is she, my shy little rabbit, not only hours ago and is now beckoning me to lie with her on the bed?

Ripping my tunic off my body, leaving on my trousers, I opened the blankets while scooping her into my side. Her raven hair fell on her cheek while I brushed it away. "My Rose, I'm so glad to have found you." Kissing her cheek, her head came closer to my lips so I wouldn't let go.

"Me too. It was most welcome." Her voice was a low whisper as her breath tickled my chest. Our lips were close, too close not to touch, but I was anxious.

The Alaneo, nervous. Who would have thought?

Before I made my move, she jerked up and claimed my lips. Her lips were hot as she pushed me down onto the mattress. My shy Rose moved her lips feverously as I had now snapped out of my stupor. Juliet was ravishing.

Juliet became shy and stiff as my hands went to glide around her back and pulled her impossibly closer. She leaned back while I captured the side of her neck as she sighed and rolled onto her back. The short little pants had my dick twitching as her red eyes stared into mine.

"I'm sorry. I don't know what came over me to jump you like that." A small purr came from my chest as I cupped her face.

"Your animalistic side is hungry for blood and our bond has you itching to drink from me." My heart soared thinking of her wanting me.

Like any other Fae in primary school, I had spent my time learning the ways of each culture. More so as I took on as second-in-command as Osirus' advisor. Vampires rarely visited The Golden Light Kingdom, but they always fascinate me. Not only does a vampire crave their mate's blood, but they also do sexually. Almost impossible to hold back when their mates were nearby. She was still young when she was captured. Juliet might not have learned this.

"Do you understand, my Rose?" Her head tilted to the side, and she shook her head no. I didn't want to spend my time explaining vampire anatomy, so I gave her the best advice I could give her. "Just follow your primal instincts...." I whispered. No anatomy lesson on how vampires mated. I would guide her and hope for the best. Thankfully, her eyes closed and leaned up towards me as I licked her lips so I could partake in the sweetest taste.

No ambrosia could compare to the sweet lips these give, and I couldn't wait to try another set of lips as she became bolder. Her fang nicked my lip, which caused me to growl. I've always had a kink for pain, and this could not have been a better match.

Juliet paused as she tasted my blood. Licking her lips, she sucked on the cut as I palmed her voluminous ass. Kneading it, caressing it, and dare I say maybe hit it later with my dick, she moaned into my mouth. My shirt came off her body quickly as I ripped it on the seam. A quick yelp, and I jumped on top of her. I caught her off guard, and the lust in her eyes told me it was all right.

Her hands roamed my torso with her claws, scratching my hip bone as she tugged at my trousers. "Patience, my little flower," I sucked her neck on her marking spot while she thrust her hips upwards. Juliet's fangs were growing, and the growl in her throat let me know she wasn't one for patience. My head dipped as my fangs nicked around her pert nipples while she gasped, holding my head to her bosom.

Juliet was gifted. She had a round ass and just as enticing breasts as I kneaded one and sucked on the other. I bit a little too hard as one of my fangs grazed the side, and blood trickled. I have never been one to taste blood but my gods. She tasted amazing. "Lick me," she purred as I stared into her eyes as slid my tongue across it.

"Exquisite," I moaned while trailing my tongue to the other breast. I couldn't like the left breast to be too greedy, now, could I? Juliet's hips thrust into my chest, rubbing her sweet spot on my abs. I couldn't tease and taunt her too much. She was still weak, but I had to have a taste of her nectar.

Her pussy dripped onto the sheets. I prayed to the gods it would always remain there so I could rub my body in her sweet scent. She wasn't completely bare. She had a small amount of trimmed hair near her pussy, but I loved it. It was soft with a bit of curl as I nuzzled my nose into it. My tongue parted her folds as licked her clit lovingly.

"Alaneo," she cried as she fisted her hands into my hair. The claws scraped my scalp that gave an instant shudder to my cock. I was leaking, gods how embarrassing I could cum right now with Juliet just petting my head. It had a mind of its own, wanting to be buried balls deep within my mate, but I had to prepare. She was a virgin, that was for sure, and I would take much pleasure in her being her first.

My soul ached at what I had done. I should have waited, I should have waited for her, but I never thought she would come to me. I will beg for forgiveness for the rest of our lives and drive her pussy into oblivion.

My tongue teased her opening as I tried to have her cream into my mouth; my tongue was fruitful as her nectar slid on my rough tongue. I swallowed as she continued to pour into my mouth; her silent scream made me grip her thighs and haul them over my shoulder. I would feast and eat her almost raw before I made her take my aching cock.

"Alaneo." Juliet's chest heaved as her large breast bounced. "It's too much!" she cried again as she tried to wiggle away from me. Taking a break from my tongue, I took a finger and entered her cavern.

So slick, almost ready. I needed to stretch Juliet so she could take me. Being gentle wasn't part of my nature when it came to fucking, but I wasn't fucking. I was making damn love to my mate. With one finger, she was tight. How the hell am I going to thrust into this vice?

Two fingers I pushed through, and she wiggled while she grabbed her own breasts. Gods, she was breathtaking. "Take control, Juliet. What do you want?" Her lips were moving, but no sound came out. I must be doing my job. I thrust the two fingers into her gingerly as her body moved. Breasts and thighs jiggled on the bed while she plucked her nipples.

I can't take it anymore. My cock can't. I was going to spill my seed onto the bed, and that would be a damn waste. I lunged to the top of the bed as I smashed my lips against hers. Juliet took my tongue without question and held me close to her body. Claws scratched down my back, I could feel the blood drip, but dear gods, it was hot as fuck. A growl ripped through Juliet as she threw me onto my back. Damn, she was feisty.

She rolled me over as she licked my back. Her tongue shook as she tried with all her might not to sink her fangs into me. The drip from her slick coated my legs as I fisted the sheets with my aching hands. "I need to bury myself into you, my Rose. Before I lose myself," I gritted my teeth as she cleaned my back. Her venom had already healed me. There was no more blood or pain. Fuck, she can do that every day if she wants.

Flipping her over, blood covered her mouth as she tried to lick the remnants. I licked her cheek, tasting myself. It didn't taste like blood at all, not that terrible metallic taste.

Once we bonded, I could suck her blood as well, my fangs would hollow, and we would feed on each other. The most intimate thing a vampire could do besides mating. The way she tasted made my cock twitch again, ready to take her.

"I'm going to deflower you," her breath tethered as I lined my cock to her hole. "It will hurt at first-"

"Shut up and fuck me, mate." The blood lust had already started. Her eyes were glowing, and her fangs were ready to sink into me. One quick thrust, and I broke her innocence. A sharp scream and my stillness over her body made it even more intimate as I cooed her. My brave little bloodsucker waited for me or was instead forced to wait.

I'll still cherish this moment as she gazed into my eyes. "So damn beautiful you are." I stroked her hair as she ground her hips.

"Move Alaneo, make me yours," Juliet whispered into my lips as my hips as I continued to thrust. All the way out and back in, we went at our own rhythm.

Making love to her is hard, trying to go slow. Juliet met me thrust to thrust with her hips, and I lost it. "I'm going to fuck you. I can't hold back." I gritted my teeth.

"More!" She screamed into my ear as I fucked her into oblivion. Her legs went around my waist, and her heels dug into my back. Forcing me to go harder into her. Juliet's claws sunk into my biceps, scratching down my arms as blood dropped to the sheets. Her head hung back as she screamed my name over and over as she reached her high several times.

I wanted to hold out, show her how damn good I was, but I was losing it. I couldn't last. "Come for me one last time, so I can make you mine."

"Mine," she growled as my fangs itched to bite her skin. Her eyes dilated as her orgasm ripped through her, and she sunk her teeth into me. Her fangs hit the bone as I went to her shoulder and did the same. She screamed in pleasure as I continued to pump into her, spilling my seed into her womb.

Slowing down, her arms dropped as my body quivered. Not wanting to put all my weight on her luscious body, I fell to the side and pulled her to me. "Drink, my Rose. You need it." Blood was coming out of the bite I gave her, as well as the blood on my shoulder. She didn't hesitate and latched onto me.

Juliet was so exhausted. I felt her lean on me for support as she sucked. I licked the blood on her shoulder. It tasted of the most exotic pies of the elves that I craved so much during the Light Source Celebration. As she continued, I felt my eyes droop, and her breathing had slowed as well. Licking my wounds closed, she nudged her head undermine as I held her tight with one arm around her shoulder and the other on her breast.

It was my new security blanket, yet it was tits. I'll always love holding them, but most of all, her.

Chapter 62

Melina

After the initial shock a boy named Cricket was Elaine's son, I grabbed my father as he spun around to look at me. Elaine's eyes had tears threatening to spill at the thought of her daughter not being her own. I couldn't imagine what Elaine was thinking. Her heart was broken that Daphne was beyond redemption, and now she has another chance to even raise her own son, her blood.

Quickly explaining how I knew the boy named Cricket at the orphanage with my wild hand gestures, Elaine's features brightened. She wiggled to get down from my father's hold, but he quickly gathered her up. "You are too weak, my love. Let Melina go fetch him while you rest." Elaine continued to look at both of us back and forth until she realized she wouldn't win this fight. She really was weak, but her heart was so full that she didn't know a proper solution that would bring both of her men into her life.

Without a second thought, I grabbed Lucca to come with me when Osirus stopped me. The glare on his face let me know he would not let me go alone with Lucca. With only days away from the coronation and binding ceremony, Daphne's plan was still rolling until we told her that her supposed mother was in the palace. Osirus gripped my hand tightly as I gave Lucca a small eye roll, to which he snickered. Lucca held his index finger and thumb together to form a circle and took his other hand and stuck a finger through the hole. I gasped as he started laughing while Father nudged him to cut it out.

Osirus led me up the stairs as we walked down the grand hallway while motioning for Finley to grab the others. Do we really need that much of an entourage? Then again, we had witches working for Daphne, and who knows what they could do? I internally shivered, thinking how powerful some could be. If they get ahold of shifter Dragon blood, we would all be in some trouble, especially in the wrong hands. My mood instantly soured, and my shoulder slumped.

Why couldn't things go slower? I remembered when I told Osirus how I wanted things to continue with us to be slow, to date and court like an average human would do, but then again, I wasn't human anymore. I was a Fae/Siren hybrid that couldn't control her voice and just looked pretty when my wings were hanging out. I had little going for me right now, and I just wanted to spend time with Osirus and get to know him more. I barely knew anything about his childhood, his hopes, and dreams for his kingdom once all of this was settled. What if he wasn't King? What would he have wanted to do with his life?

"Since Cricket knows you, I'll allow you to go, but I'm coming, too." Osirus continued to hold me close to his side as we walked down the hallway. As his skin touched mine, he immediately stopped in the hallway and looked down at me. His gaze burned my cheeks as I continued to look forward. I was supposed to be strong. Heck, I was strong before him, but this was all becoming too much. Being strong so long can only last until you crumble.

"Darling," he cooed as his hands cupped my face, tilting it so I could look up at his tall form. "What is wrong?" A little sniff came from my nose as I tried to itch away from the tears.

"Nothing, everything is fine." A lie that he instantly saw through didn't shake the concern he held in his eyes. My heart felt immediately warm as he buried my face in his chest, his head resting on my head.

"It's a lot, isn't it?" I sighed heavily while nodding and wrapping my arms around him.

"We have to keep going, though." I tightened my grip on his tunic as he ran his fingers through my white hair.

"Darling, it will be over soon. I know this isn't the best situation, but it won't always be like this, I promise." I wanted to believe the promise he gave, but so far, everything had been nothing but a whirlwind, from the first kiss down to the mating. Don't get me wrong, I wanted it, and I want him still, but could I really handle being Queen? Would I even see him at all once I was given specific duties?

Could I just be his princess and sit and look pretty? I was tired of taking care of myself and others; I just wanted a bit of me-time. However, people looked up to him, and I had to be his support and work through it all alongside him. I had to get Cricket to Elaine, stop Daphne from taking my King away from me, and stop the witches all at once. A small sob wrecked through me as Osirus picked me up. I clutched to him like a small panda.

"Let's take some time together before we pick up Cricket. How about a nap?" I nodded my head as I felt a cramp come to my stomach. It was not a welcoming cramp as I realized I was due for something very monthly. I rolled my head back and groaned. Great, just great.

Osirus' nose flared. Please, goddess, tell me he can't smell that. Osirus kissing me on the forehead and nuzzling his nose into my neck, let me know he did and led me to our room. If I was lucky, and I mean really lucky, it would pass before our celebration. On the plus side, I wasn't pregnant because I think I might cry if that was put on me right now.

"I didn't expect you to be pregnant yet, darling. Our mating marks wouldn't allow it since your body went through such a change, being half-human. It was a blank canvas that had to redirect certain parts of your body." I gripped him tighter as I felt more cramps coming on. Maybe Finley, Everett, and Braxton could fetch Cricket because I don't think I wanted to leave the bed today.

Osirus took me to our room while he called for several women servants to help while he left me, letting me have my privacy. Thankfully, things weren't much different from Earth, except everything was made of biodegradable cotton and some funky-looking pad things. Thank the goddess because it was all I could do to contain the mess as I finally dragged myself to the bed in my now comfortable clothes.

Osirus had ordered the most delicate silk that brushed over my skin. It was cool as my body became hot and flustered at the situation.

It hit me hard and fast; the emotion that was all swirling around me was, in fact, a severe case of PMS and pain. I've never had my monthly light, and I knew the next couple of days were going to be a roller coaster not only for me but for all the other events happening.

Being unlike myself since I arrived in this strange world, I cried to myself silently. These girls weren't Peoni and Primrose, but they were indeed lovely, trying to comfort me while getting me physically comfortable. They tucked me into bed as a few tears left me. I continued to think of all the things that could go wrong this week. My body cursing me for not getting pregnant was not helping the overwhelming feeling of doom lurking over my head.

Before I could curse myself more, I felt the bed dip behind me as I stayed curled up in the fetal position. Osirus was bare-chested as I felt the heat from his body immediately as he spooned me. His hand went immediately to my stomach, and the touch of tingles and warmth of his hand calmed me. The tears stopped, but my face was wet and sticky from the mascara I had attempted to put on this morning.

"It will be all right," Osirus whispered in my ear as he

kissed the shell of my ear. "We have an entire kingdom that will help us; we aren't alone." The words were soothing as he rubbed my terrible cramps away.

"I'm sorry, I whispered. "It could be just my hormones, but I'm just tired of pushing, fighting, fearing the unknown. Everything has been so… rushed." Osirus hummed in my ear as my eyes fluttered closed.

"I know it hasn't been the best." His finger pulled my hair behind my ear. "I wanted to court you the way you would have liked. Take you on your dates, pamper, love you. It is a lot, and it won't always be like this. We have forever." I hummed, listening to the calming of his voice. The pain was drifting away as he hummed a strange song while I fell asleep.

Osirus

I hummed a lullaby that was often sung to me as a child. It was something so common among The Golden Light Kingdom, but I knew that Melina would have never heard it. It could put the most challenging child to sleep, and once we had our own children, her own singing would lull them to sleep. May it be the song or her commanding singing abilities.

I couldn't help myself but be a little disappointed that Melina wasn't carrying our child. It was selfish of me to think that way, but she was right; this all was too much for her. The thought of having little Sirens or Fae running around thrilled me. Usually, if two different species are combined in a mating, a child will hold true to either one species or the other, causing the mixture of the species to remain pure. However, if Melina gives birth to a Siren child, I worry she would have to spend time in the sea. Mating Siren to Fae hasn't been recorded, but I have left it up to the fates and the gods. Once that bridge breached our horizon, then we will deal with it.

Within a month, everything she had known to be the truth of our existence was granted real, and she was caught in the middle of it. Her heart still held onto the human she was raised to, and I couldn't fault her for it. I would have liked to have taken things slower, but the war, battles, and now a whole national takeover were in our midst with the Blood Coven. Vermillion was still oblivious and sending messengers at this point seemed too dangerous.

As Melina's breath evened out, I laid back on the pillow, keeping my hand on her stomach. Our bond was the best medicine to control her pain. I would have to make it up to her, take things slow after the coronation and make sure she gets to experience all Bergarian. A long 'honeymoon' is what Luna Clara said is when a pair of freshly bonded go off and spend time together on a vacation. I would do that for her. We could take a trip to the Northern Winter Palace and spend a month there just being with each other, away from duties. With my father now back in the picture, I'm sure he would have no problems taking over for that stent of time.

A light knock at the door stirred me from my thoughts as I saw it crack open. It was Finley. He had taken it upon himself to become second in command as Alaneo took care of his new mate. I've been happy for him. He deserved it, but at the same time, it could have been the absolute worst timing for everyone to be getting their mates.

Gods, please wait until this mess is over before anyone else finds one.

The gods were trying to make me fret. Reluctantly leaving Melina, I sat up from bed and made my way to the door. Not one damn moment of peace.

"Finley, what seems to be the problem?" Finley backed away from the door as he had one hand on his sword.

"Your Majesty, His Majesty Girard has asked about the boy, Cricket, and when he will be brought to the palace. Both he and Her Majesty Elaine saw Melina was taken immediately to her room instead of leaving. They also want to know about her welfare." I groaned while scratching the stubble on my chin. At this rate, I will grow a full-grown beard by the time this is over.

"She's resting. She isn't feeling well. I believe all the commotion has her body tired and forcing her to rest. I need you and your brothers to retrieve the boy. Melina mentioned at one time you were with her while you met the child?" Finley nodded.

"Yes, a bright lad, very caring. I'll gather the others and let Melina's Father know of the situation. I've been briefed why the boy is to be here and make sure he is treated like the prince he is." Finley nodded his head in a curt bow and almost skipped out of the room.

"Finley?" I called, and he stopped to turn around. "What has you in such a joyful mood?"

"Nothing, Your Majesty. Just the view is most pleasant by the orphanage." Finley left the room before I could utter another sentence.

Chapter 63

Finley

I dashed out the door as quickly as I could. I didn't need Osirus asking me more questions why I was so happy. It wasn't any of his business, and he had enough on his plate as it was. I was just pleased that I could fetch the boy that Melina had grown so fond of. To think that he was now her younger brother made it all the sweeter.

I went to my room. First, I threw on my more excellent uniform and made sure the buttons were shined and the slit in the back was open, so I could have easy access to my wings when needed. Fae women, way back when used to awe over a suitable set of wings. Mine were strong, and my heritage showed through with tiny bits of red swirled in the patterns. I straightened my coat and combed my hair back, and put on a dash of musk enhancer, all while trimming my beard. I wanted to look sharp for this visit to gain her attention.

"Finley," Everett bellowed as he walked into our communal bathroom. "Ah, you must be going to the orphanage again." He rolled his eyes as he put on his trousers. It was true. I had been sneaking by the orphanage to get a glimpse of the beautiful Fae I had met not too long ago with Melina. She was a sight, but it wasn't her looks that caught me, but the forceful personality that she tried to hide. She was a mystery I wanted to unravel, a perfect package of a warrior Fae that was hiding something.

"She'll never fall for you," Everett joked as he ran his hands through his red hair. "I know it because she wouldn't dare look at me, and we all know who is the most handsome." I rolled my eyes, not caring to fight. Everett was the most muscular of us all, but I had the charm. I'd do my best to flirt with her and get to know her. She had been so stand-offish, not wanting to get to know me, which drove me mad.

"She'll come to me," I boasted.

I had caught her staring as I would fly by. At first, she would glare at me, but I knew something was there. I piqued her interest, whether she knew it or not. When I had a moment to spare, I would try to speak with her, but she could sense me. As soon as I was in the area, she would gather the children and head inside. My heart wished for her to be my mate, but when I looked into her eyes at a distance, my soul could not figure her out. A mystery.

Not today, Nana. I will have to speak with you with orders from the King. I checked myself one more time before Everett grabbed Braxton, who was making out with some fairy servant. He needed to grow up if he ever planned to find his own mate. Everett had calmed down considerably since Osirus had his mate, and now Alaneo. We were both getting antsy, but Braxton continued to overcompensate for his need for desire.

"Let's go." My beard was trimmed, my hair pulled back in a lower tail, and we were off to the one place my heart had been aching to go. Braxton shoved the female off his lap while she gave a loud whine about why he was leaving. Braxton snickered and waved her off.

We flew over the marketplace with ease. The Fae and several Elves spoke with each other as we passed. Many of the Fae were nobles that had split from their chosen partners who looked for their mates, and the marketplace was the perfect community spot to seek them. There was slight chaos at the beginning, but things have simmered down. Many couples took it as having no hard feelings, while others had a difficult time with the split. They had created their own bond with their chosen and had become good friends, but that was all it was. Friends.

Once they find their mate, they would feel complete and feel more joy than they ever could have with their chosen. Then why am I obsessing over Nana? She wasn't my mate, but I was drawn to her. It wasn't just her beauty. I felt that didn't matter. It was just her, her aura. I could almost see a golden glow around her as she walked and took care of the orphaned children.

As we arrived, our three cousins greeted us as they were hanging up the daily laundry. They spoke about how excited they were. They no longer had to work for coinage and concentrated on having the children adopted. There had already been several parents coming by to adopt children with their newly formed bonds. Thank the goddess I saw Cricket trying to fly up a nearby jumba tree instead of being taken away by new parents.

"We are actually here on business, ladies. Is Nana around?" The girls all elbowed each other and pointed to the house. I gave them a bow, and they laughed at my silliness and headed inside.

Nana must not have heard me because she was in the kitchen, washing dishes and humming a tune. An old nursery rhyme that I heard Osirus humming to Queen Melina just this afternoon. Nana was as radiant as the day I saw her as we approached the orphanage to return Cricket from the marketplace. I cleared my throat, and Nana turned around, startled.

"Oh, um, Commander Finley, can I help you?" Her eyes wouldn't look at me as I walked toward her. She was hiding her fierceness; I could feel it.

"I'm here to pick up Cricket. We have found his mother,

and she desperately wants him back." Nana's face fell as she grabbed the dishrag.

"Y-you can't. Cricket is mine." This perked my attention. This morning, I was informed that Cricket was Elaine's. The mother who had been given Cricket as compensation for her birthed baby was no longer around. Her identity must have been changed, but, of course, Cosmo kept tabs on the boy.

"Have you known Cricket since his birth?" I inquired. Nana nodded her head as she wrung out the towel. Her hands were shaking, and her demeanor changed. Taking her hand, I felt the sparks fly across my skin, the classic sign of a mate. Gods, she was my mate. Why could I not see it in her soul? Taking my hand away, she looked up at me and held her hand to her mouth.

"I-I'm sorry. I-I can't." Nana stepped away, but I took another step closer.

"Opal? Are you Opal?" Her eyes glistened as she gripped her body. Out of instinct, I grabbed her and pulled her into my arms. Holding her while she cried, I held her head close to my body, not daring to let her go. Everett and Braxton entered the room but quickly left, seeing the state Nana was in.

After a few moments of crying, she looked up into my eyes. If I had just gotten closer to her sooner, I could see the sparkle in her eyes. Her soul was reaching for me. I felt the bond within her. Why do I have to be this close? Sensing my questioning gaze, "It's a spell," she choked. "I did it to hide from Cosmo."

She was hiding from the bastard. Opal may have thought he would come back to rape her, and I bet the damn fool would have too. I'll crush his bones the way he has ruined so many lives.

"I hid, but the downside of using a glamour spell is that it would hide me, and I could not find a second chance mate if I was granted one," she sobbed. "How did you find me?" I wiped a tear away from her cheek and smiled down at her.

"I always find what I am looking for, and I have looked for

you for centuries." I wanted to kiss her, ravish her, and take care of all the ailments she had gone through. Her heart had been broken by a mate, and I wasn't about to do it to her. Opal doesn't know how a mate should be treated, so we will take it slow and prove my worth. I will be valiant and defend her honor. "Cosmo is captured and will die a painful death. You do not have to hide any longer," I cooed in her ear. "May I see my future blushing bride?"

"I have the undoing potion in my room." Opal's blush scattered across her face, and the tiny freckles glowed brightly. Opal continued to look into my eyes. Neither one of us wanted to let go, but until I gaze at my beautiful mate in her true form, the itch will always be there.

"Be quick," I spoke in a hushed voice, and with a reluctant look, she ran up the stairs. My heart thudded in my chest. Even with a glamor potion, I could find her. It took me a lot longer to see her since she had hidden in the forest with the orphanage, along with her own glamor spell. The real question would be if she had an antidote for the boy, Cricket, so he could grow and stop being a boy. Melina would want that for him as well as his birth mother.

Opal will face hardships once I bring her back to the palace. She already knew her daughter Daphne whom she birthed had grown to be the villain in this story, along with her ex-mate. Hell, I remembered when Daphne walked into the orphanage, not more than a month ago demanding money from her to pay taxes. Did she really know? There was obvious hurt in her eyes, but maybe she never saw Daphne as her daughter. She never raised her, and she never held her in her arms.

Opal jumped down the stairs in her dull dress with a brown smock. I would dress her in the finest clothes. I have waited for her and saved for my mate to have the best. The small potion was dusty, and with one quick swig of the drink, she set it on the table and stepped away from me.

The lifeless hair started changing from root to tip. Spirals of chestnut hair strung down to her waist, her green eyes were brightened, and her face no longer looked pale. Opal looked rested and beautiful, but most of all, what I noticed was our bond and how strong it was. It was a damn waterfall with the water pounding me into the rocks.

I ran to her and picked her up, spinning her around while she laughed and held me by my shoulders. "We will take it slow. I know you have been through much." My urge to kiss her still sat in the forefront of my mind and her licking her lips didn't help.

"I know of your honor, Finley. I've watched you a long time." Her finger brushed my short beard. "We won't go too terribly slow," she winked and leaned her lips to mine. I leaned down and pressed to hers, and our bodies instantly touched each other. Her breasts were about to spill out of her dress as I held her close. With one hand on her back and the other at the curve of her back, I let her feel how much I wanted her. So much for going slow.

The door opened wide, and a confused Cricket walked in. "Where's Nana?!" Opal laughed and ran to him and grabbed his hands. "It is me, Cricket. I'm Nana, well I'm Opal. I've had a glamor spell on me, and I have a spell on you too, my little heart." Cricket looked up, confused, with his mouth hanging open.

"You know how you never grow?" Cricket stared back with amusement.

"Yeah, you said I didn't eat enough vegetables," he pouted. We both laughed, and Opal shook her head.

"I did it to keep you safe from someone, but you are safe now. When you were a baby, I had a powerful witch cast a spell on you so you wouldn't grow older than 8 years old." Cricket squinted his eyes at her.

"Okay, so what now? Can I grow up all at once? That would be so cool!" Opal laughed again and shook her head no.

"No, you will grow slowly once we give you the potion. We need to do it in front of a witch to make sure the spell and the potion are done properly. Now, go pack your bags. You are going to go meet your mother today." Cricket let out an enormous scream and ran up the stairs. I was happy that Opal will let Cricket go, but the pain in her heart will be great once his birth mother leaves for Atlantis.

I will fill her heart, and we will create our own children in our own likeness.

Everett and Braxton came barging in with swords pulled out, ready for a battle. Pulling Opal close, I had her head buried into my neck. "Everything is fine," I yelled at them playfully. Opal leaned up and pecked my lips again.

"What the hell did I miss?" Braxton sheathed his sword and walked to both of us. "Nana?" he questioned when he looked at her. Opal gave me another hug as my heart warmed. Even with Opal's bitter beginning while she hid from Cosmo, she was still willing to give us a try. I guess watching me from afar, knowing who I was, gave her the extra confidence to even consider having me as a mate. I prided myself I didn't let other women try to seduce me.

I would have to explain it to Braxton later as he continues his frivolous encounters with random Fae women.

"It's a long story. Once we gather Cricket and head back to the palace, we will tell you all about it," I smirked while holding on to my mate. Opal was worth the wait, and I would cherish her and treat her like a queen like Osirus treated his mate, Melina.

Chapter 64

Melina

Osirus curled me around his arms for the rest of the night until the sun hit the horizon the next day. I wasn't feeling as terrible as yesterday, but then again, I had only been awake for a few minutes. Osirus' face was buried in my neck, and I took a deep sigh and cuddled closer.

The entire night, Osirus was by my side. He would rub my belly to keep the pain away. There were times he even went and retrieved a hot water bottle and asked if I wanted chocolate. I couldn't help but laugh at him and almost shed tears of joy.

No more tears.

I knew hormones played a big part in my breakdown yesterday, but could anyone blame me? I've been holding everything inside, trying not to break. All the emotion came crashing down in an instant of how much responsibility I would carry in our near future.

Osirus' breath hitched as he rolled over on his back. His muscles rippled on his skin as he stretched. Even in the terrible predicament I was in, I still wanted to lick up his entire torso with my tongue. Touching him gave me pleasure, and he didn't need to touch me to provide me with the feelings that stirred in my belly. Osirus' head relaxed in the pillow while one arm was wrapped around me and the other held the back of his head. I could feel myself automatically rubbing my thighs together.

Down girl, down. Let's concentrate on taking care of him.

My mouth didn't think twice, and my lips connected with his muscular chest. I kissed, licked, and nipped at his nipples as he groaned and took the hand behind his head, and grabbed the back of my head. "Darling," his raspy voice flowed straight to my nether regions. Goddess, why does his voice have to sound so darn sexy in the morning? I wanted him to say my name over and over in that smooth voice.

My lips trailed lower as I sucked near his hip bone; his hips flexed as I pulled his trousers down below his shaft. His morning wood was already at attention, so I didn't have to work so hard. Then again, he was always hard. However, I wanted to tease a bit. Osirus' eyes were still closed as I cupped his balls and licked the tip of his dick. "Baby," he growled, one hand still on my head as he tried to guide me lower.

My teasing didn't last long as he pushed my head straight down on his shaft. A grunt left his throat as I bobbed it up and down on his velvet skin. "Goddess," he moaned. His eyes were now staring into mine as I hummed into his cock. The vibrations set him off, and he jerked his hips up while I sucked him, so his dick hit the back of my throat.

"Baby, do you like my cock that much? Do you like to suck?" I let a little growl out of my throat as I bobbed harder and massaged his balls. The skin below his balls loved to be stroked. It made him go crazy. I wasn't sure what it was with this area, but I was going to take advantage. Using some spit that had dripped from my mouth, I took my wet finger and massaged it under his balls. His head threw back as I swirled my tongue around his head.

"Fucking Goddess baby, just like that!" I slammed my mouth down again, bobbing feverishly, and to my surprise, Osirus ripped his load into my mouth. I swallowed the sweet tasting cum he allowed me to have as he pulled me to his chest. Osirus' arms instantly went around my body as he peppered kisses on my forehead.

"Darling, you are sick. You didn't need to do that, but goddess, it was welcomed." I giggled and kissed his neck while he massaged my back with one of his large hands. "Are you feeling better today, then?" I nodded yes silently until he used his hand to have me look at him. "Words, darling."

"Yes, much better." His stern look went to a happy one as he wrapped his legs around my body.

"Let's get you showered. I have a lot of work to do today, but I want you to stay here and rest." I pouted. I didn't want him to go. "Darling, just a few more days, then we will go on a 'honeymoon.'" My ears instantly perked up at the word, 'honeymoon,' and I wrapped my arms around his neck.

"Really? A honeymoon? You know what that is?" My excitement led to bouncing on the bed while he threw his head back and gave a glorious laugh.

"Yes, darling. I am trying to keep up with the customs you are used to." I stood frozen for a moment before dashing off into the bathroom to get ready for the day. "Now quickly, I heard a messenger came bringing news of Tulip." His voice faded as I put my head under the warm water.

Rest my butt. I'm coming with him!

Osirus was already dressed by the time I emerged from the bathroom in his full royal Fae attire. It only made me hot and needy, but there was nothing I could do about that. His hand reached for mine as we walked hand in hand to the tearoom.

His mother and father sat beside each other, whispering, and kissing before we approached. Along with my father and his new mate, Elaine, they sat closely with one another as they sipped on their own beverages.

Elaine already looked much better. Her eyes no longer held bags under them, and there was a twinkle in her eye as she stared longingly at my father. I was exceedingly happy for both; they deserved each other.

"Princess, you look better today." My father stood up to give me a hug, and I gave one in return. "You have been working too hard, haven't you? Or is your mate not taking care of you?" My father gave Osirus a glare while Osirus clenched his fists, wanting to strike back.

"No, no," I waved my hands. "Osirus takes terrific care of me. I'm just not feeling my best, is all." Elaine came behind me to put her hand on my shoulder.

"Melina's mate is doing fine, Girard. She is dealing with something different entirely." Gosh, everyone can smell me; I'm surprised my father hasn't. Elaine gave a long look at my father, who then took a deep breath in.

"Don't do that!" I squealed, running away into Osirus' arms.

"Oh, I didn't realize." My father blushed as he walked away. "I don't go smelling my own daughter's pheromones. I don't need to smell her mate all over her. She's still my princess," he apologized.

This was utterly embarrassing.

"At least you aren't pregnant before the bonding," he kept adding. The awkwardness continued to seep into the room until Elaine patted his arm and shook her head.

"Just stop, dear; you are embarrassing our daughter."

My heart instantly warmed as Elaine called me hers. We knew little about each other, but she was willing to adopt me as her own. Cricket came to mind; she would get a chance to raise her very own son even after trying to raise Daphne. It explained a lot since she couldn't stay with her daughter and continue to watch her grow. Elaine didn't have a bond connected to Daphne, so her heart weakened the more the days passed dealing with Cosmo.

The question was, where was Daphne's real mother, and would she be willing to help us with Daphne once we told her the truth?

Another Dark Pixie flew into the room and dropped a

small letter of parchment. He had the same haircut and dark wings as I had first met, but he didn't stay. It was a drop-and-go departure as soon as he had delivered his message. Not one bow or recognition from the others as he flew into the morning light through the window.

Alec was standing in the room's corner, observing. He had been quiet, just wandering the halls of the palace like a lost puppy. Alec and Tulip hadn't been mated for long, and the effects were taking a toll on him and his Wolf.

Osirus and my father grunted at the blatant disrespect of the Dark Pixie while I picked up the small note. It was a deep-colored parchment paper, and the handwriting was not of Tulip's. My heart stopped beating for a fleeting moment as I read.

Osirus,

You have my mother, and I have your mate's friend. I'll give you an even trade. Meet me at Progronie Creek tomorrow at noon. No guards, no spells. Come with an open mind.

Daphne.

Well, this positioned us with several problems. One, I would not let Osirus go alone. That bish was going to do something sneaky and put a spell on him and make him come with her. I wouldn't put it past those witches to do something from afar. Two, my father would NOT let Elaine go alone. He'd die before that happened.

Hot, sticky, uncomfortable, formidable mess this was.

Instantly, there was arguing, along with Osirus' father and mother, who had walked into the room. There was so much royal tension going on that it about made my head explode. Little banter led to yelling, and the yelling led to full-out growls and roars. Alec was doing his best to keep his Wolf in control and not rip a royal's head off to protect his mate.

"My mate will not dare go near there!" My father gritted

his teeth. His fins pierced through his royal blue blazer as Elaine tried to calm him. "I don't trust the bitch, she will have the Blood Coven with her, and you know it!"

Nyx got in on the action yelling that a future king does not work with traditor scum, and they needed to cut their losses and let Tulip take the wrap. Osirus started arguing that Tulip was my sister and Alec's mate. Tulip now had the same rights as a royal and should be saved accordingly. The room grew louder, and everyone was talking over each other. The growl in my throat grew into a gentle hum as I tried to calm myself. Closing my eyes, I let the song come from my body as I imagined peace by the sea.

I hadn't had time to spend much time with my father in his kingdom, but the thoughts of the waves, the cool water, and the fish brought me to my calm as I breathed slowly. The outward sounds of the noise and the fighting were no longer around me, and it was just me and the gentle breeze of the sea.

I could almost feel the ocean spray glisten on my face as I felt a warm hand on my arm. My eyes flew open to see Osirus smiling at me and bringing me into his arms. The sea faded away, and I was brought back to the tearoom with two other couples and Alec staring at me intently. I buried my face into Osirus' chest, to his amusement as he petted my head.

"Sorry, princess, this isn't normally how we conduct meetings," my father said apologetically. "My need to protect my unmarked mate got the best of me." My father pressed his lips to Elaine's forehead as he held her close.

"I think it is understandable. We all have someone to take care of. But, darling, you soothed some of the most powerful supernaturals in all Bergarian. I'm impressed."

"I didn't mean to. I was just tired of the yelling, so I tried to zone out. I'm sorry."

"Don't be," Nyx stood up and buttoned his blazer. "It was needed. Your instincts kicked in, and we needed it."

"Now." Osirus pulled me to his lap at the head of the

table and snaked his arms around my waist. I still had a few cramps leftovers from yesterday, but thankfully they had subsided substantially. I'm thanking Osirus and the bond for that. I'm sure he had something to do with it because I am usually in bed for days. "For us to proceed, I think we need to take one thing at a time..."

As Osirus spoke, Finley and a beautiful Fae woman with spiraled chestnut curls stepped into the room. She looked vaguely familiar as she walked up to the table. Finley was gazing at her with such an adoring look. I couldn't help but smile. His hand was on her lower back, and she stared at him longingly.

"Your Majesty," she bowed at both Osirus and me. "My name used to be Nana. I have been hiding and taking care of the boy, Cricket, as my own. My real name is Opal." Elaine took in a deep breath and held her hands to her mouth.

"Goddess," she whispered. Opal took a glance at Elaine, who was equally stunned. "I'm so sorry about what happened, I-"Opal walked towards Elaine and held out her arms, in which both Elaine and Opal wept. "I swear I didn't want him," Elaine cried. Opal held her tightly again and nodded her head in understanding.

"He's evil, an evil beast," Opal agreed. Finley growled and pulled Opal back. Phew, the sexual claiming tension in here was stifling.

"I will go to Daphne," Opal declared. "I believe she has felt a bond between us, but she doesn't understand it. This nonsense needs to stop, and I will tell her that." Finley turned her around and grasped her arms.

"No, I won't allow it! What if she turns on you?"

Opal stood up straighter and brushed her hair back. "I am her birth mother, and she will come to realize it. We just need to get a few witches to put a cloaking spell on your warriors. Do you honestly think she will play fair? She has no heart because of that evil winged bat. I've seen how she has tortured innocent people over the years; there is no turning back for her as much as I want to believe. I've got some witch friends that could possibly help."

"They aren't from the Blood Coven, are they?" Alaneo walked into the room with his new mate, Juliet. Both sporting large mating bites for all the world to see. I wanted to run up to Alaneo, but I knew better. Osirus spoke last night about how territorial vampires could be. Standing still in awe of her beauty and curves, I couldn't believe I stood in the same room as a vampire.

"This is better than Twilight," I whispered to no one in particular. Juliet giggled and waved.

"Vampires that sparkle. Really?" Her voice rang like bells as she replied to me with a toothy grin.

"No, most witches stay away from the Blood Coven. Their practices are unethical," Opal replied confidently.

"Good, because they are in a heap of trouble, and the entire coven is going to be wiped from the entire face of Bergarian," Osirus stated.

Chapter 65

Osirus

"No, Osirus, I'm coming too!" Melina had not stopped whining since coming back from our planning meeting yesterday.

Opal was to come with me as we traveled to Progronie Creek. The warriors we were bringing would not be small in numbers. The cloaking spells of Opal's witching friends said their cloaking spell was strong enough to hold one hundred warriors. The witches laughed at how the Blood Coven wouldn't see us coming until it was too late. I dared not ask how they could accomplish this large spell as they snickered, poking, and prodding each other.

I don't want or need to know how they have a spell more potent than another coven. I needed to know it will work. Daphne and Tulip are the only people that will see Opal and I. Girard and Elaine were to stay back at the palace to monitor Melina because I know my mate is as stubborn as a mule. She will try to evade the "Red Fury" and fly to make sure Daphne doesn't take hold of me. No spell could keep me from my mate, and I would make sure of it.

However, if our roles were reversed, I would do the same. I'm doing my job protecting my mate and my kingdom, and if I must handcuff her to the bed, I will. Her father in the room or not.

Alaneo was also coming, leaving his mate Juliet behind. The wounds were too fresh for Juliet as much as she wanted to help. During the few days that Alaneo and Juliet bonded, Juliet would often wake up in a cold sweat, fearing that the coven leader, Prinna, was coming to take more samples of her blood.

Blood of any race will help reach a higher potency level in potions, spells, and curses. Vampire blood was among the weakest to use, but anything to increase their power would do. No race was to give witches their blood unless cleared with a royal, and obviously, the Blood Coven was not following that protocol.

In my short time with Juliet, along with Melina, we learned of specific spells they were trying to cast. Some were simple like regenerating food, but their spiritual power dwindled quickly once it was used. Vampire blood helped replenishes their spirits to continue to cast at a higher rate.

Some spells were more complicated in which they would need the most potent blood of all, Dragons' blood. The Dragons had long left besides Horus, who was too powerful to get to, so the shifter-Dragons were the next best thing. The most extensive spell they were trying to cast was that of dimension trans teleportation. Instead of using the portals that were heavily guarded, they were trying to make their own. For what, Juliet wasn't sure.

Daphne was only playing a minor role when it came to all of this, but her puny mind couldn't see through it. They would give her the throne, but it would only be for show. Once she was decreed as a queen, the Dragon Shifters were no longer protected under our joint alliance with the Cerulean Moon Kingdom, and they would be able to overthrow the Dragons. Numbers mattered in this war, and they were not expecting The Golden Light Kingdom and the Cerulean Moon Kingdom to come together just a month ago.

Melina rolled her eyes again as she sat cross-legged on the

bed. I had just put on my battle armor in our room. She eyed me up and down several times, and it was all I could do to keep the smirk on my face away from her. My cock twitched a bit, knowing that she liked how I looked. Even with all the lovemaking, we have been doing, she still wanted me.

Curse the gods that I had to wait. It would only make our Binding Ceremony that much of a thrill once I take her to bed.

"Please, Osirus, let me go!"

"I've told you no. If there are other Blood Coven members present, they would smell you. They have blood-hunting warlocks in their coven and would pick you out right away and give away the surprise. You would put everyone in danger!" I sternly told her, as she immediately crouched back.

"I'm sorry I yelled." I came and sat on the bed and pulled her face to mine. I knew all of this was too much, but what could I do? This had to be done swiftly, so she was safe during the coronation. "If all goes well, this will be put behind us, and Tulip will be here with you. Alec is coming and will be sure she will come home."

"But what about you?" Her eyes softened. "I can't lose you. Especially to her." We grabbed each other, and I kissed her cheek.

"I always come back. There hasn't been a battle or spar I haven't won. I will come back to you."

"You better!" She pushed me on the shoulder. I didn't budge. "You got me all hyped up being with you forever; you can't go breaking promises now." I tackled her to the bed, my sword poking her side, and I don't mean the one I was used to battling evil entities with.

***

Montu trotted alongside Opal and her mare, Apples. The orphanage had one horse to travel within case a child needed medical attention. Being worried at first about the small mare and lack of strength, I was surprised it kept up with

Montu well. Both the horses looked at one another, and I couldn't help but let out a chuckle.

"What?" Opal looked at me, dazed. She was still tired, no doubt from ridding herself of the spell she had cast on her for years. Finley wouldn't leave her side and was walking alongside her in the cloaking spell. Often, Opal would jerk her hand and give small little bits of laughter. If it weren't for Finley walking alongside her, I would have thought she went crazy.

"Our horses, I believe they have struck a bit of liking to each other." Montu snorted and bobbed his head while Opal laughed.

"I believe they have, haven't you Apples?" She groaned in agreement as we carried on.

The creek was a reasonable distance from the palace and closer to the Blood Coven's territory. The Golden Light Kingdom went dark from view as we entered the Southern Forest that bordered the Dark Forest. An area that I had fought in not too long ago with rogues trying to steal Luna Clara's healing abilities.

The trees that grew here were massive; one could not put their arms around a tree, it took over five men to reach around. Some trees that had died were hollowed out to make homes for dark Pixies and Fae that preferred the darkness. Their own light generated enough for them to power themselves.

"I don't like this place," Opal spoke aloud. The warriors and several witches that were holding the spell crept behind us. The sounds of the stream were coming closer, and Opal fidgeted with the reigns.

The entire forest had a darkness that should not have been there. The leaves that branched over the sparsely spaced trees stretched wide, so even the floor was covered in darkness. No wandering forest sprites or small animals were about gathering food. There also were no insects to be heard; something was wrong.

I raised my hand to signal to stop. Opal pulled at the reins and looked at me. "What's wrong?" she whispered, eying the stream in front of us. Taking in the view, I scanned the area. There was no sign of Daphne or Tulip, and all was quiet except the stream.

"Stay mounted. If I tell you to run, you take Apples and run back." I grabbed my sword, not yet wanting to unsheathe it. My chest was bare to show no ill intentions, but I still wasn't going in without a weapon. Stepping near the stream, I scanned my surroundings again, and behind one tree, I saw Tulip strolling towards me with her hands bound in silver.

Werewolves were proud creatures. She did not hold her head down, instead, holding it up defiantly as she walked toward us. Hoping it was truly Tulip, I still could not trust this scene. "Halt." Tulip stopped and held up her hands. There were burns and scars on her arms. Her leather pants were torn, and her shirt barely covered her breasts. "What were you and Melina doing the last night of our stay in the Crimson Shadows Pack?" Tulip smiled and chuckled.

"Skinny dipping, but the poor thing wouldn't take off her bra and underwear." I let go of my sword and went to Tulip and ripped the weak ropes from her body. A slow clap came from behind the tree as Daphne stepped out.

"Congratulations, you have your Tulip. Now give me my mother." Opal dismounted her horse and put her hand on my shoulder to walk towards Daphne. Daphne let out a huff in disgust. "You are not my mother. Did you go back on your word, Osirus?"

"I did not. I just brought your true mother," I stated. Finley was behind me. His breath was on my neck. He wanted to tear Daphne to pieces if she did anything to harm his mate.

"You feel it, don't you?" Opal took a step forward. "You have always felt it, but you ignored it." Another step ahead, and Daphne released her hardened stance. "You felt it at the orphanage each time you came, but you couldn't explain it." Daphne stepped back a few steps.

"Nana..."

"It confused you, hurt you when you saw me hurt, but you continued to wreak your wrath on others around you. Your anger only grew when you realized when you hurt me, you only hurt yourself." Daphne backed up into the tree; she had nowhere to go. Opal held out her hand to touch her daughter's cheek.

"I am your mother, Daphne. Your father tricked me into sleeping with him and got me pregnant. He took you from me the day you were born. It broke me." Opal's firm voice quivered. "I love you, and I wanted to take you away, but I had become too weak because I had rejected him."

"Now is your last chance to ask for forgiveness. There will still be punished, and with enough time to make amends. Make this right. I will nurture you to be the beautiful, soulful, wonderful daughter I know you can be. Let me love you as I should have. Please." Opal's aura could be felt even twenty feet away from me. The love Opal had for a daughter she never raised was undeniably strong. Opal was indeed as strong as Nyx made her out to be. I had high hopes that Daphne would take the offer.

Daphne's eyes glistened as tears tried to escape. "Mother? You are my mother?" Opal nodded and put both of her hands on her daughter's face. As I relaxed and motioned Tulip to mount Montu, the ear-piercing scream rushed to my ears.

"OPAL!" Finley screamed, and his spell was broken on him, unable to keep his position a secret. Looking back at Opal, there was a dagger stabbed right in the middle of Opal's torso. Her hands grabbed the dagger as she fell backward to her knees. Finley ran towards her. A warrior's battle cry was heard as his sword was drawn. I instantly took my hand to mine as we rushed to Daphne, who smiled evilly and, in a swift motion, lifted her arm with a straight up and down motion.

At least eighty witches and sorcerers stood behind the tree line Daphne had leaned against. The one hundred warriors I had brought may be an even match with magic, but we would need more help.

Alaneo, sensing my unease, reared back his horse as another witch dropped his cloaking and blew on the Shifter Horn. Any shifter within a five-mile radius could hear it and aid us if they were able. The witches kept our warriors cloaked so they could fight without detection. Unless they have a more powerful witch than the ones cloaking my men to rid the spell, we may last the battle.

My sword let out its cry as I started plunging it into our enemy. I stayed with Finley as he held Opal, who was barely clinging to life. Several witches came to grab Daphne, but Alaneo stopped them with a quick swipe of the sword. Then Alaneo plunged his sword beside Daphne's head into the tree, trapping her. Her face twitched in fear. She thought I would be of honor and keep my word of not having my men, but she was mistaken.

"Let me go, or I'll make sure Melina suffers the worst by the time it's over," she seethed.

"It is over!" I growled and plunged my sword deep into her chest. I gripped the handle and twisted, making sure there would be no recovery. The light in her eyes faded, mouth agape at the rash decision I had made. Daphne started a war, and I was to end it. I wanted nothing more than to torture her, but I would not give myself the satisfaction. I am ridding the problem once and for all and not prolonging it.

Pulling my sword from the tree, she slumped over as her head fell on a nearby rock. Alaneo had already mounted his horse as his sword swung at warlocks, throwing fire. Slowly, our warriors appeared on the battlefield; a sorcerer must have found our witches. Our witches were holding their own, backing up behind each other, covering each other from all sides. They wielded webs of electricity that took down several at a time, but the Blood Coven was stronger. They had the vampire blood running through their veins, helping them recover quickly.

Our witches were becoming weaker in their magic, using too much of their spirit.

Finley was on the ground, holding Opal to his chest. The knife was still stuck in her belly as the blood poured from the wound. She was in obvious distress. The color from her face was draining, and her eyes are becoming dull. Finley was beside himself, not using the proper tools or training he had been given.

"Finley, snap out of it. Treat her as a warrior. Remove the knife!" Finley's shaky hand pulled the knife from Opal, and she gasped a cry as I held my hand over her stomach. Alaneo was nearby, using his skills to evade any attacks while we stayed somewhat hidden from the chaos. I pulled my satchel off my hip and grabbed the small vial containing a small amount of healing agent.

"Finley, pull back the wound," I ordered. Several Fae doctors made the healing agent. It helped slow down the bleeding of deep wounds, enough to get our wounded to a safe place. Finley pulled the skin apart as Opal struggled with the blood seeping from her mouth. "This will sting," I tried to warn soothingly as it dripped into her stomach. Finley then gripped her stomach again. Our best course of action was to get her to the palace, but during a warlock battle might be tricky.

A loud howl came from the side of the woods. It shook the ground, and the dead leaves from the trees fell. I knew that howl from anywhere, one of the strongest Werewolves known in the history books. His half-shifted form came stomping out of the woods. Alpha Kane roared again as hundreds of wolves poured into the battleground. Chomping, ripping, and yipping filled the air as the coven retreated.

Alpha Kane, now Torin, his Wolf, stood over us.

"We end this," he growled as he and his wolves marched through the Blood Coven territory. The coven wasn't large, but if Prinna was still alive, there would always be a chance for them to regain their strength. We had to destroy their territory, their coven, and their leader.

Chapter 66

Melina

"This has to be the most boring thing I have ever done," I yawned as my father and Elaine continued to play chess. It wasn't an ordinary chessboard. It had unique pieces, such as an actual Fae king and queen and distinct ranks of generals and warriors. They had been at it for the past hour, and they both have given each other googly eyes.

I loved them both already in the short time I've known them, but this was getting ridiculous. I didn't need to see my parents wanting to do each other over a chess game. The way they 'accidentally' touch each other's hands and have some crude little jokes secretly made me want to scream. "Can I leave?" I whined, and my father rolled his eyes.

"No, we can't have you going after Osirus. You are my blood, and if I know anything about our family, you can be stubborn. Besides, you have absolutely no combat training."

"It's not my fault. I thought I was a full human." I crossed my arms as I leaned back in the overly decorated chair dramatically. "If I had known I was some supernatural, I would have trained more with the Werewolves, or better yet, joined the swim team." Father let out a grunt of disapproval. He was still upset that he never knew about me, let alone being raised by Wolves. My father was grateful that I was protected by the Wolves. I've already noticed my father's old ways could not help the bit of hostility he still has towards them. The Shifter War didn't just involve those with shifters, but with the Fae, the Sirens, and a few Elves. It was a differences war, no one understood each other, and they preferred to stay to themselves. Land territories were fought over, innocent lives were lost during that time. It reminded me of the early days when Europeans tried to take over the Americas and the racism that Earth still dealt with.

Lucca walked in the room glancing at Father, but his stature slacked once his eyes set on me. "Melina! Want to go for a walk around the palace? I haven't checked it out." I jumped from my chair and stood over the chessboard. They hadn't noticed that Lucca had walked in, too busy sucked into each other's eyes.

It made me jealous that Osirus wasn't here. It made me worry. My parents weren't worried at all, and it was ticking me off. Did they not care?

I could feel the pain in my heart, how much I missed Osirus. I complained about how bored I was while they played chess together, but I worried. Complaining about something different entirely gave me something else to think about.

My shoulder slumped, and Lucca came over to embrace me in a hug. His head drooped and cuddled into my neck. I started laughing while my father and Elaine looked up. A few tears were threatening to fall, but I held my own. I would not cry. I had to be the darn queen soon.

"Father, we won't leave the palace," Lucca pleaded as he took my hand. Father gave a small smile and brought me into his embrace.

"Osirus is strong. He will be fine. Even though he is a Fae," he joked. Giving a little sniff and a nod, he let me go. "Don't leave the palace. Everett and Braxton are assisting in the guard changes, and I don't want to hear you both being reckless while they are gone."

"You forget who the best at sparring is, Father." Lucca puffed out his chest. "Besides, the brothers are all in the palace assisting. What makes you think we will have time to do anything fun with those twats walking around all noble?"

Lucca raced me out of the room, gripping my hand tightly while laughing loudly. Once we were halfway down the hall, we looked in every room. I hadn't had a chance to even look through the rooms of the palace. Osirus always had me by his side, and I never wanted to leave his.

"How are you doing?" His voice went somber as I opened another door. This room was filled with stuffed animals, and I'm not talking about the cute, cuddly kind you take to bed. These animals were vicious-looking, and the taxidermist did a great job showing how ferocious they could be. My fingers wanted to touch the armor-plated lizards, but I held back. It only reminded me of the snake that Daphne was. Was Osirus going to be all right?

I gripped the shawl that Osirus had given me this morning. It matched the color of his battle trousers and shirt. The designs on his armor also showed on the light blanket that covered me. Concentrating really hard, I could almost smell the musky scent he left as he kissed me on the pillow before he left.

Goddess, I missed him. I prayed for an even trade, and Daphne could come to her senses. I had a horrible feeling that it would not be the case.

"I'm fine," I lied as I touched the soft pelt of a saber-tooth-like bear.

"That was a horrible lie," Lucca joked. "Do you think Osirus hunted all these?"

"Osirus says whatever they kill, they eat. However, I noticed that full-blooded Fae like to eat lighter meats. I can't tell you how much I miss eating cows." Lucca scratched his scalp in question.

"Cow? Ohhhh! The animal on Earth. They say 'moo,' right? We have several textbooks about Earth animals. I heard they have excellent meat if bred and fed correctly. I'm getting sick of fish myself."

"Yes, they do, and I need me a good steak every once in and while. Amora from a Dragon Shifter tribe says she is willing to send me one since they farm them. If you are good to me, maybe I'll let you have some," I chided as I pushed him towards the door.

Lucca turned suddenly away from the conversation. "Do you smell that?"

"Huh? Smell what? Did talking about juicy steaks trigger you? I know I could go for one right- "

"Shh," Lucca put his hand over my mouth while grabbing me with the other hand. We ran out of the room and down several hallways.

"Lucca, what are you doing?"

"Goddess, it smells amazing," he breathed in again.

"The kitchen is on the opposite—oh gods," I breathed. Could Sirens smell their mate? Fae look into the eyes of the soul. Werewolves could smell. Can a Siren?

"Quick, look around the corner. Tell me what you see," Lucca ordered. We were both pinned up by the wall, wheezing by the sprint he made me keep up with. His eyes were dilated to a vertical slit, like a freaking shark. Can my eyes do that?

Putting my hand over my beating heart, I looked around the corner to see who his mate could possibly be.

Sean. He was guarding Carson and Peoni's door.

Holy Mother of Pearl, Sean was Lucca's mate.

"Lucca, are you gay?" I asked, surprised. He has never told me he was. I just assumed he was straight, which was dumb on my part. He kept saving the women from the land, so I automatically thought...

"I... I..." Lucca fumbled with his words as I turned to him. I grabbed his hands and held them close to me.

"It's all right if you are. I would love and care for you all the same. Is that what you are worried about?" Lucca's eyes wouldn't look into mine as he chewed on his bottom lip. Lucca was a beautiful Siren. The blue streaks in his hair and the few scales that appeared on his neck were gorgeous. He was embarrassed, but he shouldn't be. This was how he was born and wired. Why would I shame him for it? Would Father? He couldn't go back on what the goddess had given him.

"Lucca, go to him. Sean has looked for a long time for his mate." I gave a gentle squeeze.

"Sean?" he whispered. A large growl behind my ear startled me. I felt the hot breath of an animal tickle my ear. Instantly realizing the situation, I stood to the side, letting Sean look into the eyes of his mate.

Sean's eyes were black. His Wolf came forward as Lucca looked longingly at him. Not wanting to ruin the moment, I backed away, and Lucca grabbed my hand. Lucca trembled as he held it. Squeezing his hand in return, I tried to let go. "It's all right. Sean is a good Wolf. He will take care of you." I almost wanted to cry. My big bro just got his mate, and to a decent Wolf too!

"Mine," Sean pulled Lucca into his embrace. Sean's muscles were much more significant than Lucca's and certainly towered over him. Crazy Wolf genetics. Sean immediately put his head on Lucca's neck while Lucca stiffened at the sudden intrusion.

I need to get out of here before they mate in the hallway.

Pulling my hand from Lucca's with a bit of force, Sean glanced at me, giving me a thankful smile. Backing away, I readied myself for the long walk back to the room that Osirus and I shared.

The palace grew so much more significant when you are alone.

It was well into the late afternoon. Time had flown being with Lucca, and now I'm stuck with my thoughts of Osirus and how he was doing. Taking my time walking back, I glanced in mostly guest quarters, storage, and even maid and butler supply rooms. Having an entire room dedicated to bed linens is funny, but it made sense on the grand scale of things. Turning away from the rooms, I headed to the large stained-glass window. The tops of the windows had bright colors that cast a beautiful painting on the marbled floors as the suns began their descents across the horizon.

It crossed my mind to visit Juliet. She must have felt the loneliness too. Alaneo refused to let her leave, and she didn't mind. She had fought for a long time and was still recovering herself. Being sure of my decision, I went to leave when I had an eerie feeling. The back of my head burned like someone was watching me.

Turning around quickly, I see one door to a guest bedroom being cracked open. Squinting and taking slow steps to the gold and white decorative door, I covered myself with my shawl a little tighter. The heat of my face was still on fire. Osirus' smell engulfed me, giving me the extra bravery, I needed to check on the other side.

The heat grew to blazing scorch as I touched the door to open it until a large hand gripped my shoulder and pulled me back. An enormous scream was thrown from my mouth as I turned around and punched the intruder in the jaw. I kept swinging as I heard them groan and kicked them in the crotch. I was too afraid to open my eyes and kept swinging.

"Oi! Melina stop!" My eyes flew open, only to see a jumbled mess of red hair on the face of the brute.

"Everett! I am so sorry!" I reached for his hand, but he pushed back and scooted his butt across the floor.

"Ey, stay where you are! You are dangerous! What the fuck was that about!? You about kicked my cave hunter clean off!" Everett grabbed his crotch and moaned. I had completely forgotten about the door as it stood there, wide open. The burning stare I felt was no longer there.

"I'm so sorry!" I turned around to get on my knees. "I thought you were someone else!" Everett's face was scrunched up with pain as I helped lift him off the floor. "Let's get you to a chair and rest." Everett put his arm around me as I helped guide him to a sitting room before I took one last glance at the darkroom door.

There was nothing there. Was it all just my imagination? I could feel the heat linger on my cheeks as I sat Everett down. A nearby servant was dusting a vase as I approached her. "Can you please get us some ice? I might have kicked Everett in his private area." The servant girl glanced over and started giggling. With a quick nod, she ran from the room to get some ice.

Heading back over to Everett, I felt a sharp pain in my shoulder. A scream left me as the pain radiated from my body. Grabbing my shoulder, I looked for blood. There was nothing, but there had to be something wrong!

"Melina, what's wrong?" My father had run down the hall. We weren't far from my room, and my cries must have startled them. Everett had stood up, hand still on his crotch as he was reaching for me.

"AHH!" I screamed again; the pain was now at my other shoulder as I collapsed to the floor. "What is wrong with me?" I yelled as I violently thrashed. "I can't get up!" The pressure was unbearable. Both shoulders stung as the pressure let up.

"Osirus, he's hurt," Elaine whispered as my father picked me up from the floor as my head dangled from his embrace. I thrashed a bit, yelling to let me go. I felt my strength returning as my father sat me on the couch.

"I must go to him! Let me go! He needs me!" Everett put both hands on my shoulders to keep me in place. Several of my brothers rushed into the room.

"Go find Osirus and his warriors. Take the horses from the royal stable! Something is wrong!" he bellowed. My brothers fled the room, slinging on their tridents on their backs. My heart was racing, telling me to follow, but the strength that Everett had surpassed my own. I continued to struggle as my father glared at me.

"You cannot go, Melina. You will stay here where it is safe. Osirus will handle this, he has his finest warriors and Alaneo and his father."

"Last chance, Everett or I will drive you nuts to the floor," I growled. Nothing was going to stop me from getting to Osirus.

Everett chuckled. "Wrong side of the couch, sweetheart." I huffed as a slight grin formed.

I took in a deep breath and concentrated with all my will for them to freeze and began to hum a forceful tune, thinking what I wanted them to do.

Everyone in the room froze. My father looked at me in panic, I ripped my arm from Everett's hold and sprung my wings out with a flip of my hair.

My shawl fell to the floor as I flew down the hallway, leaving my frozen parents behind. I wasn't about to sit around and wait for Osirus to come home or wait until he succumbed to some power-hungry bitch. I was going to take back what was mine.

Chapter 67

Lucca

I held onto Melina's hand, squeezing it tightly. I could feel my palms getting sweaty as she tried to break away from me, but I couldn't let her. I didn't want to be alone with him just yet. My body and soul knew what to do; it screamed for me to run into his muscular arms and let him have me. Finally, be connected to the soul that was destined to be mine, but I panicked. My mind was controlling my body, and it did not want me to move.

Fear enveloped me. He was dominating, more so than I could ever be. But will he be gentle too?

I could hear the soft words that Melina was cooing in my ear. A gentle squeeze later, she let go of my hand while the Werewolf named Sean gripped my hips closer to his. Melina gave a modest nod to Sean while he gave her a grateful smile. Melina knew him, so he must be a good Wolf, right?

I've heard stories. The beasts in them have large sexual appetites, and it was common for them to have multiple partners before finding their mates. The thought made me angry, but I didn't know a thing about him, which gave me less right to judge.

Melina's compact form walked quickly down the hallway

and out of sight. I could see the slump of her shoulders, probably thinking of her mate that was putting his life in danger for the sake of their own relationship. Sean's large hand gripped my chin to look back at him. His facial features were robust, a rigid jawline, broad shoulders, and a muscular neck. It was thick, veiny-like from the hours he must have put into working his body.

Sure, I was muscular, but it was lean from swimming all my calories away. I was also shorter than my mate, a good head shorter, but he was just so damn tall. How could a powerful Wolf-like him want a small fish like me?

"Mate," he growled within his chest as he pulled me closer. My nerves were shot as his hands wrapped around the lower part of my back. His head dipped into my neck again, and he took in a large breath. I wasn't upset by it. In fact, it instead turned me on at the woodsy smell he produced. It was wild and free, and I wanted nothing more for him to take me to his forest home.

"I hope you weren't planning on making me wait." One hand gripped my ass, and the other trailed up my back. It was seductive, torturous that my mate could touch me this way and render me speechless. "Because I'm going to claim you...now." My lungs wouldn't release into the air. I desperately needed to switch out for ample oxygen. He grabbed my arm and ran me down the hall to a free guest bedroom.

The room was dimly lit as he held onto my wrist; he shut the door, locking it from the inside so we wouldn't be disturbed. Backing away slowly, he immediately pulled off his shirt. His chest was adorned with tattoos of wolves, moons, and several tribal bands. One caught my attention that had a red fox in front of a moon with the word "Clara" written around the moon.

"The fuck is that?" I yelled. "Looks like your body is already marked with some woman." I scoffed and folded my arms. Sean stood confused as he put his hand to his chest. It was located on his left pectoral muscle. His hand stroked it as his eyes softened.

"This is in honor of my Luna of our pack. Most warriors and trackers placed her name here after battling an evil rogue that wanted to destroy the peace we had worked so hard for. She is mated with the strongest Werewolf to date. She is not mine." His voice was laced with conviction and love for his Luna. I had only studied bits and pieces of Wolves, but I knew the significance of the Alpha and Luna. My tense shoulders relaxed as Sean came toward me.

"I would claim no one other than my mate. I have yet to taste the skin of another man. I've waited for you." Sean's fingers fumbled with the tie of my tunic. Once it untied, I slipped it over my head, revealing not only my pale skin but a few scales I couldn't help to hide. Sean was making me drop all my defenses. The bond was genuinely strong for me to deny, and I wanted nothing more than to show him who I was, but would he accept?

"Show me," he growled. "I want to see you, all of you." My scales rippled on my calves and forearms as my fins also came through. Slowly taking off my lower linens, my sharp, pointed teeth came to a point. My slitted golden eyes bore into his dark amber ones. "Fucking amazing." Sean leaned down and captured my lips without warning.

I had never kissed a man, only the occasional female Siren, but it never got me hard like this. His lips were powerful, demanding as he sought to enter my mouth; letting him through, he nicked his tongue on one of my fangs, which only made me groan. The metallic taste filled my mouth as my cock pressed against his belly. His was the same as mine, maybe even bigger. The way he pushed harder against my dick made me let out a groan of enjoyment.

Sean picked me up and threw me on the bed. My trousers were halfway down my ass as he threw his pants off. His dick had sprung to life as it strained against his boxers. My mouth instantly watered; I wonder how he tasted.

My mouth must have been drooling because the enormous smile thrown on his face was sexy as hell. Pulling off his boxers, his cock bounced as it hit his muscular torso. Fuck, I wanted to drive my hands around his body and squeeze the life out of him.

Sean hovered over me, kissing my stomach all the way to my lips, and sucked my tongue out of my mouth. I groaned as his hand trailed down and gripped my throbbing member. I could feel the pre-cum leak out of the tip as he swirled his thump at the top. "Fuck," I whispered as he sucked on the side of my neck.

"I'm going to suck you off, fuck you, and mark you as mine. You belong to me now." The vibrations reverberated into my crotch as I felt the sharp nips of kisses and bites go down my body.

His head was directly above my dick. First, he spread my legs wide and started nibbling on my balls. That about made me cum right there. "Damn!" I fisted the sheets beneath me; his other hand went south to my puckered hole as I felt him spit on his thumb. He probed the area as his mouth came to the tip of my cock and licked the spice from it.

A hum left his lips. "You taste so fucking good, Mate. I can't wait to swallow you whole." His mouth dove onto my cock as his thumb slipped into my backside. Feeling so full made me moan as I put my hands in his hair. The tighter I held onto him, the more vibrations left his mouth. His thumb continued to go in and out of me, no doubt to prepare me for what was to come. I felt my orgasm coming as I began moaning out his name.

"Sean," I breathed, "Fuck, I'm going to--" I spewed my warm seed into his mouth. His mouth bobbed continuously as he sucked me dry. He licked the cum that escaped down my balls. His mouth came to me again as I tasted myself, and I have to say, with his own taste and mine intertwined, it didn't taste half bad.

"Rollover," he commanded, and I complied. My dick was still hard and sensitive as I felt cool sheets beneath me trail up the bed. Sean widened my stance as he pulled me up to my knees. I heard a click. Looking back, he had a bottle of lube that came from a nearby drawer.

Kinky-ass Fae.

Sean kissed down my back, leaving trails of sparks as he palmed and massaged my ass. Several times he gripped my balls and hummed as his torso laid flat on my back. "Fuck, I love these. They are damn huge." My dick hardened painfully. I had never felt this before. It was almost unbearable. I wanted to release myself right then.

His dick prodded my puckered hole. I was worried; I'd done no penetration, and Sean wasn't a tiny Wolf. His girth was enormous, and he just might break me, but I would do anything to make him happy. "Slow and steady," he ruffed as the tip slid into me. My hole refused, wanting to push him out.

"Relax, my little shark," Sean whispered in my ear. "I'll take care of you." I released a breath as I let him guide himself in. Slowly, ever so slowly, he pushed farther until I eventually took his entire length. Full, I felt so complete.

Sean gripped my length, lube still on his palm as he began to slowly thrust into me. It was slow and tedious, making sure I was comfortable. "So, fucking tight, little shark. I could spew right now." His thrusts became more demanding as I moaned at the feeling of his enormous shaft. The slaps of our wet skin fueled the fire of the need for him. Poseidon, it feels like heaven! His hand matched his thrusts and jacked me off at the same rhythm.

My ass backed up, meeting him thrust for thrust. It was hot, and heavy, and our sweat made our bodies slick. We were both holding out, giving each other as much pleasure as we could. My ass was feeling exquisitely sore, but I wanted more.

"Fuck, I will not last much longer, little shark." Our breaths were panting; my hand job was getting reckless as I felt his cock contract in my ass. As he released, I released too, and the tickle of his canines brushed my neck. His torso was flat on me as he bit into the soft tissue of my shoulder. I let out a scream of ecstasy as I came over and over, drenching the sheets below me. Sean let go of the last grunt as he filled me and pulled out slowly, falling to the bed. His cock was covered in his own seed as I straddled him, nibbling his neck while his cock continued to drip.

Finding my marking spot, I licked it twice and plunged my own fangs into his shoulder. He moaned my name while his cock twitched and leaked again.

Our pants filled the room as he wrapped me in his arms and buried his nose into my neck. "Mine," he breathed harshly. Our liquids were all over each other, only reminding me of the pure pleasure a mate can really give.

"And you are mine," I breathed as his lips captured mine again in a slow, tantalizing kiss.

Our bodies continue to quiver under the sheets that Sean threw over us. Touching was going to be our thing. We couldn't get enough. Either my hand was on his face or chest, while his hands were around my waist or ass. I was at a place I never wanted to leave. Unfortunately, our bliss didn't last for long.

"Son, are you in there?" There was a loud knock at the door. My father's booming voice came from the doorway.

"Shit," I whispered. I wrapped a sheet around my body, and Sean stayed in bed, leaning back against the headboard. His muscles rippled as he put his arms behind his head. I almost wanted a second round. Sean winked and nodded to the door.

Opening it, I found my father breathing harshly with his face pale. "Melina has gone off to find Osirus!" he spat out.

"What!? That's insane! I'll get dressed and..."

"Lucca? Did you find your mate?" Father pointed to my shoulder. It was red, and I honestly felt weak. I swayed a bit as I put my hand on the doorway. Sean quickly ran up behind me, with his boxers on, to steady me.

"Are you?" My father's questioning gaze wanted to ask

what he already knew. Looking at both of us, he gave a smile.

"The goddess doesn't make mistakes." He patted my good shoulder while shaking Sean's hand. "Welcome to the family. Now, you can't help because you have both been marked. Go bond. Your brothers are heading out. I'm going myself."

"Father, no! I'll go! I'm the strongest of us!"

"No!" my father said sternly. "Don't. You are weak after a bonding. Melina would be furious. Now go, take care of my son."

Without another word, my father left me with Sean to go find my little sister.

Chapter 68

Osirus

Kane led the charge as the witches ran deeper into the wood. The trees grew sparse as their trunks widened. I had mounted Montu as I continued to venture further inward. Alaneo was behind me while Finley took his mate, Opal, back to the palace.

Now that the threat had retreated from the area, he could fly her back safely. The bleeding had stopped for the moment, but her body was still pale. Opal drifted in and out of consciousness as Finley lifted her to his body. "Finley, take her back and stay with her. The bond will help her heal." Finley gave a grateful nod and spread his wings to fly her back.

Kane headed the charge. The Wolves howled in victory, which could be too soon for comfort. Their ways of torture and magic were almost unbearable. If you thought the Fae were tricky and sneaky creatures, just wait until you have a vengeful witch after your neck. They could singe your nerves, inflict their injury, and bring your nerves back to life in a matter of seconds, so the pain hit you all at once.

Kane howled, his half Wolf-human form, scaring any remaining animals that were in the area. His black fur sprouted over his body, and his claws were thickened with blood. Enormous teeth lengthened over his muscular jaw as he licked them, slowly savoring the taste of his enemies. As much as I have messed with him in our past encounters, he scared the shit out of me. I'll never let him know that, though.

Clara would never let harm come to me. She and I had a sibling-like bond, but Kane didn't feel that way. He would rip my throat out in an instant the moment I ever upset his mate.

The claws of the wolves penetrated the dirt, flying upwards as our horses strode alongside. Howls from the trackers and runners had found the source of the coven. As our horses arrived, we saw several warlocks run right into a brick fence that was six feet tall. It was overgrown with vines and thorns and dirt, and muck covered any scent of the magical wards that encompassed it.

"What now?" I heard one Wolf say. "Charge it?" Kane grunted as he walked closer to the wall. The wall had been there for many years, erected during the Shifter War to keep Fae and shifters on their side of the land.

Kane took his claw, meaning to slice through the vines only to have his hand sucked into the ward. "It's penetrable," his Wolf Torin growled. "But this is too easy." Several Wolves growled as they pawed the ground, mouths still dripping with blood from the previous battle.

As a group, we had taken down at least half of their own warriors; the question was how many were left inside. This could be a trap, and even numbers wouldn't be able to save us.

"There aren't that many," Tulip strode out with Alec by her side. She had on just an oversized shirt over her body while Alec sported his birthing attire. "There aren't that many unethical witches, and the ones who were driven to power hid here. There may be 120 witches in total, but they are powerful."

Alec held onto Tulip by her waist. Not wanting to let her go again. I didn't blame him; he almost lost her. "You shouldn't be back here Tulip, we came to rescue you, and you now come back to join the fight?" Tulip laughed while standing in front of Alec so she could hide his growing erection for her.

"I was a warrior in my pack, and now being mated to one of the strongest warriors of Alpha Kane's pack, it was an easy decision. I live for the fight," she snarled. "Now, let's kick some ass so my sister can get hitched," Kane growled in approval while I unsheathed my sword as I jumped from my horse.

"What are we getting into, Tulip?"

Tulip stood in front of the supposed doorway. "Once you enter, you will find yourself in their courtyard. It is built like a castle on the inside. Four walls surround the perimeter. The basement holds the potions and spell books. Prinna is usually situated down there, but it has the most protection spells in that area. You won't be able to regenerate. Don't go down there if you can't handle being wounded. Shots fatal to humans will be fatal to you."

"Understood?" Kane growled as he licked his maw. Men and women shifted back into their wolves and growled in agreement. Kane, again, led the charge. We all burst into the courtyard that was swimming with witches and warlocks. Many held fireballs, ice streams, and some had electricity dancing on their fingers. The pure hatred in their eyes was daunting, but we never wavered.

Within seconds, hell broke loose as the wolves, and my men battled. My men were encouraged to use their gifted powers, and it didn't disappoint. Several Fae had force-fields that glowed around their bodies, and no spell could touch them. Some had strength that matched an ogre. several even spout out their own electricity from their chests. Swords swung and claws ripped into bare flesh as the witches and warlocks tried to maintain the fight.

My sword swung as a jolt of electricity was flung at my back. Slitting the opponent's throat in front of me, the witch behind me took it as an opportunity to dig her nails into my back. Shaking my head, I pushed myself off the ground, causing the witch to fall backward as I lunged forward and impaled her with my sword. Not waiting to see if the light left her eyes, I pulled it out to head to the basement.

I was going to kill the queen of this operation. Once the queen of this evil hive was destroyed, then all hope for the coven to revive itself later would be lost. Kane was howling, taking on three or four witches at a time. Their spells had no effect as he swiped at them once, causing them to fall to the floor.

Tulip called for me at the corner of the courtyard. Rushing to her, I saw the dried blood on her chest. Alec wasn't far, he was keeping the Witches preoccupied so they would not detect us. "Down here," she rushed. "Prinna is hiding there. She doesn't think anyone will get in. There is a ward hiding her smell, but I know she is there," Tulip panted. "That's where she kept them." She let out a whimper. "They are all gone, all the prisoners. Alec won't let me go down, but Alpha will join you in a moment."

"Leave Tulip, your job is done." Before she said another word, I rushed down the stairs, my hair flying about as the wind blew upward. The stairs were dark, wet, and the smell of mold tickled my nose. Drips of water hit the puddles as I quickly stomped through the mess.

The smell of urine, blood, and feces became stronger as I passed by a few cells. Pixies laid dead in the corner. I tightened my grip around the sword. They took all the blood their little bodies had. I would make Prinna suffer. I would drain her of her own blood and let the Dragon Shifters eat her body.

As I rounded the corner, there was chanting. The loose locks of her hair covered her face as Prinna sat with her legs crossed around a pentagram circle on the floor. Candles surrounded her as a newborn fawn laid dead on one side of the ring and a live snake on the other. It hissed and coiled up as it saw me as I approached the lighted room.

My footsteps were light as I came forward. My tunic was

ripped down the middle as my chest was shown bear to the light. I tried to will myself to absorb as much light as the candles could give me. Her aura was dark, the darkest black and purples I had ever seen. This witch was a new type of evil; it almost surpassed the Rogue King Clara had fought a few months ago.

Her melancholy laugh echoed through the basement walls. "Welcome, Fae King. Where is your little mate?" My fangs emerged as I held a tightened grip with both hands on my sword. "You know that little bitch ruined my damn plans, right?"

Prinna's body lifted off the floor without moving her muscles; her body was limp as she floated closer to me. The long hair had her face completely covered as it hungover on the front of her chest. "I haven't lost yet, Fae King. I still have my ways of getting what I want. I just will need to be less diplomatic." I went to swing my sword, and it hovered over my head and held its place in the air. The more I tried to move my arms, the more pain I felt in my wrists.

My whole body was shaking as I now tried to move my legs. They were stuck to the floor, like a fly on sticky paper. Prinna laughed cruelly as she approached. Her hair showed the left side of her old face. Prinna was once said to be beautiful, but the black magic she used took her appearance. Black magic gave you the power, but it took something in return until its just dues were paid back.

"I'm this close," her fingers showed a pinching motion, "this close to getting the blood I need to make this coven unstoppable. While you bid your time hunting us down, I have my best warlocks finding your Dragon in his lonely cave," she cackled. "That had to be the easiest diversion I've ever imagined!"

This Bitch...

"So, you would sacrifice half your coven for a diversion?" I spat.

"Of course, only a witch of my caliber would understand

such sacrifices. Only the strong will be left, and once the Dragon's blood has been obtained, I'll fix my looks and take control of not only Bergarian, but Earth as well."

Prinna's rotten teeth gleamed in the low light as she continued her insults; I, on the other hand, was working on releasing something darker than she thought. Prinna used dark magic to expel her power, and with most Fae being that of light, magic could cripple us instantly. I felt my darker power surge forth, wrapping around my light and storing it until I could use it once again. Feeling my aura change from a sunny yellow to a bright red, my wings blackened behind me. Prinna stopped laughing as she saw my brightened skin become tan as I twitched my fingers.

It took me time to switch over. I haven't had the chance to enhance my skill, but I was faring better than anticipated. Prinna hiked her skirt as I could move one of my legs and took out a dagger; being able to dodge at the last moment, she pushed the blade into my right shoulder. I howled out in pain, gripping the bloodied wound. Before I repositioned myself, she stabbed the other shoulder and pushed me to the ground.

"Impossible, you are a light Fae!" Prinna sat above me as I struggled to complete my new form; I could feel the whites of my eyes grow dark, and hers widened. She pulled the knife from my arm as I wrestled her. Two shoulders were maimed, and I was now the same physical strength as this witch. I pushed her off me, but the pressure she had on my chest became unbearable.

"Do you hear that?" She smirked as she held the knife at my throat. The wolves began howling, whimpering, and yipping. "That is the anti-healing surge. I completed it before you arrived, and it is now just kicking in. Your wolves will no longer regenerate while my coven can.

A shot of adrenaline fueled my anger as I threw her off me. I had to destroy her on my own. I could no longer wait for Kane while he saved his own Wolves. The dagger at my side brushed my thigh as I pulled it from its smaller sheath. Prinna's nails elongated with black sludge dripping from them.

I felt my chest tighten as I took a knee. My body had almost completed itself, and the darkness was too much to bear. A nearby mirror showed black veins coming from my chest as it seeped through my neck. Prinna gritted her teeth as she lunged to my weakening form.

Holding my arm out for the brace of impact, her body stopped with the dagger still hanging in the air. She continued to push through, but to no avail did she wrestle with the invisible barrier she was under.

"No," she growled. "You can't!"

"Fight fire with fire, huh, Prinna? The goddess thinks so." I stood up to a standing position and concentrated on healing my wounds as she stood unmoving. Her body continued to twitch her way out, but she was trapped and wouldn't leave this basement alive.

Grabbing my sword, I went to stab her through the gut, only for it to pause as it gently poked her black corset. "Ha, I have my own ways to protect myself. Your Elven steel won't touch me."

Dust rained on us as I dropped my sword. A loud roar came from above. It was loud enough to loosen a few bricks and rock in the basement. I knew that roar. I smirked back at Prinna, who was even more furious. The face was red as her wicked face contorted in pure loathing.

Screams were heard as I felt Horus land in the middle of the courtyard. Witches were shouting spells instead of casting them through their minds, only strengthening them. The Wolves' claws scratched the cobblestone as they ran out of the coven, no doubt hurt and trying to get away. Kane's roar was heard, letting me know of their retreat.

Kane just doesn't give up. It wasn't in his nature. I bit my bottom lip as I wondered what was going to happen.

Witches continued to yell and scream, and I heard Horus'

loud growl shook the ground. Feeling significant vibration and the heat that sunk into the basement, Horus blew out his fire. It reached halfway down the stairs, searing all the lost prisoners.

All was silent after the fire had receded until I heard a voice that was all too familiar.

"Come out, you dumb bitch, and give me my mate!"

She's getting spanked for this.

Chapter 69

Melina

I flew out of the palace like my rear was on fire. I got halfway up to the top of the trees until I realized I had no weapon with me. I was donned in just the dress that Osirus had left me in. A baby blue lace dress with an intricate weaving of baby's breath at the hems. My boobs were basically falling out. No doubt Osirus wanted a glimpse at them when he got home. Going into battle looking like a child would be hilarious, and no one was going to take me seriously. On top of that, I have no fighting experience and no weapon to yield, as explained by my father.

I needed a plan and a good one.

I flew up to the largest tree next to the palace to think. I couldn't fly in guns blazing because, in fact, there were no guns. Scratching my chin, trying to think my way into this predicament by not getting blown up to bits, I heard some arguing.

Perking my head up and flying to the very top, I poked my head from the branches and saw three warlocks standing out by Horus's cave.

Poo on a stick. They were screwed. Don't wake a sleeping Dragon.

The three men continued to argue. "Well, how in the hell was I supposed to know the spell wouldn't work? Prinna gave it to me," he yelled at the other two.

"Just go in there and jab the syringe in between his scales, pull what we need, and let's get out. We can't bring the whole Dragon," said the shorter of the three.

"Are you nuts? That thing will wake up and blow me to bits. I should have stayed back and got in on the fighting. This recon shit ain't my forte." The last warlock scoffed and grabbed the small dagger.

"Since you idiots couldn't do a levitation spell right, I'll go in and extract the blood, but I'm taking the credit. I've got a numbing spell, and he won't feel a damn thing."

That got my attention. If he gets Horus's blood, we were all screwed. We would have a bunch of crazy spelling casting mess in Bergarian, and who knows where else. I landed softly on the ground and tip-toed to the cave. My back was completely flat to the wall while the other two stood guard, kicking dirt and telling each other what idiots they were.

Since they said they were, in fact, idiots, I grabbed a rock and chucked it to the other side of the clearing. Their heads both perked up, and they both looked at each other and then behind them, completely opposite of where the rock landed.

Son of Bitchachos.

"Look what we have here," said the taller one. Wow, that was a completely terrible line. Might as well say, 'did you fall from heaven because you look like an angel.'

"Hey gorgeous, did you fall from heaven because-"I put my hand up to stop his excessive talking.

Goddess, they are idiots.

I needed to change my tactic and get to Horus and fast.

"No, actually, I'm a snowflake," I swayed my hips as I approached them, making sure I flutter my wings for good measure. "Because I think I'm falling for you." I make sure not to look either in the eye, otherwise, I would burst out laughing. Both straightened up and adjusted their robes as

I circled around to get a good glimpse inside the cave. The other warlock's lantern was heading down the long cave. He hadn't reached Horus yet.

Both warlocks stepped forward while nudging each other, annoyed that they each approached. "I'm sorry, my little snowflake. Which one were you speaking to?" They both glared at each other while I played with my necklace.

"I was hoping both," I cringed internally. The thought of anyone other than my mate made me physically sick. They kept walking towards me, whispering to each other when I realized this was as far as I could go to get them away from the cave. I started humming, thinking of having them fall asleep just beside the cave making no noise.

"What a pretty melody," one yawned as they continued closer. It wasn't strong enough. I would have to actually sing something, but my mind was shot. No lyrics were coming to me, so I did the next best thing I have dubbed the name, 'the Ariel." My mind went to the scene where she sang to the evil witch who could suck in her voice in the tiny shell necklace. Concentrating on the melody and having them be lulled to sleep, it started working. They both sat beside the cave, leaning on each other. Both of them curled up like babies, and once their breaths evened out, I sprinted to the mouth of the cave.

The light was still swaying back and forth; dang, this was a deep cave. Horus would sleep, so I started screaming for him to wake up. "Horus! You are in danger! Wake up!!" I yelled as I sprinted on the jagged rocks.

There was a growl and a high-pitched scream from the other warlock as I heard a loud snap. The ground below me rumbled as I felt the heavy breaths of Horus ascending the cave. Running back out into the light, Horus stood tall in all his glory. His scales shined as a drip of blood left his lips.

"D-did you eat him?" I cried, not really wanting to know the answer. Horus gave a stiff nod and took his snake-like tongue to clean up the mess. Gagging a bit, I shook my head and came back to the real reason for what we needed to do. Get Osirus.

"Horus, Osirus is in trouble. The Blood Coven is hidden, and I don't know where they are, but he needs help." Horus huffed and crouched down so I could mount. Gripping ahold of his horns, I stiffened and remembered that the witches would want his blood.

"You can't get hurt, Horus. The witches want your blood to make their magic stronger..." Before I could finish, Horus reared back his head and gave a laugh. A dang laugh, this Dragon was laughing at me. He shook his head and jumped in mid-air as we flew through the sky.

I had no clue where I was going, but Horus sure did. With three large flaps with his wings, he was in the air, high above the trees. The trees around the palace became small as the trees up ahead were taller than the palace. As we were flying, I could imagine the trunks of the tree being vast. What fun it would be to run through that forest!

Howling came from up ahead as I saw wolves falling out of a brick wall; there must be a spell barricading them in. Horus huffed at me as if he knew what I thought as he dove closer to the ground. His feet landed with a thump while leaving large claw indentions in the dirt.

"Your Majesty!" I sat up straight as one of Osirus' warriors appeared from the fence. "You shouldn't be here. His Majesty-" I put my hand up like Osirus does when he wants people to shut up.

"Your King isn't here, is he? I am, so where are they? What's going on?" I clipped.

"T-they are inside. There is a spell blocking healing abilities, and everyone will be slaughtered!" I nodded my head as Horus looked behind himself, giving me a wink. He wanted in, and he wanted to steal the show.

"Get back in there and get everyone out. We are coming in, and Horus will torch the place." The warrior fell to the ground before launching himself back into the wall. Backing up, Horus took a running start and dove through the barrier. Horus's roar was so loud it shook the walls of the fake castle they made. The bricks crumbled as everyone stared at the massive Dragon before them.

Looking at the half-Wolf, half-human beast in front of me, I instantly knew it was Alpha Kane. They said he was terrifying, and no doubt my once brave face held worry. Kane growled for an answer while everyone started running away from Horus. "We're gonna torch it, get everyone out." I didn't yell, but I didn't have to because of Kane's incredible hearing.

The warrior I had sent in had gathered up the rest of Osirus' warriors as Horus began shaking the ground with the stomps of his caws. His wings flapped, hitting several warlocks to the ground, and guarding the door. The vibrations from Horus's throat let me know something was coming from it, and it was going to be big. Kane looked one more time my way before I threw a thumbs up and Horus let out his grunty breath.

Flames seared the entire walls. Warlocks were screaming, several still on fire as they tried to leave through the exit. Horus chomped on several warlocks, blood smearing the cobblestone pathway. No one was getting out alive in this secret hideaway. The fire had already consumed the drapes, tables, and furniture that was laid out recklessly. Bodies were charred and left lifeless on the floor. It reminded me of the movie Kill Bill when she takes on almost the whole restaurant of fighters. Except I wasn't bloody, and I had a dang Dragon instead of a sword.

My scene was better.

Horus puffed out his chest, happy with the result until I heard footsteps coming from behind us. A sizeable crowd entered, and Horus didn't seem worried. My father and my brothers, minus Lucca, came marching in with their tridents and swords. My father took one look at me and let out a sigh of relief.

"Look, Dad! I'm riding a Dragon!" My father rolled his eyes

as he stuck his trident in the ground and took off his armored gloves.

"Hey, at least she isn't riding Osirus?" one of my brothers jeered while my father smacked up upside the head.

"Owie."

Horus walked forward, sniffing, and putting his head near a basement door or what was left of a door. A large, charred opening was left. I dismounted and felt my heart pull to the bottom of the basement. It was dark, dreary, and thankfully dry since Horus's flames went halfway down. Still, I wasn't going down there. I've watched too many horror movies, and that is where you end up dead.

"Hey!" I yelled down to the basement. "Come out, you dumb bitch, and give me my mate!" I smiled triumphantly at my fantastic Joan Of Arc words while my father shook his head.

"Princesses don't cuss," he grumbled as he pulled me away from the entryway.

"Well, good, because I'm not a princess. I'm a damn queen!"

"Right on!" one brother replied and gave me a high five.

One set of footsteps came up the stairs; the light cast a shadow so no one could see who it was. I did, though. My heart palpated as Osirus emerged from the depths of the basement. Dried blood was on his tunic, and his skin was no longer white but a light tan with his black wings. His black obsidian eyes glared into the sun until he looked at me.

Uh, I hope he wasn't mad that I saved his butt. His eyes lightened instantly, and his dark wings and skin vanished. He ran up to me and engulfed me in an enormous hug. "My darling, what did I tell you!" he cried as he buried his face in my neck.

"To behave?" I whispered.

"And you didn't," he growled.

"That was one rule I was willing to break for punishment." I put both of my hands on his face and gave him a searing kiss. A few of my brothers groaned as Osirus snaked his arms around my waist. Horus gave a little bite to my tush as I squealed.

"Right, right," I pulled away, but Osirus didn't let go of my hand. "I think Horus wants to eat the witch down there." I pointed to the entrance. My brothers nodded as Osirus told them how to bring her up.

She was frozen, unable to move, but she could talk. Boy, could she talk. There were phrases and words I had never heard of before. My father came behind me to cover my ears as they brought Prinna in front of Horus. Horus's eyes gleamed with excitement as Prinna tried to back away.

"He gets stronger the more magical entities he eats," Osirus explained. "You helping him consume a coven Witch has only put him in further debt with us, even though I tell him he can leave." Horus eyed me and gave his little Dragon bow he does while I clung to Osirus. "I thought the witches would get to him. That's why I left him out of the fight, but I guess you knew better, darling."

"Yup—" I popped the p. "I did." No, I didn't. I had no clue what I was doing. Osirus pitched my butt as I rubbed the pain away.

Osirus grabbed me and pulled me to his chest while I heard the screams quiet, and the cracking of bones invade my ears. The sound alone was going to give me nightmares, let alone all the burned bodies.

Chapter 70

Melina

After the adrenaline slowly left my body, I understood everything I saw. It was so much blood and carnage. The crisp figures lying in the courtyard made my stomach churn. I had not grown up with so much violence and this being my first battlefield, was shocking, and I knew I was not made for this kind of life. Now that Osirus was back with my family and me by my side, I could finally relax.

Until the dang coronation.

Tulip was safe, we were safe, and it was all said and done. Letting out an enormous sigh, Osirus put his hand on the small of my back. My father started directing orders for my brothers to check for anyone left alive around the area and take care of it before anyone healed.

"Let's get you home, darling," Osirus spoke as he waved for Horus to come around. Horus stood triumphant as he licked his lips after obtaining a coven witch in his belly. A few glides later, he stood before us and leaned his neck down. I mounted first with Osirus' help, and he sat behind me, holding my waist. Horus walked through the barrier that was now crumbling, and there stood behind us was a large stone structure of what was the Blood Coven. The glamour spell had broken. It was attached to a great stone wall that had been there for centuries.

"This building connected to the wall served as border control between the two nations during the Shifter War. The Vampires' nation is on the other side; it's best to steer clear of them now." I hummed in acknowledgment, not wanting to have a history lesson at the moment. I still had to store the memories of what happened just this afternoon, and that was going to take a bit to get over.

Horus took to the sky, with long gentle strokes of his wings. The scales shone brighter as he ascended the clouds. "You know, you are still not without punishment." My body stiffened a bit at his words. "I told you to behave, and you deliberately put yourself in danger."

"I think you liked it I disobeyed you. I think you wanted to spank me," I chided. His grip around my waist grew tighter as his lips brushed my ear.

"I would love nothing more than to spank you, but what you did deserves more than that." His voice was husky and low as he bit my ear a little too hard. I immediately clamped my legs around Horus's neck, and he started growling lowly. Osirus let out a loud laugh as he kissed the temple of my head.

Once we arrived close to the palace, we saw Cricket running around with Elaine. She looked happy, healthy even. Her smile was wide, and her skin had lost the terrible grey color. Her wings were out as she showed Cricket how to use them to make him run faster since his wings were not large enough to fly.

"That's it!" She laughed heartedly as he began flapping feverishly. "Keep going!" Cricket saw us in the sky as Horus started his descent into the front courtyard. The flowers and leaves blew, causing petals to fly about as he landed. Horus kept his talons in as he landed on the soft grass, being sure not to destroy the lawn.

"Melina!" Cricket screamed as he hugged my legs. "You

found my mama!" I hugged him tightly as Everett and Braxton approached.

"Eye, that she did," Everett bragged. "And to think all she did was save the boy from getting his hand cut off by the baker." Elaine gasped as she grabbed hold of Cricket again.

"What happened?" she cried.

"It was nothing," I sighed as I pet Cricket's head. "The orphanage didn't have enough money for food, but we made sure it was corrected. Cricket was just trying to feed the younger children." Elaine kissed Cricket's cheeks, calling him his brave boy while he tried to push her away.

"Not around my friends, mama!" Elaine's eyes investigated the distance as if she was looking for someone.

"It was Daphne, wasn't it? She taxed them heavily, didn't she?" Osirus grabbed me by the waist with one hand and rubbed my arm with the other. I nodded my head solemnly as she clutched one hand to her chest.

"I'm sorry," I nodded in confirmation.

"Is she…?" Osirus put me behind him as he stepped forward.

"She is no longer with us." He put his arm over his heart and bowed slightly. Elaine gripped him tightly in a hug while Osirus stiffened. Elaine let out a few tears clutching Osirus and nodded into his chest.

"It was for the best." Wiping a few tears, Cricket came up and wrapped his little arms around Elaine. Petting his hair lovingly, she grabbed his hand and smiled. "Let's go inside, hmm? Papa will be back soon." Cricket jumped excitedly and raced to the palace while Elaine walked after him.

My shoulders slumped as she walked away. Elaine had been through so much and now dealing with the loss of a daughter that wanted nothing more than to get the power her father wanted.

The suns were setting as the warriors began emerging from the trees. Some were bloodied from battle, but their wounds were healing. They weren't healing as fast as the

Werewolves, but they would be good as new in time. The Wolves had left to go back to their pack to prepare for the upcoming coronation ceremony here at the palace.

More stress. Yay!

As we walked in, there was chaos running through the hallways. Several maids and butlers were running with flowers, linens, bed sheets, candles, and one group of men were carrying an entire throne. Osirus rolled his eyes and pulled me towards our hallway.

"What's going on?" I questioned as he continued to pull me while I watched the chaos. One woman dropped a stack of plates that crashed to the floor. Nissa came running by and checked the maid before her voice changed an octave higher. "Quick! Someone needs to go to the pottery store and have fifty royal plates made. They must be in light mint green! I don't care about the price!" Two servants left while another group swept up the mess.

"Now that the threat has been done and over with, my mother is frantic trying to prepare the Coronation and Binding Ceremony. The guest wings need to be prepared, decorations need to be hung, and food. Gods, the food," he whined. "I forgot to have you pick your favorite flavor sponge cake for a surprise."

I gave him a disgusting look. "Are you serious right now? I know I love food and all, but we just got back from the worst blood bath I had ever seen, and you are worried about my favorite sponge cake?" Lifting one of my eyebrows, Osirus rubbed his forehead.

"You're right," he sighed.

"But if you are asking," I chimed in, "almond flavor with the strawberry syrup and chocolate shavings." Osirus chuckled. "Aaaand whipped cream."

We found our family hallway swarming with maids. There was a new plush white carpet laid down the hallway. Enormous flowers were flanking each doorway. They were beautiful blues, purples, and even hints of yellow in every bunch. Tiny Pixies were dusting each petal with small pieces of glitter, and when the light caught the tip of one, its sparkle touched the high ceilings with light.

The aroma also filled the hallway as we walked by each bouquet. We headed to our room where dinner was waiting for us, but I still had not seen my father or brothers return. I had seen no one besides Braxton and Everett. "Where is Finley?" I asked. Osirus opened the door and led me to our private dining room and had me sit down.

"Opal was stabbed by Daphne." I gasped while Osirus lifted the covering to my food. To my surprise, it was a large steak, just like the one I had at the Shifter Dragon's territory. My heart wanted to burst. He remembered how much I loved eating steak. His plate was filled with the same, along with mashed potatoes and asparagus.

"Opal is healing well. She will be up and ready for the ceremony. Finley is with her." Osirus took his fork and pointed to my food. "Please eat." His demeanor went cold as I began cutting and eating my food. I wanted to ask about the others, but the mood of the room didn't allow it.

Little moans left my lips as I tasted my medium-cooked steak. I wondered if Horus thought Prinna tasted like a steak? I snuffed a giggle as Osirus eyed me suspiciously. Clearing my throat, I began eating again. Someone was in a mood.

I patted my lips when I was done and touched one petal on the flower arrangement on the table. I couldn't get over how soft it felt. Osirus sat there, staring at me like a hunter to prey. His eyes weren't the deep amber color but were covered in black. Osirus stood up without warning, startling me as he walked to the door. Sitting dumbfounded, I sat as he opened our bedroom door.

"Go shower." His voice was low as I slowly got up. My eyes never left his as he held the door and ushered me in. Osirus walked to our large window. The moon was climbing high. I grabbed my nightwear and walked to the bathroom. A few light Pixies flew by the window, letting trails of glitter and sparkle fall to the ground. Osirus stood there, hands behind his back while gazing over the sea as he waited for me to leave the room.

Shutting the door quietly and stripping out of my clothes, I felt a slight shiver. The room felt colder than usual, but maybe it was because Osirus was sore with me. I disobeyed him by going off and finding him, but I wasn't just going to sit and wait while I felt his pain. Besides, I had Horus with me. He wouldn't let any harm come to me. "I helped," I whispered to myself while I checked the temperature of the water.

Three heads rained down warm water as I entered. I was grateful that my monthly had slowed down to a barely-there trickle. Today's stress made my body suck whatever I had in me back up into my body. My body thought I would need all the blood I could get because I was going to die. There you go; my body couldn't even trust me.

I sighed heavily, my body facing the wall as my hair became drenched with water. The icy shiver I had returned. My ears perked up, and I felt a few scales release on my body when I felt a warm hand wrap around my stomach and another around my throat. My body relaxed slightly. Tingles erupted on my skin.

Osirus' erection was pressed up against my butt. He moved in closer, almost burying it between my ass. I was pushed up against the shower wall, my nipples tightened as the coolness of the wall tickled around me. Osirus' lips brushed up against my ear while he tightened his hand around my neck. "You disobeyed me, darling." His breath was ragged as the hand on my stomach now lowered and traced my inner thigh. My body shivered while I let out a breathy moan.

Feeling Osirus' lips smirk on my skin gave me whole new wetness to my pussy. "Now, I want you to call me, 'Sir,' you lost your privilege to call me daddy." I whimpered. The hand caressing my inner thigh left me cold as he pulled away, and instead, a large smack was left on my ass. The wet skin and the echo of the shower made it sound worse than it really was. His grip on my neck was tight, but it was delightfully so. It turned me on more the way he had control.

That was one of the many things I loved about Osirus. He knew how to push my buttons. Osirus could take complete control and let me experience things and know he would never hurt me. I didn't have to think, only feel the pleasure he was giving me.

Another smack woke me from my thoughts as he bit down on my mark. Trickles of red trailed down to my naval as the spike of pleasure was felt at my core. My legs wanted to give out, but he twisted me to face him. "What happened to my strong little queen?" he growled before he impaled his tongue in my mouth. His kiss was painful, pleasurable, and so damn hot. My hands left my body as I went to put my hands in his hair, only for him to grab my hands and put them above me. The water trickled down our bodies as I struggled to get free.

"You are mine, darling." His other hand went straight to my ass and squeezed it tight. "If I say not to follow me into a battle, you listen." Another smack echoed through the shower. "You are not to cum," he growled as he grabbed my leg and threw it over his hip. In one quick thrust, he entered me. It was achingly delicious as he thrust into my weepy core.

The head of his cock and the position he was holding me hit my g-spot just right. It was rough, and intense, and I wanted to cream all over him. If we weren't in a shower, I would have been just as wet from sweat. He was relentless. His muscles tightened as his chest rose and fell with his heated breaths.

"Osirus, please," I begged, but was met with another slap under the leg he was holding. My other leg was becoming weak, trying to hold myself up.

"What do you call me?" He fucked me harder. In and out and pushed until another slap, more brutal than the others,

VERA FOXX

came down on me.

A moan left my lips. "Sir, please," I begged quietly, and that devilish Fae smirk fell on his lips.

"Not yet." He fucked me three more times until he pulled out. His cock was glistening with juices. It bobbed as he turned me around. The bench in the large shower was to our left as he forced me over. "Hands-on the bench and bend over." Before I could spread my legs, he was already inside me.

His claws lengthened as I felt them scratch my skin. "Holy shit, baby." His legs started shaking. His resolve was wavering. He was going to come, and my body was begging, no pleading with me to let it go. Holding it on, I let out a frustrated scream. My clit was pounding. I was surprised he couldn't feel it on his own cock as he slipped in and out of me.

"Please!" I cried again as I held onto the bench. He was just too damn good. Osirus yelled out my name over and over as I felt him rip ropes of his cum inside me. He came so hard.

I swore I could feel it in my throat. Osirus' thrust became longer and slower. My pussy was frustrated as it tingled for a release. He came before I could, and I wanted to hit him for it. He left me high and dry!

But I disobeyed him. I gritted my teeth. I kept quiet. My body demanded it as his flaccid cock fell out of me. I kept my hands on the bench, waiting for his following command. My ass was sore from the hefty slaps on my skin. Osirus' chest leaned on my back while I kept my body hunched over. "Such a great job you did," he cooed, "taking your punishment like the queen you are." He kissed my shoulder, and my knees buckled, getting ready to land on the hard floor. Once my knees hit, I fell into something soft. Osirus had placed a towel so my knees wouldn't get bruised. If I wasn't so angry, I would think it would be the sweetest thing.

"Since you did so well, I think I'll reward you." Feeling the tip of something vibrating made me straighten my back. Osirus pushed the foreign object into my body. It felt like an average penis but not the warm cock I usually felt. Between being on the edge of an orgasm and the vibrations of this object moving in and out of my body, I crashed. I crashed and burned like the witches from the Blood Coven. I let out a battle cry as Osirus' grip held onto me as he continued to pump it in and out of my pussy.

I felt another wave crash down on me while he held me up. Once it passed, he pulled it from me. From a glimpse, I saw nothing but a blue vibrating fake cock. As much as I enjoyed my release, I wanted Osirus, not a damn substitute. Plus, it wasn't as big as my mate.

"Behave, and you can cum on the real thing, my darling." I sighed, defeated, as he pulled me to sit on the bench.

Osirus washed my hair as I worked on regaining my strength from the strenuous activity. Who knew standing there to get fucked would wear you out so much?

He combed my hair and dried it all while drying both of our bodies. He carried me with one arm around my back and one under my legs and led me to the bed. One of his freshly cleaned tunics was laid out, and he put it over my head so he could tuck me in. Osirus didn't put on anything and scooted behind me, holding our exhausted bodies.

Trails of his kisses on my shoulder made me hum in contentment. "Tomorrow will be a busy day, darling. I need you to get plenty of rest and enjoy yourself tomorrow." I hummed, half listening. I was halfway to dreamland before I felt his cock rub up against my ass while the other hand grabbed my breast as we both fell asleep.

Chapter 71

Osirus

What have I done?

I growled as soon as I felt Melina's body slumped in my arms. Her breathing was steady as I felt the tiny breaths on my arm. She was sleeping peacefully while I had too many thoughts running through my mind.

I lost control today. I don't lose control when it comes to my love, and here I was, only a month into our relationship, and I fucking lost it. I grew up learning to control my emotions. Entrap them in the corner of my mind and never let it out. I was the next in line to be king. It was required of me to be the stoic, fearless leader. Everyone feared me, respected, and listened and obeyed.

Not my Melina. My mate.

When Melina rode in on Horus, I knew the majestic beast would keep her safe, and he would not have brought her if he thought otherwise. Still, Melina disobeyed a direct order from me. I told her to behave, sit tight, and wait for my return, yet she still came for me. She doesn't understand the mate bond very well. Her education is limited. The striking pain she felt in her body when I was hit would only make her jump into action.

My actual anger should be to whoever told her I was in danger. They made her worry and jump to a ridiculous plan. I gripped her a little tighter, causing her to fall back into my chest.

Melina was in real danger today, and there would have been nothing for me to do to stop it if she were in trouble. She came in triumphant, thankfully, on a beast she had ridden only a handful of times. The battle cry she yelled for me and the worry and want made me swell with pride that she would risk her life for me. Melina wanted the sorceress or Daphne as dead as the rest of us.

There she was, trying to come to save me. She would have nothing to fear, because I told her I would protect her from the beginning. I would battle the demon king himself and any other creature that stood in our way of being together. I should be flattered, honored even that my mate, who had no fighting experience, no muscles to compete in physical sparring, would come for me.

Melina showed how much she cared for and how much she loved me, and I spat it back in her face because of my pride and my terrible personality trait for complete control. Melina liked control from how I picked out her clothes and babied her each morning; she wanted to be taken care of, especially in the bedroom. But she disobeyed me purposefully and came into harm's way.

I didn't like it. She didn't listen, but Melina was her own person. She lets me do things to her I never thought possible. The once closed-off, stubborn, and independent woman broke down her walls for me and let me care for her, love her, and protect her, all while not understanding anything in this world. Melina surrendered herself, and I have not yet submitted myself to her.

My chest tightens at the thought of me being too rough with her this evening. I wanted to put her in her place, let her know I was in control, and I feared it was too much.

The hours have slipped by, and I still cannot sleep. My

thoughts wandering what my darling is dreaming and thinking. I swore I wouldn't invade her dreams after being apart from her. I couldn't invade her privacy now. There was no distress in her sleeping as she nuzzled closer into my neck. But why did I feel the heaviness in my heart?

Guilt.

It overwhelmed me. I'm angry at myself and the situation I've put us both in. I wanted her safe, but I still had to give her the independence she has spoken of from the beginning. Melina's getting ready to take on a role so vital to the kingdom, being strapped down to one place and taking on a great responsibility she never knew she would have.

Melina would be at my side, ruling an entire nation. She's given up her freedom to be attached to a devilish Fae, and I go and take her orgasm from her.

Fuck.

The frustration became too much, and I could feel damn tears pool in my eyes. I don't remember the last time I cried. It could have been when I was just a little thing sparing with my brothers. Melina has to wake up. She has to tell me she was all right. I needed to depend on her now to hold me together, or I would fall apart.

"Melina," I whispered in her ear. I dropped a kiss to her cheek as she stirred. The window lightened as I saw several light Pixies dust the window. They could sense their king was upset, something I rarely show, if ever. I waved them away, but they still sat quietly on the balcony edge.

"Darling, please wake up," I pleaded like a child. Melina stirred and rubbed the sleep from her eyes.

"Osirus? What's wrong?" Her voice was rough as she looked up. Her hair was a mess, and her cheeks were red from lying up against my chest.

"I'm sorry," was all I could mutter as I gripped her tightly. "Goddess, I am so sorry."

"Osirus." Her voice was muffled as her lips tickled my chest. "What are you sorry for? Are you all right?"

"I'm sorry," I muttered again. "I shouldn't have taken my anger out on you like that." Melina sat in the bed while I held back a sob. Tears were forming now, and they were too heavy to stay in my eyes.

"Osirus," she cooed as she smiled. "There isn't anything to be sorry about. Why are you so upset?" I buried my face in her stomach and clasped her. Her hands brushed my hair, smoothing out the knots.

"I was too rough with you earlier. I was so angry with you coming to the middle of a battle. I worried for your safety, and you didn't listen to me. I did what I did to show you I was in control, and I regret every moment. I shouldn't deny you anything...."

Melina started shushing me and tickled my bareback. "First, you did not hurt me physically. I was mad you didn't let me orgasm with you. That's kind of our thing, so I missed that." Her hands grabbed both sides of my face and lifted me up to her face. A quick kiss and adoration from her eyes gave me a bit of relief.

"I liked everything else, though," she winked. "I know you need control, and you don't like it when I get my spurt of 'I do what I want' attitude. But I think that is why the goddess put us both together. We both need to be evened out a bit, don't you think?" Melina smiled brightly at me and kissed my lips softly. "Just know if you are ever in danger, I'll find you just as you will find me. We can both be thrown into the wrestling ring of passion until both of our desires are met. How does that sound?" Her eyes lit up like the summer solstice.

"How about we both just stay out of danger but still do the lovemaking?" I sucked back a sniff. She threw her head back and laughed.

"Of course, as long as you still are the dominating one in bed." Her voice grew a few octaves lower than made my lower region stir.

"How about I make it up to you then, let you cum around my cock?" I sat up and grabbed her bottom lip and gave it a suck. A breathy moan left her lips as she met me back with her needy lips.

"I would like that," she breathed. Her eyes were filled with wonderful love. I kissed her softly, our mouths entangled with one another, just like our first kiss. We explored each other, tasted, and savored. She was my main course and dessert all into one.

One of her hands ran through my hair while the other wiped away my tears as I felt her body against me. Her tunic was discarded as we caressed each other softly. Gently tugging each other's hair, getting lost in our touches. Heaven couldn't compare to the traces she left on my skin.

We slowed our kiss as she pulled away and softly kissed both my eyes. My eyes continued to water, not of anger or guilt, but of the pure love I had for her. How could a bond be this powerful? How could a love like this exist?

I could feel the wetness pool between her legs. Her hand trailed down my right side as our breaths evened out as our bare bodies lightly touched each other.

"Make love to me," she whispered. What my queen wants, she gets. I parted her legs and positioned the tip of my cock at her entrance. She gasped as I slowly sank into her. It was like making love to her for the first time as I slid slowly into her wet cavern. Both of our eyes shut so we could feel the ways our bodies became one. Her pussy was tight as it took my girth. I felt every crevice of her body as I slowly pulled back.

Slowly, sensually, we rubbed our bodies together. The sheets were the only thing coving our bodies as both of my elbows entrapped my destined one. "Osirus," she moaned as I captured her hips. My movements became faster as she met me thrust for thrust with her hips.

"My darling," I spoke strained as my hair trapped us in our own canopy around our faces. "I love you," and I felt her core tightening.

"I love you, Osirus, so much." The grip she had on my biceps made me want to pull closer. Melina's moan shook me as she rose to her peak.

"Melina!" I groaned as we both came around each other, our bodies hot and wet. We finished with one final passionate kiss as I fell to her side. Her legs wrapped around mine as our pants became slow whimpers as sleep finally took me, with my love in my arms.

***

It was early morning, the light sprites had disappeared for the night, and the light sources were rising. Melina was still sleeping peacefully in my arms, and I didn't want to leave. There hadn't been twenty four hours for us to even lie in bed to worship each other. Now that we were this close to our binding ceremony, I know it would all be downhill.

The following day we would be in the throne room, our loved one's surrounding us as the sun rises and hits the stain-glassed window. The light sources would paint a beautiful portrait of my darling on the marbled floor. I've had glaziers working through the night, so Melina would overlook part of her surprise. Not that she would have had time to notice, anyway.

I rose from the bed, grabbing the closest pair of trousers I could find. Melina would be with her new mother and friends for the day. Prepping her body, the dress, and hopefully just relaxing. I grabbed the blue rose from the neighboring vase and left it on my empty pillow. Writing a quick note, I laid it beside her. Melina's hair was strung all over the pillows as she snored softly.

Going to the far-left corner of our room, I moved the large painting of Montu to the side and slipped through the surprise that I had waiting for her after our day of celebration.

Chapter 72

Melina

Stretching out like a starfish, I felt my back pop in multiple places. Groaning at how good it felt, I felt beside my body to feel for Osirus. We aren't usually this far away from each other, and I got confused since I stretched so far. Popping my head up quickly, I looked to the right side of the bed that he has dubbed as "his."

Instead of finding his god-like body in all his naked glory, I'm met with a royal blue rose that had hints of sparkle on the tips of its petals. Grinning like a little schoolgirl, I picked it up to smell its scent. It smelled like blueberries and tangerines, an odd combination, but it was nice. A paper had fallen onto the mattress held by the mysterious rose, so I picked it up to read it.

Good morning, darling,

As per the tradition of the Fae people, we are not to see each other for twenty-four hours before the celebration. I long to see your beauty as you walk to me during our moment together. You will have a busy day preparing for tomorrow. Please be safe and know I am not that far away. I love you.

Love,
Your Destined One

I sighed and flopped my head onto the pillow, holding the parchment paper to my chest. A month ago, I would have dreaded this day, but now I couldn't be more excited.

A loud bang knocked on the door and swung open. I took the sheets to cover my bare chest because let's face it, I was about as dressed as a naked mole-rat. "Melina!!" The screech went over the throngs of people walking into the bedroom.

"I am naked!" I squealed, trying to cover myself up with more layers of blankets. Amora came pouncing in and tries to wrestle the sheets off my body. "Amora! What are you doing here!!" The excitement of her being here overshadowed my nakedness as I drew her in for a hug.

"Phew, girl, you stank of the Fae!" Tulip jumped to the other side of the bed until she quickly bounced back off. "And sex, oh my gosh, how long did you do it last night?" Tulip held her nose and waved her hand in the air.

"Um, sorry." My face turned six different shades of red. How brazen everyone is talking about sex like it is no big deal. At least be a little modest about it.

An aura of calmness swept the room as the last person entered. As I glanced up, it was none other than Luna Clara from the Crimson Shadows pack carrying a baby in her arms. "Melina!" she spoke calmly, so she didn't wake the baby.

Walking over quickly to the bed, she started giggling. "Osirus had to have you one last time this morning, didn't he?" I groaned and threw the sheets over my head. "Oh, it is completely normal. He will probably adhere to the Fae tradition and not see you tonight, so it is to be expected. Come on and get up so we can prepare you."

"Prepare me? How do we do that? Just shower?" Tulip and Amora started laughing and threw a robe toward me.

"Your father wants you prepared like an Atlantean princess before the day of her bonding, so we get to go to Atlantis!" The women cheered at the excitement of traveling to a kingdom that visitors rarely get to visit.

Once we were at the water's edge, Elaine summoned a bubble chariot for her, since she had not yet bonded with my father. He boarded with her as well as Tulip, Clara, and Amora. Lucca walked up with Sean, and they both greeted me with a hug. "Are you ready to swim?" I nodded my head, excited to let the water run over my hot skin.

Father had brought me a ceremonial outfit that my grandmother had worn on her bonding day. It was a short, glowing white wrap-around skirt, enough to keep my cheeks from falling out, wrapped in pearls and shells. The top was adorned with iridescent clamshells to keep my chest covered. Diamonds and bits of emerald and sapphires decorated it in an intricate pattern. My hair laid loosely around my waist, and my blue highlights complemented the outfit.

"You look gorgeous," my father patted my head as he headed to the bubble orb. "Just follow us, swim around the kingdom one full turn, and wave to your subjects. Lucca will keep you company." Sean gave Lucca a passionate kiss and joined the rest of the caravan. I internally fangirled at them.

"The eldest brother is supposed to swim with you for this tradition, but he gave me that honor since you haven't got to know him well enough. I hope that is all right?" Lucca smiled as he grabbed my hand.

"That was sweet of him. I'm glad he let you." We both entered the water, and the tide rose around us. Lucca's blue and green tail sparkled as he jumped out of the water. My two legs wouldn't be as fast as his tail, but I was still quicker than any other supernatural in the water.

We followed the bubble. As father commanded, I swam around the giant orb of Atlantis that kept it primarily dry. Everyone waved, and some swam out to follow behind me. I didn't know these people, but they were celebrating as if I was here all along. A national family of sorts. It made me laugh as several dolphins came my way as I latched on with one of my hands. They jetted me through the water to keep up with Lucca and landed me just outside the water portal.

Lucca led me through the shell and spongy material of the streets. One hand was behind my back, and Father joined us as soon as his large sphere carriage was ported. Elaine, as well as the rest of the attendants, left to go to the palace. It was tradition for a princess to walk through the streets after mating with some of her family as acceptance.

The crowd cheered as father and Lucca stuck to my side like glue. They gave me encouraging words to wave and smile as I tried to shy away. My father's bare chest was adorned with achievements of brightly colored metals and shells as he kept his trident by his side. Lucca continued to rub my back as the crowds became closer to get a better look. Several men tried to approach and give me a better offer of being their mate, but who better than Osirus? He was the King of the Golden Light Kingdom who stole my heart. I was appalled they would think that I would give that up.

My father stood in front of them, arms crossed. Besides my brothers, they would be the best suiters in the kingdom. Their wealth indeed showed as the cloth that hid their manhood was made of a fancy leather. "You dare think you are best for my daughter?" he growled as they stepped back.

"But Your Majesty, think of her being able to stay here instead of with the land dwellers? You just found her for her only to be taken away. Wouldn't this be a better proposition?" One of them gave me a wink while I stuck his tongue out at him. Father noticed and gave a scoff.

"Who better than to take care of my princess than a king?" I smiled and grabbed his arm to walk away from the stuck-up snobs. Lucca started snickering. "To think I thought they were the motion of the ocean at one time." Father rolled his eyes as we continued down the pathway.

Unlike the last time I visited the Atlantean palace, the gates were opened wide for us as we walked in. Servants and guards stood on each side of the pathway to the main doors. Father kissed my forehead and told me to have fun while Lucca grabbed my hand to lead me away for my pampering session.

Tulip and I used to have pretend spa days when we were little. We would try to massage each other, but it ended up in a wrestling match when it was over. Lucca led me to the bedroom I stayed in for a few hours the last time I was here. When you finally met your father and your brothers for the first time, they all talked until the clock hit midnight, and even then, they followed me to my room and talked for a few more hours.

The light purples and blues made the room peaceful, and I instantly yawned. I hardly got any sleep last night, and with that exciting day and a few rounds of lovemaking, I was spent.

"Oh no, you don't!" Tulip popped out of the bathroom. She had a few different colored bottles of oils in her hands, as well as a few towels. "Go strip. It's massage time." I looked at her warily until she started snorting. "No, silly, I won't give you the massage. They have special people do that here." I let out a breath of relief that there would be no sisterly massages.

Lucca joined us as well. He said he spent a lot of time in the spa portion of the palace while growing up. Yet he didn't know he was rooting for the other team? Or did it not cross his mind? Either way, he enjoyed the massage so much he ended up falling asleep while the rest of us got our manicures and pedicures. His soft snores only made me joyful inside. Poor Sean had been wearing him out since yesterday.

Sean continued to pop his head in from time to time to check on Lucca. With a bunch of us naked women walking around, he didn't seem to mind when he finally saw Sean face down and asleep on the table. Picking him up gently, Sean wrapped him in a blanket and took him to the room they were staying in. Whether or not he let Lucca continue to sleep, I wasn't sure.

The girls continued their treatment on my body. I was rubbed with a sugar scrub to rip off any dead skin, then dipped into a mineral clay. On top of that, they wrapped me up in seaweed and put cucumbers on my eyes. "I'm hungry," I groaned. This relaxing stuff was hard work. We had been at it for six hours, and I had yet to see my dress.

Amora came in with champagne and small crab cakes and placed one in my mouth. I moaned how marvelous it tasted. "More!" I mumbled before I could even swallow.

"Yeah, that is what you are going to be saying tomorrow night!" Tulip chided, while Clara snickered in the corner, feeding Evelyn.

"We probably shouldn't drink much," Amora stated, as she had her second glass. "I kinda got in trouble last time." Amora leaned close to my ear. "My mate doesn't enjoy talking about our 'private times.'"

"Yeah, Osirus doesn't want me to discuss how big his little king is, but let me tell you, it isn't little," I added while Clara burst into laughter.

"You both are awful!" whispered Clara as she covered her mouth.

"Are we talking about one-eyed nightcrawlers?" poked Tulip.

"No, magic sticks," Amora deadpanned.

"Oh, you mean a womb raider!" Tulip yelled out loud, only to have my father walk into the room. We all sat wide-eyed in our robes, holding onto our champagne flutes, and he immediately walked back out the door.

***

Evelyn was a doll. Every chance I could, I held her in my arms. She was only a month old but had the strength of a 6- or 7-month-old. She was sitting up and almost crawling! Clara commented that the supernatural have more robust bodies than humans, and I should expect to see the same thing with Osirus and I's children. As much as I wanted to have children, we had a long time before Osirus, and I had to supply an heir. We had forever to have babies, and I wanted to explore this world more before we started bringing in little stubborn and dominating children.

I was finally stripped off the wrap and shoved into the shower. My skin had turned into silk and almost glowed porcelain as the water instantly beaded off. The hot water felt amazing, but it only made me tired. We had been at it too long, and my mind was ready to shut off. The alcohol, crab cakes, and way too much honeymoon information on positions had me sore at my sides from laughing.

Evelyn was asleep on one side of the bed while I lay on the other. Coming out in just a robe, the lights were dimmed low, and Clara was the only one left in the room. Soft little pants came out of Evelyn's mouth as she dreamed of her mother, most likely.

I yawned quietly as I laid my head on my arm. Clara radiated that peace that Tulip spoke about. Not once did Evelyn cry around her mother, and that was when Kane was the calmest. "We didn't wear you out, did we?" Clara poked fun as she massaged her finger on Evelyn's hand. She stirred, but quickly went back to sleep.

"A little," I whispered. "But I've had a lot of fun. Everyone seems like family here." Clara hummed in response.

"We are. I'm glad Osirus found you. I've been worried since I met him. He was such a lost soul. I felt like he had given up on life." I wrapped a blanket around my body to listen to Clara more closely.

"When I met him, I was angry at Kane over something silly, but he was right there to help me realize I was stronger than what Kane thought of me to be. I wasn't his worthless mate. I was strong physically when Kane thought otherwise, even after fighting my own battles. What I mean to tell you is... Just know you are stronger than you think, Melina."

Clara laid beside Evelyn and covered her with the blanket. I blinked a few times, meeting up at her gaze. "You are strong physically, too. You don't always need Osirus or a Dragon to save you. Osirus will always be there to help you, but don't you dare give up on yourself. You are more than what you make yourself to be."

"How can you read me so well?" I whispered.

"It was a gift given to me by the gods. Plus, you are totally easy to read. You don't think you are worth it being here in this palace. You are, and you're strong. Now that you are with Osirus, you are stronger."

I wanted to believe her words, but I still needed to prove it to myself. Even with a Dragon, I was scared to death to lose Osirus, and if I had gone in alone, I surely would have died. I'm no fighter.

"You are a fighter, Melina."

"Cut that out. It is weirding me out," I cried. Clara gave a smile and pushed a piece of long hair that fell into my eyes.

"Just remember that." Her eyes darted at me mischievously.

"I need to tell you, though, as the Queen of the Golden Light Kingdom, that we are having trouble with Vermillion." I sat up on my elbow while Clara continued to tickle Evelyn's belly. "The Queen and the Crowned Prince are having trouble regulating rogue Vampires and Witches in their kingdom. You saw that yesterday while our Wolves came to assist. For now, things are stable, but my mother sees another war brewing. With your association with your father, you may have to call upon his help, too."

I frowned. A war? We just took care of the Blood Coven. How many other powerful entities could there be?

"Do not worry, Melina. We have some time before anything happens. You are a woman who likes to plan, so I thought I would give a heads up." Clara laid on her back to close her eyes.

"And I will have to do the same," she whispered so faintly I barely heard it.

The future queen of the Werewolves spoke of the war of vampires with a warning, and all I could do was think about how I was going to help her. After the coronation, I would train with Osirus and become his fiercest warrior if I had to. To protect our home, new life, and whatever family we create together.

"Melina, sleep. I had to tell you now because we are both busy women," she giggled as she rolled over. My eyes slipped a few times before I felt a strong feeling of drowsiness hover over my eyes.

Chapter 73

Osirus

The men gathered in the smoking-room. It was filled with darker wood furniture and paintings of old warriors with nothing but pelts of animals and warrior regalia. Darker greens and reds kept the room ominous, which is why I stayed away from this room. My father and Cosmo used to use this place as a war room, or should I say Cosmo used to sway my father's decisions about the kingdom. Using filthy words of the deceit of how it would better the people.

Now it was being used for the first time in ages as a bachelor pad. There weren't really any bachelors, but Luna Clara said the men should get together just to "hang out" while the women do their thing.

Kane was sitting in the corner, sulking. The guy had some issues he needed to work on his own. His mate can't be up his ass all the time. Every few minutes, you could hear a growl from his Wolf in disapproval of being away from Clara.

Then again, who am I to judge? I want Melina all to myself, but hell, I just found her, and I didn't want to let her go. Doesn't that give me more reason to be possessive?

"So, what does one do at a 'bachelor party?'" Alaneo took a sip of his wine as he sat gracefully on the couch. Kane threw back a shot of Werewine, rolled his eyes, and planted both hands on the bar behind the sofa.

"Girls, man, there are usually girls," Braxton had his head leaned back in his chair in boredom and tossed a grape in the air, catching it flawlessly. "Like strippers and shit, maybe some lap dances?" Everett scoffed in the corner, his arms crossed with a disappointed look towards his brother..

"Eye, we are the only unmated men in the room," Everett smacked his brother. "Besides, you should prepare yourself for your mate. I've got a good feeling we will meet them soon." Everett's smile crept upon his lips as he chewed his cheek. "If my mate is as sweet as Opal, I would be a fortunate man."

"Whatever, brother," Braxton scoffed. Braxton had long given up on finding his mate. Thus, his dick had become the head of the operation to any fantasies he wanted. If he wasn't careful, his mate would catch him in the act with someone else.

My father walked into the room with a sizeable golden-colored box. Setting it on the table, he fiddled with the lock, and the container squeaked open. Inside there were several pipes along with a few bags of herbs of various colors. Each pipe he set out on a felt pad with the utmost care as he fiddled with the herbs and stuffed each one.

"I do not know what a 'bachelor party' is but I will tell you one thing. It is a tradition to smoke these pipes the day before the binding ceremony. Even though you are already mated, Osirus, I still feel like we just uphold this in honor of your grandfathers." I nodded at him. I still wanted to keep up on certain traditions, which seemed very important for a binding ceremony. There were enough pipes for all of us. Braxton took the first and inhaled the substance; he tilted his head with his eyebrows raised, looking pleased as he sat back down.

Alaneo, Kane, and Everett followed suit, and Finley would have to take a rain check since he was still tending to Opal in the sick ward. My pipe was the largest, with a family crest embossed on the side. I took a puff as the room filled with smoke clouds.

"I feel funny," Braxton leaned back on the couch. "I feel like I'm floating." Braxton took his hands and waved them around his face and started giggling. Others had different reactions, such as Kane, who only seemed antsier. He was pacing the room as soon as he took three puffs of the stuff. There was growling and a bit of swearing.

Alaneo sat stoically, along with a faint grin on his face, while he looked out the window. Several sighs left him as he finished his pipe. I felt alert and more in tune with my body. My heart felt like it was being pulled out of my chest. I followed the pull, and it led me to the window where Alaneo was staring.

Juliet was in the garden sitting with several women. They were tending to her hair, and they were putting flowers in the braid. Juliet had opted to stay at the palace because she was freshly mated, and the thought of being too far away from Alaneo hurt her. My heart still would not rest. It was beating out of my chest that I wanted to scratch off my tunic.

Kane joined me at the window. "Clara isn't here," he growled. "Where the fuck is my mate?" Kane grabbed my arm, but I quickly let the deep Fae magic seep from me that scalded his hand. "The hell?" He wiped his hand on his shirt, leaving black smudges.

Concentrating, I could feel Melina was not here either. "Where are our mates? Where are the warriors?" I spat as I went to the door. My father stopped me and put his hand on my shoulder.

"Easy there, son, they are all right. They went to Atlantis to partake in her people's traditions. Clara went willingly as well as your Melina." The room shook as Kane growled in frustration.

"Bring them back," he whispered. His claws were becoming exposed. Worrying about him shifting right here in front of a bunch of high-ranking warriors high as a kite, my father waved the smoke around the room with a large fan.

"The herb is called Caspis. They are found in the Western mountains. Their properties when you inhale, let your body take on your emotions to get you drunk on your desires."

"Damnit, father, you can't give that shit to Kane." I took Kane's pipe and shoved it back into the box. Those with mates had raging boners, and Braxton had fallen asleep.

"It's unbearable." Everett grabbed his knees. "I don't have a mate, and I yearn for her. This was fucked up." Everett stood up and left the room while I scowled at my father.

"Why would you give that to him?" I growled out at him, but he only laughed.

"It only means his mate is nearby. It can also make the pull stronger if you haven't been mated. She must be in the palace somewhere." My father had a sick sense of humor.

"Then I'm guessing it does nothing to those that don't have mates and are not near?"

Father laughed while scratching his head. "Yeah, who knows where his mate is," Father laughed. "Come on, it's a funny prank that has been done for generations! Live a little!"

Kane continued growling; a few sprigs of Torin's hair poked through. "Well, you just gave some of your herbal stuff to the most possessive Werewolf to date. That's the future king of the Cerulean Moon Kingdom."

Father stepped back a few feet, "oh, well, that's not good."

"Do you not keep up with times, old man!?" I yelled as Kane's bones began breaking.

"Where is she?" he growled as his shirt tore.

"Clara is in Atlantis! She's with Melina, calm down and go back to your human form and I'll have a witch show you!" Kane licked his fangs as he stopped panting.

Luckily, a witch was walking down the hall, and I pulled her in. "I need you to find someone for me," I looked back at Kane. "And fast." The witch nodded and sat at the desk.

"Who do you want to see?" Her bag popped open as a

glass orb was set on the table with a stand. "Luna Clara of the Warrior Pack, future Queen of The Cerulean Moon Kingdom." Kane's chest purred hearing her name while my father packed up the herbal shit that got us into this mess. I barely got a puff out of it, but the way everyone was acting, I was glad I didn't.

"I need something of hers. Do you have anything, Alpha?" The witch's voice shook. Kane reached into his pants pocket and pulled out a bright pink pair of lace underwear. No one dared laugh or said a word as the witch gently took the item and placed it on the ball.

Kane stood stoically still as he stared at the piece of cloth-like it was a lifeline. Thank gods I'm not this bad. In my mind, I was just roaring in laughter.

A few enchantments of words and the ball threw a picture inside. Clara, Evelyn, and Melina were sleeping on the bed. Both adults were curled around Evelyn, keeping her in a little nest.

Once Kane saw his two precious girls were safe, he snatched the underwear, put it back in his pocket, and sat down in the corner to sulk.

Thanking the Witch as she left, the others came out of their drug trance and shook their heads in confusion. After a quick summary of what happened, they were all pissed at my father, and I didn't blame them. He could have given a warning. However, he was now laughing with a red face and all almost on the floor.

Never had I seen him act like a child, but something had happened since Cosmo was no longer in control. He had given up his past life and was now moving forward. I wasn't sure how I felt about this prankster in him, but whatever works.

The rest of the day we spent separately. Many wanted to spend time with their mates here, and Kane wanted to make sure his warriors were up to guarding the palace, giving my warriors a rest. There was talk about another uprising in the

South, but that would have to be dealt with later. I had too many things on my mind, and the biggest one of all was Melina.

Crowds of people, primarily unmated, were attending the ceremony tomorrow. Melina wanted it to be a 'mating fest' so people could find their mates.

I marched back to our room. The bed had already been made from this morning, and I could still smell her faint scent. Her bags had been packed by the maids, ready for our departure tomorrow evening after the party. We were going to be flying to the winter palace so she could experience actual Bergarian snow. Instead of the white snow covering the Earth, Bergarian snow had faint bits of colors in its snowflakes that give it an iridescent look.

A knock at the door moved me from my thoughts as I placed her bags by the servant's quarter doors. As I opened it, I saw Finley standing there with a small cage. The Frost Fairy Fox, from when Melina had first visited the marketplace, had been kept in a safe place by the servant's children. She had been well tamed and taught by several of the animal-loving children.

"I'm glad you got her this. This was the only thing that caught her eye in the entire market. She passed by the jewelry and clothes and only wanted the little furball."

"Thank you, Finley," I grabbed his shoulder and pulled him in for a hug. Finley would be the godfather to our children once we had them. Even though I wanted them now, Melina wanted to wait.

I've already started taking my herbal sterilizer to keep us safe for the month, so I know she will be happy not to do anything on her side of fertility. She had gone through enough, so why not the man take care of not having children too soon?

Taking the Frost Fairy Fox, I opened its cage and let it on the bed. I would stay here for the night while Melina would return soon and staying in the bridal chambers. The fox curled up in the bed on Melina's side, probably already sensing that she would be her master. Finley spoke about how the fox liked her just through the cage.

My heart filled with warmth as I felt Melina set foot in the palace. The bustling of people walking down the hallway had piqued my interest, but I continued to lie still. I could feel Melina's presence as she stood at the door. I wanted to jump up and take her to bed with me, but one night of a tradition my mother thought was so important took root in me. Taking every bit of my will, I stayed in bed as the fox whimpered at my distress.

I felt Melina press on as people ushered her down the hall. This was going to be a long night until I saw her at sunrise.

***

After several hours of sleeping, I felt a pull at my chest. Distress, I felt Melina was in pain. I flung the sheets off the bed, and as soon as I stepped onto the floor, I felt a stab in my leg, causing me to fall to the floor.

"Damn!" I looked down at my leg, and there was nothing there that could only mean one thing.

I started screaming for warriors on the other side of the doorway. I gripped my sword with nothing on but my trousers as I burst through the living room. Warriors looked in panic as my disheveled self-approached. "Check the bridal chambers!" I barked as we all ran.

The hall continued to become longer as we ran. Her room was across the palace grounds as we stepped outside into the darkened night. The extensive building, mainly suited for traveling royalty, held her room. It was heavily guarded on the outside, but no one was concerned. As I approached with my warriors, they all stood at attention and questioned.

"Melina is hurt. Where is she?" The guards stood confused as I brushed past them. Running up the stairway, I found her room to be closed and locked. Pushing it forward, it wouldn't budge. Banging on the door with the butt of my sword, I called for her. "Melina!! Open the door!"

No sounds.

"BREAK IT DOWN!" I roared, my wings exploded from my back, and black sludge dripped down my claws. Once we entered, the room was not disheveled, and there were no signs of life. My heart continued to pull in pain as I felt a sharp prick in my neck.

"She's here, in the palace. Split up and FIND HER!" Wolves started howling while Clara and Kane approached me outside.

"Melina is missing. She is here on the palace grounds. I feel her!" Clara's calming aura swept over me as the grip on my sword became light.

"We're on it. Let's go, Kane." Clara shifted, ripped her nightdress to pieces, and began running in the small red fox form of a Wolf. I followed not far behind her as Kane turned half form to secure the perimeter.

Another flame of pain ripped through my arm, and I gripped it tightly. Clara looked back, only to beckon me to follow her. Clara must have her scent if she is this determined.

My heart became heavier, feeling Melina's emotions of hopelessness. She was giving up. She was going to leave me if I didn't get there in time. I spread fury through my feelings, praying she could feel it. My desperation to find her, take her with me, and never let her out of my sight consumed my soul. I would reach her, and whatever the hell took her from me will pay dearly.

Clara stopped at the stairway to the dungeons. Fuck no.

We both ran to the bottom, now Fae and Wolf warriors behind us. Snarling, growls, and angry men clogged the hallways. Passing by Cosmo, he only let out a low laugh as I passed his cell.

"Good luck," he sang.

Chapter 74

Melina

After our brief nap, the servants grabbed a few of our bags of clothing we had brought and packed them up to be taken back to the Golden Light Kingdom. There was a particularly large bag hanging in the room's corner that I wasn't there before. Sitting up from the bed, Evelyn stirred and woke up to cling to Clara.

"Let's get you fitted for your dress," Elaine popped in, holding Cricket's hand. "Your father is eager for you to try it on. He had it made specifically for the binding and coronation ceremony." Slowly rising from the bed, Amora and Tulip gathered around me and helped me take off my clothes. All the extra attention had me wanting to cover up my body, but they all scoffed.

"We were naked before. Why are you shy now?" Amora patted my shoulder. Cricket was turned around, eating a giant lollipop Elaine had brought him to keep him occupied.

"I'm just nervous. I know I'm already mated, but now it will be official I will be a queen. I just hope to live up to the expectations."

"You will," Clara came over to squeeze my hand. "Don't forget what I told you. You are strong. You are a warrior." I nodded, still not believing it entirely.

The dress was gently pulled out of the bag, and the giant mirror was covered, so I couldn't see the dress until it was on my body entirely. Stepping in from the top, it slid across my body. The silky-smooth feeling cooled my body as it finally reached the top of my chest. It was strapless, and the back was a corset, so it would be easy to adjust the waist size. It fit like a glove, holding in all my curves yet still giving me ample room to breathe.

The dress was covered in sheer white tulle and shaped into petals. It held a hint of blue at the bottom that gently faded as it rose to my waist. Tiny blue pearls outline my breast area while diamonds twinkled in small clusters.

The mirror covering was removed, and I stood in awe. I didn't look like myself. This dress was made for a queen, and I certainly didn't feel like one. As I walked, the layers of the dress swayed. The diamonds twinkled. The headpiece was a small coral crown with tiny shining shells that held a large sapphire in the middle. It was gorgeous; it was all too much.

My emotions caught up with me as I clutched my stomach. My father walked in behind me and smiled as he put both his hands on my shoulders. "You look stunning, Melina, my daughter." He kissed my cheek, and Elaine handed him a small flat rectangular box. Diamond teardrop earrings and a teardrop necklace with a diamond and a dolphin wrapped around it. "My mother wore this on her coronation day." His breath hitched as I clutched the pendant.

"It's so beautiful," I whispered.

"You are so beautiful, Melina. I'm so proud of how far you have come and so grateful to have you in my life. Just promise me you won't forget about your old man and visit often."

"I would never forget you." He pulled me into his embrace as we both sobbed quietly. I had just found my father, but I had almost lost him, too. We will have time to be together, but never experience him raising me as his daughter. Once I have children, I'm sure he will want to help raise them to get a piece of me to raise.

"I'm glad it fits." He stepped back, wiping away a tear. "But we need to get you back. We don't need your mate throwing a fit because you are too tired in the morning for the ceremony." I acknowledged and quickly undressed.

The ride back was uneventful. We all rode back in the magical sphere carriage for which I still didn't have a name. Several times I nodded off, only for Lucca to wake me up. Sean always had a hand on Lucca, and Lucca always looked at Sean so lovingly. Their bond was already so strong, and I was exceedingly excited my father was so accepting.

Many human adoptive parents would be upset, especially in the human world. However, with Selene doing the matchmaking and Bergarian being so adamant about listening to the goddesses' matchmaking abilities, no one ever questioned it. If only Earth could accept of all kinds of love.

Once we arrived at the shore, we stepped out of the carriage. Many Wolves from Clara's pack were there and were ordered to take her immediately to Kane. The girls started giggling and waved goodbye as Clara rolled her eyes.

Tulip and Amora led me down the hallway where Osirus and I stayed. We had to travel down this hallway to reach another part of the palace grounds that held royal suites and the bridal chambers. I stopped at Osirus' door. I could feel him in our room on the other side. I wondered if he could feel me too? My heart called out to him as I put my hand on the door. I wanted to walk in and just curl up in his arms, and we could prepare for the day together.

"Come on, you will see him soon enough." Tulip pulled my arm while my fingers traced the door being as I was pulled away.

Once we arrived at the bridal suite, both Wolf and Fae warriors surrounded the building, which made me feel safe as we walked up the long stairwell. "Do you need anything?" Amora spoke calmly as she pulled the sheets from the bed. I shook my head no and climbed in the sheets.

"You sure I can't go to Osirus?" I chuckled. Amora smiled and spooned me in the bed.

"I know it's hard to sleep. Just do the best you can. Do you want me to stay?" Amora lovingly pushed my hair away from my face.

"Yes, we can stay, and you can wake up to this pretty face," Tulip fluttered her eyelashes while I started laughing.

"No, both of you go to your mates. I can't make you guys suffer, too. I'll be fine. Just six hours to wake up, right?"

"Right," they both said at the same time.

Both left as I curled myself further into the plush comforter. The entire room was white, representing purity. If only they knew how unpure I was with Osirus already. I internally snickered, remembering all the fun times we had already.

My eyes were half-closed when I felt a chill in the room. I wrapped myself tighter into the comforter. The cold became stronger, and I sat up to look at the window and see if it was open. Before I slid out of bed, an arm wrapped around my waist, and a cloth was shoved to my nose. I wrestled with whoever was trying to grab me, but they were unbelievably strong. The longer I tried to wrestle away, the tiny breaths I was taking made me sleepy.

I pushed with my knees on the bed and slammed them back on the mattress. My arms were stuck to my body as someone kept them pinned with one arm. I continue to wiggle and struggle, only for them to squeeze me tighter.

"Shhhh, just sleep," his voice sounded eerily familiar. My eyes tried to widen, but whatever was on the cloth had me falling asleep too quickly. I didn't give up until, finally, I succumbed to the exhaustion.

***

I woke up with a burn in my throat. It felt scratchy as I tried to clear it. Shaking my head, I felt the surface beneath me only to find a thin mattress spread on a stone floor. Sitting up on my elbow, I could feel the hardness of the stones. What had happened? Being disoriented, I tried to stand up, only to fumble back to the ground.

The thin nightgown didn't keep the cold out, nor did it give me enough coverage to conceal myself from unwanted eyes. Damn Osirus and his negligee fetish.

A metal door opened with a loud moan and shut quickly. The person took the key and instantly locked it from the inside and put it on top of the barely-there doorframe. The steps were slow and calculated as the door widow's light cast a shadow on their face. Whoever this person was, was big.

The muscles were outlined in a stretched-out navy blue t-shirt, and ripped jeans clung to his hips. The bottom of the pant legs was ripped to shreds, and they were completely barefoot. A low growl rippled through the room as I stood up and backed up to the wall.

"Hello, Melina." The voice spoke, and it finally hit me. Esteban.

"E-Esteban?"

"I'm surprised you remembered my name. Did you even think of what happened to me the day they took me away?"

Honestly, no, but I would not say that. I'm a smart mouth, but I'm not stupid. He went bat-shit crazy. I was ready to forget that mess.

"I wondered if you were all right," I spoke.

"Really, even when you are off fucking some Fairy?" he growled. "A Fairy, Melina! I offered you a chance of a lifetime, and you threw it away for a Fairy!"

"Um, actually, he is a Fae...." I started until his hand went back, and I flinched. He held his hand in the air and dropped it to his side. "Melina, you are the first woman to ever reject me. Do you know what that does to me?"

"N-no?" Esteban came closer to me. My back was flushed against the wall.

Leaning in, he moved my hair and whispered in my ear.

"It infuriates me. However, my Wolf finds the chase excit-ing." I gasped as I pushed his chest away from me. He started chuckling as I scampered to the other side of the room.

"Oh, Melina, always running." Esteban took slow steps toward me as he lifted his shirt. "I knew I wanted you the day you moved into our pack territory. Yet you wouldn't give me the time a day. I didn't know if it was just a quick fuck I wanted or something more."

My breathing started escalating as my heart was felt in my throat.

"So, I waited. I waited to see what could develop all these years, but now it has become an obsession. My Wolf craved you because you didn't want us. Hell, I felt the tingles when we touched. My Wolf wanted to conquer you, and now I do, too. I even wanted you as my mate, but you rejected that idea right at the get-go when you got some Fairy swooning over you. But I won't blame you, no... I won't." Esteban's eyes flickered from brown to black, his fangs quickly growing.

"I fucked girls right in front of you to get you jealous, and you did nothing, not even a hint of jealousy, only disgust." I swallowed the ball of spit in my throat.

"What do you want, Esteban?" I tried keeping my com-posure.

"What fire you have, Melina."

"Stop this, Esteban, and let me go! Osirus will find me!"

"Oh, he will find you, and that is what I'm hoping. I didn't follow you around the past month to give up my prize so easily."

"The cold? The heated stares yesterday?" I questioned. Trying to keep him talking, I scooted towards the door, hop-ing he would stay in place, but he chased me like the little rabbit I was.

"A little side-effect on the cloaking spell I had on me but not enough to fool you, right?" he smirked.

"Were you in the..." I wanted to say bathroom before Os-irus came in, but it was stuck on the tip of my tongue. "You wouldn't..."

"Oh, I did, and I saw the little show you and Osirus put on. Didn't know you liked it quite that rough. Maybe I will enjoy myself."

A sob wracked my chest as I went to put my hand on the handle of the door. Quickly, Esteban grabbed my hand and slung me back onto the mattress. "No! Let go of me!" I was thrown rapidly down trying to stand up, and Esteban's pants were passed down his knees. Not like this, not like this.

"I'm giving you a choice. Let me mark you. You can have both of us. You are royalty," he gritted his teeth as he held my hands above my head.

"Never!" I spat in his face.

"Accept my bite, and I won't kill you!" I wrestled again, trying to get my knee to hit his groin, but he was too heavy.

"NO!" I screamed as a burst of energy grew from my body. Falling to the floor and rolling near the door, Esteban stood back up. My claws grew as my wings burst forth out of my back with enough strength that it pushed Esteban off me. My wings were shaking with fear, and my claws grew longer. I will not give up now. I was a warrior.

Esteban and I circled one another until he leaped towards me and ripped a large wound down the top of my leg with one claw. I screamed as I tried to back away, but the pressure and weight of the leg were too much. Falling to the floor, I gripped my leg to stop the bleeding. Esteban was chuckling in the corner.

"Best give up now, Melina. We need to get you stitched up before you bleed out." I growled at him as my fangs pierced my lips.

"So feisty," he grinned. Esteban picked me up while I struggled and put me on the mattress, taking his shirt and wiping the blood.

I'm going to die trying to get out of this. I wanted to give up. Esteban had tracked me down and watched me from the very beginning, and he was going to continue to do what he wanted until the job was done. Why did I have to deal with his shit?

Esteban tried to give the utmost care to my wound. He wrapped it with his shirt and put a bit of pressure. I wanted to kill him. I wanted him to suffer, so no other woman had to deal with this prick. But who am I? I can't even get away from him, and Osirus can't protect me, either. Esteban has practically lived in the palace with us, and we didn't know the wiser.

Hopeless. Osirus won't feel me missing. That's why he drug me down to the dungeons to make it feel like I was still in bed. Would Osirus feel my pain like I felt him? Would he wake up to rescue me? Warmth flooded my chest as the feeling of wanting to give up and not fight left. I felt love, fierce and undying love across my body. I became heated with Osirus' determination. I felt him.

Osirus was telling me not to give up as much as I wanted to. "Are you ready to calm down now?" Esteban laid me on the mattress, my head feeling the floor beneath it. As soon as Esteban relaxed, I took my claw and ripped him right across the chest. He roared and pushed his hand to my neck as I felt one sharp fang pierce the skin. In a knee-jerk reaction, my wings pushed my back up with force as he flung on the floor.

My neck was bleeding, but I felt no connection to him. It didn't work. He completed nothing if that was what he was going for. "I'll never give up Esteban, just accept it and leave. Last warning." He stood up, unaffected, when I started singing random notes. I willed myself for him to feel pain, but he still stood up walking. I growled out again in frustration. Why wasn't it working?

"Did you know the bulbs of a Naraco plant can keep even the strongest Siren songs at bay? Just one small bulb in each ear, and I'm safe. Now, doll, how about you stop the nonsense, and I'll try to forgive you?" Esteban held out his hand as the wound on his chest healed. Think again, douche.

I charged him as my wings pushed me forward. Gripping his neck and having my claws scrape across important arteries proved nothing as he grabbed my upper arm, leaving deep indentions. Along with one leg and one arm out of the game, I was ultimately screwed.

I tried wiggling from his grasp, only for him to grunt in satisfaction and push me back to the mattress. "Fine, you die, but not before I had my fun." His dirty hand went up to my leg and moved my nightdress. One hand was around my neck, enough to cut off the oxygen. I was being pushed down too hard to use my wings as a springboard. As Esteban concentrated on my lower half, I swung my other leg that wasn't occupied over his waist, causing him to be flat on his back while I straddled him.

"If this is what you wanted, you should have said so!" He grabbed my hips, expecting me to leave, but I ground my hips into his erection, causing him to close his eyes and groan. "Stupid Wolf," I muttered as my fangs grew, and I leaned over and grabbed his windpipe with my fangs. His trachea was crushed, and blood spewed into my mouth. He began gurgling, drinking his own blood spilling from his neck.

I jumped off, not wanting to get any more blood on my hands, but he had one more move in him. His claws scratched my stomach, ripping my nightdress and leaving three long gashes in my stomach. I wailed in pain as I fell over. Esteban was still coughing and gurgling. There was no way I was going to let him heal. I took my claws and continued to claw at his throat while I cried, lying next to him.

I was too weak to move. I could feel wetness pool around us. I no longer had the strength to keep clawing Esteban' neck.

Large bangs were heard on the door, but they continued to fade as I tried to finish the job. Esteban was going to be no more, and he would never hurt or use another woman again. I clawed at him one last time when I heard Osirus' voice.

My hearing was muffled as I heard screaming for a doctor. Osirus' arms picked me up and cradled me to his bare chest. He was so warm while I was feeling cold. "Stay with me, Melina. I'm getting you help, Okay, darling? You can't leave me."

"I'm not leaving, Osirus." I gasped "I need you to stitch me up so we can go on our honeymoon." Osirus laughed as I felt him climbing the stairs. Noises faded in and out as I heard wolves howling and my father screaming.

"Sorry, I made a mess," I whispered.

Osirus gripped me tighter. "Only you would think of something like that."

I felt my body being laid down on a firm surface, Fae physicians gathered around. Osirus didn't let go of my good arm as they worked on me. I felt salves and hands-on my cuts and then the faint hint of incense in the room.

"Breathe it in, Your Majesty. It will help you sleep," one healer spoke.

"I can't, can't leave Osirus." I gently squeezed his hand. Osirus petted my cheek with his thumb.

"It's all right now. You are going to be fine. You can sleep, and I will be here when you wake up."

"But the ceremony," I whispered.

"Sleep. They can't throw a party without us." Osirus' lips tickled mine as he left kisses on me as I fell asleep.

Chapter 75

Everett

Dawn had come and gone. The chairs in the throne room sat empty as everyone worried about the future Queen of the Fae Kingdom. Even though His Majesty said she would make a full recovery, the people still worried for her. Melina had become part of our world in such a short time and touched so many lives she wasn't even aware of.

Melina, just being with her mate, the King, helped the kingdom in ways she will never understand. She helped grant us our freedom, along with saving Osirus' ass with a Dragon.

Servants walked by, watering flowers in the aisles of rows of chairs. Chairs were continuing to be dusted, and the palace kitchen cooked hordes of food to feed those who were guests in the palace of top ranks. The subjects outside opened their homes to those visiting and were planning on celebrating in the streets. The kingdom had come together to supply each other and take care of the outsiders, which will make Osirus very proud.

Melina's fight just a few hours before gave the entire palace a shake when we realized someone had taken her. Witches came to find only traces of a spell newly constructed of different herbs and scents one would not pick up right away. The witches grew wary when they realized another coven must have an unjustified coven leader. No witch or coven would have given away such a spell to hide a scent along with the invisibility properties of anyone but under a royal's command. The art of this spell practiced too much dark magic. Each spell has hints of its origin, and it led to one that resided in Vermillion.

This only confirms suspicions of Queen Diana not being able to control the rogues that are multiplying. Soon the vampires will feed on the innocent and not wait for their blood supply bags to reach them and instead go to the source of those unwilling.

I threw my sword back on my hips as I adjusted the straps. My waist had become thicker since training twice a day. Finley, the ringleader of our brotherhood, attended to Opal, who was now in stable condition in their room. It won't be long before he claimed her, officially leaving just two of the 'Red Fury' alone. Braxton had continued sulking, and once the announcement was granted that the ceremony would take place three days from now, he headed off on horseback to get some bonding time with Neolla. His black mare was the only one that could comfort him, and a few nights under the stars would rejuvenate him.

The drug we were given by King Nyx had done a number on both of us. I felt nothing but pain in my heart and the pull that would lead me nowhere. I wandered the palace grounds to follow the nagging pull, and as I got closer, it would pull away too fast for me to follow.

Many guards were placed throughout the city. Osirus had announced for those who were unmated to hunt the city to find mates. Since Fae could now leave their chosen mates to seek their true mate, many came from miles around. They trickled in from the Northern mountains to the Eastern Sea, and I felt myself become more unnerved.

What if she doesn't come? What if she was dead? What

if her chosen one refused to let her go? Too many questions for me. I've never been a thinking man. I would rather act and scourge into battle as I devour my enemies. This thinking had already been too much for my feeble mind.

Maybe she wouldn't be Fae at all? There had been many inter-species mating around here. More than I last remember. It was a good thing both species could bring much to the table in their relationship to restore a kingdom once deprived of love. There was a time when species collided with each other in harmony, but Cosmo stopped that.

What was interesting were the children. Children would take on one species of their parents instead of producing a mixed child. At first, we found it strange, but we no longer questioned what the goddess had planned. Children would grow up and find a mate, may it be their own species or not.

There was one child that had resisted that norm, and it was now Queen Diana of Vermillion. She was a mix of Witch and Vampire in an unholy union that had taken place when an old king of the vampires had been previously mated. This may be the downfall of Vermillion since a full-blooded vampire was not sitting on its throne. The reasoning for her mixed blood is unknown. She had been created as a powerful being, but was it powerful enough to fight off a nation?

Walking through the streets, several carriages were passing. Kids screamed and played as they kicked a ball around with their feet and hands. Running through their playground on the main street, I kicked the ball right into one of their nets as some screamed in laughter. I pulled my red beard aside and scratched my chin and smiled at the lot of them.

I was heading for the outskirts of town, following the nagging pulling that kept me awake. I'm not expecting to find what I look for, but it will ease my aching mind. Up ahead is the large well that many everyday folks use. Buckets lay outside as one woman walks up. She's singing an old song, one that is older than my years on this land.

Her eyes were as purple as the light source's sunset, and her skin was the color of caramel. Her black silk hair hung loosely on her back with a braid wound tightly with leather straps. She's too busy humming, knowing my approach, but I fear she will hear my heart beating heart as I came closer.

The woman's long tan dress scraped the ground and was full of mud, and the smock she wore was full of stone fruits that were about to topple over. Her cheeks were dirtied from her time fetching food from the dirt, but my soul stirs, seeing her content.

I stood still as I watched her fill up the cup near the well and drink it down. Water spilled from the corner of her mouth and dripped down her neck. Droplets disappeared in between her breasts.

Cleaning my voice, she stopped drinking to look at me in the eyes, and that was when we felt it. The pull.

Dropping her cup, she grasps her apron, waiting for a movement from me. She looked timid as she cowered back. "Please, I won't hurt you," I reached my hand out, still not moving my feet. Her delicate hand went to her lips to cover them.

"How can this be?" she whispered so softly I barely made it out.

"What is my little forest Nymph?" Her wings fluttered softly as her face lost its initial shock.

"I lost my mate so long ago," she spoke louder. "I'm sorry, I, I didn't think I would have a mate again."

A bit of jealousy rose in me knowing she had a mate before me, but the comfort I had knowing she had no mark on her neck broke me of my selfish thoughts.

"You had a mate before?" I walked around the well as she stood still, looking straight up at me. I was significantly taller than her, even though she was taller than future Queen Melina.

"We grew up together. The day he turned eighteen, he said I was his mate, but he was called to war. Since I wasn't eighteen yet, we couldn't solidify a bond. He died out in battle." Her face lowered sadly while I took my hand to lift her head back to me.

"I'm so sorry for your loss," I sympathized with her. "I can promise you when I go to war, I will never die, not when you are beckoning me in my dreams to come home." A slight hitch in her throat left her speechless as the sparks flew down our bodies. Immediately, I stepped closer to her to put her in my embrace, but she pulled away. My heart stung at the rejection, but I held on.

"You can't promise that. He promised me that too." She held her arms to her stomach as she sat on the well. "You can't promise something you have no control over." Kneeling in front of her, I put my hand on her knee.

"I have been through two wars and an infinite number of battles, just as two days ago, and I will fight through that many more because the thought of finding you was too great. Now that I have you, I will never let you go." Two silent tears dropped to my hand, and I kissed them with my lips.

"Now, please tell me, my forest Nymph, what is your name?" Her eyes fluttered to mine, almost accepting me. Squeezing her hand to listen to the first time she would speak her name, the word left her lips.

"Sundew," she breathed.

Sundew led me back to her cabin in the woods. She had spent most of the summer months in the Northern mountains, and this cabin was her sisters' who had already found a mate and were living elsewhere.

It was a small cabin with one bedroom, a small kitchen, and a few sitting areas. It was perfect for a single person, or better yet, a newly mated couple. While walking over to the cabin, I noticed Sundew was a bit on the skinny side, but I would afford to give her the most delicate foods with the money I had saved over the years. As much as I liked the palace, I really liked her tiny cabin in the woods.

It was quiet, and away from prying eyes. Sundew led me

inside and asked if I wanted some tea, but I quickly declined. I wanted to know everything about her and let her know I was never leaving.

"Come sit with me," I beckoned her. I took up most of the room on the small couch where I sat, so it was a perfect excuse for me to touch her. She sighed as I put my arm around her.

"Do you know how long I've waited for you?" I leaned in closer. Her heart was racing, but I couldn't feel any fear radiating off her. Sundew had been staring at me, I could feel her heated stare as I walked into the cabin. She especially enjoyed my open tunic, and I had to do a bit of flexing to make her want me more.

It's like a damn bird dance. I'm puffing my chest out like an idiot because I wanted to seem more immense, more intimidating when I was one of the most giant warriors. Sundew gave a shy smile as I grabbed her hand. "Do you feel this?" I put her hand on my chest as she gasped. My muscles tightened at her touch. "It beats for you," I whispered, and pulled her face closer.

I had never wanted a woman more than this moment. I wanted to show her the pleasure that no woman had ever experienced from me.

Our lips brushed each other, and I felt the warmth of my soul coming back to life.

Braxton

Neolla's hooves drove into the ground as I kicked her lightly. She was one of the fastest horses in Bergarian, besides Montu. Noella would hardly sweat as she pounded the dirt with her fury. She was on edge, as I was. I was tired of hunting, fighting, and regretting.

I had given up. I had given up on finding my mate. Sure, my King and two brothers had found theirs, but I had seen mine long ago. She was in the Shifter War fighting against us. Her body was ravishing as she stood naked with her pride. A black panther.

Her skin was the color of cocoa that had a sheen of gold. Her eyes were bright green, and her fangs were glorious. I wanted to march right across the field and claim her as mine, let everyone watch as I took her to bed. I was elated and began starving the very moment her eyes laid on me. I smiled at her, letting her know I was friendly and wanted her.

The only problem was this was a war, and we were on the opposite sides. Her pride had sneaked into our campsite at night, slashing many Fae and Elves in their sleep. A cold tactic, but all is fair in war, I suppose.

When our eyes locked, I was ready for a truce, even if the rest of the nation didn't see it. Stopping the war and being with her would have made my life happier. Until the smile on my face had faded because her hiss shot me down cold. Quickly changing into her panther form, she raced towards me. Not able to use my wings I held out my blade to block her attack, only to have her dart away and slash me in the shoulder.

I could feel my voice calling to her, "mate, wait!" I begged and pleaded with her to stop as she wrestled with me on the ground. Her growls, hisses, and swipes to my neck made my soul break more. Maybe she had become rabid or didn't feel the bond? Holding her maw away from my neck, I could still feel the sparks in my hands despite the fur. "Mate, stop!" I cried as I tried to let up and be gentle, but she never relented.

My brothers came to my side. Everett used his boulder of a body to knock her off as she whimpered, skidding to a stop ten feet away. Shaking off the dust of her fur, she charged again. Holding my sword in front of me, bracing for impact, I felt my brother push me forward, causing me to take a knee, and my sword impaled her through the underside of her body, straight through her heart.

My heart was crushed at the moment of impact as she lay

beside me. Everett walked away to help Finley, but I couldn't leave my shifter mate alone. "Why couldn't you stop?" I cried as I petted her head. "Why? Were our differences too much?" She let out a groan, and her body shifted back to her human. The sword was empaled straight through her heart. Gasping for air, her eyes landed on me. The bright green stole my soul again.

"Not...with....a... Fae. Never...a... Fae." Her last words rung in my head as her body stopped moving.

Noella continued to pound the dirt until we came to our favorite spot. Times when I needed to be alone, I would travel to the Glowing Cavity. A cave that used to be the home of hundreds of Dragons. My own brothers don't know if this spot, I always told them I sleep under the stars. Novella trotted in the cave, leaving loud hoof echoes. I dismounted and unhooked her bridal, and she immediately left the cave, searching for sweet grass on the outside.

It had been a few years since I had been here. Osirus had needed too much help, and his mental state was not well before he had Melina. My brothers and I were on constant guard as he continued to deteriorate.

Heading to my storage chest, I opened it only to find a few bottles of wine left. The dried food I had stored, however, was gone. "What the fuck!?" I cried out as I pulled everything out of the chest. Huffing in annoyance and putting my hands on my hips, I walked down the cave more. The light at the end of the cave came from the many glowing pools of water. Light fairies would come here to nest in the many crevices in the rocks. Between their glow and the reflection of the water, it gave the cave a glorious shine.

I finally reached the end, and the pool was as clear as a mountain spring. It looked refreshing, so I knelt into the water to take a sip when I saw a glimpse of something moving from the corner of my eye. Standing up quickly, I unsheathed my sword. A strong pull came to my chest as I rounded the large lake. My heart hurt worse as I neared but kept my feet moving.

A small indention in the cave, almost like a hollowed-out nest, came into view. I saw none other than my blankets covering something or someone. A small whimper came from the blanket, so I used my sword to toss it to the side. As soon as I did, a girl popped her head up to look behind her and saw me.

"Please don't hurt me!" she cried and scooted to the back of the cave. My heart was bursting inside me, and my soul was screaming. The bright, golden eyes of a small Elven girl had claimed me. "I'll leave peacefully. Please let me go!" She cried again.

My mate was a girl, not a woman. My heart was too excited to care. When she turned eighteen, she would realize who I was, and until then, I could take care of her.

"I would never hurt you." I softened my stature and put my sword away. "I'm Braxton. What's your name?" I held out my hand to take, but she curled up into her ball tighter.

"Emilee," she whispered.

"Emilee, beautiful name for a pretty girl," I cooed. "Can you tell me how old you are?"

"Ten," she whispered again. I smiled, and she gave me a small one back.

I spent the next hour asking her questions and how she got here. Her Uncle and Aunt had raised her for as long as she could remember. Emilee couldn't remember the last time she had fun because she was expected to do chores for the family. She knew how to cook, clean, and even sew and would be expected to do extra tasks each day. Emilee only ate the scraps from the table, which wasn't much since her 'siblings' were very greedy.

Emilee had had enough and ran away. She had no plan but to run, and she felt a pounding in her chest to lead her here and stay. She felt safe for the first time, and the food and water rations kept her stable for the past two weeks.

After she came closer to me, I saw handprints on her arms

from someone trying to grab hold of her. Her arms were skinny, and the clothes she wore were nothing but rags.

Anger welled within me as she told me the punishments she would receive. The thought of having her live with a family, to grow up and have an everyday family life crossed my mind, but I wanted to be selfish. I was the only one that could genuinely keep her safe and make sure she could live a healthy life. I could send her to school and help her grow up and be the person she wanted to be.

It will be a complex situation if I keep her. Once she felt for me, when the bond awakened in her, she will be shocked and confused that her caregiver was her mate. The emotional repercussions may be too significant.

Fuck. I don't want to be away from her. I want to know she's happy and healthy.

I've never heard of a supernatural finding their mate before they turned of age, but I suppose it was possible. Things were changing all the time in Bergarian. I know I didn't have any physical desires for her; I felt unconditional love and the need to protect her. That was all I wanted for her. Protection. Seeing her smile and grow up with other children. She needed me.

She should have a mother and a father with siblings, though. Emilee should grow up and have a normal life before me. I just found her too soon. The ache in my chest grew heavy as I thought about giving her up. Letting her go would be the most painful thing, mainly since I had just found her. I saw Emilee becoming uncomfortable. "What's wrong little, one?"

"Chest hurts." She soothingly rubbed her chest. Running my hand through my hair, I let out a gruff.

Shit, the bond is there.

I would have to take her back to the palace and get some advice from some bonding experts, preferably some Witches that understood it well. Only then I could figure out what to do. Keep her with me and raise her or give her to a close family that will treat her well until she is of age.

"How about I take you to a special place, hm?" Her short red curls covered her cheeks as she played with her fingers.

"You promise not to hurt me, Braxton?" My eyes stung as she called me by my name.

"Never, I promise nothing will ever happen to you ever again." Emilee quickly crawled up in my lap as she sighed contently, and I carried her out of the cave.

Chapter 76

Osirus

I almost didn't make it.

Hell, it was too close.

I swung the door open to reveal a bloodied Esteban, the bastard that tried to steal Melina the first time I laid eyes on her. He wanted her, and I knew he did. I saw the possessive look in his eyes, but in the past month, I heard nothing of his whereabouts. Esteban was supposed to be on Earth, back in his home pack, but he escaped.

How did his Alpha not know he was missing? Could he not sense when a pack member was missing from his pack? Putting thoughts aside, I saw my darling covered in blood, and it wasn't just Esteban' but her own as well.

"Melina!" I screamed as I burst through the door. Clara immediately pulled Esteban by the leg to pull him away. He sputtered and leaked blood from his neck until Clara cracked his neck, causing him to stop his frantic movements. Melina had done a number on him, slashes down his face, and bite marks near crucial arteries. Even though she was not trained for any type of hand-to-hand combat, she knew the vital points where she needed to make a dent in a Wolf.

Wolves' necks were a crucial organ. It was soft and not

entirely covered in muscle and bone, with significant arteries running through; you should have a good chance at getting an excellent shot.

Melina was now lying in my arms. Her leg was bleeding, but she had a shirt wrapped tightly around her leg. The bleeding had slowed, but her abdominal muscles and arms were still bleeding heavily. Picking her up, she continued to sob as I held her close to my chest. I was covered in her blood, and terrible scenarios played through my head. What if she didn't make it?

Running up the stairs, there was utter chaos. Kane was yelling for warriors to retrieve the body to be sure the fucker was dead. A few rounds of my soldiers ran through to the dungeon and checked for any remnants of magic that could cause some other uprising here in the palace. We didn't know if Esteban was working with anyone, but you could never be too sure.

Upon arriving in the healers' quarters, the bed was already prepared for her. The firm surface was quickly covered in her blood as three healers attacked her wounds. Several bottles of antiseptic were poured on her leg and arm. Another started using sealing magic to heal the inside of her body.

"Her womb is still intact, Your Majesty," I grunted in understanding. That was the least of my worries. If she couldn't give me children, to hell with it. All I needed was her. Melina continued to moan out for me, telling me she was sorry for making a mess. Like anyone cared. She was my warrior queen and a damn strong one, too.

She took on a high-ranking warrior with years of skills under his belt while she had nothing. The healers threw some incense on a burner beside her head and wafted the smoke to her nostrils. Her eyes drooped as she complained about being ready for our ceremony. There would be no ceremony today. She needed her strength, and I needed her.

"Just sleep, darling. The party will wait for us." Melina

quickly succumbed to her darkness as I sighed out in relief. She was no longer in pain.

"She will recover. These wounds are deep, but no vital organs were struck. In fact, with her Siren and Fae abilities, she should be healed in three days when she wakes up and can carry out the ceremonies." The healer bowed as he cleaned up the blood. Attendants lifted her body so they could place medicine on her lips, and she instantly swallowed.

Once she was cleaned, I stayed in the room with her. I wasn't planning on leaving her. I'd answer questions as they came and decide about crucial matters with the kingdom right at her bedside.

Melina was now dressed in a long purple nightgown that made it easily accessible to her wounds. I had initially bought it for her to be easily assessable in other ways, but this worked just too. I smirked as her hand twitched towards mine. Grabbing it, I brought her hand to my lips while I kissed her knuckles.

***

A few days went by, and Melina barely moved. Healers removed bandages, and each day they closed more and more. The bruises left on her neck were gone, and the scrapes on her shoulder and leg had healed. What remained were a few light scratches on her torso.

Becoming anxious, I hovered over her. Each slight twitch made my heart jump, thinking she was waking up to me. My mind raced how she would react to what happened to her. Would she leave me because I couldn't protect her? Trying to push the thought away, I kept my anger towards Esteban. He was indeed dead, and the kingdom made an enormous bonfire and threw his remnants into the burning flames to make sure of it.

Many demanded Cosmo to be burned alongside the traitor. I was hoping to reserve a trial for him, point out every single flaw to ruin the name he had spent so many years try-ing to build for himself. Still, I had been too preoccupied with my thoughts of Melina and her recovery.

"I'll take care of it," my father growled. "Your people de-mand justice, and I will see to it." My father, the previous ruler, taking Cosmo to his grave was a good thing. Father had Cosmo stripped of his wings in front of a crowd of roaring fans. Wolves included started howling with glee, watching the primary leader of all their sufferings fall. My father com-prised a small list of all of Cosmo's wrongdoings, such as lies and treason of false information of the King.

Cosmo was then tied to a post while the people gathered clothes that were made to keep their wings concealed around his feet. This didn't silence the people as they threw their torches into the growing pile of wood, clothing, and tax papers. Cosmo continued to struggle, calling them all hope-less, and the downfall of The Golden Light Kingdom was near until his last breath.

Lost in thought, I wiped Melina's head with a wet cloth until I heard footsteps near.

"Your Majesty," Everett stepped in our bedchambers. I had Melina moved as soon as the rapid healing took place. I wanted her comfortable and away from the noise of the bust-ling of the palace. It had become too noisy for my liking, and I knew she would appreciate being in our room together when she woke.

"Yes, Everett?" Everett smiled up at me and pulled along a small Fae woman with sleek, dark hair. "This is my mate, Sundew. I wanted you to be the first to meet her." I stood up and warmly smiled. He wanted to let me greet his mate first before his brothers. An honor itself. Then again, we were all brothers, not by blood.

"It is certainly nice to meet you," I bowed slightly as she bowed almost too low.

"It is my honor, Your Majesty!" Her face flushed and hid half her body behind Everett.

Everett held his hand behind her back to move her forward, but she stuck to him like honey. "I would also like to tell you, Braxton has found his mate, but it is certainly unorthodox. He wants an audience with the Witches who understand the scientific properties of bonding." Everett gave a sad smile as I questioned.

"She is only a child. He found her in a cave running away from an abusive family." My face went to immediate understanding. A few times in my life, I had witnessed a mate being older than another when one did not have the bond activated yet in their soul. The most senior mate would have to wait until it was recognized before anything could transpire.

"How old is the child?"

"She's ten, Your Majesty."

"Hmm, eight years he will have to wait. I can tell you right now he cannot be around her long periods until the bond takes place," I deadpanned. "She's getting ready to go through her bodily change to become a woman, and what little bond is there would cause disastrous results." Everett nodded and gripped Sundew's hand.

"I think he is worried about who she will end up with. He had a feeling this would be the best route. She was abused before, and his protective instincts are strong for her. He will want a family he knows he can trust to take care of her." Before I could speak of a few ideas I had, Finley and Opal walked up to the room.

"Your Majesty, if I may, Finley and I would like to take the child." Finley smiled and gave Opal a gentle squeeze. "I am still in charge of running the orphanage and being a teacher. I think this little girl would benefit from having others to play with and grow up. The girl would ultimately come home with Finley and me to our home, and Braxton could come to visit once a week to check on her so they can know each other." Opal smiled as Finley looked into his mate's eyes. It was better than the plans that I had thought, which were to send her with Melina's family back to Atlantis.

"If Braxton is fine with it, then that is what we will do. He can't raise her. It wouldn't be right," I spoke firmly. Everyone nodded while I heard a small voice from our bed. Melina was sitting up, wiping the sleep from her eyes as she looked for me. "Darling." I rushed to the bed while she giggled into my arms. "I was so worried about you." Kissing her forehead, she reached under and kissed my neck.

"As scary as it was, I kicked some major ass." Melina tried to hide the shiver, but I knew better. It scared her to death. "Blood was everywhere!"

"It's all right to be scared, love. What you did was amazing, but I refuse to let you do that again," I warned.

Melina crossed her arms. "Nuh-uh, you are going to train me, and I'm gonna learn to fight on my own. I may have kicked that Wolf's tail, but I need some serious training. I'm going to be a warrior queen, damnit." I laughed and tackled her to the bed, trailing kisses up her neck.

"Never again will we spend a night apart," I whispered in her ear.

"Never again will I allow it," she replied, nipping at my neck. "So, when do we get this show on the road? My body doesn't even hurt anymore, and I want our guests to hurry and get out of the palace."

Lifting away the sheets revealed her smooth, creamy skin. There wasn't a scar left on her, no evidence of the struggle she had just a few days before. "Whenever you are ready, you have slept three days." Melina gasped at the audacity.

"All right, at dawn tomorrow then!" The sun was setting, and she grinned up at me. "But screw your traditions of sleeping away from me. We go to bed and wake up together from now on, you hear me?" Melina lectured.

"Fae honor," I crossed my chest with my arm as I bowed.

Melina climbed out of bed and sashayed to the bathroom. When I thought she was gone, I stood up to let the servants announce the new itinerary for tomorrow. Melina's head popped out beside the door and had a mischievous grin. "I think I need a shower. I'm a bit dirty," she winked. "But I don't think I can do it... alone." Her head left the doorway, only leaving her beckoning hand.

Screw the announcers. I'll tell them after.

I didn't walk seductively. I ran to her. Her contagious laughter filled the washroom with a loud echo as I pushed her to the shower wall. Steam had already covered the glass as I lifted one of her legs, so my crotch nestled perfectly to her core.

The thoughts of her ever having to fight again filled me with grief. This wasn't the life I wanted to give her. I wanted to pamper her, love her, and make crude love to her whenever she let me. Melina was her own person and needed parts of her independence, even if I wasn't a fan. We will learn to work with our relationship, and when she let me take care of her when she feels overwhelmed, I will welcome it with open arms.

"Osirus," she breathed as her hands went messily through my hair. Gods, I missed her, the three days asleep, and the day she was pampered. I wanted her and her body like I needed air. Melina continued to pull down my pants as I placed hot, sucking kisses on her neck. Her chest heaved as her nightdress fell to the floor. The water had drenched our clothes quickly. Her breasts looked rounder, perkier than I last remember; then again, it had been four damn days.

I lifted her with my arms and had her thighs between my head. She weighed as light as a feather as I dove my tongue beneath her folds as she squealed at the sudden height she gained. "Osirus!" Her moans and mewls made my dick stand to attention. Melina's hands dove into my hair, pulling and kneading it until she released her thick desire into my face. Her nails scraped my upper back, causing me to shutter.

As she came down from her high, I kissed her so she could taste the sweet honey I collected from her hive. Breaking the kiss, she kissed down my neck and pushed me to the wall. It was cold on my hot skin as the water tricked down my abdomen. "Did I tell you how much I love these?" Her tongue traced each abdominal muscle as she trailed down to my cock. Her hands wrapped around my arse, and her nails dug in tightly. Fuck.

"And this too," Melina licked the tip, and my hips jerked for her to take more, but she took it a step further. Licking down my shaft and to my balls, she took each one into her mouth. Massaging and sucking until it was driving me mad. With a slight pop sound, she took her tongue and trailed just underneath my balls and licked between my balls and ass.

"Gods!" I growled as I tried to pull her up. It was sensitive, electrifying. I couldn't stand it. My dick even hitched, ready to spew my seed all into her hair. Coming back up, she sucked in my cock with her mouth and hummed. Watching her bob her head made my balls squeeze up close to my body.

"I want you to cum in my mouth, Osirus. You can only have this pussy after the ceremony." Her mouth dove back down as I leaned my head back.

I could take her over my knee right now, but fuck, I loved how she said she was going to deny me. That would make taking her cunt so much sweeter. "Darling, fuck!" I wailed as I spurted into her mouth. She continued to swallow as my load unfurled and my breath calmed. Standing back up, she came up to me and sucked my bottom lip as we kissed nice and slow until the shower ran cold.

"I love you, Osirus, with all my heart and soul."

"And I love you, darling, my precious little queen."

Chapter 77

Melina

The night was slowly fading, and I knew I had to rise early before the dawn approached. My dreams would have been filled with nightmares if Osirus didn't stay last night. I don't think we will ever be away from each other from now on. The thought of being taken away infuriated me and how weak I had been. I fought to the end, though, making sure that Esteban felt every bit of my claws rake across his pathetic neck. It ended up better than expected for a warrior to be beaten by someone who has never fought a day in her life. My legs and arms were completely healed, thanks to Fae and Siren speed, and my stomach only had a few bruises left over. By this evening, I wouldn't be surprised if they were gone entirely.

All along, I thought I was weak, but Clara was right. I was strong. She was wiser than her years, as they all say. The calm she could radiate in a room certainly helped me throw away my deafening thoughts of being a failure. Now that I had battled my very own battle and alone, I felt a little more worthy. I had a long way to prove that I could be a warrior queen, but it was a step in the right direction.

Before I could move, Osirus' tight arms held me, grabbing my breasts as he chuckled into my ear. "Still tired?" he rasped, and I wiggled my rear end to let him know I was feeling friskier than anything. "Don't do that, darling, or we will never get this ceremony over with." Giggling with my eyes closed, I felt something wet and cold touch my nose. My eyes popped open to be greeted with large blue eyes and a white furry face.

"You didn't!" I squealed. I wiggled out of Osirus' arms to grab the adorable fox I saw just a few weeks ago. It was the size of a fluffy raccoon, and its three tails all wagged happily as I nuzzled into it. The feelings were mutual. We both thought of each other as equally adorable. "Osirus!" I gasped again as it licked my nose. "He's so cute!" I squealed as it jumped around the bed and burrow under the covers.

"He's for you. Finley said this was the only thing that made you smile at the marketplace the day you visited." The light blue ears flicked back and forth, looking at Osirus, but clumsily rolled back to my side of the bed.

"He's adorable. I love him!" Around its neck was a beautiful diamond studded collar with a blank nameplate.

"Figured you would want to name him," Osirus sat up with his head propped up with his elbow.

"How about Toki? He seems he has a fun little personality!" Osirus was still completely naked, and my attention to my new pet was diverted quickly back to him. Osirus grabbed the back of my head and pulled me in for a passionate kiss as I toppled on top of him. He greedily forced his tongue in my mouth while I straddled my legs over his morning wood.

"Osirus," I breathed as I ground my bare pussy against it. I was already wet. Those few days of sleeping had awoken a sex goddess, and I was ready to pounce.

I traced my finger across his chiseled jaw, his amber eyes darkened with lust. A few of his fangs tickled his lips. My heartbeat quickened, wanting nothing more than for him to bite me on my mark. Banging on the door ensued before anything more heated could happen, and we both woke from our lustful haze.

"Time to get ready, darling." Osirus stood from the bed in all his naked glory, not even bothering to cover himself. His erection sprang free and bounced as he walked to a picture on the far side of the room and moved it. "See you soon, my sexy queen." I licked my lips, and Osirus was gone as the picture moved back into place. Holy crap, that was awesome. Why haven't I seen that before!? I wanted to sneak over and move the picture, but the door broke free of the lock.

Tulip came bouncing in along with Elaine, Amora, and Clara. "Time to get you dressed, my little sex addict! I'm so proud," Tulip cooed. Rolling my eyes and covering my chest, they helped me out of bed and made sure I washed any remnants from last night from my body. They scrubbed it one more time, full of lavender and bath salts, to make my body shine again.

In record time, I was dressed in my beautiful petal dress. The light blue reverse ombre dress made me smile as I swished it back and forth across the floor. I really was a Fairy princess. I snickered.

My father entered the room to watch them put the final touches as they put clusters of light blue starfish in my long, thick white hair. It was curled and put in a loose braid that hung on the right side of my shoulder. The corset hung low, so my wings could be free, something my father was proud of since my wings held the colors of my people so well. They were also one of a kind; no other Fae had colors of this magnitude on their wings.

"It shows you are certainly a royal Siren Fae," he joked as he looked at them. "There are even small hints of scales on them. I bet you could use them as fins in the water." Since I didn't have a tail, I think it would make sense to try. I could keep up with Lucca in the water when we went on swims.

There would be no crown on my head since I will bear the Fae crown, so my father retrieved an intricate diamond and sapphire necklace in the shape of a dolphin. Father was disappointed I wouldn't wear the crown he had initially been picked out, but I was being placed as a Fae Queen and not a Siren. The necklace was small and delicate, nothing that would be considered over the top, which I loved.

I would also walk barefoot, as a representation of Atlantis, as most Atlanteans didn't wear shoes, and I was happy I didn't have to walk around in tall stilettos. My toenails had been painted white with tiny silver sparkles.

My heart jumped a few times as I saw the sun break the surface of the water. Osirus and I certainly had the best room in all the castle. Waking up with the sea and the sun was a sight to adore, especially since my roots led back to the sea.

"Are you ready?" Lucca walked in with Sean. All my brothers were donned in their traditional uniforms, which meant no shirts, just shells of metals and seashell necklaces. They were wearing trousers that fitted their bodies and a large blue leather sash that dangled to the floor. Their hair was gelled back, and small crowns were set on their heads. I had my fingers crossed. They would all find their mates today. The crowds outside had gathered to dance in the streets as the people inside witnessed firsthand.

Sean continued to gawk at his mate while wearing his warrior regalia which looked like a human uniform of tans and greens. Sean's tattoos poked through above the collar of his uniform, and Lucca kept tracing his finger, causing Sean to shiver. I snickered, and my father bumped my shoulder to keep quiet. I couldn't help it, my big bro got his mate, and he was so happy!

"Ready as I will ever be," I replied to Lucca as I grabbed a single blue rose from the vase. There were no enormous bouquets of flowers, just one rose that would be joined with Osirus' once I arrived at both thrones. Each flower would be put together in one single vase, symbolizing our coming together to create a new beauty of a nation.

I took one sniff of the flower while my father held out his arm for me to take. Tulip, Amora, and Clara walked down the aisle in front of us, not as bridesmaids but as viewers of the ceremony. Their mates gripped them tightly and had them sit on their laps, a great way to save on seating.

My father and I had halted at the door, waiting for the opening music to start. I saw Tulip's mother and her mate, Elm. Both smiled and gave me loving waves. I bet they never guessed their adoptive daughter would now be the queen of land they had hidden from me for so many years.

The room was dark, but I could see tall decorative trees that scaled the room. Some were as high as the distant ceiling and held tiny fairy lights and many Pixies that glowed, giving the room a romantic dim hue. Some trees had ropes of tulle of pale whites, blues, and creams, making the throne room not seem so vastly large but more intimate.

Many looked back to stare at both me and my father, King of Atlantis. His classic royal blue suit with his metals of battles and honor stood proudly. He was the Atlantean with the most clothing in the crowd. His dark hair and scruffy beard were neatly trimmed for such an occasion, while Elaine smiled seductively at him from afar.

"Breathe, dad," I joked as he started growling at her. I was sensing a mating night soon.

The throne room was still dark, with the crowd holding candles to their bodies. The suns were close to rising, and that was when we would begin our long walk through the throngs of people. Osirus stood tall in his white decorative suit. Gold and silver outlined every battle he had won, which was many. His cape was touching the floor and slightly dragging. Unique gold leaves outlined his cloak that trailed off the edges, giving it an organic look. Somehow, he could still leave his tunic open to let his chest shine in tune with the sun.

Taking a shaky breath, my father gave me a gentle squeeze with his hand. "I'm so proud of you, princess. You've grown to be the daughter I've always dreamed of."

I glanced at the silent tears that were threatening to leave his eyes. "You will always be my father and expect a lot of visits, Okay?"

Father took a shaky sigh and gripped me tighter. "I'm holding it to you, princess." The harps played as the sun skipped the horizon. Bright colors danced on the floor of blues, greens, and purples for the people in the room to murmur and aweing over. Taking my attention from the floor to the stained-glass window, I saw Osirus and me. We were in each other's embrace with my wings fully extending. The floor was now covered in bright colors as the light went through the window. It was the most beautiful piece of artwork I had ever seen; how he could get someone to construct something like this in such a short amount of time was awe-inspiring.

"It's so beautiful," I whispered. The harp music continued to play, and my new fairy fox hopped down the aisle with me. He brushed my dress that made the light blue at the bottom swish across the floor. Several children started giggling while my new pet sat in front of Osirus proudly. Osirus' eyes met mine, and his face held such affection my heart was going to explode. His eyes were glassy; hell, mine was too, as he reached for my hand.

My father took my hand, kissed it, and handed me over to a crying Osirus. His tears left his face as he pulled me to him, and I kissed each one that trailed his cheeks. "Don't cry; we are together now," I chided. Osirus gave a small smile and pecked my lips as he held me so tightly no one could ever come between us.

The officiator, who was a high-ranking light coven witch, conducted the ceremony. I honestly couldn't tell you what she said, because I was looking at my mate the entire time. He radiated so much love and affection and the brilliance of light that shone from him left me blinded in love for him. I could feel him swimming in my soul. Who would have thought I would be here today with a man I had so much love for? I didn't know what love was until I met him. I didn't know what it meant to feel until him. Thank the goddess for a bond because, without it, I would have indeed been lost forever.

Osirus, feeling my sadness, pulled my hand up to kiss it as the official continued to talk about the importance of the relationship between a king and queen.

"Melina, princess of the Atlantean Kingdom, do you officially take your mate, Osirus, King of the Fae Kingdom as your mate and life partner, the queen of this nation and all the responsibilities that go with it?"

Without hesitation, "I do."

"And Osirus-"Osirus cut her off before another word was spoken, "I do damnit," and he pulled me into his mouth into a knee-bending kiss. He leaned over my body and pressed against my breasts as he held me up with one arm wrapped around my waist and the other behind my head. The suns had finally risen, and the entire room was engulfed with bursts of light. Pixies started cheering, and small bursts of glitter, white feathers, and bubbles exploded into the air.

Cheers were heard throughout the room. Peoni was sitting on Carson's lap, both looking much better after their own brush with death. Rex was sucking face with Primrose, and Lucca and Sean held onto each other, gazing into each other's eyes. I started laughing at how happy everyone was, but as selfish as I was being, I was more excited about being with Osirus. No one else mattered, just him and I in our own little world.

While the cheering was exploding over the throne room, the officiator came over and had both Osirus and I sit on our respective thrones. First, Osirus was given an enormous ornamental crown that was not for everyday use. He sat with a grin on his face as he held my hand, and another crown was placed on my head. It was silver with hints of gold, amber stones, and blue sapphire in the middle.

Osirus gave a tight squeeze to my hand and pulled me out of the chair and straight onto his lap.

The cheers from outside the palace walls shook the floors. Fairies and Pixies had flown up into the windows to get a glimpse of their new king and queen on their throne. Banging on windows, and stomps of the floors, the sounds became overwhelming as I nuzzled into my mate's neck.

This day could not get any more perfect. I sighed contentedly. The people whom I love the most were in this very room. I've made new friends, found family, and now my life felt complete. That is, until we made our own little prince and princesses when the time was right.

"The fun is just getting started, darling," he whispered in my ear as his hand tried to trail up my dress.

"Oh, I'm counting on it," I joked back as he leaned me back into the chair and kissed me senselessly.

Chapter 78

Melina

The crowd dispersed as Alaneo directed everyone to the beach outside. The ocean was part of my blood, so the reception was held next to the sea to integrate both the Fae and Siren cultures. Many of my father's subjects could attend and walk out of the water and hopefully find a mate.

"Come with me." Osirus tickled my ear with his lips as he grabbed my hand. My petal dress flowed with the wind as he led me down a dark hallway. The petal dress parted, and my legs were out for a show, only giving Osirus a devious grin. He pulled me into an abandoned closet and pushed me against the wall. Linens began falling around us as his hands touched my chest. Pulling down, he took one swipe with his thumb on one nipple, and his mouth took the other. My fingers dug into his hair as he hit it harshly. "I can never get enough of these," he bit me.

His hand parted the petal folds of the dress and rubbed my bundle of nerves as his mouth went back up to my lips. "You are always ready for me, my love." His finger dipped into my core as he rubbed back up my slit to rub my clit. "But you are always ready for pleasure, aren't you?" His teeth nipped my neck as my claws ripped part of his cloak.

"Whoops," I whispered, as he chuckled darkly. His hand left my clit, causing me to whine at the lack of his heat when he pulled something from his trousers. Osirus' hand rubbed my core again with two fingers and inserted an egg-like device. I squeaked at the sudden feeling, trying to push it from my body.

"Keep it there," he whispered into my neck. "I'll punish you if you take it out."

"What if I want to be punished?" I growled back, and he sucked my bottom lip.

"You wouldn't like this kind of punishment, darling, trust me. Don't deny yourself on our official binding ceremony day." Osirus nipped at my lip and pulled away. Pouting, he pulled me from the closet.

I walked out, pulling my dress up to cover my breasts. As I walked, I felt the object in my pussy rolling around, hitting places that caused little bursts of pleasure. "Ugh, Osirus," I whined as I tried to walk.

"I can't wait to have fun with you today," he whispered.

Tulip walked up and scowled at Osirus. "No, no, no, she needs to get ready for the reception. You can bang each other later. Come on, Melina." Alec smirked at Osirus as they both went down the hallway, hands in pockets, leaving us alone.

"What now?" I whined as she dragged me back to the bridal suite.

"You can't very well dance with that big puffy thing. It's time to put on your party dress. Let me just say your Siren family does not care about nudity...." Tulip trailed off as she shoved me into the room.

Tulip handed me my undergarments that comprised a black lace thong and bra set. The top was just a silver sequenced halter, with the bottom part of my breast showing down to my hipbones. The skirt covered more, down to my knees, but was skintight that there was nothing left to the imagination. My ass looked pretty damn good; I have to say so myself.

Tulip came up and grabbed my rear. "Damn girl, those sponge cakes did you some good. Osirus' got a lot to grab!" I slapped Tulip's hand while she laughed and led me back to the beach. The egg device kept rubbing me and caused my face to flush. I was drenched, and I don't know how long my black lacy thong would stay dry because I thought I felt a bit of me drip down my thigh.

All while walking, Tulip took my braid out, so my messy curls flowed endlessly down my back. The light blue star-fish hung on tightly. My skirt kept riding up, and my thong was drenched. It was terribly uncomfortable, so taking it off would be the best thing. Smirking, I waved at Tulip to wait a minute as I ducked into an empty room. I slid off the perpetrator for my uncomfortable core and devised an evil plan to get back at Osirus. Stuffing it in my bra, I came back outside with Tulip lifting an eyebrow.

"What did you do?" she crossed her arms. "I can smell you from here."

I tsked as I walked by. "You'll see."

Walking outside, it was now noon, with the sun high in the sky. Buffet tables were set up, a sizeable make-shift floor, so no one had to sink into the sand. Potted trees were brought in for shade as sprites burst glitter in the air as they saw couples making out or dancing to the beat of the music. It was loud, deafening. I wouldn't be surprised if the entire Bergarian continent heard this party.

Several of my unmated brothers seemed to have found their mates. Their head was buried in their necks while they cupped their butts leading them to the ocean. Some were other Sirens, and several were Elves and Fae. What pretty babies they are going to make! I squealed in my head, thinking how awesome of an aunt I was going to be. I'd have hundreds of little nieces and nephews to coo over.

Tulip left my side with a promise to save her dance for later. Goddess knows what she had planned.

I felt the heated stare on my body, knowing it may be of

my mate. I clenched my thighs together as I felt a warming sensation in my core. Gentle vibrations pulsed through my pussy, and I had to lean on a pillar to keep myself steady. The beats became stronger as I closed my eyes to calm any orgasm trying to build.

"Mm, my mate looks like she is in trouble." Osirus came up behind me, putting the palm of his hand on my stomach. His erection dug into me, and the heat of his cock filled my body with warmth.

"This isn't fair," I said, letting out a breathy moan. "You can't do this in the open."

"That I can, and I can't wait to watch you orgasm in front of all these people." Gritting my teeth, his cock rubbed against me once more while another hand holding a small remote came into view. He squeezed my breast closest to the pillar away from prying eyes.

"Princess." My father approached as Osirus let go of my tit he was pinching. "I think it's time for our dance, hmm?" Gently wiping the glistening sweat from my forehead, I nodded enthusiastically. I gave a death glare to Osirus, who calmed down the raging vibrations. My father studied at Osirus and back to me, giving Osirus a stern look.

Taking my father's hand, the floor cleared, and Osirus' mother came into view, holding onto Osirus. We both danced with our parents as people talked silently on the sidelines. Many were eating, drinking, and laughing. The entire kingdom was at peace and at rest. The thoughts of an upcoming war still bothered me. Osirus had come so far to bring his kingdom the happiness it deserved, the freedom and love of mates. I didn't want to see one soul have to die to protect what we all fought so hard to keep.

"Your mind is wandering, princess," my father spoke, taking me away from my thoughts. He twirled me and dipped me low to the ground while I giggled.

"Just thinking of the future," I said breathlessly while he used his fancy footwork to lead me to the sidelines as other couples joined our slow song.

"Would you take the advice from one of royalty to another?" My father's eyes glistened their dark blue while he gave me a sad smile. "Live in the now. It is good to plan and prepare, but if you constantly worry about the 'what ifs,' your life will bring you nothing but sadness. The gods will protect those who are just. It will take time and maybe lives, but the light will always prevail whether the darkness realizes this." I hummed as he pulled me close.

"It's a large job making decisions, but the goddess doesn't make mistakes when it comes to choosing mates. You are an amazing queen, and you and Osirus will help guide the people back to its long-standing of peace once it is all said and done."

The song ended, and father stepped back to give me a bow while I curtsied. Running up to him, not caring about the formalities, I gave him a big kiss on his furry cheek. "I love you, dad," he gave me a bigger squeeze and let go gently, off to find his mate. Osirus still stood on the dance floor, heated eyes on me. Osirus' hands reached out and took mine, pulling me flush against his body.

The trees that went around the perimeter of the large dance floor swayed together and covered the sun from view. As the leaves and branches grew, it turned into a rainforest-like canopy. Now it looked like a fantasy dance club. The mood was set as many unmated as well as newly mated couples walked to the floor. The beat of the music played, and Pixies lit up the floor.

Heated bodies rubbed against each other. Osirus grasped me and pulled my ass to his throbbing erection. Everyone was in their own world with their mates that we were in our own bubble. Osirus opened his tunic, exposing his body to the world.

The vibration in my pussy filled me as he cranked up the volume. "Do you like that?" My head leaned back on his chest as his hand rubbed the outside of my mound. I groaned, and he chuckled darkly in my ear. "Hmm, I thought so." He rubbed his erection more on my ass while I fell over and over in excess. His hot breath fanned my neck as I shook my head.

"Too much, too much," I whined as he turned off the vibration.

"What an amazing mate I have," he whispered as he turned me around and explored my mouth. My hands went around his neck as I pulled him closer. Osirus' hands encompassed my waist pulling me closer, rubbing me. "Gods, you are so beautiful," he moaned. "You are my perfect match, my perfect sun, my perfect everything." I blushed, leaning into him more.

"I love you, Osirus," I cupped his cheek while his forehead touched mine. "You always know how to keep me under your spell." I went to kiss him again until I felt a tap on my shoulder.

"Hate to interrupt," Alaneo cleared his throat with Juliet hanging onto his arm. "But we need a decision if we can open up more ambrosia reserves." Osirus kissed my lips.

"I'll be back, darling. Don't go anywhere," he winked as Alaneo walked away. Juliet gave me a small wave as she followed her mate.

Tulip was right behind me and pulled me to her. "Did he stick something in you?" she demanded.

"I'm sorry, what?" I snorted. "He sticks it in me all the time and more if people would stop interrupting!"

"That egg thing? Did he stick that in you?" Tulip's temper was rising.

"Yeah, how did you know that?" I replied, confused.

"There must be some male gift basket thing going on because Amora got one, too. Kane had one for Clara, but Kane refused to put it in her because he said the only thing that belonged in her was his own dick." I burst out laughing as she pulled me to Amora, who was also fuming.

"Kane is jealous of a vibrator?" I giggled as I pulled Tulip around to look at me.

"Oh yeah, he is one jealous Alpha. We tried to get her to dance with us, but Kane won't even let her dance with other women besides his sister."

"He keeps turning it off and on," Amora cried. "I tried to talk with some neighboring Elves of our tribe, and I started orgasming right there!" I started laughing again, but they both crossed their arms.

"We are going to get them back for humiliating us," Tulip huffed. "And you are helping."

I pointed to myself, "Me?"

"Yeah, come with us," again Tulip and Amora pulled me to the darkened corner of the make-shift club and started grinding on me.

"Whoa, what is this?" I waved my hands back as Tulip stuck her ass out to me.

"We are going to dance together and make them hot and bothered!" Amora shouted as she started rubbing her breasts

"I hate to break it to you, but my mate is already hot and bothered," I snickered. "But sure, I'll play your game as long as the rest of the dance floor can't see. I don't need the entire kingdom thinking I'm cheating on my mate." Tulip scoffed.

"Yeah, yeah. I mind-linked Alec. He's bringing our mates. Now act like you are all hot for me."

"Tulip, I see you as a sister. That's kinda gross. Let's make Amora the middle," I laughed.

We all started dancing. Amora slipped part of her top off, so one of her breasts showed, but I kept covered. I wanted to be spanked but not denied anything later. I'm not stupid. I'm laughing at the situation, not really acting seductive at all. Tulip is rubbing Amora's ass, and I'm making this dry hump motion near Amora, not touching her. Sorry, I just cannot get into that.

I felt the vibration surge through me again, and my pussy instantly dripped. I stopped dancing and started looking for Osirus, who is smirking like Hades himself. He walked up to me with the small remote in hand, and I grabbed my breasts and rubbed them intently. I had almost forgotten when I felt the lace thong. The vibrator got kicked up a notch, and I stumbled, only to feel Osirus catch me. Osirus was the one I wanted, and come hell or high water, I was going to do anything to get my mouth on that delicious body of his.

"I see what you did there," he pulled me into my arms. "You didn't engage in their stupid ploy to anger their mates." Osirus' hand trailed down my side and gripped my ass. "Maybe you should get a reward." His hand lifted the back of my skirt where part of my cheek was showing. It was far less than what Amora was showing now. Her top was completely down, and Tulip wasn't far behind. Their mates grabbed both of them, threw them over their shoulders, and stomped out of the party.

"I know when to push my limits," I answered seductively. Pulling out the thong between my breasts, I stuffed it in Osirus' mouth. His eyes widened as I grabbed his crotch. "So, when are you going to reward me?"

Pulling it out of his mouth, he grabbed my arm and left the club scene. Spreading his wings, he pulled me to his chest and flew straight up the palace walls. The higher he went, the smaller the people became, and the music faded, and the only thing that could be heard was the flutter of his wings and the waves of the sea.

Flying through an open window surrounded by nothing other large, opened windows laid a bed with an enormous mattress on the floor. It reminded me of the time we spent in the Elven territory in Osirus' old treehouse. The sun was brightly showing, and the potted plants granted us enough shade to keep the room cool with the other open windows. My hair flew in my face, and as I removed my hair, Osirus' mouth hit mine.

"Fuck, you are perfect," he licked my lips as he nipped my cheek. "How did I get so damn lucky?" His member brushed up against my leg as I went to grab him through his trousers.

"What about the party?" I teased as his kisses trailed

down my neck and to my breasts. He roughly pulled my dress down to expose the black lace bra that barely hid my womanly features.

"We have our own party, darling. And I'm going to make love to you while there is an orgy going on down there."

It was true. The dance party had become one massive sex fest. It reeked of hormones and sweat, and I was ready to get out of there. My brothers had left with their mates, my family had waved goodbye to me long ago as they trekked home. The only soul I saw left was Braxton, sitting solemnly at a table. Finley and Opal had taken Emilee home and he would be granted to visit every Saturday. My heart ached for Braxton, but this would be the time to show his love for her by waiting and cleansing his soul for her.

"I like the sound of that," I whispered as my dress slid down my body. Osirus parted my legs wide as he took a deep breath of my aroma. Osirus pulled out the vibrator and tossed it to the side.

"I want to be the only one to pleasure you," Osirus growled as he licked me from the bottom to the top of my clit. His tongue circled around me as I wiggled in his grasp. I moaned as he forcefully held my hips still, and I dug my fingers into his scalp. "Harder," I rasped. "Suck harder!" Osirus obliged and sucked the ever-living shit out of me. I came undone, cumming in his face forcefully as he lapped me up.

Before I had time to recover myself, I took my legs and squeezed his head, and rolled him over. He let out a slight yelp in surprise as his hands went to my ass. "Fuck, that was hot, baby." My pussy was right in his face as he continued to assault me with his tongue.

He kneaded my ass as I rode his face until I came again, my legs shaking; I went down his body to line my pussy against his painfully large cock. "Ride me, Melina. Gods, I need you to," Osirus strained as he aligned my hips. The tip of his dick was dripping with pre-cum as I lowered myself. Today felt like the first time. I was almost too tight at this angle as I pushed myself onto him.

"Fucking hell!" He growled as the rest of his trousers were kicked from his ankles. "Please move," he begged me, and move I did. I didn't start slow; I wanted it hard and fast. My breasts bounced as he had one hand on my hip and one on my tit, squeezing and letting go. Osirus' abs contracted as I felt the slapping of our skins.

Osirus grunted as his growl rumbled through my tits. Sitting up, he puts his mouth on my other breast, sucking so hard I swear I saw stars. I moaned and pushed his head further into my breasts, which he quickly sucked, marking me.

I felt my high coming, and Osirus put both his hands on either ass cheeks. "Now, baby, cum all over me," he yelled as we both felt each other's pleasure. Both of our mouths went to our respective marks and bit again, only solidifying the bond we already shared. The euphoria continued as we held each other.

Coming down, Osirus laid back into the soft plush cushions, stroking my shoulder. Our mouths left the marks, and Osirus and I fell into a deep sleep with him still pulsing inside me.

Chapter 79

Osirus

I couldn't sleep. My mate was finally mine. She was my Queen, and I would treat her as such for the rest of eternity. Melina laid face down on the mattress, her head slightly turned to the left as she cuddled into the sheets. Back bare, I could see the tiny goosebumps that tickled her skin as I rubbed small circles in her back.

She had been sleeping for well over an hour, and I knew if we wanted to head to our final destination, 'our honeymoon,' as she put it, I would have to wake her soon. The light sources had descended, the reception was still blazing with music with another wave of travelers that had heard of the massive unmated party. I could hear the growls, screams, and cheers as many supernaturals found their mates.

It was all Melina's idea to turn her classical reception into a raging party so mates would be found. She opposed the idea just a month ago. I'm glad now she was a powerful advocate for finding mates.

Tickling her on her sides, she started to smile but nuzzled back into the sheets. The sheet came down low on her lower back as I now hovered over her. My hair tickled her sides as I started planting small kisses down her skin.

"Mmm, five more minutes?" she whined as she grabbed a decorative pillow and shoved it in her face.

"I would, darling, but the second part of our honeymoon is waiting." Melina's eyes popped open as she leaned up on her forearms. Her breasts tickled the sheets as I reached around to cup them.

Giggling, she spat, "I thought we had places to go, my King?"

I groaned at the question. Of course, we do.

We both quickly dressed, and I pulled her into my arms as we glided down to the ground. Warriors were standing around Horus, who was already packed with our belongings for two weeks. We would have clothes in the mountains, but I had many gifts to give Melina, and I knew I wouldn't find them in the cold tundra of the Northern Mountains.

"Are you ready, darling?" I turned to her as I finished tightening the straps of our cargo. Melina turned to me, and the light hit her face just right, making her look like the Goddess Aphrodite herself. She was wearing tight-fitting leather pants with a warm overcoat, but it didn't cover her cleavage as she picked the smallest brassiere, she could find to tease me.

"I'm ready, my King," she said, sultry as I pulled her to me. With a quick kiss on her forehead, I pushed her up onto Horus' back, who purred gently. Horus had a soft spot for her, as well as every other animal. Toki hopped outside and immediately shrunk down to the size of a small hamster and jumped into her front pocket.

"Toki is freaking adorable! Look at this wittle face!" she cooed as she petted his head. "And he can get big too, right?"

"Big enough to ride," I joked as her eyes lit up. "In a few years, darling, he is still a kit." Nodding in understanding, I made Melina hold on to my back for the two-hour flight to the Northern Palace.

If we had flown ourselves, it would have taken well over six hours, and on foot or carriage, it would have been days, but Horus and his speed were unmatched. He flew high in the sky, away from the bustling of fairies and Fae fluttering about. His wings would glide long and hard as he strode with the wind.

Every so often, I would hear Melina's awe over the scenery. From the forest area where we lived to the foothills of the elves and the more mountainous terrain of the Dragon shifters, we flew on. Several areas were unclaimed territory, which some rogues used as their own. They were those without packs or families that remained outside of kingdom protection, not wanting anything to do with others.

Not all rogues were evil, but many were. The term rogue had earned itself a bad name. It only meant they were without companions for one reason or another. It could have been for an evil crime, rebellious against kingdoms, or having ill understanding of their own kind. There could also be packs of rogues, which lead to nothing but trouble.

The weather became cold as we neared the tallest of mountains. Many frost Pixies and fairies stayed here, unable to bear the heat of the light sources for long summers. They would visit when we had our own 'winter' in The Golden Light Kingdom, which lasted three weeks out of the year.

Snow had recently fallen. Stags, bears, and winter fairy foxes were following the shadow of Horus. His bright scales proved to be a treasure they wanted to seek. If only they knew they would be dinner once landed if they dared to follow further.

Melina gripped me tighter as the wind picked up; her cheek was cold against my own, and Toki was even chattering his tiny teeth. "I thought he was supposed to be a winter fox thing?" Melina joked as she nestled him into her jacket.

"He has spent too much time in the Golden Light Kingdom. He's become acclimated to our weather."

The snow fell again as we approached. The palace sat on the side of a mountain; it wasn't as large as back home but still beautiful in all its grandeur. As the snow fell around us, I heard Melina squeal and pull out her hand. Small flakes with an iridescent sparkle melted into her palm.

"It's like a pastel rainbow on each flake!" She laughed as Horus landed on the large balcony overlooking the snowy tundra. As we dismounted, winter Fae came close to us to unload our bags. It was now sunset, and Melina ran to the side of the balcony to get a better look. After beckoning the servants to ready our room, I followed her while Toki jumped out of her pocket and ran inside.

Even he was cold.

"Osirus, I've seen nothing like this!" The forest was covered in white powder, the wildlife was abundant, perfect for hunting. The snow garden had beautiful bright flowers that only thrived in cold climates already blooming. Winter flowers could be fickle, with too much snow on their petals. Trolls that lived in the nearby caves were handsomely paid for their help in keeping them alive. Melina continued to frantically look about, trying to bring in the entire sight.

"Do you like it here?" I wrapped my hands around her waist. Her head leaned back on my shoulder while she smiled.

"It's so beautiful. I can't imagine anything more perfect," she sighed.

"I think I can," I whispered in her ear as I turned her around to face me. "If you could see the way I see you, you would know how perfect you are for me." My thumb traced her cheek as she leaned over and gave me a sweet and gentle kiss.

Leading her inside the palace, it differed greatly from at home. Its ceilings were high, but thick red drapes hung over the windows, and animal rugs decorated the floor. The entire palace radiated warmth, as each room had a roaring fire keeping us warm.

Our bags were already emptied and place in their respective closets; thick winter furs and clothing were also waiting for us. The gigantic bed held a snow beast fur, the head no longer attached, knowing it would upset my mate seeing such an evil face. Melina's hands brushed the fur as her face glowed by the fire.

"I'm scared I'm living a dream, and I'm going to wake up alone again," she choked as I walked up to her. Pushing back her messy hair from our flight, I cupped her cheek.

"Do you feel this?" The sparks flew across my hand and her cheek, and she nodded sadly. "This is not a dream, and you will not wake up without me. I will be here when we go to sleep, hold you every night, and when we wake, I'll make love to you every morning so that silly thought of yours is gone."

Melina smiled as a pink blush dusted her cheeks. "I'm going to hold you to that, my King." I hummed and kissed her forehead.

"We have a busy day tomorrow. We can explore the palace and the grounds so you can become familiar with it and then maybe see some wildlife. How does that sound?"

"Wonderful," she breathed. Feeling her heart race, I knew she was thinking of something other than a tour.

"I'll go get ready for bed." Her hand trailed down my chest as she left.

The Goddess blessed me with a mate that could keep up with my stamina; at first, I was afraid she would be too shy, but that proved wrong far too quickly. I stripped my overcoat and left nothing but my trousers and my bare feet. Pulling the pillows off the bed and pulling the covers, I hear a light clearing of Melina's dainty throat.

She's dressed in a baby doll pink lingerie set. Her navel had a dangling mini-chandelier piece that flickered in the light. I groaned internally, not wanting to ruin the moment. She wore a thigh-high garter belt with a matching thong. She looked like a goddess, a sex goddess that would put any female to shame. The love I have for her only swelled more in my chest. Melina has given herself to me many times over the past few weeks, but this was the ultimate gift.

The smile, the love, and humor she has about love were incomparable to any other woman I had ever had the chance of knowing. If all the women of the planet had disappeared, I would never know because my eyes would always be on her, my Queen. It wasn't often I was left in shock, but this stunning beauty before me had once again proved me wrong. Melina's hand was setting on the doorway, waiting for me to beckon her towards me.

"Come," I rasped as I walked around the bed, slow and steady. Like hunter to prey, or was it really hunter to hunter? We both had lust in our eyes, raking through each other's bodies and souls. She was my soul. I could never live without her. "You are everything my heart desires," I gasped as I pulled her close.

I raised the silk fabric above her hips as I felt the backside of her body. Melina was already wearing too many clothes.

Leading her to the bed, I picked her up and laid her down like she was a precious work of art. I hovered over her, kissing her forehead, cheeks, and chin, and finally her lips as I grabbed her hair. She pressed her laced chest up my body as I unclipped her bra in one stroke. Pooling into my hands, I squeezed and flicked her glorious nipples as her hands touched my face.

Each finger stroke left the sparks trail down my body. Our hands explored each other like it would be the last time we would see each other. Memorizing every detail, every indentation of her skin, my hands trailed down to her luscious thighs. I wanted to be in her. It was as simple as that.

Taking a large breath, I smelled her arousal; it was thick and heavy of lust. My cock gently brushed her slit as she moaned my name. Tickling her as I wiggled inside her, her pussy clenched instantly. Tightly, she squeezed my girth as I slid in and out of her.

Neither of us begged. Neither of us demanded anything from each other. Just the soft touches, the gentle pull of our nether regions, kept us sated. We stared into each other's eyes as our bodies moved in sync with one another. "I love you," she groaned as her eyes started to roll back into her head. Her hair spread throughout the pillow as I pulled both of her legs around my hips.

Getting a better angle, I sped up my motion, pulsing in her. Within a few seconds, I had already released myself. Her body and mine glistened with sweat. I kept myself inside her wet cavern as I pulled her to my chest while laying on my side.

"And I love you, darling," I panted. "Forever, I will."

"Through thick and thin and whatever future Bergarian throws at us," she whispered. Knowing there would be a war coming, the double meaning behind it brought me back down from heaven.

"For now, we are in our own paradise, and I will make sure you will always have one." I rested my chin over her head as we both dreamed about our beautiful future together.

Chapter 80

"Tell us about the story where you slashed all the warlocks' throats!" Thicket screamed as he pounced on the bed. His dogwood sword in hand, he waved it about as King Osirus smiled at the enthusiasm of his five-year-old. "Tell us how you gutted them like fish!"

"Hey!" Pandora screamed in defense. "You can't stay stuff like that. Mama said so! It is racist!" Pandora sat on the bed opposite her brother, who was still jumping around the room.

Osirus nodded as he went to calm his son down. "Thicket, Pandora is right. You can't say such things. You have a bit of your mother in you as well, don't forget that. Just because you took genes of a Fae doesn't mean it isn't part of your genealogy." Thicket sighed and plopped on the bed.

Thicket and Pandora were twins, born twenty years exactly after King Osirus and Queen Melina's honeymoon. Osirus made sure his queen could cover all Bergarian in their many adventures. He even took her farther that any supernatural had traveled in their realm, all the way to the abandoned deserts.

Melina had also become one of the top warriors, surpassing even the Red Fury, who had, mostly, retired spending time with their mates and their respective families. Brendon, the last one to claim his mate Emilee, was still in their own honeymoon phase since she had become of age just a few years before.

"Yeah," Pandora quipped. "I'm just more like mama, a fearless warrior both on land and sea!"

Thicket crossed his arms, unamused by his sisters' ramblings. "I'll be better than you, just wait and see. Once Mama allows it, I'll be in the ring the same day!"

Osirus laughed as his beautiful queen entered the room. She was swollen with their third child and was due in just a few weeks. "There will be no fighting until you are at least ten," she scolded. "That is the age where all Fae and Sirens start their training. Any earlier, I won't allow it." Melina sat beside Osirus, who only pulled her to his lap. His hand immediately caressed her belly as she played with his hair.

"So, what are we arguing about before this debate happened?" She smiled at both of her children.

"On which story dad was going to tell," Pandora answered, her eyes shining brightly. "I wanted to hear the story of how you both met. It isn't like the other mating stories I have heard from the servants."

Melina giggled, "No, it's not. But it's our story. Your father needed to realize I would not swoon into his arms and give myself to him. Sexy looks can't get you everything." Melina winked at Osirus, who only tickled her sides in return.

"Ewww," Thicket groaned. "I wanted to hear a war story! Like the Warlock battle where mama came in riding Horus! Or the war against the rogue Vampires in Vermillion!" Melina frowned and rubbed her chest. There was a deep scar running from the top left of her body to the bottom right. Melina almost lost her life that day. Osirus was a mess. He carried her bloodied body over an enormous battlefield of raging gore and violence to get her back to their tent. The healers looked on in fear, fear of not only the queen's life but of Osirus' fury on theirs.

He was tainted black, the blackest skin he had ever conjured. His wings sparkled an onyx-colored glitter. As each speck fell to the ground, a puff of smoke would arise. Osirus laid her on the table, the sword still on his mate's side. "Fix her," he commanded, and they tried. For twenty-four hours, they tried to heal her wounds, only for her veins and arteries to turn black. When all hope was lost, the healers laid their faces on the ground, ready to lose their lives until one soul came to save her.

Creed. The Dragon that had been shunned by his own kind. Creed's dark presence hushed the tent as many looked on at his sudden appearance. Blood dripped from his lower extremities. He was naked from being in his Dragon form, but that did not deter him. He owed his life to the queen, and this was his repayment. Creed never spoke a word, just cut his palm, and leaked his blood into a cup sitting on the side of the bed. One of the Witch healers rushed to him, thanking him for his magical blood. Creed looked Osirus square in the eye and nodded and left the tent as quickly as he came.

The blood magnified the healing powers one hundredfold for the Witch. It was enough to seal the wound and get rid of the poisons, but not without cost. Her womb had been cut, the poison had seeped through, and there was no guarantee that she would bear any children. The large scar was light but still noticeable to even a Fae. The healing powers of a Fae were no match for a demon's dagger.

It took several months until Melina could even walk again, but Osirus was with her every step of the way. He bathed her, clothed her, read to her, and even took her flying to get fresh air. He loved his queen, and he loved her stubbornness to not give up.

It took fifteen years after the war to bear the two beautiful twins they had now. The magic in the Death Sword carried by a rogue demon that pledged his allegiance with the vampires just about ended it all for the couple.

"How about we skip that story?" Melina was still upset to this very day. Her brush with death, being separated by her mate from this world to the next, almost killed her heart right there. She was a fighter; she always was. Melina went to say more but felt a strong jab in her belly. Grunting, she doubled over in pain as Osirus held her up from hitting the floor.

"Are you all right, mama!?" Pandora squealed as her feet hit the floor. Thicket threw down his play sword and ran to get a nearby servant to fetch the doctor.

"A few weeks early," Melina joked as she held her stomach. Osirus lifted her in his arms as he kissed her forehead. He knew from the last time she gave birth that panicking was something she didn't need. Melina would smack him every time he asked the doctor if something was normal. Melina needed the calm. He would create a quiet room around them as she gave birth.

The family strode down the hallway as a healer had met them halfway to the healing room. Checking her pulse, timing her contractions, they continued down to the brightly lit room. The bath was being prepared in case it would be another Siren and a bed if it was a Fae child. Osirus laid her on the bed as she held her stomach. The children looked on in worry as the royal nanny came in just in her nightclothes and cap.

"Come, children, let's wait out here. It might be a bit before your sibling is born." Melina let out a groan and gripped Osirus' arm. "Siren, it's a Siren." Melina knew the difference between races of her children when they were born. She had no trouble giving birth to Thicket on the bed, but there had been a roaring pain she felt in her back and her lightly colored scales ached when Pandora was entering the world. Instinct drew her to the water, and the tub was filled just in time for her daughter's arrival. Osirus ripped the clothes off her body and gently set her in the tub, listening to his queen's cries.

Osirus did the same, pulling off his tunic and leaving nothing but his trousers on as he slid in behind her. Counting and petting her cheek with words of encouragement, the pain lessened to just an ordinary birth.

Since giving birth to the twins, pushing out a singleton would be a piece of cake. She gripped the sides of the tub as another contraction ripped through her. When one would typically hear the soft cries of a baby being born, there was a large splash. Their Siren son had emerged and took his first swim, tail, and all. He swam to the surface as the healer grabbed the baby, checking scales and breathing.

A Siren baby had to spend most of their time in the water the first week before they could transform their legs properly. Melina had a hard time splitting her time between children until Pandora could wear the necklace that Callista had created for all the royal Siren family to spend as much time out of the water as possible. Once the tiny necklace that Pandora now wore was created, it made life as a mother of twins much more enjoyable.

"A boy," Osirus whispered as he kissed Melina's cheek. Osirus was immensely proud of his mate. Against all odds, she could give them both three beautiful children. Their lives could not get any more perfect.

"What should we name him?" she whispered as she tried to feed him. The boy wiggled its tail against his mother as he began suckling.

"How about Athos?" Osirus continued to pet his son's cheek. Melina hummed in contentment as she leaned her head back into Osirus' chest.

"I love it," she signed. "And I love you, my King."

"And I will continue to love you, my queen, even when the time finally stops."

Printed in Great Britain
by Amazon

79821283R00356